A STORM OF SWORDS
Part Two: Blood and Gold

George R.R. Martin is the author of fourteen novels, including five volumes of *A Song of Ice and Fire*, several collections of short stories and numerous screen plays for television drama and feature films. He lives in Santa Fe, New Mexico.

Praise for *A Song of Ice and Fire*:

'This is one of those rare and effortless reads.'   ROBIN HOBB

'George R.R. Martin is one of our very best writers, and this is one of his very best books.'   RAYMOND E. FEIST

'Such a splendid tale. I read my eyes out—I couldn't stop till I'd finished and it was dawn.'   ANNE MCCAFFREY

'George R.R. Martin is assuredly a new master craftsman in the guild of heroic fantasy.'   KATHARINE KERR

'Few created worlds are as imaginative and diverse.'   JANNY WURTS

By George R.R. Martin

A SONG OF ICE AND FIRE
Book One: *A Game of Thrones*
Book Two: *A Clash of Kings*
Book Three: part one: *A Storm of Swords: Steel and Snow*
Book Three: part two: *A Storm of Swords: Blood and Gold*
Book Four: *A Feast for Crows*
Book Five: part one: *A Dance with Dragons: Dreams and Dust*
Book Five: part two: *A Dance with Dragons: After the Feast*

Fevre Dream
The Armageddon Rag
Tuf Voyaging
Dying of the Light
Sandkings
Portraits of His Children
A Song for Lya
Songs of Stars and Shadows
Windhaven (with Lisa Tuttle)
Nightflyers

A STORM OF SWORDS

PART TWO: BLOOD AND GOLD

BOOK THREE OF
A Song of Ice and Fire

GEORGE R.R. MARTIN

HARPER
Voyager

HarperVoyager
An imprint of HarperCollins*Publishers*
77–85 Fulham Palace Road,
Hammersmith, London W6 8JB

www.harpercollins.co.uk

This paperback edition 2011
35

Previously published in paperback by Voyager in 2001, 2003

First published in Great Britain by Voyager in 2000

A catalogue record for this book
is available from the British Library

ISBN 978-0-00-744785-5

Set in Minion by Palimpsest Book Production Limited,
Falkirk, Stirlingshire

Printed and bound in Great Britain by
Clays Ltd, St Ives plc

MIX
Paper from
responsible sources
FSC® C007454

FSC is a non-profit international organisation established
to promote the responsible management of the world's forests.
Products carrying the FSC label are independently certified
to assure consumers that they come from forests that are managed
to meet the social, economic and ecological needs
of present and future generations.

Find out more about HarperCollins and the environment at
www.harpercollins.co.uk/green

For Phyllis
who made me put the dragons in

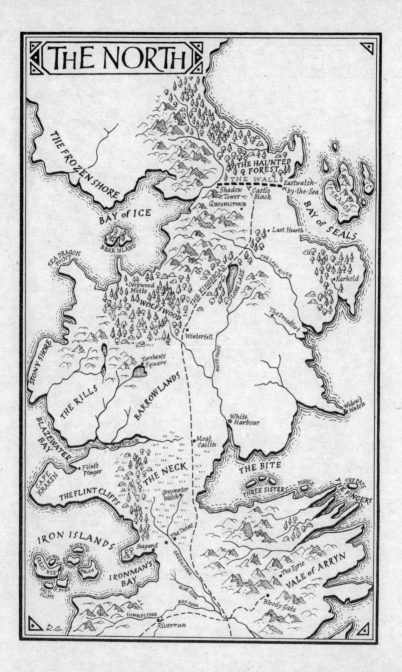

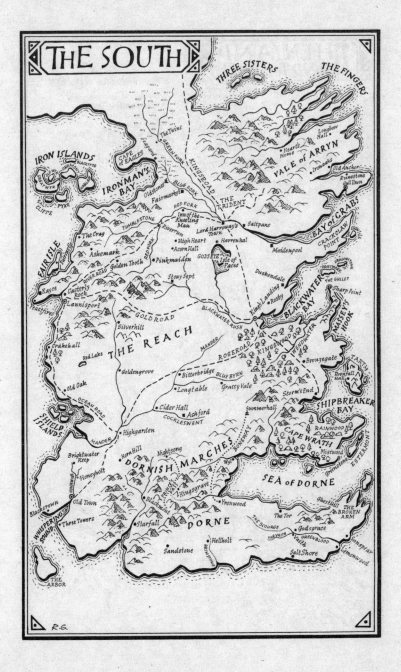

THE SOUTH

THREE SISTERS

THE FINGERS

IRON ISLANDS

ORKMONT
BLACKTYDE
GREAT WYK
HARLAW
PYKE
OLD WYK
SALT CLIFFE

CAPE
of EAGLES

IRONMAN'S
BAY

Seagard

The Twins

Oldstones

Fairmarket

BLUE FORK

THE TWINS

GREENFORK

KINGSROAD

Hill
Hill
Hill
Hill
Hill
Hill

Hearts
Home

Longbow
Hall

VALE of ARRYN

Ironoaks

Old Anchor

Redfort
Gulltown

BAY of CRABS

RED FORK

Inn of the
Kneeling
Man

THE
TRIDENT

Saltpans

Lord Harroway's
Town

Harrenhal

Maidenpool

CRACKCLAW
POINT

Claw I.

THE CRAG

TUMBLESTONE

Riverrun

RED FORK

High Heart

Acorn Hall

GODSEYE Isle of
Faces

Duskendale

DRIFTMARK
DRAGONSTONE

THE GULLET

FAIRISLE

Faircastle

Ashemark

Golden Tooth

RIVER ROAD

Pinkmaiden

Stony Sept

Sharp Point

Kayce

Casterly
Rock

Lannisport

GOLD ROAD

BLACKWATER RUSH

King's Landing

Rosby

BLACKWATER
BAY

Feastfires

MASSEY'S
HOOK

Silverhill

THE REACH

MANDER

ROSEROAD

KINGSWOOD

WEIRWOOD

Bronzegate

TARTH

Evenfall
Hall

Crakehall

Red Lake

Goldengrove

Old Oak

OCEAN ROAD

Bitterbridge

Longtable

BLUE BYRN

Grassy Vale

Storm's End

SHIPBREAKER
BAY

Cider Hall

Ashford

COCKLESWENT

Summerhall

CAPE
WRATH

RAINWOOD

MANDER

Highgarden

DORNISH MARCHES

Nightsong

Wyl

BONEWAY

Mistwood

Grimstone

ESTERMONT

SHIELD
ISLANDS

Brightwater
Keep

Honeyholt

Horn Hill

Blackmont

Kingsgrave

Yronwood

SEA of DORNE

SUNHOUSE

Blackcrown

Old Town

Three Towers

Starfall

PRINCE'S PASS

DORNE

The Tor

THE SCOURGE

Godsgrace

THE VAITH

Vaith

GREENBLOOD

THE
BROKEN
ARM

Ghaston

Hellholt

Sandstone

BRIMSTONE

Saltshore

Lemonwood

Yellowyard

WHISPERING
SOUND

THE
ARBOR

R.G.

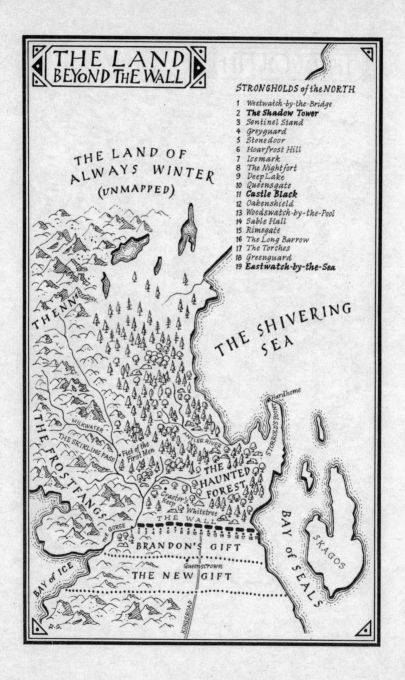

THE LAND BEYOND THE WALL

STRONGHOLDS of the NORTH

1 Westwatch-by-the-Bridge
2 **The Shadow Tower**
3 Sentinel Stand
4 Greyguard
5 Stonedoor
6 Hoarfrost Hill
7 Icemark
8 The Nightfort
9 Deep Lake
10 Queensgate
11 **Castle Black**
12 Oakenshield
13 Woodswatch-by-the-Pool
14 Sable Hall
15 Rimegate
16 The Long Barrow
17 The Torches
18 Greenguard
19 **Eastwatch-by-the-Sea**

THE LAND OF ALWAYS WINTER
(UNMAPPED)

THENN

THE SHIVERING SEA

MILKWATER

THE SKIRLING PASS

Fist of the First Men

ANTLER RIVER

Hardhome

STORROLD'S POINT

THE FROSTFANGS

THE HAUNTED FOREST

Craster's Keep

Whitetree

THE GORGE

THE WALL

1 2 3 4 5 6 7 8 9 10 11 12 13 14 15 16 17 18 19

BRANDON'S GIFT

BAY of SEALS

SKAGOS

BAY of ICE

Queenscrown

THE NEW GIFT

KINGSROAD

R.G.

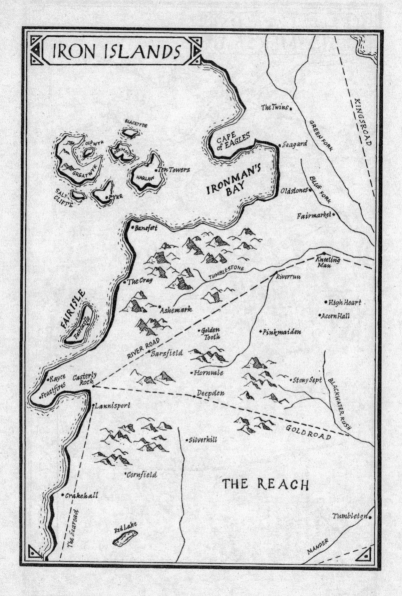

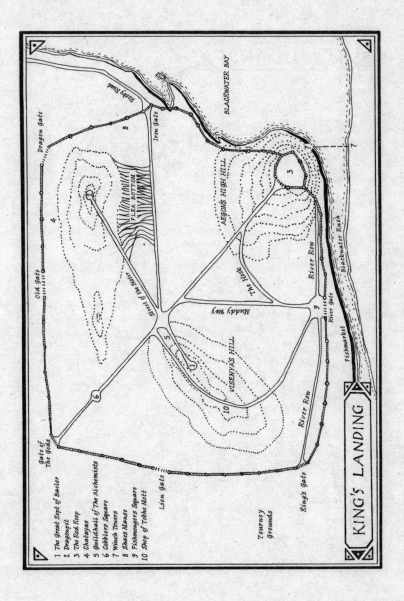

KING'S LANDING

1 The Great Sept of Baelor
2 Dragonpit
3 The Red Keep
4 Chataqyas
5 Guildhall of The Alchemists
6 Cobblers Square
7 Winch Towers
8 Shoes Manse
9 Fishmongers Square
10 Shop of Tobho Mott

DAENERYS

Her Dothraki scouts had told her how it was, but Dany wanted to see for herself. Ser Jorah Mormont rode with her through a birchwood forest and up a slanting sandstone ridge. "Near enough," he warned her at the crest.

Dany reined in her mare and looked across the fields, to where the Yunkish host lay athwart her path. Whitebeard had been teaching her how best to count the numbers of a foe. "Five thousand," she said after a moment.

"I'd say so." Ser Jorah pointed. "Those are sellswords on the flanks. Lances and mounted bowmen, with swords and axes for the close work. The Second Sons on the left wing, the Stormcrows to the right. About five hundred men apiece. See the banners?"

Yunkai's harpy grasped a whip and iron collar in her talons instead of a length of chain. But the sellswords flew their own standards beneath those of the city they served: on the right four crows between crossed thunderbolts, on the left a broken sword. "The Yunkai'i hold the center themselves," Dany noted. Their officers looked indistinguishable from Astapor's at a distance; tall bright helms and cloaks sewn with flashing copper disks. "Are those slave soldiers they lead?"

"In large part. But not the equal of Unsullied. Yunkai is known for training bed slaves, not warriors."

"What say you? Can we defeat this army?"

"Easily," Ser Jorah said.

"But not bloodlessly." Blood aplenty had soaked into the bricks of Astapor the day that city fell, though little of it belonged to her or hers. "We might win a battle here, but at such cost we cannot take the city."

"That is ever a risk, *Khaleesi*. Astapor was complacent and vulnerable. Yunkai is forewarned."

Dany considered. The slaver host seemed small compared to her own numbers, but the sellswords were ahorse. She'd ridden too long with Dothraki not to have a healthy respect for what mounted warriors could do to foot. *The Unsullied could withstand their charge, but my freedmen will be slaughtered.* "The slavers like to talk," she said. "Send word that I will hear them this evening in my tent. And invite the captains of the sellsword companies to call on me as well. But not together. The Stormcrows at midday, the Second Sons two hours later."

"As you wish," Ser Jorah said. "But if they do not come—"

"They'll come. They will be curious to see the dragons and hear what I might have to say, and the clever ones will see it for a chance to gauge my strength." She wheeled her silver mare about. "I'll await them in my pavilion."

Slate skies and brisk winds saw Dany back to her host. The deep ditch that would encircle her camp was already half dug, and the woods were full of Unsullied lopping branches off birch trees to sharpen into stakes. The eunuchs could not sleep in an unfortified camp, or so Grey Worm insisted. He was there watching the work. Dany halted a moment to speak with him. "Yunkai has girded up her loins for battle."

"This is good, Your Grace. These ones thirst for blood."

When she had commanded the Unsullied to choose officers from amongst themselves, Grey Worm had been their overwhelming choice for the highest rank. Dany had put Ser Jorah over him to train him for command, and the exile knight said that so far the young eunuch was hard but fair, quick to learn, tireless, and utterly unrelenting in his attention to detail.

"The Wise Masters have assembled a slave army to meet us."

"A slave in Yunkai learns the way of seven sighs and the sixteen seats of pleasure, Your Grace. The Unsullied learn the way of the three spears. Your Grey Worm hopes to show you."

One of the first things Dany had done after the fall of Astapor was abolish the custom of giving the Unsullied new slave names every day. Most of those born free had returned to their birth names; those who still remembered them, at least. Others had called themselves after heroes or gods, and sometimes weapons, gems, and even flowers, which resulted in soldiers with some very peculiar names, to Dany's ears. Grey Worm had remained Grey Worm. When she asked him why, he said, "It is a lucky name. The name this one was born to was accursed. That was the name he had when he was taken for a slave. But Grey Worm is the name this one drew the day Daenerys Stormborn set him free."

"If battle is joined, let Grey Worm show wisdom as well as valor," Dany told him. "Spare any slave who runs or throws down his weapon. The fewer slain, the more remain to join us after."

"This one will remember."

"I know he will. Be at my tent by midday. I want you there with my other officers when I treat with the sellsword captains." Dany spurred her silver on to camp.

Within the perimeter the Unsullied had established, the tents were going up in orderly rows, with her own tall golden pavilion at the center. A second encampment lay close beyond her own; five times the size, sprawling and chaotic, this second camp had no ditches, no tents, no sentries, no horselines. Those who had horses or mules slept beside them, for fear they might be stolen. Goats, sheep, and half-starved dogs wandered freely amongst hordes of women, children, and old men. Dany had left Astapor in the hands of a council of former slaves led by a healer, a scholar, and a priest. Wise men all, she thought, and just. Yet even so, tens of thousands preferred to follow her to Yunkai, rather than remain behind in Astapor. *I gave them the city, and most of them were too frightened to take it.*

The raggle-taggle host of freedmen dwarfed her own, but they were more burden than benefit. Perhaps one in a hundred had a donkey, a camel, or an ox; most carried weapons looted from some slaver's armory, but only one in ten was strong enough to fight, and none was trained. They ate the land bare as they passed, like locusts in sandals. Yet Dany could not bring herself to abandon them as Ser Jorah and her bloodriders urged. *I told them they were free. I cannot tell them now they are not free to join me.* She gazed at the smoke rising from their cookfires and swallowed a sigh. She might have the best footsoldiers in the world, but she also had the worst.

Arstan Whitebeard stood outside the entrance of her tent, while Strong Belwas sat crosslegged on the grass nearby, eating a bowl of figs. On the march, the duty of guarding her fell upon their shoulders. She had made Jhogo, Aggo, and Rakharo her *ko*s as well as her bloodriders, and just now she needed them more to command her Dothraki than to protect her person. Her *khalasar* was tiny, some thirty-odd mounted warriors, and most of them braidless boys and bentback old men. Yet they were all the horse she had, and she dared not go without them. The Unsullied might be the finest infantry in all the world, as Ser Jorah claimed, but she needed scouts and outriders as well.

"Yunkai will have war," Dany told Whitebeard inside the pavilion. Irri and Jhiqui had covered the floor with carpets while Missandei lit a stick of incense to sweeten the dusty air. Drogon and Rhaegal were asleep atop some cushions, curled about each other, but Viserion perched on the edge of her empty bath. "Missandei, what language will these Yunkai'i speak, Valyrian?"

"Yes, Your Grace," the child said. "A different dialect than Astapor's, yet close enough to understand. The slavers name themselves the Wise Masters."

"Wise?" Dany sat crosslegged on a cushion, and Viserion spread his white-and-gold wings and flapped to her side. "We shall see how wise they are," she said as she scratched the dragon's scaly head behind the horns.

Ser Jorah Mormont returned an hour later, accompanied by three captains of the Stormcrows. They wore black feathers on their polished helms, and claimed to be all equal in honor and authority. Dany studied them as Irri and Jhiqui poured the wine. Prendahl na Ghezn was a thickset Ghiscari with a broad face and dark hair going grey; Sallor the Bald had a twisting scar across his pale Qartheen cheek; and Daario Naharis was flamboyant even for a Tyroshi. His beard was cut into three prongs and dyed blue, the same color as his eyes and the curly hair that fell to his collar. His pointed mustachios were painted gold. His clothes were all shades of yellow; a foam of Myrish lace the color of butter spilled from his collar and cuffs, his doublet was sewn with brass medallions in the shape of dandelions, and ornamental goldwork crawled up his high leather boots to his thighs. Gloves of soft yellow suede were tucked into a belt of gilded rings, and his fingernails were enameled blue.

But it was Prendahl na Ghezn who spoke for the sellswords. "You would do well to take your rabble elsewhere," he said. "You took Astapor by treachery, but Yunkai shall not fall so easily."

"Five hundred of your Stormcrows against ten thousand of my Unsullied," said Dany. "I am only a young girl and do not understand the ways of war, yet these odds seem poor to me."

"The Stormcrows do not stand alone," said Prendahl.

"Stormcrows do not stand at all. They fly, at the first sign of thunder. Perhaps you should be flying now. I have heard that sellswords are notoriously unfaithful. What will it avail you to be staunch, when the Second Sons change sides?"

"That will not happen," Prendahl insisted, unmoved. "And if it did, it would not matter. The Second Sons are nothing. We fight beside the stalwart men of Yunkai."

"You fight beside bed-boys armed with spears." When she turned her head, the twin bells in her braid rang softly. "Once battle is joined, do not think to ask for quarter. Join me now, however, and you shall keep the gold the Yunkai'i paid you and claim a share of the plunder besides, with greater rewards later when I come into my kingdom. Fight for the Wise Masters, and your wages will be death. Do you imagine that Yunkai will open its gates when my Unsullied are butchering you beneath the walls?"

"Woman, you bray like an ass, and make no more sense."

"*Woman?*" She chuckled. "Is that meant to insult me? I would return the slap, if I took you for a man." Dany met his stare. "I am

Daenerys Stormborn of House Targaryen, the Unburnt, Mother of Dragons, *khaleesi* to Drogo's riders, and queen of the Seven Kingdoms of Westeros."

"What you are," said Prendahl na Ghezn, "is a horselord's whore. When we break you, I will breed you to my stallion."

Strong Belwas drew his *arakh*. "Strong Belwas will give his ugly tongue to the little queen, if she likes."

"No, Belwas. I have given these men my safe conduct." She smiled. "Tell me this—are the Stormcrows slave or free?"

"We are a brotherhood of free men," Sallor declared.

"Good." Dany stood. "Go back and tell your brothers what I said, then. It may be that some of them would sooner sup on gold and glory than on death. I shall want your answer on the morrow."

The Stormcrow captains rose in unison. "Our answer is no," said Prendahl na Ghezn. His fellows followed him out of the tent . . . but Daario Naharis glanced back as he left, and inclined his head in polite farewell.

Two hours later the commander of the Second Sons arrived alone. He proved to be a towering Braavosi with pale green eyes and a bushy red-gold beard that reached nearly to his belt. His name was Mero, but he called himself the Titan's Bastard.

Mero tossed down his wine straightaway, wiped his mouth with the back of his hand, and leered at Dany. "I believe I fucked your twin sister in a pleasure house back home. Or was it you?"

"I think not. I would remember a man of such magnificence, I have no doubt."

"Yes, that is so. No woman has ever forgotten the Titan's Bastard." The Braavosi held out his cup to Jhiqui. "What say you take those clothes off and come sit on my lap? If you please me, I might bring the Second Sons over to your side."

"If you bring the Second Sons over to my side, I might not have you gelded."

The big man laughed. "Little girl, another woman once tried to geld me with her teeth. She has no teeth now, but my sword is as long and thick as ever. Shall I take it out and show you?"

"No need. After my eunuchs cut it off, I can examine it at my leisure." Dany took a sip of wine. "It is true that I am only a young girl, and do not know the ways of war. Explain to me how you propose to defeat ten thousand Unsullied with your five hundred. Innocent as I am, these odds seem poor to me."

"The Second Sons have faced worse odds and won."

"The Second Sons have faced worse odds and run. At Qohor, when the Three Thousand made their stand. Or do you deny it?"

"That was many and more years ago, before the Second Sons were led by the Titan's Bastard."

"So it is from you they get their courage?" Dany turned to Ser Jorah. "When the battle is joined, kill this one first."

The exile knight smiled. "Gladly, Your Grace."

"Of course," she said to Mero, "you could run again. We will not stop you. Take your Yunkish gold and go."

"Had you ever seen the Titan of Braavos, foolish girl, you would know that it has no tail to turn."

"Then stay, and fight for me."

"You are worth fighting for, it is true," the Braavosi said, "and I would gladly let you kiss my sword, if I were free. But I have taken Yunkai's coin and pledged my holy word."

"Coins can be returned," she said. "I will pay you as much and more. I have other cities to conquer, and a whole kingdom awaiting me half a world away. Serve me faithfully, and the Second Sons need never seek hire again."

The Braavosi tugged on his thick red beard. "As much and more, and perhaps a kiss besides, eh? Or more than a kiss? For a man as magnificent as me?"

"Perhaps."

"I will like the taste of your tongue, I think."

She could sense Ser Jorah's anger. *My black bear does not like this talk of kissing.* "Think on what I've said tonight. Can I have your answer on the morrow?"

"You can." The Titan's Bastard grinned. "Can I have a flagon of this fine wine to take back to my captains?"

"You may have a tun. It is from the cellars of the Good Masters of Astapor, and I have wagons full of it."

"Then give me a wagon. A token of your good regard."

"You have a big thirst."

"I am big all over. And I have many brothers. The Titan's Bastard does not drink alone, *Khaleesi*."

"A wagon it is, if you promise to drink to my health."

"Done!" he boomed. "And done, and done! Three toasts we'll drink you, and bring you an answer when the sun comes up."

But when Mero was gone, Arstan Whitebeard said, "That one has an evil reputation, even in Westeros. Do not be misled by his manner, Your Grace. He will drink three toasts to your health tonight, and rape you on the morrow."

"The old man's right for once," Ser Jorah said. "The Second Sons are an old company, and not without valor, but under Mero they've turned near as bad as the Brave Companions. The man is as dangerous to his employers as to his foes. That's why you find him out here. None of the Free Cities will hire him any longer."

"It is not his reputation that I want, it's his five hundred horse. What of the Stormcrows, is there any hope there?"

"No," Ser Jorah said bluntly. "That Prendahl is Ghiscari by blood. Likely he had kin in Astapor."

"A pity. Well, perhaps we will not need to fight. Let us wait and hear what the Yunkai'i have to say."

The envoys from Yunkai arrived as the sun was going down; fifty men on magnificent black horses and one on a great white camel. Their helms were twice as tall as their heads, so as not to crush the bizarre twists and towers and shapes of their oiled hair beneath. They dyed their linen skirts and tunics a deep yellow, and sewed copper disks to their cloaks.

The man on the white camel named himself Grazdan mo Eraz. Lean and hard, he had a white smile such as Kraznys had worn until Drogon burned off his face. His hair was drawn up in a unicorn's horn that jutted from his brow, and his *tokar* was fringed with golden Myrish lace. "Ancient and glorious is Yunkai, the queen of cities," he said when Dany welcomed him to her tent. "Our walls are strong, our nobles proud and fierce, our common folk without fear. Ours is the blood of ancient Ghis, whose empire was old when Valyria was yet a squalling child. You were wise to sit and speak, *Khaleesi*. You shall find no easy conquest here."

"Good. My Unsullied will relish a bit of a fight." She looked to Grey Worm, who nodded.

Grazdan shrugged expansively. "If blood is what you wish, let it flow. I am told you have freed your eunuchs. Freedom means as much to an Unsullied as a hat to a haddock." He smiled at Grey Worm, but the eunuch might have been made of stone. "Those who survive we shall enslave again, and use to retake Astapor from the rabble. We can make a slave of you as well, do not doubt it. There are pleasure houses in Lys and Tyrosh where men would pay handsomely to bed the last Targaryen."

"It is good to see you know who I am," said Dany mildly.

"I pride myself on my knowledge of the savage senseless west." Grazdan spread his hands, a gesture of conciliation. "And yet, why should we speak thus harshly to one another? It is true that you committed savageries in Astapor, but we Yunkai'i are a most forgiving people. Your quarrel is not with us, Your Grace. Why squander your strength against our mighty walls when you will need every man to regain your father's throne in far Westeros? Yunkai wishes you only well in that endeavor. And to prove the truth of that, I have brought you a gift." He clapped his hands, and two of his escort came forward bearing a heavy cedar chest bound in bronze and gold. They set it at her feet. "Fifty thousand golden marks," Grazdan said smoothly. "Yours, as a gesture of friendship from the Wise Masters of Yunkai. Gold given freely is better than plunder bought with blood, surely? So I say to you, Daenerys Targaryen, take this chest, and go."

Dany pushed open the lid of the chest with a small slippered foot. It was full of gold coins, just as the envoy said. She grabbed a handful and let them run through her fingers. They shone brightly as they tumbled and fell; new minted, most of them, stamped with a stepped pyramid on one face and the harpy of Ghis on the other. "Very pretty. I wonder how many chests like this I shall find when I take your city?"

He chuckled. "None, for that you shall never do."

"I have a gift for you as well." She slammed the chest shut. "Three days. On the morning of the third day, send out your slaves. All of them. Every man, woman, and child shall be given a weapon, and as much food, clothing, coin, and goods as he or she can carry. These they shall be allowed to choose freely from among their masters' possessions, as payment for their years of servitude. When all the slaves have departed, you will open your gates and allow my Unsullied to enter and search your city, to make certain none remain in bondage. If you do this, Yunkai will not be burned or plundered, and none of your people shall be molested. The Wise Masters will have the peace they desire, and will have proved themselves wise indeed. What say you?"

"I say, you are mad."

"Am I?" Dany shrugged, and said, "*Dracarys.*"

The dragons answered. Rhaegal *hiss*ed and smoked, Viserion snapped, and Drogon spat swirling red-black flame. It touched the drape of Grazdan's *tokar*, and the silk caught in half a heartbeat. Golden marks spilled across the carpets as the envoy stumbled over the chest, shouting curses and beating at his arm until Whitebeard flung a flagon of water over him to douse the flames. "You swore I should have safe conduct!" the Yunkish envoy wailed.

"Do all the Yunkai'i whine so over a singed *tokar*? I shall buy you a new one . . . if you deliver up your slaves within three days. Elsewise, Drogon shall give you a warmer kiss." She wrinkled her nose. "You've soiled yourself. Take your gold and go, and see that the Wise Masters hear my message."

Grazdan mo Eraz pointed a finger. "You shall rue this arrogance, whore. These little lizards will not keep you safe, I promise you. We will fill the air with arrows if they come within a league of Yunkai. Do you think it is so hard to kill a dragon?"

"Harder than to kill a slaver. Three days, Grazdan. Tell them. By the end of the third day, I will be in Yunkai, whether you open your gates for me or no."

Full dark had fallen by the time the Yunkai'i departed from her camp. It promised to be a gloomy night; moonless, starless, with a chill wet wind blowing from the west. *A fine black night*, thought Dany. The fires burned all around her, small orange stars strewn across hill and field. "Ser Jorah," she said, "summon my bloodriders." Dany seated herself on a mound of cushions to await them, her dragons all about her. When they were assembled, she said, "An hour past midnight should be time enough."

"Yes, *Khaleesi*," said Rakharo. "Time for what?"

"To mount our attack."

Ser Jorah Mormont scowled. "You told the sellswords—"

"—that I wanted their answers on the morrow. I made no promises about tonight. The Stormcrows will be arguing about my offer. The Second Sons will be drunk on the wine I gave Mero. And the Yunkai'i believe they have three days. We will take them under cover of this darkness."

"They will have scouts watching for us."

"And in the dark, they will see hundreds of campfires burning," said Dany. "If they see anything at all."

"*Khaleesi*," said Jhogo, "I will deal with these scouts. They are no riders, only slavers on horses."

"Just so," she agreed. "I think we should attack from three sides. Grey Worm, your Unsullied shall strike at them from right and left, while my *kos* lead my horse in wedge for a thrust through their center. Slave soldiers will never stand before mounted Dothraki." She smiled. "To be sure, I am only a young girl and know little of war. What do you think, my lords?"

"I think you are Rhaegar Targaryen's sister," Ser Jorah said with a rueful half smile.

"Aye," said Arstan Whitebeard, "and a queen as well."

It took an hour to work out all the details. *Now begins the most dangerous time*, Dany thought as her captains departed to their commands. She could only pray that the gloom of the night would hide her preparations from the foe.

Near midnight, she got a scare when Ser Jorah bulled his way past Strong Belwas. "The Unsullied caught one of the sellswords trying to sneak into the camp."

"A spy?" That frightened her. If they'd caught one, how many others might have gotten away?

"He claims to come bearing gifts. It's the yellow fool with the blue hair."

Daario Naharis. "That one. I'll hear him, then."

When the exile knight delivered him, she asked herself whether two men had ever been so different. The Tyroshi was fair where Ser Jorah was swarthy; lithe where the knight was brawny; graced with flowing locks where the other was balding, yet smooth-skinned where Mormont was hairy. And her knight dressed plainly while this other made a peacock look drab, though he had thrown a heavy black cloak over his bright yellow finery for this visit. He carried a heavy canvas sack slung over one shoulder.

"*Khaleesi*," he cried, "I bring gifts and glad tidings. The Stormcrows are yours." A golden tooth gleamed in his mouth when he smiled. "And so is Daario Naharis!"

Dany was dubious. If this Tyroshi had come to spy, this declaration might be no more than a desperate plot to save his head. "What do Prendahl na Ghezn and Sallor say of this?"

"Little." Daario upended the sack, and the heads of Sallor the Bald and Prendahl na Ghezn spilled out upon her carpets. "My gifts to the dragon queen."

Viserion sniffed the blood leaking from Prendahl's neck, and let loose a gout of flame that took the dead man full in the face, blackening and blistering his bloodless cheeks. Drogon and Rhaegal stirred at the smell of roasted meat.

"You did this?" Dany asked queasily.

"None other." If her dragons discomfited Daario Naharis, he hid it well. For all the mind he paid them, they might have been three kittens playing with a mouse.

"Why?"

"Because you are so beautiful." His hands were large and strong, and there was something in his hard blue eyes and great curving nose that suggested the fierceness of some splendid bird of prey. "Prendahl talked too much and said too little." His garb, rich as it was, had seen hard wear; salt stains patterned his boots, the enamel of his nails was chipped, his lace was soiled by sweat, and she could see where the end of his cloak was fraying. "And Sallor picked his nose as if his snot was gold." He stood with his hands crossed at the wrists, his palms resting on the pommels of his blades; a curving Dothraki *arakh* on his left hip, a Myrish stiletto on his right. Their hilts were a matched pair of golden women, naked and wanton.

"Are you skilled in the use of those handsome blades?" Dany asked him.

"Prendahl and Sallor would tell you so, if dead men could talk. I count no day as lived unless I have loved a woman, slain a foeman, and eaten a fine meal . . . and the days that I have lived are as numberless as the stars in the sky. I make of slaughter a thing of beauty, and many a tumbler and fire dancer has wept to the gods that they might be half so quick, a quarter so graceful. I would tell you the names of all the men I have slain, but before I could finish your dragons would grow large as castles, the walls of Yunkai would crumble into yellow dust, and winter would come and go and come again."

Dany laughed. She liked the swagger she saw in this Daario Naharis. "Draw your sword and swear it to my service."

In a blink, Daario's *arakh* was free of its sheath. His submission was as outrageous as the rest of him, a great swoop that brought his face down to her toes. "My sword is yours. My life is yours. My love is yours. My blood, my body, my songs, you own them all. I live and die at your command, fair queen."

"Then live," Dany said, "and fight for me tonight."

"That would not be wise, my queen." Ser Jorah gave Daario a cold, hard stare. "Keep this one here under guard until the battle's fought and won."

She considered a moment, then shook her head. "If he can give us the Stormcrows, surprise is certain."

"And if he betrays you, surprise is lost."

Dany looked down at the sellsword again. He gave her such a smile that she flushed and turned away. "He won't."

"How can you know that?"

She pointed to the lumps of blackened flesh the dragons were consuming, bite by bloody bite. "I would call that proof of his sincerity. Daario Naharis, have your Stormcrows ready to strike the Yunkish rear when my attack begins. Can you get back safely?"

"If they stop me, I will say I have been scouting, and saw nothing." The Tyroshi rose to his feet, bowed, and swept out.

Ser Jorah Mormont lingered. "Your Grace," he said, too bluntly, "that was a mistake. We know nothing of this man—"

"We know that he is a great fighter."

"A great talker, you mean."

"He brings us the Stormcrows." *And he has blue eyes.*

"Five hundred sellswords of uncertain loyalty."

"All loyalties are uncertain in such times as these," Dany reminded him. *And I shall be betrayed twice more, once for gold and once for love.*

"Daenerys, I am thrice your age," Ser Jorah said. "I have seen how false men are. Very few are worthy of trust, and Daario Naharis is not one of them. Even his beard wears false colors."

That angered her. "Whilst you have an honest beard, is that what you are telling me? You are the only man I should ever trust?"

He stiffened. "I did not say that."

"You say it every day. Pyat Pree's a liar, Xaro's a schemer, Belwas a braggart, Arstan an assassin ... do you think I'm still some virgin girl, that I cannot hear the words behind the words?"

"Your Grace—"

She bulled over him. "You have been a better friend to me than any I have known, a better brother than Viserys ever was. You are the first of my Queensguard, the commander of my army, my most valued counselor, my good right hand. I honor and respect and cherish you—but I do not desire you, Jorah Mormont, and I am weary of your trying to push every other man in the world away from me, so I must needs rely on you and you alone. It will not serve, and it will not make me love you any better."

Mormont had flushed red when she first began, but by the time Dany was done his face was pale again. He stood still as stone. "If my queen commands," he said, curt and cold.

Dany was warm enough for both of them. "She does," she said. "She *commands*. Now go see to your Unsullied, ser. You have a battle to fight and win."

When he was gone, Dany threw herself down on her pillows beside her dragons. She had not meant to be so sharp with Ser Jorah, but his endless suspicion had finally woken her dragon.

He will forgive me, she told herself. *I am his liege.* Dany found herself wondering whether he was right about Daario. She felt very lonely all of a sudden. Mirri Maz Duur had promised that she would never bear a living child. *House Targaryen will end with me.* That made her sad. "You must be my children," she told the dragons, "my three fierce children. Arstan says dragons live longer than men, so you will go on after I am dead."

Drogon looped his neck around to nip at her hand. His teeth were very sharp, but he never broke her skin when they played like this. Dany laughed, and rolled him back and forth until he roared, his tail lashing like a whip. *It is longer than it was,* she saw, *and tomorrow it will be longer still. They grow quickly now, and when they are grown I shall have my wings.* Mounted on a dragon, she could lead her own men into battle, as she had in Astapor, but as yet they were still too small to bear her weight.

A stillness settled over her camp when midnight came and went. Dany remained in her pavilion with her maids, while Arstan Whitebeard and Strong Belwas kept the guard. *The waiting is the hardest part.* To sit in her tent with idle hands while her battle was being fought without her made Dany feel half a child again.

The hours crept by on turtle feet. Even after Jhiqui rubbed the knots from her shoulders, Dany was too restless for sleep. Missandei offered to sing her a lullaby of the Peaceful People, but Dany shook her head. "Bring me Arstan," she said.

When the old man came, she was curled up inside her *hrakkar* pelt, whose musty smell still reminded her of Drogo. "I cannot sleep when men are dying for me, Whitebeard," she said. "Tell me more of my brother Rhaegar, if you would. I liked the tale you told me on the ship, of how he decided that he must be a warrior."

"Your Grace is kind to say so."

"Viserys said that our brother won many tourneys."

Arstan bowed his white head respectfully. "It is not meet for me to deny His Grace's words . . ."

"But?" said Dany sharply. "Tell me. I command it."

"Prince Rhaegar's prowess was unquestioned, but he seldom entered the lists. He never loved the song of swords the way that

Robert did, or Jaime Lannister. It was something he had to do, a task the world had set him. He did it well, for he did everything well. That was his nature. But he took no joy in it. Men said that he loved his harp much better than his lance."

"He won *some* tourneys, surely," said Dany, disappointed.

"When he was young, His Grace rode brilliantly in a tourney at Storm's End, defeating Lord Steffon Baratheon, Lord Jason Mallister, the Red Viper of Dorne, and a mystery knight who proved to be the infamous Simon Toyne, chief of the kingswood outlaws. He broke twelve lances against Ser Arthur Dayne that day."

"Was he the champion, then?"

"No, Your Grace. That honor went to another knight of the Kingsguard, who unhorsed Prince Rhaegar in the final tilt."

Dany did not want to hear about Rhaegar being unhorsed. "But what tourneys did my brother *win*?"

"Your Grace." The old man hesitated. "He won the greatest tourney of them all."

"Which was that?" Dany demanded.

"The tourney Lord Whent staged at Harrenhal beside the Gods Eye, in the year of the false spring. A notable event. Besides the jousting, there was a mêlée in the old style fought between seven teams of knights, as well as archery and axe-throwing, a horse race, a tournament of singers, a mummer show, and many feasts and frolics. Lord Whent was as open handed as he was rich. The lavish purses he proclaimed drew hundreds of challengers. Even your royal father came to Harrenhal, when he had not left the Red Keep for long years. The greatest lords and mightiest champions of the Seven Kingdoms rode in that tourney, and the Prince of Dragonstone bested them all."

"But that was the tourney when he crowned Lyanna Stark as queen of love and beauty!" said Dany. "Princess Elia was there, his wife, and yet my brother gave the crown to the Stark girl, and later stole her away from her betrothed. How could he do that? Did the Dornish woman treat him so ill?"

"It is not for such as me to say what might have been in your brother's heart, Your Grace. The Princess Elia was a good and gracious lady, though her health was ever delicate."

Dany pulled the lion pelt tighter about her shoulders. "Viserys said once that it was my fault, for being born too late." She had denied it hotly, she remembered, going so far as to tell Viserys that it was his fault for not being born a girl. He beat her cruelly for that insolence. "If I had been born more timely, he said, Rhaegar would have married me instead of Elia, and it would all have come out different. If Rhaegar had been happy in his wife, he would not have needed the Stark girl."

"Perhaps so, Your Grace." Whitebeard paused a moment. "But I am not certain it was in Rhaegar to be happy."

"You make him sound so sour," Dany protested.

"Not sour, no, but . . . there was a melancholy to Prince Rhaegar, a sense . . ." The old man hesitated again.

"Say it," she urged. "A sense . . .?"

". . . of doom. He was born in grief, my queen, and that shadow hung over him all his days."

Viserys had spoken of Rhaegar's birth only once. Perhaps the tale saddened him too much. "It was the shadow of Summerhall that haunted him, was it not?"

"Yes. And yet Summerhall was the place the prince loved best. He would go there from time to time, with only his harp for company. Even the knights of the Kingsguard did not attend him there. He liked to sleep in the ruined hall, beneath the moon and stars, and whenever he came back he would bring a song. When you heard him play his high harp with the silver strings and sing of twilights and tears and the death of kings, you could not but feel that he was singing of himself and those he loved."

"What of the Usurper? Did he play sad songs as well?"

Arstan chuckled. "Robert? Robert liked songs that made him laugh, the bawdier the better. He only sang when he was drunk, and then it was like to be 'A Cask of Ale' or 'Fifty-Four Tuns' or 'The Bear and the Maiden Fair.' Robert was much—"

As one, her dragons lifted their heads and roared.

"Horses!" Dany leapt to her feet, clutching the lion pelt. Outside, she heard Strong Belwas bellow something, and then other voices, and the sounds of many horses. "Irri, go see who . . ."

The tent flap pushed open, and Ser Jorah Mormont entered. He was dusty, and spattered with blood, but otherwise none the worse for battle. The exile knight went to one knee before Dany and said, "Your Grace, I bring you victory. The Stormcrows turned their cloaks, the slaves broke, and the Second Sons were too drunk to fight, just as you said. Two hundred dead, Yunkai'i for the most part. Their slaves threw down their spears and ran, and their sellswords yielded. We have several thousand captives."

"Our own losses?"

"A dozen. If that many."

Only then did she allow herself to smile. "Rise, my good brave bear. Was Grazdan taken? Or the Titan's Bastard?"

"Grazdan went to Yunkai to deliver your terms." Ser Jorah got to his feet. "Mero fled, once he realized the Stormcrows had turned. I have men hunting him. He shouldn't escape us long."

"Very well," Dany said. "Sellsword or slave, spare all those who will pledge me their faith. If enough of the Second Sons will join us, keep the company intact."

The next day, they marched the last three leagues to Yunkai. The city was built of yellow bricks instead of red; elsewise it was Astapor all over again, with the same crumbling walls and high stepped pyramids, and a great harpy mounted above its gates. The wall and towers swarmed with crossbowmen and slingers. Ser Jorah and Grey Worm deployed her men, Irri and Jhiqui raised her pavilion, and Dany sat down to wait.

On the morning of the third day, the city gates swung open and a line of slaves began to emerge. Dany mounted her silver to greet them. As they passed, little Missandei told them that they owed their freedom to Daenerys Stormborn, the Unburnt, Queen of the Seven Kingdoms of Westeros and Mother of Dragons.

"*Mhysa!*" a brown-skinned man shouted out at her. He had a child on his shoulder, a little girl, and she screamed the same word in her thin voice. "*Mhysa! Mhysa!*"

Dany looked at Missandei. "What are they shouting?"

"It is Ghiscari, the old pure tongue. It means 'Mother.' "

Dany felt a lightness in her chest. *I will never bear a living child,* she remembered. Her hand trembled as she raised it. Perhaps she smiled. She must have, because the man grinned and shouted again, and others took up the cry. "*Mhysa!*" they called. "*Mhysa! MHYSA!*" They were all smiling at her, reaching for her, kneeling before her. "*Maela*," some called her, while others cried, "*Aelalla*" or "*Qathei*" or "*Tato*," but whatever the tongue it all meant the same thing. *Mother. They are calling me Mother.*

The chant grew, spread, swelled. It swelled so loud that it frightened her horse, and the mare backed and shook her head and lashed her silvergrey tail. It swelled until it seemed to shake the yellow walls of Yunkai. More slaves were streaming from the gates every moment, and as they came they took up the call. They were running toward her now, pushing, stumbling, wanting to touch her hand, to stroke her horse's mane, to kiss her feet. Her poor bloodriders could not keep them all away, and even Strong Belwas grunted and growled in dismay.

Ser Jorah urged her to go, but Dany remembered a dream she had dreamed in the House of the Undying. "They will not hurt me," she told him. "They are my children, Jorah." She laughed, put her heels into her horse, and rode to them, the bells in her hair ringing sweet victory. She trotted, then cantered, then broke into a gallop, her braid streaming behind. The freed slaves parted before her. "Mother," they called from a hundred throats, a thousand, ten thousand. "Mother," they sang, their fingers brushing her legs as she flew by. "Mother, Mother, Mother!"

ARYA

When Arya saw the shape of a great hill looming in the distance, golden in the afternoon sun, she knew it at once. They had come all the way back to High Heart.

By sunset they were at the top, making camp where no harm could come to them. Arya walked around the circle of weirwood stumps with Lord Beric's squire Ned, and they stood on top of one watching the last light fade in the west. From up here she could see a storm raging to the north, but High Heart stood *above* the rain. It wasn't above the wind, though; the gusts were blowing so strongly that it felt like someone was behind her, yanking on her cloak. Only when she turned, no one was there.

Ghosts, she remembered. *High Heart is haunted.*

They built a great fire atop the hill, and Thoros of Myr sat cross-legged beside it, gazing deep into the flames as if there was nothing else in all the world.

"What is he doing?" Arya asked Ned.

"Sometimes he sees things in the flames," the squire told her. "The past. The future. Things happening far away."

Arya squinted at the fire to see if she could see what the red priest was seeing, but it only made her eyes water and before long she turned away. Gendry was watching the red priest as well. "Can you truly see the future there?" he asked suddenly.

Thoros turned from the fire, sighing. "Not here. Not now. But some days, yes, the Lord of Light grants me visions."

Gendry looked dubious. "My master said you were a sot and a fraud, as bad a priest as there ever was."

"That was unkind." Thoros chuckled. "True, but unkind. Who was this master of yours? Did I know you, boy?"

"I was 'prenticed to the master armorer Tobho Mott, on the Street of Steel. You used to buy your swords from him."

"Just so. He charged me twice what they were worth, then scolded me for setting them afire." Thoros laughed. "Your master had it right. I was no very holy priest. I was born youngest of eight, so my father gave me over to the Red Temple, but it was not the path I would have chosen. I prayed the prayers and I spoke the spells, but I would also lead raids on the kitchens, and from time to time they found girls in my bed. Such wicked girls, I never knew how they got there.

"I had a gift for tongues, though. And when I gazed into the flames, well, from time to time I saw things. Even so, I was more bother than I was worth, so they sent me finally to King's Landing to bring the Lord's light to seven-besotted Westeros. King Aerys so loved fire it was thought he might make a convert. Alas, his pyromancers knew better tricks than I did.

"King Robert was fond of me, though. The first time I rode into a mêlée with a flaming sword, Kevan Lannister's horse reared and threw him and His Grace laughed so hard I thought he might rupture." The red priest smiled at the memory. "It was no way to treat a blade, though, your master had the right of that too."

"Fire consumes." Lord Beric stood behind them, and there was something in his voice that silenced Thoros at once. "It *consumes*, and when it is done there is nothing left. *Nothing*."

"Beric. Sweet friend." The priest touched the lightning lord on the forearm. "What are you saying?"

"Nothing I have not said before. Six times, Thoros? Six times is too many." He turned away abruptly.

That night the wind was howling almost like a wolf and there were some real wolves off to the west giving it lessons. Notch, Anguy, and Merrit o' Moontown had the watch. Ned, Gendry, and many of the others were fast asleep when Arya spied the small pale shape creeping behind the horses, thin white hair flying wild as she leaned upon a gnarled cane. The woman could not have been more than three feet tall. The firelight made her eyes gleam as red as the eyes of Jon's wolf. *He was a ghost too.* Arya stole closer, and knelt to watch.

Thoros and Lem were with Lord Beric when the dwarf woman sat down uninvited by the fire. She squinted at them with eyes like hot coals. "The Ember and the Lemon come to honor me again, and His Grace the Lord of Corpses."

"An ill-omened name. I have asked you not to use it."

"Aye, you have. But the stink of death is fresh on you, my lord." She had but a single tooth remaining. "Give me wine or I will go. My bones are old. My joints ache when the winds do blow, and up here the winds are always blowing."

"A silver stag for your dreams, my lady," Lord Beric said, with solemn courtesy. "Another if you have news for us."

"I cannot eat a silver stag, nor ride one. A skin of wine for my dreams, and for my news a kiss from the great oaf in the yellow cloak." The little woman cackled. "Aye, a sloppy kiss, a bit of tongue. It has been too long, too long. His mouth will taste of lemons, and mine of bones. I am too old."

"Aye," Lem complained. "Too old for wine and kisses. All you'll get from me is the flat of my sword, crone."

"My hair comes out in handfuls and no one has kissed me for a thousand years. It is hard to be so old. Well, I will have a song then. A song from Tom o' Sevens, for my news."

"You will have your song from Tom," Lord Beric promised. He gave her the wineskin himself.

The dwarf woman drank deep, the wine running down her chin. When she lowered the skin, she wiped her mouth with the back of a wrinkled hand and said, "Sour wine for sour tidings, what could be more fitting? The king is dead, is that sour enough for you?"

Arya's heart caught in her throat.

"*Which* bloody king is dead, crone?" Lem demanded.

"The wet one. The kraken king, m'lords. I dreamt him dead and he died, and the iron squids now turn on one another. Oh, and Lord

Hoster Tully's died too, but you know that, don't you? In the hall of kings, the goat sits alone and fevered as the great dog descends on him." The old woman took another long gulp of wine, squeezing the skin as she raised it to her lips.

The great dog. Did she mean the Hound? Or maybe his brother, the Mountain That Rides? Arya was not certain. They bore the same arms, three black dogs on a yellow field. Half the men whose deaths she prayed for belonged to Ser Gregor Clegane; Polliver, Dunsen, Raff the Sweetling, the Tickler, and Ser Gregor himself. *Maybe Lord Beric will hang them all.*

"I dreamt a wolf howling in the rain, but no one heard his grief," the dwarf woman was saying. "I dreamt such a clangor I thought my head might burst, drums and horns and pipes and screams, but the saddest sound was the little bells. I dreamt of a maid at a feast with purple serpents in her hair, venom dripping from their fangs. And later I dreamt that maid again, slaying a savage giant in a castle built of snow." She turned her head sharply and smiled through the gloom, right at Arya. "You cannot hide from me, child. Come closer, now."

Cold fingers walked down Arya's neck. *Fear cuts deeper than swords,* she reminded herself. She stood and approached the fire warily, light on the balls of her feet, poised to flee.

The dwarf woman studied her with dim red eyes. "I see you," she whispered. "I see you, wolf child. Blood child. I thought it was the lord who smelled of death ..." She began to sob, her little body shaking. "You are cruel to come to my hill, cruel. I gorged on grief at Summerhall, I need none of yours. Begone from here, dark heart. *Begone!*"

There was such fear in her voice that Arya took a step backward, wondering if the woman was mad. "Don't frighten the child," Thoros protested. "There's no harm in her."

Lem Lemoncloak's finger went to his broken nose. "Don't be so bloody sure of that."

"She will leave on the morrow, with us," Lord Beric assured the little woman. "We're taking her to Riverrun, to her mother."

"Nay," said the dwarf. "You're not. The black fish holds the rivers now. If it's the mother you want, seek her at the Twins. For there's to be a *wedding*." She cackled again. "Look in your fires, pink priest, and you will see. Not now, though, not here, you'll see nothing here. This place belongs to the old gods still ... they linger here as I do, shrunken and feeble but not yet dead. Nor do they love the flames. For the oak recalls the acorn, the acorn dreams the oak, the stump lives in them both. And they remember when the First Men came with fire in their fists." She drank the last of the wine in four long swallows, flung the skin aside, and pointed her stick at Lord Beric. "I'll have my payment now. I'll have the song you promised me."

And so Lem woke Tom Sevenstrings beneath his furs, and brought him yawning to the fireside with his woodharp in hand. "The same song as before?" he asked.

"Oh, aye. My Jenny's song. Is there another?"

And so he sang, and the dwarf woman closed her eyes and rocked slowly back and forth, murmuring the words and crying. Thoros took Arya firmly by the hand and drew her aside. "Let her savor her song in peace," he said. "It is all she has left."

I wasn't going to hurt her, Arya thought. "What did she mean about the Twins? My mother's at Riverrun, isn't she?"

"She was." The red priest rubbed beneath his chin. "A wedding, she said. We shall see. Wherever she is, Lord Beric will find her, though."

Not long after, the sky opened. Lightning cracked and thunder rolled across the hills, and the rain fell in blinding sheets. The dwarf woman vanished as suddenly as she had appeared, while the outlaws gathered branches and threw up crude shelters.

It rained all through that night, and come morning Ned, Lem, and Watty the Miller awoke with chills. Watty could not keep his breakfast down, and young Ned was feverish and shivering by turns, with skin clammy to the touch. There was an abandoned village half a day's ride to the north, Notch told Lord Beric; they'd find better shelter there, a place to wait out the worst of the rains. So they dragged themselves back into the saddles and urged their horses down the great hill.

The rains did not let up. They rode through woods and fields, fording swollen streams where the rushing water came up to the bellies of their horses. Arya pulled up the hood of her cloak and hunched down, sodden and shivering but determined not to falter. Merrit and Mudge were soon coughing as bad as Watty, and poor Ned seemed to grow more miserable with every mile. "When I wear my helm, the rain beats against the steel and gives me headaches," he complained. "But when I take it off, my hair gets soaked and sticks to my face and in my mouth."

"You have a knife," Gendry suggested. "If your hair annoys you so much, shave your bloody head."

He doesn't like Ned. The squire seemed nice enough to Arya; maybe a little shy, but good-natured. She had always heard that Dornishmen were small and swarthy, with black hair and small black eyes, but Ned had big blue eyes, so dark that they looked almost purple. And his hair was a pale blond, more ash than honey.

"How long have you been Lord Beric's squire?" she asked, to take his mind from his misery.

"He took me for his page when he espoused my aunt." He coughed. "I was seven, but when I turned ten he raised me to squire. I won a prize once, riding at rings."

"I never learned the lance, but I could beat you with a sword," said Arya. "Have you killed anyone?"

That seemed to startle him. "I'm only twelve."

I killed a boy when I was eight, Arya almost said, but she thought she'd better not. "You've been in battles, though."

"Yes." He did not sound very proud of it. "I was at the Mummer's Ford. When Lord Beric fell into the river, I dragged him up onto the bank so he wouldn't drown and stood over him with my sword. I never had to fight, though. He had a broken lance sticking out of him, so no one bothered us. When we regrouped, Green Gergen helped pull his lordship back onto a horse."

Arya was remembering the stableboy at King's Landing. After him there'd been that guard whose throat she cut at Harrenhal, and Ser Amory's men at that holdfast by the lake. She didn't know if Weese and Chiswyck counted, or the ones who'd died on account of the weasel soup . . . all of a sudden, she felt very sad. "My father was called Ned too," she said.

"I know. I saw him at the Hand's tourney. I wanted to go up and speak with him, but I couldn't think what to say." Ned shivered beneath his cloak, a sodden length of pale purple. "Were you at the tourney? I saw your sister there. Ser Loras Tyrell gave her a rose."

"She told me." It all seemed so long ago. "Her friend Jeyne Poole fell in love with your Lord Beric."

"He's promised to my aunt." Ned looked uncomfortable. "That was before, though. Before he . . ."

. . . *died?* she thought, as Ned's voice trailed off into an awkward silence. Their horses' hooves made sucking sounds as they pulled free of the mud.

"My lady?" Ned said at last. "You have a baseborn brother . . . Jon Snow?"

"He's with the Night's Watch on the Wall." *Maybe I should go to the Wall instead of Riverrun. Jon wouldn't care who I killed or whether I brushed my hair . . .* "Jon looks like me, even though he's bastard-born. He used to muss my hair and call me 'little sister.' " Arya missed Jon most of all. Just saying his name made her sad. "How do you know about Jon?"

"He is my milk brother."

"Brother?" Arya did not understand. "But you're from Dorne. How could you and Jon be blood?"

"*Milk* brothers. Not blood. My lady mother had no milk when I was little, so Wylla had to nurse me."

Arya was lost. "Who's Wylla?"

"Jon Snow's mother. He never told you? She's served us for years and years. Since before I was born."

"Jon never knew his mother. Not even her name." Arya gave Ned a wary look. "You know her? Truly?" *Is he making mock of me?* "If you lie I'll punch your face."

"Wylla was my wetnurse," he repeated solemnly. "I swear it on the honor of my House."

"You have a House?" That was stupid; he was a squire, of course he had a House. "Who *are* you?"

"My lady?" Ned looked embarrassed. "I'm Edric Dayne, the . . . the Lord of Starfall."

Behind them, Gendry groaned. "Lords and ladies," he proclaimed in a disgusted tone. Arya plucked a withered crabapple off a passing branch and whipped it at him, bouncing it off his thick bull head. "Ow," he said. "That hurt." He felt the skin above his eye. "What kind of lady throws crabapples at people?"

"The bad kind," said Arya, suddenly contrite. She turned back to Ned. "I'm sorry I didn't know who you were. My lord."

"The fault is mine, my lady." He was very polite.

Jon has a mother. Wylla, her name is Wylla. She would need to remember so she could tell him, the next time she saw him. She wondered if he would still call her "little sister." *I'm not so little anymore. He'd have to call me something else.* Maybe once she got to Riverrun she could write Jon a letter and tell him what Ned Dayne had said. "There was an Arthur Dayne," she remembered. "The one they called the Sword of the Morning."

"My father was Ser Arthur's elder brother. Lady Ashara was my aunt. I never knew her, though. She threw herself into the sea from atop the Palestone Sword before I was born."

"Why would she do that?" said Arya, startled.

Ned looked wary. Maybe he was afraid that she was going to throw something at him. "Your lord father never spoke of her?" he said. "The Lady Ashara Dayne, of Starfall?"

"No. Did he know her?"

"Before Robert was king. She met your father and his brothers at Harrenhal, during the year of the false spring."

"Oh." Arya did not know what else to say. "Why did she jump in the sea, though?"

"Her heart was broken."

Sansa would have sighed and shed a tear for true love, but Arya just thought it was stupid. She couldn't say that to Ned, though, not about his own aunt. "Did someone break it?"

He hesitated. "Perhaps it's not my place . . ."

"*Tell me.*"

He looked at her uncomfortably. "My aunt Allyria says Lady Ashara and your father fell in love at Harrenhal—"

"That's not so. He loved my lady mother."

"I'm sure he did, my lady, but—"

"She was the *only* one he loved."

"He must have found that bastard under a cabbage leaf, then," Gendry said behind them.

Arya wished she had another crabapple to bounce off his face. "My father had *honor*," she said angrily. "And we weren't talking to *you* anyway. Why don't you go back to Stoney Sept and ring that girl's stupid bells?"

Gendry ignored that. "At least your father *raised* his bastard, not like mine. I don't even know my father's name. Some smelly drunk, I'd wager, like the others my mother dragged home from the alehouse. Whenever she got mad at me, she'd say, 'If your father was here, he'd beat you bloody.' That's all I know of him." He spat. "Well, if he was here now, might be I'd beat *him* bloody. But he's dead, I figure, and your father's dead too, so what does it matter who he lay with?"

It mattered to Arya, though she could not have said why. Ned was trying to apologize for upsetting her, but she did not want to hear it. She pressed her heels into her horse and left them both. Anguy the Archer was riding a few yards ahead. When she caught up with him, she said, "Dornishmen lie, don't they?"

"They're famous for it." The bowman grinned. "Of course, they say the same of us marchers, so there you are. What's the trouble now? Ned's a good lad . . ."

"He's just a stupid liar." Arya left the trail, leapt a rotten log and splashed across a streambed, ignoring the shouts of the outlaws behind her. *They just want to tell me more lies.* She thought about trying to get away from them, but there were too many and they knew these lands too well. What was the use of running if they caught you?

It was Harwin who rode up beside her, in the end. "Where do you think you're going, milady? You shouldn't run off. There are wolves in these woods, and worse things."

"I'm not afraid," she said. "That boy Ned said . . ."

"Aye, he told me. Lady Ashara Dayne. It's an old tale, that one. I heard it once at Winterfell, when I was no older than you are now." He took hold of her bridle firmly and turned her horse around. "I doubt there's any truth to it. But if there is, what of it? When Ned met this Dornish lady, his brother Brandon was still alive, and it was him betrothed to Lady Catelyn, so there's no stain on your father's honor. There's nought like a tourney to make the blood run hot, so maybe some words were whispered in a tent of a night, who can say? Words or kisses, maybe more, but where's the harm in that? Spring had come, or so they thought, and neither one of them was pledged."

"She killed herself, though," said Arya uncertainly. "Ned says she jumped from a tower into the sea."

"So she did," Harwin admitted, as he led her back, "but that was for grief, I'd wager. She'd lost a brother, the Sword of the Morning." He shook his head. "Let it lie, my lady. They're dead, all of them. Let it lie . . . and please, when we come to Riverrun, say naught of this to your mother."

The village was just where Notch had promised it would be. They took shelter in a grey stone stable. Only half a roof remained, but that was half a roof more than any other building in the village. *It's not a village, it's only black stones and old bones.* "Did the Lannisters kill the people who lived here?" Arya asked as she helped Anguy dry the horses.

"No." He pointed. "Look at how thick the moss grows on the stones. No one's moved them for a long time. And there's a tree growing out of the wall there, see? This place was put to the torch a long time ago."

"Who did it, then?" asked Gendry.

"Hoster Tully." Notch was a stooped thin grey-haired man, born in these parts. "This was Lord Goodbrook's village. When Riverrun declared for Robert, Goodbrook stayed loyal to the king, so Lord Tully came down on him with fire and sword. After the Trident, Goodbrook's son made his peace with Robert and Lord Hoster, but that didn't help the dead none."

A silence fell. Gendry gave Arya a queer look, then turned away to brush his horse. Outside the rain came down and down. "I say we need a fire," Thoros declared. "The night is dark and full of terrors. And wet too, eh? Too very wet."

Jack-Be-Lucky hacked some dry wood from a stall, while Notch and Merrit gathered straw for kindling. Thoros himself struck the spark, and Lem fanned the flames with his big yellow cloak until they roared and swirled. Soon it grew almost hot inside the stable. Thoros sat before it crosslegged, devouring the flames with his eyes just as he had atop High Heart. Arya watched him closely, and once his lips moved, and she thought she heard him mutter, "Riverrun." Lem paced back and forth, coughing, a long shadow matching him stride for stride, while Tom o' Sevens pulled off his boots and rubbed his feet.

"I must be mad, to be going back to Riverrun," the singer complained. "The Tullys have never been lucky for old Tom. It was that Lysa sent me up the high road, when the moon men took my gold and my horse and all my clothes as well. There's knights in the Vale still telling how I came walking up to the Bloody Gate with only my harp to keep me modest. They made me sing 'The Name Day Boy' and 'The King Without Courage' before they opened that gate. My only solace was that three of them died laughing. I haven't been back to the Eyrie since, and I won't sing 'The King Without Courage' either, not for all the gold in Casterly—"

"*Lannisters*," Thoros said. "Roaring red and gold." He lurched to his feet and went to Lord Beric. Lem and Tom wasted no time joining them. Arya could not make out what they were saying, but the singer kept glancing at her, and one time Lem got so angry he pounded a fist against the wall. That was when Lord Beric gestured for her to come closer. It was the last thing she wanted to do, but Harwin put a hand in the small of her back and pushed her forward. She took two steps and hesitated, full of dread. "My lord." She waited to hear what Lord Beric would say.

"Tell her," the lightning lord commanded Thoros.

The red priest squatted down beside her. "My lady," he said, "the Lord granted me a view of Riverrun. An island in a sea of fire, it seemed. The flames were leaping lions with long crimson claws. And how they roared! A sea of Lannisters, my lady. Riverrun will soon come under attack."

Arya felt as though he'd punched her in the belly. "*No!*"

"Sweetling," said Thoros, "the flames do not lie. Sometimes I read them wrongly, blind fool that I am. But not this time, I think. The Lannisters will soon have Riverrun under siege."

"Robb will beat them." Arya got a stubborn look. "He'll beat them like he did before."

"Your brother may be gone," said Thoros. "Your mother as well. I did not see them in the flames. This wedding the old one spoke of, a wedding on the Twins . . . she has her own ways of knowing things, that one. The weirwoods whisper in her ear when she sleeps. If she says your mother is gone to the Twins . . ."

Arya turned on Tom and Lem. "If you hadn't caught me, I would have *been* there. I would have been *home*."

Lord Beric paid no heed to her outburst. "My lady," he said with weary courtesy, "would you know your grandfather's brother by sight? Ser Brynden Tully, called the Blackfish? Would he know you, perchance?"

Arya shook her head miserably. She had heard her mother speak of Ser Brynden Blackfish, but if she had ever met him herself it had been when she was too little to remember.

"Small chance the Blackfish will pay good coin for a girl he doesn't know," said Tom. "Those Tullys are a sour, suspicious lot, he's like to think we're selling him false goods."

"We'll convince him," Lem Lemoncloak insisted. "*She* will, or Harwin. Riverrun is closest. I say we take her there, get the gold, and be bloody well done with her."

"And if the lions catch us inside the castle?" said Tom. "They'd like nothing better than to hang his lordship in a cage from the top of Casterly Rock."

"I do not mean to be taken," said Lord Beric. A final word hung unspoken in the air. *Alive.* They all heard it, even Arya, though it never passed his lips. "Still, we dare not go blindly here. I want to know where the armies are, the wolves and lions both. Sharna will know something, and Lord Vance's maester will know more. Acorn Hall's not far. Lady Smallwood will shelter us for a time while we send scouts ahead to learn . . ."

His words beat at her ears like the pounding of a drum, and suddenly it was more than Arya could stand. She wanted Riverrun, not Acorn Hall; she wanted her mother and her brother Robb, not Lady Smallwood or some uncle she never knew. Whirling, she broke for the door, and when Harwin tried to grab her arm she spun away from him quick as a snake.

Outside the stables the rain was still falling, and distant lightning flashed in the west. Arya ran as fast as she could. She did not know where she was going, only that she wanted to be alone, away from all the voices, away from their hollow words and broken promises. *All I wanted was to go to Riverrun.* It was her own fault, for taking Gendry and Hot Pie with her when she left Harrenhal. She would have been better alone. If she had been alone, the outlaws would never have caught her, and she'd be with Robb and her mother by now. *They were never my pack. If they had been, they wouldn't leave me.* She splashed through a puddle of muddy water. Someone was shouting her name, Harwin probably, or Gendry, but the thunder drowned them out as it rolled across the hills, half a heartbeat behind the lightning. *The lightning lord,* she thought angrily. Maybe he couldn't die, but he could lie.

Somewhere off to her left a horse whinnied. Arya couldn't have gone more than fifty yards from the stables, yet already she was soaked to the bone. She ducked around the corner of one of the tumbledown houses, hoping the mossy walls would keep the rain off, and almost bowled right into one of the sentries. A mailed hand closed hard around her arm.

"You're *hurting* me," she said, twisting in his grasp. "Let *go*, I was going to go back, I . . ."

"Back?" Sandor Clegane's laughter was iron scraping over stone. "Bugger that, wolf girl. You're *mine*." He needed only one hand to yank her off her feet and drag her kicking toward his waiting horse. The cold rain lashed them both and washed away her shouts, and all that Arya could think of was the question he had asked her. *Do you know what dogs do to wolves?*

JAIME

Though his fever lingered stubbornly, the stump was healing clean, and Qyburn said his arm was no longer in danger. Jaime was anxious to be gone, to put Harrenhal, the Bloody Mummers, and Brienne of Tarth all behind him. A real woman waited for him in the Red Keep.

"I am sending Qyburn with you, to look after you on the way to King's Landing," Roose Bolton said on the morn of their departure. "He has a fond hope that your father will force the Citadel to give him back his chain, in gratitude."

"We all have fond hopes. If he grows me back a hand, my father will make him Grand Maester."

Steelshanks Walton commanded Jaime's escort; blunt, brusque, brutal, at heart a simple soldier. Jaime had served with his sort all his life. Men like Walton would kill at their lord's command, rape when their blood was up after battle, and plunder wherever they could, but once the war was done they would go back to their homes, trade their spears for hoes, wed their neighbors' daughters, and raise a pack of squalling children. Such men obeyed without question, but the deep malignant cruelty of the Brave Companions was not a part of their nature.

Both parties left Harrenhal the same morning, beneath a cold grey sky that promised rain. Ser Aenys Frey had marched three days before, striking northeast for the kingsroad. Bolton meant to follow him. "The Trident is in flood," he told Jaime. "Even at the ruby ford, the crossing will be difficult. You will give my warm regards to your father?"

"So long as you give mine to Robb Stark."

"That I shall."

Some Brave Companions had gathered in the yard to watch them leave. Jaime trotted over to where they stood. "Zollo. How kind of you to see me off. Pyg. Timeon. Will you miss me? No last jest to share, Shagwell? To lighten my way down the road? And Rorge, did you come to kiss me goodbye?"

"Bugger off, cripple," said Rorge.

"If you insist. Rest assured, though, I will be back. A Lannister always pays his debts." Jaime wheeled his horse around and rejoined Steelshanks Walton and his two hundred.

Lord Bolton had accoutred him as a knight, preferring to ignore the missing hand that made such warlike garb a travesty. Jaime rode with sword and dagger on his belt, shield and helm hung from his saddle, chainmail under a dark brown surcoat. He was not such a fool as to show the lion of Lannister on his arms, though, nor the plain white blazon that was his right as a Sworn Brother of the Kingsguard. He found an old shield in the armory, battered and splintered, the chipped paint still showing most of the great black bat of House Lothston upon a field of silver and gold. The Lothstons held Harrenhal before the Whents and had been a powerful family in their day, but they had died out ages ago, so no one was likely to object to him bearing their arms. He would be no one's cousin, no one's enemy, no one's sworn sword . . . in sum, no one.

They left through Harrenhal's smaller eastern gate, and took their leave of Roose Bolton and his host six miles farther on, turning south to follow along the lake road for a time. Walton meant to avoid the kingsroad as long as he could, preferring the farmer's tracks and game trails near the Gods Eye.

"The kingsroad would be faster." Jaime was anxious to return to Cersei as quickly as he could. If they made haste, he might even arrive in time for Joffrey's wedding.

"I want no trouble," said Steelshanks. "Gods know who we'd meet along that kingsroad."

"No one you need fear, surely? You have two hundred men."

"Aye. But others might have more. M'lord said to bring you safe to your lord father, and that's what I mean to do."

I have come this way before, Jaime reflected a few miles further on, when they passed a deserted mill beside the lake. Weeds now grew where once the miller's daughter had smiled shyly at him, and the miller himself had shouted out, "The tourney's back the other way, ser." *As if I had not known.*

King Aerys made a great show of Jaime's investiture. He said his vows before the king's pavilion, kneeling on the green grass in white armor while half the realm looked on. When Ser Gerold Hightower raised him up and put the white cloak about his shoulders, a roar went up that Jaime still remembered, all these years later. But that very night Aerys had turned sour, declaring that he had no need of *seven* Kingsguard here at Harrenhal. Jaime was commanded to return to King's Landing to guard the queen and little Prince Viserys, who'd remained behind. Even when the White Bull offered to take that duty himself, so Jaime might compete in Lord Whent's tourney, Aerys had refused. "He'll win no glory here," the king had said. "He's mine now, not Tywin's. He'll serve as I see fit. I am the king. I rule, and he'll obey."

That was the first time that Jaime understood. It was not his skill with sword and lance that had won him his white cloak, nor any feats of valor he'd performed against the Kingswood Brotherhood. Aerys had chosen him to spite his father, to rob Lord Tywin of his heir.

Even now, all these years later, the thought was bitter. And that day, as he'd ridden south in his new white cloak to guard an empty castle, it had been almost too much to stomach. He would have ripped the cloak off then and there if he could have, but it was too late. He had said the words whilst half the realm looked on, and a Kingsguard served for life.

Qyburn fell in beside him. "Is your hand troubling you?"

"The lack of my hand is troubling me." The mornings were the hardest. In his dreams Jaime was a whole man, and each dawn he would lie half-awake and feel his fingers move. *It was a nightmare,* some part of him would whisper, refusing to believe even now, *only a nightmare.* But then he would open his eyes.

"I understand you had a visitor last night," said Qyburn. "I trust that you enjoyed her?"

Jaime gave him a cool look. "She did not say who sent her."

The maester smiled modestly. "Your fever was largely gone, and I thought you might enjoy a bit of exercise. Pia is quite skilled, would you not agree? And so ... willing."

She had been that, certainly. She had slipped in his door and out of her clothes so quickly that Jaime had thought he was still dreaming.

It hadn't been until the woman slid in under his blankets and put his good hand on her breast that he roused. *She was a pretty little thing, too.* "I was a slip of a girl when you came for Lord Whent's tourney and the king gave you your cloak," she confessed. "You were so handsome all in white, and everyone said what a brave knight you were. Sometimes when I'm with some man, I close my eyes and pretend it's you on top of me, with your smooth skin and gold curls. I never truly thought I'd have you, though."

Sending her away had not been easy after that, but Jaime had done it all the same. *I have a woman,* he reminded himself. "Do you send girls to everyone you leech?" he asked Qyburn.

"More often Lord Vargo sends them to me. He likes me to examine them, before ... well, suffice it to say that once he loved unwisely, and he has no wish to do so again. But have no fear, Pia is quite healthy. As is your maid of Tarth."

Jaime gave him a sharp look. "Brienne?"

"Yes. A strong girl, that one. And her maidenhead is still intact. As of last night, at least." Qyburn gave a chuckle.

"He sent you to examine her?"

"To be sure. He is ... fastidious, shall we say?"

"Does this concern the ransom?" Jaime asked. "Does her father require proof she is still maiden?"

"You have not heard?" Qyburn gave a shrug. "We had a bird from Lord Selwyn. In answer to mine. The Evenstar offers three hundred dragons for his daughter's safe return. I had told Lord Vargo there were no sapphires on Tarth, but he will not listen. He is convinced the Evenstar intends to cheat him."

"Three hundred dragons is a fair ransom for a knight. The goat should take what he can get."

"The goat is Lord of Harrenhal, and the Lord of Harrenhal does not haggle."

The news irritated him, though he supposed he should have seen it coming. *The lie spared you awhile, wench. Be grateful for that much.* "If her maidenhead's as hard as the rest of her, the goat will break his cock off trying to get in," he jested. Brienne was tough enough to survive a few rapes, Jaime judged, though if she resisted too vigorously Vargo Hoat might start lopping off her hands and feet. *And if he does, why should I care? I might still have a hand if she had let me have my cousin's sword without getting stupid.* He had almost taken off her leg himself with that first stroke of his, but after that she had given him more than he wanted. *Hoat may not know how freakish strong she is. He had best be careful, or she'll snap that skinny neck of his, and wouldn't that be sweet?*

Qyburn's companionship was wearing on him. Jaime trotted toward the head of the column. A round little tick of a northman name of Nage went before Steelshanks with the peace banner; a rainbow-striped flag with seven long tails, on a staff topped by a seven-pointed star. "Shouldn't you northmen have a different sort of peace banner?" he asked Walton. "What are the Seven to you?"

"Southron gods," the man said, "but it's a southron peace we need, to get you safe to your father."

My father. Jaime wondered whether Lord Tywin had received the goat's demand for ransom, with or without his rotted hand. *What is a swordsman worth without his sword hand? Half the gold in Casterly Rock? Three hundred dragons? Or nothing?* His father had never been unduly swayed by sentiment. Tywin Lannister's own father Lord Tytos had once imprisoned an unruly bannerman, Lord Tarbeck. The redoubtable Lady Tarbeck responded by capturing three Lannisters, including young Stafford, whose sister was betrothed to cousin Tywin. "Send back my lord and love, or these three shall answer for any harm that comes him," she had written to Casterly Rock. Young Tywin suggested his father oblige by sending back Lord Tarbeck in three pieces. Lord Tytos was a gentler sort of lion, however, so Lady Tarbeck won a few more years for her muttonheaded lord, and Stafford wed and bred and blundered on till Oxcross. But Tywin Lannister endured, eternal as Casterly Rock. *And now you have a cripple for a son as well as a dwarf, my lord. How you will hate that . . .*

The road led them through a burned village. It must have been a year or more since the place had been put to torch. The hovels stood blackened and roofless, but weeds were growing waist high in all the surrounding fields. Steelshanks called a halt to allow them to water the horses. *I know this place too*, Jaime thought as he waited by the well. There had been a small inn where only a few foundation stones and a chimney now stood, and he had gone in for a cup of ale. A dark-eyed serving wench brought him cheese and apples, but the innkeep had refused his coin. "It's an honor to have a knight of the Kingsguard under my roof, ser," the man had said. "It's a tale I'll tell my grandchildren." Jaime looked at the chimney poking out of the weeds and wondered whether he had ever gotten those grandchildren. *Did he tell them the Kingslayer once drank his ale and ate his cheese and apples, or was he ashamed to admit he fed the likes of me?* Not that he would ever know; whoever burned the inn had likely killed the grandchildren as well.

He could feel his phantom fingers clench. When Steelshanks said that perhaps they should have a fire and a bit of food, Jaime shook his head. "I mislike this place. We'll ride on."

By evenfall, they had left the lake to follow a rutted track through a wood of oak and elm. Jaime's stump was throbbing dully when Steelshanks decided to make camp. Qyburn had brought a skin of dreamwine, thankfully. While Walton set the watches, Jaime stretched out near the fire and propped a rolled-up bearskin against a stump as a pillow for his head. The wench would have told him he had to eat before he slept, to keep his strength up, but he was more tired than hungry. He closed his eyes, and hoped to dream of Cersei. The fever dreams were all so vivid . . .

Naked and alone he stood, surrounded by enemies, with stone

walls all around him pressing close. *The Rock*, he knew. He could feel the immense weight of it above his head. He was home. He was home and whole.

He held his right hand up and flexed his fingers to feel the strength in them. It felt as good as sex. As good as swordplay. *Four fingers and a thumb.* He had dreamed that he was maimed, but it wasn't so. Relief made him dizzy. *My hand, my good hand.* Nothing could hurt him so long as he was whole.

Around him stood a dozen tall dark figures in cowled robes that hid their faces. In their hands were spears. "Who are you?" he demanded of them. "What business do you have in Casterly Rock?"

They gave no answer, only prodded him with the points of their spears. He had no choice but to descend. Down a twisting passageway he went, narrow steps carved from the living rock, down and down. *I must go up*, he told himself. *Up, not down. Why am I going down?* Below the earth his doom awaited, he knew with the certainty of dream; something dark and terrible lurked there, something that wanted him. Jaime tried to halt, but their spears prodded him on. *If only I had my sword, nothing could harm me.*

The steps ended abruptly on echoing darkness. Jaime had the sense of vast space before him. He jerked to a halt, teetering on the edge of nothingness. A spearpoint jabbed at the small of the back, shoving him into the abyss. He shouted, but the fall was short. He landed on his hands and knees, upon soft sand and shallow water. There were watery caverns deep below Casterly Rock, but this one was strange to him. "What place is this?"

"Your place." The voice echoed; it was a hundred voices, a thousand, the voices of all the Lannisters since Lann the Clever, who'd lived at the dawn of days. But most of all it was his father's voice, and beside Lord Tywin stood his sister, pale and beautiful, a torch burning in her hand. Joffrey was there as well, the son they'd made together, and behind them a dozen more dark shapes with golden hair.

"Sister, why has Father brought us here?"

"Us? This is your place, Brother. This is your darkness." Her torch was the only light in the cavern. Her torch was the only light in the world. She turned to go.

"Stay with me," Jaime pleaded. "Don't leave me here alone." But they were leaving. "*Don't leave me in the dark!*" Something terrible lived down here. "Give me a sword, at least."

"I gave you a sword," Lord Tywin said.

It was at his feet. Jaime groped under the water until his hand closed upon the hilt. *Nothing can hurt me so long as I have a sword.* As he raised the sword a finger of pale flame flickered at the point and crept up along the edge, stopping a hand's breath from the hilt. The fire took on the color of the steel itself so it burned with a silvery-blue light, and the gloom pulled back. Crouching, listening, Jaime moved in a circle, ready for anything that might come out of the darkness. The water flowed into his boots, ankle deep and bitterly cold. *Beware the water*, he told himself. *There may be creatures living in it, hidden deeps . . .*

From behind came a great splash. Jaime whirled toward the sound . . . but the faint light revealed only Brienne of Tarth, her hands bound in heavy chains. "I swore to keep you safe," the wench said stubbornly. "I swore an oath." Naked, she raised her hands to Jaime. "Ser. Please. If you would be so good."

The steel links parted like silk. "A sword," Brienne begged, and there it was, scabbard, belt, and all. She buckled it around her thick waist. The light was so dim that Jaime could scarcely see her, though they stood a scant few feet apart. *In this light she could almost be a beauty*, he thought. *In this light she could almost be a knight.* Brienne's sword took flame as well, burning silvery blue. The darkness retreated a little more.

"The flames will burn so long as you live," he heard Cersei call. "When they die, so must you."

"*Sister!*" he shouted. "Stay with me. *Stay!*" There was no reply but the soft sound of retreating footsteps.

Brienne moved her longsword back and forth, watching the silvery flames shift and shimmer. Beneath her feet, a reflection of the burning blade shone on the surface of the flat black water. She was as tall and strong as he remembered, yet it seemed to Jaime that she had more of a woman's shape now.

"Do they keep a bear down here?" Brienne was moving, slow and wary, sword to hand; step, turn, and listen. Each step made a little splash. "A cave lion? Direwolves? Some bear? Tell me, Jaime. What lives here? What lives in the darkness?"

"Doom." *No bear*, he knew. *No lion.* "Only doom."

In the cool silvery-blue light of the swords, the big wench looked pale and fierce. "I mislike this place."

"I'm not fond of it myself." Their blades made a little island of light, but all around them stretched a sea of darkness, unending. "My feet are wet."

"We could go back the way they brought us. If you climbed on my shoulders you'd have no trouble reaching that tunnel mouth."

Then I could follow Cersei. He could feel himself growing hard at the thought, and turned away so Brienne would not see.

"Listen." She put a hand on his shoulder, and he trembled at the sudden touch. *She's warm.* "Something comes." Brienne lifted her sword to point off to his left. "There."

He peered into the gloom until he saw it too. Something was moving through the darkness, he could not quite make it out . . .

"A man on a horse. No, two. Two riders, side by side."

"Down here, beneath the Rock?" It made no sense. Yet there came two riders on pale horses, men and mounts both armored. The destriers emerged from the blackness at a slow walk. *They make no sound*, Jaime realized. *No splashing, no clink of mail nor clop of hoof.* He remembered Eddard Stark, riding the length of Aerys's throne room wrapped in silence. Only his eyes had spoken; a lord's eyes, cold and grey and full of judgment.

"Is it you, Stark?" Jaime called. "Come ahead. I never feared you living, I do not fear you dead."

Brienne touched his arm. "There are more."

He saw them too. They were armored all in snow, it seemed to him, and ribbons of mist swirled back from their shoulders. The visors of their helms were closed, but Jaime Lannister did not need to look upon their faces to know them.

Five had been his brothers. Oswell Whent and Jon Darry. Lewyn Martell, a prince of Dorne. The White Bull, Gerold Hightower. Ser Arthur Dayne, Sword of the Morning. And beside them, crowned in mist and grief with his long hair streaming behind him, rode Rhaegar Targaryen, Prince of Dragonstone and rightful heir to the Iron Throne.

"You don't frighten me," he called, turning as they split to either side of him. He did not know which way to face. "I will fight you one by one or all together. But who is there for the wench to duel? She gets cross when you leave her out."

"I swore an oath to keep him safe," she said to Rhaegar's shade. "I swore a holy oath."

"We all swore oaths," said Ser Arthur Dayne, so sadly.

The shades dismounted from their ghostly horses. When they drew their longswords, it made not a sound. "He was going to burn the city," Jaime said. "To leave Robert only ashes."

"He was your king," said Darry.

"You swore to keep him safe," said Whent.

"And the children, them as well," said Prince Lewyn.

Prince Rhaegar burned with a cold light, now white, now red, now dark. "I left my wife and children in your hands."

"I never thought he'd hurt them." Jaime's sword was burning less brightly now. "I was with the king . . ."

"Killing the king," said Ser Arthur.

"Cutting his throat," said Prince Lewyn.

"The king you had sworn to die for," said the White Bull.

The fires that ran along the blade were guttering out, and Jaime remembered what Cersei had said. *No.* Terror closed a hand about his throat. Then his sword went dark, and only Brienne's burned, as the ghosts came rushing in.

"No," he said, "no, no, no. *Noooooooooo!*"

Heart pounding, he jerked awake, and found himself in starry darkness amidst a grove of trees. He could taste bile in his mouth, and he was shivering with sweat, hot and cold at once. When he looked down for his sword hand, his wrist ended in leather and linen, wrapped snug around an ugly stump. He felt sudden tears well up in his eyes. *I felt it, I felt the strength in my fingers, and the rough leather of the sword's grip. My hand . . .*

"My lord." Qyburn knelt beside him, his fatherly face all crinkly with concern. "What is it? I heard you cry out."

Steelshanks Walton stood above them, tall and dour. "What is it? Why did you scream?"

"A dream ... only a dream." Jaime stared at the camp around him, lost for a moment. "I was in the dark, but I had my hand back." He looked at the stump and felt sick all over again. *There's no place like that beneath the Rock*, he thought. His stomach was sour and empty, and his head was pounding where he'd pillowed it against the stump.

Qyburn felt his brow. "You still have a touch of fever."

"A fever dream." Jaime reached up. "Help me." Steelshanks took him by his good hand and pulled him to his feet.

"Another cup of dreamwine?" asked Qyburn.

"No. I've dreamt enough this night." He wondered how long it was till dawn. Somehow he knew that if he closed his eyes, he would be back in that dark wet place again.

"Milk of the poppy, then? And something for your fever? You are still weak, my lord. You need to sleep. To rest."

That is the last thing I mean to do. The moonlight glimmered pale upon the stump where Jaime had rested his head. The moss covered it so thickly he had not noticed before, but now he saw that the wood was white. It made him think of Winterfell, and Ned Stark's heart tree. *It was not him*, he thought. *It was never him.* But the stump was dead and so was Stark and so were all the others, Prince Rhaegar and Ser Arthur and the children. *And Aerys. Aerys is most dead of all.* "Do you believe in ghosts, Maester?" he asked Qyburn.

The man's face grew strange. "Once, at the Citadel, I came into an empty room and saw an empty chair. Yet I knew a woman had been there, only a moment before. The cushion was dented where she'd sat, the cloth was still warm, and her scent lingered in the air. If we leave our smells behind us when we leave a room, surely something of our souls must remain when we leave this life?" Qyburn spread his hands. "The archmaesters did not like my thinking, though. Well, Marwyn did, but he was the only one."

Jaime ran his fingers through his hair. "Walton," he said, "saddle the horses. I want to go back."

"Back?" Steelshanks regarded him dubiously.

He thinks I've gone mad. And perhaps I have. "I left something at Harrenhal."

"Lord Vargo holds it now. Him and his Bloody Mummers."

"You have twice the men he does."

"If I don't serve you up to your father as commanded, Lord Bolton will have my hide. We press on to King's Landing."

Once Jaime might have countered with a smile and a threat, but one-handed cripples do not inspire much fear. He wondered what his brother would do. *Tyrion would find a way.* "Lannisters lie, Steelshanks. Didn't Lord Bolton tell you that?"

The man frowned suspiciously. "What if he did?"

"Unless you take me back to Harrenhal, the song I sing my father may not be one the Lord of the Dreadfort would wish to hear. I might even say it was Bolton ordered my hand cut off, and Steelshanks Walton who swung the blade."

Walton gaped at him. "That isn't so."

"No, but who will my father believe?" Jaime made himself smile, the way he used to smile when nothing in the world could frighten him. "It will be so much easier if we just go back. We'd be on our way again soon enough, and I'd sing such a sweet song in King's Landing you'll never believe your ears. You'd get the girl, and a nice fat purse of gold as thanks."

"Gold?" Walton liked that well enough. "How much gold?"

I have him. "Why, how much would you want?"

And by the time the sun came up, they were halfway back to Harrenhal.

Jaime pushed his horse much harder than he had the day before, and Steelshanks and the northmen were forced to match his pace. Even so, it was midday before they reached the castle on the lake. Beneath a darkening sky that threatened rain, the immense walls and five great towers stood black and ominous. *It looks so dead.* The walls were empty, the gates closed and barred. But high above the barbican, a single banner hung limp. *The black goat of Qohor*, he knew. Jaime cupped his hands to shout. "You in there! Open your gates, or I'll kick them down!"

It was not until Qyburn and Steelshanks added their voices that a head finally appeared on the battlements above them. He goggled down at them, then vanished. A short time later, they heard the portcullis being drawn upward. The gates swung open, and Jaime Lannister spurred his horse through the walls, scarcely glancing at the murder holes as he passed beneath them. He had been worried that the goat might not admit them, but it seemed as if the Brave Companions still thought of them as allies. *Fools.*

The outer ward was deserted; only the long slate-roofed stables showed any signs of life, and it was not horses that interested Jaime just then. He reined up and looked about. He could hear sounds from somewhere behind the Tower of Ghosts, and men shouting in half a dozen tongues. Steelshanks and Qyburn rode up on either side. "Get what you came back for, and we'll be gone again," said Walton. "I want no trouble with the Mummers."

"Tell your men to keep their hands on their sword hilts, and the Mummers will want no trouble with you. Two to one, remember?" Jaime's head jerked round at the sound of a distant roar, faint but ferocious. It echoed off the walls of Harrenhal, and the laughter swelled up like the sea. All of a sudden, he knew what was happening. *Have we come too late?* His stomach did a lurch, and he slammed his spurs into his horse, galloping across the outer ward, beneath an arched stone bridge, around the Wailing Tower, and through the Flowstone Yard.

They had her in the bear pit.

King Harren the Black had wished to do even his bear-baiting in lavish style. The pit was ten yards across and five yards deep, walled in stone, floored with sand, and encircled by six tiers of marble benches. The Brave Companions filled only a quarter of the seats, Jaime saw as he swung down clumsily from his horse. The sellswords were so fixed on the spectacle beneath that only those across the pit noticed their arrival.

Brienne wore the same ill-fitting gown she'd worn to supper with Roose Bolton. No shield, no breastplate, no chainmail, not even boiled leather, only pink satin and Myrish lace. Maybe the goat thought she was more amusing when dressed as a woman. Half her gown was hanging off in tatters, and her left arm dripped blood where the bear had raked her.

At least they gave her a sword. The wench held it one-handed, moving sideways, trying to put some distance between her and the bear. *That's no good, the ring's too small.* She needed to attack, to make a quick end to it. Good steel was a match for any bear. But the wench seemed afraid to close. The Mummers showered her with insults and obscene suggestions.

"This is none of our concern," Steelshanks warned Jaime. "Lord Bolton said the wench was theirs, to do with as they liked."

"Her name's Brienne." Jaime descended the steps, past a dozen startled sellswords. Vargo Hoat had taken the lord's box in the lowest tier. "Lord Vargo," he called over the shouts.

The Qohorik almost spilt his wine. "*Kingthlayer?*" The left side of his face was bandaged clumsily, the linen over his ear spotted with blood.

"Pull her out of there."

"Thay out of thith, Kingthlayer, unleth you'd like another thump." He waved a wine cup. "Your thee-mouth bit oth my ear. Thmall wonder her father will not ranthom thuch a freak."

A roar turned Jaime back around. The bear was eight feet tall. *Gregor Clegane with a pelt,* he thought, *though likely smarter.* The beast did not have the reach the Mountain had with that monster greatsword of his, though.

Bellowing in fury, the bear showed a mouth full of great yellow teeth, then fell back to all fours and went straight at Brienne. *There's your chance,* Jaime thought. *Strike! Now!*

Instead, she poked out ineffectually with the point of her blade. The bear recoiled, then came on, rumbling. Brienne slid to her left and poked again at the bear's face. This time he lifted a paw to swat the sword aside.

He's wary, Jaime realized. *He's gone up against other men. He knows swords and spears can hurt him. But that won't keep him off her long.* "Kill him!" he shouted, but his voice was lost amongst all the other shouts. If Brienne heard, she gave no sign. She moved around the pit, keeping the wall at her back. *Too close. If the bear pins her by the wall . . .*

The beast turned clumsily, too far and too fast. Quick as a cat,

Brienne changed direction. *There's the wench I remember*. She leapt in to land a cut across the bear's back. Roaring, the beast went up on his hind legs again. Brienne scrambled back away. *Where's the blood?* Then suddenly he understood. Jaime rounded on Hoat. "You gave her a tourney sword."

The goat brayed laughter, spraying him with wine and spittle. "Of courth."

"*I'll* pay her bloody ransom. Gold, sapphires, whatever you want. Pull her out of there."

"You want her? Go get her."

So he did.

He put his good hand on the marble rail and vaulted over, rolling as he hit the sand. The bear turned at the *thump*, sniffing, watching this new intruder warily. Jaime scrambled to one knee. *Well, what in seven hells do I do now?* He filled his fist with sand. "Kingslayer?" he heard Brienne say, astonished.

"Jaime." He uncoiled, flinging the sand at the bear's face. The bear mauled the air and roared like blazes.

"What are you *doing* here?"

"Something stupid. Get behind me." He circled toward her, putting himself between Brienne and the bear.

"*You* get behind. I have the sword."

"A sword with no point and no edge. *Get behind me!*" He saw something half-buried in the sand, and snatched it up with his good hand. It proved to be a human jawbone, with some greenish flesh still clinging to it, crawling with maggots. *Charming*, he thought, wondering whose face he held. The bear was edging closer, so Jaime whipped his arm around and flung bone, meat, and maggots at the beast's head. He missed by a good yard. *I ought to lop my left hand off as well, for all the good it does me.*

Brienne tried to dart around, but he kicked her legs out from under her. She fell in the sand, clutching the useless sword. Jaime straddled her, and the bear came charging.

There was a deep *twang*, and a feathered shaft sprouted suddenly beneath the beast's left eye. Blood and slaver ran from his open mouth, and another bolt took him in the leg. The bear roared, reared. He saw Jaime and Brienne again and lumbered toward them. More crossbows fired, the quarrels ripping through fur and flesh. At such short range, the bowmen could hardly miss. The shafts hit as hard as maces, but the bear took another step. *The poor dumb brave brute.* When the beast swiped at him, he danced aside, shouting, kicking sand. The bear turned to follow his tormentor, and took another two quarrels in the back. He gave one last rumbling growl, settled back onto his haunches, stretched out on the bloodstained sand, and died.

Brienne got back to her knees, clutching the sword and breathing short ragged breaths. Steelshanks's archers were winding their crossbows and reloading while the Bloody Mummers shouted curses and threats at them. Rorge and Three Toes had swords out, Jaime saw, and Zollo was uncoiling his whip.

"You thlew my bear!" Vargo Hoat shrieked.

"And I'll serve you the same if you give me trouble," Steelshanks threw back. "We're taking the wench."

"Her name is Brienne," Jaime said. "Brienne, the maid of Tarth. You *are* still maiden, I hope?"

Her broad homely face turned red. "Yes."

"Oh, good," Jaime said. "I only rescue maidens." To Hoat he said, "You'll have your ransom. For both of us. A Lannister pays his debts. Now fetch some ropes and get us out of here."

"Bugger that," Rorge growled. "Kill them, Hoat. Or you'll bloody well wish you had!"

The Qohorik hesitated. Half his men were drunk, the northmen stone sober, and there were twice as many. Some of the crossbowmen had reloaded by now. "Pull them out," Hoat said, and then, to Jaime, "I hath chothen to be merthiful. Tell your lord father."

"I will, my lord." *Not that it will do you any good.*

Not until they were half a league from Harrenhal and out of range of archers on the walls did Steelshanks Walton let his anger show. "Are you *mad*, Kingslayer? Did you mean to die? No man can fight a bear with his bare hands!"

"One bare hand and one bare stump," Jaime corrected. "But I hoped you'd kill the beast before the beast killed me. Elsewise, Lord Bolton would have peeled you like an orange, no?"

Steelshanks cursed him roundly for a fool of Lannister, spurred his horse, and galloped away up the column.

"Ser Jaime?" Even in soiled pink satin and torn lace, Brienne looked more like a man in a gown than a proper woman. "I am grateful, but . . . you were well away. Why come back?"

A dozen quips came to mind, each crueler than the one before, but Jaime only shrugged. "I dreamed of you," he said.

CATELYN

Robb bid farewell to his young queen thrice. Once in the godswood before the heart tree, in sight of gods and men. The second time beneath the portcullis, where Jeyne sent him forth with a long embrace and a longer kiss. And finally an hour beyond the Tumblestone, when the girl came galloping up on a well-lathered horse to plead with her young king to take her along.

Robb was touched by that, Catelyn saw, but abashed as well. The day was damp and grey, a drizzle had begun to fall, and the last thing he wanted was to call a halt to his march so he could stand in the wet and console a tearful young wife in front of half his army. *He speaks her gently,* she thought as she watched them together, *but there is anger underneath.*

All the time the king and queen were talking, Grey Wind prowled around them, stopping only to shake the water from his coat and bare his teeth at the rain. When at last Robb gave Jeyne one final kiss, dispatched a dozen men to take her back to Riverrun, and mounted his horse once more, the direwolf raced off ahead as swift as an arrow loosed from a longbow.

"Queen Jeyne has a loving heart, I see," said Lame Lothar Frey to Catelyn. "Not unlike my own sisters. Why, I would wager a guess that even now Roslin is dancing round the Twins chanting 'Lady *Tully*, Lady *Tully*, Lady *Roslin* Tully.' By the morrow she'll be holding swatches of Riverrun red-and-blue to her cheek to picture how she'll look in her bride's cloak." He turned in the saddle to smile at Edmure. "But you are strangely quiet, Lord Tully. How do *you* feel, I wonder?"

"Much as I did at the Stone Mill just before the warhorns sounded," Edmure said, only half in jest.

Lothar gave a good-natured laugh. "Let us pray your marriage ends as happily, my lord."

And may the gods protect us if it does not. Catelyn pressed her heels into her horse, leaving her brother and Lame Lothar to each other's company.

It had been her who had insisted that Jeyne remain at Riverrun, when Robb would sooner have kept her by his side. Lord Walder might well construe the queen's absence from the wedding as another slight, yet her presence would have been a different sort of insult, salt in the old man's wound. "Walder Frey has a sharp tongue and a long memory," she had warned her son. "I do not doubt that you are strong enough to suffer an old man's rebukes as the price of his allegiance, but you have too much of your father in you to sit there while he insults Jeyne to her face."

Robb could not deny the sense of that. *Yet all the same, he resents me for it,* Catelyn thought wearily. *He misses Jeyne already, and some part of him blames me for her absence, though he knows it was good counsel.*

Of the six Westerlings who had come with her son from the Crag, only one remained by his side; Ser Raynald, Jeyne's brother, the royal banner-bearer. Robb had dispatched Jeyne's uncle Rolph Spicer to deliver young Martyn Lannister to the Golden Tooth the very day he received Lord Tywin's assent to the exchange of captives. It was deftly done. Her son was relieved of his fear for Martyn's safety, Galbart Glover was relieved to hear that his brother Robett had been put on a ship at Duskendale, Ser Rolph had important and honorable employment . . . and Grey Wind was at the king's side once more. *Where he belongs.*

Lady Westerling had remained at Riverrun with her children; Jeyne, her little sister Eleyna, and young Rollam, Robb's squire, who complained bitterly about being left. Yet that was wise as well. Olyvar

Frey had squired for Robb previously, and would doubtless be present for his sister's wedding; to parade his replacement before him would be as unwise as it was unkind. As for Ser Raynald, he was a cheerful young knight who swore that no insult of Walder Frey's could possibly provoke him. *And let us pray that insults are all we need to contend with.*

Catelyn had her fears on that score, though. Her lord father had never trusted Walder Frey after the Trident, and she was ever mindful of that. Queen Jeyne would be safest behind the high, strong walls of Riverrun, with the Blackfish to protect her. Robb had even created him a new title, Warden of the Southern Marches. Ser Brynden would hold the Trident if any man could.

All the same, Catelyn would miss her uncle's craggy face, and Robb would miss his counsel. Ser Brynden had played a part in every victory her son had won. Galbart Glover had taken command of the scouts and outriders in his place; a good man, loyal and steady, but without the Blackfish's brilliance.

Behind Glover's screen of scouts, Robb's line of march stretched several miles. The Greatjon led the van. Catelyn traveled in the main column, surrounded by plodding warhorses with steelclad men on their backs. Next came the baggage train, a procession of wayns laden with food, fodder, camp supplies, wedding gifts, and the wounded too weak to walk, under the watchful eye of Ser Wendel Manderly and his White Harbor knights. Herds of sheep and goats and scrawny cattle trailed behind, and then a little tail of footsore camp followers. Even farther back was Robin Flint and the rearguard. There was no enemy in back of them for hundreds of leagues, but Robb would take no chances.

Thirty-five hundred they were, thirty-five hundred who had been blooded in the Whispering Wood, who had reddened their swords at the Battle of the Camps, at Oxcross, Ashemark, and the Crag, and all through the gold-rich hills of the Lannister west. Aside from her brother Edmure's modest retinue of friends, the lords of the Trident had remained to hold the riverlands while the king retook the north. Ahead awaited Edmure's bride and Robb's next battle . . . *and for me, two dead sons, an empty bed, and a castle full of ghosts.* It was a cheerless prospect. *Brienne, where are you? Bring my girls back to me, Brienne. Bring them back safe.*

The drizzle that had sent them off turned into a soft steady rain by midday, and continued well past nightfall. The next day the northmen never saw the sun at all, but rode beneath leaden skies with their hoods pulled up to keep the water from their eyes. It was a heavy rain, turning roads to mud and fields to quagmires, swelling the rivers and stripping the trees of their leaves. The constant patter made idle chatter more bother than it was worth, so men spoke only when they had something to say, and that was seldom enough.

"We are stronger than we seem, my lady," Lady Maege Mormont said as they rode. Catelyn had grown fond of Lady Maege and her eldest daughter, Dacey; they were more understanding than most in the matter of Jaime Lannister, she had found. The daughter was tall and lean, the mother short and stout, but they dressed alike in mail and leather, with the black bear of House Mormont on shield and surcoat. By Catelyn's lights, that was queer garb for a lady, yet Dacey and Lady Maege seemed more comfortable, both as warriors and as women, than ever the girl from Tarth had been.

"I have fought beside the Young Wolf in every battle," Dacey Mormont said cheerfully. "He has not lost one yet."

No, but he has lost everything else, Catelyn thought, but it would not do to say it aloud. The northmen did not lack for courage, but they were far from home, with little enough to sustain them but for their faith in their young king. That faith must be protected, at all costs. *I must be stronger*, she told herself. *I must be strong for Robb. If I despair, my grief will consume me.* Everything would turn on this marriage. If Edmure and Roslin were happy in one another, if the Late Lord Frey could be appeased and his power once more wedded to Robb's . . . *Even then, what chance will we have, caught between Lannister and Greyjoy?* It was a question Catelyn dared not dwell on, though Robb dwelt on little else. She saw how he studied his maps whenever they made camp, searching for some plan that might win back the north.

Her brother Edmure had other cares. "You don't suppose *all* Lord Walder's daughters look like him, do you?" he wondered, as he sat in his tall striped pavilion with Catelyn and his friends.

"With so many different mothers, a few of the maids are bound to turn up comely," said Ser Marq Piper, "but why should the old wretch give you a pretty one?"

"No reason at all," said Edmure in a glum tone.

It was more than Catelyn could stand. "Cersei Lannister is comely," she said sharply. "You'd be wiser to pray that Roslin is strong and healthy, with a good head and a loyal heart." And with that she left them.

Edmure did not take that well. The next day he avoided her entirely on the march, preferring the company of Marq Piper, Lymond Goodbrook, Patrek Mallister, and the young Vances. *They do not scold him, except in jest,* Catelyn told herself when they raced by her that afternoon with nary a word. *I have always been too hard with Edmure, and now grief sharpens my every word.* She regretted her rebuke. There was rain enough falling from the sky without her making more. And was it really such a terrible thing, to want a pretty wife? She remembered her own childish disappointment, the first time she had laid eyes on Eddard Stark. She had pictured him as a younger version of his brother Brandon, but that was wrong. Ned was shorter and plainer of face, and so somber. He spoke courteously enough, but beneath the words she sensed a coolness that was all at odds with Brandon, whose mirths had been as wild as his rages. Even when he took her maidenhood, their love had more of duty to it than of passion. *We made Robb that night, though; we made a king together. And after the war, at Winterfell, I had love enough for any woman, once I found the good sweet heart beneath Ned's solemn face. There is no reason Edmure should not find the same, with his Roslin.*

As the gods would have it, their route took them through the Whispering Wood where Robb had won his first great victory. They followed the course of the twisting stream on the floor of that pinched narrow valley, much as Jaime Lannister's men had done that fateful night. *It was warmer then,* Catelyn remembered, *the trees were still green, and the stream did not overflow its banks.* Fallen leaves choked the flow now and lay in sodden snarls among the rocks and roots, and the trees that had once hidden Robb's army had exchanged their green raiment for leaves of dull gold spotted with brown, and a red that reminded her of rust and dry blood. Only the spruce and the soldier pines still showed green, thrusting up at the belly of the clouds like tall dark spears.

More than the trees have died since then, she reflected. On the night of the Whispering Wood, Ned was still alive in his cell beneath Aegon's High Hill, Bran and Rickon were safe behind the walls of Winterfell. *And Theon Greyjoy fought at Robb's side, and boasted of how he had almost crossed swords with the Kingslayer. Would that he had. If Theon had died in place of Lord Karstark's sons, how much ill would have been undone?*

As they passed through the battleground, Catelyn glimpsed signs of the carnage that had been; an overturned helm filling with rain, a splintered lance, the bones of a horse. Stone cairns had been raised over some of the men who had fallen here, but scavengers had already been at them. Amidst the tumbles of rock, she spied brightly colored cloth and bits of shiny metal. Once she saw a face peering out at her, the shape of the skull beginning to emerge from beneath the melting brown flesh.

It made her wonder where Ned had come to rest. The silent sisters had taken his bones north, escorted by Hallis Mollen and a small honor guard. Had Ned ever reached Winterfell, to be interred beside his brother Brandon in the dark crypts beneath the castle? Or did the door slam shut at Moat Cailin before Hal and the sisters could pass?

Thirty-five hundred riders wound their way along the valley floor through the heart of the Whispering Wood, but Catelyn Stark had seldom felt lonelier. Every league she crossed took her farther from Riverrun, and she found herself wondering whether she would ever see the castle again. Or was it lost to her forever, like so much else?

Five days later, their scouts rode back to warn them that the rising waters had washed out the wooden bridge at Fairmarket. Galbart Glover and two of his bolder men had tried swimming their mounts across the turbulent Blue Fork at Ramsford. Two of the horses had been swept under and drowned, and one of the riders; Glover himself managed to cling to a rock until they could pull him in. "The river hasn't run this high since spring," Edmure said. "And if this rain keeps falling, it will go higher yet."

"There's a bridge further upstream, near Oldstones," remembered Catelyn, who had often crossed these lands with her father. "It's older and smaller, but if it still stands—"

"It's gone, my lady," Galbart Glover said. "Washed away even before the one at Fairmarket."

Robb looked to Catelyn. "Is there another bridge?"

"No. And the fords will be impassable." She tried to remember. "If we cannot cross the Blue Fork, we'll have to go around it, through Sevenstreams and Hag's Mire."

"Bogs and bad roads, or none at all," warned Edmure. "The going will be slow, but we'll get there, I suppose."

"Lord Walder will wait, I'm sure," said Robb. "Lothar sent him a bird from Riverrun, he knows we are coming."

"Yes, but the man is prickly, and suspicious by nature," said Catelyn. "He may take this delay as a deliberate insult."

"Very well, I'll beg his pardon for our tardiness as well. A sorry king I'll be, apologizing with every second breath." Robb made a wry face. "I hope Bolton got across the Trident before the rains began. The kingsroad runs straight north, he'll have an easy march. Even afoot, he should reach the Twins before us."

"And when you've joined his men to yours and seen my brother married, what then?" Catelyn asked him.

"North." Robb scratched Grey Wind behind an ear.

"By the causeway? Against Moat Cailin?"

He gave her an enigmatic smile. "That's one way to go," he said, and she knew from his tone that he would say no more. *A wise king keeps his own counsel*, she reminded herself.

They reached Oldstones after eight more days of steady rain, and made their camp upon the hill overlooking the Blue Fork, within a ruined stronghold of the ancient river kings. Its foundations remained amongst the weeds to show where the walls and keeps had stood, but the local smallfolk had long ago made off with most of the stones to raise their barns and septs and holdfasts. Yet in the center of what once would have been the castle's yard, a great carved sepulcher still rested, half hidden in waist-high brown grass amongst a stand of ash.

The lid of the sepulcher had been carved into a likeness of the man whose bones lay beneath, but the rain and the wind had done their work. The king had worn a beard, they could see, but otherwise his face was smooth and featureless, with only vague suggestions of a mouth, a nose, eyes, and the crown about the temples. His hands folded over the shaft of a stone warhammer that lay upon his chest. Once the warhammer would have been carved with runes that told its name and history, but all that the centuries had worn away. The stone itself was cracked and crumbling at the corners, discolored here and there by spreading white splotches of lichen, while wild roses crept up over the king's feet almost to his chest.

It was there that Catelyn found Robb, standing somber in the gathering dusk with only Grey Wind beside him. The rain had stopped for once, and he was bareheaded. "Does this castle have a name?" he asked quietly, when she came up to him.

"Oldstones, all the smallfolk called it when I was a girl, but no doubt it had some other name when it was still a hall of kings." She had camped here once with her father, on their way to Seagard. *Petyr was with us too . . .*

"There's a song," he remembered. "'Jenny of Oldstones, with the flowers in her hair.'"

"We're all just songs in the end. If we are lucky." She had played at being Jenny that day, had even wound flowers in her hair. And Petyr had pretended to be her Prince of Dragonflies. Catelyn could not have been more than twelve, Petyr just a boy.

Robb studied the sepulcher. "Whose grave is this?"

"Here lies Tristifer, the Fourth of His Name, King of the Rivers and the Hills." Her father had told her his story once. "He ruled from the Trident to the Neck, thousands of years before Jenny and her prince, in the days when the kingdoms of the First Men were falling one after the other before the onslaught of the Andals. The Hammer of Justice, they called him. He fought a hundred battles and won nine-and-ninety, or so the singers say, and when he raised this castle it was the strongest in Westeros." She put a hand on her son's shoulder. "He died in his hundredth battle, when seven Andal kings joined forces against him. The fifth Tristifer was not his equal, and soon the kingdom was lost, and then the castle, and last of all the line. With

Tristifer the Fifth died House Mudd, that had ruled the riverlands for a thousand years before the Andals came."

"His heir failed him." Robb ran a hand over the rough weathered stone. "I had hoped to leave Jeyne with child . . . we tried often enough, but I'm not certain . . ."

"It does not always happen the first time." *Though it did with you.* "Nor even the hundredth. You are very young."

"Young, and a king," he said. "A king must have an heir. If I should die in my next battle, the kingdom must not die with me. By law Sansa is next in line of succession, so Winterfell and the north would pass to her." His mouth tightened. "To her, and her lord husband. Tyrion Lannister. I cannot allow that. I *will* not allow that. That dwarf must never have the north."

"No," Catelyn agreed. "You must name another heir, until such time as Jeyne gives you a son." She considered a moment. "Your father's father had no siblings, but his father had a sister who married a younger son of Lord Raymar Royce, of the junior branch. They had three daughters, all of whom wed Vale lordlings. A Waynwood and a Corbray, for certain. The youngest . . . it might have been a Templeton, but . . ."

"Mother." There was a sharpness in Robb's tone. "You forget. My father had four sons."

She had not forgotten; she had not wanted to look at it, yet there it was. "A Snow is not a Stark."

"Jon's more a Stark than some lordlings from the Vale who have never so much as set eyes on Winterfell."

"Jon is a brother of the Night's Watch, sworn to take no wife and hold no lands. Those who take the black serve for life."

"So do the knights of the Kingsguard. That did not stop the Lannisters from stripping the white cloaks from Ser Barristan Selmy and Ser Boros Blount when they had no more use for them. If I send the Watch a hundred men in Jon's place, I'll wager they find some way to release him from his vows."

He is set on this. Catelyn knew how stubborn her son could be. "A bastard cannot inherit."

"Not unless he's legitimized by a royal decree," said Robb. "There is more precedent for that than for releasing a Sworn Brother from his oath."

"Precedent," she said bitterly. "Yes, Aegon the Fourth legitimized all his bastards on his deathbed. And how much pain, grief, war, and murder grew from that? I know you trust Jon. But can you trust his sons? Or *their* sons? The Blackfyre pretenders troubled the Targaryens for five generations, until Barristan the Bold slew the last of them on the Stepstones. If you make Jon legitimate, there is no way to turn him bastard again. Should he wed and breed, any sons you may have by Jeyne will never be safe."

"Jon would never harm a son of mine."

"No more than Theon Greyjoy would harm Bran or Rickon?"

Grey Wind leapt up atop King Tristifer's crypt, his teeth bared. Robb's own face was cold. "That is as cruel as it is unfair. Jon is no Theon."

"So you pray. Have you considered your sisters? What of *their* rights? I agree that the north must not be permitted to pass to the Imp, but what of Arya? By law, she comes after Sansa . . . your own sister, trueborn . . ."

". . . and *dead*. No one has seen or heard of Arya since they cut Father's head off. Why do you lie to yourself? Arya's gone, the same as Bran and Rickon, and they'll kill Sansa too once the dwarf gets a child from her. Jon is the only brother that remains to me. Should I die without issue, I want him to succeed me as King in the North. I had hoped you would support my choice."

"I cannot," she said. "In all else, Robb. In everything. But not in this . . . this folly. Do not ask it."

"I don't have to. I'm the king." Robb turned and walked off, Grey Wind bounding down from the tomb and loping after him.

What have I done? Catelyn thought wearily, as she stood alone by Tristifer's stone sepulcher. *First, I anger Edmure, and now Robb, but all I have done is speak the truth. Are men so fragile they cannot bear to hear it?* She might have wept then, had not the sky begun to do it for her. It was all she could do to walk back to her tent, and sit there in the silence.

In the days that followed, Robb was everywhere and anywhere;

riding at the head of the van with the Greatjon, scouting with Grey Wind, racing back to Robin Flint and the rearguard. Men said proudly that the Young Wolf was the first to rise each dawn and the last to sleep at night, but Catelyn wondered whether he was sleeping at all. *He grows as lean and hungry as his direwolf.*

"My lady," Maege Mormont said to her one morning as they rode through a steady rain, "you seem so somber. Is aught amiss?"

My lord husband is dead, as is my father. Two of my sons have been murdered, my daughter has been given to a faithless dwarf to bear his vile children, my other daughter is vanished and likely dead, and my last son and my only brother are both angry with me. What could possibly be amiss? That was more truth than Lady Maege would wish to hear, however. "This is an evil rain," she said instead. "We have suffered much, and there is more peril and more grief ahead. We need to face it boldly, with horns blowing and banners flying bravely. But this rain beats us down. The banners hang limp and sodden, and the men huddle under their cloaks and scarcely speak to one another. Only an evil rain would chill our hearts when most we need them to burn hot."

Dacey Mormont looked up at the sky. "I would sooner have water raining down on me than arrows."

Catelyn smiled despite herself. "You are braver than I am, I fear. Are all your Bear Island women such warriors?"

"She-bears, aye," said Lady Maege. "We have needed to be. In olden days the ironmen would come raiding in their longboats, or wildlings from the Frozen Shore. The men would be off fishing, like as not. The wives they left behind had to defend themselves and their children, or else be carried off."

"There's a carving on our gate," said Dacey. "A woman in a bearskin, with a child in one arm suckling at her breast. In the other hand she holds a battleaxe. She's no proper lady, that one, but I always loved her."

"My nephew Jorah brought home a proper lady once," said Lady Maege. "He won her in a tourney. How she hated that carving."

"Aye, and all the rest," said Dacey. "She had hair like spun gold, that Lynesse. Skin like cream. But her soft hands were never made for axes."

"Nor her teats for giving suck," her mother said bluntly.

Catelyn knew of whom they spoke; Jorah Mormont had brought his second wife to Winterfell for feasts, and once they had guested for a fortnight. She remembered how young the Lady Lynesse had been, how fair, and how unhappy. One night, after several cups of wine, she had confessed to Catelyn that the north was no place for a Hightower of Oldtown. "There was a Tully of Riverrun who felt the same once," she had answered gently, trying to console, "but in time she found much here she could love."

All lost now, she reflected. *Winterfell and Ned, Bran and Rickon, Sansa, Arya, all gone. Only Robb remains.* Had there been too much of Lynesse Hightower in her after all, and too little of the Starks? *Would that I had known how to wield an axe, perhaps I might have been able to protect them better.*

Day followed day, and still the rain kept falling. All the way up the Blue Fork they rode, past Sevenstreams where the river unraveled into a confusion of rills and brooks, then through Hag's Mire, where glistening green pools waited to swallow the unwary and the soft ground sucked at the hooves of their horses like a hungry babe at its mother's breast. The going was worse than slow. Half the wayns had to be abandoned to the muck, their loads distributed amongst mules and draft horses.

Lord Jason Mallister caught up with them amidst the bogs of Hag's Mire. There was more than an hour of daylight remaining when he rode up with his column, but Robb called a halt at once, and Ser Raynald Westerling came to escort Catelyn to the king's tent. She found her son seated beside a brazier, a map across his lap. Grey Wind slept at his feet. The Greatjon was with him, along with Galbart Glover, Maege Mormont, Edmure, and a man that Catelyn did not know, a fleshy balding man with a cringing look to him. *No lordling, this one,* she knew the moment she laid eyes on the stranger. *Not even a warrior.*

Jason Mallister rose to offer Catelyn his seat. His hair had almost as much white in it as brown, but the Lord of Seagard was still a handsome man; tall and lean, with a chiseled clean-shaven face, high cheekbones, and fierce blue-grey eyes. "Lady Stark, it is ever a pleasure. I bring good tidings, I hope."

"We are in sore need of some, my lord." She sat, listening to the rain patter down noisily against the canvas overhead.

Robb waited for Ser Raynald to close the tent flap. "The gods have heard our prayers, my lords. Lord Jason has brought us the captain of the *Myraham*, a merchanter out of Oldtown. Captain, tell them what you told me."

"Aye, Your Grace." He licked his thick lips nervously. "My last port of call afore Seagard, that was Lordsport on Pyke. The ironmen kept me there more'n half a year, they did. King Balon's command. Only, well, the long and the short of it is, he's dead."

"Balon Greyjoy?" Catelyn's heart skipped a beat. "You are telling us that Balon Greyjoy is dead?"

The shabby little captain nodded. "You know how Pyke's built on a headland, and part on rocks and islands off the shore, with bridges between? The way I heard it in Lordsport, there was a blow coming in from the west, rain and thunder, and old King Balon was crossing one of them bridges when the wind got hold of it and just tore the thing to pieces. He washed up two days later, all bloated and broken. Crabs ate his eyes, I hear."

The Greatjon laughed. "King crabs, I hope, to sup upon such royal jelly, eh?"

The captain bobbed his head. "Aye, but that's not all of it, no!" He leaned forward. "The *brother's* back."

"Victarion?" asked Galbart Glover, surprised.

"Euron. Crow's Eye, they call him, as black a pirate as ever raised a sail. He's been gone for years, but Lord Balon was no sooner cold than there he was, sailing into Lordsport in his *Silence*. Black sails and a red hull, and crewed by mutes. He'd been to Asshai and back, I heard. Wherever he was, though, he's home now, and he marched right into Pyke and sat his arse in the Seastone Chair, and drowned Lord Botley in a cask of seawater when he objected. That was when I ran back to *Myraham* and slipped anchor, hoping I could get away whilst things were confused. And so I did, and here I am."

"Captain," said Robb when the man was done, "you have my thanks, and you will not go unrewarded. Lord Jason will take you back to your ship when we are done. Pray wait outside."

"That I will, Your Grace. That I will."

No sooner had he left the king's pavilion than the Greatjon began to laugh, but Robb silenced him with a look. "Euron Greyjoy is no man's notion of a king, if half of what Theon said of him was true. Theon is the rightful heir, unless he's dead . . . but Victarion commands the Iron Fleet. I can't believe he would remain at Moat Cailin while Euron Crow's Eye holds the Seastone Chair. He *has* to go back."

"There's a daughter as well," Galbart Glover reminded him. "The one who holds Deepwood Motte, and Robett's wife and child."

"If she stays at Deepwood Motte that's *all* she can hope to hold," said Robb. "What's true for the brothers is even more true for her. She will need to sail home to oust Euron and press her own claim." Her son turned to Lord Jason Mallister. "You have a fleet at Seagard?"

"A fleet, Your Grace? Half a dozen longships and two war galleys. Enough to defend my own shores against raiders, but I could not hope to meet the Iron Fleet in battle."

"Nor would I ask it of you. The ironborn will be setting sail toward Pyke, I expect. Theon told me how his people think. Every captain a king on his own deck. They will all want a voice in the succession. My lord, I need two of your longships to sail around the Cape of Eagles and up the Neck to Greywater Watch."

Lord Jason hesitated. "A dozen streams drain the wetwood, all shallow, silty, and uncharted. I would not even call them rivers. The channels are ever drifting and changing. There are endless sandbars, deadfalls, and tangles of rotting trees. And Greywater Watch *moves*. How are my ships to find it?"

"Go upriver flying my banner. The crannogmen will find you. I want two ships to double the chances of my message reaching Howland Reed. Lady Maege shall go on one, Galbart on the second." He turned to the two he'd named. "You'll carry letters for those lords of mine who remain in the north, but all the commands within will be false, in case you have the misfortune to be taken. If that happens, you must tell them that you were sailing for the north. Back to Bear Island, or for the Stony Shore." He tapped a finger on the map. "Moat Cailin is the key. Lord Balon knew that, which is why he sent his brother Victarion there with the hard heart of the Greyjoy strength."

"Succession squabbles or no, the ironborn are not such fools as to abandon Moat Cailin," said Lady Maege.

"No," Robb admitted. "Victarion will leave the best part of his garrison, I'd guess. Every man he takes will be one less man we need to fight, however. And he *will* take many of his captains, count on that. The leaders. He will need such men to speak for him if he hopes to sit the Seastone Chair."

"You cannot mean to attack up the causeway, Your Grace," said Galbart Glover. "The approaches are too narrow. There is no way to deploy. No one has ever taken the Moat."

"From the south," said Robb. "But if we can attack from the north and west simultaneously, and take the ironmen in the rear while they are beating off what they think is my main thrust up the causeway, then we have a chance. Once I link up with Lord Bolton and the Freys, I will have more than twelve thousand men. I mean to divide them into three battles and start up the causeway a half-day apart. If the Greyjoys have eyes south of the Neck, they will see my whole strength rushing headlong at Moat Cailin.

"Roose Bolton will have the rearguard, while I command the center. Greatjon, you shall lead the van against Moat Cailin. Your attack must be so fierce that the ironborn have no leisure to wonder if anyone is creeping down on them from the north."

The Greatjon chuckled. "Your creepers best come fast, or my men will swarm those walls and win the Moat before you show your face. I'll make a gift of it to you when you come dawdling up."

"That's a gift I should be glad to have," said Robb.

Edmure was frowning. "You talk of attacking the ironmen in the rear, sire, but how do you mean to get north of them?"

"There are ways through the Neck that are not on any map, Uncle. Ways known only to the crannogmen—narrow trails between the bogs, and wet roads through the reeds that only boats can follow." He turned to his two messengers. "Tell Howland Reed that he is to send guides to me, two days after I have started up the causeway. To the *center* battle, where my own standard flies. Three hosts will leave the Twins, but only two will reach Moat Cailin. Mine own battle will melt away into the Neck, to reemerge on the Fever. If we move swiftly once my uncle's wed, we can all be in position by year's end. We will fall upon the Moat from three sides on the first day of the new century, as the ironmen are waking with hammers beating at their heads from the mead they'll quaff the night before."

"I like this plan," said the Greatjon. "I like it well."

Galbart Glover rubbed his mouth. "There are risks. If the crannogmen should fail you . . ."

"We will be no worse than before. But they will not fail. My father knew the worth of Howland Reed." Robb rolled up the map, and only then looked at Catelyn. "Mother."

She tensed. "Do you have some part in this for me?"

"Your part is to stay safe. Our journey through the Neck will be dangerous, and naught but battle awaits us in the north. But Lord Mallister has kindly offered to keep you safe at Seagard until the war is done. You will be comfortable there, I know."

Is this my punishment for opposing him about Jon Snow? Or for being a woman, and worse, a mother? It took her a moment to realize that they were all watching her. They had *known*, she realized. Catelyn should not have been surprised. She had won no friends by freeing the Kingslayer, and more than once she had heard the Greatjon say that women had no place on a battlefield.

Her anger must have blazed across her face, because Galbart Glover spoke up before she said a word. "My lady, His Grace is wise. It's best you do not come with us."

"Seagard will be brightened by your presence, Lady Catelyn," said Lord Jason Mallister.

"You would make me a prisoner," she said.

"An honored guest," Lord Jason insisted.

Catelyn turned to her son. "I mean no offense to Lord Jason," she said stiffly, "but if I cannot continue on with you, I would sooner return to Riverrun."

"I left my wife at Riverrun. I want my mother elsewhere. If you keep all your treasures in one purse, you only make it easier for those who would rob you. After the wedding, you shall go to Seagard, that is my royal command." Robb stood, and as quick as that, her fate was settled. He picked up a sheet of parchment. "One more matter. Lord

Balon has left chaos in his wake, we hope. I would not do the same. Yet I have no son as yet, my brothers Bran and Rickon are dead, and my sister is wed to a Lannister. I've thought long and hard about who might follow me. I command you now as my true and loyal lords to fix your seals to this document as witnesses to my decision."

A king indeed, Catelyn thought, defeated. She could only hope that the trap he'd planned for Moat Cailin worked as well as the one in which he'd just caught her.

SAMWELL

Whitetree, Sam thought. *Please, let this be Whitetree.* He remembered Whitetree. Whitetree was on the maps he'd drawn, on their way north. If this village was Whitetree, he knew where they were. *Please, it has to be.* He wanted that so badly that he forgot his feet for a little bit, he forgot the ache in his calves and his lower back and the stiff frozen fingers he could scarcely feel. He even forgot about Lord Mormont and Craster and the wights and the Others. *Whitetree*, Sam prayed, to any god that might be listening.

All wildling villages looked much alike, though. A huge weirwood grew in the center of this one ... but a white tree did not mean Whitetree, necessarily. Hadn't the weirwood at Whitetree been bigger than this one? Maybe he was remembering it wrong. The face carved into the bone pale trunk was long and sad; red tears of dried sap leaked from its eyes. *Was that how it looked when we came north?* Sam couldn't recall.

Around the tree stood a handful of one-room hovels with sod roofs, a longhall built of logs and grown over with moss, a stone well, a sheepfold ... but no sheep, nor any people. The wildlings had gone to join Mance Rayder in the Frostfangs, taking all they owned except their houses. Sam was thankful for that. Night was coming on, and it would be good to sleep beneath a roof for once. He was so tired. It seemed as though he had been walking half his life. His boots were falling to pieces, and all the blisters on his feet had burst and turned to callus, but now he had new blisters *under* the callus, and his toes were getting frostbitten.

But it was either walk or die, Sam knew. Gilly was still weak from childbirth and carrying the babe besides; she needed the horse more than he did. The second horse had died on them three days out from Craster's Keep. It was a wonder she lasted that long, poor half-starved thing. Sam's weight had probably done for her. They might have tried riding double, but he was afraid the same thing would happen again. *It's better that I walk.*

Sam left Gilly in the longhall to make a fire while he poked his head into the hovels. She was better at making fires; he could never seem to get the kindling to catch, and the last time he'd tried to strike a spark off flint and steel he managed to cut himself on his knife. Gilly bound up the gash for him, but his hand was stiff and sore, even clumsier than it had been before. He knew he should wash the wound and change the binding, but he was afraid to look at it. Besides, it was so cold that he hated taking off his gloves.

Sam did not know what he hoped to find in the empty houses. Maybe the wildlings had left some food behind. He had to take a look. Jon had searched the huts at Whitetree, on their way north. Inside one hovel Sam heard a rustling of rats from a dark corner, but otherwise there was nothing in any of them but old straw, old smells, and some ashes beneath the smoke hole.

He turned back to the weirwood and studied the carved face a moment. *It is not the face we saw*, he admitted to himself. *The tree's not half as big as the one at Whitetree.* The red eyes wept blood, and he didn't remember that either. Clumsily, Sam sank to his knees. "Old gods, hear my prayer. The Seven were my father's gods but I said my words to you when I joined the Watch. Help us now. I fear we might be lost. We're hungry too, and so cold. I don't know what gods I believe in now, but . . . please, if you're there, help us. Gilly has a little son." That was all that he could think to say. The dusk was deepening, the leaves of the weirwood rustling softly, waving like a thousand blood-red hands. Whether Jon's gods had heard him or not he could not say.

By the time he returned to the longhall, Gilly had the fire going. She sat close to it with her furs opened, the babe at her breast. *He's as hungry as we are*, Sam thought. The old women had smuggled out food for them from Craster's, but they had eaten most of it by now. Sam had been a hopeless hunter even at Horn Hill, where game was plentiful and he had hounds and huntsmen to help him; here in this endless empty forest, the chances of him catching anything were remote. His efforts at fishing the lakes and half-frozen streams had been dismal failures as well.

"How much longer, Sam?" Gilly asked. "Is it far, still?"

"Not so far. Not so far as it was." Sam shrugged out of his pack, eased himself awkwardly to the floor, and tried to cross his legs. His back ached so abominably from the walking that he would have liked to lean up against one of the carved wooden pillars that supported the roof, but the fire was in the center of the hall beneath the smoke hole and he craved warmth even more than comfort. "Another few days should see us there."

Sam had his maps, but if this wasn't Whitetree then they weren't going to be much use. *We went too far east to get around that lake*, he fretted, *or maybe too far west when I tried to double back*. He was coming to hate lakes and rivers. Up here there was never a ferry or bridge, which meant walking all the way around the lakes and searching for places to ford the rivers. It was easier to follow a game trail than to struggle through the brush, easier to circle a ridge instead of climbing it. *If Bannen or Dywen were with us we'd be at Castle Black by now, warming our feet in the common room.* Bannen was dead, though, and Dywen gone with Grenn and Dolorous Edd and the others.

The Wall is three hundred miles long and seven hundred feet high, Sam reminded himself. If they kept going south, they *had* to find it, sooner or later. And he was certain that they had been going south. By day he took directions from the sun, and on clear nights they could follow the Ice Dragon's tail, though they hadn't traveled much by night since the second horse had died. Even when the moon was full it was too dark beneath the trees, and it would have been so easy for Sam or the last garron to break a leg. *We have to be well south by now, we have to be.*

What he wasn't so certain of was how far east or west they might have strayed. They would reach the Wall, yes . . . in a day or a fortnight, it couldn't be farther than that, surely, surely . . . but *where?* It was the gate at Castle Black they needed to find; the only way through the Wall for a hundred leagues.

"Is the Wall as big as Craster used to say?" Gilly asked.

"Bigger." Sam tried to sound cheerful. "So big you can't even see the castles hidden behind it. But they're there, you'll see. The Wall is all ice, but the castles are stone and wood. There are tall towers and deep vaults and a huge longhall with a great fire burning in the hearth, day and night. It's so hot in there, Gilly, you'll hardly believe it."

"Could I stand by the fire? Me and the boy? Not for a long time, just till we're good and warm?"

"You can stand by the fire as long as you like. You'll have food and drink, too. Hot mulled wine and a bowl of venison stewed with onions, and Hobb's bread right out of the oven, so hot it will burn your fingers." Sam peeled a glove off to wriggle his own fingers near the flames, and soon regretted it. They had been numb with cold, but as feeling returned they hurt so much he almost cried. "Sometimes one of the brothers will sing," he said, to take his mind off the pain. "Dareon sang best, but they sent him to Eastwatch. There's still Halder, though. And Toad. His real name is Todder, but he looks like a toad, so we call him that. He likes to sing, but he has an awful voice."

"Do you sing?" Gilly rearranged her furs, and she moved the babe from one breast to the other.

Sam blushed. "I . . . I know some songs. When I was little I liked to sing. I danced too, but my lord father never liked me to. He said if I wanted to prance around I should do it in the yard with a sword in my hand."

"Could you sing some southron song? For the babe?"

"If you like." Sam thought for a moment. "There's a song our septon used to sing to me and my sisters, when we were little and it was time for us to go to sleep. 'The Song of the Seven,' it's called." He cleared his throat and softly sang:

The Father's face is stern and strong,
        he sits and judges right from wrong.
He weighs our lives, the short and long,
        and loves the little children.

The Mother gives the gift of life,
        and watches over every wife.
Her gentle smile ends all strife,
        and she loves her little children.

The Warrior stands before the foe,
        protecting us where e'er we go.
With sword and shield and spear and bow,
        he guards the little children.

The Crone is very wise and old,
        and sees our fates as they unfold.
She lifts her lamp of shining gold,
        to lead the little children.

The Smith, he labors day and night,
        to put the world of men to right.
With hammer, plow, and fire bright,
        he builds for little children.

The Maiden dances through the sky,
        she lives in every lover's sigh,
Her smiles teach the birds to fly,
        and give dreams to little children.

The Seven Gods who made us all,
        are listening if we should call.
So close your eyes, you shall not fall,
        they see you, little children,
Just close your eyes, you shall not fall,
        they see you, little children.

Sam remembered the last time he'd sung the song with his mother, to lull baby Dickon to sleep. His father had heard their voices and come barging in, angry. "I will have no more of that," Lord Randyll told his wife harshly. "You ruined one boy with those soft septon's songs, do you mean to do the same to this babe?" Then he looked at Sam and said, "Go sing to your sisters, if you must sing. I don't want you near my son."

Gilly's babe had gone to sleep. He was such a tiny thing, and so quiet that Sam feared for him. He didn't even have a name. He had asked Gilly about that, but she said it was bad luck to name a child before he was two. So many of them died.

She tucked her nipple back inside her furs. "That was pretty, Sam. You sing good."

"You should hear Dareon. His voice is sweet as mead."

"We drank the sweetest mead the day Craster made me a wife. It was summer then, and not so cold." Gilly gave him a puzzled look. "Did you only sing of six gods? Craster always told us you southrons had seven."

"Seven," he agreed, "but no one sings of the Stranger." The Stranger's face was the face of death. Even talking of him made Sam uncomfortable. "We should eat something. A bite or two."

Nothing was left but a few black sausages, as hard as wood. Sam sawed off a few thin slices for each of them. The effort made his wrist ache, but he was hungry enough to persist. If you chewed the slices long enough they softened up, and tasted good. Craster's wives seasoned them with garlic.

After they had finished, Sam begged her pardon and went out to relieve himself and look after the horse. A biting wind was blowing from the north, and the leaves in the trees rattled at him as he passed. He had to break the thin scum of ice on top of the stream so the horse could get a drink. *I had better bring her inside.* He did not want to wake up at break of day to find that their horse had frozen to death during the night. *Gilly would keep going even if that happened.* The girl was very brave, not like him. He wished he knew what he was going to do with her back at Castle Black. She kept saying how she'd be his wife if he wanted, but black brothers didn't keep wives; besides, he was a Tarly of Horn Hill, he could never wed a wildling. *I'll have to think of something. So long as we reach the Wall alive, the rest doesn't matter, it doesn't matter one little bit.*

Leading the horse to the longhall was simple enough. Getting her through the door was not, but Sam persisted. Gilly was already dozing by the time he got the garron inside. He hobbled the horse in a corner, fed some fresh wood to the fire, took off his heavy cloak, and wriggled down under the furs beside the wildling woman. His cloak was big enough to cover all three of them and keep in the warmth of their bodies.

Gilly smelled of milk and garlic and musty old fur, but he was used to that by now. They were good smells, so far as Sam was concerned. He liked sleeping next to her. It made him remember times long past, when he had shared a huge bed at Horn Hill with two of his sisters. That had ended when Lord Randyll decided it was making him soft as a girl. *Sleeping alone in my own cold cell never made me any harder or braver, though.* He wondered what his father would say if he could see him now. *I killed one of the Others, my lord,* he imagined saying. *I stabbed him with an obsidian dagger, and my Sworn Brothers call me Sam the Slayer now.* But even in his fancies, Lord Randyll only scowled, disbelieving.

His dreams were strange that night. He was back at Horn Hill, at the castle, but his father was not there. It was Sam's castle now. Jon Snow was with him. Lord Mormont too, the Old Bear, and Grenn and Dolorous Edd and Pyp and Toad and all his other brothers from the Watch, but they wore bright colors instead of black. Sam sat at the high table and feasted them all, cutting thick slices off a roast with his father's greatsword Heartsbane. There were sweet cakes to eat and honeyed wine to drink, there was singing and dancing, and everyone was warm. When the feast was done he went up to sleep; not to the lord's bedchamber where his mother and father lived but to the room he had once shared with his sisters. Only instead of his sisters it was Gilly waiting in the huge soft bed, wearing nothing but a big shaggy fur, milk leaking from her breasts.

He woke suddenly, in cold and dread.

The fire had burned down to smouldering red embers. The air

itself seemed frozen, it was so cold. In the corner the garron was whinnying and kicking the logs with her hind legs. Gilly sat beside the fire, hugging her babe. Sam sat up groggy, his breath puffing pale from his open mouth. The longhall was dark with shadows, black and blacker. The hair on his arms was standing up.

It's nothing, he told himself. *I'm cold, that's all.* Then, by the door, one of the shadows moved. A big one. *This is still a dream*, Sam prayed. *Oh, make it that I'm still asleep, make it a nightmare. He's dead, he's dead, I saw him die.* "He's come for the babe," Gilly wept. "He smells him. A babe fresh-born stinks o' life. He's come for the life."

The huge dark shape stooped under the lintel, into the hall, and shambled toward them. In the dim light of the fire, the shadow became Small Paul.

"Go away," Sam croaked. "We don't want you here."

Paul's hands were coal, his face was milk, his eyes shone a bitter blue. Hoarfrost whitened his beard, and on one shoulder hunched a raven, pecking at his cheek, eating the dead white flesh. Sam's bladder let go, and he felt the warmth running down his legs. "Gilly, calm the horse and lead her out. You do that."

"You—" she started.

"I have the knife. The dragonglass dagger." He fumbled it out as he got to his feet. He'd given the first knife to Grenn, but thankfully he'd remembered to take Lord Mormont's dagger before fleeing Craster's Keep. He clutched it tight, moving away from the fire, away from Gilly and the babe. "Paul?" He meant to sound brave, but it came out in a squeak. "Small Paul. Do you know me? I'm Sam, fat Sam, Sam the Scared, you saved me in the woods. You carried me when I couldn't walk another step. No one else could have done that, but you did." Sam backed away, knife in hand, sniveling. *I am such a coward.* "Don't hurt us, Paul. Please. Why would you want to hurt us?"

Gilly scrabbled backward across the hard dirt floor. The wight turned his head to look at her, but Sam shouted "*NO!*" and he turned back. The raven on his shoulder ripped a strip of flesh from his pale ruined cheek. Sam held the dagger before him, breathing like a blacksmith's bellows. Across the longhall, Gilly reached the garron. *Gods give me courage*, Sam prayed. *For once, give me a little courage. Just long enough for her to get away.*

Small Paul moved toward him. Sam backed off until he came up against a rough log wall. He clutched the dagger with both hands to hold it steady. The wight did not seem to fear the dragonglass. Perhaps he did not know what it was. He moved slowly, but Small Paul had never been quick even when he'd been alive. Behind him, Gilly murmured to calm the garron and tried to urge it toward the door. But the horse must have caught a whiff of the wight's queer cold scent. Suddenly she balked, rearing, her hooves lashing at the frosty air. Paul swung toward the sound, and seemed to lose all interest in Sam.

There was no time to think or pray or be afraid. Samwell Tarly threw himself forward and plunged the dagger down into Small Paul's back. Half-turned, the wight never saw him coming. The raven gave a shriek and took to the air. "You're dead!" Sam screamed as he stabbed. "You're dead, you're dead." He stabbed and screamed, again and again, tearing huge rents in Paul's heavy black cloak. Shards of dragonglass flew everywhere as the blade shattered on the iron mail beneath the wool.

Sam's wail made a white mist in the black air. He dropped the useless hilt and took a hasty step backwards as Small Paul twisted around. Before he could get out his other knife, the steel knife that every brother carried, the wight's black hands locked beneath his chins. Paul's fingers were so cold they seemed to burn. They burrowed deep into the soft flesh of Sam's throat. *Run, Gilly, run*, he wanted to scream, but when he opened his mouth only a choking sound emerged.

His fumbling fingers finally found the dagger, but when he slammed it up into the wight's belly the point skidded off the iron links, and the blade went spinning from Sam's hand. Small Paul's fingers tightened inexorably, and began to twist. *He's going to rip my head off*, Sam thought in despair. His throat felt frozen, his lungs on fire. He punched and pulled at the wight's wrists, to no avail. He kicked Paul between the legs, uselessly. The world shrank to two blue stars, a terrible crushing pain, and a cold so fierce that his tears froze over his eyes. Sam squirmed and pulled, desperate . . . and then he lurched forward.

Small Paul was big and powerful, but Sam still outweighed him, and the wights were clumsy, he had seen that on the Fist. The sudden shift sent Paul staggering back a step, and the living man and the dead one went crashing down together. The impact knocked one hand from Sam's throat, and he was able to suck in a quick breath of air before the icy black fingers returned. The taste of blood filled his mouth. He twisted his neck around, looking for his knife, and saw a dull orange glow. *The fire!* Only ember and ashes remained, but still . . . he could not breathe, or think . . . Sam wrenched himself sideways, pulling Paul with him . . . his arms flailed against the dirt floor, groping, reaching, scattering the ashes, until at last they found something hot . . . a chunk of charred wood, smouldering red and orange within the black . . . his fingers closed around it, and he smashed it into Paul's mouth, so hard he felt teeth shatter.

Yet even so the wight's grip did not loosen. Sam's last thoughts were for the mother who had loved him and the father he had failed. The longhall was spinning around him when he saw the wisp of smoke rising from between Paul's broken teeth. Then the dead man's face burst into flame, and the hands were gone.

Sam sucked in air, and rolled feebly away. The wight was burning, hoarfrost dripping from his beard as the flesh beneath blackened. Sam heard the raven shriek, but Paul himself made no sound. When his mouth opened, only flames came out. And his eyes . . . *It's gone, the blue glow is gone.*

He crept to the door. The air was so cold that it hurt to breathe, but such a fine sweet hurt. He ducked from the longhall. "Gilly?" he called. "Gilly, I killed it. Gil—"

She stood with her back against the weirwood, the boy in her arms. The wights were all around her. There were a dozen of them, a score, more . . . some had been wildlings once, and still wore skins and hides . . . but more had been his brothers. Sam saw Lark the Sisterman, Softfoot, Ryles. The wen on Chett's neck was black, his boils covered with a thin film of ice. And that one looked like Hake, though it was hard to know for certain with half his head missing. They had torn the poor garron apart, and were pulling out her entrails with dripping red hands. Pale steam rose from her belly.

Sam made a whimpery sound. "It's not fair . . ."

"*Fair*." The raven landed on his shoulder. "*Fair, far, fear.*" It flapped its wings, and screamed along with Gilly. The wights were almost on her. He heard the dark red leaves of the weirwood rustling, whispering to one another in a tongue he did not know. The starlight itself seemed to stir, and all around them the trees groaned and creaked. Sam Tarly turned the color of curdled milk, and his eyes went wide as plates. *Ravens!* They were in the weirwood, hundreds of them, thousands, perched on the bone-white branches, peering between the leaves. He saw their beaks open as they screamed, saw them spread their black wings. Shrieking, flapping, they descended on the wights in angry clouds. They swarmed round Chett's face and pecked at his blue eyes, they covered the Sisterman like flies, they plucked gobbets from inside Hake's shattered head. There were so many that when Sam looked up, he could not see the moon.

"*Go*," said the bird on his shoulder. "*Go, go, go.*"

Sam ran, puffs of frost exploding from his mouth. All around him the wights flailed at the black wings and sharp beaks that assailed them, falling in an eerie silence with never a grunt nor cry. But the ravens ignored Sam. He took Gilly by the hand and pulled her away from the weirwood. "We have to go."

"But where?" Gilly hurried after him, holding her baby. "They killed our horse, how will we . . ."

"*Brother!*" The shout cut through the night, through the shrieks of a thousand ravens. Beneath the trees, a man muffled head to heels in mottled blacks and greys sat astride an elk. "*Here*," the rider called. A hood shadowed his face.

He's wearing blacks. Sam urged Gilly toward him. The elk was huge, a great elk, ten feet tall at the shoulder, with a rack of antlers near as wide. The creature sank to his knees to let them mount. "Here," the rider said, reaching down with a gloved hand to pull Gilly up behind him. Then it was Sam's turn. "My thanks," he puffed. Only when he grasped the offered hand did he realize that the rider wore no glove. His hand was black and cold, with fingers hard as stone.

ARYA

When they reached the top of the ridge and saw the river, Sandor Clegane reined up hard and cursed.

The rain was falling from a black iron sky, pricking the green and brown torrent with ten thousand swords. *It must be a mile across*, Arya thought. The tops of half a hundred trees poked up out the swirling waters, their limbs clutching for the sky like the arms of drowning men. Thick mats of sodden leaves choked the shoreline, and farther out in the channel she glimpsed something pale and swollen, a deer or perhaps a dead horse, moving swiftly downstream. There was a sound too, a low rumble at the edge of hearing, like the sound a dog makes just before he growls.

Arya squirmed in the saddle and felt the links of the Hound's mail digging into her back. His arms encircled her; on the left, the burned arm, he'd donned a steel vambrace for protection, but she'd seen him change the dressings, and the flesh beneath was still raw and seeping. If the burns pained him, though, Sandor Clegane gave no hint of it.

"Is this the Blackwater Rush?" They had ridden so far in rain and darkness, through trackless woods and nameless villages, that Arya had lost all sense of where they were.

"It's a river we need to cross, that's all you need to know." Clegane would answer her from time to time, but he had warned her not to talk back. He had given her a lot of warnings that first day. "The next time you hit me, I'll tie your hands behind your back," he'd said. "The next time you try and run off, I'll bind your feet together. Scream or shout or bite me again, and I'll gag you. We can ride double, or I can throw you across the back of the horse trussed up like a sow for slaughter. Your choice."

She had chosen to ride, but the first time they made camp she'd waited until she thought he was asleep, and found a big jagged rock to smash his ugly head in. *Quiet as a shadow*, she told herself as she crept toward him, but that wasn't quiet enough. The Hound hadn't been asleep after all. Or maybe he'd woken. Whichever it was, his eyes opened, his mouth twitched, and he took the rock away from her as if she were a baby. The best she could do was kick him. "I'll give you that one," he said, when he flung the rock into the bushes. "But if you're stupid enough to try again, I'll hurt you."

"Why don't you just *kill* me like you did Mycah?" Arya had screamed at him. She was still defiant then, more angry than scared.

He answered by grabbing the front of her tunic and yanking her within an inch of his burned face. "The next time you say that name I'll beat you so bad you'll *wish* I killed you."

After that, he rolled her in his horse blanket every night when he went to sleep, and tied ropes around her top and bottom so she was bound up as tight as a babe in swaddling clothes.

It has to be the Blackwater, Arya decided as she watched the rain lash the river. The Hound was Joffrey's dog; he was taking her back to the Red Keep, to hand to Joffrey and the queen. She wished that the sun would come out, so she could tell which way they were going. The more she looked at the moss on the trees the more confused she got. *The Blackwater wasn't so wide at King's Landing, but that was before the rains.*

"The fords will all be gone," Sandor Clegane said, "and I wouldn't care to try and swim over neither."

There's no way across, she thought. *Lord Beric will catch us for sure.* Clegane had pushed his big black stallion hard, doubling back thrice to throw off pursuit, once even riding half a mile up the center of a swollen stream ... but Arya still expected to see the outlaws every time she looked back. She had tried to help them by scratching her name on the trunks of trees when she went in the bushes to make water, but the fourth time she did it he caught her, and that was the end of that. *It doesn't matter*, Arya told herself, *Thoros will find me in his flames.* Only he hadn't. Not yet, anyway, and once they crossed the river . . .

"Harroway town shouldn't be far," the Hound said. "Where Lord Roote stables Old King Andahar's two-headed water horse. Maybe we'll ride across."

Arya had never heard of Old King Andahar. She'd never seen a horse with two heads either, especially not one who could run on water, but she knew better than to ask. She held her tongue and sat stiff as the Hound turned the stallion's head and trotted along the ridgeline, following the river downstream. At least the rain was at their backs this way. She'd had enough of it stinging her eyes half-blind and washing down her cheeks like she was crying. *Wolves never cry*, she reminded herself again.

It could not have been much past noon, but the sky was dark as dusk. They had not seen the sun in more days than she could count. Arya was soaked to the bone, saddle-sore, sniffling, and achy. She had a fever too, and sometimes shivered uncontrollably, but when she'd told the Hound that she was sick he'd only snarled at her. "Wipe your nose and shut your mouth," he told her. Half the time he slept in the saddle now, trusting his stallion to follow whatever rutted farm track or game trail they were on. The horse was a heavy courser, almost as big as a destrier but much faster. *Stranger*, the Hound called him. Arya had tried to steal him once, when Clegane was taking a piss against a tree, thinking she could ride off before he could catch her. Stranger had almost bitten her face off. He was gentle as an old gelding with his master, but otherwise he had a temper as black as he was. She had never known a horse so quick to bite or kick.

They rode beside the river for hours, splashing across two muddy vassal streams before they reached the place that Sandor Clegane had spoken of. "Lord Harroway's Town," he said, and then, when he saw it, "*Seven hells!*" The town was drowned and desolate. The rising waters had overflowed the riverbanks. All that remained of Harroway town was the upper story of a daub-and-wattle inn, the seven-sided dome of a sunken sept, two-thirds of a stone roundtower, some moldy thatch roofs, and a forest of chimneys.

But there was smoke coming from the tower, Arya saw, and below one arched window a wide flat-bottomed boat was chained up tight. The boat had a dozen oarlocks and a pair of great carved wooden horse heads mounted fore and aft. *The two-headed horse*, she realized. There was a wooden house with a sod roof right in the middle of the deck, and when the Hound cupped his hands around his mouth and shouted two men came spilling out. A third appeared in the window of the roundtower, clutching a loaded crossbow. "*What do you want?*" he shouted across the swirling brown waters.

"*Take us over*," the Hound shouted back.

The men in the boat conferred with one another. One of them, a grizzled grey-haired man with thick arms and a bent back, stepped to the rail. "*It will cost you.*"

"*Then I'll pay.*"

With what? Arya wondered. The outlaws had taken Clegane's gold, but maybe Lord Beric had left him some silver and copper. A ferry ride shouldn't cost more than a few coppers . . .

The ferrymen were talking again. Finally the bent-backed one turned away and gave a shout. Six more men appeared, pulling up hoods to keep the rain off their heads. Still more squirmed out the holdfast window and leapt down onto the deck. Half of them looked enough like the bent-backed man to be his kin. Some of them undid the chains and took up long poles, while the others slid heavy wide-bladed oars through the locks. The ferry swung about and began to creep slowly toward the shallows, oars stroking smoothly on either side. Sandor Clegane rode down the hill to meet it.

When the aft end of the boat slammed into the hillside, the ferrymen opened a wide door beneath the carved horse's head, and extended a heavy oaken plank. Stranger balked at the water's edge, but the Hound put his heels into the courser's flank and urged him up the gangway. The bent-backed man was waiting for them on deck. "Wet enough for you, ser?" he asked, smiling.

The Hound's mouth gave a twitch. "I need your boat, not your bloody wit." He dismounted, and pulled Arya down beside him. One of the boatmen reached for Stranger's bridle. "I wouldn't," Clegane said, as the horse kicked. The man leapt back, slipped on the rain-slick deck, and crashed onto his arse, cursing.

The ferryman with the bent back wasn't smiling any longer. "We can get you across," he said sourly. "It will cost you a gold piece. Another for the horse. A third for the boy."

"Three dragons?" Clegane gave a bark of laughter. "For three dragons I should own the bloody ferry."

"Last year, might be you could. But with this river, I'll need extra hands on the poles and oars just to see we don't get swept a hundred miles out to sea. Here's your choice. Three dragons, or you teach that hellhorse how to walk on water."

"I like an honest brigand. Have it your way. Three dragons . . . when you put us ashore safe on the north bank."

"I'll have them now, or we don't go." The man thrust out a thick, callused hand, palm up.

Clegane rattled his longsword to loosen the blade in the scabbard. "Here's *your* choice. Gold on the north bank, or steel on the south."

The ferryman looked up at the Hound's face. Arya could tell that he didn't like what he saw there. He had a dozen men behind him, strong men with oars and hardwood poles in their hands, but none of them were rushing forward to help him. Together they could overwhelm Sandor Clegane, though he'd likely kill three or four of them before they took him down. "How do I know you're good for it?" the bent-backed man asked, after a moment.

He's not, she wanted to shout. Instead she bit her lip.

"Knight's honor," the Hound said, unsmiling.

He's not even a knight. She did not say that either.

"That will do." The ferryman spat. "Come on then, we can have you across before dark. Tie the horse up, I don't want him spooking when we're under way. There's a brazier in the cabin if you and your son want to get warm."

"*I'm not his stupid son!*" said Arya furiously. That was even worse than being taken for a boy. She was so angry that she might have told them who she *really* was, only Sandor Clegane grabbed her by the back of the collar and hoisted her one-handed off the deck. "How many times do I need to tell you to *shut your bloody mouth*?" He shook her so hard her teeth rattled, then let her fall. "Get in there and get dry, like the man said."

Arya did as she was told. The big iron brazier was glowing red, filling the room with a sullen suffocating heat. It felt pleasant to stand beside it, to warm her hands and dry off a little bit, but as soon as she felt the deck move under her feet she slipped back out through the forward door.

The two-headed horse eased slowly through the shallows, picking its way between the chimneys and rooftops of drowned Harroway. A dozen men labored at the oars while four more used the long poles to push off whenever they came too close to a rock, a tree, or a sunken house. The bent-backed man had the rudder. Rain pattered against the smooth planks of the deck and splashed off the tall carved horse-heads fore and aft. Arya was getting soaked again, but she didn't care. She wanted to see. The man with the crossbow still stood in the window of the roundtower, she saw. His eyes followed her as the ferry slid by underneath. She wondered if he was this Lord Roote that the Hound had mentioned. *He doesn't look much like a lord.* But then, she didn't look much like a lady either.

Once they were beyond the town and out in the river proper, the current grew much stronger. Through the grey haze of rain Arya could make out a tall stone pillar on the far shore that surely marked the ferry landing, but no sooner had she seen it than she realized that they were being pushed away from it, downstream. The oarsmen were rowing more vigorously now, fighting the rage of the river. Leaves and broken branches swirled past as fast as if they'd been fired from a scorpion. The men with the poles leaned out and shoved away anything that came too close. It was windier out here, too. Whenever she turned to look upstream, Arya got a face full of blowing rain. Stranger was screaming and kicking as the deck moved underfoot.

If I jumped over the side, the river would wash me away before the Hound even knew that I was gone. She looked back over a shoulder, and saw Sandor Clegane struggling with his frightened horse, trying to calm him. She would never have a better chance to get away from him. *I might drown, though.* Jon used to say that she swam like a fish, but even a fish might have trouble in this river. Still, drowning might be better than King's Landing. She thought about Joffrey and crept up to the prow. The river was murky brown with mud and lashed by rain, looking more like soup than water. Arya wondered how cold it would be. *I couldn't get much wetter than I am now.* She put a hand on the rail.

But a sudden shout snapped her head about before she could leap. The ferrymen were rushing forward, poles in hand. For a moment, she did not understand what was happening. Then she saw it: an uprooted tree, huge and dark, coming straight at them. A tangle of roots and limbs poked up out of the water as it came, like the reaching arms of a great kraken. The oarsmen were backing water frantically, trying to avoid a collision that could capsize them or stove their hull in. The old man had wrenched the rudder about, and the horse at the prow was swinging downstream, but too slowly. Glistening brown and black, the tree rushed toward them like a battering ram.

It could not have been more than ten feet from their prow when two of the boatmen somehow caught it with their long poles. One snapped, and the long splintering *craaaack* made it sound as if the ferry were breaking up beneath them. But the second man managed to give the trunk a hard shove, just enough to deflect it away from them. The tree swept past the ferry with inches to spare, its branches scrabbling like claws against the horsehead. Only just when it seemed as if they were clear, one of the monster's upper limbs dealt them a glancing thump. The ferry seemed to shudder, and Arya slipped, landing painfully on one knee. The man with the broken pole was not so lucky. She heard him shout as he stumbled over the side. Then the raging brown water closed over him, and he was gone in the time it took Arya to climb back to her feet. One of the other boatmen snatched up a coil of rope, but there was no one to throw it to.

Maybe he'll wash up someplace downstream, Arya tried to tell herself, but the thought had a hollow ring. She had lost all desire to go swimming. When Sandor Clegane shouted at her to get back inside before he beat her bloody, she went meekly. The ferry was fighting to turn back on course by then, against a river that wanted nothing more than to carry it down to the sea.

When they finally came ashore, it was a good two miles downriver of their usual landing. The boat slammed into the bank so hard that another pole snapped, and Arya almost lost her feet again. Sandor Clegane lifted her onto Stranger's back as if she weighed no more than a doll. The boatmen stared at them with dull, exhausted eyes, all but the bent-backed man, who held his hand out. "Six dragons," he demanded. "Three for the passage, and three for the man I lost."

Sandor Clegane rummaged in his pouch and shoved a crumpled wad of parchment into the boatman's palm. "There. Take ten."

"Ten?" The ferryman was confused. "What's this, now?"

"A dead man's note, good for nine thousand dragons or near-abouts." The Hound swung up into the saddle behind Arya, and smiled down unpleasantly. "Ten of it is yours. I'll be back for the rest one day, so see you don't go spending it."

The man squinted down at the parchment. "Writing. What good's writing? You promised gold. Knight's honor, you said."

"Knights have no bloody honor. Time you learned that, old man." The Hound gave Stranger the spur and galloped off through the rain. The ferrymen threw curses at their backs, and one or two threw stones. Clegane ignored rocks and words alike, and before long they were lost in the gloom of the trees, the river a dwindling roar behind them. "The ferry won't cross back till morning," he said, "and that lot won't be taking paper promises from the next fools to come along. If your friends are chasing us, they're going to need to be bloody strong swimmers."

Arya huddled down and held her tongue. *Valar morghulis*, she thought sullenly. *Ser Ilyn, Ser Meryn, King Joffrey, Queen Cersei. Dunsen, Polliver, Raff the Sweetling, Ser Gregor and the Tickler. And the Hound, the Hound, the Hound.*

By the time the rain stopped and the clouds broke, she was shivering and sneezing so badly that Clegane called a halt for the night, and even tried to make a fire. The wood they gathered proved too wet, though. Nothing he tried was enough to make the spark catch. Finally he kicked it all apart in disgust. "Seven bloody hells," he swore. "I hate fires."

They sat on damp rocks beneath an oak tree, listening to the slow patter of water dripping from the leaves as they ate a cold supper of hardbread, moldy cheese, and smoked sausage. The Hound sliced the meat with his dagger, and narrowed his eyes when he caught Arya looking at the knife. "Don't even think about it."

"I wasn't," she lied.

He snorted to show what he thought of *that*, but he gave her a thick slice of sausage. Arya worried it with her teeth, watching him all the while. "I never beat your sister," the Hound said. "But I'll beat you if you make me. Stop trying to think up ways to kill me. None of it will do you a bit of good."

She had nothing to say to that. She gnawed on the sausage and stared at him coldly. *Hard as stone*, she thought.

"At least you look at my face. I'll give you that, you little she-wolf. How do you like it?"

"I don't. It's all burned and ugly."

Clegane offered her a chunk of cheese on the point of his dagger. "You're a little fool. What good would it do you if you *did* get away? You'd just get caught by someone worse."

"I would *not*," she insisted. "There is no one worse."

"You never knew my brother. Gregor once killed a man for snoring. His own man." When he grinned, the burned side of his face pulled tight, twisting his mouth in a queer unpleasant way. He had no lips on that side, and only the stump of an ear.

"I did so know your brother." Maybe the Mountain *was* worse, now that Arya thought about it. "Him and Dunsen and Polliver, and Raff the Sweetling and the Tickler."

The Hound seemed surprised. "And how would Ned Stark's precious little daughter come to know the likes of them? Gregor never brings his pet rats to court."

"I know them from the village." She ate the cheese, and reached for a hunk of hardbread. "The village by the lake where they caught Gendry, me, and Hot Pie. They caught Lommy Greenhands too, but Raff the Sweetling killed him because his leg was hurt."

Clegane's mouth twitched. "Caught you? My brother *caught* you?" That made him laugh, a sour sound, part rumble and part snarl. "Gregor never knew what he had, did he? He couldn't have, or he would have dragged you back kicking and screaming to King's Landing and dumped you in Cersei's lap. Oh, that's bloody sweet. I'll be sure and tell him that, before I cut his heart out."

It wasn't the first time he had talked of killing the Mountain. "But he's your brother," Arya said dubiously.

"Didn't you ever have a brother you wanted to kill?" He laughed again. "Or maybe a sister?" He must have seen something in her face then, for he leaned closer. "Sansa. That's it, isn't it? The wolf bitch wants to kill the pretty bird."

"No," Arya spat back at him. "I'd like to kill *you*."

"Because I hacked your little friend in two? I've killed a lot more than him, I promise you. You think that makes me some monster. Well, maybe it does, but I saved your sister's life too. The day the mob pulled her off her horse, I cut through them and brought her back to the castle, else she would have gotten what Lollys Stokeworth got. And she sang for me. You didn't know that, did you? Your sister sang me a sweet little song."

"You're lying," she said at once.

"You don't know half as much as you think you do. The *Blackwater*? Where in seven hells do you think we are? Where do you think we're going?"

The scorn in his voice made her hesitate. "Back to King's Landing," she said. "You're bringing me to Joffrey and the queen." That was wrong, she realized all of a sudden, just from the way he asked the questions. But she had to say *something*.

"Stupid blind little wolf bitch." His voice was rough and hard as an iron rasp. "Bugger Joffrey, bugger the queen, and bugger that twisted little gargoyle she calls a brother. I'm done with their city, done with their Kingsguard, done with Lannisters. What's a dog to do with lions, I ask you?" He reached for his waterskin, took a long pull. As he wiped his mouth, he offered the skin to Arya and said, "The river was the Trident, girl. The *Trident*, not the Blackwater. Make the map in your head, if you can. On the morrow we should reach the kingsroad. We'll make good time after that, straight up to the Twins. It's going to be me who hands you over to that mother of yours. Not the noble lightning lord or that flaming fraud of a priest, the monster."

He grinned at the look on her face. "You think your outlaw friends are the only ones can smell a ransom? Dondarrion took my gold, so I took you. You're worth twice what they stole from me, I'd say. Maybe even more if I sold you back to the Lannisters like you fear, but I won't. Even a dog gets tired of being kicked. If this Young Wolf has the wits the gods gave a toad, he'll make me a lordling and beg me to enter his service. He *needs* me, though he may not know it yet. Maybe I'll even kill Gregor for him, he'd like that."

"He'll never take you," she spat back. "Not *you*."

"Then I'll take as much gold as I can carry, laugh in his face, and ride off. If he doesn't take me, he'd be wise to kill me, but he won't. Too much his father's son, from what I hear. Fine with me. Either way I win. And so do you, she-wolf. So stop whimpering and snapping at me, I'm sick of it. Keep your mouth shut and do as I tell you, and maybe we'll even be in time for your uncle's bloody wedding."

JON

The mare was blown, but Jon could not let up on her. He had to reach the Wall before the Magnar. He would have slept in the saddle if he'd had one; lacking that, it was hard enough to stay ahorse while awake. His wounded leg grew ever more painful. He dare not rest long enough to let it heal. Instead he ripped it open anew each time he mounted up.

When he crested a rise and saw the brown rutted kingsroad before him wending its way north through hill and plain, he patted the mare's neck and said, "Now all we need do is follow the road, girl. Soon the Wall." His leg had gone as stiff as wood by then, and fever had made him so light-headed that twice he found himself riding in the wrong direction.

Soon the Wall. He pictured his friends drinking mulled wine in the common hall. Hobb would be with his kettles, Donal Noye at his forge, Maester Aemon in his rooms beneath the rookery. *And the Old Bear? Sam, Grenn, Dolorous Edd, Dywen with his wooden teeth . . .* Jon could only pray that some had escaped the Fist.

Ygritte was much in his thoughts as well. He remembered the smell of her hair, the warmth of her body . . . and the look on her face as she slit the old man's throat. *You were wrong to love her,* a voice whispered. *You were wrong to leave her,* a different voice insisted. He wondered if his father had been torn the same way, when he'd left

Jon's mother to return to Lady Catelyn. *He was pledged to Lady Stark, and I am pledged to the Night's Watch.*

He almost rode through Mole's Town, so feverish that he did not know where he was. Most of the village was hidden underground, only a handful of small hovels to be seen by the light of the waning moon. The brothel was a shed no bigger than a privy, its red lantern creaking in the wind, a bloodshot eye peering through the blackness. Jon dismounted at the adjoining stable, half-stumbling from the mare's back as he shouted two boys awake. "I need a fresh mount, with saddle and bridle," he told them, in a tone that brooked no argument. They brought him that; a skin of wine as well, and half a loaf of brown bread. "Wake the village," he told them. "Warn them. There are wildlings south of the Wall. Gather your goods and make for Castle Black." He pulled himself onto the black gelding they'd given him, gritting his teeth at the pain in his leg, and rode hard for the north.

As the stars began to fade in the eastern sky, the Wall appeared before him, rising above the trees and the morning mists. Moonlight glimmered pale against the ice. He urged the gelding on, following the muddy slick road until he saw the stone towers and timbered halls of Castle Black huddled like broken toys beneath the great cliff of ice. By then the Wall glowed pink and purple with the first light of dawn.

No sentries challenged him as he rode past the outbuildings. No one came forth to bar his way. Castle Black seemed as much a ruin as Greyguard. Brown brittle weeds grew between cracks in the stones of the courtyards. Old snow covered the roof of the Flint Barracks and lay in drifts against the north side of Hardin's Tower, where Jon used to sleep before being made the Old Bear's steward. Fingers of soot streaked the Lord Commander's Tower where the smoke had boiled from the windows. Mormont had moved to the King's Tower after the fire, but Jon saw no lights there either. From the ground he could not tell if there were sentries walking the Wall seven hundred feet above, but he saw no one on the huge switchback stair that climbed the south face of the ice like some great wooden thunderbolt.

There was smoke rising from the chimney of the armory, though; only a wisp, almost invisible against the grey northern sky, but it was enough. Jon dismounted and limped toward it. Warmth poured out the open door like the hot breath of summer. Within, one-armed Donal Noye was working his bellows at the fire. He looked up at the noise. "Jon Snow?"

"None else." Despite fever, exhaustion, his leg, the Magnar, the old man, Ygritte, Mance, despite it all, Jon smiled. It was good to be back, good to see Noye with his big belly and pinned-up sleeve, his jaw bristling with black stubble.

The smith released his grip on the bellows. "Your face . . ."

He had almost forgotten about his face. "A skinchanger tried to rip out my eye."

Noye frowned. "Scarred or smooth, it's a face I thought I'd seen the last of. We heard you'd gone over to Mance Raydar."

Jon grasped the door to stay upright. "Who told you that?"

"Jarman Buckwell. He returned a fortnight past. His scouts claim they saw you with their own eyes, riding along beside the wildling column and wearing a sheepskin cloak." Noye eyed him. "I see the last part's true."

"It's all true," Jon confessed. "As far as it goes."

"Should I be pulling down a sword to gut you, then?"

"No. I was acting on orders. Qhorin Halfhand's last command. Noye, where is the garrison?"

"Defending the Wall against your wildling friends."

"Yes, but *where*?"

"Everywhere. Harma Dogshead was seen at Woodswatch-by-the-Pool, Rattleshirt at Long Barrow, the Weeper near Icemark. All along the Wall . . . they're here, they're there, they're climbing near Queensgate, they're hacking at the gates of Greyguard, they're massing against Eastwatch . . . but one glimpse of a black cloak and they're gone. Next day they're somewhere else."

Jon swallowed a groan. "Feints. Mance wants us to spread ourselves thin, don't you see?" *And Bowen Marsh has obliged him.* "The gate is here. The attack is here."

Noye crossed the room. "Your leg is drenched in blood."

Jon looked down dully. It was true. His wound had opened again. "An arrow wound . . ."

"A wildling arrow." It was not a question. Noye had only one arm, but that was thick with muscle. He slid it under Jon's to help support him. "You're white as milk, and burning hot besides. I'm taking you to Aemon."

"There's no time. There are wildlings *south* of the Wall, coming up from Queenscrown to open the gate."

"How many?" Noye half-carried Jon out the door.

"A hundred and twenty, and well armed for wildlings. Bronze armor, some bits of steel. How many men are left here?"

"Forty odd," said Donal Noye. "The crippled and infirm, and some green boys still in training."

"If Marsh is gone, who did he name as castellan?"

The armorer laughed. "Ser Wynton, gods preserve him. Last knight in the castle and all. The thing is, Stout seems to have forgotten and no one's been rushing to remind him. I suppose I'm as much a commander as we have now. The meanest of the cripples."

That was for the good, at least. The one-armed armorer was hard headed, tough, and well seasoned in war. Ser Wynton Stout, on the other hand . . . well, he had been a good man once, everyone agreed, but he had been eighty years a ranger, and both strength and wits were gone. Once, he'd fallen asleep at supper and almost drowned in a bowl of pea soup.

"Where's your wolf?" Noye asked as they crossed the yard.

"Ghost. I had to leave him when I climbed the Wall. I'd hoped he'd make his way back here."

"I'm sorry, lad. There's been no sign of him." They limped up to the maester's door, in the long wooden keep beneath the rookery. The armorer gave it a kick. "*Clydas!*"

After a moment, a stooped, round-shouldered little man in black peered out. His small pink eyes widened at the sight of Jon. "Lay the lad down, I'll fetch the maester."

A fire was burning in the hearth, and the room was almost stuffy. The warmth made Jon sleepy. As soon as Noye eased him down onto his back, he closed his eyes to stop the world from spinning. He could hear the ravens *quork*ing and complaining in the rookery above. "*Snow*," one bird was saying. "*Snow, snow, snow*." That was Sam's doing, Jon remembered. Had Samwell Tarly made it home safely, he wondered, or only the birds?

Maester Aemon was not long in coming. He moved slowly, one spotted hand on Clydas's arm as he shuffled forward with small careful steps. Around his thin neck his chain hung heavy, gold and silver links glinting amongst iron, lead, tin, and other base metals. "Jon Snow," he said, "you must tell me all you've seen and done when you are stronger. Donal, put a kettle of wine on the fire, and my irons as well. I will want them red-hot. Clydas, I shall need that good sharp knife of yours." The maester was more than a hundred years old; shrunken, frail, hairless, and quite blind. But if his milky eyes saw nothing, his wits were still as sharp as they had ever been.

"There are wildlings coming," Jon told him, as Clydas ran a blade up the leg of his breeches, slicing the heavy black cloth, crusty with old blood and sodden with new. "From the south. We climbed the Wall . . ."

Maester Aemon gave Jon's crude bandage a sniff when Clydas cut it away. "We?"

"I was with them. Qhorin Halfhand commanded me to join them." Jon winced as the maester's finger explored his wound, poking and prodding. "The Magnar of Thenn—*aaaaah*, that hurts." He clenched his teeth. "Where is the Old Bear?"

"Jon . . . it grieves me to say, but Lord Commander Mormont was murdered at Craster's Keep, at the hands of his Sworn Brothers."

"Bro . . . *our own men?*" Aemon's words hurt a hundred times worse than his fingers. Jon remembered the Old Bear as last he'd seen him, standing before his tent with his raven on his arm croaking for corn. *Mormont gone?* He had feared it ever since he'd seen the aftermath of battle on the Fist, yet it was no less a blow. "Who was it? Who turned on him?"

"Garth of Oldtown, Ollo Lophand, Dirk . . . thieves, cowards and killers, the lot of them. We should have seen it coming. The Watch is not what it was. Too few honest men to keep the rogues in line." Donal Noye turned the maester's blades in the fire. "A dozen true men made it back. Dolorous Edd, Giant, your friend the Aurochs. We had the tale from them."

Only a dozen? Two hundred men had left Castle Black with Lord Commander Mormont, two hundred of the Watch's best. "Does this mean Marsh is Lord Commander, then?" The Old Pomegranate was amiable, and a diligent First Steward, but he was woefully ill-suited to face a wildling host.

"For the nonce, until we can hold a choosing," said Maester Aemon. "Clydas, bring me the flask."

A choosing. With Qhorin Halfhand and Ser Jaremy Rykker both dead and Ben Stark still missing, who was there? Not Bowen Marsh or Ser Wynton Stout, that was certain. Had Thoren Smallwood survived the Fist, or Ser Ottyn Wythers? *No, it will be Cotter Pyke or Ser Denys Mallister. Which, though?* The commanders at the Shadow Tower and Eastwatch were good men, but very different; Ser Denys courtly and cautious, as chivalrous as he was elderly, Pyke younger, bastard-born, rough-tongued, and bold to a fault. Worse, the two men despised each other. The Old Bear had always kept them far apart, at opposite ends of the Wall. The Mallisters had a bone-deep mistrust of the ironborn, Jon knew.

A stab of pain reminded him of his own woes. The maester squeezed his hand. "Clydas is bringing milk of the poppy."

Jon tried to rise. "I don't need—"

"You do," Aemon said firmly. "This will hurt."

Donal Noye crossed the room and shoved Jon back onto his back. "Be still, or I'll tie you down." Even with only one arm, the smith handled him as if he were a child. Clydas returned with a green flask and a rounded stone cup. Maester Aemon poured it full. "Drink this."

Jon had bitten his lip in his struggles. He could taste blood mingled with the thick, chalky potion. It was all he could do not to retch it back up.

Clydas brought a basin of warm water, and Maester Aemon washed the pus and blood from his wound. Gentle as he was, even the lightest touch made Jon want to scream. "The Magnar's men are disciplined, and they have bronze armor," he told them. Talking helped keep his mind off his leg.

"The Magnar's a lord on Skagos," Noye said. "There were Skagossons at Eastwatch when I first came to the Wall, I remember hearing them talk of him."

"Jon was using the word in its older sense, I think," Maester Aemon said, "not as a family name but as a title. It derives from the Old Tongue."

"It means lord," Jon agreed. "Styr is the Magnar of some place called Thenn, in the far north of the Frostfangs. He has a hundred of his own men, and a score of raiders who know the Gift almost as well as we do. Mance never found the horn, though, that's something. The Horn of Winter, that's what he was digging for up along the Milkwater."

Maester Aemon paused, washcloth in hand. "The Horn of Winter is an ancient legend. Does the King-beyond-the-Wall truly believe that such a thing exists?"

"They all do," said Jon. "Ygritte said they opened a hundred graves ... graves of kings and heroes, all over the valley of the Milkwater, but they never ..."

"Who is *Ygritte*?" Donal Noye asked pointedly.

"A woman of the free folk." How could he explain Ygritte to them? *She's warm and smart and funny and she can kiss a man or slit his throat.* "She's with Styr, but she's not ... she's young, only a girl, in truth, wild, but she ..." *She killed an old man for building a fire.* His tongue felt thick and clumsy. The milk of the poppy was clouding his wits. "I broke my vows with her. I never meant to, but ..." *It was wrong. Wrong to love her, wrong to leave her ...* "I wasn't strong enough. The Halfhand commanded me, ride with them, watch, I must not balk, I ..." His head felt as if it were packed with wet wool.

Maester Aemon sniffed Jon's wound again. Then he put the bloody cloth back in the basin and said, "Donal, the hot knife, if you please. I shall need you to hold him still."

I will not scream, Jon told himself when he saw the blade glowing red hot. But he broke that vow as well. Donal Noye held him down, while Clydas helped guide the maester's hand. Jon did not move, except to pound his fist against the table, again and again and again. The pain was so huge he felt small and weak and helpless inside it, a child whimpering in the dark. *Ygritte*, he thought, when the stench of burning flesh was in his nose and his own shriek echoing in her ears. *Ygritte, I had to.* For half a heartbeat the agony started to ebb. But then the iron touched him once again, and he fainted.

When his eyelids fluttered open, he was wrapped in thick wool and floating. He could not seem to move, but that did not matter. For a time he dreamed that Ygritte was with him, tending him with gentle hands. Finally he closed his eyes and slept.

The next waking was not so gentle. The room was dark, but under the blankets the pain was back, a throbbing in his leg that turned into a hot knife at the least motion. Jon learned that the hard way when he tried to see if he still had a leg. Gasping, he swallowed a scream and made another fist.

"Jon?" A candle appeared, and a well-remembered face was looking down on him, big ears and all. "You shouldn't move."

"Pyp?" Jon reached up, and the other boy clasped his hand and gave it a squeeze. "I thought you'd gone . . ."

". . . with the Old Pomegranate? No, he thinks I'm too small and green. Grenn's here too."

"I'm here too." Grenn stepped to the other side of the bed. "I fell asleep."

Jon's throat was dry. "Water," he gasped. Grenn brought it, and held it to his lips. "I saw the Fist," he said, after a long swallow. "The blood, and the dead horses . . . Noye said a dozen made it back . . . who?"

"Dywen did. Giant, Dolorous Edd, Sweet Donnel Hill, Ulmer, Left Hand Lew, Garth Greyfeather. Four or five more. Me."

"Sam?"

Grenn looked away. "He killed one of the Others, Jon. I saw it. He stabbed him with that dragonglass knife you made him, and we started calling him Sam the Slayer. He hated that."

Sam the Slayer. Jon could hardly imagine a less likely warrior than Sam Tarly. "What happened to him?"

"We left him." Grenn sounded miserable. "I shook him and screamed at him, even slapped his face. Giant tried to drag him to his feet, but he was too heavy. Remember in training how he'd curl up on the ground and lie there whimpering? At Craster's, he wouldn't even whimper. Dirk and Ollo were tearing up the walls looking for food, Garth and Garth were fighting, some of the others were raping Craster's wives. Dolorous Edd figured Dirk's bunch would kill all the loyal men to keep us from telling what they'd done, and they had us two to one. We left Sam with the Old Bear. He wouldn't *move*, Jon."

You were his brother, he almost said. *How could you leave him amongst wildlings and murderers?*

"He might still be alive," said Pyp. "He might surprise us all and come riding up tomorrow."

"With Mance Rayder's head, aye." Grenn was trying to sound cheerful, Jon could tell. "Sam the Slayer!"

Jon tried to sit again. It was as much a mistake as the first time. He cried out, cursing.

"Grenn, go wake Maester Aemon," said Pyp. "Tell him Jon needs more milk of the poppy."

Yes, Jon thought. "No," he said. "The Magnar . . ."

"We know," said Pyp. "The sentries on the Wall have been told to keep one eye on the south, and Donal Noye dispatched some men to Weatherback Ridge to watch the kingsroad. Maester Aemon's sent birds to Eastwatch and the Shadow Tower too."

Maester Aemon shuffled to the bedside, one hand on Grenn's shoulder. "Jon, be gentle with yourself. It is good that you have woken, but you must give yourself time to heal. We drowned the wound with boiling wine, and closed you up with a poultice of nettle, mustard seed and moldy bread, but unless you rest . . ."

"I can't." Jon fought through the pain to sit. "Mance will be here soon . . . thousands of men, giants, mammoths . . . has word been sent to Winterfell? To the king?" Sweat dripped off his brow. He closed his eyes a moment.

Grenn gave Pyp a strange look. "He doesn't know."

"Jon," said Maester Aemon, "much and more happened while you were away, and little of it good. Balon Greyjoy has crowned himself again and sent his longships against the north. Kings sprout like weeds at every hand and we have sent appeals to all of them, yet none will come. They have more pressing uses for their swords, and we are far off and forgotten. And Winterfell ... Jon, be strong ... Winterfell is no more ..."

"No more?" Jon stared at Aemon's white eyes and wrinkled face. "My brothers are at Winterfell. Bran and Rickon ..."

The maester touched his brow. "I am so very sorry, Jon. Your brothers died at the command of Theon Greyjoy, after he took Winterfell in his father's name. When your father's bannermen threatened to retake it, he put the castle to the torch."

"Your brothers were avenged," Grenn said. "Bolton's son killed all the ironmen, and it's said he's flaying Theon Greyjoy inch by inch for what he did."

"I'm sorry, Jon." Pyp squeezed his shoulder. "We are all."

Jon had never liked Theon Greyjoy, but he had been their father's ward. Another spasm of pain twisted up his leg, and the next he knew he was flat on his back again. "There's some mistake," he insisted. "At Queenscrown, I saw a direwolf, a *grey* direwolf ... grey ... *it knew me*." If Bran was dead, could some part of him live on in his wolf, as Orell lived within his eagle?

"Drink this." Grenn held a cup to his lips. Jon drank. His head was full of wolves and eagles, the sound of his brothers' laughter. The faces above him began to blur and fade. *They can't be dead. Theon would never do that. And Winterfell ... grey granite, oak and iron, crows wheeling around the towers, steam rising off the hot pools in the godswood, the stone kings sitting on their thrones ... how could Winterfell be gone?*

When the dreams took him, he found himself back home once more, splashing in the hot pools beneath a huge white weirwood that had his father's face. Ygritte was with him, laughing at him, shedding her skins till she was naked as her name day, trying to kiss him, but he couldn't, not with his father watching. He was the blood of Winterfell, a man of the Night's Watch. *I will not father a bastard*, he told her. *I will not. I will not.* "You know nothing, Jon Snow," she whispered, her skin dissolving in the hot water, the flesh beneath sloughing off her bones until only skull and skeleton remained, and the pool bubbled thick and red.

CATELYN

They heard the Green Fork before they saw it, an endless susurrus, like the growl of some great beast. The river was a boiling torrent, half again as wide as it had been last year, when Robb had divided his army here and vowed to take a Frey to bride as the price of his crossing. *He needed Lord Walder and his bridge then, and he needs them even more now.* Catelyn's heart was full of misgivings as she watched the murky green waters swirl past. *There is no way we will ford this, nor swim across, and it could be a moon's turn before these waters fall again.*

As they neared the Twins, Robb donned his crown and summoned Catelyn and Edmure to ride beside him. Ser Raynald Westerling bore his banner, the direwolf of Stark on its ice-white field.

The gatehouse towers emerged from the rain like ghosts, hazy grey apparitions that grew more solid the closer they rode. The Frey stronghold was not one castle but two; mirror images in wet stone standing on opposite sides of the water, linked by a great arched bridge. From the center of its span rose the Water Tower, the river running straight and swift below. Channels had been cut from the banks, to form moats that made each twin an island. The rains had turned the moats to shallow lakes.

Across the turbulent waters, Catelyn could see several thousand men encamped around the eastern castle, their banners hanging like so many drowned cats from the lances outside their tents. The rain made it impossible to distinguish colors and devices. Most were grey, it seemed to her, though beneath such skies the whole world seemed grey.

"Tread lightly here, Robb," she cautioned her son. "Lord Walder has a thin skin and a sharp tongue, and some of these sons of his will doubtless take after their father. You must not let yourself be provoked."

"I know the Freys, Mother. I know how much I wronged them, and how much I *need* them. I shall be as sweet as a septon."

Catelyn shifted her seat uncomfortably. "If we are offered refreshment when we arrive, on no account refuse. Take what is offered, and eat and drink where all can see. If nothing is offered, ask for bread and cheese and a cup of wine."

"I'm more wet than hungry ..."

"Robb, *listen to me.* Once you have eaten of his bread and salt, you have the guest right, and the laws of hospitality protect you beneath his roof."

Robb looked more amused than afraid. "I have an army to protect me, Mother, I don't need to trust in bread and salt. But if it pleases Lord Walder to serve me stewed crow smothered in maggots, I'll eat it and ask for a second bowl."

Four Freys rode out from the western gatehouse, wrapped in heavy cloaks of thick grey wool. Catelyn recognized Ser Ryman, son of the late Ser Stevron, Lord Walder's firstborn. With his father dead, Ryman was heir to the Twins. The face she saw beneath his hood was fleshy, broad, and stupid. The other three were likely his own sons, Lord Walder's great grandsons.

Edmure confirmed as much. "Edwyn is eldest, the pale slender man with the constipated look. The wiry one with the beard is Black Walder, a nasty bit of business. Petyr is on the bay, the lad with the unfortunate face. Petyr Pimple, his brothers call him. Only a year or two older than Robb, but Lord Walder married him off at ten to a woman thrice his age. Gods, I hope Roslin doesn't take after *him.*"

They halted to let their hosts come to them. Robb's banner drooped on its staff, and the steady sound of rainfall mingled with the rush of the swollen Green Fork on their right. Grey Wind edged forward, tail stiff, watching through slitted eyes of dark gold. When the Freys were a half-dozen yards away Catelyn heard him growl, a deep rumble that seemed almost one with rush of the river. Robb looked startled. "Grey Wind, to me. To *me*!"

Instead the direwolf leapt forward, snarling.

Ser Ryman's palfrey shied off with a whinny of fear, and Petyr Pimple's reared and threw him. Only Black Walder kept his mount in hand. He reached for the hilt of his sword. "*No!*" Robb was shouting. "Grey Wind, here. *Here*." Catelyn spurred between the direwolf and the horses. Mud spattered from the hooves of her mare as she cut in front of Grey Wind. The wolf veered away, and only then seemed to hear Robb calling.

"Is this how a Stark makes amends?" Black Walder shouted, with naked steel in hand. "A poor greeting I call it, to set your wolf upon us. Is this why you've come?"

Ser Ryman had dismounted to help Petyr Pimple back to his feet. The lad was muddy, but unhurt.

"I've come to make my apology for the wrong I did your House, and to see my uncle wed." Robb swung down from the saddle. "Petyr, take my horse. Yours is almost back to the stable."

Petyr looked to his father and said, "I can ride behind one of my brothers."

The Freys made no sign of obeisance. "You come late," Ser Ryman declared.

"The rains delayed us," said Robb. "I sent a bird."

"I do not see the woman."

By *the woman* Ser Ryman meant Jeyne Westerling, all knew. Lady Catelyn smiled apologetically. "Queen Jeyne was weary after so much travel, sers. No doubt she will be pleased to visit when times are more settled."

"My grandfather will be displeased." Though Black Walder had sheathed his sword, his tone was no friendlier. "I've told him much of the lady, and he wished to behold her with his own eyes."

Edwyn cleared his throat. "We have chambers prepared for you in the Water Tower, Your Grace," he told Robb with careful courtesy, "as well as for Lord Tully and Lady Stark. Your lords bannermen are also welcome to shelter under our roof and partake of the wedding feast."

"And my men?" asked Robb.

"My lord grandfather regrets that he cannot feed nor house so large a host. We have been sore pressed to find fodder and provender for our own levies. Nonetheless, your men shall not be neglected. If they will cross and set up their camp beside our own, we will bring out enough casks of wine and ale for all to drink the health of Lord Edmure and his bride. We have thrown up three great feast tents on the far bank, to provide them with some shelter from the rains."

"Your lord father is most kind. My men will thank him. They have had a long wet ride."

Edmure Tully edged his horse forward. "When shall I meet my betrothed?"

"She waits for you within," promised Edwyn Frey. "You will forgive her if she seems shy, I know. She has been awaiting this day most anxiously, poor maid. But perhaps we might continue this out of the rain?"

"Truly." Ser Ryman mounted up again, pulling Petyr Pimple up behind him. "If you would follow me, my father awaits." He turned the palfrey's head back toward the Twins.

Edmure fell in beside Catelyn. "The Late Lord Frey might have seen fit to welcome us in person," he complained. "I am his liege lord as well as his son-to-be, and Robb's his king."

"When you are one-and-ninety, Brother, see how eager *you* are to go riding in the rain." Yet she wondered if that was the whole truth of it. Lord Walder normally went about in a covered litter, which would have kept the worst of the rain off him. *A deliberate slight?* If so, it might be the first of many yet to come.

There was more trouble at the gatehouse. Grey Wind balked in the middle of the drawbridge, shook the rain off, and howled at the portcullis. Robb whistled impatiently. "Grey Wind. What is it? Grey Wind, with me." But the direwolf only bared his teeth. *He does not like this place*, Catelyn thought. Robb had to squat and speak softly to the wolf before he would consent to pass beneath the portcullis. By then Lame Lothar and Walder Rivers had come up. "It's the sound of the water he fears," Rivers said. "Beasts know to avoid the river in flood."

"A dry kennel and a leg of mutton will see him right again," said Lothar cheerfully. "Shall I summon our master of hounds?"

"He's a direwolf, not a dog," said Robb, "and dangerous to men he does not trust. Ser Raynald, stay with him. I won't take him into Lord Walder's hall like this."

Deftly done, Catelyn decided. *Robb keeps the Westerling out of Lord Walder's sight as well.*

Gout and brittle bones had taken their toll of old Walder Frey. They found him propped up in his high seat with a cushion beneath him and an ermine robe across his lap. His chair was black oak, its back carved into the semblance of two stout towers joined by an arched bridge, so massive that its embrace turned the old man into a grotesque child. There was something of the vulture about Lord Walder, and rather more of the weasel. His bald head, spotted with age, thrust out from his scrawny shoulders on a long pink neck. Loose skin dangled beneath his receding chin, his eyes were runny and clouded, and his toothless mouth moved constantly, sucking at the empty air as a babe sucks at his mother's breast.

The eighth Lady Frey stood beside Lord Walder's high seat. At his feet sat a somewhat younger version of himself, a stooped thin man of fifty whose costly garb of blue wool and grey satin was strangely accented by a crown and collar ornamented with tiny brass bells. The likeness between him and his lord was striking, save for their eyes; Lord Frey's small, dim, and suspicious, the other's large, amiable, and vacant. Catelyn recalled that one of Lord Walder's brood had fathered a halfwit long years ago. During past visits, the Lord of the Crossing had always taken care to hide this one away. *Did he always wear a fool's crown, or is that meant as mockery of Robb?* It was a question she dare not ask.

Frey sons, daughters, children, grandchildren, husbands, wives, and servants crowded the rest of the hall. But it was the old man who spoke. "You will forgive me if I do not kneel, I know. My legs no longer work as they did, though that which hangs between 'em serves well enough, *heh*." His mouth split in a toothless smile as he eyed

Robb's crown. "Some would say it's a poor king who crowns himself with bronze, Your Grace."

"Bronze and iron are stronger than gold and silver," Robb answered. "The old Kings of Winter wore such a sword-crown."

"Small good it did them when the dragons came. *Heh*." That *heh* seemed to please the lackwit, who bobbed his head from side to side, jingling crown and collar. "Sire," Lord Walder said, "forgive my Aegon the noise. He has less wits than a crannogman, and he's never met a king before. One of Stevron's boys. We call him Jinglebell."

"Ser Stevron mentioned him, my lord." Robb smiled at the lackwit. "Well met, Aegon. Your father was a brave man."

Jinglebell jingled his bells. A thin line of spit ran from one corner of his mouth when he smiled.

"Save your royal breath. You'd do as well talking to a chamberpot." Lord Walder shifted his gaze to the others. "Well, Lady Catelyn, I see you have returned to us. And young Ser Edmure, the victor of the Stone Mill. Lord Tully now, I'll need to remember that. You're the fifth Lord Tully I've known. I outlived the other four, *heh*. Your bride's about here somewhere. I suppose you want a look at her."

"I would, my lord."

"Then you'll have it. But clothed. She's a modest girl, and a maid. You won't see her naked till the bedding." Lord Walder cackled. "*Heh*. Soon enough, soon enough." He craned his head about. "Benfrey, go fetch your sister. Be quick about it, Lord Tully's come all the way from Riverrun." A young knight in a quartered surcoat bowed and took his leave, and the old man turned back to Robb. "And where's *your* bride, Your Grace? The fair Queen Jeyne. A Westerling of the Crag, I'm told, *heh*."

"I left her at Riverrun, my lord. She was too weary for more travel, as we told Ser Ryman."

"That makes me grievous sad. I wanted to behold her with mine own weak eyes. We all did, *heh*. Isn't that so, my lady?"

Pale wispy Lady Frey seemed startled that she would be called upon to speak. "Y-yes, my lord. We all so wanted to pay homage to Queen Jeyne. She must be fair to look on."

"She is most fair, my lady." There was an icy stillness in Robb's voice that reminded Catelyn of his father.

The old man either did not hear it or refused to pay it any heed. "Fairer than my own get, *heh*? Elsewise how could her face and form have made the King's Grace forget his solemn promise."

Robb suffered the rebuke with dignity. "No words can set that right, I know, but I have come to make my apologies for the wrong I did your House, and to beg for your forgiveness, my lord."

"Apologies, *heh*. Yes, you vowed to make one, I recall. I'm old, but I don't forget such things. Not like some kings, it seems. The young remember nothing when they see a pretty face and a nice firm pair of teats, isn't that so? I was the same. Some might say I still am, *heh heh*. They'd be wrong, though, wrong as you were. But now you're here to make amends. It was my girls you spurned, though. Mayhaps it's them should hear you beg for pardon, Your Grace. My maiden girls. Here, have a look at them." When he waggled his fingers, a flurry of femininity left their places by the walls to line up beneath the dais. Jinglebell started to rise as well, his bells ringing merrily, but Lady Frey grabbed the lackwit's sleeve and tugged him back down.

Lord Walder named the names. "My daughter Arwyn," he said of a girl of fourteen. "Shirei, my youngest trueborn daughter. Ami and Marianne are granddaughters. I married Ami to Ser Pate of Sevenstreams, but the Mountain killed the oaf so I got her back. That's a Cersei, but we call her Little Bee, her mother's a Beesbury. More granddaughters. One's a Walda, and the others ... well, they have names, whatever they are ..."

"I'm Merry, Lord Grandfather," one girl said.

"You're noisy, that's for certain. Next to Noisy is my daughter Tyta. Then another Walda. Alyx, Marissa ... are you Marissa? I thought you were. She's not always bald. The maester shaved her hair off, but he swears it will soon grow back. The twins are Serra and Sarra." He squinted down at one of the younger girls. "*Heh*, are you another Walda?"

The girl could not have been more than four. "I'm Ser Aemon Rivers's Walda, lord great grandfather." She curtsied.

"How long have you been talking? Not that you're like to have anything sensible to say, your father never did. He's a bastard's son besides, *heh*. Go away, I wanted only Freys up here. The King in the North has no interest in base stock." Lord Walder glanced to Robb, as Jinglebell bobbed his head and chimed. "There they are, all maidens. Well, and one widow, but there's some who like a woman broken in. You might have had any one of them."

"It would have been an impossible choice, my lord," said Robb with careful courtesy. "They're all too lovely."

Lord Walder snorted. "And they say *my* eyes are bad. Some will do well enough, I suppose. Others . . . well, it makes no matter. They weren't good enough for the King in the North, *heh*. Now what is it you have to say?"

"My ladies." Robb looked desperately uncomfortable, but he had known this moment must come, and he faced it without flinching. "All men should keep their word, kings most of all. I was pledged to marry one of you and I broke that vow. The fault is not in you. What I did was not done to slight you, but because I loved another. No words can set it right, I know, yet I come before you to ask forgiveness, that the Freys of the Crossing and the Starks of Winterfell may once again be friends."

The smaller girls fidgeted anxiously. Their older sisters waited for Lord Walder on his black oak throne. Jinglebell rocked back and forth, bells chiming on collar and crown.

"Good," the Lord of the Crossing said. "That was very good, Your Grace. 'No words can set it right,' *heh*. Well said, well said. At the wedding feast I hope you will not refuse to dance with my daughters. It would please an old man's heart, *heh*." He bobbed his wrinkled pink head up and down, in much the same way his lackwit grandson did, though Lord Walder wore no bells. "And here she is, Lord Edmure. My daughter Roslin, my most precious little blossom, *heh*."

Ser Benfrey led her into the hall. They looked enough alike to be full siblings. Judging from their age, both were children of the sixth Lady Frey; a Rosby, Catelyn seemed to recall.

Roslin was small for her years, her skin as white as if she had just risen from a milk bath. Her face was comely, with a small chin, delicate nose, and big brown eyes. Thick chestnut hair fell in loose waves to a waist so tiny that Edmure would be able to put his hands around it. Beneath the lacy bodice of her pale blue gown, her breasts looked small but shapely.

"Your Grace." The girl went to her knees. "Lord Edmure, I hope I am not a disappointment to you."

Far from it, thought Catelyn. Her brother's face had lit up at the sight of her. "You are a delight to me, my lady," Edmure said. "And ever will be, I know."

Roslin had a small gap between two of her front teeth that made her shy with her smiles, but the flaw was almost endearing. *Pretty enough*, Catelyn thought, *but so small, and she comes of Rosby stock.* The Rosbys had never been robust. She much preferred the frames of some of the older girls in the hall; daughters or granddaughters, she could not be sure. They had a Crakehall look about them, and Lord Walder's third wife had been of that House. *Wide hips to bear children, big breasts to nurse them, strong arms to carry them. The Crakehalls have always been a big-boned family, and strong.*

"My lord is kind," the Lady Roslin said to Edmure.

"My lady is beautiful." Edmure took her hand and drew her to her feet. "But why are you crying?"

"For joy," Roslin said. "I weep for joy, my lord."

"*Enough*," Lord Walder broke in. "You may weep and whisper after you're wed, *heh*. Benfrey, see your sister back to her chambers, she has a wedding to prepare for. And a bedding, *heh*, the sweetest part. For all, for all." His mouth moved in and out. "We'll have music, such sweet music, and wine, *heh*, the red will run, and we'll put some wrongs aright. But now you're weary, and wet as well, dripping on my floor. There's fires waiting for you, and hot mulled wine, and baths if you want 'em. Lothar, show our guests to their quarters."

"I need to see my men across the river, my lord," Robb said.

"They shan't get lost," Lord Walder complained. "They've crossed before, haven't they? When you came down from the north. You wanted crossing and I gave it to you, and you never said mayhaps, *heh*. But suit yourself. Lead each man across by the hand if you like, it's naught to me."

"*My lord!*" Catelyn had almost forgotten. "Some food would be most welcome. We have ridden many leagues in the rain."

Walder Frey's mouth moved in and out. "Food, *heh*. A loaf of bread, a bite of cheese, mayhaps a sausage."

"Some wine to wash it down," Robb said. "And salt."

"Bread and salt. *Heh*. Of course, of course." The old man clapped his hands together, and servants came into the hall, bearing flagons of wine and trays of bread, cheese, and butter. Lord Walder took a cup of red himself, and raised it high with a spotted hand. "My guests," he said. "My honored guests. Be welcome beneath my roof, and at my table."

"We thank you for your hospitality, my lord," Robb replied. Edmure echoed him, along with the Greatjon, Ser Marq Piper, and the others. They drank his wine and ate his bread and butter. Catelyn tasted the wine and nibbled at some bread, and felt much the better for it. *Now we should be safe*, she thought.

Knowing how petty the old man could be, she had expected their rooms to be bleak and cheerless. But the Freys had made more than ample provision for them, it seemed. The bridal chamber was large and richly appointed, dominated by a great featherbed with corner posts carved in the likeness of castle towers. Its draperies were Tully red and blue, a nice courtesy. Sweet-smelling carpets covered a plank floor, and a tall shuttered window opened to the south. Catelyn's own room was smaller, but handsomely furnished and comfortable, with a fire burning in the hearth. Lame Lothar assured them that Robb would have an entire suite, as befit a king. "If there is anything you require, you need only tell one of the guards." He bowed and withdrew, limping heavily as he made his way down the curving steps.

"We should post our own guards," Catelyn told her brother. She would rest easier with Stark and Tully men outside her door. The audience with Lord Walder had not been as painful as she feared, yet all the same she would be glad to be done with this. *A few more days, and Robb will be off to battle, and me to a comfortable captivity at*

Seagard. Lord Jason would show her every courtesy, she had no doubt, but the prospect still depressed her.

She could hear the sounds of horses below as the long column of mounted men wound their way across the bridge from castle to castle. The stones rumbled to the passage of heavy-laden wayns. Catelyn went to the window and gazed out, to watch Robb's host emerge from the eastern twin. "The rain seems to be lessening."

"Now that we're inside." Edmure stood before the fire, letting the warmth wash over him. "What did you make of Roslin?"

Too small and delicate. Childbirth will go hard on her. But her brother seemed well pleased with the girl, so all she said was, "Sweet."

"I believe she liked me. Why was she crying?"

"She's a maid on the eve of her wedding. A few tears are to be expected." Lysa had wept lakes the morning of their own wedding, though she had managed to be dry-eyed and radiant when Jon Arryn swept his cream-and-blue cloak about her shoulders.

"She's prettier than I dared hope." Edmure raised a hand before she could speak. "I know there are more important things, spare me the sermon, septa. Even so . . . did you see some of those other maids Frey trotted out? The one with the twitch? Was that the shaking sickness? And those twins had more craters and eruptions on their faces than Petyr Pimple. When I saw that lot, I knew Roslin would be bald and one-eyed, with Jinglebell's wits and Black Walder's temper. But she seems gentle as well as fair." He looked perplexed. "Why would the old weasel refuse to let me choose unless he meant to foist off someone hideous?"

"Your fondness for a pretty face is well known," Catelyn reminded him. "Perhaps Lord Walder actually wants you to be happy with your bride." *Or more like, he did not want you balking over a boil and upsetting all his plans.* "Or it may be that Roslin is the old man's favorite. The Lord of Riverrun is a much better match than most of his daughters can hope for."

"True." Her brother still seemed uncertain, however. "Is it possible the girl is barren?"

"Lord Walder wants his grandson to inherit Riverrun. How would it serve him to give you a barren wife?"

"It rids him of a daughter no one else would take."

"Small good that will do him. Walder Frey is a peevish man, not a stupid one."

"Still . . . it *is* possible?"

"Yes," Catelyn conceded, reluctantly. "There are illnesses a girl can have in childhood that leave her unable to conceive. There's no reason to believe that Lady Roslin was so afflicted, though." She looked round the room. "The Freys have received us more kindly than I had anticipated, if truth be told."

Edmure laughed. "A few barbed words and some unseemly gloating. From him that's courtesy. I expected the old weasel to piss in our wine and make us praise the vintage."

The jest left Catelyn strangely disquieted. "If you will excuse me, I should change from these wet clothes.

"As you wish." Edmure yawned. "I may nap an hour."

She retreated to her own room. The chest of clothes she'd brought from Riverrun had been carried up and laid at the foot of the bed. After she'd undressed and hung her wet clothing by the fire, she donned a warm wool dress of Tully red and blue, washed and brushed her hair and let it dry, and went in search of Freys.

Lord Walder's black oak throne was empty when she entered the hall, but some of his sons were drinking by the fire. Lame Lothar rose clumsily when he saw her. "Lady Catelyn, I thought you would be resting. How may I be of service?"

"Are these your brothers?" she asked.

"Brothers, half-brothers, good brothers, and nephews. Raymund and I shared a mother. Lord Lucias Vypren is my half-sister Lythene's husband, and Ser Damon is their son. My half-brother Ser Hosteen I believe you know. And this is Ser Leslyn Haigh and his sons, Ser Harys and Ser Donnel."

"Well met, sers. Is Ser Perwyn about? He helped escort me to Storm's End and back, when Robb sent me to speak with Lord Renly. I was looking forward to seeing him again."

"Perwyn is away," Lame Lothar said. "I shall give him your regards. I know he will regret having missed you."

"Surely he will return in time for Lady Roslin's wedding?"

"He had hoped to," said Lame Lothar, "but with this rain . . . you saw how the rivers ran, my lady."

"I did indeed," said Catelyn. "I wonder if you would be so good as to direct me to your maester?"

"Are you unwell, my lady?" asked Ser Hosteen, a powerful man with a square strong jaw.

"A woman's complaint. Nothing to concern you, ser."

Lothar, ever gracious, escorted her from the hall, up some steps, and across a covered bridge to another stair. "You should find Maester Brenett in the turret on the top, my lady."

Catelyn half expected that the maester would be yet another son of Walder Frey's, but Brenett did not have the look. He was a great fat man, bald and double-chinned and none too clean, to judge from the raven droppings that stained the sleeves of his robes, yet he seemed amiable enough. When she told him of Edmure's concerns about Lady Roslin's fertility, he chuckled. "Your lord brother need have no fear, Lady Catelyn. She's small, I'll grant you, and narrow in the hips, but her mother was the same, and Lady Bethany gave Lord Walder a child every year."

"How many lived past infancy?" she asked bluntly.

"Five." He ticked them off on fingers plump as sausages. "Ser Perwyn. Ser Benfrey. Maester Willamen, who took his vows last year and now serves Lord Hunter in the Vale. Olyvar, who squired for your son. And Lady Roslin, the youngest. Four boys to one girl. Lord Edmure will have more sons than he knows what to do with."

"I am sure that will please him." So the girl was like to be fertile as well as fair of face. *That should put Edmure's mind at ease.* Lord Walder had left her brother no cause for complaint, so far as she could see.

Catelyn did not return to her own room after leaving the maester; instead she went to Robb. She found Robin Flint and Ser Wendel Manderly with him, along with the Greatjon and his son, who was still called the Smalljon though he threatened to overtop his father. They were all damp. Another man, still wetter, stood before the fire in a pale pink cloak trimmed with white fur. "Lord Bolton," she said.

"Lady Catelyn," he replied, his voice faint, "it is a pleasure to look on you again, even in such trying times."

"You are kind to say so." Catelyn could feel gloom in the room. Even the Greatjon seemed somber and subdued. She looked at their grim faces and said, "What's happened?"

"Lannisters on the Trident," said Ser Wendel unhappily. "My brother is taken again."

"And Lord Bolton has brought us further word of Winterfell," Robb added. "Ser Rodrik was not the only good man to die. Cley Cerwyn and Leobald Tallhart were slain as well."

"Cley Cerwyn was only a boy," she said, saddened. "Is this true, then? All dead, and Winterfell gone?"

Bolton's pale eyes met her own. "The ironmen burned both castle and winter town. Some of your people were taken back to the Dreadfort by my son, Ramsay."

"Your bastard was accused of grievous crimes," Catelyn reminded him sharply. "Of murder, rape, and worse."

"Yes," Roose Bolton said. "His blood is tainted, that cannot be denied. Yet he is a good fighter, as cunning as he is fearless. When the ironmen cut down Ser Rodrik, and Leobald Tallhart soon after, it fell to Ramsay to lead the battle, and he did. He swears that he shall not sheathe his sword so long as a single Greyjoy remains in the north. Perhaps such service might atone in some small measure for whatever crimes his bastard blood has led him to commit." He shrugged. "Or not. When the war is done, His Grace must weigh and judge. By then I hope to have a trueborn son by Lady Walda."

This is a cold man, Catelyn realized, not for the first time.

"Did Ramsay mention Theon Greyjoy?" Robb demanded. "Was he slain as well, or did he flee?"

Roose Bolton removed a ragged strip of leather from the pouch at his belt. "My son sent this with his letter."

Ser Wendel turned his fat face away. Robin Flint and Smalljon Umber exchanged a look, and the Greatjon snorted like a bull. "Is that . . . skin?" said Robb.

"The skin from the little finger of Theon Greyjoy's left hand. My son is cruel, I confess it. And yet . . . what is a little skin, against the lives of two young princes? You were their mother, my lady. May I offer you this . . . small token of revenge?"

Part of Catelyn wanted to clutch the grisly trophy to her heart, but she made herself resist. "Put it away. Please."

"Flaying Theon will not bring my brothers back," Robb said. "I want his head, not his skin."

"He is Balon Greyjoy's only living son," Lord Bolton said softly, as if they had forgotten, "and now rightful King of the Iron Islands. A captive king has great value as a hostage."

"Hostage?" The word raised Catelyn's hackles. Hostages were oft exchanged. "Lord Bolton, I hope you are not suggesting that we *free* the man who killed my sons."

"Whoever wins the Seastone Chair will want Theon Greyjoy dead," Bolton pointed out. "Even in chains, he has a better claim than any of his uncles. Hold him, I say, and demand concessions from the ironborn as the price of his execution."

Robb considered that reluctantly, but in the end he nodded. "Yes. Very well. Keep him alive, then. For the present. Hold him secure at the Dreadfort till we've retaken the north."

Catelyn turned back to Roose Bolton. "Ser Wendel said something of Lannisters on the Trident?"

"He did, my lady. I blame myself. I delayed too long before leaving Harrenhal. Aenys Frey departed several days before me and crossed the Trident at the ruby ford, though not without difficulty. But by the time we came up the river was a torrent. I had no choice but to ferry my men across in small boats, of which we had too few. Two-thirds of my strength was on the north side when the Lannisters attacked those still waiting to cross. Norrey, Locke, and Burley men chiefly, with Ser Wylis Manderly and his White Harbor knights as rear guard. I was on the wrong side of the Trident, powerless to help them. Ser Wylis rallied our men as best he could, but Gregor Clegane attacked with heavy horse and drove them into the river. As many drowned as were cut down. More fled, and the rest were taken captive."

Gregor Clegane was always ill news, Catelyn reflected. Would Robb need to march south again to deal with him? Or was the Mountain coming here? "Is Clegane across the river, then?"

"No." Bolton's voice was soft, but certain. "I left six hundred men at the ford. Spearmen from the rills, the mountains, and the White

Knife, a hundred Hornwood longbows, some freeriders and hedge knights, and a strong force of Stout and Cerwyn men to stiffen them. Ronnel Stout and Ser Kyle Condon have the command. Ser Kyle was the late Lord Cerwyn's right hand, as I'm sure you know, my lady. Lions swim no better than wolves. So long as the river runs high, Ser Gregor will not cross."

"The last thing we need is the Mountain at our backs when we start up the causeway," said Robb. "You did well, my lord."

"Your Grace is too kind. I suffered grievous losses on the Green Fork, and Glover and Tallhart worse at Duskendale."

"*Duskendale.*" Robb made the word a curse. "Robett Glover will answer for that when I see him, I promise you."

"A folly," Lord Bolton agreed, "but Glover was heedless after he learned that Deepwood Motte had fallen. Grief and fear will do that to a man."

Duskendale was done and cold; it was the battles still to come that worried Catelyn. "How many men have you brought my son?" she asked Roose Bolton pointedly.

His queer colorless eyes studied her face a moment before he answered. "Some five hundred horse and three thousand foot, my lady. Dreadfort men, in chief, and some from Karhold. With the loyalty of the Karstarks so doubtful now, I thought it best to keep them close. I regret there are not more."

"It should be enough," said Robb. "You will have command of my rear guard, Lord Bolton. I mean to start for the Neck as soon as my uncle has been wedded and bedded. We're going home."

ARYA

The outriders came on them an hour from the Green Fork, as the wayn was slogging down a muddy road. "Keep your head down and your mouth shut," the Hound warned her as the three spurred toward them; a knight and two squires, lightly armored and mounted on fast palfreys. Clegane cracked his whip at the team, a pair of old drays that had known better days. The wayn was creaking and swaying, its two huge wooden wheels squeezing mud up out of the deep ruts in the road with every turn. Stranger followed, tied to the wagon.

The big bad-tempered courser wore neither armor, barding, nor harness, and the Hound himself was garbed in splotchy green roughspun and a soot-grey mantle with a hood that swallowed his head. So long as he kept his eyes down you could not see his face, only the whites of his eyes peering out. He looked like some down-at-heels farmer. A *big* farmer, though. And under the roughspun was boiled leather and oiled mail, Arya knew. She looked like a farmer's son, or maybe a swineherd. And behind them were four squat casks of salt pork and one of pickled pigs' feet.

The riders split and circled them for a look before they came up close. Clegane drew the wayn to a halt and waited patiently on their pleasure. The knight bore spear and sword while his squires carried longbows. The badges on their jerkins were smaller versions of the sigil sewn on their master's surcoat; a black pitchfork on a golden bar sinister, upon a russet field. Arya had thought of revealing herself to the first outriders they encountered, but she had always pictured grey-cloaked men with the direwolf on their breasts. She might have risked it even if they'd worn the Umber giant or the Glover fist, but she did not know this pitchfork knight or whom he served. The closest thing to a pitchfork she had ever seen at Winterfell was the trident in the hand of Lord Manderly's merman.

"You have business at the Twins?" the knight asked.

"Salt pork for the wedding feast, if it please you, ser." The Hound mumbled his reply, his eyes down, his face hidden.

"Salt pork never pleases me." The pitchfork knight gave Clegane only the most cursory glance, and paid no attention at all to Arya, but he looked long and hard at Stranger. The stallion was no plow horse, that was plain at a glance. One of the squires almost wound up in the mud when the big black courser bit at his own mount. "How did you come by this beast?" the pitchfork knight demanded.

"M'lady told me to bring him, ser," Clegane said humbly. "He's a wedding gift for young Lord Tully."

"What lady? Who is it you serve?"

"Old Lady Whent, ser."

"Does she think she can buy Harrenhal back with a horse?" the knight asked. "Gods, is there any fool like an old fool?" Yet he waved them down the road. "Go on with you, then."

"Aye, m'lord." The Hound snapped his whip again, and the old drays resumed their weary trek. The wheels had settled deep into the mud during the halt, and it took several moments for the team to pull them free again. By then the outriders were riding off. Clegane gave them one last look and snorted. "Ser Donnel Haigh," he said. "I've taken more horses off him than I can count. Armor as well. Once I near killed him in a mêlée."

"How come he didn't know you, then?" Arya asked.

"Because knights are fools, and it would have been beneath him to look twice at some poxy peasant." He gave the horses a lick with the whip. "Keep your eyes down and your tone respectful and say *ser* a lot, and most knights will never see you. They pay more mind to horses than to smallfolk. He might have known Stranger if he'd ever seen me ride him."

He would have known your face, though. Arya had no doubt of that. Sandor Clegane's burns would not be easy to forget, once you saw them. He couldn't hide the scars behind a helm, either; not so long as the helm was made in the shape of a snarling dog.

That was why they'd needed the wayn and the pickled pigs' feet. "I'm not going to be dragged before your brother in chains," the Hound had told her, "and I'd just as soon not have to cut through his men to get to him. So we play a little game."

A farmer chance-met on the kingsroad had provided them with wayn, horses, garb, and casks, though not willingly. The Hound had taken them at swordpoint. When the farmer cursed him for a robber, he said, "No, a forager. Be grateful you get to keep your smallclothes. Now take those boots off. Or I'll take your legs off. Your choice." The farmer was as big as Clegane, but all the same he chose to give up his boots and keep his legs.

Evenfall found them still trudging toward the Green Fork and Lord Frey's twin castles. *I am almost there,* Arya thought. She knew she ought to be excited, but her belly was all knotted up tight. Maybe that was just the fever she'd been fighting, but maybe not. Last night, she'd had a bad dream, a *terrible* dream. She couldn't remember what she'd dreamed of now, but the feeling had lingered all day. If anything, it had only gotten stronger. *Fear cuts deeper than swords.* She had to be strong now, the way her father told her. There was nothing between her and her mother but a castle gate, a river, and an army . . . but it was *Robb's* army, so there was no real danger there. Was there?

Roose Bolton was one of them, though. The Leech Lord, as the outlaws called him. That made her uneasy. She had fled Harrenhal to get away from Bolton as much as from the Bloody Mummers, and she'd had to cut the throat of one of his guards to escape. Did he know she'd done that? Or did he blame Gendry or Hot Pie? Would he have told her mother? What would he do if he saw her? *He probably won't even know me.* She looked more like a drowned rat than a lord's cupbearer these days. A drowned *boy* rat. The Hound had hacked handfuls of her hair off only two days past. He was an even worse barber than Yoren, and he'd left her half bald on one side. *Robb won't know me either, I bet. Or even Mother.* She had been a little girl the last time she saw them, the day Lord Eddard Stark left Winterfell.

They heard the music before they saw the castle; the distant rattle of drums, the brazen blare of horns, the thin skirling of pipes faint beneath the growl of the river and the sound of the rain beating on their heads. "We've missed the wedding," the Hound said, "but it sounds as though the feast is still going. I'll be rid of you soon."

No, I'll be rid of you, Arya thought.

The road had been running mostly northwest, but now it turned due west between an apple orchard and a field of drowned corn beaten down by the rain. They passed the last of the apple trees and crested a rise, and the castles, river, and camps all appeared at once. There were hundreds of horses and thousands of men, most of them milling about the three huge feast tents that stood side by side facing the castle gates, like three great canvas longhalls. Robb had made his camp well back from the walls, on higher, drier ground, but the Green Fork had overflown its bank and even claimed a few carelessly placed tents.

The music from the castles was louder here. The sound of the drums and horns rolled across the camp. The musicians in the nearer castle were playing a different song than the ones in the castle on the far bank, though, so it sounded more like a battle than a song. "They're not very good," Arya observed.

The Hound made a sound that might have been a laugh. "There's old deaf women in Lannisport complaining of the din, I'll warrant. I'd heard Walder Frey's eyes were failing, but no one mentioned his bloody ears."

Arya found herself wishing it were day. If the sun was out and the wind was blowing, she would have been able to see the banners better. She would have looked for the direwolf of Stark, or maybe the Cerwyn battleaxe or the Glover fist. But in the gloom of night all the colors looked grey. The rain had dwindled down to a fine drizzle, almost a mist, but an earlier downpour had left the banners wet as dishrags, sodden and unreadable.

A hedge of wagons and carts had been drawn up along the

perimeter to make a crude wooden wall against any attack. That was where the guards stopped them. The lantern their sergeant carried shed enough light for Arya to see that his cloak was a pale pink, spotted with red teardrops. The men under him had the Leech Lord's badge sewn over their hearts, the flayed man of the Dreadfort. Sandor Clegane gave them the same tale he'd used on the outriders, but the Bolton sergeant was a harder sort of nut than Ser Donnel Haigh had been. "Salt pork's no fit meat for a lord's wedding feast," he said scornfully.

"Got pickled pigs' feet too, ser."

"Not for the feast, you don't. The feast's half done. And I'm a northman, not some milksuck southron knight."

"I was told to see the steward, or the cook . . ."

"Castle's closed. The lordlings are not to be disturbed." The sergeant considered a moment. "You can unload by the feast tents, there." He pointed with a mailed hand. "Ale makes a man hungry, and old Frey won't miss a few pigs' feet. He don't have the teeth for such anyhow. Ask for Sedgekins, he'll know what's to be done with you." He barked a command, and his men rolled one of the wagons aside for them to enter.

The Hound's whip spurred the team toward the tents. No one seemed to pay them any mind. They splashed past rows of brightly colored pavilions, their walls of wet silk lit up like magic lanterns by lamps and braziers inside; pink and gold and green they glimmered, striped and fretty and chequy, emblazoned with birds and beasts, chevrons and stars, wheels and weapons. Arya spotted a yellow tent with six acorns on its panels, three over two over one. *Lord Smallwood*, she knew, remembering Acorn Hall so far away, and the lady who'd said she was pretty.

But for every shimmering silk pavilion there were two dozen of felt or canvas, opaque and dark. There were barracks tents too, big enough to shelter two score footsoldiers, though even those were dwarfed by the three great feast tents. The drinking had been going on for hours, it seemed. Arya heard shouted toasts and the clash of cups, mixed in with all the usual camp sounds, horses whinnying and dogs barking, wagons rumbling through the dark, laughter and curses, the clank and clatter of steel and wood. The music grew still louder as they approached the castle, but under that was a deeper, darker sound: the river, the swollen Green Fork, growling like a lion in its den.

Arya twisted and turned, trying to look everywhere at once, hoping for a glimpse of a direwolf badge, for a tent done up in grey and white, for a face she knew from Winterfell. All she saw were strangers. She stared at a man relieving himself in the reeds, but he wasn't Alebelly. She saw a half-dressed girl burst from a tent laughing, but the tent was pale blue, not grey like she'd thought at first, and the man who went running after her wore a treecat on his doublet, not a wolf. Beneath a tree, four archers were slipping waxed strings over the notches of their longbows, but they were not her father's archers. A maester crossed their path, but he was too young and thin to be Maester Luwin. Arya gazed up at the Twins, their high tower windows glowing softly wherever a light was burning. Through the haze of rain, the castles looked spooky and mysterious, like something from one of Old Nan's tales, but they weren't Winterfell.

The press was thickest at the feast tents. The wide flaps were tied back, and men were pushing in and out with drinking horns and tankards in their hands, some with camp followers. Arya glanced inside as the Hound drove past the first of the three, and saw hundreds of men crowding the benches and jostling around the casks of mead and ale and wine. There was hardly room to move inside, but none of them seemed to mind. At least they were warm and dry. Cold wet Arya envied them. Some were even singing. The fine misty rain was steaming all around the door from the heat escaping from inside. "Here's to Lord Edmure and Lady Roslin," she heard a voice shout. They all drank, and someone yelled, "Here's to the Young Wolf and Queen Jeyne."

Who is Queen Jeyne? Arya wondered briefly. The only queen she knew was Cersei.

Firepits had been dug outside the feast tents, sheltered beneath rude canopies of woven wood and hides that kept the rain out, so long as it fell straight down. The wind was blowing off the river, though, so the drizzle came in anyway, enough to make the fires hiss and swirl. Serving men were turning joints of meat on spits above the flames. The smells made Arya's mouth water. "Shouldn't we stop?" she asked Sandor Clegane. "There's northmen in the tents." She knew them by their beards, by their faces, by their cloaks of bearskin and sealskin, by their half-heard toasts and the songs they sang; Karstarks and Umbers and men of the mountain clans. "I bet there are Winterfell men too." Her father's men, the Young Wolf's men, the direwolves of Stark.

"Your brother will be in the castle," he said. "Your mother too. You want them or not?"

"Yes," she said. "What about Sedgekins?" The sergeant had told them to ask for Sedgekins.

"Sedgekins can bugger himself with a hot poker." Clegane shook out his whip, and sent it hissing through the soft rain to bite at a horse's flank. "It's your bloody brother I want."

CATELYN

The drums were pounding, pounding, pounding, and her head with them. Pipes wailed and flutes trilled from the musicians' gallery at the foot of the hall; fiddles screeched, horns blew, the skins skirled a lively tune, but the drumming drove them all. The sounds echoed off the rafters, whilst the guests ate, drank, and shouted at one another below. *Walder Frey must be deaf as a stone to call this music.* Catelyn sipped a cup of wine and watched Jinglebell prance to the sounds of "Alysanne." At least she thought it was meant to be "Alysanne." With these players, it might as easily have been "The Bear and the Maiden Fair."

Outside, the rain still fell, but within the Twins the air was thick and hot. A fire roared in the hearth and rows of torches burned smokily from iron sconces on the walls. Yet most of the heat came off the bodies of the wedding guests, jammed in so thick along the benches that every man who tried to lift his cup poked his neighbor in the ribs.

Even on the dais they were closer than Catelyn would have liked. She had been placed between Ser Ryman Frey and Roose Bolton, and had gotten a good noseful of both. Ser Ryman drank as if Westeros was about to run short of wine, and sweated it all out under his arms. He had bathed in lemonwater, she judged, but no lemon could mask so much sour sweat. Roose Bolton had a sweeter smell to him, yet no more pleasant. He sipped hippocras in preference to wine or mead, and ate but little.

Catelyn could not fault him for his lack of appetite. The wedding feast began with a thin leek soup, followed by a salad of green beans, onions, and beets, river pike poached in almond milk, mounds of mashed turnips that were cold before they reached the table, jellied calves' brains, and a leche of stringy beef. It was poor fare to set before a king, and the calves' brains turned Catelyn's stomach. Yet Robb ate it uncomplaining, and her brother was too caught up with his bride to pay much attention.

You would never guess Edmure complained of Roslin all the way from Riverrun to the Twins. Husband and wife ate from a single plate, drank from a single cup, and exchanged chaste kisses between sips. Most of the dishes Edmure waved away. She could not blame him for that. She remembered little of the food served at her own wedding feast. *Did I even taste it? Or spend the whole time gazing at Ned's face, wondering who he was?*

Poor Roslin's smile had a fixed quality to it, as if someone had sewn it onto her face. *Well, she is a maid wedded, but the bedding's yet to come. No doubt she's as terrified as I was.* Robb was seated between Alyx Frey and Fair Walda, two of the more nubile Frey maidens. "At the wedding feast I hope you will not refuse to dance with my daughters," Walder Frey had said. "It would please an old man's heart." His heart should be well pleased, then; Robb had done his duty like a king. He had danced with each of the girls, with Edmure's bride and the eighth Lady Frey, with the widow Ami and Roose Bolton's wife Fat Walda, with the pimply twins Serra and Sarra, even with Shirei, Lord Walder's youngest, who must have been all of six. Catelyn wondered whether the Lord of the Crossing would be satisfied, or if he would find cause for complaint in all the other daughters and granddaughters who had not had a turn with the king. "Your sisters dance very well," she said to Ser Ryman Frey, trying to be pleasant.

"They're aunts and cousins." Ser Ryman drank a swallow of wine, the sweat trickling down his cheek into his beard.

A sour man, and in his cups, Catelyn thought. The Late Lord Frey might be niggardly when it came to feeding his guests, but he did not stint on the drink. The ale, wine, and mead were flowing as fast as the river outside. The Greatjon was already roaring drunk. Lord Walder's son Merrett was matching him cup for cup, but Ser Whalen Frey had passed out trying to keep up with the two of them. Catelyn would sooner Lord Umber had seen fit to stay sober, but telling the Greatjon not to drink was like telling him not to breathe for a few hours.

Smalljon Umber and Robin Flint sat near Robb, to the other side of Fair Walda and Alyx, respectively. Neither of them was drinking; along with Patrek Mallister and Dacey Mormont, they were her son's guards this evening. A wedding feast was not a battle, but there were always dangers when men were in their cups, and a king should never be unguarded. Catelyn was glad of that, and even more glad of the swordbelts hanging on pegs along the walls. *No man needs a longsword to deal with jellied calves' brains.*

"Everyone thought my lord would choose Fair Walda," Lady Walda Bolton told Ser Wendel, shouting to be heard above the music. Fat Walda was a round pink butterball of a girl with watery blue eyes, limp yellow hair, and a huge bosom, yet her voice was a fluttering squeak. It was hard to picture her in the Dreadfort in her pink lace and cape of vair. "My lord grandfather offered Roose his bride's weight in silver as a dowry, though, so my lord of Bolton picked *me.*" The girl's chins jiggled when she laughed. "I weigh six stone more than Fair Walda, but that was the first time I was glad of it. I'm Lady Bolton now and my cousin's still a maid, and she'll be *nineteen* soon, poor thing."

The Lord of the Dreadfort paid the chatter no mind, Catelyn saw. Sometimes he tasted a bite of this, a spoon of that, tearing bread from the loaf with short strong fingers, but the meal could not distract him. Bolton had made a toast to Lord Walder's grandsons when the wedding feast began, pointedly mentioning that Walder and Walder were in the care of his bastard son. From the way the old man had squinted at him, his mouth sucking at the air, Catelyn knew he had heard the unspoken threat.

Was there ever a wedding less joyful? she wondered, until she remembered her poor Sansa and her marriage to the Imp. *Mother take mercy on her. She has a gentle soul.* The heat and smoke and noise were making her sick. The musicians in the gallery might be numerous and loud, but they were not especially gifted. Catelyn took another swallow of wine and allowed a page to refill her cup. *A few more hours, and the worst will be over.* By this hour tomorrow, Robb would be off to another battle, this time with the ironmen at Moat Cailin. Strange, how that prospect seemed almost a relief. *He will win his battle. He wins all his battles, and the ironborn are without a king. Besides, Ned taught him well.* The drums were pounding. Jinglebell hopped past her once again, but the music was so loud she could scarcely hear his bells.

Above the din came a sudden snarling as two dogs fell upon each other over a scrap of meat. They rolled across the floor, snapping and biting, as a howl of mirth went up. Someone doused them with a flagon of ale and they broke apart. One limped toward the dais. Lord Walder's toothless mouth opened in a bark of laughter as the dripping wet dog shook ale and hair all over three of his grandsons.

The sight of the dogs made Catelyn wish once more for Grey Wind, but Robb's direwolf was nowhere to be seen. Lord Walder had refused to allow him in the hall. "Your wild beast has a taste for human flesh, I hear, *heh*," the old man had said. "Rips out throats, yes. I'll have no such creature at my Roslin's feast, amongst women and little ones, all my sweet innocents."

"Grey Wind is no danger to them, my lord," Robb protested. "Not so long as I am there."

"You were there at my gates, were you not? When the wolf attacked the grandsons I sent to greet you? I heard all about that, don't think I didn't, *heh*."

"No harm was done—"

"No harm, the king says? No harm? Petyr fell from his horse, *fell*. I lost a wife the same way, falling." His mouth worked in and out. "Or was she just some strumpet? Bastard Walder's mother, yes, now I recall. She fell off her horse and cracked her head. What would Your Grace do if Petyr had broken his neck, *heh*? Give me another apology in place of a grandson? No, no, no. Might be you're king, I won't say you're not, the King in the North, *heh*, but under my roof, my rule. Have your wolf or have your wedding, sire. You'll not have both."

Catelyn could tell that her son was furious, but he yielded with as much courtesy as he could summon. *If it pleases Lord Walder to serve me stewed crow smothered in maggots*, he'd told her, *I'll eat it and ask for a second bowl.* And so he had.

The Greatjon had drunk another of Lord Walder's brood under the table, Petyr Pimple this time. *The lad has a third his capacity, what did he expect?* Lord Umber wiped his mouth, stood, and began to sing. "*A bear there was, a bear, a BEAR! All black and brown and covered with hair!*" His voice was not at all bad, though somewhat thick from drink. Unfortunately, the fiddlers and drummers and flutists up above were playing "Flowers of Spring," which suited the words of "The Bear and the Maiden Fair" as well as snails might suit a bowl of porridge. Even poor Jinglebell covered his ears at the cacophony.

Roose Bolton murmured some words too soft to hear and went off in search of a privy. The cramped hall was in a constant uproar of guests and servants coming and going. A second feast, for knights and lords of somewhat lesser rank, was roaring along in the other castle, she knew. Lord Walder had exiled his baseborn children and their offspring to that side of the river, so that Robb's northmen had taken to referring to it as "the bastard feast." Some guests were no doubt stealing off to see if the bastards were having a better time than they were. Some might even be venturing as far as the camps. The Freys had provided wagons of wine, ale, and mead, so the common soldiers could drink to the wedding of Riverrun and the Twins.

Robb sat down in Bolton's vacant place. "A few more hours and this farce is done, Mother," he said in a low voice, as the Greatjon sang of the maid with honey in her hair. "Black Walder's been mild as a lamb for once. And Uncle Edmure seems well content in his bride." He leaned across her. "Ser Ryman?"

Ser Ryman Frey blinked and said, "Sire. Yes?"

"I'd hoped to ask Olyvar to squire for me when we march north," said Robb, "but I do not see him here. Would he be at the other feast?"

"Olyvar?" Ser Ryman shook his head. "No. Not Olyvar. Gone . . . gone from the castles. Duty."

"I see." Robb's tone suggested otherwise. When Ser Ryman offered nothing more, the king got to his feet again. "Would you care for a dance, Mother?"

"Thank you, but no." A dance was the last thing she needed, the way her head was throbbing. "No doubt one of Lord Walder's daughters would be pleased to partner you."

"Oh, no doubt." His smile was resigned.

The musicians were playing "Iron Lances" by then, while the Greatjon sang "The Lusty Lad." *Someone should acquaint them with each other, it might improve the harmony.* Catelyn turned back to Ser Ryman. "I had heard that one of your cousins was a singer."

"Alesander. Symond's son. Alyx is his sister." He raised a cup toward where she danced with Robin Flint.

"Will Alesander be playing for us tonight?"

Ser Ryman squinted at her. "Not him. He's away." He wiped sweat from his brow and lurched to his feet. "Pardons, my lady. Pardons." Catelyn watched him stagger toward the door.

Edmure was kissing Roslin and squeezing her hand. Elsewhere in the hall, Ser Marq Piper and Ser Danwell Frey played a drinking game, Lame Lothar said something amusing to Ser Hosteen, one of the younger Freys juggled three daggers for a group of giggly girls, and Jinglebell sat on the floor sucking wine off his fingers. The servers were bringing out huge silver platters piled high with cuts of juicy pink lamb, the most appetizing dish they'd seen all evening. And Robb was leading Dacey Mormont in a dance.

When she wore a dress in place of a hauberk, Lady Maege's eldest daughter was quite pretty; tall and willowy, with a shy smile that made her long face light up. It was pleasant to see that she could be as graceful on the dance floor as in the training yard. Catelyn wondered if Lady Maege had reached the Neck as yet. She had taken her other daughters with her, but as one of Robb's battle companions Dacey had chosen to remain by his side. *He has Ned's gift for inspiring loyalty.* Olyvar Frey had been devoted to her son as well. Hadn't Robb said that Olyvar wanted to remain with him even *after* he'd married Jeyne?

Seated betwixt his black oak towers, the Lord of the Crossing clapped his spotted hands together. The noise they made was so faint that even those on the dais scarce heard it, but Ser Aenys and Ser Hosteen saw and began to pound their cups on the table. Lame Lothar joined them, then Marq Piper and Ser Danwell and Ser Raymund. Half the guests were soon pounding. Finally, even the mob of musicians in the gallery took note. The piping, drumming, and fiddling trailed off into quiet.

"Your Grace," Lord Walder called out to Robb, "the septon has prayed his prayers, some words have been said, and Lord Edmure's wrapped my sweetling in a fish cloak, but they are not yet man and wife. A sword needs a sheath, *heh,* and a wedding needs a bedding. What does my sire say? Is it meet that we should bed them?"

A score or more of Walder Frey's sons and grandsons began to bang their cups again, shouting, "To bed! To bed! *To bed with them!*" Roslin had gone white. Catelyn wondered whether it was the prospect of losing her maidenhead that frightened the girl, or the bedding itself. With so many siblings, she was not like to be a stranger to the custom, but it was different when you were the one being bedded. On Catelyn's own wedding night, Jory Cassell had torn her gown in his haste to get her out of it, and drunken Desmond Grell kept apologizing for every bawdy joke, only to make another. When Lord Dustin had beheld her naked, he'd told Ned that her breasts were enough to make him wish he'd never been weaned. *Poor man,* she thought. He had ridden south with Ned, never to return. Catelyn wondered how many of the men here tonight would be dead before the year was done. *Too many, I fear.*

Robb raised a hand. "If you think the time is meet, Lord Walder, by all means let us bed them."

A roar of approval greeted his pronouncement. Up in the gallery, the musicians took up their pipes and horns and fiddles again, and began to play "The Queen Took Off Her Sandal, the King Took Off His Crown." Jinglebell hopped from foot to foot, his own crown ringing. "I hear Tully men have trout between their legs instead of cocks," Alyx Frey called out boldly. "Does it take a worm to make them rise?" To which Ser Marq Piper threw back, "*I* hear that Frey women have two gates in place of one!" and Alyx said, "Aye, but both are closed and barred to little things like you!" A gust of laughter followed, until Patrek Mallister climbed up onto a table to propose a toast to Edmure's one-eyed fish. "And a mighty pike it is!" he proclaimed. "Nay, I'll wager it's a minnow," Fat Walda Bolton shouted out from Catelyn's side. Then the general cry of "*Bed them! Bed them!*" went up again.

The guests swarmed the dais, the drunkest in the forefront as ever. The men and boys surrounded Roslin and lifted her into the air whilst the maids and mothers in the hall pulled Edmure to his feet and began tugging at his clothing. He was laughing and shouting bawdy jokes back at them, though the music was too loud for Catelyn to hear. She heard the Greatjon, though. "Give this little bride to me," he bellowed as he shoved through the other men and threw Roslin over one shoulder. "Look at this little thing! No meat on her at all!"

Catelyn felt sorry for the girl. Most brides tried to return the banter, or at least pretended to enjoy it, but Roslin was stiff with terror, clutching the Greatjon as if she feared he might drop her. *She's crying too*, Catelyn realized as she watched Ser Marq Piper pull off one of the bride's shoes. *I hope Edmure is gentle with the poor child.* Jolly, bawdy music still poured down from the gallery; the queen was taking off her kirtle now, and the king his tunic.

She knew she should join the throng of women round her brother, but she would only ruin their fun. The last thing she felt just now was bawdy. Edmure would forgive her absence, she did not doubt; much jollier to be stripped and bedded by a score of lusty, laughing Freys than by a sour, stricken sister.

As man and maid were carried from the hall, a trail of clothing behind them, Catelyn saw that Robb had also remained. Walder Frey was prickly enough to see some insult to his daughter in that. *He should join in Roslin's bedding, but is it my place to tell him so?* She tensed, until she saw that others had stayed as well. Petyr Pimple and Ser Whalen Frey slept on, their heads on the table. Merrett Frey poured himself another cup of wine, while Jinglebell wandered about stealing bites off the plates of those who'd left. Ser Wendel Manderly was lustily attacking a leg of lamb. And of course Lord Walder was far too feeble to leave his seat without help. *He will expect Robb to go, though.* She could almost hear the old man asking why His Grace did not want to see his daughter naked. The drums were pounding again, pounding and pounding and pounding.

Dacey Mormont, who seemed to be the only woman left in the hall besides Catelyn, stepped up behind Edwyn Frey, and touched him lightly on the arm as she said something in his ear. Edwyn wrenched himself away from her with unseemly violence. "No," he said, too loudly. "I'm done with dancing for the nonce." Dacey paled and turned away. Catelyn got slowly to her feet. *What just happened there?* Doubt gripped her heart, where an instant before had been only weariness. *It is nothing,* she tried to tell herself, *you are seeing grumkins in the woodpile, you are become an old silly woman sick with grief and fear.* But something must have shown on her face. Even Ser Wendel Manderly took note. "Is something amiss?" he asked, the leg of lamb in his hands.

She did not answer him. Instead she went after Edwyn Frey. The players in the gallery had finally gotten both king and queen down to their name-day suits. With scarcely a moment's respite, they began to play a very different sort of song. No one sang the words, but Catelyn knew "The Rains of Castamere" when she heard it. Edwyn was hurrying toward a door. She hurried faster, driven by the music. Six quick strides and she caught him. *And who are you, the proud lord said, that I must bow so low?* She grabbed Edwyn by the arm to turn him and went cold all over when she felt the iron rings beneath his silken sleeve.

Catelyn slapped him so hard she broke his lip. *Olyvar,* she thought, *and Perwyn, Alesander, all absent. And Roslin wept . . .*

Edwyn Frey shoved her aside. The music drowned all other sound, echoing off the walls as if the stones themselves were playing. Robb gave Edwyn an angry look and moved to block his way . . . and staggered suddenly as a quarrel sprouted from his side, just beneath the shoulder. If he screamed then, the sound was swallowed by the pipes and horns and fiddles. Catelyn saw a second bolt pierce his leg, saw him fall. Up in the gallery, half the musicians had crossbows in their hands instead of drums or lutes. She ran toward her son, until something punched in the small of the back and the hard stone floor came up to slap her. "*Robb!*" she screamed. She saw Smalljon Umber wrestle a table off its trestles. Crossbow bolts thudded into the wood, one two three, as he flung it down on top of his king. Robin Flint was ringed by Freys, their daggers rising and falling. Ser Wendel Manderly rose ponderously to his feet, holding his leg of lamb. A quarrel went in his open mouth and came out the back of his neck. Ser Wendel crashed forward, knocking the table off its trestles and sending cups, flagons, trenchers, platters, turnips, beets, and wine bouncing, spilling, and sliding across the floor.

Catelyn's back was on fire. *I have to reach him.* The Smalljon bludgeoned Ser Raymund Frey across the face with a leg of mutton. But when he reached for his swordbelt a crossbow bolt drove him to his knees. *In a coat of gold or a coat of red, a lion still has claws.* She saw Lucas Blackwood cut down by Ser Hosteen Frey. One of the Vances was hamstrung by Black Walder as he was wrestling with Ser Harys Haigh. *And mine are long and sharp, my lord, as long and sharp as yours.* The crossbows took Donnel Locke, Owen Norrey, and half a dozen more. Young Ser Benfrey had seized Dacey Mormont by the arm, but Catelyn saw her grab up a flagon of wine with her other hand, smash it full in his face, and run for the door. It flew open before she reached it. Ser Ryman Frey pushed into the hall, clad in steel from helm to heel. A dozen Frey men-at-arms packed the door behind him. They were armed with heavy longaxes.

"*Mercy!*" Catelyn cried, but horns and drums and the clash of steel smothered her plea. Ser Ryman buried the head of his axe in Dacey's stomach. By then men were pouring in the other doors as well, mailed men in shaggy fur cloaks with steel in their hands. *Northmen!* She took them for rescue for half a heartbeat, till one of them struck the Smalljon's head off with two huge blows of his axe. Hope blew out like a candle in a storm.

In the midst of slaughter, the Lord of the Crossing sat on his carved oaken throne, watching greedily.

There was a dagger on the floor a few feet away. Perhaps it had skittered there when the Smalljon knocked the table off its trestles, or perhaps it had fallen from the hand of some dying man. Catelyn crawled toward it. Her limbs were leaden, and the taste of blood was in her mouth. *I will kill Walder Frey*, she told herself. Jinglebell was closer to the knife, hiding under a table, but he only cringed away as she snatched up the blade. *I will kill the old man, I can do that much at least.*

Then the tabletop that the Smalljon had flung over Robb shifted, and her son struggled to his knees. He had an arrow in his side, a second in his leg, a third through his chest. Lord Walder raised a hand, and the music stopped, all but one drum. Catelyn heard the crash of distant battle, and closer the wild howling of a wolf. *Grey Wind*, she remembered too late. "*Heh*," Lord Walder cackled at Robb, "the King in the North arises. Seems we killed some of your men, Your Grace. Oh, but I'll make you an *apology*, that will mend them all again, *heh*."

Catelyn grabbed a handful of Jinglebell Frey's long grey hair and dragged him out of his hiding place. "Lord Walder!" she shouted. "*LORD WALDER!*" The drum beat slow and sonorous, *doom boom doom*. "Enough," said Catelyn. "*Enough*, I say. You have repaid betrayal with betrayal, let it end." When she pressed her dagger to Jinglebell's throat, the memory of Bran's sickroom came back to her, with the feel of steel at her own throat. The drum went *boom doom boom doom boom doom*. "Please," she said. "He is my son. My first son, and my last. Let him go. Let him go and I swear we will forget this ... forget all you've done here. I swear it by the old gods and new, we ... we will take no vengeance ..."

Lord Walder peered at her in mistrust. "Only a fool would believe such blather. D'you take me for a fool, my lady?"

"I take you for a father. Keep me for a hostage, Edmure as well if you haven't killed him. But let Robb go."

"No." Robb's voice was whisper faint. "Mother, no ..."

"Yes. Robb, get up. Get up and walk out, please, *please*. Save yourself ... if not for me, for Jeyne."

"Jeyne?" Robb grabbed the edge of the table and forced himself to stand. "Mother," he said, "Grey Wind ..."

"Go to him. Now. Robb, *walk out of here*."

Lord Walder snorted. "And why would I let him do that?"

She pressed the blade deeper into Jinglebell's throat. The lackwit rolled his eyes at her in mute appeal. A foul stench assailed her nose, but she paid it no more mind than she did the sullen ceaseless pounding of that drum, *boom doom boom doom boom doom*. Ser Ryman and Black Walder were circling round her back, but Catelyn did not care. They could do as they wished with her; imprison her, rape her, kill her, it made no matter. She had lived too long, and Ned was waiting. It was Robb she feared for.

"On my honor as a Tully," she told Lord Walder, "on my honor as a Stark, I will trade your boy's life for Robb's. A son for a son." Her hand shook so badly she was ringing Jinglebell's head.

Boom, the drum sounded, *boom doom boom doom*. The old man's lips went in and out. The knife trembled in Catelyn's hand, slippery with sweat. "A son for a son, *heh*," he repeated. "But that's a grandson . . . and he never was much use."

A man in dark armor and a pale pink cloak spotted with blood stepped up to Robb. "Jaime Lannister sends his regards." He thrust his longsword through her son's heart, and twisted.

Robb had broken his word, but Catelyn kept hers. She tugged hard on Aegon's hair and sawed at his neck until the blade grated on bone. Blood ran hot over her fingers. His little bells were ringing, ringing, ringing, and the drum went *boom doom boom*.

Finally, someone took the knife away from her. The tears burned like vinegar as they ran down her cheeks. Ten fierce ravens were raking her face with sharp talons and tearing off strips of flesh, leaving deep furrows that ran red with blood. She could taste it on her lips.

It hurts so much, she thought. *Our children, Ned, all our sweet babes. Rickon, Bran, Arya, Sansa, Robb . . . Robb . . . please, Ned, please, make it stop, make it stop hurting . . .* The white tears and the red ones ran together until her face was torn and tattered, the face that Ned had loved. Catelyn Stark raised her hands and watched the blood run down her long fingers, over her wrists, beneath the sleeves of her gown. Slow red worms crawled along her arms and under her clothes. *It tickles*. That made her laugh until she screamed. "Mad," someone said, "she's lost her wits," and someone else said,

"Make an end," and a hand grabbed her scalp just as she'd done with Jinglebell, and she thought, *No, don't, don't cut my hair, Ned loves my hair.* Then the steel was at her throat, and its bite was red and cold.

ARYA

The feast tents were behind them now. They squished over wet clay and torn grass, out of the light and back into the gloom. Ahead loomed the castle gatehouse. She could see torches moving on the walls, their flames dancing and blowing in the wind. The light shone dully against the wet mail and helms. More torches were moving on the dark stone bridge that joined the Twins, a column of them streaming from the west bank to the east.

"The castle's not closed," Arya said suddenly. The sergeant had said it would be, but he was wrong. The portcullis was being drawn upward even as she watched, and the drawbridge had already been lowered to span the swollen moat. She had been afraid that Lord Frey's guardsmen would refuse to let them in. For half a heartbeat she chewed her lip, too anxious to smile.

The Hound reined up so suddenly that she almost fell off the wayn. "Seven bloody buggering hells," Arya heard him curse, as their left wheel began to sink in soft mud. The wayn tilted slowly. "Get *down*," Clegane roared at her, slamming the heel of his hand into her shoulder to knock her sideways. She landed light, the way Syrio had taught her, and bounced up at once with a face full of mud. "*Why did you do that?*" she screamed. The Hound had leapt down as well. He tore the seat off the front of the wayn and reached in for the swordbelt he'd hidden beneath it.

It was only then that she heard the riders pouring out the castle gate in a river of steel and fire, the thunder of their destriers crossing the drawbridge almost lost beneath the drumming from the castles. Men and mounts wore plate armor, and one in every ten carried a torch. The rest had axes, longaxes with spiked heads and heavy bone-crushing armor-smashing blades.

Somewhere far off she heard a wolf howling. It wasn't very loud compared to the camp noise and the music and the low ominous growl of the river running wild, but she heard it all the same. Only maybe it wasn't her ears that heard it. The sound shivered through Arya like a knife, sharp with rage and grief. More and more riders were emerging from the castle, a column four wide with no end to it, knights and squires and freeriders, torches and longaxes. And there was noise coming from behind as well.

When Arya looked around, she saw that there were only two of the huge feast tents where once there had been three. The one in the middle had collapsed. For a moment she did not understand what she was seeing. Then the flames went licking up from the fallen tent, and now the other two were collapsing, heavy oiled cloth settling down on the men beneath. A flight of fire arrows streaked through the air. The second tent took fire, and then the third. The screams grew so loud she could hear words through the music. Dark shapes moved in front of the flames, the steel of their armor shining orange from afar.

A battle, Arya knew. *It's a battle. And the riders . . .*

She had no more time to watch the tents then. With the river overflowing its banks, the dark swirling waters at the end of the drawbridge reached as high as a horse's belly, but the riders splashed through them all the same, spurred on by the music. For once, the same song was coming from both castles. *I know this song*, Arya realized suddenly. Tom o' Sevens had sung it for them, that rainy night the outlaws had sheltered in the brewhouse with the brothers. *And who are you, the proud lord said, that I must bow so low?*

The Frey riders were struggling through the mud and reeds, but some of them had seen the wayn. She watched as three riders left the main column, pounding through the shallows. *Only a cat of a different coat, that's all the truth I know.*

Clegane cut Stranger loose with a single slash of his sword and leapt onto his back. The courser knew what was wanted of him. He pricked up his ears and wheeled toward the charging destriers. *In a coat of gold or a coat of red, a lion still has claws. And mine are long and sharp, my lord, as long and sharp as yours.* Arya had prayed a hundred hundred times for the Hound to die, but now . . . there was a rock in her hand, slimy with mud, and she didn't even remember picking it up. *Who do I throw it at?*

She jumped at the clash of metal as Clegane turned aside the first longaxe. While he was engaged with the first man, the second circled behind him and aimed a blow for the small of his back. Stranger was wheeling, so the Hound took only a glancing blow, enough to rip a great gash in his baggy peasant's blouse and expose the mail below. *He is one against three.* Arya still clutched her rock. *They're sure to kill him.* She thought of Mycah, the butcher's boy who had been her friend so briefly.

Then she saw the third rider coming her way. Arya moved behind the wayn. *Fear cuts deeper than swords.* She could hear drums and warhorns and pipes, stallions trumpeting, the shriek of steel on steel, but all the sounds seemed so far away. There was only the oncoming horseman and the longaxe in his hand. He wore a surcoat over his armor and she saw the two towers that marked him for a Frey. She did not understand. Her uncle was marrying Lord Frey's daughter, the Freys were her brother's friends. "*Don't!*" she screamed as he rode around the wayn, but he paid no mind.

When he charged Arya threw the rock, the way she'd once thrown a crabapple at Gendry. She'd gotten Gendry right between the eyes, but this time her aim was off, and the stone caromed sideways off his temple. It was enough to break his charge, but no more. She retreated, darting across the muddy ground on the balls of her feet, putting the wayn between them once more. The knight followed at a trot, only darkness behind his eyeslit. She hadn't even dented his helm. They went round once, twice, a third time. The knight cursed her. "*You can't run for—*"

The axehead caught him square in the back of the head, crashing through his helm and the skull beneath and sending him flying face first from his saddle. Behind him was the Hound, still mounted on Stranger. *How did you get an axe?* she almost asked, before she saw. One of the other Freys was trapped beneath his dying horse, drowning in a foot of water. The third man was sprawled on his back, unmoving. He hadn't worn a gorget, and a foot of broken sword jutted from beneath his chin.

"Get my helm," Clegane growled at her.

It was stuffed at the bottom of a sack of dried apples, in the back of the wayn behind the pickled pigs' feet. Arya upended the sack and tossed it to him. He snatched it one-handed from the air and lowered it over his head, and where the man had sat only a steel dog remained, snarling at the fires.

"My brother . . ."

"Dead," he shouted back at her. "Do you think they'd slaughter his men and leave him alive?" He turned his head back toward the camp. "Look. *Look,* damn you."

The camp had become a battlefield. *No, a butcher's den.* The flames from the feasting tents reached halfway up the sky. Some of the barracks tents were burning too, and half a hundred silk pavilions. Everywhere swords were singing. *And now the rains weep o'er his hall, with not a soul to hear.* She saw two knights ride down a running man. A wooden barrel came crashing onto one of the burning tents and burst apart, and the flames leapt twice as high. *A catapult,* she knew. The castle was flinging oil or pitch or something.

"Come with me." Sandor Clegane reached down a hand. "We have to get away from here, and now." Stranger tossed his head impatiently, his nostrils flaring at the scent of blood. The song was done. There was only one solitary drum, its slow monotonous beats echoing across the river like the pounding of some monstrous heart. The black sky wept, the river grumbled, men cursed and died. Arya had mud in her teeth and her face was wet. *Rain. It's only rain. That's all it is.* "We're *here,*" she shouted. Her voice sounded thin and scared, a little girl's voice. "Robb's just in the castle, and my mother. The gate's even open." There were no more Freys riding out. *I came so far.* "We have to go get my *mother.*"

"Stupid little bitch." Fires glinted off the snout of his helm, and made the steel teeth shine. "You go in there, you won't come out. Maybe Frey will let you kiss your mother's corpse."

"Maybe we can *save* her . . ."

"Maybe you can. I'm not done living yet." He rode toward her, crowding her back toward the wayn. "Stay or go, she-wolf. Live or die. Your—"

Arya spun away from him and darted for the gate. The portcullis was coming down, but slowly. *I have to run faster.* The mud slowed her, though, and then the water. *Run fast as a wolf.* The drawbridge had begun to lift, the water running off it in a sheet, the mud falling in heavy clots. *Faster.* She heard loud splashing and looked back to see Stranger pounding after her, sending up gouts of water with every stride. She saw the longaxe too, still wet with blood and brains. And Arya ran. Not for her brother now, not even for her mother, but for herself. She ran faster than she had ever run before, her head down and her feet churning up the river, she ran from him as Mycah must have run.

His axe took her in the back of the head.

TYRION

They supped alone, as they did so often.

"The pease are overcooked," his wife ventured once.

"No matter," he said. "So is the mutton."

It was a jest, but Sansa took it for criticism. "I am sorry, my lord."

"Why? Some cook should be sorry. Not you. The pease are not your province, Sansa."

"I . . . I am sorry that my lord husband is displeased."

"Any displeasure I'm feeling has naught to do with pease. I have Joffrey and my sister to displease me, and my lord father, and three hundred bloody Dornishmen." He had settled Prince Oberyn and his lords in a cornerfort facing the city, as far from the Tyrells as he could put them without evicting them from the Red Keep entirely. It was not nearly far enough. Already there had been a brawl in a Flea Bottom pot-shop that left one Tyrell man-at-arms dead and two of Lord Gargalen's scalded, and an ugly confrontation in the yard when Mace Tyrell's wizened little mother called Ellaria Sand "the serpent's whore." Every time he chanced to see Oberyn Martell, the prince asked when the justice would be served. Overcooked pease were the least of Tyrion's troubles, but he saw no point in burdening his young wife with any of that. Sansa had enough griefs of her own.

"The pease suffice," he told her curtly. "They are green and round, what more can one expect of pease? Here, I'll have another serving, if it please my lady." He beckoned, and Podrick Payne spooned so many pease onto his plate that Tyrion lost sight of his mutton. *That was stupid*, he told himself. *Now I have to eat them all, or she'll be sorry all over again.*

The supper ended in a strained silence, as so many of their suppers did. Afterward, as Pod was removing the cups and platters, Sansa asked Tyrion for leave to visit the godswood.

"As you wish." He had become accustomed to his wife's nightly devotions. She prayed at the royal sept as well, and often lit candles to Mother, Maid, and Crone. Tyrion found all this piety excessive, if truth be told, but in her place he might want the help of the gods as well. "I confess, I know little of the old gods," he said, trying to be pleasant. "Perhaps someday you might enlighten me. I could even accompany you."

"No," Sansa said at once. "You ... you are kind to offer, but ... there are no *devotions*, my lord. No priests or songs or candles. Only trees, and silent prayer. You would be bored."

"No doubt you're right." *She knows me better than I thought.* "Though the sound of rustling leaves might be a pleasant change from some septon droning on about the seven aspects of grace." Tyrion waved her off. "I won't intrude. Dress warmly, my lady, the wind is brisk out there." He was tempted to ask what she prayed for, but Sansa was so dutiful she might actually tell him, and he didn't think he wanted to know.

He went back to work after she left, trying to track some golden dragons through the labyrinth of Littlefinger's ledgers. Petyr Baelish had not believed in letting gold sit about and grow dusty, that was for certain, but the more Tyrion tried to make sense of his accounts the more his head hurt. It was all very well to talk of breeding dragons instead of locking them up in the treasury, but some of these ventures smelled worse than week-old fish. *I wouldn't have been so quick to let Joffrey fling the Antler Men over the walls if I'd known how many of the bloody bastards had taken loans from the crown.* He would have to send Bronn to find their heirs, but he feared that would prove as fruitful as trying to squeeze silver from a silverfish.

When the summons from his lord father arrived, it was the first time Tyrion could ever recall being pleased to see Ser Boros Blount. He closed the ledgers gratefully, blew out the oil lamp, tied a cloak around his shoulders, and waddled across the castle to the Tower of the Hand. The wind *was* brisk, just as he'd warned Sansa, and there was a smell of rain in the air. Perhaps when Lord Tywin was done with him he should go to the godswood and fetch her home before she got soaked.

But all that went straight out of his head when he entered the Hand's solar to find Cersei, Ser Kevan, and Grand Maester Pycelle gathered about Lord Tywin and the king. Joffrey was almost bouncing, and Cersei was savoring a smug little smile, though Lord Tywin looked as grim as ever. *I wonder if he could smile even if he wanted to.* "What's happened?" Tyrion asked.

His father offered him a roll of parchment. Someone had flattened it, but it still wanted to curl. "*Roslin caught a fine fat trout,*" the message read. "*Her brothers gave her a pair of wolf pelts for her wedding.*" Tyrion turned it over to inspect the broken seal. The wax was silvery-grey, and pressed into it were the twin towers of House Frey. "Does the Lord of the Crossing imagine he's being poetic? Or is this meant to confound us?" Tyrion snorted. "The trout would be Edmure Tully, the pelts . . ."

"He's *dead*!" Joffrey sounded so proud and happy you might have thought he'd skinned Robb Stark himself.

First Greyjoy and now Stark. Tyrion thought of his child wife, praying in the godswood even now. *Praying to her father's gods to bring her brother victory and keep her mother safe, no doubt.* The old gods paid no more heed to prayer than the new ones, it would seem. Perhaps he should take comfort in that. "Kings are falling like leaves this autumn," he said. "It would seem our little war is winning itself."

"Wars do not win themselves, Tyrion," Cersei said with poisonous sweetness. "Our lord father won this war."

"Nothing is won so long as we have enemies in the field," Lord Tywin warned them.

"The river lords are no fools," the queen argued. "Without the northmen they cannot hope to stand against the combined power of

Highgarden, Casterly Rock, and Dorne. Surely they will choose submission rather than destruction."

"Most," agreed Lord Tywin. "Riverrun remains, but so long as Walder Frey holds Edmure Tully hostage, the Blackfish dare not mount a threat. Jason Mallister and Tytos Blackwood will fight on for honor's sake, but the Freys can keep the Mallisters penned up at Seagard, and with the right inducement Jonos Bracken can be persuaded to change his allegiance and attack the Blackwoods. In the end they will bend the knee, yes. I mean to offer generous terms. Any castle that yields to us will be spared, save one."

"Harrenhal?" said Tyrion, who knew his sire.

"The realm is best rid of these Brave Companions. I have commanded Ser Gregor to put the castle to the sword."

Gregor Clegane. It appeared as if his lord father meant to mine the Mountain for every last nugget of ore before turning him over to Dornish justice. The Brave Companions would end as heads on spikes, and Littlefinger would stroll into Harrenhal without so much as a spot of blood on those fine clothes of his. He wondered if Petyr Baelish had reached the Vale yet. *If the gods are good, he ran into a storm at sea and sank.* But when had the gods ever been especially good?

"They should all be put to the sword," Joffrey declared suddenly. "The Mallisters and Blackwoods and Brackens ... all of them. They're traitors. I want them killed, Grandfather. I won't have any *generous terms.*" The king turned to Grand Maester Pycelle. "And I want Robb Stark's head too. Write to Lord Frey and tell him. The king commands. I'm going to have it served to Sansa at my wedding feast."

"Sire," Ser Kevan said, in a shocked voice, "the lady is now your aunt by marriage."

"A jest." Cersei smiled. "Joff did not mean it."

"Yes I did," Joffrey insisted. "He was a traitor, and I want his stupid head. I'm going to make Sansa kiss it."

"*No.*" Tyrion's voice was hoarse. "Sansa is no longer yours to torment. Understand that, monster."

Joffrey sneered. "You're the monster, Uncle."

"Am I?" Tyrion cocked his head. "Perhaps you should speak more softly to me, then. Monsters are dangerous beasts, and just now kings seem to be dying like flies."

"I could have your tongue out for saying that," the boy king said, reddening. "I'm the king."

Cersei put a protective hand on her son's shoulder. "Let the dwarf make all the threats he likes, Joff. I want my lord father and my uncle to see what he is."

Lord Tywin ignored that; it was Joffrey he addressed. "Aerys also felt the need to remind men that he was king. And he was passing fond of ripping tongues out as well. You could ask Ser Ilyn Payne about that, though you'll get no reply."

"Ser Ilyn never dared provoke Aerys the way your Imp provokes Joff," said Cersei. "You heard him. 'Monster,' he said. To the King's Grace. And he threatened him . . ."

"Be quiet, Cersei. Joffrey, when your enemies defy you, you must serve them steel and fire. When they go to their knees, however, you must help them back to their feet. Elsewise no man will ever bend the knee to you. And any man who must say 'I am the king' is no true king at all. Aerys never understood that, but you will. When I've won your war for you, we will restore the king's peace and the king's justice. The only head that need concern you is Margaery Tyrell's maidenhead."

Joffrey had that sullen, sulky look he got. Cersei had him firmly by the shoulder, but perhaps she should have had him by the throat. The boy surprised them all. Instead of scuttling safely back under his rock, Joff drew himself up defiantly and said, "You talk about Aerys, Grandfather, but you were scared of him."

Oh, my, hasn't this gotten interesting? Tyrion thought.

Lord Tywin studied his grandchild in silence, gold flecks shining in his pale green eyes. "Joffrey, apologize to your grandfather," said Cersei.

He wrenched free of her. "Why should I? Everyone knows it's true. My father won all the battles. He killed Prince Rhaegar and took the crown, while *your* father was hiding under Casterly Rock." The boy gave his grandfather a defiant look. "A *strong* king acts boldly, he doesn't just talk."

"Thank you for that wisdom, Your Grace," Lord Tywin said, with a courtesy so cold it was like to freeze their ears off. "Ser Kevan, I can see the king is tired. Please see him safely back to his bedchamber. Pycelle, perhaps some gentle potion to help His Grace sleep restfully?"

"Dreamwine, my lord?"

"I don't want any dreamwine," Joffrey insisted.

Lord Tywin would have paid more heed to a mouse squeaking in the corner. "Dreamwine will serve. Cersei, Tyrion, remain."

Ser Kevan took Joffrey firmly by the arm and marched him out the door, where two of the Kingsguard were waiting. Grand Maester Pycelle scurried after them as fast as his shaky old legs could take him. Tyrion remained where he was.

"Father, I am sorry," Cersei said, when the door was shut. "Joff has always been willful, I did warn you . . ."

"There is a long league's worth of difference between willful and stupid. 'A strong king acts boldly?' Who told him that?"

"Not me, I promise you," said Cersei. "Most like it was something he heard Robert say . . ."

"The part about you hiding under Casterly Rock does sound like Robert." Tyrion didn't want Lord Tywin forgetting that bit.

"Yes, I recall now," Cersei said, "Robert *often* told Joff that a king must be bold."

"And what were *you* telling him, pray? I did not fight a war to seat Robert the Second on the Iron Throne. You gave me to understand the boy cared nothing for his father."

"Why would he? Robert ignored him. He would have *beat* him if I'd allowed it. That brute you made me marry once hit the boy so hard he knocked out two of his baby teeth, over some mischief with a cat. I told him I'd kill him in his sleep if he ever did it again, and he never did, but sometimes he would say things . . ."

"It appears things needed to be said." Lord Tywin waved two fingers at her, a brusque dismissal. "Go."

She went, seething.

"Not Robert the Second," Tyrion said. "Aerys the Third."

"The boy is thirteen. There is time yet." Lord Tywin paced to the window. That was unlike him; he was more upset than he wished to show. "He requires a sharp lesson."

Tyrion had gotten his own sharp lesson at thirteen. He felt almost sorry for his nephew. On the other hand, no one deserved it more. "Enough of Joffrey," he said. "Wars are won with quills and ravens, wasn't that what you said? I must congratulate you. How long have you and Walder Frey been plotting this?"

"I mislike that word," Lord Tywin said stiffly.

"And I mislike being left in the dark."

"There was no reason to tell you. You had no part in this."

"Was Cersei told?" Tyrion demanded to know.

"No one was told, save those who had a part to play. And they were only told as much as they needed to know. You ought to know that there is no other way to keep a secret—here, especially. My object was to rid us of a dangerous enemy as cheaply as I could, not to indulge your curiosity or make your sister feel important." He closed the shutters, frowning. "You have a certain cunning, Tyrion, but the plain truth is *you talk too much*. That loose tongue of yours will be your undoing."

"You should have let Joff tear it out," suggested Tyrion.

"You would do well not to tempt me," Lord Tywin said. "I'll hear no more of this. I have been considering how best to appease Oberyn Martell and his entourage."

"Oh? Is this something I'm allowed to know, or should I leave so you can discuss it with yourself?"

His father ignored the sally. "Prince Oberyn's presence here is unfortunate. His brother is a cautious man, a *reasoned* man, subtle, deliberate, even indolent to a degree. He is a man who weighs the consequences of every word and every action. But Oberyn has always been half-mad."

"Is it true he tried to raise Dorne for Viserys?"

"No one speaks of it, but yes. Ravens flew and riders rode, with what secret messages I never knew. Jon Arryn sailed to Sunspear to return Prince Lewyn's bones, sat down with Prince Doran, and ended all the talk of war. But Robert never went to Dorne thereafter, and Prince Oberyn seldom left it."

"Well, he's here now, with half the nobility of Dorne in his tail, and he grows more impatient every day," said Tyrion. "Perhaps I should show him the brothels of King's Landing, that might distract him. A tool for every task, isn't that how it works? My tool is yours, Father. Never let it be said that House Lannister blew its trumpets and I did not respond."

Lord Tywin's mouth tightened. "Very droll. Shall I have them sew you a suit of motley, and a little hat with bells on it?"

"If I wear it, do I have leave to say anything I want about His Grace King Joffrey?"

Lord Tywin seated himself again and said, "I was made to suffer my father's follies. I will not suffer yours. Enough."

"Very well, as you ask so pleasantly. The Red Viper is *not* going to be pleasant, I fear ... nor will he content himself with Ser Gregor's head alone."

"All the more reason not to give it to him."

"*Not* to ...?" Tyrion was shocked. "I thought we were agreed that the woods were full of beasts."

"Lesser beasts." Lord Tywin's fingers laced together under his chin. "Ser Gregor has served us well. No other knight in the realm inspires such terror in our enemies."

"Oberyn *knows* that Gregor was the one who ..."

"He knows nothing. He has heard tales. Stable gossip and kitchen calumnies. He has no crumb of proof. Ser Gregor is certainly not about to confess to him. I mean to keep him well away for so long as the Dornishmen are in King's Landing."

"And when Oberyn demands the justice he's come for?"

"I will tell him that Ser Amory Lorch killed Elia and her children," Lord Tywin said calmly. "So will you, if he asks."

"Ser Amory Lorch is dead," Tyrion said flatly.

"Precisely. Vargo Hoat had Ser Amory torn apart by a bear after the fall of Harrenhal. That ought to be sufficiently grisly to appease even Oberyn Martell."

"You may call that justice ..."

"It *is* justice. It was Ser Amory who brought me the girl's body, if you must know. He found her hiding under her father's bed, as if she believed Rhaegar could still protect her. Princess Elia and the babe were in the nursery a floor below."

"Well, it's a tale, and Ser Amory's not like to deny it. What will you tell Oberyn when he asks who gave Lorch his orders?"

"Ser Amory acted on his own in the hope of winning favor from the new king. Robert's hatred for Rhaegar was scarcely a secret."

It might serve, Tyrion had to concede, *but the snake will not be happy.* "Far be it from me to question your cunning, Father, but in your place I do believe I'd have let Robert Baratheon bloody his own hands."

Lord Tywin stared at him as if he had lost his wits. "You deserve that motley, then. We had come late to Robert's cause. It was necessary to demonstrate our loyalty. When I laid those bodies before the throne, no man could doubt that we had forsaken House Targaryen forever. And Robert's relief was palpable. As stupid as he was, even he knew that Rhaegar's children had to die if his throne was ever to be secure. Yet he saw himself as a hero, and heroes do not kill children." His father shrugged. "I grant you, it was done too brutally. Elia need not have been harmed at all, that was sheer folly. By herself she was nothing."

"Then why did the Mountain kill her?"

"Because I did not tell him to spare her. I doubt I mentioned her at all. I had more pressing concerns. Ned Stark's van was rushing south from the Trident, and I feared it might come to swords between us. And it was in Aerys to murder Jaime, with no more cause than spite. That was the thing I feared most. That, and what Jaime himself might do." He closed a fist. "Nor did I yet grasp what I had in Gregor Clegane, only that he was huge and terrible in battle. The rape ... even you will not accuse me of giving *that* command, I would hope. Ser Amory was almost as bestial with Rhaenys. I asked him afterward why it had required half a hundred thrusts to kill a girl of ... two? Three? He said she'd kicked him and would not stop screaming. If Lorch had half the wits the gods gave a turnip, he would have calmed her with a few sweet words and used a soft silk pillow." His mouth twisted in distaste. "The blood was in him."

But not in you, Father. There is no blood in Tywin Lannister. "Was it a soft silk pillow that slew Robb Stark?"

"It was to be an arrow, at Edmure Tully's wedding feast. The boy was too wary in the field. He kept his men in good order, and surrounded himself with outriders and bodyguards."

"So Lord Walder slew him under his own roof, at his own table?" Tyrion made a fist. "What of Lady Catelyn?"

"Slain as well, I'd say. *A pair of wolfskins.* Frey had intended to keep her captive, but perhaps something went awry."

"So much for guest right."

"The blood is on Walder Frey's hands, not mine."

"Walder Frey is a peevish old man who lives to fondle his young wife and brood over all the slights he's suffered. I have no doubt he hatched this ugly chicken, but he would never have dared such a thing without a promise of protection."

"I suppose you would have spared the boy and told Lord Frey you had no need of his allegiance? That would have driven the old fool right back into Stark's arms and won you another year of war. Explain to me why it is more noble to kill ten thousand men in battle than a dozen at dinner." When Tyrion had no reply to that, his father continued. "The price was cheap by any measure. The crown shall grant Riverrun to Ser Emmon Frey once the Blackfish yields. Lancel and Daven must marry Frey girls, Joy is to wed one of Lord Walder's natural sons when she's old enough, and Roose Bolton becomes Warden of the North and takes home Arya Stark."

"*Arya* Stark?" Tyrion cocked his head. "And Bolton? I might have known Frey would not have the stomach to act alone. But Arya ... Varys and Ser Jacelyn searched for her for more than half a year. Arya Stark is surely dead."

"So was Renly, until the Blackwater."

"What does that mean?"

"Perhaps Littlefinger succeeded where you and Varys failed. Lord Bolton will wed the girl to his bastard son. We shall allow the Dreadfort to fight the ironborn for a few years, and see if he can bring Stark's other bannermen to heel. Come spring, all of them should be at the end of their strength and ready to bend the knee. The north will go to your son by Sansa Stark ... if you ever find enough manhood in you to breed one. Lest you forget, it is not only Joffrey who must needs take a maidenhead."

I had not forgotten, though I'd hoped you had. "And when do you imagine Sansa will be at her most fertile?" Tyrion asked his father in tones that dripped acid. "Before or after I tell her how we murdered her mother and her brother?"

DAVOS

For a moment it seemed as though the king had not heard. Stannis showed no pleasure at the news, no anger, no disbelief, not even relief. He stared at his Painted Table with teeth clenched hard. "You are certain?" he asked.

"I am not seeing the body, no, Your Kingliness," said Salladhor Saan. "Yet in the city, the lions prance and dance. *The Red Wedding*, the smallfolk are calling it. They swear Lord Frey had the boy's head hacked off, sewed the head of his direwolf in its place, and nailed a crown about his ears. His lady mother was slain as well, and thrown naked in the river."

At a wedding, thought Davos. *As he sat at his slayer's board, a guest beneath his roof. These Freys are cursed.* He could smell the burning blood again, and hear the leech hissing and spitting on the brazier's hot coals.

"It was the Lord's wrath that slew him," Ser Axell Florent declared. "It was the hand of R'hllor!"

"*Praise the Lord of Light!*" sang out Queen Selyse, a pinched thin hard woman with large ears and a hairy upper lip.

"Is the hand of R'hllor spotted and palsied?" asked Stannis. "This sounds more Walder Frey's handiwork than any god's."

"R'hllor chooses such instruments as he requires." The ruby at Melisandre's throat shone redly. "His ways are mysterious, but no man may withstand his fiery will."

"*No man may withstand him!*" the queen cried.

"Be quiet, woman. You are not at a nightfire now." Stannis considered the Painted Table. "The wolf leaves no heirs, the kraken too many. The lions will devour them unless . . . Saan, I will require your fastest ships to carry envoys to the Iron Islands and White Harbor. I shall offer pardons." The way he snapped his teeth showed how little he liked that word. "Full pardons, for all those who repent of treason and swear fealty to their rightful king. They must see . . ."

"They will not." Melisandre's voice was soft. "I am sorry, Your Grace. This is not an end. More false kings will soon rise to take up the crowns of those who've died."

"More?" Stannis looked as though he would gladly have throttled her. "More usurpers? *More* traitors?"

"I have seen it in the flames."

Queen Selyse went to the king's side. "The Lord of Light sent Melisandre to guide you to your glory. Heed her, I beg you. R'hllor's holy flames do not lie."

"There are lies and lies, woman. Even when these flames speak truly, they are full of tricks, it seems to me."

"An ant who hears the words of a king may not comprehend what he is saying," Melisandre said, "and all men are ants before the fiery face of god. If sometimes I have mistaken a warning for a prophecy or a prophecy for a warning, the fault lies in the reader, not the book. But this I know for a certainty—envoys and pardons will not serve you now, no more than leeches. You must show the realm a sign. A sign that proves your power!"

"*Power?*" The king snorted. "I have thirteen hundred men on Dragonstone, another three hundred at Storm's End." His hand swept over the Painted Table. "The rest of Westeros is in the hands of my foes. I have no fleet but Salladhor Saan's. No coin to hire sellswords. No prospect of plunder or glory to lure freeriders to my cause."

"Lord husband," said Queen Selyse, "you have more men than Aegon did three hundred years ago. All you lack are dragons."

The look Stannis gave her was dark. "Nine mages crossed the sea to hatch Aegon the Third's cache of eggs. Baelor the Blessed prayed over his for half a year. Aegon the Fourth built dragons of wood and iron. Aerion Brightflame drank wildfire to transform himself. The mages failed, King Baelor's prayers went unanswered, the wooden dragons burned, and Prince Aerion died screaming."

Queen Selyse was adamant. "None of these was the chosen of R'hllor. No red comet blazed across the heavens to herald their coming. None wielded Lightbringer, the red sword of heroes. And none of them paid the price. Lady Melisandre will tell you, my lord. Only death can pay for life."

"The boy?" The king almost spat the words.

"The boy," agreed the queen.

"The boy," Ser Axell echoed.

"I was sick unto death of this wretched boy before he was even born," the king complained. "His very name is a roaring in my ears and a dark cloud upon my soul."

"Give the boy to me and you need never hear his name spoken again," Melisandre promised.

No, but you'll hear him screaming when she burns him. Davos held his tongue. It was wiser not to speak until the king commanded it.

"Give me the boy for R'hllor," the red woman said, "and the ancient prophecy shall be fulfilled. Your dragon shall awaken and spread his stony wings. The kingdom shall be yours."

Ser Axell went to one knee. "On bended knee I beg you, sire. Wake the stone dragon and let the traitors tremble. Like Aegon you begin as Lord of Dragonstone. Like Aegon you shall conquer. Let the false and the fickle feel your flames."

"Your own wife begs as well, lord husband." Queen Selyse went down on both knees before the king, hands clasped as if in prayer. "Robert and Delena defiled our bed and laid a curse upon our union. This boy is the foul fruit of their fornications. Lift his shadow from my womb and I will bear you many trueborn sons, I know it." She threw her arms around his legs. "He is only one boy, born of your brother's lust and my cousin's shame."

"He is mine own blood. Stop clutching me, woman." King Stannis put a hand on her shoulder, awkwardly untangling himself from her grasp. "Perhaps Robert did curse our marriage bed. He swore to me that he never meant to shame me, that he was drunk and never knew which bedchamber he entered that night. But does it matter? The boy was not at fault, whatever the truth."

Melisandre put her hand on the king's arm. "The Lord of Light cherishes the innocent. There is no sacrifice more precious. From his king's blood and his untainted fire, a dragon shall be born."

Stannis did not pull away from Melisandre's touch as he had from his queen's. The red woman was all Selyse was not; young, full-bodied, and strangely beautiful, with her heart-shaped face, coppery hair, and unearthly red eyes. "It would be a wondrous thing to see stone come to life," he admitted, grudging. "And to mount a dragon ... I remember the first time my father took me to court, Robert had to hold my hand. I could not have been older than four, which would have made him five or six. We agreed afterward that the king had been as noble as the dragons were fearsome." Stannis snorted. "Years later, our father told us that Aerys had cut himself on the throne that morning, so his Hand had taken his place. It was Tywin Lannister who'd so impressed us." His fingers touched the surface of the table, tracing a path lightly across the varnished hills. "Robert took the skulls down when he donned the crown, but he could not bear to have them destroyed. Dragon wings over Westeros ... there would be such a ..."

"*Your Grace!*" Davos edged forward. "Might I speak?"

Stannis closed his mouth so hard his teeth snapped. "My lord of the Rainwood. Why do you think I made you Hand, if not to speak?" The king waved a hand. "Say what you will."

Warrior, make me brave. "I know little of dragons and less of gods ... but the queen spoke of curses. No man is as cursed as the kinslayer, in the eyes of gods and men."

"There are no gods save R'hllor and the Other, whose name must not be spoken." Melisandre's mouth made a hard red line. "And small men curse what they cannot understand."

"I am a small man," Davos admitted, "so tell me why you need this boy Edric Storm to wake your great stone dragon, my lady." He was determined to say the boy's name as often as he could.

"Only death can pay for life, my lord. A great gift requires a great sacrifice."

"Where is the greatness in a baseborn child?"

"He has kings' blood in his veins. You have seen what even a little of that blood could do—"

"I saw you burn some leeches."

"And two false kings are dead."

"Robb Stark was murdered by Lord Walder of the Crossing, and we have heard that Balon Greyjoy fell from a bridge. Who did your leeches kill?"

"Do you doubt the power of R'hllor?"

No. Davos remembered too well the living shadow that had squirmed from out her womb that night beneath Storm's End, its black hands pressing at her thighs. *I must go carefully here, or some shadow may come seeking me as well.* "Even an onion smuggler knows two onions from three. You are short a king, my lady."

Stannis gave a snort of laughter. "He has you there, my lady. Two is not three."

"To be sure, Your Grace. One king might die by chance, even two ... but three? If Joffrey should die in the midst of all his power, surrounded by his armies and his Kingsguard, would not that show the power of the Lord at work?"

"It might." The king spoke as if he grudged each word.

"Or not." Davos did his best to hide his fear.

"Joffrey *shall* die," Queen Selyse declared, serene in her confidence.

"It may be that he is dead already," Ser Axell added.

Stannis looked at them with annoyance. "Are you trained crows, to croak at me in turns? Enough."

"Husband, hear me—" the queen entreated.

"Why? Two is not three. Kings can count as well as smugglers. You may go." Stannis turned his back on them.

Melisandre helped the queen to her feet. Selyse swept stiffly from the chamber, the red woman trailing behind. Ser Axell lingered long enough to give Davos one last look. *An ugly look on an ugly face,* he thought as he met the stare.

After the others had gone, Davos cleared his throat. The king looked up. "Why are you still here?"

"Sire, about Edric Storm ..."

Stannis made a sharp gesture. "Spare me."

Davos persisted. "Your daughter takes her lessons with him, and plays with him every day in Aegon's Garden."

"I know that."

"Her heart would break if anything ill should—"

"I know that as well."

"If you would only see him—"

"I have seen him. He looks like Robert. Aye, and worships him. Shall I tell him how often his beloved father ever gave him a thought? My brother liked the making of children well enough, but after birth they were a bother."

"He asks after you every day, he—"

"You are making me angry, Davos. I will hear no more of this bastard boy."

"His name is Edric Storm, sire."

"I know his name. Was there ever a name so apt? It proclaims his bastardy, his high birth, and the turmoil he brings with him. Edric Storm. There, I have said it. Are you satisfied, my lord Hand?"

"Edric—" he started.

"—is *one boy*! He may be the best boy who ever drew breath and it would not matter. My duty is to the realm." His hand swept across the Painted Table. "How many boys dwell in Westeros? How many girls? How many men, how many women? The darkness will devour them all, she says. The night that never ends. She talks of prophecies . . . a hero reborn in the sea, living dragons hatched from dead stone . . . she speaks of *signs* and swears they point to me. I never asked for this, no more than I asked to be king. Yet dare I disregard her?" He ground his teeth. "We do not choose our destinies. Yet we must . . . we must do our duty, no? Great or small, *we must do our duty*. Melisandre swears that she has seen me in her flames, facing the dark with Lightbringer raised on high. *Lightbringer!*" Stannis gave a derisive snort. "It glimmers prettily, I'll grant you, but on the Blackwater this magic sword served me no better than any common steel. A dragon would have turned that battle. Aegon once stood here as I do, looking down on this table. Do you think we would name him Aegon the Conqueror today if he had not had *dragons*?"

"Your Grace," said Davos, "the cost . . ."

"*I know the cost!* Last night, gazing into that hearth, I saw things in the flames as well. I saw a king, a crown of fire on his brows, burning . . . *burning*, Davos. His own crown consumed his flesh and turned him into ash. Do you think I need Melisandre to tell me what that means? Or *you*?" The king moved, so his shadow fell upon King's Landing. "If Joffrey should die . . . what is the life of one bastard boy against a kingdom?"

"Everything," said Davos, softly.

Stannis looked at him, jaw clenched. "Go," the king said at last, "before you talk yourself back into the dungeon."

Sometimes the storm winds blow so strong a man has no choice but to furl his sails. "Aye, Your Grace." Davos bowed, but Stannis had seemingly forgotten him already.

It was chilly in the yard when he left the Stone Drum. A wind blew briskly from the east, making the banners snap and flap noisily along the walls. Davos could smell salt in the air. *The sea.* He loved that smell. It made him want to walk a deck again, to raise his canvas and sail off south to Marya and his two small ones. He thought of them most every day now, and even more at night. Part of him wanted nothing so much as to take Devan and go home. *I cannot. Not yet. I am a lord now, and the King's Hand, I must not fail him.*

He raised his eyes to gaze up at the walls. In place of merlons, a thousand grotesques and gargoyles looked down on him, each different from all the others; wyverns, griffins, demons, manticores, minotaurs, basilisks, hellhounds, cockatrices, and a thousand queerer creatures sprouted from the castle's battlements as if they'd grown there. And the dragons were everywhere. The Great Hall was a dragon lying on its belly. Men entered through its open mouth. The kitchens were a dragon curled up in a ball, with the smoke and steam of the ovens vented through its nostrils. The towers were dragons hunched above the walls or poised for flight; the Windwyrm seemed to scream defiance, while Sea Dragon Tower gazed serenely out across the waves. Smaller dragons framed the gates. Dragon claws emerged from walls to grasp at torches, great stone wings enfolded the smith and armory, and tails formed arches, bridges, and exterior stairs.

Davos had often heard it said that the wizards of Valyria did not cut and chisel as common masons did, but worked stone with fire and magic as a potter might work clay. But now he wondered. *What if they were real dragons, somehow turned to stone?*

"If the red woman brings them to life, the castle will come crashing down, I am thinking. What kind of dragons are full of rooms and stairs and furniture? And windows. And chimneys. And privy shafts."

Davos turned to find Salladhor Saan beside him. "Does this mean you have forgiven my treachery, Salla?"

The old pirate wagged a finger at him. "Forgiving, yes. Forgetting, no. All that good gold on Claw Isle that might have been mine, it makes me old and tired to think of it. When I die impoverished, my wives and concubines will curse you, Onion Lord. Lord Celtigar had many fine wines that now I am not tasting, a sea eagle he had trained to fly from the wrist, and a magic horn to summon krakens from the deep. Very useful such a horn would be, to pull down Tyroshi and other vexing creatures. But do I have this horn to blow? No, because the king made my old friend his Hand." He slipped his arm through Davos's and said, "The queen's men love you not, old friend. I am hearing that a certain Hand has been making friends of his own. This is true, yes?"

You hear too much, you old pirate. A smuggler had best know men as well as tides, or he would not live to smuggle long. The queen's men might remain fervent followers of the Lord of Light, but the lesser folk of Dragonstone were drifting back to the gods they'd known all their lives. They said Stannis was ensorceled, that Melisandre had turned him away from the Seven to bow before some demon out of shadow, and ... worst sin of all ... that she and her god had failed him. And there were knights and lordlings who felt the same. Davos had sought them out, choosing them with the same care with which he'd once picked his crews. Ser Gerald Gower fought stoutly on the Blackwater, but afterward had been heard to say that R'hllor must be a feeble god to let his followers be chased off by a dwarf and a dead man. Ser Andrew Estermont was the king's cousin, and had served as his squire years ago. The Bastard of Nightsong had commanded the rearguard that allowed Stannis to reach the safety of Salladhor

Saan's galleys, but he worshiped the Warrior with a faith as fierce as he was. *King's men, not queen's men.* But it would not do to boast of them.

"A certain Lysene pirate once told me that a good smuggler stays out of sight," Davos replied carefully. "Black sails, muffled oars, and a crew that knows how to hold their tongues."

The Lyseni laughed. "A crew with no tongues is even better. Big strong mutes who cannot read or write." But then he grew more somber. "But I am glad to know that someone watches your back, old friend. Will the king give the boy to the red priestess, do you think? One little dragon could end this great big war."

Old habit made him reach for his luck, but his fingerbones no longer hung about his neck, and he found nothing. "He will not do it," said Davos. "He could not harm his own blood."

"Lord Renly will be glad to hear this."

"Renly was a traitor in arms. Edric Storm is innocent of any crime. His Grace is a just man."

Salla shrugged. "We shall be seeing. Or you shall. For myself, I am returning to sea. Even now, rascally smugglers may be sailing across the Blackwater Bay, hoping to avoid paying their lord's lawful duties." He slapped Davos on the back. "Take care. You with your mute friends. You are grown so very great now, yet the higher a man climbs the farther he has to fall."

Davos reflected on those words as he climbed the steps of Sea Dragon Tower to the maester's chambers below the rookery. He did not need Salla to tell him that he had risen too high. *I cannot read, I cannot write, the lords despise me, I know nothing of ruling, how can I be the King's Hand? I belong on the deck of a ship, not in a castle tower.*

He had said as much to Maester Pylos. "You are a notable captain," the maester replied. "A captain rules his ship, does he not? He must navigate treacherous waters, set his sails to catch the rising wind, know when a storm is coming and how best to weather it. This is much the same."

Pylos meant it kindly, but his assurances rang hollow. "It is not at all the same!" Davos had protested. "A kingdom's not a ship . . . and a good thing, or this kingdom would be sinking. I know wood and rope and water, yes, but how will that serve me now? Where do I find the wind to blow King Stannis to his throne?"

The maester laughed at that. "And there you have it, my lord. Words are wind, you know, and you've blown mine away with your good sense. His Grace knows what he has in you, I think."

"Onions," said Davos glumly. "That is what he has in me. The King's Hand should be a highborn lord, someone wise and learned, a battle commander or a great knight . . ."

"Ser Ryam Redwyne was the greatest knight of his day, and one of the worst Hands ever to serve a king. Septon Murmison's prayers worked miracles, but as Hand he soon had the whole realm praying for his death. Lord Butterwell was renowned for wit, Myles Smallwood for courage, Ser Otto Hightower for learning, yet they failed as Hands, every one. As for birth, the dragonkings oft chose Hands from amongst their own blood, with results as various as Baelor Breakspear and Maegor the Cruel. Against this, you have Septon Barth, the black-smith's son the Old King plucked from the Red Keep's library, who gave the realm forty years of peace and plenty." Pylos smiled. "Read your history, Lord Davos, and you will see that your doubts are groundless."

"How can I read history, when I cannot read?"

"Any man can read, my lord," said Maester Pylos. "There is no magic needed, nor high birth. I am teaching the art to your son, at the king's command. Let me teach you as well."

It was a kindly offer, and not one that Davos could refuse. And so every day he repaired to the maester's chambers high atop Sea Dragon Tower, to frown over scrolls and parchments and great leather tomes and try to puzzle out a few more words. His efforts often gave him headaches, and made him feel as big a fool as Patchface besides. His son Devan was not yet twelve, yet he was well ahead of his father, and for Princess Shireen and Edric Storm reading seemed as natural as breathing. When it came to books, Davos was more a child than any of them. Yet he persisted. He was the King's Hand now, and a King's Hand should read.

The narrow twisting steps of Sea Dragon Tower had been a sore trial to Maester Cressen after he broke his hip. Davos still found himself missing the old man. He thought Stannis must as well. Pylos seemed clever and diligent and well-meaning, but he was so young, and the king did not confide in him as he had in Cressen. The old man had been with Stannis so long ... *Until he ran afoul of Melisandre, and died for it.*

At the top of the steps Davos heard a soft jingle of bells that could only herald Patchface. The princess's fool was waiting outside the maester's door for her like a faithful hound. Dough-soft and slump-shouldered, his broad face tattooed in a motley pattern of red and green squares, Patchface wore a helm made of a rack of deer antlers strapped to a tin bucket. A dozen bells hung from the tines and rang when he moved ... which meant constantly, since the fool seldom stood still. He jingled and jangled his way everywhere he went; small wonder that Pylos had exiled him from Shireen's lessons. "Under the sea the old fish eat the young fish," the fool muttered at Davos. He bobbed his head, and his bells clanged and chimed and sang. "I know, I know, oh oh oh."

"Up here the young fish teach the old fish," said Davos, who never felt so ancient as when he sat down to try and read. It might have been different if aged Maester Cressen had been the one teaching him, but Pylos was young enough to be his son.

He found the maester seated at his long wooden table covered with books and scrolls, across from the three children. Princess Shireen sat between the two boys. Even now Davos could take great pleasure in the sight of his own blood keeping company with a princess and a king's bastard. *Devan will be a lord now, not merely a knight. The Lord of the Rainwood.* Davos took more pride in that than in wearing the title himself. *He reads too. He reads and he writes, as if he had been born to it.* Pylos had naught but praise for his diligence, and the master-at-arms said Devan was showing promise with sword and lance as well. *And he is a godly lad, too.* "My brothers have ascended to the Hall of Light, to sit beside the Lord," Devan had said when his father told him how his four elder brothers had died. "I will pray for them at the nightfires, and for you as well, Father, so you might walk in the Light of the Lord till the end of your days."

"Good morrow to you, Father," the boy greeted him. *He looks so much like Dale did at his age,* Davos thought. His eldest had never dressed so fine as Devan in his squire's raiment, to be sure, but they shared the same square plain face, the same forthright brown eyes, the same thin brown flyaway hair. Devan's cheeks and chin were dusted with blond hair, a fuzz that would have shamed a proper peach, though the boy was fiercely proud of his "beard." *Just as Dale was proud of his, once.* Devan was the oldest of the three children at the table.

Yet Edric Storm was three inches taller and broader in the chest and shoulders. He was his father's son in that; nor did he ever miss a morning's work with sword and shield. Those old enough to have known Robert and Renly as children said that the bastard boy had more of their look than Stannis had ever shared; the coal-black hair, the deep blue eyes, the mouth, the jaw, the cheekbones. Only his ears reminded you that his mother had been a Florent.

"Yes, good morrow, my lord," Edric echoed. The boy could be fierce and proud, but the maesters and castellans and masters-at-arms who'd raised him had schooled him well in courtesy. "Do you come from my uncle? How fares His Grace?"

"Well," Davos lied. If truth be told, the king had a haggard, haunted look about him, but he saw no need to burden the boy with his fears. "I hope I have not disturbed your lesson."

"We had just finished, my lord," Maester Pylos said.

"We were reading about King Daeron the First." Princess Shireen was a sad, sweet, gentle child, far from pretty. Stannis had given her his square jaw and Selyse her Florent ears, and the gods in their cruel wisdom had seen fit to compound her homeliness by afflicting her with greyscale in the cradle. The disease had left one cheek and half her neck grey and cracked and hard, though it had spared both her life and her sight. "He went to war and conquered Dorne. The Young Dragon, they called him."

"He worshiped false gods," said Devan, "but he was a great king otherwise, and very brave in battle."

"He was," agreed Edric Storm, "but my father was braver. The Young Dragon never won three battles in a day."

The princess looked at him wide-eyed. "Did Uncle Robert win three battles in a day?"

The bastard nodded. "It was when he'd first come home to call his banners. Lords Grandison, Cafferen, and Fell planned to join their strength at Summerhall and march on Storm's End, but he learned their plans from an informer and rode at once with all his knights and squires. As the plotters came up on Summerhall one by one, he defeated each of them in turn before they could join up with the others. He slew Lord Fell in single combat and captured his son Silveraxe."

Devan looked to Pylos. "Is that how it happened?"

"I *said* so, didn't I?" Edric Storm said before the maester could reply. "He smashed all three of them, and fought so bravely that Lord Grandison and Lord Cafferen became his men afterward, and Silveraxe too. No one ever beat my father."

"Edric, you ought not boast," Maester Pylos said. "King Robert suffered defeats like any other man. Lord Tyrell bested him at Ashford, and he lost many a tourney tilt as well."

"He won more than he lost, though. And he killed Prince Rhaegar on the Trident."

"That he did," the maester agreed. "But now I must give my attention to Lord Davos, who has waited so patiently. We will read more of King Daeron's *Conquest of Dorne* on the morrow."

Princess Shireen and the boys said their farewells courteously. When they had taken their leaves, Maester Pylos moved closer to Davos. "My lord, perhaps you would like to try a bit of *Conquest of Dorne* as well?" He slid the slender leather-bound book across the table. "King Daeron wrote with an elegant simplicity, and his history is rich with blood, battle, and bravery. Your son is quite engrossed."

"My son is not quite twelve. I am the King's Hand. Give me another letter, if you would."

"As you wish, my lord." Maester Pylos rummaged about his table, unrolling and then discarding various scraps of parchment. "There are no new letters. Perhaps an old one . . ."

Davos enjoyed a good story as well as any man, but Stannis had not named him Hand for his enjoyment, he felt. His first duty was to help his king rule, and for that he must needs understand the words the ravens brought. The best way to learn a thing was to do it, he had found; sails or scrolls, it made no matter.

"This might serve our purpose." Pylos passed him a letter.

Davos flattened down the little square of crinkled parchment and squinted at the tiny crabbed letters. Reading was hard on the eyes, that much he had learned early. Sometimes he wondered if the Citadel offered a champion's purse to the maester who wrote the smallest hand. Pylos had laughed at the notion, but . . .

"To the . . . five kings," read Davos, hesitating briefly over *five*, which he did not often see written out. "The king . . . be . . . the king . . . beware?"

"*Beyond*," the maester corrected.

Davos grimaced. "The King beyond the Wall comes . . . comes *south*. He leads a . . . a . . . fast . . ."

"Vast."

". . . a *vast* host of wil . . . wild . . . wildlings. Lord M . . . Mmmor . . . Mormont sent a . . . raven from the . . . ha . . . ha . . ."

"Haunted. The *haunted forest*." Pylos underlined the words with the point of his finger.

". . . the haunted forest. He is . . . *under* a . . . attack?"

"Yes."

Pleased, he plowed onward. "Oth . . . other birds have come since, with no words. We . . . fear . . . Mormont slain with all . . . with all his . . . stench . . . no, *strength*. We fear Mormont slain with all his strength . . ." Davos suddenly realized just what he was reading. He turned the letter over, and saw that the wax that had sealed it had been black. "This is from the Night's Watch. Maester, has King Stannis seen this letter?"

"I brought it to Lord Alester when it first arrived. He was the Hand then. I believed he discussed it with the queen. When I asked him if he wished to send a reply, he told me not to be a fool. 'His Grace lacks the men to fight his own battles, he has none to waste on wildlings,' he said to me."

That was true enough. And this talk of five kings would certainly have angered Stannis. "Only a starving man begs bread from a beggar," he muttered.

"Pardon, my lord?"

"Something my wife said once." Davos drummed his shortened fingers against the tabletop. The first time he had seen the Wall he had been younger than Devan, serving aboard the *Cobblecat* under Roro Uhoris, a Tyroshi known up and down the narrow sea as the Blind Bastard, though he was neither blind nor baseborn. Roro had sailed past Skagos into the Shivering Sea, visiting a hundred little coves that had never seen a trading ship before. He brought steel; swords, axes, helms, good chainmail hauberks, to trade for furs, ivory, amber, and obsidian. When the *Cobblecat* turned back south her holds were stuffed, but in the Bay of Seals three black galleys came out to herd her into Eastwatch. They lost their cargo and the Bastard lost his head, for the crime of trading weapons to the wildlings.

Davos had traded at Eastwatch in his smuggling days. The black brothers made hard enemies but good customers, for a ship with the right cargo. But while he might have taken their coin, he had never forgotten how the Blind Bastard's head had rolled across the *Cobblecat*'s deck. "I met some wildlings when I was a boy," he told Maester Pylos. "They were fair thieves but bad hagglers. One made off with our cabin girl. All in all, they seemed men like any other men, some fair, some foul."

"Men are men," Maester Pylos agreed. "Shall we return to our reading, my lord Hand?"

I am the Hand of the King, yes. Stannis might be the King of Westeros in name, but in truth he was the King of the Painted Table. He held Dragonstone and Storm's End, and had an ever-more-uneasy alliance with Salladhor Saan, but that was all. How could the Watch have looked to him for help? *They may not know how weak he is, how lost his cause.* "King Stannis never saw this letter, you are quite certain? Nor Melisandre?"

"No. Should I bring it to them? Even now?"

"No," Davos said at once. "You did your duty when you brought it to Lord Alester." *If Melisandre knew of this letter . . .* What was it she had said? *One whose name may not be spoken is marshaling his power, Davos Seaworth. Soon comes the cold, and the night that never ends . . .* And Stannis had seen a vision in the flames, a ring of torches in the snow with terror all around.

"My lord, are you unwell?" asked Pylos.

I am frightened, Maester, he might have said. Davos was remembering a tale Salladhor Saan had told him, of how Azor Ahai tempered Lightbringer by thrusting it through the heart of the wife he loved. *He slew his wife to fight the dark. If Stannis is Azor Ahai come again, does that mean Edric Storm must play the part of Nissa Nissa?* "I was thinking, Maester. My pardons." *What harm if some wildling king conquers the north?* It was not as though Stannis *held* the north. His Grace could scarcely be expected to defend people who refused to acknowledge him as king. "Give me another letter," he said abruptly. "This one is too . . ."

". . . difficult?" suggested Pylos.

Soon comes the cold, whispered Melisandre, *and the night that never ends.* "Troubling," said Davos. "Too . . . troubling. A different letter, please."

JON

They woke to the smoke of Mole's Town burning.

Atop the King's Tower, Jon Snow leaned on the padded crutch that Maester Aemon had given him and watched the grey plume rise. Styr had lost all hope of taking Castle Black unawares when Jon escaped him, yet even so, he need not have warned of his approach so bluntly. *You may kill us,* he reflected, *but no one will be butchered in their beds. That much I did, at least.*

His leg still hurt like blazes when he put his weight on it. He'd needed Clydas to help him don his fresh-washed blacks and lace up his boots that morning, and by the time they were done he'd wanted to drown himself in the milk of the poppy. Instead, he had settled for half a cup of dreamwine, a chew of willow bark, and the crutch. The beacon was burning on Weatherback Ridge, and the Night's Watch had need of every man.

"I can fight," he insisted when they tried to stop him.

"Your leg's healed, is it?" Noye snorted. "You won't mind me giving it a little kick, then?"

"I'd sooner you didn't. It's stiff, but I can hobble around well enough, and stand and fight if you have need of me."

"I have need of every man who knows which end of the spear to stab into the wildlings."

"The pointy end." Jon had told his little sister something like that once, he remembered.

Noye rubbed the bristle on his chin. "Might be you'll do. We'll put you on a tower with a longbow, but if you bloody well fall off don't come crying to me."

He could see the kingsroad wending its way south through stony brown fields and over windswept hills. The Magnar would be coming up that road before the day was done, his Thenns marching behind him with axes and spears in their hands and their bronze-and-leather shields on their backs. *Grigg the Goat, Quort, Big Boil, and the rest will be coming as well. And Ygritte.* The wildlings had never been his friends, he had not *allowed* them to be his friends, but her . . .

He could feel the throb of pain where her arrow had gone through the meat and muscle of his thigh. He remembered the old man's eyes too, and the black blood rushing from his throat as the storm cracked overhead. But he remembered the grotto best of all, the look of her naked in the torchlight, the taste of her mouth when it opened under his. *Ygritte, stay away. Go south and raid, go hide in one of those roundtowers you liked so well. You'll find nothing here but death.*

Across the yard, one of the bowmen on the roof of the old Flint Barracks had unlaced his breeches and was pissing through a crenel. *Mully*, he knew from the man's greasy orange hair. Men in black cloaks were visible on other roofs and tower tops as well, though nine of every ten happened to be made of straw. "The scarecrow sentinels," Donal Noye called them. *Only we're the crows,* Jon mused, *and most of us were scared enough.*

Whatever you called them, the straw soldiers had been Maester Aemon's notion. They had more breeches and jerkins and tunics in the storerooms than they'd had men to fill them, so why not stuff some with straw, drape a cloak around their shoulders, and set them to standing watches? Noye had placed them on every tower and in half the windows. Some were even clutching spears, or had crossbows cocked under their arms. The hope was that the Thenns would see them from afar and decide that Castle Black was too well defended to attack.

Jon had six scarecrows sharing the roof of the King's Tower with him, along with two actual breathing brothers. Deaf Dick Follard sat in a crenel, methodically cleaning and oiling the mechanism of his crossbow to make sure the wheel turned smoothly, while the Oldtown boy wandered restlessly around the parapets, fussing with the clothes on straw men. *Maybe he thinks they will fight better if they're posed just right. Or maybe this waiting is fraying his nerves the way it's fraying mine.*

The boy claimed to be eighteen, older than Jon, but he was green as summer grass for all that. Satin, they called him, even in the wool and mail and boiled leather of the Night's Watch; the name he'd gotten in the brothel where he'd been born and raised. He was pretty as a girl with his dark eyes, soft skin, and raven's ringlets. Half a year at Castle Black had toughened up his hands, however, and Noye said he was passable with a crossbow. Whether he had the courage to face what was coming, though . . .

Jon used the crutch to limp across the tower top. The King's Tower was not the castle's tallest—the high, slim, crumbling Lance held that honor, though Othell Yarwyck had been heard to say it might topple any day. Nor was the King's Tower strongest—the Tower of Guards beside the kingsroad would be a tougher nut to crack. But it was tall enough, strong enough, and well placed beside the Wall, overlooking the gate and the foot of the wooden stair.

The first time he had seen Castle Black with his own eyes, Jon had wondered why anyone would be so foolish as to build a castle without walls. How could it be defended?

"It can't," his uncle told him. "That is the point. The Night's Watch is pledged to take no part in the quarrels of the realm. Yet over the centuries certain Lords Commander, more proud than wise, forgot their vows and near destroyed us all with their ambitions. Lord Commander Runcel Hightower tried to bequeathe the Watch to his bastard son. Lord Commander Rodrik Flint thought to make himself King-beyond-the-Wall. Tristan Mudd, Mad Marq Rankenfell, Robin Hill . . . did you know that six hundred years ago, the commanders at Snowgate and the Night-fort went to war *against each other*? And when the Lord Commander tried to stop them, they joined forces to murder him? The Stark in Winterfell had to take a hand . . . and both their heads. Which he did easily, because *their strongholds were not defensible.* The Night's Watch had nine hundred and ninety-six Lords Commander before Jeor Mormont, most of them men of courage and honor . . . but we have had cowards and fools as well, our tyrants and our madmen. We survive because the lords and kings of the Seven Kingdoms know that we pose no threat to them, no matter *who* should lead us. Our only foes are to the north, and to the north we have the Wall."

Only now those foes have gotten past the Wall to come up from the south, Jon reflected, *and the lords and kings of the Seven Kingdoms have forgotten us. We are caught between the hammer and the anvil.* Without a wall Castle Black could not be held; Donal Noye knew that as well as any. "The castle does them no good," the armorer told his little garrison. "Kitchens, common hall, stables, even the towers . . . let them take it all. We'll empty the armory and move what stores we can to the top of the Wall, and make our stand around the gate."

So Castle Black had a wall of sorts at last, a crescent-shaped barricade ten feet high made of stores; casks of nails and barrels of salt mutton, crates, bales of black broadcloth, stacked logs, sawn timbers, fire-hardened stakes, and sacks and sacks of grain. The crude rampart enclosed the two things most worth defending; the gate to the north, and the foot of the great wooden switchback stair that clawed and climbed its way up the face of the Wall like a drunken thunderbolt, supported by wooden beams as big as tree trunks driven deep into the ice.

The last few moles were still making the long climb, Jon saw, urged on by his brothers. Grenn was carrying a little boy in his arms, while Pyp, two flights below, let an old man lean upon his shoulder. The oldest villagers still waited below for the cage to make its way back down to them. He saw a mother pulling along two children, one on either hand, as an older boy ran past her up the steps. Two hundred feet above them, Sky Blue Su and Lady Meliana (who was no lady, all her friends agreed) stood on a landing, looking south. They had a better view of the smoke than he did, no doubt. Jon wondered about the villagers who had chosen not to flee. There were always a few, too stubborn or too stupid or too brave to run, a few who preferred to fight or hide or bend the knee. Maybe the Thenns would spare them.

The thing to do would be to take the attack to them, he thought. *With fifty rangers well mounted, we could cut them apart on the road.* They did not have fifty rangers, though, nor half as many horses. The garrison had not returned, and there was no way to know just where they were, or even whether the riders that Noye had sent out had reached them.

We are the garrison, Jon told himself, *and look at us.* The brothers Bowen Marsh had left behind were old men, cripples, and green boys, just as Donal Noye had warned him. He could see some wrestling barrels up the steps, others on the barricade; stout old Kegs, as slow as ever, Spare Boot hopping along briskly on his carved wooden leg, half-mad Easy who fancied himself Florian the Fool reborn, Dornish Dilly, Red Alyn of the Rosewood, Young Henly (well past fifty), Old Henly (well past seventy), Hairy Hal, Spotted Pate of Maidenpool. A couple of them saw Jon looking down from atop the King's Tower and waved up at him. Others turned away. *They still think me a turncloak.* That was a bitter draft to drink, but Jon could not blame them. He was a bastard, after all. Everyone knew that bastards were wanton and treacherous by nature, having been born of lust and deceit. And he had made as many enemies as friends at Castle Black . . . Rast, for one. Jon had once threatened to have Ghost rip his throat out unless he stopped tormenting Samwell Tarly, and Rast did not forget things like that. He was raking dry leaves into piles under the stairs just now, but every so often he stopped long enough to give Jon a nasty look.

"No," Donal Noye roared at three of the Mole's Town men, down below. "The pitch goes to the hoist, the oil up the steps, crossbow bolts to the fourth, fifth, and sixth landings, spears to first and second. Stack the lard under the stair, yes, there, behind the planks. The casks of meat are for the barricade. *Now*, you poxy plow pushers, *NOW*!"

He has a lord's voice, Jon thought. His father had always said that in battle a captain's lungs were as important as his sword arm. "It does not matter how brave or brilliant a man is, if his commands cannot be heard," Lord Eddard told his sons, so Robb and he used to climb the towers of Winterfell to shout at each other across the yard. Donal Noye could have drowned out both of them. The moles all went in terror of him, and rightfully so, since he was always threatening to rip their heads off.

Three-quarters of the village had taken Jon's warning to heart and come to Castle Black for refuge. Noye had decreed that every man still spry enough to hold a spear or swing an axe would help defend the barricade, else they could damn well go home and take their chances with the Thenns. He had emptied the armory to put good steel in their hands; big double-bladed axes, razor-sharp daggers, longswords, maces, spiked morningstars. Clad in studded leather jerkins and mail hauberks, with greaves for their legs and gorgets to keep their heads on their shoulders, a few of them even looked like soldiers. *In a bad light. If you squint.*

Noye had put the women and children to work as well. Those too young to fight would carry water and tend the fires, the Mole's Town midwife would assist Clydas and Maester Aemon with any wounded, and Three-Finger Hobb suddenly had more spit boys, kettle stirrers, and onion choppers than he knew what to do with. Two of the whores had even offered to fight, and had shown enough skill with the crossbow to be given a place on the steps forty feet up.

"It's cold." Satin stood with his hands tucked into his armpits under his cloak. His cheeks were bright red.

Jon made himself smile. "The Frostfangs are cold. This is a brisk autumn day."

"I hope I never see the Frostfangs then. I knew a girl in Oldtown who liked to ice her wine. That's the best place for ice, I think. In wine." Satin glanced south, frowned. "You think the scarecrow sentinels scared them off, my lord?"

"We can hope." It was possible, Jon supposed ... but more likely the wildlings had simply paused for a bit of rape and plunder in Mole's Town. Or maybe Styr was waiting for nightfall, to move up under cover of darkness.

Midday came and went, with still no sign of Thenns on the kingsroad. Jon heard footsteps inside the tower, though, and Owen the Oaf popped up out of the trapdoor, red-faced from the climb. He had a basket of buns under one arm, a wheel of cheese under the other, a bag of onions dangling from one hand. "Hobb said to feed you, in case you're stuck up here awhile."

That, or for our last meal. "Thank him for us, Owen."

Dick Follard was deaf as a stone, but his nose worked well enough.

The buns were still warm from the oven when he went digging in the basket and plucked one out. He found a crock of butter as well, and spread some with his dagger. "Raisins," he announced happily. "Nuts, too." His speech was thick, but easy enough to understand once you got used to it.

"You can have mine too," said Satin. "I'm not hungry."

"Eat," Jon told him. "There's no knowing when you'll have another chance." He took two buns himself. The nuts were pine nuts, and besides the raisins there were bits of dried apple.

"Will the wildlings come today, Lord Snow?" Owen asked.

"You'll know if they do," said Jon. "Listen for the horns."

"Two. Two is for wildlings." Owen was tall, towheaded, and amiable, a tireless worker and surprisingly deft when it came to working wood and fixing catapults and the like, but as he'd gladly tell you, his mother had dropped him on his head when he was a baby, and half his wits had leaked out through his ear.

"You remember where to go?" Jon asked him.

"I'm to go to the stairs, Donal Noye says. I'm to go up to the third landing and shoot my crossbow down at the wildlings if they try to climb over the barrier. The *third* landing, one two three." His head bobbed up and down. "If the wildlings attack, the king will come and help us, won't he? He's a mighty warrior, King Robert. He's sure to come. Maester Aemon sent him a bird."

There was no use telling him that Robert Baratheon was dead. He would forget it, as he'd forgotten it before. "Maester Aemon sent him a bird," Jon agreed. That seemed to make Owen happy.

Maester Aemon had sent a lot of birds . . . not to one king, but to four. *Wildlings at the gate,* the message ran. *The realm in danger. Send all the help you can to Castle Black.* Even as far as Oldtown and the Citadel the ravens flew, and to half a hundred mighty lords in their castles. The northern lords offered their best hope, so to them Aemon had sent two birds. To the Umbers and the Boltons, to Castle Cerwyn and Torrhen's Square, Karhold and Deepwood Motte, to Bear Island, Oldcastle, Widow's Watch, White Harbor, Barrowton, and the Rills, to the mountain fastnesses of the Liddles, the Burleys, the Norreys, the Harclays, and the Wulls, the black birds brought their plea. *Wildlings at the gate. The north in danger. Come with all your strength.*

Well, ravens might have wings, but lords and kings do not. If help was coming, it would not come today.

As morning turned to afternoon, the smoke of Mole's Town blew away and the southern sky was clear again. *No clouds,* thought Jon. That was good. Rain or snow could doom them all.

Clydas and Maester Aemon rode the winch cage up to safety at the top of the Wall, and most of the Mole's Town wives as well. Men in black cloaks paced restlessly on the tower tops and shouted back and forth across the courtyards. Septon Cellador led the men on the barricade in a prayer, beseeching the Warrior to give them strength. Deaf Dick Follard curled up beneath his cloak and went to sleep. Satin walked a hundred leagues in circles, round and round the crenellations. The Wall wept and the sun crept across a hard blue sky. Near evenfall, Owen the Oaf returned with a loaf of black bread and a pail of Hobb's best mutton, cooked in a thick broth of ale and onions. Even Dick woke up for that. They ate every bit of it, using chunks of bread to wipe the bottom of the pail. By the time they were done the sun was low in the west, the shadows sharp and black throughout the castle. "Light the fire," Jon told Satin, "and fill the kettle with oil."

He went downstairs himself to bar the door, to try and work some of the stiffness from his leg. That was a mistake, and Jon soon knew it, but he clutched the crutch and saw it through all the same. The door to the King's Tower was oak studded with iron. It might delay the Thenns, but it would not stop them if they wanted to come in. Jon slammed the bar down in its notches, paid a visit to the privy—it might well be his last chance—and hobbled back up to the roof, grimacing at the pain.

The west had gone the color of a blood bruise, but the sky above was cobalt blue, deepening to purple, and the stars were coming out. Jon sat between two merlons with only a scarecrow for company and watched the Stallion gallop up the sky. Or was it the Horned Lord? He wondered where Ghost was now. He wondered about Ygritte as well, and told himself that way lay madness.

They came in the night, of course. *Like thieves*, Jon thought. *Like murderers.*

Satin pissed himself when the horns blew, but Jon pretended not to notice. "Go shake Dick by the shoulder," he told the Oldtown boy, "else he's liable to sleep through the fight."

"I'm frightened." Satin's face was a ghastly white.

"So are they." Jon leaned his crutch up against a merlon and took up his longbow, bending the smooth thick Dornish yew to slip a bowstring through the notches. "Don't waste a quarrel unless you know you have a good clean shot," he said when Satin returned from waking Dick. "We have an ample supply up here, but *ample* doesn't mean inexhaustible. And step behind a merlon to reload, don't try and hide in back of a scarecrow. They're made of straw, an arrow will punch through them." He did not bother telling Dick Follard anything. Dick could read your lips if there was enough light and he gave a damn what you were saying, but he knew it all already.

The three of them took up positions on three sides of the round-tower. Jon hung a quiver from his belt and pulled an arrow. The shaft was black, the fletching grey. As he notched it to his string, he remembered something that Theon Greyjoy had once said after a hunt. "The boar can keep his tusks and the bear his claws," he had declared, smiling that way he did. "There's nothing half so mortal as a grey goose feather."

Jon had never been half the hunter that Theon was, but he was no stranger to the longbow either. There were dark shapes slipping around the armory, backs against the stone, but he could not see them well enough to waste an arrow. He heard distant shouts, and saw the archers on the Tower of Guards loosing shafts at the ground. That was too far off to concern Jon. But when he glimpsed three shadows detach themselves from the old stables fifty yards away, he stepped up to the crenel, raised his bow, and drew. They were running, so he led them, waiting, waiting . . .

The arrow made a soft *hiss* as it left his string. A moment later there was a grunt, and suddenly only two shadows were loping across the yard. They ran all the faster, but Jon had already pulled a second arrow from his quiver. This time he hurried the shot too much, and missed. The wildlings were gone by the time he nocked again. He searched for another target, and found four, rushing around the empty shell of the Lord Commander's Keep. The moonlight glimmered off their spears and axes, and the gruesome devices on their round leathern shields; skulls and bones, serpents, bear claws, twisted demonic faces. *Free folk*, he knew. The Thenns carried shields of black boiled leather with bronze rims and bosses, but theirs were plain and unadorned. These were the lighter wicker shields of raiders.

Jon pulled the goose feather back to his ear, aimed, and loosed the arrow, then nocked and drew and loosed again. The first shaft pierced the bearclaw shield, the second one a throat. The wildling screamed as he went down. He heard the deep *thrum* of Deaf Dick's crossbow to his left, and Satin's a moment later. "I got one!" the boy cried hoarsely. "I got one in the chest."

"Get another," Jon called.

He did not have to search for targets now; only choose them. He dropped a wildling archer as he was fitting an arrow to his string, then sent a shaft toward the axeman hacking at the door of Hardin's Tower. That time he missed, but the arrow quivering in the oak made the wildling reconsider. It was only as he was running off that Jon recognized Big Boil. Half a heartbeat later, old Mully put an arrow through his leg from the roof of the Flint Barracks, and he crawled off bleeding. *That will stop him bitching about his boil,* Jon thought.

When his quiver was empty, he went to get another, and moved to a different crenel, side by side with Deaf Dick Follard. Jon got off three arrows for every bolt Deaf Dick discharged, but that was the advantage of the longbow. The crossbow penetrated better, some insisted, but it was slow and cumbersome to reload. He could hear the wildlings shouting to each other, and somewhere to the west a warhorn blew. The world was moonlight and shadow, and time became an endless round of notch and draw and loose. A wildling arrow ripped through the throat of the straw sentinel beside him, but

Jon Snow scarcely noticed. *Give me one clean shot at the Magnar of Thenn*, he prayed to his father's gods. The Magnar at least was a foe that he could hate. *Give me Styr.*

His fingers were growing stiff and his thumb was bleeding, but still Jon notched and drew and loosed. A gout of flame caught his eye, and he turned to see door of the common hall afire. It was only a few moments before the whole great timbered hall was burning. Three-Finger Hobb and his Mole's Town helpers were safe atop the Wall, he knew, but it felt like a punch in the belly all the same. "*JON*," Deaf Dick yelled in his thick voice, "*the armory.*" They were on the roof, he saw. One had a torch. Dick hopped up on the crenel for a better shot, jerked his crossbow to his shoulder, and sent a quarrel thrumming toward the torch man. He missed.

The archer down below him didn't.

Follard never made a sound, only toppled forward headlong over the parapet. It was a hundred feet to the yard below. Jon heard the thump as he was peering round a straw soldier, trying to see where the arrow had come from. Not ten feet from Deaf Dick's body, he glimpsed a leather shield, a ragged cloak, a mop of thick red hair. *Kissed by fire*, he thought, *lucky.* He brought his bow up, but his fingers would not part, and she was gone as suddenly as she'd appeared. He swiveled, cursing, and loosed a shaft at the men on the armory roof instead, but he missed them as well.

By then the east stables were afire too, black smoke and wisps of burning hay pouring from the stalls. When the roof collapsed, a flames rose up roaring, so loud they almost drowned out the warhorns of the Thenns. Fifty of them were pounding up the kingsroad in tight column, their shields held up above their heads. Others were swarming through the vegetable garden, across the flagstone yard, around the old dry well. Three had hacked their way through the doors of Maester Aemon's apartments in the timber keep below the rookery, and a desperate fight was going on atop the Silent Tower, longswords against bronze axes. None of that mattered. *The dance has moved on*, he thought.

Jon hobbled across to Satin and grabbed him by the shoulder. "With me," he shouted. Together they moved to the north parapet, where the King's Tower looked down on the gate and Donal Noye's makeshift wall of logs and barrels and sacks of corn. The Thenns were there before them.

They wore halfhelms, and had thin bronze disks sewn to their long leather shirts. Many wielded bronze axes, though a few were chipped stone. More had short stabbing spears with leaf-shaped heads that gleamed redly in the light from the burning stables. They were screaming in the Old Tongue as they stormed the barricade, jabbing with their spears, swinging their bronze axes, spilling corn and blood with equal abandon while crossbow quarrels and arrows rained down on them from the archers that Donal Noye had posted on the stair.

"What do we *do*?" Satin shouted.

"We kill them," Jon shouted back, a black arrow in his hand.

No archer could have asked for an easier shot. The Thenns had their backs to the King's Tower as they charged the crescent, clambering over bags and barrels to reach the men in black. Both Jon and Satin chanced to choose the same target. He had just reached the top of the barricade when an arrow sprouted from his neck and a quarrel between his shoulder blades. Half a heartbeat later a longsword took him in the belly and he fell back onto the man behind him. Jon reached down to his quiver and found it empty again. Satin was winding back his crossbow. He left him to it and went for more arrows, but he hadn't taken more than three steps before the trap slammed open three feet in front of him. *Bloody hell, I never even heard the door break.*

There was no time to think or plan or shout for help. Jon dropped his bow, reached back over his shoulder, ripped Longclaw from its sheath, and buried the blade in the middle of the first head to pop out of the tower. Bronze was no match for Valyrian steel. The blow sheared right through the Thenn's helm and deep into his skull, and he went crashing back down where he'd come from. There were more behind him, Jon knew from the shouting. He fell back and called to Satin. The next man to make the climb got a quarrel through his cheek. He vanished too. "The oil," Jon said. Satin nodded. Together they snatched up the thick quilted pads they'd left beside the fire, lifted the heavy kettle of boiling oil, and dumped it down the hole on the Thenns below. The shrieks were as bad as anything he had ever heard, and Satin looked as though he was going to be sick. Jon kicked the trapdoor shut, set the heavy iron kettle on top of it, and gave the boy with the pretty face a hard shake. "Retch later," Jon yelled. "*Come.*"

They had only been gone from the parapets for a few moments, but everything below had changed. A dozen black brothers and a few Mole's Town men still stood atop the crates and barrels, but the wildlings were swarming over all along the crescent, pushing them back. Jon saw one shove his spear up through Rast's belly so hard he lifted him into the air. Young Henly was dead and Old Henly was dying, surrounded by foes. He could see Easy spinning and slashing, laughing like a loon, his cloak flapping as he leapt from cask to cask. A bronze axe caught him just below the knee and the laughter turned into a bubbling shriek.

"They're breaking," Satin said.

"No," said Jon, "they're broken."

It happened quickly. One mole fled and then another, and suddenly all the villagers were throwing down their weapons and abandoning the barricade. The brothers were too few to hold alone. Jon watched them try and form a line to fall back in order, but the Thenns washed over them with spear and axe, and then they were fleeing too. Dornish Dilly slipped and went down on his face, and a wildling planted a spear between his shoulder blades. Kegs, slow and short of breath, had almost reached the bottom step when a Thenn caught the end of his cloak and yanked him around ... but a crossbow quarrel dropped the man before his axe could fall. "*Got* him," Satin crowed, as Kegs staggered to the stair and began to crawl up the steps on hands and knees.

The gate is lost. Donal Noye had closed and chained it, but it was there for the taking, the iron bars glimmering red with reflected firelight, the cold black tunnel behind. No one had fallen back to defend it; the only safety was on top of the Wall, seven hundred feet up the crooked wooden stairs.

"What gods do you pray to?" Jon asked Satin.

"The Seven," the boy from Oldtown said.

"Pray, then," Jon told him. "Pray to your new gods, and I'll pray to my old ones." It all turned here.

With the confusion at the trapdoor, Jon had forgotten to fill his quiver. He limped back across the roof and did that now, and picked up his bow as well. The kettle had not moved from where he'd left it, so it seemed as though they were safe enough for the nonce. *The dance has moved on, and we're watching from the gallery*, he thought as he hobbled back. Satin was loosing quarrels at the wildlings on the steps, then ducking down behind a merlon to cock the crossbow. *He may be pretty, but he's quick.*

The real battle was on the steps. Noye had put spearmen on the two lowest landings, but the headlong flight of the villagers had panicked them and they had joined the flight, racing up toward the third landing with the Thenns killing anyone who fell behind. The archers and crossbowmen on the higher landings were trying to drop shafts over their heads. Jon nocked an arrow, drew, and loosed, and was pleased when one of the wildlings went rolling down the steps. The heat of the fires was making the Wall weep, and the flames danced and shimmered against the ice. The steps shook to the footsteps of men running for their lives.

Again, Jon notched and drew and loosed, but there was only one of him and one of Satin, and a good sixty or seventy Thenns pounding up the stairs, killing as they went, drunk on victory. On the fourth landing, three brothers in black cloaks stood shoulder to shoulder with longswords in their hands, and battle was joined again, briefly. But there were only three and soon enough the wildling tide washed over them, and their blood dripped down the steps. "A man is never so vulnerable in battle as when he flees," Lord Eddard had told Jon once. "A running man is like a wounded animal to a soldier. It gets his bloodlust up." The archers on the fifth landing fled before the battle even reached them. It was a rout, a red rout.

"Fetch the torches," Jon told Satin. There were four of them stacked beside the fire, their heads wrapped in oily rags. There were a dozen fire arrows too. The Oldtown boy thrust one torch into the fire until it was blazing brightly, and brought the rest back under his arm, unlit. He looked frightened again, as well he might. Jon was frightened too.

It was then that he saw Styr. The Magnar was climbing up the barricade, over the gutted corn sacks and smashed barrels and the bodies of friends and foe alike. His bronze scale armor gleamed darkly in the firelight. Styr had taken off his helm to survey the scene of his triumph, and the bald earless whoreson was smiling. In his hand was a long weirwood spear with an ornate bronze head. When he saw the gate, he pointed the spear at it and barked something in the Old Tongue to the half-dozen Thenns around him. *Too late*, Jon thought. *You should have led your men over the barricade, you might have been able to save a few.*

Up above, a warhorn sounded, long and low. Not from the top of the Wall, but from the ninth landing, some two hundred feet up, where Donal Noye was standing.

Jon notched a fire arrow to his bowstring, and Satin lit it from the torch. He stepped to the parapet, drew, aimed, loosed. Ribbons of flame trailed behind as the shaft sped downward and thudded into its target, crackling.

Not Styr. The steps. Or more precisely, the casks and kegs and sacks that Donal Noye had piled up *beneath* the steps, as high as the first landing; the barrels of lard and lamp oil, the bags of leaves and oily rags, the split logs, bark, and wood shavings. "Again," said Jon, and, "Again," and, "Again." Other longbowmen were firing too, from every tower top in range, some sending their arrows up in high arcs to drop before the Wall. When Jon ran out of fire arrows, he and Satin began to light the torches and fling them from the crenels.

Up above, another fire was blooming. The old wooden steps had drunk up oil like a sponge, and Donal Noye had drenched them from the ninth landing all the way down to the seventh. Jon could only hope that most of their own people had staggered up to safety before Noye threw the torches. The black brothers at least had known the plan, but the villagers had not.

Wind and fire did the rest. All Jon had to do was watch. With flames below and flames above, the wildlings had nowhere to go. Some continued upward, and died. Some went downward, and died. Some stayed where they were. They died as well. Many leapt from the steps before they burned, and died from the fall. Twenty-odd

Thenns were still huddled together between the fires when the ice cracked from the heat, and the whole lower third of the stair broke off, along with several tons of ice. That was the last that Jon Snow saw of Styr, the Magnar of Thenn. *The Wall defends itself*, he thought.

Jon asked Satin to help him down to the yard. His wounded leg hurt so badly that he could hardly walk, even with the crutch. "Bring the torch," he told the boy from Oldtown. "I need to look for someone." It had been mostly Thenns on the steps. Surely, some of the free folk had escaped. Mance's people, not the Magnar's. She might have been one. So they climbed down past the bodies of the men who'd tried the trapdoor, and Jon wandered through the dark with his crutch under one arm, and the other around the shoulders of a boy who'd been a whore in Oldtown.

The stables and the common hall had burned down to smoking cinders by then, but the fire still raged along the wall, climbing step by step and landing by landing. From time to time they'd hear a groan and then a *craaaack*, and another chunk would come crashing off the Wall. The air was full of ash and ice crystals.

He found Quort dead, and Stone Thumbs dying. He found some dead and dying Thenns he had never truly known. He found Big Boil, weak from all the blood he'd lost but still alive.

He found Ygritte sprawled across a patch of old snow beneath the Lord Commander's Tower, with an arrow between her breasts. The ice crystals had settled over her face, and in the moonlight it looked as though she wore a glittering silver mask.

The arrow was black, Jon saw, but it was fletched with white duck feathers. *Not mine*, he told himself, *not one of mine*. But he felt as if it were.

When he knelt in the snow beside her, her eyes opened. "Jon Snow," she said, very softly. It sounded as though the arrow had found a lung. "Is *this* a proper castle now? Not just a tower?"

"It is." Jon took her hand.

"Good," she whispered. "I wanted t' see one proper castle, before ... before I ..."

"You'll see a hundred castles," he promised her. "The battle's done. Maester Aemon will see to you." He touched her hair. "You're kissed by fire, remember? Lucky. It will take more than an arrow to kill you. Aemon will draw it out and patch you up, and we'll get you some milk of the poppy for the pain."

She just smiled at that. "D'you remember that cave? We should have stayed in that cave. I told you so."

"We'll go back to the cave," he said. "You're not going to die, Ygritte. You're not."

"Oh." Ygritte cupped his cheek with her hand. "You know nothing, Jon Snow," she sighed, dying.

BRAN

"It is only another empty castle," Meera Reed said as she gazed across the desolation of rubble, ruins, and weeds.

No, thought Bran, *it is the Nightfort, and this is the end of the world*. In the mountains, all he could think of was reaching the Wall and finding the three-eyed crow, but now that they were here he was filled with fears. The dream he'd had . . . the dream *Summer* had had . . . *No, I mustn't think about that dream.* He had not even told the Reeds, though Meera at least seemed to sense that something was wrong. If he never talked of it maybe he could forget he ever dreamed it, and then it wouldn't have happened and Robb and Grey Wind would still be . . .

"Hodor." Hodor shifted his weight, and Bran with it. He was tired. They had been walking for hours. *At least he's not afraid.* Bran was scared of this place, and almost as scared of admitting it to the Reeds. *I'm a prince of the north, a Stark of Winterfell, almost a man grown, I have to be as brave as Robb.*

Jojen gazed up at him with his dark green eyes. "There's nothing here to hurt us, Your Grace."

Bran wasn't so certain. The Nightfort had figured in some of Old Nan's scariest stories. It was here that Night's King had reigned, before his name was wiped from the memory of man. This was where the Rat Cook had served the Andal king his prince-and-bacon pie, where the seventy-nine sentinels stood their watch, where brave young Danny Flint had been raped and murdered. This was the castle where King Sherrit had called down his curse on the Andals of old, where the 'prentice boys had faced the thing that came in the night, where blind Symeon Star-Eyes had seen the hellhounds fighting. Mad Axe had once walked these yards and climbed these towers, butchering his brothers in the dark.

All that had happened hundreds and thousands of years ago, to be sure, and some maybe never happened at all. Maester Luwin always said that Old Nan's stories shouldn't be swallowed whole. But once his uncle came to see Father, and Bran asked about the Nightfort. Benjen Stark never said the tales were true, but he never said they weren't; he only shrugged and said, "We left the Nightfort two hundred years ago," as if that was an answer.

Bran forced himself to look around. The morning was cold but bright, the sun shining down from a hard blue sky, but he did not like the *noises*. The wind made a nervous whistling sound as it shivered through the broken towers, the keeps groaned and settled, and he could hear rats scrabbling under the floor of the great hall. *The Rat Cook's children running from their father*. The yards were small forests where spindly trees rubbed their bare branches together and dead leaves scuttled like roaches across patches of old snow. There were trees growing where the stables had been, and a twisted white weirwood pushing up through the gaping hole in the roof of the domed kitchen. Even Summer was not at ease here. Bran slipped inside his skin, just for an instant, to get the smell of the place. He did not like that either.

And there was no way through.

Bran had told them there wouldn't be. He had told them and *told* them, but Jojen Reed had insisted on seeing for himself. He had had a green dream, he said, and his green dreams did not lie. *They don't open any gates either*, thought Bran.

The gate the Nightfort guarded had been sealed since the day the black brothers had loaded up their mules and garrons and departed for Deep Lake; its iron portcullis lowered, the chains that raised it carried off, the tunnel packed with stone and rubble all frozen together until they were as impenetrable as the Wall itself. "We should have followed Jon," Bran said when he saw it. He thought of his bastard brother often, since the night that Summer had watched him ride off through the storm. "We should have found the kingsroad and gone to Castle Black."

"We dare not, my prince," Jojen said. "I've told you why."

"But there are *wildlings*. They killed some man and they wanted to kill Jon too. Jojen, there were a *hundred* of them."

"So you said. We are four. You helped your brother, if that was him in truth, but it almost cost you Summer."

"I know," said Bran miserably. The direwolf had killed three of them, maybe more, but there had been too many. When they formed a tight ring around the tall earless man, he had tried to slip away through the rain, but one of their arrows had come flashing after him, and the sudden stab of pain had driven Bran out of the wolf's skin and back into his own. After the storm finally died, they had huddled in the dark without a fire, talking in whispers if they talked at all, listening to Hodor's heavy breathing and wondering if the wildlings might try and cross the lake in the morning. Bran had reached out for Summer time and time again, but the pain he found drove him back, the way a red-hot kettle makes you pull your hand back even when you mean to grab it. Only Hodor slept that night, muttering "Hodor, hodor," as he tossed and turned. Bran was terrified that Summer was off dying in the darkness. *Please, you old gods*, he prayed, *you took Winterfell, and my father, and my legs, please don't take Summer too. And watch over Jon Snow too, and make the wildlings go away.*

No weirwoods grew on that stony island in the lake, yet somehow the old gods must have heard. The wildlings took their sweet time about departing the next morning, stripping the bodies of their dead and the old man they'd killed, even pulling a few fish from the lake, and there was a scary moment when three of them found the causeway and started to walk out ... but the path turned and they didn't, and two of them nearly drowned before the others pulled them out. The tall bald man yelled at them, his words echoing across the water in some tongue that even Jojen did not know, and a little while later they gathered up their shields and spears and marched off north by east, the same way Jon had gone. Bran wanted to leave too, to look for Summer, but the Reeds said no. "We will stay another night," said Jojen, "put some leagues between us and the wildlings. You don't want to meet them again, do you?" Late that afternoon Summer returned from wherever he'd been hiding, dragging his back leg. He ate parts of the bodies in the inn, driving off the crows, then swam out to the island. Meera had drawn the broken arrow from his leg and rubbed the wound with the juice of some plants she found growing around the base of the tower. The direwolf was still limping, but a little less each day, it seemed to Bran. The gods had heard.

"Maybe we should try another castle," Meera said to her brother. "Maybe we could get through the gate somewhere else. I could go scout if you wanted, I'd make better time by myself."

Bran shook his head. "If you go east there's Deep Lake, then Queensgate. West is Icemark. But they'll be the same, only smaller. All the gates are sealed except the ones at Castle Black, Eastwatch, and the Shadow Tower."

Hodor said, "Hodor," to that, and the Reeds exchanged a look. "At least I should climb to the top of the Wall," Meera decided. "Maybe I'll see something up there."

"What could you hope to see?" Jojen asked.

"*Something*," said Meera, and for once she was adamant.

It should be me. Bran raised his head to look up at the Wall, and imagined himself climbing inch by inch, squirming his fingers into cracks in the ice and kicking footholds with his toes. That made him smile in spite of everything, the dreams and the wildlings and Jon and *everything*. He had climbed the walls of Winterfell when he was little, and all the towers too, but none of them had been so high, and they were only stone. The Wall could *look* like stone, all grey and pitted, but then the clouds would break and the sun would hit it differently, and all at once it would transform, and stand there white and blue and glittering. It was the end of the world, Old Nan always said. On the other side were monsters and giants and ghouls, but they could not pass so long as the Wall stood strong. *I want to stand on top with Meera*, Bran thought. *I want to stand on top and see.*

But he was a broken boy with useless legs, so all he could do was watch from below as Meera went up in his stead.

She wasn't really *climbing*, the way he used to climb. She was only walking up some steps that the Night's Watch had hewn hundreds and thousands of years ago. He remembered Maester Luwin saying the Nightfort was the only castle where the steps had been cut from the ice of the Wall itself. Or maybe it had been Uncle Benjen. The newer castles had wooden steps, or stone ones, or long ramps of earth and gravel. *Ice is too treacherous*. It was his uncle who'd told him that. He said that the outer surface of the Wall wept icy tears sometimes, though the core inside stayed frozen hard as rock. The steps must have melted and refrozen a thousand times since the last black brothers left the castle, and every time they did they shrunk a little and got smoother and rounder and more treacherous.

And smaller. *It's almost like the Wall was swallowing them back into itself.* Meera Reed was very surefooted, but even so she was going slowly, moving from nub to nub. In two places where the steps were hardly there at all she got down on all fours. *It will be worse when she comes down*, Bran thought, watching. Even so, he wished it was him up there. When she reached the top, crawling up the icy knobs that were all that remained of the highest steps, Meera vanished from his sight.

"When will she come down?" Bran asked Jojen.

"When she is ready. She will want to have a good look . . . at the Wall and what's beyond. We should do the same down here."

"Hodor?" said Hodor, doubtfully.

"We might find something," Jojen insisted.

Or something might find us. Bran couldn't say it, though; he did not want Jojen to think he was craven.

So they went exploring, Jojen Reed leading, Bran in his basket on Hodor's back, Summer padding by their side. Once the direwolf bolted through a dark door and returned a moment later with a grey rat between his teeth. *The Rat Cook*, Bran thought, but it was the wrong color, and only as big as a cat. The Rat Cook was white, and almost as huge as a sow . . .

There were a lot of dark doors in the Nightfort, and a lot of rats. Bran could hear them scurrying through the vaults and cellars, and the maze of pitch-black tunnels that connected them. Jojen wanted to go poking around down there, but Hodor said "*Hodor*" to that, and Bran said "No." There were worse things than rats down in the dark beneath the Nightfort.

"This seems an old place," Jojen said as they walked down a gallery where the sunlight fell in dusty shafts through empty windows.

"Twice as old as Castle Black," Bran said, remembering. "It was the first castle on the Wall, and the largest." But it had also been the first abandoned, all the way back in the time of the Old King. Even then it had been three-quarters empty and too costly to maintain. Good Queen Alysanne had suggested that the Watch replace it with a smaller, newer castle at a spot only seven miles east, where the Wall curved along the shore of a beautiful green lake. Deep Lake had been paid for by the queen's jewels and built by the men the Old King had sent north, and the black brothers had abandoned the Nightfort to the rats.

That was two centuries past, though. Now Deep Lake stood as empty as the castle it had replaced, and the Nightfort ...

"There are ghosts here," Bran said. Hodor had heard all the stories before, but Jojen might not have. "*Old* ghosts, from before the Old King, even before Aegon the Dragon, seventy-nine deserters who went south to be outlaws. One was Lord Ryswell's youngest son, so when they reached the barrowlands they sought shelter at his castle, but Lord Ryswell took them captive and returned them to the Nightfort. The Lord Commander had holes hewn in the top of the Wall and he put the deserters in them and sealed them up alive in the ice. They have spears and horns and they all face north. The seventy-nine sentinels, they're called. They left their posts in life, so in death their watch goes on forever. Years later, when Lord Ryswell was old and dying, he had himself carried to the Nightfort so he could take the black and stand beside his son. He'd sent him back to the Wall for honor's sake, but he loved him still, so he came to share his watch."

They spent half the day poking through the castle. Some of the towers had fallen down and others looked unsafe, but they climbed the bell tower (the bells were gone) and the rookery (the birds were gone). Beneath the brewhouse they found a vault of huge oaken casks that boomed hollowly when Hodor knocked on them. They found a library (the shelves and bins had collapsed, the books were gone, and rats were everywhere).

They found a dank and dim-lit dungeon with cells enough to hold five hundred captives, but when Bran grabbed hold of one of the rusted bars it broke off in his hand. Only one crumbling wall remained of the great hall, the bathhouse seemed to be sinking into the ground, and a huge thornbush had conquered the practice yard outside the armory where black brothers had once labored with spear and shield and sword. The armory and the forge still stood, however, though cobwebs, rats, and dust had taken the places of blades, bellows, and anvil. Sometimes Summer would hear sounds that Bran seemed deaf to, or bare his teeth at nothing, the fur on the back of his neck bristling ... but the Rat Cook never put in an appearance, nor the seventy-nine sentinels, nor Mad Axe. Bran was much relieved. *Maybe it is only a ruined empty castle.*

By the time Meera returned, the sun was only a sword's breath above the western hills. "What did you see?" her brother Jojen asked her.

"I saw the haunted forest," she said in a wistful tone. "Hills rising wild as far as the eye can see, covered with trees that no axe has ever touched. I saw the sunlight glinting off a lake, and clouds sweeping in from the west. I saw patches of old snow, and icicles long as pikes. I even saw an eagle circling. I think he saw me too. I waved at him."

"Did you see a way down?" asked Jojen.

She shook her head. "No. It's a sheer drop, and the ice is so smooth ... I might be able to make the descent if I had a good rope and an axe to chop out handholds, but ..."

"... but not us," Jojen finished.

"No," his sister agreed. "Are you sure this is the place you saw in your dream? Maybe we have the wrong castle."

"No. This is the castle. There is a gate here."

Yes, thought Bran, *but it's blocked by stone and ice.*

As the sun began to set the shadows of the towers lengthened and the wind blew harder, sending gusts of dry dead leaves rattling through the yards. The gathering gloom put Bran in mind of another of Old Nan's stories, the tale of Night's King. He had been the thirteenth man to lead the Night's Watch, she said; a warrior who knew no fear. "And that was the fault in him," she would add, "for all men must know fear." A woman was his downfall; a woman glimpsed from atop the Wall, with skin as white as the moon and eyes like blue stars. Fearing nothing, he chased her and caught her and loved her, though her skin was cold as ice, and when he gave his seed to her he gave his soul as well.

He brought her back to the Nightfort and proclaimed her a queen and himself her king, and with strange sorceries he bound his Sworn Brothers to his will. For thirteen years they had ruled, Night's King and his corpse queen, till finally the Stark of Winterfell and Joramun of the wildlings had joined to free the Watch from bondage. After his fall, when it was found he had been sacrificing to the Others, all records of Night's King had been destroyed, his very name forbidden.

"Some say he was a Bolton," Old Nan would always end. "Some say a Magnar out of Skagos, some say Umber, Flint, or Norrey. Some would have you think he was a Woodfoot, from them who ruled Bear Island before the ironmen came. He never was. He was a Stark, the brother of the man who brought him down." She always pinched Bran on the nose then, he would never forget it. "He was a Stark of Winterfell, and who can say? Mayhaps his name was *Brandon*. Mayhaps he slept in this very bed in this very room."

No, Bran thought, *but he walked in this castle, where we'll sleep tonight.* He did not like that notion very much at all. Night's King was only a man by light of day, Old Nan would always say, but the night was his to rule. *And it's getting dark.*

The Reeds decided that they would sleep in the kitchens, a stone octagon with a broken dome. It looked to offer better shelter than most of the other buildings, even though a crooked weirwood had burst up through the slate floor beside the huge central well, stretching slantwise toward the hole in the roof, its bone-white branches reaching for the sun. It was a queer kind of tree, skinnier than any other weirwood that Bran had ever seen and faceless as well, but it made him feel as if the old gods were with him here, at least.

That was the only thing he liked about the kitchens, though. The roof was mostly there, so they'd be dry if it rained again, but he didn't think they would ever get *warm* here. You could feel the cold seeping up through the slate floor. Bran did not like the shadows either, or the huge brick ovens that surrounded them like open mouths, or the rusted meat hooks, or the scars and stains he saw in the butcher's block along one wall. *That was where the Rat Cook chopped the prince to pieces*, he knew, *and he baked the pie in one of these ovens.*

The well was the thing he liked the least, though. It was a good twelve feet across, all stone, with *steps* built into its side, circling down and down into darkness. The walls were damp and covered with niter, but none of them could see the water at the bottom, not even Meera with her sharp hunter's eyes. "Maybe it doesn't have a bottom," Bran said uncertainly.

Hodor peered over the knee-high lip of the well and said, "*HODOR!*" The word echoed down the well, "Hodorhodorhodorhodor," fainter and fainter, "hodorhodorhodorhodor," until it was less than a whisper. Hodor looked startled. Then he laughed, and bent to scoop a broken piece of slate off the floor.

"Hodor, *don't!*" said Bran, but too late. Hodor tossed the slate over the edge. "You shouldn't have done that. You don't know what's down there. You might have hurt something, or . . . or woken something up."

Hodor looked at him innocently. "Hodor?"

Far, far, far below, they heard the sound as the stone found water. It wasn't a *splash*, not truly. It was more a *gulp*, as if whatever was below had opened a quivering gelid mouth to swallow Hodor's stone. Faint echoes traveled up the well, and for a moment Bran thought he heard something moving, thrashing about in the water. "Maybe we shouldn't stay here," he said uneasily.

"By the well?" asked Meera. "Or in the Nightfort?"

"Yes," said Bran.

She laughed, and sent Hodor out to gather wood. Summer went too. It was almost dark by then, and the direwolf wanted to hunt.

Hodor returned alone with both arms full of deadwood and broken branches. Jojen Reed took his flint and knife and set about lighting a fire while Meera boned the fish she'd caught at the last stream they'd crossed. Bran wondered how many years had passed since there had last been a supper cooked in the kitchens of the Nightfort. He wondered who had cooked it too, though maybe it was better not to know.

When the flames were blazing nicely Meera put the fish on. *At least it's not a meat pie.* The Rat Cook had cooked the son of the Andal king in a big pie with onions, carrots, mushrooms, lots of pepper and salt, a rasher of bacon, and a dark red Dornish wine. Then he served him to his father, who praised the taste and had a second slice. Afterward, the gods transformed the cook into a monstrous white rat who could only eat his own young. He had roamed the Nightfort ever since, devouring his children, but still his hunger was not sated. "It was not for murder that the gods cursed him," Old Nan said, "nor for serving the Andal king his son in a pie. A man has a right to vengeance. But he slew a *guest* beneath his roof, and that the gods cannot forgive."

"We should sleep," Jojen said solemnly, after they were full. The fire was burning low. He stirred it with a stick. "Perhaps I'll have another green dream to show us the way."

Hodor was already curled up and snoring lightly. From time to time he thrashed beneath his cloak, and whimpered something that might have been "Hodor." Bran wriggled closer to the fire. The warmth felt good, and the soft crackling of flames soothed him, but sleep would not come. Outside the wind was sending armies of dead leaves marching across the courtyards to scratch faintly at the doors and windows. The sounds made him think of Old Nan's stories. He could almost hear the ghostly sentinels calling to each other atop the Wall and winding their ghostly warhorns. Pale moonlight slanted down through the hole in the dome, painting the branches of the weirwood as they strained up toward the roof. It looked as if the tree was trying to catch the moon and drag it down into the well. *Old gods,* Bran prayed, *if you hear me, don't send a dream tonight. Or if you do, make it a good dream.* The gods made no answer.

Bran made himself close his eyes. Maybe he even slept some, or maybe he was just drowsing, floating the way you do when you are half awake and half asleep, trying not to think about Mad Axe or the Rat Cook or the thing that came in the night.

Then he heard the noise.

His eyes opened. *What was that?* He held his breath. *Did I dream it? Was I having a stupid nightmare?* He didn't want to wake Meera and Jojen for a bad dream, but ... *there* ... a soft scuffling sound, far off ... *Leaves, it's leaves rattling off the walls outside and rustling together ... or the wind, it could be the wind ...* The sound wasn't coming from outside, though. Bran felt the hairs on his arm start to rise. *The sound's inside, it's in here with us, and it's getting louder.* He pushed himself up onto an elbow, listening. There *was* wind, and blowing leaves as well, but this was something else. *Footsteps.* Someone was coming this way. Some*thing* was coming this way.

It wasn't the sentinels, he knew. The sentinels never left the Wall. But there might be other ghosts in the Nightfort, ones even more terrible. He remembered what Old Nan had said of Mad Axe, how he took his boots off and prowled the castle halls barefoot in the dark, with never a sound to tell you where he was except for the drops of blood that fell from his axe and his elbows and the end of his wet red beard. Or maybe it wasn't Mad Axe at all, maybe it was the thing that came in the night. The 'prentice boys all saw it, Old Nan said, but afterward when they told their Lord Commander every description had been different. *And three died within the year, and the fourth went mad, and a hundred years later when the thing had come again, the 'prentice boys were seen shambling along behind it, all in chains.*

That was only a story, though. He was just scaring himself. There was no thing that comes in the night, Maester Luwin had said so. If there had ever been such a thing, it was gone from the world now, like giants and dragons. *It's nothing*, Bran thought.

But the sounds were louder now.

It's coming from the well, he realized. That made him even more afraid. Something was coming up from under the ground, coming up out of the dark. *Hodor woke it up. He woke it up with that stupid piece of slate, and now it's coming.* It was hard to hear over Hodor's snores and the thumping of his own heart. Was that the sound blood made dripping from an axe? Or was it the faint, far-off rattling of ghostly chains? Bran listened harder. *Footsteps.* It was definitely footsteps, each one a little louder than the one before. He couldn't tell how many, though. The well made the sounds echo. He didn't hear any dripping, or chains either, but there *was* something else . . . a high thin whimpering sound, like someone in pain, and heavy muffled breathing. But the footsteps were loudest. The footsteps were coming closer.

Bran was too frightened to shout. The fire had burned down to a few faint embers and his friends were all asleep. He almost slipped his skin and reached out for his wolf, but Summer might be miles away. He couldn't leave his friends helpless in the dark to face whatever was coming up out of the well. *I told them not to come here,* he thought miserably. *I told them there were ghosts. I told them that we should go to Castle Black.*

The footfalls sounded heavy to Bran, slow, ponderous, scraping against the stone. *It must be huge.* Mad Axe had been a big man in Old Nan's story, and the thing that came in the night had been monstrous. Back in Winterfell, Sansa had told him that the demons of the dark couldn't touch him if he hid beneath his blanket. He almost did that now, before he remembered that he was a prince, and almost a man grown.

Bran wriggled across the floor, dragging his dead legs behind him until he could reach out and touch Meera on the foot. She woke at once. He had never known anyone to wake as quick as Meera Reed, or to be so alert so fast. Bran pressed a finger to his mouth so she'd know not to speak. She heard the sound at once, he could see that on her face; the echoing footfalls, the faint whimpering, the heavy breathing.

Meera rose to her feet without a word and reclaimed her weapons. With her three-pronged frog spear in her right hand and the folds of her net dangling from her left, she slipped barefoot toward the well. Jojen dozed on, oblivious, while Hodor muttered and thrashed in restless sleep. She kept to the shadows as she moved, stepped around the shaft of moonlight as quiet as a cat. Bran was watching her all the while, and even he could barely see the faint sheen of her spear. *I can't let her fight the thing alone*, he thought. Summer was far away, but . . .

. . . he slipped his skin, and reached for Hodor.

It was not like sliding into Summer. That was so easy now that Bran hardly thought about it. This was harder, like trying to pull a left boot on your right foot. It fit all wrong, and the boot was *scared* too, the boot didn't know what was happening, the boot was pushing the foot away. He tasted vomit in the back of *Hodor's* throat, and that was almost enough to make him flee. Instead, he squirmed and shoved, sat up, gathered his legs under him—his huge strong legs—and rose. *I'm standing.* He took a step. *I'm walking.* It was such a strange feeling that he almost fell. He could see himself on the cold stone floor, a little broken thing, but he wasn't broken now. He grabbed Hodor's longsword. The breathing was as loud as a blacksmith's bellows.

From the well came a wail, a piercing *creech* that went through him like a knife. A huge black shape heaved itself up into the darkness and lurched toward the moonlight, and the fear rose up in Bran so thick that before he could even *think* of drawing Hodor's sword the way he'd meant to, he found himself back on the floor again with Hodor roaring, "*Hodor hodor HODOR,*" the way he had in the lake tower whenever the lightning flashed. But the thing that came in the night was screaming too, and thrashing wildly in the folds of Meera's net. Bran saw her spear dart out of the darkness to snap at it, and the thing staggered and fell, struggling with the net. The wailing was still coming from the well, even louder now. On the floor the black thing flopped and fought, screeching, "*No, no, don't, please, DON'T . . .*"

Meera stood over him, the moonlight shining silver off the prongs of her frog spear. "Who are you?" she demanded.

"I'm *SAM,*" the black thing sobbed. "Sam, Sam, I'm Sam, let me *out*, you *stabbed* me . . ." He rolled through the puddle of moonlight, flailing and flopping in the tangles of Meera's net. Hodor was still shouting, "Hodor hodor hodor."

It was Jojen who fed the sticks to the fire and blew on them until the flames leapt up crackling. Then there was light, and Bran saw the pale thin-faced girl by the lip of the well, all bundled up in furs and skins beneath an enormous black cloak, trying to shush the screaming baby in her arms. The thing on the floor was pushing an arm through the net to reach his knife, but the loops wouldn't let him. He wasn't any monster beast, or even Mad Axe drenched in gore; only a big fat man dressed up in black wool, black fur, black leather, and black mail. "He's a black brother," said Bran. "Meera, he's from the Night's Watch."

"Hodor?" Hodor squatted down on his haunches to peer at the man in the net. "Hodor," he said again, hooting.

"The Night's Watch, yes." The fat man was still breathing like a bellows. "I'm a brother of the Watch." He had one cord under his chins, forcing his head up, and others digging deep into his cheeks. "I'm a crow, please. Let me out of this."

Bran was suddenly uncertain. "Are you the three-eyed crow?" *He can't be the three-eyed crow.*

"I don't think so." The fat man rolled his eyes, but there were only two of them. "I'm only Sam. Samwell Tarly. Let me *out*, it's hurting me." He began to struggle again.

Meera made a disgusted sound. "Stop flopping around. If you tear my net, I'll throw you back down the well. Just lie still and I'll untangle you."

"Who are you?" Jojen asked the girl with the baby.

"Gilly," she said. "For the gillyflower. He's Sam. We never meant to scare you." She rocked her baby and murmured at it, and finally it stopped crying.

Meera was untangling the fat brother. Jojen went to the well and peered down. "Where did you come from?"

"From Craster's," the girl said. "Are you the one?"

Jojen turned to look at her. "The one?"

"He said that Sam wasn't the one," she explained. "There was someone else, he said. The one he was sent to find."

"Who said?" Bran demanded.

"Coldhands," Gilly answered softly.

Meera peeled back one end of her net, and the fat man managed to sit up. He was shaking, Bran saw, and still struggling to catch his breath. "He said there would be people," he huffed. "People in the castle.

I didn't know you'd be right at the top of the steps, though. I didn't know you'd throw a net on me or stab me in the stomach." He touched his belly with a black-gloved hand. "Am I bleeding? I can't see."

"It was just a poke to get you off your feet," said Meera. "Here, let me have a look." She went to one knee, and felt around his navel. "You're wearing *mail*. I never got near your skin."

"Well, it hurt all the same," Sam complained.

"Are you *really* a brother of the Night's Watch?" Bran asked.

The fat man's chins jiggled when he nodded. His skin looked pale and saggy. "Only a steward. I took care of Lord Mormont's ravens." For a moment he looked like he was going to cry. "I lost them at the Fist, though. It was my fault. I got us lost too. I couldn't even find the Wall. It's a hundred leagues long and seven hundred feet high and *I couldn't find it*!"

"Well, you've found it now," said Meera. "Lift your rump off the ground, I want my net back."

"How did you get through the Wall?" Jojen demanded as Sam struggled to his feet. "Does the well lead to an underground river, is that where you came from? You're not even wet . . ."

"There's a gate," said fat Sam. "A hidden gate, as old as the Wall itself. *The Black Gate*, he called it."

The Reeds exchanged a look. "We'll find this gate at the bottom of the well?" asked Jojen.

Sam shook his head. "*You* won't. I have to take you."

"Why?" Meera demanded. "If there's a gate . . ."

"You won't find it. If you did it wouldn't open. Not for you. It's the *Black* Gate." Sam plucked at the faded black wool of his sleeve. "Only a man of the Night's Watch can open it, he said. A Sworn Brother who has said his words."

"*He* said." Jojen frowned. "This . . . Coldhands?"

"That wasn't his true name," said Gilly, rocking. "We only called him that, Sam and me. His hands were cold as ice, but he saved us from the dead men, him and his ravens, and he brought us here on his elk."

"His elk?" said Bran, wonderstruck.

"His elk?" said Meera, startled.

"His *ravens*?" said Jojen.

"Hodor?" said Hodor.

"Was he green?" Bran wanted to know. "Did he have antlers?"

The fat man was confused. "The elk?"

"*Coldhands*," said Bran impatiently. "The green men ride on elks, Old Nan used to say. Sometimes they have antlers too."

"He wasn't a green man. He wore blacks, like a brother of the Watch, but he was pale as a wight, with hands so cold that at first I was afraid. The wights have blue eyes, though, and they don't have tongues, or they've forgotten how to use them." The fat man turned to Jojen. "He'll be waiting. We should go. Do you have anything warmer to wear? The Black Gate is cold, and the other side of the Wall is even colder. You—"

"Why didn't he come with you?" Meera gestured toward Gilly and her babe. "*They* came with you, why not him? Why didn't you bring him through this Black Gate too?"

"He . . . he can't."

"Why not?"

"The Wall. The Wall is more than just ice and stone, he said. There are spells woven into it . . . old ones, and strong. He cannot pass beyond the Wall."

It grew very quiet in the castle kitchen then. Bran could hear the soft crackle of the flames, the wind stirring the leaves in the night, the creak of the skinny weirwood reaching for the moon. *Beyond the gates the monsters live, and the giants and the ghouls,* he remembered Old Nan saying, *but they cannot pass so long as the Wall stands strong. So go to sleep, my little Brandon, my baby boy. You needn't fear. There are no monsters here.*

"I am not the one you were told to bring," Jojen Reed told fat Sam in his stained and baggy blacks. "*He* is."

"Oh." Sam looked down at him uncertainly. It might have been just then that he realized Bran was crippled. "I don't . . . I'm not strong enough to carry you, I . . ."

"Hodor can carry me." Bran pointed at his basket. "I ride in that, up on his back."

Sam was staring at him. "You're Jon Snow's brother. The one who fell . . ."

"No," said Jojen. "That boy is dead."

"Don't tell," Bran warned. "Please."

Sam looked confused for a moment, but finally he said, "I . . . I can keep a secret. Gilly too." When he looked at her, the girl nodded. "Jon . . . Jon was *my* brother too. He was the best friend I ever had, but he went off with Qhorin Halfhand to scout the Frostfangs and never came back. We were waiting for him on the Fist when . . . when . . ."

"Jon's here," Bran said. "Summer saw him. He was with some wildlings, but they killed a man and Jon took his horse and escaped. I bet he went to Castle Black."

Sam turned big eyes on Meera. "You're certain it was Jon? You saw him?"

"I'm Meera," Meera said with a smile. "Summer is . . ."

A shadow detached itself from the broken dome above and leapt down through the moonlight. Even with his injured leg, the wolf landed as light and quiet as a snowfall. The girl Gilly made a frightened sound and clutched her babe so hard against her that it began to cry again.

"He won't hurt you," Bran said. "*That*'s Summer."

"Jon said you all had wolves." Sam pulled off a glove. "I know Ghost." He held out a shaky hand, the fingers white and soft and fat as little sausages. Summer padded closer, sniffed them, and gave the hand a lick.

That was when Bran made up his mind. "We'll go with you."

"All of you?" Sam seemed surprised by that.

Meera ruffled Bran's hair. "He's our prince."

Summer circled the well, sniffing. He paused by the top step and looked back at Bran. *He wants to go.*

"Will Gilly be safe if I leave her here till I come back?" Sam asked them.

"She should be," said Meera. "She's welcome to our fire."

Jojen said, "The castle is empty."

Gilly looked around. "Craster used to tell us tales of castles, but I never knew they'd be so big."

It's only the kitchens. Bran wondered what she'd think when she saw Winterfell, if she ever did.

It took them a few minutes to gather their things and hoist Bran into his wicker seat on Hodor's back. By the time they were ready to go, Gilly sat nursing her babe by the fire. "You'll come back for me," she said to Sam.

"As soon as I can," he promised, "then we'll go somewhere warm." When he heard that, part of Bran wondered what he was doing. *Will I ever go someplace warm again?*

"I'll go first, I know the way." Sam hesitated at the top. "There's just so many *steps*," he sighed, before he started down. Jojen followed, then Summer, then Hodor with Bran riding on his back. Meera took the rear, with her spear and net in hand.

It was a long way down. The top of the well was bathed in moonlight, but it grew smaller and dimmer every time they went around. Their footsteps echoed off the damp stones, and the water sounds grew louder. "Should we have brought torches?" Jojen asked.

"Your eyes will adjust," said Sam. "Keep one hand on the wall and you won't fall."

The well grew darker and colder with every turn. When Bran finally lifted his head around to look back up the shaft, the top of the well was no bigger than a half-moon. "*Hodor*," Hodor whispered. "*Hodorhodorhodorhodorhodorhodor*," the well whispered back. The water sounds were close, but when Bran peered down he saw only blackness.

A turn or two later Sam stopped suddenly. He was a quarter of the way around the well from Bran and Hodor and six feet farther down, yet Bran could barely see him. He could see the door, though. *The Black Gate*, Sam had called it, but it wasn't black at all.

It was white weirwood, and there was a face on it.

A glow came from the wood, like milk and moonlight, so faint it scarcely seemed to touch anything beyond the door itself, not even Sam standing right before it. The face was old and pale, wrinkled and shrunken. *It looks dead.* Its mouth was closed, and its eyes; its cheeks were sunken, its brow withered, its chin sagging. *If a man could live for a thousand years and never die but just grow older, his face might come to look like that.*

The door opened its eyes.

They were white too, and blind. "Who are you?" the door asked, and the well whispered, "*Who-who-who-who-who-who-who*."

"I am the sword in the darkness," Samwell Tarly said. "I am the watcher on the walls. I am the fire that burns against the cold, the light that brings the dawn, the horn that wakes the sleepers. I am the shield that guards the realms of men."

"Then pass," the door said. Its lips opened, wide and wider and wider still, until nothing at all remained but a great gaping mouth in a ring of wrinkles. Sam stepped aside and waved Jojen through ahead of him. Summer followed, sniffing as he went, and then it was Bran's turn. Hodor ducked, but not low enough. The door's upper lip brushed softly against the top of Bran's head, and a drop of water fell on him and ran slowly down his nose. It was strangely warm, and salty as a tear.

DAENERYS

Meereen was as large as Astapor and Yunkai combined. Like her sister cities she was built of brick, but where Astapor had been red and Yunkai yellow, Meereen was made with bricks of many colors. Her walls were higher than Yunkai's and in better repair, studded with bastions and anchored by great defensive towers at every angle. Behind them, huge against the sky, could be seen the top of the Great Pyramid, a monstrous thing eight hundred feet tall with a towering bronze harpy at its top.

"The harpy is a craven thing," Daario Naharis said when he saw it. "She has a woman's heart and a chicken's legs. Small wonder her sons hide behind their walls."

But the hero did not hide. He rode out the city gates, armored in scales of copper and jet and mounted upon a white charger whose striped pink-and-white barding matched the silk cloak flowing from the hero's shoulders. The lance he bore was fourteen feet long, swirled in pink and white, and his hair was shaped and teased and lacquered into two great curling ram's horns. Back and forth he rode beneath the walls of multicolored bricks, challenging the besiegers to send a champion forth to meet him in single combat.

Her bloodriders were in such a fever to go meet him that they almost came to blows. "Blood of my blood," Dany told them, "your place is here by me. This man is a buzzing fly, no more. Ignore him, he will soon be gone." Aggo, Jhogo, and Rakharo were brave warriors, but they were young, and too valuable to risk. They kept her *khalasar* together, and were her best scouts too.

"That was wisely done," Ser Jorah said as they watched from the front of her pavilion. "Let the fool ride back and forth and shout until his horse goes lame. He does us no harm."

"He does," Arstan Whitebeard insisted. "Wars are not won with swords and spears alone, ser. Two hosts of equal strength may come together, but one will break and run whilst the other stands. This hero builds courage in the hearts of his own men and plants the seeds of doubt in ours."

Ser Jorah snorted. "And if our champion were to lose, what sort of seed would that plant?"

"A man who fears battle wins no victories, ser."

"We're not speaking of battle. Meereen's gates will not open if that fool falls. Why risk a life for naught?"

"For honor, I would say."

"I have heard enough." Dany did not need their squabbling on top of all the other troubles that plagued her. Meereen posed dangers far more serious than one pink-and-white hero shouting insults, and she could not let herself be distracted. Her host numbered more than eighty thousand after Yunkai, but fewer than a quarter of them were soldiers. The rest ... well, Ser Jorah called them mouths with feet, and soon they would be starving.

The Great Masters of Meereen had withdrawn before Dany's advance, harvesting all they could and burning what they could not harvest. Scorched fields and poisoned wells had greeted her at every hand. Worst of all, they had nailed a slave child up on every milepost along the coast road from Yunkai, nailed them up still living with their entrails hanging out and one arm always outstretched to point the way to Meereen. Leading her van, Daario had given orders for the children to be taken down before Dany had to see them, but she had countermanded him as soon as she was told. "I *will* see them," she said. "I will see every one, and count them, and look upon their faces. And I will remember."

By the time they came to Meereen sitting on the salt coast beside her river, the count stood at one hundred and sixty-three. *I will have this city*, Dany pledged to herself once more.

The pink-and-white hero taunted the besiegers for an hour, mocking their manhood, mothers, wives, and gods. Meereen's defenders cheered him on from the city walls. "His name is Oznak zo Pahl," Brown Ben Plumm told her when he arrived for the war council. He was the new commander of the Second Sons, chosen by a vote of his fellow sellswords. "I was bodyguard to his uncle once, before I joined the Second Sons. The Great Masters, what a ripe lot o' maggots. The women weren't so bad, though it was worth your life to look at the wrong one the wrong way. I knew a man, Scarb, this Oznak cut his liver out. Claimed to be defending a lady's honor, he did, said Scarb had raped her with his eyes. How do you rape a wench with *eyes*, I ask you? But his uncle is the richest man in Meereen and his father commands the city guard, so I had to run like a rat before he killed me too."

They watched Oznak zo Pahl dismount his white charger, undo his robes, pull out his manhood, and direct a stream of urine in the general direction of the olive grove where Dany's gold pavilion stood among the burnt trees. He was still pissing when Daario Naharis rode up, *arakh* in hand. "Shall I cut that off for you and stuff it down his mouth, Your Grace?" His tooth shone gold amidst the blue of his forked beard.

"It's his city I want, not his meager manhood." She was growing angry, however. *If I ignore this any longer, my own people will think me weak.* Yet who could she send? She needed Daario as much as she did her bloodriders. Without the flamboyant Tyroshi, she had no hold on the Stormcrows, many of whom had been followers of Prendahl na Ghezn and Sallor the Bald.

High on the walls of Meereen, the jeers had grown louder, and now hundreds of the defenders were taking their lead from the hero and pissing down through the ramparts to show their contempt for the besiegers. *They are pissing on slaves, to show how little they fear us*, she thought. *They would never dare such a thing if it were a Dothraki khalasar outside their gates.*

"This challenge must be met," Arstan said again.

"It will be." Dany said, as the hero tucked his penis away again. "Tell Strong Belwas I have need of him."

They found the huge brown eunuch sitting in the shade of her pavilion, eating a sausage. He finished it in three bites, wiped his greasy hands clean on his trousers, and sent Arstan Whitebeard to fetch him his steel. The aged squire honed Belwas's *arakh* every evening and rubbed it down with bright red oil.

When Whitebeard brought the sword, Strong Belwas squinted down the edge, grunted, slid the blade back into its leather sheath, and tied the swordbelt about his vast waist. Arstan had brought his shield as well: a round steel disk no larger than a pie plate, which the eunuch grasped with his off hand rather than strapping to his forearm in the manner of Westeros. "Find liver and onions, Whitebeard," Belwas said. "Not for now, for after. Killing makes Strong Belwas hungry." He did not wait for a reply, but lumbered from the olive grove toward Oznak zo Pahl.

"Why that one, *Khaleesi?*" Rakharo demanded of her. "He is fat and stupid."

"Strong Belwas was a slave here in the fighting pits. If this high-born Oznak should fall to such the Great Masters will be shamed, while if he wins . . . well, it is a poor victory for one so noble, one that Meereen can take no pride in." And unlike Ser Jorah, Daario, Brown Ben, and her three bloodriders, the eunuch did not lead troops, plan battles, or give her counsel. *He does nothing but eat and boast and bellow at Arstan.* Belwas was the man she could most easily spare. And it was time she learned what sort of protector Magister Illyrio had sent her.

A thrum of excitement went through the siege lines when Belwas was seen plodding toward the city, and from the walls and towers of Meereen came shouts and jeers. Oznak zo Pahl mounted up again, and waited, his striped lance held upright. The charger tossed his head impatiently and pawed the sandy earth. As massive as he was, the eunuch looked small beside the hero on his horse.

"A chivalrous man would dismount," said Arstan.

Oznak zo Pahl lowered his lance and charged.

Belwas stopped with legs spread wide. In one hand was his small

round shield, in the other the curved *arakh* that Arstan tended with
such care. His great brown stomach and sagging chest were bare above
the yellow silk sash knotted about his waist, and he wore no armor
but his studded leather vest, so absurdly small that it did not even
cover his nipples. "We should have given him chainmail," Dany said,
suddenly anxious.

"Mail would only slow him," said Ser Jorah. "They wear no armor
in the fighting pits. It's blood the crowds come to see."

Dust flew from the hooves of the white charger. Oznak thundered
toward Strong Belwas, his striped cloak streaming from his shoulders.
The whole city of Meereen seemed to be screaming him on. The
besiegers' cheers seemed few and thin by comparison; her Unsullied
stood in silent ranks, watching with stone faces. Belwas might have
been made of stone as well. He stood in the horse's path, his vest
stretched tight across his broad back. Oznak's lance was leveled at the
center of his chest. Its bright steel point winked in the sunlight. *He's
going to be impaled*, she thought ... as the eunuch spun sideways.
And quick as the blink of an eye the horseman was beyond him,
wheeling, raising the lance. Belwas made no move to strike at him. The
Meereenese on the walls screamed even louder. "What is he doing?"
Dany demanded.

"Giving the mob a show," Ser Jorah said.

Oznak brought the horse around Belwas in a wide circle, then dug
in with his spurs and charged again. Again Belwas waited, then spun
and knocked the point of the lance aside. She could hear the eunuch's
booming laughter echoing across the plain as the hero went past him.
"The lance is too long," Ser Jorah said. "All Belwas needs do is avoid
the point. Instead of trying to spit him so prettily, the fool should ride
right over him."

Oznak zo Pahl charged a third time, and now Dany could see
plainly that he was riding *past* Belwas, the way a Westerosi knight
might ride at an opponent in a tilt, rather than *at* him, like a Dothraki
riding down a foe. The flat level ground allowed the charger to get
up a good speed, but it also made it easy for the eunuch to dodge
the cumbersome fourteen-foot lance.

Meereen's pink-and-white hero tried to anticipate this time, and swung his lance sideways at the last second to catch Strong Belwas when he dodged. But the eunuch had anticipated too, and this time he dropped down instead of spinning sideways. The lance passed harmlessly over his head. And suddenly Belwas was rolling, and bringing the razor-sharp *arakh* around in a silver arc. They heard the charger scream as the blade bit into his legs, and then the horse was falling, the hero tumbling from the saddle.

A sudden silence swept along the brick parapets of Meereen. Now it was Dany's people who were screaming and cheering.

Oznak leapt clear of his horse and managed to draw his sword before Strong Belwas was on him. Steel sang against steel, too fast and furious for Dany to follow the blows. It could not have been a dozen heartbeats before Belwas's chest was awash in blood from a slice below his breasts, and Oznak zo Pahl had an *arakh* planted right between his ram's horns. The eunuch wrenched the blade loose and parted the hero's head from his body with three savage blows to the neck. He held it up high for the Meereenese to see, then flung it toward the city gates and let it bounce and roll across the sand.

"So much for the hero of Meereen," said Daario, laughing.

"A victory without meaning," Ser Jorah cautioned. "We will not win Meereen by killing its defenders one at a time."

"No," Dany agreed, "but I'm pleased we killed this one."

The defenders on the walls began firing their crossbows at Belwas, but the bolts fell short or skittered harmlessly along the ground. The eunuch turned his back on the steel-tipped rain, lowered his trousers, squatted, and shat in the direction of the city. He wiped himself with Oznak's striped cloak, and paused long enough to loot the hero's corpse and put the dying horse out of his agony before trudging back to the olive grove.

The besiegers gave him a raucous welcome as soon as he reached the camp. Her Dothraki hooted and screamed, and the Unsullied sent up a great clangor by banging their spears against their shields. "Well done," Ser Jorah told him, and Brown Ben tossed the eunuch a ripe plum and said, "A sweet fruit for a sweet fight." Even her Dothraki handmaids had words of praise. "We would braid your hair and hang a bell in it, Strong Belwas," said Jhiqui, "but you have no hair to braid."

"Strong Belwas needs no tinkly bells." The eunuch ate Brown Ben's plum in four big bites and tossed aside the stone. "Strong Belwas needs liver and onions."

"You shall have it," said Dany. "Strong Belwas is hurt." His stomach was red with the blood sheeting down from the meaty gash beneath his breasts.

"It is nothing. I let each man cut me once, before I kill him." He slapped his bloody belly. "Count the cuts and you will know how many Strong Belwas has slain."

But Dany had lost Khal Drogo to a similar wound, and she was not willing to let it go untreated. She sent Missandei to find a certain Yunkish freedman renowned for his skill in the healing arts. Belwas howled and complained, but Dany scolded him and called him a big bald baby until he let the healer stanch the wound with vinegar, sew it shut, and bind his chest with strips of linen soaked in fire wine. Only then did she lead her captains and commanders inside her pavilion for their council.

"I must have this city," she told them, sitting crosslegged on a pile of cushions, her dragons all about her. Irri and Jhiqui poured wine. "Her granaries are full to bursting. There are figs and dates and olives growing on the terraces of her pyramids, and casks of salt fish and smoked meat buried in her cellars."

"And fat chests of gold, silver, and gemstones as well," Daario reminded them. "Let us not forget the gemstones."

"I've had a look at the landward walls, and I see no point of weakness," said Ser Jorah Mormont. "Given time, we might be able to mine beneath a tower and make a breach, but what do we eat while we're digging? Our stores are all but exhausted."

"No weakness in the *landward* walls?" said Dany. Meereen stood on a jut of sand and stone where the slow brown Skahazadhan flowed into Slaver's Bay. The city's north wall ran along the riverbank, its west along the bay shore. "Does that mean we might attack from the river or the sea?"

"With three ships? We'll want to have Captain Groleo take a good look at the wall along the river, but unless it's crumbling that's just a wetter way to die."

"What if we were to build siege towers? My brother Viserys told tales of such, I know they can be made."

"From wood, Your Grace," Ser Jorah said. "The slavers have burnt every tree within twenty leagues of here. Without wood, we have no trebuchets to smash the walls, no ladders to go over them, no siege towers, no turtles, and no rams. We can storm the gates with axes, to be sure, but . . ."

"Did you see them bronze heads above the gates?" asked Brown Ben Plumm. "Rows of harpy heads with open mouths? The Meereenese can squirt boiling oil out them mouths, and cook your axemen where they stand."

Daario Naharis gave Grey Worm a smile. "Perhaps the Unsullied should wield the axes. Boiling oil feels like no more than a warm bath to you, I have heard."

"This is false." Grey Worm did not return the smile. "These ones do not feel burns as men do, yet such oil blinds and kills. The Unsullied do not fear to die, though. Give these ones rams, and we will batter down these gates or die in the attempt."

"You would die," said Brown Ben. At Yunkai, when he took command of the Second Sons, he claimed to be the veteran of a hundred battles. "Though I will not say I fought bravely in all of them. There are old sellswords and bold sellswords, but no old bold sellswords." She saw that it was true.

Dany sighed. "I will not throw away Unsullied lives, Grey Worm. Perhaps we can starve the city out."

Ser Jorah looked unhappy. "We'll starve long before they do, Your Grace. There's no food here, nor fodder for our mules and horses. I do not like this river water either. Meereen shits into the Skahazadhan but draws its drinking water from deep wells. Already we've had reports of sickness in the camps, fever and brownleg and three cases of the bloody flux. There will be more if we remain. The slaves are weak from the march."

"Freedmen," Dany corrected. "They are slaves no longer."

"Slave or free, they are hungry and they'll soon be sick. The city is better provisioned than we are, and can be resupplied by water. Your three ships are not enough to deny them access to both the river and the sea."

"Then what do you advise, Ser Jorah?"

"You will not like it."

"I would hear it all the same."

"As you wish. I say, let this city be. You cannot free every slave in the world, *Khaleesi*. Your war is in Westeros."

"I have not forgotten Westeros." Dany dreamt of it some nights, this fabled land that she had never seen. "If I let Meereen's old brick walls defeat me so easily, though, how will I ever take the great stone castles of Westeros?"

"As Aegon did," Ser Jorah said, "with fire. By the time we reach the Seven Kingdoms, your dragons will be grown. And we will have siege towers and trebuchets as well, all the things we lack here . . . but the way across the Lands of the Long Summer is long and grueling, and there are dangers we cannot know. You stopped at Astapor to buy an army, not to start a war. Save your spears and swords for the Seven Kingdoms, my queen. Leave Meereen to the Meereenese and march west for Pentos."

"Defeated?" said Dany, bristling.

"When cowards hide behind great walls, it is they who are defeated, *Khaleesi*," Ko Jhogo said.

Her other bloodriders concurred. "Blood of my blood," said Rakharo, "when cowards hide and burn the food and fodder, great *khals* must seek for braver foes. This is known."

"It is known," Jhiqui agreed, as she poured.

"Not to me." Dany set great store by Ser Jorah's counsel, but to leave Meereen untouched was more than she could stomach. She could not forget the children on their posts, the birds tearing at their entrails, their skinny arms pointing up the coast road. "Ser Jorah, you say we have no food left. If I march west, how can I feed my freedmen?"

"You can't. I am sorry, *Khaleesi*. They must feed themselves or starve. Many and more will die along the march, yes. That will be hard, but there is no way to save them. We need to put this scorched earth well behind us."

Dany had left a trail of corpses behind her when she crossed the red waste. It was a sight she never meant to see again. "No," she said. "I will not march my people off to die." *My children.* "There must be *some* way into this city."

"I know a way." Brown Ben Plumm stroked his speckled grey-and-white beard. "Sewers."

"Sewers? What do you mean?"

"Great brick sewers empty into the Skahazadhan, carrying the city's wastes. They might be a way in, for a few. That was how I escaped Meereen, after Scarb lost his head." Brown Ben made a face. "The smell has never left me. I dream of it some nights."

Ser Jorah looked dubious. "Easier to go out than in, it would seem to me. These sewers empty into the river, you say? That would mean the mouths are right below the walls."

"And closed with iron grates," Brown Ben admitted, "though some have rusted through, else I would have drowned in shit. Once inside, it is a long foul climb in pitch-dark through a maze of brick where a man could lose himself forever. The filth is never lower than waist high, and can rise over your head from the stains I saw on the walls. There's *things* down there too. Biggest rats you ever saw, and worse things. Nasty."

Daario Naharis laughed. "As nasty as you, when you came crawling out? If any man were fool enough to try this, every slaver in Meereen would smell them the moment they emerged."

Brown Ben shrugged. "Her Grace asked if there was a way in, so I told her . . . but Ben Plumm isn't going down in them sewers again, not for all the gold in the Seven Kingdoms. If there's others want to try it, though, they're welcome."

Aggo, Jhogo, and Grey Worm all tried to speak at once, but Dany raised her hand for silence. "These sewers do not sound promising." Grey Worm would lead his Unsullied down the sewers if she commanded it, she knew; her bloodriders would do no less. But none of them was suited to the task. The Dothraki were horsemen, and the strength of the Unsullied was their discipline on the battlefield. *Can I send men to die in the dark on such a slender hope?* "I must think on this some more. Return to your duties."

Her captains bowed and left her with her handmaids and her dragons. But as Brown Ben was leaving, Viserion spread his pale white wings and flapped lazily at his head. One of the wings buffeted the sellsword in his face. The white dragon landed awkwardly with one foot on the man's head and one on his shoulder, shrieked, and flew off again. "He likes you, Ben," said Dany.

"And well he might." Brown Ben laughed. "I have me a drop of the dragon blood myself, you know."

"You?" Dany was startled. Plumm was a creature of the free companies, an amiable mongrel. He had a broad brown face with a broken nose and a head of nappy grey hair, and his Dothraki mother had bequeathed him large, dark, almond-shaped eyes. He claimed to be part Braavosi, part Summer Islander, part Ibbenese, part Qohorik, part Dothraki, part Dornish, and part Westerosi, but this was the first she had heard of Targaryen blood. She gave him a searching look and said, "How could that be?"

"Well," said Brown Ben, "there was some old Plumm in the Sunset Kingdoms who wed a dragon princess. My grandmama told me the tale. He lived in King Aegon's day."

"Which King Aegon?" Dany asked. "Five Aegons have ruled in Westeros." Her brother's son would have been the sixth, but the Usurper's men had dashed his head against a wall.

"Five, were there? Well, that's a confusion. I could not give you a number, my queen. This old Plumm was a lord, though, must have been a famous fellow in his day, the talk of all the land. The thing was, begging your royal pardon, he had himself a cock six foot long."

The three bells in Dany's braid tinkled when she laughed. "You mean inches, I think."

"Feet," Brown Ben said firmly. "If it was inches, who'd want to talk about it, now, Your Grace?"

Dany giggled like a little girl. "Did your grandmother claim she'd actually seen this prodigy?"

"That the old crone never did. She was half-Ibbenese and half-Qohorik, never been to Westeros, my grandfather must have told her. Some Dothraki killed him before I was born."

"And where did your grandfather's knowledge come from?"

"One of them tales told at the teat, I'd guess." Brown Ben shrugged. "That's all I know about Aegon the Unnumbered or old Lord Plumm's mighty manhood, I fear. I best see to my Sons."

"Go do that," Dany told him.

When Brown Ben left, she lay back on her cushions. "If you were grown," she told Drogon, scratching him between the horns, "I'd fly you over the walls and melt that harpy down to slag." But it would be years before her dragons were large enough to ride. *And when they are, who shall ride them? The dragon has three heads, but I have only one.* She thought of Daario. *If ever there was a man who could rape a woman with his eyes . . .*

To be sure, she was just as guilty. Dany found herself stealing looks at the Tyroshi when her captains came to council, and sometimes at night she remembered the way his gold tooth glittered when he smiled. That, and his eyes. *His bright blue eyes.* On the road from Yunkai, Daario had brought her a flower or a sprig of some plant every evening when he made his report . . . to help her learn the land, he said. Waspwillow, dusky roses, wild mint, lady's lace, daggerleaf, broom, prickly ben, harpy's gold . . . *He tried to spare me the sight of the dead children too.* He should not have done that, but he meant it kindly. And Daario Naharis made her laugh, which Ser Jorah never did.

Dany tried to imagine what it would be like if she allowed Daario to kiss her, the way Jorah had kissed her on the ship. The thought was exciting and disturbing, both at once. *It is too great a risk.* The Tyroshi sellsword was not a good man, no one needed to tell her that. Under the smiles and the jests he was dangerous, even cruel. Sallor and Prendahl had woken one morning as his partners; that very night he'd given her their heads. *Khal Drogo could be cruel as well, and there was never a man more dangerous.* She had come to love him all the same. *Could I love Daario? What would it mean, if I took him into my bed? Would that make him one of the heads of the dragon?* Ser Jorah would be angry, she knew, but he was the one who'd said she had to take two husbands. *Perhaps I should marry them both and be done with it.*

But these were foolish thoughts. She had a city to take, and dreaming of kisses and some sellsword's bright blue eyes would not help her breach the walls of Meereen. *I am the blood of the dragon*, Dany reminded herself. Her thoughts were spinning in circles, like a rat chasing its tail. Suddenly she could not stand the close confines of the pavilion another moment. *I want to feel the wind on my face, and smell the sea.* "Missandei," she called, "have my silver saddled. Your own mount as well."

The little scribe bowed. "As Your Grace commands. Shall I summon your bloodriders to guard you?"

"We'll take Arstan. I do not mean to leave the camps." She had no enemies among her children. And the old squire would not talk too much as Belwas would, or look at her like Daario.

The grove of burnt olive trees in which she'd raised her pavilion stood beside the sea, between the Dothraki camp and that of the Unsullied. When the horses had been saddled, Dany and her companions set out along the shoreline, away from the city. Even so, she could feel Meereen at her back, mocking her. When she looked over one shoulder, there it stood, the afternoon sun blazing off the bronze harpy atop the Great Pyramid. Inside Meereen the slavers would soon be reclining in their fringed *tokar*s to feast on lamb and olives, unborn puppies, honeyed dormice and other such delicacies, whilst outside her children went hungry. A sudden wild anger filled her. *I will bring you down*, she swore.

As they rode past the stakes and pits that surrounded the eunuch encampment, Dany could hear Grey Worm and his sergeants running one company through a series of drills with shield, shortsword, and heavy spear. Another company was bathing in the sea, clad only in white linen breechclouts. The eunuchs were very clean, she had noticed. Some of her sellswords smelled as if they had not washed or changed their clothes since her father lost the Iron Throne, but the Unsullied bathed each evening, even if they'd marched all day. When no water was available they cleansed themselves with sand, the Dothraki way.

The eunuchs knelt as she passed, raising clenched fists to their breasts. Dany returned the salute. The tide was coming in, and the surf foamed about the feet of her silver. She could see her ships standing out to sea. *Balerion* floated nearest; the great cog once known as *Saduleon*, her sails furled. Further out were the galleys *Meraxes* and *Vhagar*, formerly *Joso's Prank* and *Summer Sun*. They were Magister Illyrio's ships, in truth, not hers at all, and yet she had given them new names with hardly a thought. Dragon names, and more; in old Valyria before the Doom, Balerion, Meraxes, and Vhagar had been gods.

South of the ordered realm of stakes, pits, drills, and bathing eunuchs lay the encampments of her freedmen, a far noisier and more chaotic place. Dany had armed the former slaves as best she could with weapons from Astapor and Yunkai, and Ser Jorah had organized the fighting men into four strong companies, yet she saw no one drilling here. They passed a driftwood fire where a hundred people had gathered to roast the carcass of a horse. She could smell the meat and hear the fat sizzling as the spit boys turned, but the sight only made her frown.

Children ran behind their horses, skipping and laughing. Instead of salutes, voices called to her on every side in a babble of tongues. Some of the freedmen greeted her as "Mother," while others begged for boons or favors. Some prayed for strange gods to bless her, and some asked her to bless them instead. She smiled at them, turning right and left, touching their hands when they raised them, letting those who knelt reach up to touch her stirrup or her leg. Many of the freedmen believed there was good fortune in her touch. *If it helps give them courage, let them touch me*, she thought. *There are hard trials yet ahead . . .*

Dany had stopped to speak to a pregnant woman who wanted the Mother of Dragons to name her baby when someone reached up and grabbed her left wrist. Turning, she glimpsed a tall ragged man with a shaved head and a sunburnt face. "Not so hard," she started to say, but before she could finish he'd yanked her bodily from the saddle. The ground came up and knocked the breath from her, as her silver whinnied and backed away. Stunned, Dany rolled to her side and pushed herself onto one elbow . . .

. . . and then she saw the sword.

"There's the treacherous sow," he said. "I knew you'd come to get your feet kissed one day." His head was bald as a melon, his nose red and peeling, but she knew that voice and those pale green eyes. "I'm going to start by cutting off your teats." Dany was dimly aware of Missandei shouting for help. A freedman edged forward, but only a step. One quick slash, and he was on his knees, blood running down his face. Mero wiped his sword on his breeches. "Who's next?"

"I am." Arstan Whitebeard leapt from his horse and stood over her, the salt wind riffling through his snowy hair, both hands on his tall hardwood staff.

"Grandfather," Mero said, "run off before I break your stick in two and bugger you with—"

The old man feinted with one end of the staff, pulled it back, and whipped the other end about faster than Dany would have believed. The Titan's Bastard staggered back into the surf, spitting blood and broken teeth from the ruin of his mouth. Whitebeard put Dany behind him. Mero slashed at his face. The old man jerked back, cat-quick. The staff thumped Mero's ribs, sending him reeling. Arstan splashed sideways, parried a looping cut, danced away from a second, checked a third mid-swing. The moves were so fast she could hardly follow. Missandei was pulling Dany to her feet when she heard a *crack*. She thought Arstan's staff had snapped until she saw the jagged bone jutting from Mero's calf. As he fell, the Titan's Bastard twisted and lunged, sending his point straight at the old man's chest. Whitebeard swept the blade aside almost contemptuously and smashed the other end of his staff against the big man's temple. Mero went sprawling, blood bubbling from his mouth as the waves washed over him. A moment later the freedmen washed over him too, knives and stones and angry fists rising and falling in a frenzy.

Dany turned away, sickened. She was more frightened now than when it had been happening. *He would have killed me.*

"Your Grace." Arstan knelt. "I am an old man, and shamed. He should never have gotten close enough to seize you. I was lax. I did not know him without his beard and hair."

"No more than I did." Dany took a deep breath to stop her shaking. *Enemies everywhere.* "Take me back to my tent. Please."

By the time Mormont arrived, she was huddled in her lion pelt, drinking a cup of spice wine. "I had a look at the river wall," Ser Jorah started. "It's a few feet higher than the others, and just as strong. And the Meereenese have a dozen fire hulks tied up beneath the ramparts—"

She cut him off. "You might have warned me that the Titan's Bastard had escaped."

He frowned. "I saw no need to frighten you, Your Grace. I have offered a reward for his head—"

"Pay it to Whitebeard. Mero has been with us all the way from Yunkai. He shaved his beard off and lost himself amongst the freedmen, waiting for a chance for vengeance. Arstan killed him."

Ser Jorah gave the old man a long look. "A squire with a stick slew Mero of Braavos, is that the way of it?"

"A stick," Dany confirmed, "but no longer a squire. Ser Jorah, it's my wish that Arstan be knighted."

"*No.*"

The loud refusal was surprise enough. Stranger still, it came from both men at once.

Ser Jorah drew his sword. "The Titan's Bastard was a nasty piece of work. And good at killing. Who are you, old man?"

"A better knight than you, ser," Arstan said coldly.

Knight? Dany was confused. "You said you were a squire."

"I was, Your Grace." He dropped to one knee. "I squired for Lord Swann in my youth, and at Magister Illyrio's behest I have served Strong Belwas as well. But during the years between, I was a knight in Westeros. I have told you no lies, my queen. Yet there are truths I have withheld, and for that and all my other sins I can only beg your forgiveness."

"What truths have you withheld?" Dany did not like this. "You will tell me. Now."

He bowed his head. "At Qarth, when you asked my name, I said I was called Arstan. That much was true. Many men had called me by that name while Belwas and I were making our way east to find you. But it is not my true name."

She was more confused than angry. *He has played me false, just as Jorah warned me, yet he saved my life just now.*

Ser Jorah flushed red. "Mero shaved his beard, but you grew one, didn't you? No wonder you looked so bloody familiar . . ."

"You know him?" Dany asked the exile knight, lost.

"I saw him perhaps a dozen times . . . from afar most often, standing with his brothers or riding in some tourney. But every man in the Seven Kingdoms knew Barristan the Bold." He laid the point of his sword against the old man's neck. "*Khaleesi*, before you kneels Ser Barristan Selmy, Lord Commander of the Kingsguard, who betrayed your House to serve the Usurper Robert Baratheon."

The old knight did not so much as blink. "The crow calls the raven black, and *you* speak of betrayal."

"Why are you here?" Dany demanded of him. "If Robert sent you to kill me, why did you save my life?" *He served the Usurper. He betrayed Rhaegar's memory, and abandoned Viserys to live and die in exile. Yet if he wanted me dead, he need only have stood aside . . .* "I want the *whole* truth now, on your honor as a knight. Are you the Usurper's man, or mine?"

"Yours, if you will have me." Ser Barristan had tears in his eyes. "I took Robert's pardon, aye. I served him in Kingsguard and council. Served with the Kingslayer and others near as bad, who soiled the white cloak I wore. Nothing will excuse that. I might be serving in King's Landing still if the vile boy upon the Iron Throne had not cast me aside, it shames me to admit. But when he took the cloak that the White Bull had draped about my shoulders, and sent men to kill me that selfsame day, it was as though he'd ripped a caul off my eyes. That was when I knew I must find my true king, and die in his service—"

"I can grant that wish," Ser Jorah said darkly.

"Quiet," said Dany. "I'll hear him out."

"It may be that I must die a traitor's death," Ser Barristan said. "If so, I should not die alone. Before I took Robert's pardon I fought against him on the Trident. You were on the other side of that battle, Mormont, were you not?" He did not wait for an answer. "Your Grace, I am sorry I misled you. It was the only way to keep the Lannisters from learning that I had joined you. You are watched, as your brother was. Lord Varys reported every move Viserys made, for years. Whilst I sat on the small council, I heard a hundred such reports. And since the day you wed Khal Drogo, there has been an informer by your side selling your secrets, trading whispers to the Spider for gold and promises."

He cannot mean ... "You are mistaken." Dany looked at Jorah Mormont. "Tell him he's mistaken. There's no informer. Ser Jorah, tell him. We crossed the Dothraki sea together, and the red waste ..." Her heart fluttered like a bird in a trap. "Tell him, Jorah. Tell him how he got it wrong."

"The Others take you, Selmy." Ser Jorah flung his longsword to the carpet. "*Khaleesi*, it was only at the start, before I came to know you ... before I came to love ..."

"*Do not say that word!*" She backed away from him. "*How could you?* What did the Usurper promise you? Gold, was it gold?" The Undying had said she would be betrayed twice more, once for gold and once for love. "Tell me what you were promised?"

"Varys said ... I might go home." He bowed his head.

I was going to take you home! Her dragons sensed her fury. Viserion roared, and smoke rose grey from his snout. Drogon beat the air with black wings, and Rhaegal twisted his head back and belched flame. *I should say the word and burn the two of them.* Was there no one she could trust, no one to keep her safe? "Are all the knights of Westeros so false as you two? Get out, before my dragons roast you both. What does roast liar smell like? As foul as Brown Ben's sewers? *Go!*"

Ser Barristan rose stiff and slow. For the first time, he looked his age. "Where shall we go, Your Grace?"

"To hell, to serve King Robert." Dany felt hot tears on her cheeks. Drogon screamed, lashing his tail back and forth. "The Others can have you both." *Go, go away forever, both of you, the next time I see your faces I'll have your traitors' heads off.* She could not say the words, though. *They betrayed me. But they saved me. But they lied.* "You go ..." *My bear, my fierce strong bear, what will I do without him? And the old man, my brother's friend.* "You go ... go ..." *Where?*

And then she knew.

TYRION

Tyrion dressed himself in darkness, listening to his wife's soft breathing from the bed they shared. *She dreams*, he thought, when Sansa murmured something softly—a name, perhaps, though it was too faint to say—and turned onto her side. As man and wife they shared a marriage bed, but that was all. *Even her tears she hoards to herself.*

He had expected anguish and anger when he told her of her brother's death, but Sansa's face had remained so still that for a moment he feared she had not understood. It was only later, with a heavy oaken door between them, that he heard her sobbing. Tyrion had considered going to her then, to offer what comfort he could. *No*, he had to remind himself, *she will not look for solace from a Lannister.* The most he could do was to shield her from the uglier details of the Red Wedding as they came down from the Twins. Sansa did not need to hear how her brother's body had been hacked and mutilated, he decided; nor how her mother's corpse had been dumped naked into the Green Fork in a savage mockery of House Tully's funeral customs. The last thing the girl needed was more fodder for her nightmares.

It was not enough, though. He had wrapped his cloak around her shoulders and sworn to protect her, but that was as cruel a jape as the crown the Freys had placed atop the head of Robb Stark's direwolf after they'd sewn it onto his headless corpse. Sansa knew that as well. The way she looked at him, her stiffness when she climbed into their bed ... when he was with her, never for an instant could he forget who he was, or *what* he was. No more than she did. She still went nightly to the godswood to pray, and Tyrion wondered if she were praying for his death. She had lost her home, her place in the world, and everyone she had ever loved or trusted. *Winter is coming*, warned the Stark words, and truly it had come for them with a vengeance. *But it is high summer for House Lannister. So why am I so bloody cold?*

He pulled on his boots, fastened his cloak with a lion's head brooch, and slipped out into the torchlit hall. There was this much to be said for his marriage; it had allowed him to escape Maegor's Holdfast. Now that he had a wife and household, his lord father had agreed that more suitable accommodations were required, and Lord Gyles had found himself abruptly dispossessed of his spacious apartments atop the Kitchen Keep. And splendid apartments they were too, with a large bedchamber and adequate solar, a bath and dressing room for his wife, and small adjoining chambers for Pod and Sansa's maids. Even Bronn's cell by the stair had a window of sorts. *Well, more an arrow slit, but it lets in light.* The castle's main kitchen was just across the courtyard, true, but Tyrion found those sounds and smells infinitely preferable to sharing Maegor's with his sister. The less he had to see of Cersei the happier he was like to be.

Tyrion could hear Brella's snoring as he passed her cell. Shae complained of that, but it seemed a small enough price to pay. Varys had suggested the woman to him; in former days, she had run Lord Renly's household in the city, which had given her a deal of practice at being blind, deaf, and mute.

Lighting a taper, he made his way back to the servants' steps and descended. The floors below his own were still, and he heard no footsteps but his own. Down he went, to the ground floor and beyond, to emerge in a gloomy cellar with a vaulted stone ceiling. Much of the castle was connected underground, and the Kitchen Keep was no exception. Tyrion waddled along a long dark passageway until he found the door he wanted, and pushed through.

Within, the dragon skulls were waiting, and so was Shae. "I thought m'lord had forgotten me." Her dress was draped over a black tooth near as tall as she was, and she stood within the dragon's jaws, nude. *Balerion*, he thought. Or was it Vhagar? One dragon skull looked much like another.

Just the sight of her made him hard. "Come out of there."

"I won't." She smiled her wickedest smile. "M'lord will pluck me from the dragon's jaws, I know." But when he waddled closer she leaned forward and blew out the taper.

"Shae . . ." He reached, but she spun and slipped free.

"You have to catch me." Her voice came from his left. "M'lord must have played monsters and maidens when he was little."

"Are you calling me a monster?"

"No more than I'm a maiden." She was behind him, her steps soft against the floor. "You need to catch me all the same."

He did, finally, but only because she let herself be caught. By the time she slipped into his arms, he was flushed and out of breath from stumbling into dragon skulls. All that was forgotten in an instant when he felt her small breasts pressed against his face in the dark, her stiff little nipples brushing lightly over his lips and the scar where his nose had been. Tyrion pulled her down onto the floor. "My giant," she breathed as he entered her. "My giant's come to save me."

After, as they lay entwined amongst the dragon skulls, he rested his head against her, inhaling the smooth clean smell of her hair. "We should go back," he said reluctantly. "It must be near dawn. Sansa will be waking."

"You should give her dreamwine," Shae said, "like Lady Tanda does with Lollys. A cup before she goes to sleep, and we could fuck in bed beside her without her waking." She giggled. "Maybe we should, some night. Would m'lord like that?" Her hand found his shoulder, and began to knead the muscles there. "Your neck is hard as stone. What troubles you?"

Tyrion could not see his fingers in front of his face, but he ticked his woes off on them all the same. "My wife. My sister. My nephew. My father. The Tyrells." He had to move to his other hand. "Varys. Pycelle. Littlefinger. The Red Viper of Dorne." He had come to his last finger. "The face that stares back out of the water when I wash."

Shae kissed his maimed scarred nose. "A brave face. A kind and good face. I wish I could see it now."

All the sweet innocence of the world was in her voice. *Innocence? Fool, she's a whore, all she knows of men is the bit between their legs. Fool, fool.* "Better you than me." Tyrion sat. "We have a long day before us, both of us. You shouldn't have blown out that taper. How are we to find our clothing?"

She laughed. "Maybe we'll have to go naked."

And if we're seen, my lord father will hang you. Hiring Shae as one of Sansa's maids had given him an excuse to be seen talking with her, but Tyrion did not delude himself that they were safe. Varys had warned him. "I gave Shae a false history, but it was meant for Lollys and Lady Tanda. Your sister is of a more suspicious mind. If she should ask me what I know . . ."

"You will tell her some clever lie."

"No. I will tell her that the girl is a common camp follower that you acquired before the battle on the Green Fork and brought to King's Landing against your lord father's express command. I will not lie to the queen."

"You have lied to her before. Shall I tell her that?"

The eunuch sighed. "That cuts more deeply than a knife, my lord. I have served you loyally, but I must also serve your sister when I can. How long do you think she would let me live if I were of no further use to her whatsoever? I have no fierce sellsword to protect me, no valiant brother to avenge me, only some little birds who whisper in my ear. With those whisperings I must buy my life anew each day."

"Pardon me if I do not weep for you."

"I shall, but you must pardon me if I do not weep for Shae. I confess, I do not understand what there is in her to make a clever man like you act such a fool."

"You might, if you were not a eunuch."

"Is that the way of it? A man may have wits, or a bit of meat between his legs, but not both?" Varys tittered. "Perhaps I should be grateful I was cut, then."

The Spider was right. Tyrion groped through the dragon-haunted darkness for his smallclothes, feeling wretched. The risk he was taking left him tight as a drumhead, and there was guilt as well. *The Others can take my guilt,* he thought as he slipped his tunic over his head. *Why should I be guilty? My wife wants no part of me, and most especially not the part that seems to want her.* Perhaps he ought to *tell* her about Shae. It was not as though he was the first man ever to keep a concubine. Sansa's own oh-so-honorable father had given her a bastard brother. For all he knew, his wife might be thrilled to learn that he was fucking Shae, so long as it spared her his unwelcome touch.

No, I dare not. Vows or no, his wife could not be trusted. She might be maiden between the legs, but she was hardly innocent of betrayal; she had once spilled her own father's plans to Cersei. And girls her age were not known for keeping secrets.

The only safe course was to rid himself of Shae. *I might send her to Chataya,* Tyrion reflected, reluctantly. In Chataya's brothel, Shae would have all the silks and gems she could wish for, and the gentlest highborn patrons. It would be a better life by far than the one she had been living when he'd found her.

Or, if she was tired of earning her bread on her back, he might arrange a marriage for her. *Bronn, perhaps?* The sellsword had never balked at eating off his master's plate, and he was a knight now, a better match than she could elsewise hope for. *Or Ser Tallad?* Tyrion had noticed that one gazing wistfully at Shae more than once. *Why not? He's tall, strong, not hard to look upon, every inch the gifted young knight.* Of course, Tallad knew Shae only as a pretty young lady's maid in service at the castle. *If he wed her and then learned she was a whore ...*

"M'lord, where are you? Did the dragons eat you up?"

"No. Here." He groped at a dragon skull. "I have found a shoe, but I believe it's yours."

"M'lord sounds very solemn. Have I displeased you?"

"No," he said, too curtly. "You always please me." *And therein is our danger.* He might dream of sending her away at times like this, but that never lasted long. Tyrion saw her dimly through the gloom, pulling a woolen sock up a slender leg. *I can see.* A vague light was leaking through the row of long narrow windows set high in the cellar wall. The skulls of the Targaryen dragons were emerging from the darkness around them, black amidst grey. "Day comes too soon." A new day. A new year. A new century. *I survived the Green Fork and the Blackwater, I can bloody well survive King Joffrey's wedding.*

Shae snatched her dress down off the dragon's tooth and slipped it over her head. "I'll go up first. Brella will want help with the bathwater." She bent over to give him one last kiss, upon the brow. "My giant of Lannister. I love you so."

And I love you as well, sweetling. A whore she might well be, but she deserved better than what he had to give her. *I will wed her to Ser Tallad. He seems a decent man. And tall . . .*

SANSA

That was such a sweet dream, Sansa thought drowsily. She had been back in Winterfell, running through the godswood with her Lady. Her father had been there, and her brothers, all of them warm and safe. *If only dreaming could make it so . . .*

She threw back the coverlets. *I must be brave.* Her torments would soon be ended, one way or the other. *If Lady was here, I would not be afraid.* Lady was dead, though; Robb, Bran, Rickon, Arya, her father, her mother, even Septa Mordane. *All of them are dead but me.* She was alone in the world now.

Her lord husband was not beside her, but she was used to that. Tyrion was a bad sleeper and often rose before the dawn. Usually, she found him in the solar, hunched beside a candle, lost in some old scroll or leatherbound book. Sometimes the smell of the morning bread from the ovens took him to the kitchens, and sometimes he would climb up to the roof garden or wander all alone down Traitor's Walk.

She threw back the shutters and shivered as gooseprickles rose along her arms. There were clouds massing in the eastern sky, pierced by shafts of sunlight. *They look like two huge castles afloat in the morning sky.* Sansa could see their walls of tumbled stone, their mighty keeps and barbicans. Wispy banners swirled from atop their towers and reached for the fast-fading stars. The sun was coming up behind them, and she watched them go from black to grey to a thousand shades of rose and gold and crimson. Soon the wind mushed them together, and there was only one castle where there had been two.

She heard the door open as her maids brought the hot water for her bath. They were both new to her service; Tyrion said the women who'd tended to her previously had all been Cersei's spies, just as Sansa had always suspected. "Come see," she told them. "There's a castle in the sky."

They came to have a look. "It's made of gold." Shae had short dark hair and bold eyes. She did all that was asked of her, but sometimes she gave Sansa the most insolent looks. "A castle all of gold, there's a sight I'd like to see."

"A castle, is it?" Brella had to squint. "That tower's tumbling over, looks like. It's all ruins, that is."

Sansa did not want to hear about falling towers and ruined castles. She closed the shutters and said, "We are expected at the queen's breakfast. Is my lord husband in the solar?"

"No, m'lady," said Brella. "I have not seen him."

"Might be he went to see his father," Shae declared. "Might be the King's Hand had need of his counsel."

Brella gave a sniff. "Lady Sansa, you'll be wanting to get into the tub before the water gets too cool."

Sansa let Shae pull her shift up over her head and climbed into the big wooden tub. She was tempted to ask for a cup of wine, to calm her nerves. The wedding was to be at midday in the Great Sept of Baelor across the city. And come evenfall the feast would be held in the throne room; a thousand guests and seventy-seven courses, with singers and jugglers and mummers. But first came breakfast in the Queen's Ballroom, for the Lannisters and the Tyrell men—the Tyrell women would be breaking their fast with Margaery—and a hundred odd knights and lordlings. *They have made me a Lannister*, Sansa thought bitterly.

Brella sent Shae to fetch more hot water while she washed Sansa's back. "You are trembling, m'lady."

"The water is not hot enough," Sansa lied.

Her maids were dressing her when Tyrion appeared, Podrick Payne in tow. "You look lovely, Sansa." He turned to his squire. "Pod, be so good as to pour me a cup of wine."

"There will be wine at the breakfast, my lord," Sansa said.

"There's wine here. You don't expect me to face my sister sober, surely? It's a new century, my lady. The three hundredth year since Aegon's Conquest." The dwarf took a cup of red from Podrick and raised it high. "To Aegon. What a fortunate fellow. Two sisters, two wives, and three big dragons, what more could a man ask for?" He wiped his mouth with the back of his hand.

The Imp's clothing was soiled and unkempt, Sansa noticed; it looked as though he'd slept in it. "Will you be changing into fresh garb, my lord? Your new doublet is very handsome."

"The *doublet* is handsome, yes." Tyrion put the cup aside. "Come, Pod, let us see if we can find some garments to make me look less dwarfish. I would not want to shame my lady wife."

When the Imp returned a short time later, he was presentable enough, and even a little taller. Podrick Payne had changed as well, and looked almost a proper squire for once, although a rather large red pimple in the fold beside his nose spoiled the effect of his splendid purple, white, and gold raiment. *He is such a timid boy.* Sansa had been wary of Tyrion's squire at first; he was a Payne, cousin to Ser Ilyn Payne who had taken her father's head off. However, she'd soon come to realize that Pod was as frightened of her as she was of his cousin. Whenever she spoke to him, he turned the most alarming shade of red.

"Are purple, gold, and white the colors of House Payne, Podrick?" she asked him politely.

"No. I mean, yes." He blushed. "The colors. Our arms are purple and white chequy, my lady. With gold coins. In the checks. Purple and white. Both." He studied her feet.

"There's a tale behind those coins," said Tyrion. "No doubt Pod will confide it to your toes one day. Just now we are expected at the Queen's Ballroom, however. Shall we?"

Sansa was tempted to beg off. *I could tell him that my tummy was upset, or that my moon's blood had come.* She wanted nothing more than to crawl back in bed and pull the drapes. *I must be brave, like*

Robb, she told herself, as she took her lord husband stiffly by the arm.

In the Queen's Ballroom, they broke their fast on honeycakes baked with blackberries and nuts, gammon steaks, bacon, fingerfish crisped in breadcrumbs, autumn pears, and a Dornish dish of onions, cheese, and chopped eggs cooked up with fiery peppers. "Nothing like a hearty breakfast to whet one's appetite for the seventy-seven-course feast to follow," Tyrion commented as their plates were filled. There were flagons of milk and flagons of mead and flagons of a light sweet golden wine to wash it down. Musicians strolled among the tables, piping and fluting and fiddling, while Ser Dontos galloped about on his broomstick horse and Moon Boy made farting sounds with his cheeks and sang rude songs about the guests.

Tyrion scarce touched his food, Sansa noticed, though he drank several cups of the wine. For herself, she tried a little of the Dornish eggs, but the peppers burned her mouth. Otherwise she only nibbled at the fruit and fish and honeycakes. Every time Joffrey looked at her, her tummy got so fluttery that she felt as though she'd swallowed a bat.

When the food had been cleared away, the queen solemnly presented Joff with the wife's cloak that he would drape over Margaery's shoulders. "It is the cloak I donned when Robert took me for his queen, the same cloak my mother Lady Joanna wore when wed to my lord father." Sansa thought it looked threadbare, if truth be told, but perhaps because it was so used.

Then it was time for gifts. It was traditional in the Reach to give presents to bride and groom on the morning of their wedding; on the morrow they would receive more presents as a couple, but today's tokens were for their separate persons.

From Jalabhar Xho, Joffrey received a great bow of golden wood and quiver of long arrows fletched with green and scarlet feathers; from Lady Tanda a pair of supple riding boots; from Ser Kevan a magnificent red leather jousting saddle; a red gold brooch wrought in the shape of a scorpion from the Dornishman, Prince Oberyn; silver spurs from Ser Addam Marbrand; a red silk tourney pavilion from Lord Mathis Rowan. Lord Paxter Redwyne brought forth a beautiful wooden model of the war galley of two hundred oars being built even now on the Arbor. "If it please Your Grace, she will be called *King Joffrey's Valor*," he said, and Joff allowed that he was very pleased indeed. "I will make it my flagship when I sail to Dragonstone to kill my traitor uncle Stannis," he said.

He plays the gracious king today. Joffrey could be gallant when it suited him, Sansa knew, but it seemed to suit him less and less. Indeed, all his courtesy vanished at once when Tyrion presented him with their own gift: a huge old book called *Lives of Four Kings*, bound in leather and gorgeously illuminated. The king leafed through it with no interest. "And what is this, Uncle?"

A book. Sansa wondered if Joffrey moved those fat wormy lips of his when he read.

"Grand Maester Kaeth's history of the reigns of Daeron the Young Dragon, Baelor the Blessed, Aegon the Unworthy, and Daeron the Good," her small husband answered.

"A book every king should read, Your Grace," said Ser Kevan.

"My father had no time for books." Joffrey shoved the tome across the table. "If you read less, Uncle Imp, perhaps Lady Sansa would have a baby in her belly by now." He laughed . . . and when the king laughs, the court laughs with him. "Don't be sad, Sansa, once I've gotten Queen Margaery with child I'll visit your bedchamber and show my little uncle how it's done."

Sansa reddened. She glanced nervously at Tyrion, afraid of what he might say. This could turn as nasty as the bedding had at their own feast. But for once the dwarf filled his mouth with wine instead of words.

Lord Mace Tyrell came forward to present his gift: a golden chalice three feet tall, with two ornate curved handles and seven faces glittering with gemstones. "Seven faces for Your Grace's seven kingdoms," the bride's father explained. He showed them how each face bore the sigil of one of the great houses: ruby lion, emerald rose, onyx stag, silver trout, blue jade falcon, opal sun, and pearl direwolf.

"A splendid cup," said Joffrey, "but we'll need to chip the wolf off and put a squid in its place, I think."

Sansa pretended that she had not heard.

"Margaery and I shall drink deep at the feast, good father." Joffrey lifted the chalice above his head, for everyone to admire.

"The damned thing's as tall as I am," Tyrion muttered in a low voice. "Half a chalice and Joff will be falling down drunk."

Good, she thought. *Perhaps he'll break his neck.*

Lord Tywin waited until last to present the king with his own gift: a longsword. Its scabbard was made of cherrywood, gold, and oiled red leather, studded with golden lions' heads. The lions had ruby eyes, she saw. The ballroom fell silent as Joffrey unsheathed the blade and thrust the sword above his head. Red and black ripples in the steel shimmered in the morning light.

"Magnificent," declared Mathis Rowan.

"A sword to sing of, sire," said Lord Redwyne.

"A *king's* sword," said Ser Kevan Lannister.

King Joffrey looked as if he wanted to kill someone right then and there, he was so excited. He slashed at the air and laughed. "A great sword must have a great name, my lords! What shall I call it?"

Sansa remembered Lion's Tooth, the sword Arya had flung into the Trident, and Hearteater, the one he'd made her kiss before the battle. She wondered if he'd want Margaery to kiss this one.

The guests were shouting out names for the new blade. Joff dismissed a dozen before he heard one he liked. "*Widow's Wail!*" he cried. "Yes! It shall make many a widow, too!" He slashed again. "And when I face my uncle Stannis it will break his magic sword clean in two." Joff tried a downcut, forcing Ser Balon Swann to take a hasty step backward. Laughter rang through the hall at the look on Ser Balon's face.

"Have a care, Your Grace," Ser Addam Marbrand warned the king. "Valyrian steel is perilously sharp."

"I remember." Joffrey brought Widow's Wail down in a savage two-handed slice, onto the book that Tyrion had given him. The heavy leather cover parted at a stroke. "Sharp! I told you, I am no stranger to Valyrian steel." It took him half a dozen further cuts to hack the thick tome apart, and the boy was breathless by the time he was done. Sansa could feel her husband struggling with his fury as Ser Osmund Kettleblack shouted, "I pray you never turn that wicked edge on me, sire."

"See that you never give me cause, ser." Joffrey flicked a chunk of *Lives of Four Kings* off the table at swordpoint, then slid Widow's Wail back into its scabbard.

"Your Grace," Ser Garlan Tyrell said. "Perhaps you did not know. In all of Westeros there were but four copies of that book illuminated in Kaeth's own hand."

"Now there are three." Joffrey undid his old swordbelt to don his new one. "You and Lady Sansa owe me a better present, Uncle Imp. This one is all chopped to pieces."

Tyrion was staring at his nephew with his mismatched eyes. "Perhaps a knife, sire. To match your sword. A dagger of the same fine Valyrian steel ... with a dragonbone hilt, say?"

Joff gave him a sharp look. "You ... yes, a dagger to match my sword, good." He nodded. "A ... a gold hilt with rubies in it. Dragonbone is too plain."

"As you wish, Your Grace." Tyrion drank another cup of wine. He might have been all alone in his solar for all the attention he paid Sansa. But when the time came to leave for the wedding, he took her by the hand.

As they were crossing the yard, Prince Oberyn of Dorne fell in beside them, his black-haired paramour on his arm. Sansa glanced at the woman curiously. She was baseborn and unwed, and had borne two bastard daughters for the prince, but she did not fear to look even the queen in the eye. Shae had told her that this Ellaria worshiped some Lysene love goddess. "She was almost a whore when he found her, m'lady," her maid confided, "and now she's near a princess." Sansa had never been this close to the Dornishwoman before. *She is not truly beautiful*, she thought, *but something about her draws the eye.*

"I once had the great good fortune to see the Citadel's copy of *Lives of Four Kings*," Prince Oberyn was telling her lord husband. "The illuminations were wondrous to behold, but Kaeth was too kind by half to King Viserys."

Tyrion gave him a sharp look. "Too kind? He scants Viserys shamefully, in my view. It should have been *Lives of Five Kings*."

The prince laughed. "Viserys hardly reigned a fortnight."

"He reigned more than a year," said Tyrion.

Oberyn gave a shrug. "A year or a fortnight, what does it matter? He poisoned his own nephew to gain the throne and then did nothing once he had it."

"Baelor starved himself to death, fasting," said Tyrion. "His uncle served him loyally as Hand, as he had served the Young Dragon before him. Viserys might only have reigned a year, but he ruled for fifteen, while Daeron warred and Baelor prayed." He made a sour face. "And if he did remove his nephew, can you blame him? Someone had to save the realm from Baelor's follies."

Sansa was shocked. "But Baelor the Blessed was a great king. He walked the Boneway barefoot to make peace with Dorne, and rescued the Dragonknight from a snakepit. The vipers refused to strike him because he was so pure and holy."

Prince Oberyn smiled. "If you were a viper, my lady, would you want to bite a bloodless stick like Baelor the Blessed? I'd sooner save my fangs for someone juicier . . ."

"My prince is playing with you, Lady Sansa," said the woman Ellaria Sand. "The septons and singers like to say that the snakes did not bite Baelor, but the truth is very different. He was bitten half a hundred times, and should have died from it."

"If he had, Viserys would have reigned a dozen years," said Tyrion, "and the Seven Kingdoms might have been better served. Some believe Baelor was deranged by all that venom."

"Yes," said Prince Oberyn, "but I've seen no snakes in this Red Keep of yours. So how do you account for Joffrey?"

"I prefer not to." Tyrion inclined his head stiffly. "If you will excuse us. Our litter awaits." The dwarf helped Sansa up inside and clambered awkwardly after her. "Close the curtains, my lady, if you'd be so good."

"Must we, my lord?" Sansa did not want to be shut behind the curtains. "The day is so lovely."

"The good people of King's Landing are like to throw dung at the litter if they see me inside it. Do us both a kindness, my lady. Close the curtains."

She did as he bid her. They sat for a time, as the air grew warm and stuffy around them. "I was sorry about your book, my lord," she made herself say.

"It was Joffrey's book. He might have learned a thing or two if he'd read it." He sounded distracted. "I should have known better. I should have seen . . . a good many things."

"Perhaps the dagger will please him more."

When the dwarf grimaced, his scar tightened and twisted. "The boy's earned himself a dagger, wouldn't you say?" Thankfully, Tyrion did not wait for her reply. "Joff quarreled with your brother Robb at Winterfell. Tell me, was there ill feeling between Bran and His Grace as well?"

"Bran?" The question confused her. "Before he fell, you mean?" She had to try to think back. It was all so long ago. "Bran was a sweet boy. Everyone loved him. He and Tommen fought with wooden swords, I remember, but just for play."

Tyrion lapsed back into moody silence. Sansa heard the distant clank of chains from outside; the portcullis was being drawn up. A moment later there was a shout, and their litter swayed into motion. Deprived of the passing scenery, she chose to stare at her folded hands, uncomfortably aware of her husand's mismatched eyes. *Why is he looking at me that way?*

"You loved your brothers, much as I love Jaime."

Is this some Lannister trap to make me speak treason? "My brothers were traitors, and they've gone to traitors' graves. It is treason to love a traitor."

Her little husband snorted. "Robb rose in arms against his rightful king. By law, that made him a traitor. The others died too young to know what treason was." He rubbed his nose. "Sansa, do you know what happened to Bran at Winterfell?"

"Bran fell. He was always climbing things, and finally he fell. We always feared he would. And Theon Greyjoy killed him, but that was later."

"Theon Greyjoy." Tyrion sighed. "Your lady mother once accused me . . . well, I will not burden you with the ugly details. She accused me falsely. I never harmed your brother Bran. And I mean no harm to you."

What does he want me to say? "That is good to know, my lord." He wanted something from her, but Sansa did not know what it was.

He looks like a starving child, but I have no food to give him. Why won't he leave me be?

Tyrion rubbed at his scarred, scabby nose yet again, an ugly habit that drew the eye to his ugly face. "You have never asked me how Robb died, or your lady mother."

"I . . . would sooner not know. It would give me bad dreams."

"Then I will say no more."

"That . . . that's kind of you."

"Oh, yes," said Tyrion. "I am the very soul of kindness. And I know about bad dreams."

TYRION

The new crown that his father had given the Faith stood twice as tall as the one the mob had smashed, a glory of crystal and spun gold. Rainbow light flashed and shimmered every time the High Septon moved his head, but Tyrion had to wonder how the man could bear the weight. And even he had to concede that Joffrey and Margaery made a regal couple, as they stood side-by-side between the towering gilded statues of the Father and the Mother.

The bride was lovely in ivory silk and Myrish lace, her skirts decorated with floral patterns picked out in seed pearls. As Renly's widow, she might have worn the Baratheon colors, gold and black, yet she came to them a Tyrell, in a maiden's cloak made of a hundred cloth-of-gold roses sewn to green velvet. He wondered if she really was a maiden. *Not that Joffrey is like to know the difference.*

The king looked near as splendid as his bride, in his doublet of dusky rose, beneath a cloak of deep crimson velvet blazoned with his stag and lion. The crown rested easily on his curls, gold on gold. *I saved that bloody crown for him.* Tyrion shifted his weight uncomfortably from one foot to the other. He could not stand still. *Too much wine.* He should have thought to relieve himself before they set out from the Red Keep. The sleepless night he'd spent with Shae was making itself felt too, but most of all he wanted to strangle his bloody royal nephew.

I am no stranger to Valyrian steel, the boy had boasted. The septons were always going on about how the Father Above judges us all. *If the Father would be so good as to topple over and crush Joff like a dung beetle, I might even believe it.*

He ought to have seen it long ago. Jaime would never send another man to do his killing, and Cersei was too cunning to use a knife that could be traced back to her, but Joff, arrogant vicious stupid little wretch that he was . . .

He remembered a cold morning when he'd climbed down the steep exterior steps from Winterfell's library to find Prince Joffrey jesting with the Hound about killing wolves. *Send a dog to kill a wolf*, he said. Even Joffrey was not so foolish as to command Sandor Clegane to slay a son of Eddard Stark, however; the Hound would have gone to Cersei. Instead the boy found his catspaw among the unsavory lot of freeriders, merchants, and camp followers who'd attached themselves to the king's party as they made their way north. *Some poxy lackwit willing to risk his life for a prince's favor and a little coin.* Tyrion wondered whose idea it had been to wait until Robert left Winterfell before opening Bran's throat. *Joff's, most like. No doubt he thought it was the height of cunning.*

The prince's own dagger had a jeweled pommel and inlaid goldwork on the blade, Tyrion seemed to recall. At least Joff had not been stupid enough to use that. Instead he went poking among his father's weapons. Robert Baratheon was a man of careless generosity, and would have given his son any dagger he wanted . . . but Tyrion guessed that the boy had just taken it. Robert had come to Winterfell with a long tail of knights and retainers, a huge wheelhouse, and a baggage train. No doubt some diligent servant had made certain that the king's weapons went with him, in case he should desire any of them.

The blade Joff chose was nice and plain. No goldwork, no jewels in the hilt, no silver inlay on the blade. King Robert never wore it, had likely forgotten he owned it. Yet the Valyrian steel was deadly sharp . . . sharp enough to slice through skin, flesh, and muscle in one quick stroke. *I am no stranger to Valyrian steel.* But he had been, hadn't he? Else he would never have been so foolish as to pick Littlefinger's knife.

The *why* of it still eluded him. *Simple cruelty, perhaps?* His nephew had that in abundance. It was all Tyrion could do not to retch up all the wine he'd drunk, piss in his breeches, or both. He squirmed uncomfortably. He ought to have held his tongue at breakfast. *The boy knows I know now. My big mouth will be the death of me, I swear it.*

The seven vows were made, the seven blessings invoked, and the seven promises exchanged. When the wedding song had been sung and the challenge had gone unanswered, it was time for the exchange of cloaks. Tyrion shifted his weight from one stunted leg to the other, trying to see between his father and his uncle Kevan. *If the gods are just, Joff will make a hash of this.* He made certain not to look at Sansa, lest his bitterness show in his eyes. *You might have knelt, damn you. Would it have been so bloody hard to bend those stiff Stark knees of yours and let me keep a little dignity?*

Mace Tyrell removed his daughter's maiden cloak tenderly, while Joffrey accepted the folded bride's cloak from his brother Tommen and shook it out with a flourish. The boy king was as tall at thirteen as his bride was at sixteen; he would not require a fool's back to climb upon. He draped Margaery in the crimson-and-gold and leaned close to fasten it at her throat. And that easily she passed from her father's protection to her husband's. *But who will protect her from Joff?* Tyrion glanced at the Knight of Flowers, standing with the other Kingsguard. *You had best keep your sword well honed, Ser Loras.*

"With this kiss I pledge my love!" Joffrey declared in ringing tones. When Margaery echoed the words he pulled her close and kissed her long and deep. Rainbow lights danced once more about the High Septon's crown as he solemnly declared Joffrey of the Houses Baratheon and Lannister and Margaery of House Tyrell to be one flesh, one heart, one soul.

Good, that's done with. Now let's get back to the bloody castle so I can have a piss.

Ser Loras and Ser Meryn led the procession from the sept in their white scale armor and snowy cloaks. Then came Prince Tommen, scattering rose petals from a basket before the king and queen. After the royal couple followed Queen Cersei and Lord Tyrell, then the bride's mother arm-in-arm with Lord Tywin. The Queen of Thorns tottered after them with one hand on Ser Kevan Lannister's arm and the other on her cane, her twin guardsmen close behind her in case she fell. Next came Ser Garlan Tyrell and his lady wife, and finally it was their turn.

"My lady." Tyrion offered Sansa his arm. She took it dutifully, but he could feel her stiffness as they walked up the aisle together. She never once looked down at him.

He heard them cheering outside even before he reached the doors. The mob loved Margaery so much they were even willing to love Joffrey again. She had belonged to Renly, the handsome young prince who had loved them so well he had come back from beyond the grave to save them. And the bounty of Highgarden had come with her, flowing up the roseroad from the south. The fools didn't seem to remember that it had been Mace Tyrell who *closed* the roseroad to begin with, and made the bloody famine.

They stepped out into the crisp autumn air. "I feared we'd never escape," Tyrion quipped.

Sansa had no choice but to look at him then. "I . . . yes, my lord. As you say." She looked sad. "It was such a beautiful ceremony, though."

As ours was not. "It was long, I'll say that much. I need to return to the castle for a good piss." Tyrion rubbed the stump of his nose. "Would that I'd contrived some mission to take me out of the city. Littlefinger was the clever one."

Joffrey and Margaery stood surrounded by Kingsguard atop the steps that fronted on the broad marble plaza. Ser Addam and his gold cloaks held back the crowd, while the statue of King Baelor the Blessed gazed down on them benevolently. Tyrion had no choice but to queue up with the rest to offer congratulations. He kissed Margaery's fingers and wished her every happiness. Thankfully, there were others behind them waiting their turn, so they did not need to linger long.

Their litter had been sitting in the sun, and it was very warm inside the curtains. As they lurched into motion, Tyrion reclined on an elbow while Sansa sat staring at her hands. *She is just as comely as the Tyrell girl.* Her hair was a rich autumn auburn, her eyes a deep Tully blue. Grief had given her a haunted, vulnerable look; if anything, it had only made her more beautiful. He wanted to reach her, to break through the armor of her courtesy. Was that what made him speak? Or just the need to distract himself from the fullness in his bladder?

"I had been thinking that when the roads are safe again, we might journey to Casterly Rock." *Far from Joffrey and my sister.* The more he thought about what Joff had done to *Lives of Four Kings*, the more it troubled him. *There was a message there, oh yes.* "It would please me to show you the Golden Gallery and the Lion's Mouth, and the Hall of Heroes where Jaime and I played as boys. You can hear thunder from below where the sea comes in . . ."

She raised her head slowly. He knew what she was seeing; the swollen brutish brow, the raw stump of his nose, his crooked pink scar and mismatched eyes. Her own eyes were big and blue and empty. "I shall go wherever my lord husband wishes."

"I had hoped it might please you, my lady."

"It will please me to please my lord."

His mouth tightened. *What a pathetic little man you are. Did you think babbling about the Lion's Mouth would make her smile? When have you ever made a woman smile but with gold?* "No, it was a foolish notion. Only a Lannister can love the Rock."

"Yes, my lord. As you wish."

Tyrion could hear the commons shouting out King Joffrey's name. *In three years that cruel boy will be a man, ruling in his own right . . . and every dwarf with half his wits will be a long way from King's Landing.* Oldtown, perhaps. Or even the Free Cities. He had always had a yen to see the Titan of Braavos. *Perhaps that would please Sansa.* Gently, he spoke of Braavos, and met a wall of sullen courtesy as icy and unyielding as the Wall he had walked once in the north. It made him weary. Then and now.

They passed the rest of the journey in silence. After a while, Tyrion found himself hoping that Sansa would say something, anything, the merest word, but she never spoke. When the litter halted in the castle yard, he let one of the grooms help her down. "We will be expected at the feast an hour hence, my lady. I will join you shortly." He walked off stiff-legged. Across the yard, he could hear Margaery's breathless laugh as Joffrey swept her from the saddle. *The boy will be as tall and strong as Jaime one day*, he thought, *and I'll still be a dwarf beneath his feet. And one day he's like to make me even shorter . . .*

He found a privy and sighed gratefully as he relieved himself of the morning's wine. There were times when a piss felt near as good as a woman, and this was one. He wished he could relieve himself of his doubts and guilts half as easily.

Podrick Payne was waiting outside his chambers. "I laid out your new doublet. Not here. On your bed. In the bedchamber."

"Yes, that's where we keep the bed." Sansa would be in there, dressing for the feast. *Shae as well.* "Wine, Pod."

Tyrion drank it in his window seat, brooding over the chaos of the kitchens below. The sun had not yet touched the top of the castle wall, but he could smell breads baking and meats roasting. The guests would soon be pouring into the throne room, full of anticipation; this would be an evening of song and splendor, designed not only to unite Highgarden and Casterly Rock but to trumpet their power and wealth as a lesson to any who might still think to oppose Joffrey's rule.

But who would be mad enough to contest Joffrey's rule now, after what had befallen Stannis Baratheon and Robb Stark? There was still fighting in the riverlands, but everywhere the coils were tightening. Ser Gregor Clegane had crossed the Trident and seized the ruby ford, then captured Harrenhal almost effortlessly. Seagard had yielded to Black Walder Frey, Lord Randyll Tarly held Maidenpool, Duskendale, and the kingsroad. In the west, Ser Daven Lannister had linked up with Ser Forley Prester at the Golden Tooth for a march on Riverrun. Ser Ryman Frey was leading two thousand spears down from the Twins to join them. And Paxter Redwyne claimed his fleet would soon set sail from the Arbor, to begin the long voyage around Dorne and through the Stepstones. Stannis's Lyseni pirates would be outnumbered ten to one. The struggle that the maesters were calling the War of the Five Kings was all but at an end. Mace Tyrell had been heard complaining that Lord Tywin had left no victories for him.

"My lord?" Pod was at his side. "Will you be changing? I laid out the doublet. On your bed. For the feast."

"Feast?" said Tyrion sourly. "What feast?"

"The wedding feast." Pod missed the sarcasm, of course. "King Joffrey and Lady Margaery. Queen Margaery, I mean."

Tyrion resolved to get very, very drunk tonight. "Very well, young Podrick, let us go make me festive."

Shae was helping Sansa with her hair when they entered the bedchamber. *Joy and grief,* he thought when he beheld them there together. *Laughter and tears.* Sansa wore a gown of silvery satin trimmed in vair, with dagged sleeves that almost touched the floor, lined in soft purple felt. Shae had arranged her hair artfully in a delicate silver net winking with dark purple gemstones. Tyrion had never seen her look more lovely, yet she wore sorrow on those long satin sleeves. "Lady Sansa," he told her, "you shall be the most beautiful woman in the hall tonight."

"My lord is too kind."

"My lady," said Shae wistfully. "Couldn't I come serve at table? I so want to see the pigeons fly out of the pie."

Sansa looked at her uncertainly. "The queen has chosen all the servers."

"And the hall will be too crowded." Tyrion had to bite back his annoyance. "There will be musicians strolling all through the castle, though, and tables in the outer ward with food and drink for all." He inspected his new doublet, crimson velvet with padded shoulders and puffed sleeves slashed to show the black satin underlining. *A handsome garment. All it wants is a handsome man to wear it.* "Come, Pod, help me into this."

He had another cup of wine as he dressed, then took his wife by the arm and escorted her from the Kitchen Keep to join the river of silk, satin, and velvet flowing toward the throne room. Some guests had gone inside to find their places on the benches. Others were milling in front of the doors, enjoying the unseasonable warmth of the afternoon. Tyrion led Sansa around the yard, to perform the necessary courtesies.

She is good at this, he thought, as he watched her tell Lord Gyles that his cough was sounding better, compliment Elinor Tyrell on her gown, and question Jalabhar Xho about wedding customs in the Summer Isles. His cousin Ser Lancel had been brought down by Ser

Kevan, the first time he'd left his sickbed since the battle. *He looks ghastly.* Lancel's hair had turned white and brittle, and he was thin as a stick. Without his father beside him holding him up, he would surely have collapsed. Yet when Sansa praised his valor and said how good it was to see him getting strong again, both Lancel and Ser Kevan beamed. *She would have made Joffrey a good queen and a better wife if he'd had the sense to love her.* He wondered if his nephew was capable of loving anyone.

"You do look quite exquisite, child," Lady Olenna Tyrell told Sansa when she tottered up to them in a cloth-of-gold gown that must have weighed more than she did. "The wind has been at your hair, though." The little old woman reached up and fussed at the loose strands, tucking them back into place and straightening Sansa's hair net. "I was very sorry to hear about your losses," she said as she tugged and fiddled. "Your brother was a terrible traitor, I know, but if we start killing men at weddings they'll be even more frightened of marriage than they are presently. There, that's better." Lady Olenna smiled. "I am pleased to say I shall be leaving for Highgarden the day after next. I have had quite enough of this smelly city, thank you. Perhaps you would like to accompany me for a little visit, whilst the men are off having their war? I shall miss my Margaery so dreadfully, and all her lovely ladies. Your company would be such sweet solace."

"You are too kind, my lady," said Sansa, "but my place is with my lord husband."

Lady Olenna gave Tyrion a wrinkled, toothless smile. "Oh? Forgive a silly old woman, my lord, I did not mean to steal your lovely wife. I assumed you would be off leading a Lannister host against some wicked foe."

"A host of dragons and stags. The master of coin must remain at court to see that all the armies are paid for."

"To be sure. Dragons and stags, that's very clever. And dwarf's pennies as well. I have heard of these dwarf's pennies. No doubt collecting those is *such* a dreadful chore."

"I leave the collecting to others, my lady."

"Oh, do you? I would have thought you might want to tend to it yourself. We can't have the crown being cheated of its dwarf's pennies, now. Can we?"

"Gods forbid." Tyrion was beginning to wonder whether Lord Luthor Tyrell had ridden off that cliff intentionally. "If you will excuse us, Lady Olenna, it is time we were in our places."

"Myself as well. Seventy-seven courses, I daresay. Don't you find that a bit *excessive*, my lord? I shan't eat more than three or four bites myself, but you and I are very little, aren't we?" She patted Sansa's hair again and said, "Well, off with you, child, and try to be merrier. Now where have my guardsmen gone? Left, Right, where are you? Come help me to the dais."

Although evenfall was still an hour away, the throne room was already a blaze of light, with torches burning in every sconce. The guests stood along the tables as heralds called out the names and titles of the lords and ladies making their entrance. Pages in the royal livery escorted them down the broad central aisle. The gallery above was packed with musicians; drummers and pipers and fiddlers, strings and horns and skins.

Tyrion clutched Sansa's arm and made the walk with a heavy waddling stride. He could feel their eyes on him, picking at the fresh new scar that had left him even uglier than he had been before. *Let them look*, he thought as he hopped up onto his seat. *Let them stare and whisper until they've had their fill, I will not hide myself for their sake.* The Queen of Thorns followed them in, shuffling along with tiny little steps. Tyrion wondered which of them looked more absurd, him with Sansa or the wizened little woman between her seven-foot-tall twin guardsmen.

Joffrey and Margaery rode into the throne room on matched white chargers. Pages ran before them, scattering rose petals under their hooves. The king and queen had changed for the feast as well. Joffrey wore striped black-and-crimson breeches and a cloth-of-gold doublet with black satin sleeves and onyx studs. Margaery had exchanged the demure gown that she had worn in the sept for one much more revealing, a confection in pale green samite with a tight-laced bodice that bared her shoulders and the tops of her small breasts. Unbound, her soft brown hair tumbled over her white shoulders and down her back almost to her waist. Around her brows was a slim golden crown. Her smile was shy and sweet. *A lovely girl*, thought Tyrion, *and a kinder fate than my nephew deserves.*

The Kingsguard escorted them onto the dais, to the seats of honor beneath the shadow of the Iron Throne, draped for the occasion in long silk streamers of Baratheon gold, Lannister crimson, and Tyrell green. Cersei embraced Margaery and kissed her cheeks. Lord Tywin did the same, and then Lancel and Ser Kevan. Joffrey received loving kisses from the bride's father and his two new brothers, Loras and Garlan. No one seemed in any great rush to kiss Tyrion. When the king and queen had taken their seats, the High Septon rose to lead a prayer. *At least he does not drone as badly as the last one*, Tyrion consoled himself.

He and Sansa had been seated far to the king's right, beside Ser Garlan Tyrell and his wife, the Lady Leonette. A dozen others sat closer to Joffrey, which a pricklier man might have taken for a slight, given that he had been the King's Hand only a short time past. Tyrion would have been glad if there had been a hundred.

"Let the cups be filled!" Joffrey proclaimed, when the gods had been given their due. His cupbearer poured a whole flagon of dark Arbor red into the golden wedding chalice that Lord Tyrell had given him that morning. The king had to use both hands to lift it. "*To my wife the queen!*"

"*Margaery!*" the hall shouted back at him. "*Margaery! Margaery! To the queen!*" A thousand cups rang together, and the wedding feast was well and truly begun. Tyrion Lannister drank with the rest, emptying his cup on that first toast and signaling for it to be refilled as soon as he was seated again.

The first dish was a creamy soup of mushrooms and buttered snails, served in gilded bowls. Tyrion had scarcely touched the breakfast, and the wine had already gone to his head, so the food was welcome. He finished quickly. *One done, seventy-six to come. Seventy-seven dishes, while there are still starving children in this city, and men who would kill for a radish. They might not love the Tyrells half so well if they could see us now.*

Sansa tasted a spoonful of soup and pushed the bowl away. "Not to your liking, my lady?" Tyrion asked.

"There's to be so much, my lord. I have a little tummy." She fiddled nervously with her hair and looked down the table to where Joffrey sat with his Tyrell queen.

Does she wish it were her in Margaery's place? Tyrion frowned. *Even a child should have better sense.* He turned away, wanting distraction, but everywhere he looked were women, fair fine beautiful happy women who belonged to other men. Margaery, of course, smiling sweetly as she and Joffrey shared a drink from the great seven-sided wedding chalice. Her mother Lady Alerie, silver-haired and handsome, still proud beside Mace Tyrell. The queen's three young cousins, bright as birds. Lord Merryweather's dark-haired Myrish wife with her big black sultry eyes. Ellaria Sand among the Dornishmen (Cersei had placed them at their own table, just below the dais in a place of high honor but as far from the Tyrells as the width of the hall would allow), laughing at something the Red Viper had told her.

And there was one woman, sitting almost at the foot of the third table on the left . . . the wife of one of the Fossoways, he thought, and heavy with his child. Her delicate beauty was in no way diminished by her belly, nor was her pleasure in the food and frolics. Tyrion watched as her husband fed her morsels off his plate. They drank from the same cup, and would kiss often and unpredictably. Whenever they did, his hand would gently rest upon her stomach, a tender and protective gesture.

He wondered what Sansa would do if he leaned over and kissed her right now. *Flinch away, most likely.* Or be brave and suffer through it, as was her duty. *She is nothing if not dutiful, this wife of mine.* If he told her that he wished to have her maidenhead tonight, she would suffer that dutifully as well, and weep no more than she had to.

He called for more wine. By the time he got it, the second course was being served, a pastry coffyn filled with pork, pine nuts, and eggs. Sansa ate no more than a bite of hers, as the heralds were summoning the first of the seven singers.

Grey-bearded Hamish the Harper announced that he would perform "for the ears of gods and men, a song ne'er heard before in all the Seven Kingdoms." He called it "Lord Renly's Ride."

His fingers moved across the strings of the high harp, filling the throne room with sweet sound. *"From his throne of bones the Lord of Death looked down on the murdered lord,"* Hamish began, and went on to tell how Renly, repenting his attempt to usurp his nephew's crown, had defied the Lord of Death himself and crossed back to the land of the living to defend the realm against his brother.

And for this poor Symon wound up in a bowl of brown, Tyrion mused. Queen Margaery was teary-eyed by the end, when the shade of brave Lord Renly flew to Highgarden to steal one last look at his true love's face. "Renly Baratheon never repented of anything in his life," the Imp told Sansa, "but if I'm any judge, Hamish just won himself a gilded lute."

The Harper also gave them several more familiar songs. "A Rose of Gold" was for the Tyrells, no doubt, as "The Rains of Castamere" was meant to flatter his father. "Maiden, Mother, and Crone" delighted the High Septon, and "My Lady Wife" pleased all the little girls with romance in their hearts, and no doubt some little boys as well. Tyrion listened with half a ear, as he sampled sweetcorn fritters and hot oatbread baked with bits of date, apple, and orange, and gnawed on the rib of a wild boar.

Thereafter, dishes and diversions succeeded one another in a staggering profusion, buoyed along upon a flood of wine and ale. Hamish left them, his place taken by a smallish elderly bear who danced clumsily to pipe and drum while the wedding guests ate trout cooked in a crust of crushed almonds. Moon Boy mounted his stilts and strode around the tables in pursuit of Lord Tyrell's ludicrously fat fool Butterbumps, and the lords and ladies sampled roast herons and cheese-and-onion pies. A troupe of Pentoshi tumblers performed cartwheels and handstands, balanced platters on their bare feet, and stood upon each other's shoulders to form a pyramid. Their feats were accompanied by crabs boiled in fiery eastern spices, trenchers filled with chunks of chopped mutton stewed in almond milk with carrots, raisins, and onions, and fish tarts fresh from the ovens, served so hot they burned the fingers.

Then the heralds summoned another singer; Collio Quaynis of Tyrosh, who had a vermilion beard and an accent as ludicrous as Symon had promised. Collio began with his version of "The Dance of the Dragons," which was more properly a song for two singers, male and female. Tyrion suffered through it with a double helping of honey-ginger partridge and several cups of wine. A haunting ballad of two dying lovers amidst the Doom of Valyria might have pleased the hall more if Collio had not sung it in High Valyrian, which most of the guests could not speak. But "Bessa the Barmaid" won them back with its ribald lyrics. Peacocks were served in their plumage, roasted whole and stuffed with dates, while Collio summoned a drummer, bowed low before Lord Tywin, and launched into "The Rains of Castamere."

If I have to hear seven versions of that, I may go down to Flea Bottom and apologize to the stew. Tyrion turned to his wife. "So which did you prefer?"

Sansa blinked at him. "My lord?"

"The singers. Which did you prefer?"

"I . . . I'm sorry, my lord. I was not listening."

She was not eating, either. "Sansa, is aught amiss?" He spoke without thinking, and instantly felt the fool. *All her kin are slaughtered and she's wed to me, and I wonder what's amiss.*

"No, my lord." She looked away from him, and feigned an unconvincing interest in Moon Boy pelting Ser Dontos with dates.

Four master pyromancers conjured up beasts of living flame to tear at each other with fiery claws whilst the serving men ladeled out bowls of blandissory, a mixture of beef broth and boiled wine sweetened with honey and dotted with blanched almonds and chunks of capon. Then came some strolling pipers and clever dogs and sword swallowers, with buttered pease, chopped nuts, and slivers of swan poached in a sauce of saffron and peaches. ("Not swan again," Tyrion muttered, remembering his supper with his sister on the eve of battle.) A juggler kept a half-dozen swords and axes whirling through the air as skewers of blood sausage were brought sizzling to the tables, a juxtaposition that Tyrion thought passing clever, though not perhaps in the best of taste.

The heralds blew their trumpets. "To sing for the golden lute," one cried, "we give you Galyeon of Cuy."

Galyeon was a big barrel-chested man with a black beard, a bald head, and a thunderous voice that filled every corner of the throne room. He brought no fewer than six musicians to play for him. "Noble lords and ladies fair, I sing but one song for you this night," he announced. "It is the song of the Blackwater, and how a realm was saved." The drummer began a slow ominous beat.

"*The dark lord brooded high in his tower,*" Galyeon began, "*in a castle as black as the night.*"

"*Black was his hair and black was his soul,*" the musicians chanted in unison. A flute came in.

"*He feasted on bloodlust and envy, and filled his cup full up with spite,*" sang Galyeon. "*My brother once ruled seven kingdoms, he said to his harridan wife. I'll take what was his and make it all mine. Let his son feel the point of my knife.*"

"*A brave young boy with hair of gold,*" his players chanted, as a woodharp and a fiddle began to play.

"If I am ever Hand again, the first thing I'll do is hang all the singers," said Tyrion, too loudly.

Lady Leonette laughed lightly beside him, and Ser Garlan leaned over to say, "A valiant deed unsung is no less valiant."

"*The dark lord assembled his legions, they gathered around him like crows. And thirsty for blood they boarded their ships . . .*"

". . . and cut off poor Tyrion's nose," Tyrion finished.

Lady Leonette giggled. "Perhaps you should be a singer, my lord. You rhyme as well as this Galyeon."

"No, my lady," Ser Garlan said. "My lord of Lannister was made to do great deeds, not to sing of them. But for his chain and his wildfire, the foe would have been across the river. And if Tyrion's wildlings had not slain most of Lord Stannis's scouts, we would never have been able to take him unawares."

His words made Tyrion feel absurdly grateful, and helped to mollify him as Galyeon sang endless verses about the valor of the boy king and his mother, the golden queen.

"She never did that," Sansa blurted out suddenly.

"Never believe anything you hear in a song, my lady." Tyrion summoned a serving man to refill their wine cups.

Soon it was full night outside the tall windows, and still Galyeon sang on. His song had seventy-seven verses, though it seemed more like a thousand. *One for every guest in the hall.* Tyrion drank his way through the last twenty or so, to help resist the urge to stuff mushrooms in his ears. By the time the singer had taken his bows, some of the guests were drunk enough to begin providing unintentional entertainments of their own. Grand Maester Pycelle fell asleep while dancers from the Summer Isles swirled and spun in robes made of bright feathers and smoky silk. Roundels of elk stuffed with ripe blue cheese were being brought out when one of Lord Rowan's knights stabbed a Dornishman. The gold cloaks dragged them both away, one to a cell to rot and the other to get sewn up by Maester Ballabar.

Tyrion was toying with a leche of brawn, spiced with cinnamon, cloves, sugar, and almond milk, when King Joffrey lurched suddenly to his feet. "*Bring on my royal jousters!*" he shouted in a voice thick with wine, clapping his hands together.

My nephew is drunker than I am, Tyrion thought as the gold cloaks opened the great doors at the end of the hall. From where he sat, he could only see the tops of two striped lances as a pair of riders entered side by side. A wave of laughter followed them down the center aisle toward the king. *They must be riding ponies*, he concluded ... until they came into full view.

The jousters were a pair of dwarfs. One was mounted on an ugly grey dog, long of leg and heavy of jaw. The other rode an immense spotted sow. Painted wooden armor clattered and clacked as the little knights bounced up and down in their saddles. Their shields were bigger than they were, and they wrestled manfully with their lances as they clomped along, swaying this way and that and eliciting gusts of mirth. One knight was all in gold, with a black stag painted on his shield; the other wore grey and white, and bore a wolf device. Their mounts were barded likewise.

Tyrion glanced along the dais at all the laughing faces. Joffrey was red and breathless, Tommen was hooting and hopping up and down in his seat, Cersei was chuckling politely, and even Lord Tywin looked mildly amused. Of all those at the high table, only Sansa Stark was not smiling. He could have loved her for that, but if truth be told the

Stark girl's eyes were far away, as if she had not even seen the ludicrous riders loping toward her.

The dwarfs are not to blame, Tyrion decided. *When they are done, I shall compliment them and give them a fat purse of silver. And come the morrow, I will find whoever planned this little diversion and arrange for a different sort of thanks.*

When the dwarfs reined up beneath the dais to salute the king, the wolf knight dropped his shield. As he leaned over to grab for it, the stag knight lost control of his heavy lance and slammed him across the back. The wolf knight fell off his pig, and his lance tumbled over and boinked his foe on the head. They both wound up on the floor in a great tangle. When they rose, both tried to mount the dog. Much shouting and shoving followed. Finally, they regained their saddles, only mounted on each other's steed, holding the wrong shield and facing backward.

It took some time to sort that out, but in the end they spurred to opposite ends of the hall, and wheeled about for the tilt. As the lords and ladies guffawed and giggled, the little men came together with a crash and a clatter, and the wolf knight's lance struck the helm of the stag knight and knocked his head clean off. It spun through the air spattering blood to land in the lap of Lord Gyles. The headless dwarf careened around the tables, flailing his arms. Dogs barked, women shrieked, and Moon Boy made a great show of swaying perilously back and forth on his stilts, until Lord Gyles pulled a dripping red melon out of the shattered helm, at which point the stag knight poked his face up out of his armor, and another storm of laughter rocked the hall. The knights waited for it to die, circled around each other trading colorful insults, and were about to separate for another joust when the dog threw its rider to the floor and mounted the sow. The huge pig squealed in distress, while the wedding guests squealed with laughter, especially when the stag knight leapt onto the wolf knight, let down his wooden breeches, and started to pump away frantically at the other's nether portions.

"I yield, I yield," the dwarf on the bottom screamed. "Good ser, put up your sword!"

"I would, I would, if you'll stop moving the sheath!" the dwarf on the top replied, to the merriment of all.

Joffrey was snorting wine from both nostrils. Gasping, he lurched to his feet, almost knocking over his tall two-handed chalice. "A champion," he shouted. "We have a champion!" The hall began to quiet when it was seen that the king was speaking. The dwarfs untangled, no doubt anticipating the royal thanks. "Not a *true* champion, though," said Joff. "A true champion defeats *all* challengers." The king climbed up on the table. "Who else will challenge our tiny champion?" With a gleeful smile, he turned toward Tyrion. "*Uncle!* You'll defend the honor of my realm, won't you? You can ride the pig!"

The laughter crashed over him like a wave. Tyrion Lannister did not remember rising, nor climbing on his chair, but he found himself standing on the table. The hall was a torchlit blur of leering faces. He twisted his face into the most hideous mockery of a smile the Seven Kingdoms had ever seen. "Your Grace," he called, "I'll ride the pig . . . but only if you ride the dog!"

Joff scowled, confused. "Me? I'm no dwarf. Why me?"

Stepped right into the cut, Joff. "Why, you're the only man in the hall that I'm certain of defeating!"

He could not have said which was sweeter; the instant of shocked silence, the gale of laughter that followed, or the look of blind rage on his nephew's face. The dwarf hopped back to the floor well satisfied, and by the time he looked back Ser Osmund and Ser Meryn were helping Joff climb down as well. When he noticed Cersei glaring at him, Tyrion blew her a kiss.

It was a relief when the musicians began to play. The tiny jousters led dog and sow from the hall, the guests returned to their trenchers of brawn, and Tyrion called for another cup of wine. But suddenly he felt Ser Garlan's hand on his sleeve. "My lord, beware," the knight warned. "The king."

Tyrion turned in his seat. Joffrey was almost upon him, red-faced and staggering, wine slopping over the rim of the great golden wedding chalice he carried in both hands. "Your Grace," was all he had time to say before the king upended the chalice over his head. The wine washed down over his face in a red torrent. It drenched his hair, stung his eyes, burned in his wound, ran down his cheeks, and soaked the velvet of his new doublet. "How do you like that, Imp?" Joffrey mocked.

Tyrion's eyes were on fire. He dabbed at his face with the back of a sleeve and tried to blink the world back into clarity. "That was ill done, Your Grace," he heard Ser Garlan say quietly.

"Not at all, Ser Garlan." Tyrion dare not let this grow any uglier than it was, not here, with half the realm looking on. "Not every king would think to honor a humble subject by serving him from his own royal chalice. A pity the wine spilled."

"It didn't *spill*," said Joffrey, too graceless to take the retreat Tyrion offered him. "And I wasn't *serving* you, either."

Queen Margaery appeared suddenly at Joffrey's elbow. "My sweet king," the Tyrell girl entreated, "come, return to your place, there's another singer waiting."

"Alaric of Eysen," said Lady Olenna Tyrell, leaning on her cane and taking no more notice of the wine-soaked dwarf than her granddaughter had done. "I do so hope he plays us 'The Rains of Castamere.' It has been an hour, I've forgotten how it goes."

"Ser Addam has a toast he wants to make as well," said Margaery. "Your Grace, please."

"I have no wine," Joffrey declared. "How can I drink a toast if I have no wine? Uncle Imp, you can serve me. Since you won't joust you'll be my cupbearer."

"I would be most honored."

"*It's not meant to be an honor!*" Joffrey screamed. "Bend down and pick up my chalice." Tyrion did as he was bid, but as he reached for the handle Joff kicked the chalice through his legs. "Pick it *up*! Are you as clumsy as you are ugly?" He had to crawl under the table to find the thing. "Good, now fill it with wine." He claimed a flagon from a serving girl and filled the goblet three-quarters full. "No, on your knees, dwarf." Kneeling, Tyrion raised up the heavy cup, wondering if he was about to get a second bath. But Joffrey took the wedding chalice one-handed, drank deep, and set it on the table. "You can get up now, Uncle."

His legs cramped as he tried to rise, and almost spilled him again. Tyrion had to grab hold of a chair to steady himself. Ser Garlan lent him a hand. Joffrey laughed, and Cersei as well. Then others. He could not see who, but he heard them.

"Your Grace." Lord Tywin's voice was impeccably correct. "They are bringing in the pie. Your sword is needed."

"The pie?" Joffrey took his queen by the hand. "Come, my lady, it's the pie."

The guests stood, shouting and applauding and smashing their wine cups together as the great pie made its slow way down the length of the hall, wheeled along by a half-dozen beaming cooks. Two yards across it was, crusty and golden brown, and they could hear squeaks and thumpings coming from inside it.

Tyrion pulled himself back into his chair. All he needed now was for a dove to shit on him and his day would be complete. The wine had soaked through his doublet and smallclothes, and he could feel the wetness against his skin. He ought to change, but no one was permitted to leave the feast until the time came for the bedding ceremony. That was still a good twenty or thirty dishes off, he judged.

King Joffrey and his queen met the pie below the dais. As Joff drew his sword, Margaery laid a hand on his arm to restrain him. "Widow's Wail was not meant for slicing pies."

"True." Joffrey lifted his voice. "Ser Ilyn, your sword!"

From the shadows at the back of the hall, Ser Ilyn Payne appeared. *The specter at the feast*, thought Tyrion as he watched the King's Justice stride forward, gaunt and grim. He had been too young to have known Ser Ilyn before he'd lost his tongue. *He would have been a different man in those days, but now the silence is as much a part of him as those hollow eyes, that rusty chainmail shirt, and the greatsword on his back.*

Ser Ilyn bowed before the king and queen, reached back over his shoulder, and drew forth six feet of ornate silver bright with runes. He knelt to offer the huge blade to Joffrey, hilt first; points of red fire winked from ruby eyes on the pommel, a chunk of dragonglass carved in the shape of a grinning skull.

Sansa stirred in her seat. "What sword is that?"

Tyrion's eyes still stung from the wine. He blinked and looked again. Ser Ilyn's greatsword was as long and wide as Ice, but it was too silvery-bright; Valyrian steel had a darkness to it, a smokiness in its soul. Sansa clutched his arm. "What has Ser Ilyn done with my father's sword?"

I should have sent Ice back to Robb Stark, Tyrion thought. He glanced at his father, but Lord Tywin was watching the king.

Joffrey and Margaery joined hands to lift the greatsword and swung it down together in a silvery arc. When the piecrust broke, the doves burst forth in a swirl of white feathers, scattering in every direction, flapping for the windows and the rafters. A roar of delight went up from the benches, and the fiddlers and pipers in the gallery began to play a sprightly tune. Joff took his bride in his arms, and whirled her around merrily.

A serving man placed a slice of hot pigeon pie in front of Tyrion and covered it with a spoon of lemon cream. The pigeons were well and truly cooked in *this* pie, but he found them no more appetizing than the white ones fluttering about the hall. Sansa was not eating either. "You're deathly pale, my lady," Tyrion said. "You need a breath of cool air, and I need a fresh doublet." He stood and offered her his hand. "Come."

But before they could make their retreat, Joffrey was back. "Uncle, where are you going? You're my cupbearer, remember?"

"I need to change into fresh garb, Your Grace. May I have your leave?"

"No. I like the look of you this way. Serve me my wine."

The king's chalice was on the table where he'd left it. Tyrion had to climb back onto his chair to reach it. Joff yanked it from his hands and drank long and deep, his throat working as the wine ran purple down his chin. "My lord," Margaery said, "we should return to our places. Lord Buckler wants to toast us."

"My uncle hasn't eaten his pigeon pie." Holding the chalice one-handed, Joff jammed his other into Tyrion's pie. "It's ill luck not to eat the pie," he scolded as he filled his mouth with hot spiced pigeon. "See, it's good." Spitting out flakes of crust, he coughed and helped himself to another fistful. "Dry, though. Needs washing down." Joff took a swallow of wine and coughed again, more violently. "I want to see, *kof*, see you ride that, *kof kof*, pig, Uncle. I want . . ." His words broke up in a fit of coughing.

Margaery looked at him with concern. "Your Grace?"

"It's, *kof*, the pie, noth—*kof*, pie." Joff took another drink, or tried to, but all the wine came spewing back out when another spate of coughing doubled him over. His face was turning red. "I, *kof*, I can't, *kof kof kof kof* ..." The chalice slipped from his hand and dark red wine went running across the dais.

"He's choking," Queen Margaery gasped.

Her grandmother moved to her side. "Help the poor boy!" the Queen of Thorns screeched, in a voice ten times her size. "*Dolts!* Will you all stand about gaping? *Help* your king!"

Ser Garlan shoved Tyrion aside and began to pound Joffrey on the back. Ser Osmund Kettleblack ripped open the king's collar. A fearful high thin sound emerged from the boy's throat, the sound of a man trying to suck a river through a reed; then it stopped, and that was more terrible still. "Turn him over!" Mace Tyrell bellowed at everyone and no one. "Turn him over, shake him by his heels!" A different voice was calling, "Water, give him some *water!*" The High Septon began to pray loudly. Grand Maester Pycelle shouted for someone to help him back to his chambers, to fetch his potions. Joffrey began to claw at his throat, his nails tearing bloody gouges in the flesh. Beneath the skin, the muscles stood out hard as stone. Prince Tommen was screaming and crying.

He is going to die, Tyrion realized. He felt curiously calm, though pandemonium raged all about him. They were pounding Joff on the back again, but his face was only growing darker. Dogs were barking, children were wailing, men were shouting useless advice at each other. Half the wedding guests were on their feet, some shoving at each other for a better view, others rushing for the doors in their haste to get away.

Ser Meryn pried the king's mouth open to jam a spoon down his throat. As he did, the boy's eyes met Tyrion's. *He has Jaime's eyes.* Only he had never seen Jaime look so scared. *The boy's only thirteen.* Joffrey was making a dry clacking noise, trying to speak. His eyes bulged white with terror, and he lifted a hand ... reaching for his uncle, or pointing ... *Is he begging my forgiveness, or does he think I can save him?* "Noooo," Cersei wailed, "Father help him, someone help him, my son, my *son* ..."

Tyrion found himself thinking of Robb Stark. *My own wedding is looking much better in hindsight.* He looked to see how Sansa was taking this, but there was so much confusion in the hall that he could not find her. But his eyes fell on the wedding chalice, forgotten on the floor. He went and scooped it up. There was still a half-inch of deep purple wine in the bottom of it. Tyrion considered it a moment, then poured it on the floor.

Margaery Tyrell was weeping in her grandmother's arms as the old lady said, "Be brave, be brave." Most of the musicians had fled, but one last flutist in the gallery was blowing a dirge. In the rear of the throne room scuffling had broken out around the doors, and the guests were trampling on each other. Ser Addam's gold cloaks moved in to restore order. Guests were rushing headlong out into the night, some weeping, some stumbling and retching, others white with fear. It occurred to Tyrion belatedly that it might be wise to leave himself.

When he heard Cersei's scream, he knew that it was over.

I should leave. Now. Instead, he waddled toward her.

His sister sat in a puddle of wine, cradling her son's body. Her gown was torn and stained, her face white as chalk. A thin black dog crept up beside her, sniffing at Joffrey's corpse. "The boy is gone, Cersei," Lord Tywin said. He put his gloved hand on his daughter's shoulder as one of his guardsmen shooed away the dog. "Unhand him now. Let him go." She did not hear. It took two Kingsguard to pry loose her fingers, so the body of King Joffrey Baratheon could slide limp and lifeless to the floor.

The High Septon knelt beside him. "Father Above, judge our good King Joffrey justly," he intoned, beginning the prayer for the dead. Margaery Tyrell began to sob, and Tyrion heard her mother Lady Alerie saying, "He choked, sweetling. He choked on the pie. It was naught to do with you. He choked. We all saw."

"He did not choke." Cersei's voice was sharp as Ser Ilyn's sword. "My son was poisoned." She looked to the white knights standing helplessly around her. "Kingsguard, do your duty."

"My lady?" said Ser Loras Tyrell, uncertain.

"Arrest my brother," she commanded him. "He did this, the dwarf. Him and his little wife. They killed my son. Your king. *Take them!* Take them both!"

SANSA

Far across the city, a bell began to toll.

Sansa felt as though she were in a dream.

"Joffrey is dead," she told the trees, to see if that would wake her.

He had not been dead when she left the throne room. He had been on his knees, though, clawing at his throat, tearing at his own skin as he fought to breathe. The sight of it had been too terrible to watch, and she had turned and fled, sobbing. Lady Tanda had been fleeing as well. "You have a good heart, my lady," she said to Sansa. "Not every maid would weep so for a man who set her aside and wed her to a dwarf."

A good heart. I have a good heart. Hysterical laughter rose up her gullet, but Sansa choked it back down. The bells were ringing, slow and mournful. Ringing, ringing, ringing. They had rung for King Robert the same way. Joffrey was dead, he was dead, he was dead, dead, dead. Why was she crying, when she wanted to dance? Were they tears of joy?

She found her clothes where she had hidden them, the night before last. With no maids to help her, it took her longer than it should have to undo the laces of her gown. Her hands were strangely clumsy, though she was not as frightened as she ought to have been. "The gods are cruel to take him so young and handsome, at his own wedding feast," Lady Tanda had said to her.

The gods are just, thought Sansa. Robb had died at a wedding feast as well. It was Robb she wept for. *Him and Margaery.* Poor Margaery, twice wed and twice widowed. Sansa slid her arm from a sleeve, pushed down the gown, and wriggled out of it. She balled it up and shoved it into the bole of an oak, shook out the clothing she had hidden there. *Dress warmly,* Ser Dontos had told her, *and dress dark.* She had no blacks, so she chose a dress of thick brown wool. The bodice was decorated with freshwater pearls, though. *The cloak will cover them.* The cloak was a deep green, with a large hood. She slipped the dress over her head, and donned the cloak, though she left the hood down for the moment. There were shoes as well, simple and sturdy, with flat heels and square toes. *The gods heard my prayer,* she thought. She felt so numb and dreamy. *My skin has turned to porcelain, to ivory, to steel.* Her hands moved stiffly, awkwardly, as if they had never let down her hair before. For a moment she wished Shae was there, to help her with the net.

When she pulled it free, her long auburn hair cascaded down her back and across her shoulders. The web of spun silver hung from her fingers, the fine metal glimmering softly, the stones black in the moonlight. *Black amethysts from Asshai.* One of them was missing. Sansa lifted the net for a closer look. There was a dark smudge in the silver socket where the stone had fallen out.

A sudden terror filled her. Her heart hammered against her ribs, and for an instant she held her breath. *Why am I so scared, it's only an amethyst, a black amethyst from Asshai, no more than that. It must have been loose in the setting, that's all. It was loose and it fell out, and now it's lying somewhere in the throne room, or in the yard, unless . . .*

Ser Dontos had said the hair net was magic, that it would take her home. He told her she must wear it tonight at Joffrey's wedding feast. The silver wire stretched tight across her knuckles. Her thumb rubbed back and forth against the hole where the stone had been. She tried to stop, but her fingers were not her own. Her thumb was drawn to the hole as the tongue is drawn to a missing tooth. *What kind of magic?* The king was dead, the cruel king who had been her gallant prince a thousand years ago. If Dontos had lied about the hair net, had he lied about the rest as well? *What if he never comes? What if there is no ship, no boat on the river, no escape?* What would happen to her then?

She heard a faint rustle of leaves, and stuffed the silver hair net down deep in the pocket of her cloak. "Who's there?" she cried. "Who is it?" The godswood was dim and dark, and the bells were ringing Joff into his grave.

"Me." He staggered out from under the trees, reeling drunk. He caught her arm to steady himself. "Sweet Jonquil, I've come. Your Florian has come, don't be afraid."

Sansa pulled away from his touch. "You said I must wear the hair net. The silver net with . . . what sort of stones are those?"

"Amethysts. Black amethysts from Asshai, my lady."

"They're no amethysts. Are they? *Are they?* You lied."

"Black amethysts," he swore. "There was magic in them."

"There was *murder* in them!"

"Softly, my lady, softly. No murder. He choked on his pigeon pie." Dontos chortled. "Oh, tasty tasty pie. Silver and stones, that's all it was, silver and stone and magic."

The bells were tolling, and the wind was making a noise like *he* had made as he tried to suck a breath of air. "You poisoned him. You did. You took a stone from my hair . . ."

"Hush, you'll be the death of us. I did nothing. Come, we must away, they'll search for you. Your husband's been arrested."

"Tyrion?" she said, shocked.

"Do you have another husband? The Imp, the dwarf uncle, she thinks he did it." He grabbed her hand and pulled at her. "This way, we must away, quickly now, have no fear."

Sansa followed unresisting. *I could never abide the weeping of women,* Joff once said, but his mother was the only woman weeping now. In Old Nan's stories the grumkins crafted magic things that could make a wish come true. *Did I wish him dead?* she wondered, before she remembered that she was too old to believe in grumkins. "*Tyrion* poisoned him?" Her dwarf husband had hated his nephew, she knew. Could he truly have killed him? *Did he know about my hair net, about the black amethysts? He brought Joff wine.* How could you make someone choke by putting an amethyst in their wine? *If Tyrion did it, they will think I was part of it as well,* she realized with a start of fear. How not? They were man and wife, and Joff had killed her father and mocked her with her brother's death. *One flesh, one heart, one soul.*

"Be quiet now, my sweetling," said Dontos. "Outside the godswood, we must make no sound. Pull up your hood and hide your face." Sansa nodded, and did as he said.

He was so drunk that sometimes Sansa had to lend him her arm to keep him from falling. The bells were ringing out across the city, more and more of them joining in. She kept her head down and stayed in the shadows, close behind Dontos. While descending the serpentine steps he stumbled to his knees and retched. *My poor Florian,* she thought, as he wiped his mouth with a floppy sleeve. *Dress dark,* he'd said, yet under his brown hooded cloak he was wearing his old surcoat; red and pink horizontal stripes beneath a black chief bearing three gold crowns, the arms of House Hollard. "Why are you wearing your surcoat? Joff decreed it was death if you were caught dressed as a knight again, he . . . oh . . ." Nothing Joff had decreed mattered any longer.

"I wanted to be a knight. For this, at least." Dontos lurched back to his feet and took her arm. "Come. Be quiet now, no questions."

They continued down the serpentine and across a small sunken courtyard. Ser Dontos shoved open a heavy door and lit a taper. They were inside a long gallery. Along the walls stood empty suits of armor, dark and dusty, their helms crested with rows of scales that continued down their backs. As they hurried past, the taper's light made the shadows of each scale stretch and twist. *The hollow knights are turning into dragons,* she thought.

One more stair took them to an oaken door banded with iron. "Be strong now, my Jonquil, you are almost there." When Dontos lifted the bar and pulled open the door, Sansa felt a cold breeze on her face. She passed through twelve feet of wall, and then she was outside the castle, standing at the top of the cliff. Below was the river, above the sky, and one was as black as the other.

"We must climb down," Ser Dontos said. "At the bottom, a man is waiting to row us out to the ship."

"I'll fall." Bran had fallen, and he had loved to climb.

"No you won't. There's a sort of ladder, a secret ladder, carved into the stone. Here, you can feel it, my lady." He got down on his knees with her and made her lean over the edge of the cliff, groping with her fingers until she found the handhold cut into the face of the bluff. "Almost as good as rungs."

Even so, it was a long way down. "I *can't.*"

"You must."

"Isn't there another way?"

"This is the way. It won't be so hard for a strong young girl like you. Hold on tight and never look down and you'll be at the bottom in no time at all." His eyes were shiny. "Your poor Florian is fat and old and drunk, I'm the one should be afraid. I used to fall off my horse, don't you remember? That was how we began. I was drunk and fell off my horse and Joffrey wanted my fool head, but you saved me. You *saved* me, sweetling."

He's weeping, she realized. "And now you have saved me."

"Only if you go. If not, I have killed us both."

It was him, she thought. *He killed Joffrey.* She had to go, for him as much as for herself. "You go first, ser." If he *did* fall, she did not want him falling down on her head and knocking both of them off the cliff.

"As you wish, my lady." He gave her a sloppy kiss and swung his legs clumsily over the precipice, kicking about until he found a foothold. "Let me get down a bit, and come after. You will come now? You must swear it."

"I'll come," she promised.

Ser Dontos disappeared. She could hear him huffing and puffing as he began the descent. Sansa listened to the tolling of the bell, counting each ring. At ten, gingerly, she eased herself over the edge of the cliff, poking with her toes until they found a place to rest. The castle walls loomed large above her, and for a moment she wanted nothing so much as to pull herself up and run back to her warm rooms in the Kitchen Keep. *Be brave*, she told herself. *Be brave, like a lady in a song.*

Sansa dared not look down. She kept her eyes on the face of the cliff, making certain of each step before reaching for the next. The stone was rough and cold. Sometimes she could feel her fingers slipping, and the handholds were not as evenly spaced as she would have liked. The bells would not stop ringing. Before she was halfway down her arms were trembling and she knew that she was going to fall. *One more step*, she told herself, *one more step*. She had to keep moving. If she stopped, she would never start again, and dawn would find her still clinging to the cliff, frozen in fear. *One more step, and one more step*.

The ground took her by surprise. She stumbled and fell, her heart pounding. When she rolled onto her back and stared up at from where she had come, her head swam dizzily and her fingers clawed at the dirt. *I did it. I did it, I didn't fall, I made the climb and now I'm going home.*

Ser Dontos pulled her back onto her feet. "This way. Quiet now, quiet, quiet." He stayed close to the shadows that lay black and thick beneath the cliffs. Thankfully they did not have to go far. Fifty yards downriver, a man sat in a small skiff, half-hidden by the remains of a great galley that had gone aground there and burned. Dontos limped up to him, puffing. "Oswell?"

"No names," the man said. "In the boat." He sat hunched over his oars, an old man, tall and gangling, with long white hair and a great hooked nose, with eyes shaded by a cowl. "Get in, be quick about it," he muttered. "We need to be away."

When both of them were safe aboard, the cowled man slid the blades into the water and put his back into the oars, rowing them out toward the channel. Behind them the bells were still tolling the boy king's death. They had the dark river all to themselves.

With slow, steady, rhythmic strokes, they threaded their way downstream, sliding above the sunken galleys, past broken masts, burned hulls, and torn sails. The oarlocks had been muffled, so they moved almost soundlessly. A mist was rising over the water. Sansa saw the embattled ramparts of one of the Imp's winch towers looming above, but the great chain had been lowered, and they rowed un-impeded past the spot where a thousand men had burned. The shore fell away, the fog grew thicker, the sound of the bells began to fade.

Finally, even the lights were gone, lost somewhere behind them. They were out in Blackwater Bay, and the world shrank to dark water, blowing mist, and their silent companion stooped over the oars. "How far must we go?" she asked.

"No talk." The oarsman was old, but stronger than he looked, and his voice was fierce. There was something oddly familiar about his face, though Sansa could not say what it was.

"Not far." Ser Dontos took her hand in his own and rubbed it gently. "Your friend is near, waiting for you."

"*No talk!*" the oarsman growled again. "Sound carries over water, Ser Fool."

Abashed, Sansa bit her lip and huddled down in silence. The rest was rowing, rowing, rowing.

The eastern sky was vague with the first hint of dawn when Sansa finally saw a ghostly shape in the darkness ahead; a trading galley, her sails furled, moving slowly on a single bank of oars. As they drew closer, she saw the ship's figurehead, a merman with a golden crown blowing on a great seashell horn. She heard a voice cry out, and the galley swung slowly about.

As they came alongside, the galley dropped a rope ladder over the rail. The rower shipped the oars and helped Sansa to her feet. "Up now. Go on, girl, I got you." Sansa thanked him for his kindness, but received no answer but a grunt. It was much easier going up the rope ladder than it had been coming down the cliff. The oarsman Oswell followed close behind her, while Ser Dontos remained in the boat.

Two sailors were waiting by the rail to help her onto the deck. Sansa was trembling. "She's cold," she heard someone say. He took off his cloak and put it around her shoulders. "There, is that better, my lady? Rest easy, the worst is past and done."

She knew the voice. *But he's in the Vale,* she thought. Ser Lothor Brune stood beside him with a torch.

"Lord Petyr," Dontos called from the boat. "I must needs row back, before they think to look for me."

Petyr Baelish put a hand on the rail. "But first you'll want your payment. Ten thousand dragons, was it?"

"Ten thousand." Dontos rubbed his mouth with the back of his hand. "As you promised, my lord."

"Ser Lothor, the reward."

Lothor Brune dipped his torch. Three men stepped to the gunwale, raised crossbows, fired. One bolt took Dontos in the chest as he looked up, punching through the left crown on his surcoat. The others ripped into throat and belly. It happened so quickly neither Dontos nor Sansa had time to cry out. When it was done, Lothor Brune tossed the torch down on top of the corpse. The little boat was blazing fiercely as the galley moved away.

"You *killed* him." Clutching the rail, Sansa turned away and retched. Had she escaped the Lannisters to tumble into worse?

"My lady," Littlefinger murmured, "your grief is wasted on such a man as that. He was a sot, and no man's friend."

"But he *saved* me."

"He sold you for a promise of ten thousand dragons. Your disappearance will make them suspect you in Joffrey's death. The gold cloaks will hunt, and the eunuch will jingle his purse. Dontos . . . well, you heard him. He sold you for gold, and when he'd drunk it up he would have sold you again. A bag of dragons buys a man's silence for a while, but a well-placed quarrel buys it forever." He smiled sadly. "All he did he did at my behest. I dared not befriend you openly. When I heard how you saved his life at Joff's tourney, I knew he would be the perfect catspaw."

Sansa felt sick. "He said he was my Florian."

"Do you perchance recall what I said to you that day your father sat the Iron Throne?"

The moment came back to her vividly. "You told me that life was not a song. That I would learn that one day, to my sorrow." She felt tears in her eyes, but whether she wept for Ser Dontos Hollard, for Joff, for Tyrion, or for herself, Sansa could not say. "Is it *all* lies, forever and ever, everyone and everything?"

"Almost everyone. Save you and I, of course." He smiled. "*Come to the godswood tonight if you want to go home.*"

"The note . . . it was you?"

"It had to be the godswood. No other place in the Red Keep is safe from the eunuch's little birds ... or little rats, as I call them. There are trees in the godswood instead of walls. Sky above instead of ceiling. Roots and dirt and rock in place of floor. The rats have no place to scurry. Rats need to hide, lest men skewer them with swords." Lord Petyr took her arm. "Let me show you to your cabin. You have had a long and trying day, I know. You must be weary."

Already the little boat was no more than a swirl of smoke and fire behind them, almost lost in the immensity of the dawn sea. There was no going back; her only road was forward. "Very weary," she admitted.

As he led her below, he said, "Tell me of the feast. The queen took such pains. The singers, the jugglers, the dancing bear ... did your little lord husband enjoy my jousting dwarfs?"

"Yours?"

"I had to send to Braavos for them and hide them away in a brothel until the wedding. The expense was exceeded only by the bother. It is surprisingly difficult to hide a dwarf, and Joffrey ... you can lead a king to water, but with Joff one had to splash it about before he realized he could drink it. When I told him about my little surprise, His Grace said, 'Why would I want some ugly dwarfs at my feast? I hate dwarfs.' I had to take him by the shoulder and whisper, 'Not as much as your uncle will.'"

The deck rocked beneath her feet, and Sansa felt as if the world itself had grown unsteady. "They think Tyrion poisoned Joffrey. Ser Dontos said they seized him."

Littlefinger smiled. "Widowhood will become you, Sansa."

The thought made her tummy flutter. She might never need to share a bed with Tyrion again. That *was* what she'd wanted ... wasn't it?

The cabin was low and cramped, but a featherbed had been laid upon the narrow sleeping shelf to make it more comfortable, and thick furs piled atop it. "It will be snug, I know, but you shouldn't be too uncomfortable." Littlefinger pointed out a cedar chest under the porthole. "You'll find fresh garb within. Dresses, smallclothes, warm stockings, a cloak. Wool and linen only, I fear. Unworthy of a maid so beautiful, but they'll serve to keep you dry and clean until we can find you something finer."

He had this all prepared for me. "My lord, I . . . I do not understand . . . Joffrey gave you Harrenhal, made you Lord Paramount of the Trident . . . why . . ."

"Why should I wish him dead?" Littlefinger shrugged. "I had no motive. Besides, I am a thousand leagues away in the Vale. Always keep your foes confused. If they are never certain who you are or what you want, they cannot know what you are like to do next. Sometimes the best way to baffle them is to make moves that have no purpose, or even seem to work against you. Remember that, Sansa, when you come to play the game."

"What . . . what game?"

"The only game. The game of thrones." He brushed back a strand of her hair. "You are old enough to know that your mother and I were more than friends. There was a time when Cat was all I wanted in this world. I dared to dream of the life we might make and the children she would give me . . . but she was a daughter of Riverrun, and Hoster Tully. *Family, Duty, Honor,* Sansa. *Family, Duty, Honor* meant I could never have her hand. But she gave me something finer, a gift a woman can give but once. How could I turn my back upon her daughter? In a better world, you might have been mine, not Eddard Stark's. My loyal loving daughter . . . Put Joffrey from your mind, sweetling. Dontos, Tyrion, all of them. They will never trouble you again. You are safe now, that's all that matters. You are safe with me, and sailing home."

JAIME

The king is dead, they told him, never knowing that Joffrey was his son as well as his sovereign.

"The Imp opened his throat with a dagger," a costermonger declared at the roadside inn where they spent the night. "He drank his blood from a big gold chalice." The man did not recognize the bearded one-handed knight with the big bat on his shield, no more than any of them, so he said things he might otherwise have swallowed, had he known who was listening.

"It was poison did the deed," the innkeep insisted. "The boy's face turned black as a plum."

"May the Father judge him justly," murmured a septon.

"The dwarf's wife did the murder with him," swore an archer in Lord Rowan's livery. "Afterward, she vanished from the hall in a puff of brimstone, and a ghostly direwolf was seen prowling the Red Keep, blood dripping from his jaws."

Jaime sat silent through it all, letting the words wash over him, a horn of ale forgotten in his one good hand. *Joffrey. My blood. My firstborn. My son.* He tried to bring the boy's face to mind, but his features kept turning into Cersei's. *She will be in mourning, her hair in disarray and her eyes red from crying, her mouth trembling as she tries to speak. She will cry again when she sees me, though she'll fight the tears.* His sister seldom wept but when she was with him. She could not stand for others to think her weak. Only to her twin did she show her wounds. *She will look to me for comfort and revenge.*

They rode hard the next day, at Jaime's insistence. His son was dead, and his sister needed him.

When he saw the city before him, its watchtowers dark against the gathering dusk, Jaime Lannister cantered up to Steelshanks Walton, behind Nage with the peace banner.

"What's that awful stink?" the northman complained.

Death, thought Jaime, but he said, "Smoke, sweat, and shit. King's Landing, in short. If you have a good nose you can smell the treachery too. You've never smelled a city before?"

"I smelled White Harbor. It never stank like this."

"White Harbor is to King's Landing as my brother Tyrion is to Ser Gregor Clegane."

Nage led them up a low hill, the seven-tailed peace banner lifting and turning in the wind, the polished seven-pointed star shining bright upon its staff. He would see Cersei soon, and Tyrion, and their father. *Could my brother truly have killed the boy?* Jaime found that hard to believe.

He was curiously calm. Men were supposed to go mad with grief when their children died, he knew. They were supposed to tear their hair out by the roots, to curse the gods and swear red vengeance. So why was it that he felt so little? *The boy lived and died believing Robert Baratheon his sire.*

Jaime had seen him born, that was true, though more for Cersei than the child. But he had never held him. "How would it look?" his sister warned him when the women finally left them. "Bad enough Joff looks like you without you mooning over him." Jaime yielded with hardly a fight. The boy had been a squalling pink thing who demanded too much of Cersei's time, Cersei's love, and Cersei's breasts. Robert was welcome to him.

And now he's dead. He pictured Joff lying still and cold with a face black from poison, and still felt nothing. Perhaps he *was* the monster they claimed. If the Father Above came down to offer him back his son or his hand, Jaime knew which he would choose. He had a second son, after all, and seed enough for many more. *If Cersei wants another child, I'll give her one . . . and this time I'll hold him, and the Others take those who do not like it.* Robert was rotting in his grave, and Jaime was sick of lies.

He turned abruptly and galloped back to find Brienne. *Gods know why I bother. She is the least companionable creature I've ever had the misfortune to meet.* The wench rode well behind and a few feet off to the side, as if to proclaim that she was no part of them. They had found men's garb for her along the way; a tunic here, a mantle there, a pair of breeches and a cowled cloak, even an old iron breastplate. She looked more comfortable dressed as a man, but nothing would ever make her look handsome. *Nor happy.* Once out of Harrenhal, her usual pighead stubbornness had soon reasserted itself. "I want my arms and armor back," she had insisted. "Oh, by all means, let us have you back in steel," Jaime replied. "A helm, especially. We'll all be happier if you keep your mouth shut and your visor down."

That much Brienne could do, but her sullen silences soon began to fray his good humor almost as much as Qyburn's endless attempts to be ingratiating. *I never thought I would find myself missing the company of Cleos Frey, gods help me.* He was beginning to wish he had left her for the bear after all.

"King's Landing," Jaime announced when he found her. "Our journey's done, my lady. You've kept your vow, and delivered me to King's Landing. All but a few fingers and a hand."

Brienne's eyes were listless. "That was only half my vow. I told Lady Catelyn I would bring her back her daughters. Or Sansa, at the least. And now . . ."

She never met Robb Stark, yet her grief for him runs deeper than mine for Joff. Or perhaps it was Lady Catelyn she mourned. They had been at Brindlewood when they had *that* news, from a red-faced tub of a knight named Ser Bertram Beesbury, whose arms were three beehives on a field striped black and yellow. A troop of Lord Piper's men had passed through Brindlewood only yesterday, Beesbury told them, rushing to King's Landing beneath a peace banner of their own. "With the Young Wolf dead Piper saw no point to fighting on. His son is captive at the Twins." Brienne gaped like a cow about to choke on her cud, so it fell to Jaime to draw out the tale of the Red Wedding.

"Every great lord has unruly bannermen who envy him his place," he told her afterward. "My father had the Reynes and Tarbecks, the Tyrells have the Florents, Hoster Tully had Walder Frey. Only strength keeps such men in their place. The moment they smell weakness . . . during the Age of Heroes, the Boltons used to flay the Starks and wear their skins as cloaks." She looked so miserable that Jaime almost found himself wanting to comfort her.

Since that day Brienne had been like one half-dead. Even calling her "wench" failed to provoke any response. *The strength is gone from her.* The woman had dropped a rock on Robin Ryger, battled a bear with a tourney sword, bitten off Vargo Hoat's ear, and fought Jaime to exhaustion . . . but she was broken now, done. "I'll speak to my father about returning you to Tarth, if it please you," he told her. "Or if you would rather stay, I could perchance find some place for you at court."

"As a lady companion to the queen?" she said dully.

Jaime remembered the sight of her in that pink satin gown, and tried not to imagine what his sister might say of such a companion. "Perhaps a post with the City Watch . . ."

"I will not serve with oathbreakers and murderers."

Then why did you ever bother putting on a sword? he might have said, but he bit back the words. "As you will, Brienne." One-handed, he wheeled his horse about and left her.

The Gate of the Gods was open when they reached it, but two dozen wayns were lined up along the roadside, loaded with casks of cider, barrels of apples, bales of hay, and some of the biggest pumpkins Jaime had ever seen. Almost every wagon had its guards; men-at-arms wearing the badges of small lordlings, sellswords in mail and boiled leather, sometimes only a pink-cheeked farmer's son clutching a home-made spear with a fire-hardened point. Jaime smiled at them all as he trotted past. At the gate, the gold cloaks were collecting coin from each driver before waving the wagons through. "What's this?" Steelshanks demanded.

"They got to pay for the right to sell inside the city. By command of the King's Hand and the master of coin."

Jaime looked at the long line of wayns, carts, and laden horses. "Yet they still line up to pay?"

"There's good coin to be made here now that the fighting's done," the miller in the nearest wagon told them cheerfully. "It's the Lannisters hold the city now, old Lord Tywin of the Rock. They say he shits silver."

"Gold," Jaime corrected dryly. "And Littlefinger mints the stuff from goldenrod, I vow."

"The Imp is master of coin now," said the captain of the gate. "Or was, till they arrested him for murdering the king." The man looked the northmen over suspiciously. "Who are you lot?"

"Lord Bolton's men, come to see the King's Hand."

The captain glanced at Nage with his peace banner. "Come to bend the knee, you mean. You're not the first. Go straight up to the castle, and see you make no trouble." He waved them through and turned back to the wagons.

If King's Landing mourned its dead boy king, Jaime would never have known it. On the Street of Seeds a begging brother in threadbare robes was praying loudly for Joffrey's soul, but the passersby paid him no more heed than they would a loose shutter banging in the wind. Elsewhere milled the usual crowds; gold cloaks in their black mail, bakers' boys selling tarts and breads and hot pies, whores leaning out of windows with their bodices half unlaced, gutters redolent of nightsoil. They passed five men trying to drag a dead horse from the mouth of an alley, and elsewhere a juggler spinning knives through the air to delight a throng of drunken Tyrell soldiers and small children.

Riding down familiar streets with two hundred northmen, a chainless maester, and an ugly freak of a woman at his side, Jaime found he scarcely drew a second look. He did not know whether he ought to be amused or annoyed. "They do not know me," he said to Steelshanks as they rode through Cobbler's Square.

"Your face is changed, and your arms as well," the northman said, "and they have a new Kingslayer now."

The gates to the Red Keep were open, but a dozen gold cloaks armed with pikes barred the way. They lowered their points as Steelshanks came trotting up, but Jaime recognized the white knight commanding them. "Ser Meryn."

Ser Meryn Trant's droopy eyes went wide. "Ser Jaime?"

"How nice to be remembered. Move these men aside."

It had been a long time since anyone had leapt to obey him quite so fast. Jaime had forgotten how well he liked it.

They found two more Kingsguard in the outer ward; two who had not worn white cloaks when Jaime last served here. *How like Cersei to name me Lord Commander and then choose my colleagues without consulting me.* "Someone has given me two new brothers, I see," he said as he dismounted.

"We have that honor, ser." The Knight of Flowers shone so fine and pure in his white scales and silk that Jaime felt a tattered and tawdry thing by contrast.

Jaime turned to Meryn Trant. "Ser, you've been remiss in teaching our new brothers their duties."

"What duties?" said Meryn Trant defensively.

"Keeping the king alive. How many monarchs have you lost since I left the city? Two, is it?"

Then Ser Balon saw the stump. "*Your hand . . .*"

Jaime made himself smile. "I fight with my left now. It makes for more of a contest. Where will I find my lord father?"

"In the solar with Lord Tyrell and Prince Oberyn."

Mace Tyrell and the Red Viper breaking bread together? Strange and stranger. "Is the queen with them as well?"

"No, my lord," Ser Balon answered. "You'll find her in the sept, praying over King Joff—"

"*You!*"

The last of the northmen had dismounted, Jaime saw, and now Loras Tyrell had seen Brienne.

"Ser Loras." She stood stupidly, holding her bridle.

Loras Tyrell strode toward her. "Why?" he said. "You will tell me why. He treated you kindly, gave you a rainbow cloak. Why would you kill him?"

"I never did. I would have died for him."

"You will." Ser Loras drew his longsword.

"It was not me."

"Emmon Cuy swore it was, with his dying breath."

"He was outside the tent, he never saw—"

"There was no one *in* the tent but you and Lady Stark. Do you claim that old woman could cut through hardened steel?"

"There was a *shadow*. I know how mad it sounds, but ... I was helping Renly into his armor, and the candles blew out and there was blood everywhere. It was Stannis, Lady Catelyn said. His ... his shadow. I had no part in it, on my honor ..."

"You have no honor. Draw your sword. I won't have it said that I slew you while your hand was empty."

Jaime stepped between them. "Put the sword away, ser."

Ser Loras edged around him. "Are you a craven as well as a killer, Brienne? Is that why you ran, with his blood on your hands? *Draw your sword, woman!*"

"Best hope she doesn't." Jaime blocked his path again. "Or it's like to be your corpse we carry out. The wench is as strong as Gregor Clegane, though not so pretty."

"This is no concern of yours." Ser Loras shoved him aside.

Jaime grabbed the boy with his good hand and yanked him around. "I am the *Lord Commander of the Kingsguard*, you arrogant pup. *Your* commander, so long as you wear that white cloak. Now *sheathe your bloody sword*, or I'll take it from you and shove it up some place even Renly never found."

The boy hesitated half a heartbeat, long enough for Ser Balon Swann to say, "Do as the Lord Commander says, Loras." Some of the gold cloaks drew their steel then, and that made some Dreadfort men do the same. *Splendid*, thought Jaime, *no sooner do I climb down off my horse than we have a bloodbath in the yard.*

Ser Loras Tyrell slammed his sword back into its sheath.

"That wasn't so difficult, was it?"

"I want her arrested." Ser Loras pointed. "Lady Brienne, I charge you with the murder of Lord Renly Baratheon."

"For what it's worth," said Jaime, "the wench does have honor. More than I have seen from you. And it may even be she's telling it true. I'll grant you, she's not what you'd call clever, but even my horse could come up with a better lie, if it was a lie she meant to tell. As you insist, however ... Ser Balon, escort Lady Brienne to a tower cell and hold her there under guard. And find some suitable quarters for Steelshanks and his men, until such time as my father can see them."

"Yes, my lord."

Brienne's big blue eyes were full of hurt as Balon Swann and a dozen gold cloaks led her away. *You ought to be blowing me kisses, wench,* he wanted to tell her. Why must they misunderstand every bloody thing he did? *Aerys. It all grows from Aerys.* Jaime turned his back on the wench and strode across the yard.

Another knight in white armor was guarding the doors of the royal sept; a tall man with a black beard, broad shoulders, and a hooked nose. When he saw Jaime he gave a sour smile and said, "And where do you think you're going?"

"Into the sept." Jaime lifted his stump to point. "That one right there. I mean to see the queen."

"Her Grace is in mourning. And why would she be wanting to see the likes of you?"

Because I'm her lover, and the father of her murdered son, he wanted to say. "Who in seven hells are you?"

"A knight of the Kingsguard, and you'd best learn some respect, cripple, or I'll have that other hand and leave you to suck up your porridge of a morning."

"I am the queen's brother, ser."

The white knight thought that funny. "Escaped, have you? And grown a bit as well, m'lord?"

"Her *other* brother, dolt. And the Lord Commander of the Kingsguard. Now stand aside, or you'll wish you had."

The dolt took a long look this time. "Is it ... Ser Jaime." He straightened. "My pardons, milord. I did not know you. I have the honor to be Ser Osmund Kettleblack."

Where's the honor in that? "I want some time alone with my sister. See that no one else enters the sept, ser. If we're disturbed, I'll have your bloody head."

"Aye, ser. As you say." Ser Osmund opened the door.

Cersei was kneeling before the altar of the Mother. Joffrey's bier had been laid out beneath the Stranger, who led the newly dead to the other world. The smell of incense hung heavy in the air, and a hundred candles burned, sending up a hundred prayers. *Joff's like to need every one of them, too.*

His sister looked over her shoulder. "Who?" she said, then, "Jaime?" She rose, her eyes brimming with tears. "Is it truly you?" She did not come to him, however. *She has never come to me,* he thought. *She has always waited, letting me come to her. She gives, but I must ask.* "You should have come sooner," she murmured, when he took her in his arms. "Why couldn't you have come sooner, to keep him safe? My boy . . ."

Our boy. "I came as fast I could." He broke from the embrace, and stepped back a pace. "It's war out there, Sister."

"You look so thin. And your hair, your golden hair . . ."

"The hair will grow back." Jaime lifted his stump. *She needs to see.* "This won't."

Her eyes went wide. "The Starks . . ."

"No. This was Vargo Hoat's work."

The name meant nothing to her. "Who?"

"The Goat of Harrenhal. For a little while."

Cersei turned to gaze at Joffrey's bier. They had dressed the dead king in gilded armor, eerily similar to Jaime's own. The visor of the helm was closed, but the candles reflected softly off the gold, so the boy shimmered bright and brave in death. The candlelight woke fires in the rubies that decorated the bodice of Cersei's mourning dress as well. Her hair fell to her shoulders, undressed and unkempt. "He killed him, Jaime. Just as he'd warned me. One day when I thought myself safe and happy he would turn my joy to ashes in my mouth, he said."

"Tyrion said that?" Jaime had not wanted to believe it. Kinslaying was worse than kingslaying, in the eyes of gods and men. *He knew the boy was mine. I loved Tyrion. I was good to him.* Well, but for that one time . . . but the Imp did not know the truth of that. *Or did he?* "Why would he kill Joff?"

"For a whore." She clutched his good hand and held it tight in hers. "He *told* me he was going to do it. Joff knew. As he was dying, he *pointed* at his murderer. At our twisted little monster of a brother." She kissed Jaime's fingers. "You'll kill him for me, won't you? You'll avenge our son."

Jaime pulled away. "He is still my brother." He shoved his stump at her face, in case she failed to see it. "And I am in no fit state to be killing anyone."

"You have another hand, don't you? I am not asking you to best the Hound in battle. Tyrion is a *dwarf*, locked in a cell. The guards would stand aside for *you*."

The thought turned his stomach. "I must know more of this. Of how it happened."

"You shall," Cersei promised. "There's to be a trial. When you hear all he did, you'll want him dead as much as I do." She touched his face. "I was lost without you, Jaime. I was afraid the Starks would send me your head. I could not have borne that." She kissed him. A light kiss, the merest brush of her lips on his, but he could feel her tremble as he slid his arms around her. "I am not whole without you."

There was no tenderness in the kiss he returned to her, only hunger. Her mouth opened for his tongue. "No," she said weakly when his lips moved down her neck, "not here. The septons . . ."

"The Others can take the septons." He kissed her again, kissed her silent, kissed her until she moaned. Then he knocked the candles aside and lifted her up onto the Mother's altar, pushing up her skirts and the silken shift beneath. She pounded on his chest with feeble fists, murmuring about the risk, the danger, about their father, about the septons, about the wrath of gods. He never heard her. He undid his breeches and climbed up and pushed her bare white legs apart. One hand slid up her thigh and underneath her smallclothes. When he tore them away, he saw that her moon's blood was on her, but it made no difference.

"Hurry," she was whispering now, "quickly, *quickly*, now, do it now, do me now. Jaime Jaime Jaime." Her hands helped guide him. "Yes," Cersei said as he thrust, "my brother, sweet brother, yes, like that, yes, I have you, you're home now, you're home now, you're *home*." She kissed his ear and stroked his short bristly hair. Jaime lost himself in her flesh. He could feel Cersei's heart beating in time with his own, and the wetness of blood and seed where they were joined.

But no sooner were they done than the queen said, "Let me up. If we are discovered like this . . ."

Reluctantly, he rolled away and helped her off the altar. The pale marble was smeared with blood. Jaime wiped it clean with his sleeve, then bent to pick up the candles he had knocked over. Fortunately they had all gone out when they fell. *If the sept had caught fire I might never have noticed.*

"This was folly." Cersei pulled her gown straight. "With Father in the castle . . . Jaime, we must be careful."

"I am sick of being careful. The Targaryens wed brother to sister, why shouldn't we do the same? Marry me, Cersei. Stand up before the realm and say it's me you want. We'll have our own wedding feast, and make another son in place of Joffrey."

She drew back. "That's not funny."

"Do you hear me chuckling?"

"Did you leave your wits at Riverrun?" Her voice had an edge to it. "Tommen's throne derives from Robert, you know that."

"He'll have Casterly Rock, isn't that enough? Let Father sit the throne. All I want is you." He made to touch her cheek. Old habits die hard, and it was his right arm he lifted.

Cersei recoiled from his stump. "*Don't* . . . don't talk like this. You're scaring me, Jaime. Don't be *stupid*. One wrong word and you'll cost us everything. What did they do to you?"

"They cut off my hand."

"No, it's more, you're *changed*." She backed off a step. "We'll talk later. On the morrow. I have Sansa Stark's maids in a tower cell, I need to question them . . . you should go to Father."

"I crossed a thousand leagues to come to you, and lost the best part of me along the way. Don't tell me to leave."

"*Leave me*," she repeated, turning away.

Jaime laced up his breeches and did as she commanded. Weary as he was, he could not seek a bed. By now his lord father knew that he was back in the city.

The Tower of the Hand was guarded by Lannister household guards, who knew him at once. "The gods are good, to give you back to us, ser," one said, as he held the door.

"The gods had no part in it. Catelyn Stark gave me back. Her, and the Lord of the Dreadfort."

He climbed the stairs and pushed into the solar unannounced, to find his father sitting by the fire. Lord Tywin was alone, for which Jaime was thankful. He had no desire to flaunt his maimed hand for Mace Tyrell or the Red Viper just now, much less the two of them together.

"Jaime," Lord Tywin said, as if they'd last seen each other at breakfast. "Lord Bolton led me to expect you earlier. I had hoped you'd be here for the wedding."

"I was delayed." Jaime closed the door softly. "My sister outdid herself, I'm told. Seventy-seven courses and a regicide, never a wedding like it. How long have you known I was free?"

"The eunuch told me a few days after your escape. I sent men into the riverlands to look for you. Gregor Clegane, Samwell Spicer, the brothers Plumm. Varys put out the word as well, but quietly. We agreed that the fewer people who knew you were free, the fewer would be hunting you."

"Did Varys mention this?" He moved closer to the fire, to let his father see.

Lord Tywin pushed himself out of his chair, breath hissing between his teeth. "*Who did this?* If Lady Catelyn thinks—"

"Lady Catelyn held a sword to my throat and made me swear to return her daughters. This was your goat's work. Vargo Hoat, the Lord of Harrenhal!"

Lord Tywin looked away, disgusted. "No longer. Ser Gregor's taken the castle. The sellswords deserted their erstwhile captain almost to a man, and some of Lady Whent's old people opened a postern gate. Clegane found Hoat sitting alone in the Hall of a Hundred Hearths, half-mad with pain and fever from a wound that festered. His ear, I'm told."

Jaime had to laugh. *Too sweet! His ear!* He could scarcely wait to tell Brienne, though the wench wouldn't find it half so funny as he did. "Is he dead yet?"

"Soon. They have taken off his hands and feet, but Clegane seems amused by the way the Qohorik slobbers."

Jaime's smile curdled. "What about his Brave Companions?"

"The few who stayed at Harrenhal are dead. The others scattered. They'll make for ports, I'll warrant, or try and lose themselves in the woods." His eyes went back to Jaime's stump, and his mouth grew taut with fury. "We'll have their heads. Every one. Can you use a sword with your left hand?"

I can hardly dress myself in the morning. Jaime held up the hand in question for his father's inspection. "Four fingers, a thumb, much like the other. Why shouldn't it work as well?"

"Good." His father sat. "That is good. I have a gift for you. For your return. After Varys told me . . ."

"Unless it's a new hand, let it wait." Jaime took the chair across from him. "How did Joffrey die?"

"Poison. It was meant to appear as though he choked on a morsel of food, but I had his throat slit open and the maesters could find no obstruction."

"Cersei claims that Tyrion did it."

"Your brother served the king the poisoned wine, with a thousand people looking on."

"That was rather foolish of him."

"I have taken Tyrion's squire into custody. His wife's maids as well. We shall see if they have anything to tell us. Ser Addam's gold cloaks are searching for the Stark girl, and Varys has offered a reward. The king's justice will be done."

The king's justice. "You would execute your own son?"

"He stands accused of regicide and kinslaying. If he is innocent, he has nothing to fear. First we must needs consider the evidence for and against him."

Evidence. In this city of liars, Jaime knew what sort of evidence would be found. "Renly died strangely as well, when Stannis needed him to."

"Lord Renly was murdered by one of his own guards, some woman from Tarth."

"That woman from Tarth is the reason I'm here. I tossed her into a cell to appease Ser Loras, but I'll believe in Renly's ghost before I believe she did him any harm. But Stannis—"

"It was poison that killed Joffrey, not sorcery." Lord Tywin glanced at Jaime's stump again. "You cannot serve in the Kingsguard without a sword hand—"

"I can," he interrupted. "And I will. There's precedent. I'll look in the White Book and find it, if you like. Crippled or whole, a knight of the Kingsguard serves for life."

"Cersei ended that when she replaced Ser Barristan on grounds of age. A suitable gift to the Faith will persuade the High Septon to release you from your vows. Your sister was foolish to dismiss Selmy, admittedly, but now that she has opened the gates—"

"—someone needs to close them again." Jaime stood. "I am tired of having highborn women kicking pails of shit at me, Father. No one ever asked me if I wanted to be Lord Commander of the Kingsguard, but it seems I am. I have a duty—"

"You do." Lord Tywin rose as well. "A duty to House Lannister. You are the heir to Casterly Rock. That is where you should be. Tommen should accompany you, as your ward and squire. The Rock is where he'll learn to be a Lannister, and I want him away from his mother. I mean to find a new husband for Cersei. Oberyn Martell perhaps, once I convince Lord Tyrell that the match does not threaten Highgarden. And it is past time you were wed. The Tyrells are now insisting that Margaery be wed to Tommen, but if I were to offer you instead—"

"*NO!*" Jaime had heard all that he could stand. No, *more* than he could stand. He was sick of it, sick of lords and lies, sick of his father, his sister, sick of the whole bloody business. "No. No. No. No. No. How many times must I say *no* before you'll hear it? *Oberyn Martell?* The man's infamous, and not just for poisoning his sword. He has more bastards than Robert, and beds with boys as well. And if you think for one misbegotten moment that I would wed Joffrey's widow . . ."

"Lord Tyrell swears the girl's still maiden."

"She can die a maiden as far as I'm concerned. *I don't want her, and I don't want your Rock!*"

"You are my son—"

"I am a knight of the Kingsguard. The *Lord Commander* of the Kingsguard! And that's *all* I mean to be!"

Firelight gleamed golden in the stiff whiskers that framed Lord Tywin's face. A vein pulsed in his neck, but he did not speak. And did not speak. And did not speak.

The strained silence went on until it was more than Jaime could endure. "Father . . ." he began.

"You are not my son." Lord Tywin turned his face away. "You say you are the Lord Commander of the Kingsguard, and only that. Very well, ser. Go do your duty."

DAVOS

Their voices rose like cinders, swirling up into purple evening sky. "Lead us from the darkness, O my Lord. Fill our hearts with fire, so we may walk your shining path."

The nightfire burned against the gathering dark, a great bright beast whose shifting orange light threw shadows twenty feet tall across the yard. All along the walls of Dragonstone the army of gargoyles and grotesques seemed to stir and shift.

Davos looked down from an arched window in the gallery above. He watched Melisandre lift her arms, as if to embrace the shivering flames. "R'hllor," she sang in a voice loud and clear, "you are the light in our eyes, the fire in our hearts, the heat in our loins. Yours is the sun that warms our days, yours the stars that guard us in the dark of night."

"*Lord of Light, defend us. The night is dark and full of terrors.*" Queen Selyse led the responses, her pinched face full of fervor. King Stannis stood beside her, jaw clenched hard, the points of his red-gold crown shimmering whenever he moved his head. *He is with them, but not of them,* Davos thought. Princess Shireen was between them, the mottled grey patches on her face and neck almost black in the firelight.

"*Lord of Light, protect us,*" the queen sang. The king did not respond with the others. He was staring into the flames. Davos wondered what he saw there. *Another vision of the war to come? Or something closer to home?*

"R'hllor who gave us breath, we thank you," sang Melisandre. "R'hllor who gave us day, we thank you."

"We thank you for the sun that warms us," Queen Selyse and the other worshipers replied. *"We thank you for the stars that watch us. We thank you for our hearths and for our torches, that keep the savage dark at bay."* There were fewer voices saying the responses than there had been the night before, it seemed to Davos; fewer faces flushed with orange light about the fire. But would there be fewer still on the morrow . . . or more?

The voice of Ser Axell Florent rang loud as a trumpet. He stood barrel-chested and bandy-legged, the firelight washing his face like a monstrous orange tongue. Davos wondered if Ser Axell would thank him, after. The work they did tonight might well make him the King's Hand, as he dreamed.

Melisandre cried, "We thank you for Stannis, by your grace our king. We thank you for the pure white fire of his goodness, for the red sword of justice in his hand, for the love he bears his leal people. Guide him and defend him, R'hllor, and grant him strength to smite his foes."

"Grant him strength," answered Queen Selyse, Ser Axell, Devan, and the rest. *"Grant him courage. Grant him wisdom."*

When he was a boy, the septons had taught Davos to pray to the Crone for wisdom, to the Warrior for courage, to the Smith for strength. But it was the Mother he prayed to now, to keep his sweet son Devan safe from the red woman's demon god.

"Lord Davos? We'd best be about it." Ser Andrew touched his elbow gently. "My lord?"

The title still rang queer in his ears, yet Davos turned away from the window. "Aye. It's time." Stannis, Melisandre, and the queen's men would be at their prayers an hour or more. The red priests lit their fires every day at sunset, to thank R'hllor for the day just ending, and beg him to send his sun back on the morrow to banish the gathering darkness. *A smuggler must know the tides and when to seize them.* That was all he was at the end of the day; Davos the smuggler. His maimed hand rose to his throat for his luck, and found nothing. He snatched it down and walked a bit more quickly.

His companions kept pace, matching their strides to his own. The Bastard of Nightsong had a pox-ravaged face and an air of tattered chivalry; Ser Gerald Gower was broad, bluff, and blond; Ser Andrew Estermont stood a head taller, with a spade-shaped beard and shaggy brown eyebrows. They were all good men in their own ways, Davos thought. *And they will all be dead men soon, if this night's work goes badly.*

"Fire is a living thing," the red woman told him, when he asked her to teach him how to see the future in the flames. "It is always moving, always changing ... like a book whose letters dance and shift even as you try to read them. It takes years of training to see the shapes beyond the flames, and more years still to learn to tell the shapes of what will be from what may be or what was. Even then it comes hard, *hard*. You do not understand that, you men of the sunset lands." Davos asked her then how it was that Ser Axell had learned the trick of it so quickly, but to that she only smiled enigmatically and said, "Any cat may stare into a fire and see red mice at play."

He had not lied to his king's men, about that or any of it. "The red woman may see what we intend," he warned them.

"We should start by killing her, then," urged Lewys the Fishwife. "I know a place where we could waylay her, four of us with sharp swords ..."

"You'd doom us all," said Davos. "Maester Cressen tried to kill her, and she knew at once. From her flames, I'd guess. It seems to me that she is very quick to sense any threat to her own person, but surely she cannot see *everything*. If we ignore her, perhaps we might escape her notice."

"There is no honor in hiding and sneaking," objected Ser Triston of Tally Hill, who had been a Sunglass man before Lord Guncer went to Melisandre's fires.

"Is it so honorable to burn?" Davos asked him. "You saw Lord Sunglass die. Is that what you want? I don't need men of honor now. I need *smugglers*. Are you with me, or no?"

They were. Gods be good, they were.

Maester Pylos was leading Edric Storm through his sums when

Davos pushed open the door. Ser Andrew was close behind him; the others had been left to guard the steps and cellar door. The maester broke off. "That will be enough for now, Edric."

The boy was puzzled by the intrusion. "Lord Davos, Ser Andrew. We were doing sums."

Ser Andrew smiled. "I hated sums when I was your age, coz."

"I don't mind them so much. I like history best, though. It's full of tales."

"Edric," said Maester Pylos, "run and get your cloak now. You're to go with Lord Davos."

"I am?" Edric got to his feet. "Where are we going?" His mouth set stubbornly. "I won't go pray to the Lord of Light. I am a Warrior's man, like my father."

"We know," Davos said. "Come, lad, we must not dawdle."

Edric donned a thick hooded cloak of undyed wool. Maester Pylos helped him fasten it, and pulled the hood up to shadow his face. "Are you coming with us, Maester?" the boy asked.

"No." Pylos touched the chain of many metals he wore about his neck. "My place is here on Dragonstone. Go with Lord Davos now, and do as he says. He is the King's Hand, remember. What did I tell you about the King's Hand?"

"The Hand speaks with the king's voice."

The young maester smiled. "That's so. Go now."

Davos had been uncertain of Pylos. Perhaps he resented him for taking old Cressen's place. But now he could only admire the man's courage. *This could mean his life as well.*

Outside the maester's chambers, Ser Gerald Gower waited by the steps. Edric Storm looked at him curiously. As they made their descent he asked, "Where are we going, Lord Davos?"

"To the water. A ship awaits you."

The boy stopped suddenly. "A ship?"

"One of Salladhor Saan's. Salla is a good friend of mine."

"I shall go with you, Cousin," Ser Andrew assured him. "There's nothing to be frightened of."

"I am not *frightened*," Edric said indignantly. "Only . . . is Shireen coming too?"

"No," said Davos. "The princess must remain here with her father and mother."

"I have to see her then," Edric explained. "To say my farewells. Otherwise she'll be sad."

Not so sad as if she sees you burn. "There is no time," Davos said. "I will tell the princess that you were thinking of her. And you can write her, when you get to where you're going."

The boy frowned. "Are you sure I must go? Why would my uncle send me from Dragonstone? Did I displease him? I never meant to." He got that stubborn look again. "I want to see my uncle. I want to see King Stannis."

Ser Andrew and Ser Gerald exchanged a look. "There's no time for that, Cousin," Ser Andrew said.

"I want to see him!" Edric insisted, louder.

"He does not want to see you." Davos had to say something, to get the boy moving. "I am his Hand, I speak with his voice. Must I go to the king and tell him that you would not do as you were told? Do you know how angry that will make him? Have you ever seen your uncle angry?" He pulled off his glove and showed the boy the four fingers that Stannis had shortened. "I have."

It was all lies; there had been no anger in Stannis Baratheon when he cut the ends off his onion knight's fingers, only an iron sense of justice. But Edric Storm had not been born then, and could not know that. And the threat had the desired effect. "He should not have done that," the boy said, but he let Davos take him by the hand and draw him down the steps.

The Bastard of Nightsong joined them at the cellar door. They walked quickly, across a shadowed yard and down some steps, under the stone tail of a frozen dragon. Lewys the Fishwife and Omer Blackberry waited at the postern gate, two guards bound and trussed at their feet. "The boat?" Davos asked them.

"It's there," Lewys said. "Four oarsmen. The galley is anchored just past the point. *Mad Prendos.*"

Davos chuckled. *A ship named after a madman. Yes, that's fitting.* Salla had a streak of the pirate's black humor.

He went to one knee before Edric Storm. "I must leave you now," he said. "There's a boat waiting, to row you out to a galley. Then it's off across the sea. You are Robert's son so I know you will be brave, no matter what happens."

"I will. Only . . ." The boy hesitated.

"Think of this as an adventure, my lord." Davos tried to sound hale and cheerful. "It's the start of your life's great adventure. May the Warrior defend you."

"And may the Father judge you justly, Lord Davos." The boy went with his cousin Ser Andrew out the postern gate. The others followed, all but the Bastard of Nightsong. *May the Father judge me justly*, Davos thought ruefully. But it was the king's judgment that concerned him now.

"These two?" asked Ser Rolland of the guards, when he had closed and barred the gate.

"Drag them into a cellar," said Davos. "You can cut them free when Edric's safely under way."

The Bastard gave a curt nod. There were no more words to say; the easy part was done. Davos pulled his glove on, wishing he had not lost his luck. He had been a better man and a braver one with that bag of bones around his neck. He ran his shortened fingers through thinning brown hair, and wondered if it needed to be cut. He must look presentable when he stood before the king.

Dragonstone had never seemed so dark and fearsome. He walked slowly, his footsteps echoing off black walls and dragons. *Stone dragons who will never wake, I pray.* The Stone Drum loomed huge ahead of him. The guards at the door uncrossed their spears as he approached. *Not for the onion knight, but for the King's Hand.* Davos was the Hand going in, at least. He wondered what he would be coming out. *If I ever do . . .*

The steps seemed longer and steeper than before, or perhaps it was just that he was tired. *The Mother never made me for tasks like this.* He had risen too high and too fast, and up here on the mountain the air was too thin for him to breathe. As a boy he'd dreamed of riches, but that was long ago. Later, grown, all he had wanted was a few acres of good land, a hall to grow old in, a better life for his sons. The Blind Bastard used to tell him that a clever smuggler did not overreach, nor draw too much attention to himself. *A few acres, a timbered roof, a "ser" before my name, I should have been content.* If he survived this night, he would take Devan and sail home to Cape Wrath and his gentle Marya. *We will grieve together for our dead sons, raise the living ones to be good men, and speak no more of kings.*

The Chamber of the Painted Table was dark and empty when Davos entered; the king would still be at the nightfire, with Melisandre and the queen's men. He knelt and made a fire in the hearth, to drive the chill from the round chamber and chase the shadows back into their corners. Then he went around the room to each window in turn, opening the heavy velvet curtains and unlatching the wooden shutters. The wind came in, strong with the smell of salt and sea, and pulled at his plain brown cloak.

At the north window, he leaned against the sill for a breath of the cold night air, hoping to catch a glimpse of *Mad Prendos* raising sail, but the sea seemed black and empty as far as the eye could see. *Is she gone already?* He could only pray that she was, and the boy with her. A half moon was sliding in and out amongst thin high clouds, and Davos could see familiar stars. There was the Galley, sailing west; there the Crone's Lantern, four bright stars that enclosed a golden haze. The clouds hid most of the Ice Dragon, all but the bright blue eye that marked due north. *The sky is full of smugglers' stars.* They were old friends, those stars; Davos hoped that meant good luck.

But when he lowered his gaze from the sky to the castle ramparts, he was not so certain. The wings of the stone dragons cast great black shadows in the light from the nightfire. He tried to tell himself that they were no more than carvings, cold and lifeless. *This was their place, once. A place of dragons and dragonlords, the seat of House Targaryen.* The Targaryens were the blood of old Valyria . . .

The wind sighed through the chamber, and in the hearth the flames gusted and swirled. He listened to the logs crackle and spit. When Davos left the window his shadow went before him, tall and thin, and fell across the Painted Table like a sword. And there he stood for a long time, waiting. He heard their boots on the stone steps as they ascended. The king's voice went before him. ". . . is not three," he was saying.

"Three is three," came Melisandre's answer. "I swear to you, Your Grace, I saw him die and heard his mother's wail."

"In the nightfire." Stannis and Melisandre came through the door together. "The flames are full of tricks. What is, what will be, what may be. You cannot tell me for a certainty . . ."

"Your Grace." Davos stepped forward. "Lady Melisandre saw it true. Your nephew Joffrey is dead."

If the king was surprised to find him at the Painted Table, he gave no sign. "Lord Davos," he said. "He was not my nephew. Though for years I believed he was."

"He choked on a morsel of food at his wedding feast," Davos said. "It may be that he was poisoned."

"He is the third," said Melisandre.

"I can count, woman." Stannis walked along the table, past Oldtown and the Arbor, up toward the Shield Islands and the mouth of the Mander. "Weddings have become more perilous than battles, it would seem. Who was the poisoner? Is it known?"

"His uncle, it's said. The Imp."

Stannis ground his teeth. "A dangerous man. I learned that on the Blackwater. How do you come by this report?"

"The Lyseni still trade at King's Landing. Salladhor Saan has no reason to lie to me."

"I suppose not." The king ran his fingers across the table. "Joffrey . . . I remember once, this kitchen cat . . . the cooks were wont to feed her scraps and fish heads. One told the boy that she had kittens in her belly, thinking he might want one. Joffrey opened up the poor thing with a dagger to see if it were true. When he found the kittens, he brought them to show to his father. Robert hit the boy so hard I thought he'd killed him." The king took off his crown and placed it on the table. "Dwarf or leech, this killer served the kingdom well. They *must* send for me now."

"They will not," said Melisandre. "Joffrey has a brother."

"Tommen." The king said the name grudgingly.

"They will crown Tommen, and rule in his name."

Stannis made a fist. "Tommen is gentler than Joffrey, but born of the same incest. Another monster in the making. Another leech upon the land. Westeros needs a man's hand, not a child's."

Melisandre moved closer. "Save them, sire. Let me wake the stone dragons. Three is three. Give me the boy."

"Edric Storm," Davos said.

Stannis rounded on him in a cold fury. "*I know his name.* Spare me your reproaches. I like this no more than you do, but my duty is to the realm. My duty . . ." He turned back to Melisandre. "You swear there is no other way? Swear it on your life, for I promise, you shall die by inches if you lie."

"You are he who must stand against the Other. The one whose coming was prophesied five thousand years ago. The red comet was your herald. You are the prince that was promised, and if you fail the world fails with you." Melisandre went to him, her red lips parted, her ruby throbbing. "Give me this boy," she whispered, "and I will give you your kingdom."

"He can't," said Davos. "Edric Storm is gone."

"Gone?" Stannis turned. "What do you mean, *gone*?"

"He is aboard a Lyseni galley, safely out to sea." Davos watched Melisandre's pale, heart-shaped face. He saw the flicker of dismay there, the sudden uncertainty. *She did not see it!*

The king's eyes were dark blue bruises in the hollows of his face. "The bastard was taken from Dragonstone without my leave? A galley, you say? If that Lysene pirate thinks to use the boy to squeeze gold from me—"

"This is your Hand's work, sire." Melisandre gave Davos a knowing look. "You will bring him back, my lord. You will."

"The boy is out of my reach," said Davos. "And out of your reach as well, my lady."

Her red eyes made him squirm. "I should have left you to the dark, ser. Do you know what you have done?"

"My duty."

"Some might call it treason." Stannis went to the window to stare out into the night. *Is he looking for the ship?* "I raised you up from dirt, Davos." He sounded more tired than angry. "Was loyalty too much to hope for?"

"Four of my sons died for you on the Blackwater. I might have died myself. You have my loyalty, always." Davos Seaworth had thought long and hard about the words he said next; he knew his life depended on them. "Your Grace, you made me swear to give you honest counsel and swift obedience, to defend your realm against your foes, to *protect your people*. Is not Edric Storm one of your people? One of those I swore to protect? I kept my oath. How could that be treason?"

Stannis ground his teeth again. "I never asked for this crown. Gold is cold and heavy on the head, but so long as I *am* the king, I have a duty ... If I must sacrifice one child to the flames to save a million from the dark ... *Sacrifice* ... is never easy, Davos. Or it is no true sacrifice. Tell him, my lady."

Melisandre said, "Azor Ahai tempered Lightbringer with the heart's blood of his own beloved wife. If a man with a thousand cows gives one to god, that is nothing. But a man who offers the only cow he owns ..."

"She talks of cows," Davos told the king. "I am speaking of a boy, your daughter's friend, your brother's son."

"A king's son, with the power of kingsblood in his veins." Melisandre's ruby glowed like a red star at her throat. "Do you think you've saved this boy, Onion Knight? When the long night falls, Edric Storm shall die with the rest, wherever he is hidden. Your own sons as well. Darkness and cold will cover the earth. You meddle in matters you do not understand."

"There's much I don't understand," Davos admitted. "I have never pretended elsewise. I know the seas and rivers, the shapes of the coasts, where the rocks and shoals lie. I know hidden coves where a boat can land unseen. And I know that a king protects his people, or he is no king at all."

Stannis's face darkened. "Do you mock me to my face? Must I learn a king's duty from an onion smuggler?"

Davos knelt. "If I have offended, take my head. I'll die as I lived, your loyal man. But hear me first. Hear me for the sake of the onions I brought you, and the fingers you took."

Stannis slid Lightbringer from its scabbard. Its glow filled the chamber. "Say what you will, but say it quickly." The muscles in the king's neck stood out like cords.

Davos fumbled inside his cloak and drew out the crinkled sheet of parchment. It seemed a thin and flimsy thing, yet it was all the shield he had. "A King's Hand should be able to read and write. Maester Pylos has been teaching me." He smoothed the letter flat upon his knee and began to read by the light of the magic sword.

JON

He dreamt he was back in Winterfell, limping past the stone kings on their thrones. Their grey granite eyes turned to follow him as he passed, and their grey granite fingers tightened on the hilts of the rusted swords upon their laps. *You are no Stark*, he could hear them mutter, in heavy granite voices. *There is no place for you here. Go away.* He walked deeper into the darkness. "Father?" he called. "Bran? Rickon?" No one answered. A chill wind was blowing on his neck. "Uncle?" he called. "Uncle Benjen? Father? Please, Father, help me." Up above he heard drums. *They are feasting in the Great Hall, but I am not welcome there. I am no Stark, and this is not my place.* His crutch slipped and he fell to his knees. The crypts were growing darker. *A light has gone out somewhere.* "Ygritte?" he whispered. "Forgive me. Please." But it was only a direwolf, grey and ghastly, spotted with blood, his golden eyes shining sadly through the dark . . .

The cell was dark, the bed hard beneath him. His own bed, he remembered, his own bed in his steward's cell beneath the Old Bear's chambers. By rights it should have brought him sweeter dreams. Even beneath the furs, he was cold. Ghost had shared his cell before the ranging, warming it against the chill of night. And in the wild, Ygritte had slept beside him. *Both gone now.* He had burned Ygritte himself, as he knew she would have wanted, and Ghost . . . *Where are you?*

Was *he* dead as well, was that what his dream had meant, the bloody wolf in the crypts? But the wolf in the dream had been grey, not white. *Grey, like Bran's wolf.* Had the Thenns hunted him down and killed him after Queenscrown? If so, Bran was lost to him for good and all.

Jon was trying to make sense of that when the horn blew.

The Horn of Winter, he thought, still confused from sleep. But Mance never found Joramun's horn, so that couldn't be. A second blast followed, as long and deep as the first. Jon had to get up and go to the Wall, he knew, but it was so hard . . .

He shoved aside his furs and sat. The pain in his leg seemed duller, nothing he could not stand. He had slept in his breeches and tunic and smallclothes, for the added warmth, so he had only to pull on his boots and don leather and mail and cloak. The horn blew again, two long blasts, so he slung Longclaw over one shoulder, found his crutch, and hobbled down the steps.

It was the black of night outside, bitter cold and overcast. His brothers were spilling out of towers and keeps, buckling their sword-belts and walking toward the Wall. Jon looked for Pyp and Grenn, but could not find them. Perhaps one of them was the sentry blowing the horn. *It is Mance*, he thought. *He has come at last.* That was good. *We will fight a battle, and then we'll rest. Alive or dead, we'll rest.*

Where the stair had been, only an immense tangle of charred wood and broken ice remained below the Wall. The winch raised them up now, but the cage was only big enough for ten men at a time, and it was already on its way up by the time Jon arrived. He would need to wait for its return. Others waited with him; Satin, Mully, Spare Boot, Kegs, big blond Hareth with his buck teeth. Everyone called him Horse. He had been a stablehand in Mole's Town, one of the few moles who had stayed at Castle Black. The rest had run back to their fields and hovels, or their beds in the underground brothel. Horse wanted to take the black, though, the great buck-toothed fool. Zei remained as well, the whore who'd proved so handy with a crossbow, and Noye had kept three orphan boys whose father had died on the steps. They were young—nine and eight and five—but no one else seemed to want them.

As they waited for the cage to come back, Clydas brought them cups of hot mulled wine, while Three-Finger Hobb passed out chunks of black bread. Jon took a heel from him and gnawed on it.

"Is it Mance Rayder?" Satin asked anxiously.

"We can hope so." There were worse things than wildlings in the dark. Jon remembered the words the wildling king had spoken on the Fist of the First Men, as they stood amidst that pink snow. *When the dead walk, walls and stakes and swords mean nothing. You cannot fight the dead, Jon Snow. No man knows that half so well as me.* Just thinking of it made the wind seem a little colder.

Finally, the cage came clanking back down, swaying at the end of the long chain, and they crowded in silently and shut the door.

Mully yanked the bell rope three times. A moment later, they began to rise, by fits and starts at first, then more smoothly. No one spoke. At the top the cage swung sideways and they clambered out one by one. Horse gave Jon a hand down onto the ice. The cold hit him in the teeth like a fist.

A line of fires burned along the top of the Wall, contained in iron baskets on poles taller than a man. The cold knife of the wind stirred and swirled the flames, so the lurid orange light was always shifting. Bundles of quarrels, arrows, spears, and scorpion bolts stood ready on every hand. Rocks were piled ten feet high, big wooden barrels of pitch and lamp oil lined up beside them. Bowen Marsh had left Castle Black well supplied in everything save men. The wind was whipping at the black cloaks of the scarecrow sentinels who stood along the ramparts, spears in hand. "I hope it wasn't one of them who blew the horn," Jon said to Donal Noye when he limped up beside him.

"Did you hear that?" Noye asked.

There was the wind, and horses, and something else. "A mammoth," Jon said. "That was a mammoth."

The armorer's breath was frosting as it blew from his broad, flat nose. North of the Wall was a sea of darkness that seemed to stretch forever. Jon could make out the faint red glimmer of distant fires moving through the wood. It was Mance, certain as sunrise. The Others did not light torches.

"How do we fight them if we can't see them?" Horse asked.

Donal Noye turned toward the two great trebuchets that Bowen Marsh had restored to working order. "Give me *light!*" he roared.

Barrels of pitch were loaded hastily into the slings and set afire with a torch. The wind fanned the flames to a brisk red fury. "*NOW!*" Noye bellowed. The counterweights plunged downward, the throwing arms rose to *thud* against the padded crossbars. The burning pitch went tumbling through the darkness, casting an eerie flickering light upon the ground below. Jon caught a glimpse of mammoths moving ponderously through the half-light, and just as quickly lost them again. *A dozen, maybe more.* The barrels struck the earth and burst. They heard a deep bass trumpeting, and a giant roared something in the Old Tongue, his voice an ancient thunder that sent shivers up Jon's spine.

"*Again!*" Noye shouted, and the trebuchets were loaded once more. Two more barrels of burning pitch went crackling through the gloom to come crashing down amongst the foe. This time one of them struck a dead tree, enveloping it in flame. *Not a dozen mammoths,* Jon saw, *a hundred.*

He stepped to the edge of the precipice. *Careful,* he reminded himself, *it is a long way down.* Red Alyn sounded his sentry's horn once more, *Aaaaahoooooooooooooooooooooooo000000, aaaaahooooo000000000-00000000.*

And now the wildlings answered, not with one horn but with a dozen, and with drums and pipes as well. *We are come,* they seemed to say, *we are come to break your Wall, to take your lands and steal your daughters.*

The wind howled, the trebuchets creaked and thumped, the barrels flew. Behind the giants and the mammoths, Jon saw men advancing on the Wall with bows and axes. Were there twenty or twenty thousand? In the dark there was no way to tell. *This is a battle of blind men, but Mance has a few thousand more of them than we do.*

"The gate!" Pyp cried out. "They're at the *GATE!*"

The Wall was too big to be stormed by any conventional means; too high for ladders or siege towers, too thick for battering rams. No catapult could throw a stone large enough to breach it, and if you tried to set it on fire, the icemelt would quench the flames. You could climb over, as the raiders did near Greyguard, but only if you were strong and fit and sure-handed, and even then you might end up like Jarl, impaled on a tree. *They must take the gate, or they cannot pass.*

But the gate was a crooked tunnel through the ice, smaller than any castle gate in the Seven Kingdoms, so narrow that rangers must lead their garrons through single file. Three iron grates closed the inner passage, each locked and chained and protected by a murder hole. The outer door was old oak, nine inches thick and studded with iron, not easy to break through. *But Mance has mammoths,* he reminded himself, *and giants as well.*

"Must be cold down there," said Noye. "What say we warm them up, lads?" A dozen jars of lamp oil had been lined up on the precipice. Pyp ran down the line with a torch, setting them alight. Owen the Oaf followed, shoving them over the edge one by one. Tongues of pale yellow fire swirled around the jars as they plunged downward. When the last was gone, Grenn kicked loose the chocks on a barrel of pitch and sent it rumbling and rolling over the edge as well. The sounds below changed to shouts and screams, sweet music to their ears.

Yet still the drums beat on, the trebuchets shuddered and thumped, and the sound of skinpipes came wafting through the night like the songs of strange fierce birds. Septon Cellador began to sing as well, his voice tremulous and thick with wine.

> *Gentle Mother, font of mercy,*
> *save our sons from war, we pray,*
> *stay the swords and stay the arrows,*
> *let them know . . .*

Donal Noye rounded on him. "Any man here stays his sword, I'll chuck his puckered arse right off this Wall . . . starting with you, Septon. *Archers!* Do we have any bloody archers?"

"Here," said Satin.

"And here," said Mully. "But how can I find a target? It's black as the inside of a pig's belly. Where are they?"

Noye pointed north. "Loose enough arrows, might be you'll find a few. At least you'll make them fretful." He looked around the ring of firelit faces. "I need two bows and two spears to help me hold the tunnel if they break the gate." More than ten stepped forward, and the smith picked his four. "Jon, you have the Wall till I return."

For a moment Jon thought he had misheard. It had sounded as if Noye were leaving him in command. "My lord?"

"*Lord?* I'm a blacksmith. I said, the Wall is yours."

There are older men, Jon wanted to say, *better men. I am still as green as summer grass. I'm wounded, and I stand accused of desertion.* His mouth had gone bone dry. "Aye," he managed.

Afterward, it would seem to Jon Snow as if he'd dreamt that night. Side by side with the straw soldiers, with longbows or crossbows clutched in half-frozen hands, his archers launched a hundred flights of arrows against men they never saw. From time to time, a wildling arrow came flying back in answer. He sent men to the smaller catapults and filled the air with jagged rocks the size of a giant's fist, but the darkness swallowed them as a man might swallow a handful of nuts. Mammoths trumpeted in the gloom, strange voices called out in stranger tongues, and Septon Cellador prayed so loudly and drunkenly for the dawn to come that Jon was tempted to chuck him over the edge himself. They heard a mammoth dying at their feet and saw another lurch burning through the woods, trampling down men and trees alike. The wind blew cold and colder. Hobb rode up the chain with cups of onion broth, and Owen and Clydas served them to the archers where they stood, so they could gulp them down between arrows. Zei took a place among them with her crossbow. Hours of repeated jars and shocks knocked something loose on the right-hand trebuchet, and its counterweight came crashing free, suddenly and catastrophically, wrenching the throwing arm sideways with a splintering crash. The left-hand trebuchet kept throwing, but the wildlings had quickly learned to shun the place where its loads were landing.

We should have twenty trebuchets, not two, and they should be mounted on sledges and turntables so we could move them. It was a futile thought. He might as well wish for another thousand men, and maybe a dragon or three.

Donal Noye did not return, nor any of them who'd gone down with him to hold that black cold tunnel. *The Wall is mine*, Jon reminded himself whenever he felt his strength flagging. He had taken up a longbow himself, and his fingers felt crabbed and stiff, half-frozen. His fever was back as well, and his leg would tremble uncontrollably, sending a white-hot knife of pain right through him. *One more arrow, and I'll rest*, he told himself, half a hundred times. *Just one more.* Whenever his quiver was empty, one of the orphaned moles would bring him another. *One more quiver, and I'm done.* It couldn't be long until the dawn.

When morning came, none of them quite realized it at first. The world was still dark, but the black had turned to grey and shapes were beginning to emerge half-seen from the gloom. Jon lowered his bow to stare at the mass of heavy clouds that covered the eastern sky. He could see a glow behind them, but perhaps he was only dreaming. He notched another arrow.

Then the rising sun broke through to send pale lances of light across the battleground. Jon found himself holding his breath as he looked out over the half-mile swath of cleared land that lay between the Wall and the edge of the forest. In half a night they had turned it into a wasteland of blackened grass, bubbling pitch, shattered stone, and corpses. The carcass of the burned mammoth was already drawing crows. There were giants dead on the ground as well, but behind them . . .

Someone moaned to his left, and he heard Septon Cellador say, "Mother have mercy, oh. Oh, oh, oh, *Mother have mercy.*"

Beneath the trees were all the wildlings in the world; raiders and giants, wargs and skinchangers, mountain men, salt sea sailors, ice river cannibals, cave dwellers with dyed faces, dog chariots from the Frozen Shore, Hornfoot men with their soles like boiled leather, all the queer wild folk Mance had gathered to break the Wall. *This is not your land*, Jon wanted to shout at them. *There is no place for you here. Go away.* He could hear Tormund Giantsbane laughing at that. "You know nothing, Jon Snow," Ygritte would have said. He flexed his sword hand, opening and closing the fingers, though he knew full well that swords would not come into it up here.

He was chilled and feverish, and suddenly the weight of the longbow was too much. The battle with the Magnar had been nothing, he realized, and the night fight less than nothing, only a probe, a dagger in the dark to try and catch them unprepared. The real battle was only now beginning.

"I never knew there would be so *many*," Satin said.

Jon had. He had seen them before, but not like this, not drawn up in battle array. On the march the wildling column had sprawled over long leagues like some enormous worm, but you never saw all of it at once. But now . . .

"Here they come," someone said in a hoarse voice.

Mammoths centered the wildling line, he saw, a hundred or more with giants on their backs clutching mauls and huge stone axes. More giants loped beside them, pushing along a tree trunk on great wooden wheels, its end sharpened to a point. *A ram*, he thought bleakly. If the gate still stood below, a few kisses from that thing would soon turn it into splinters. On either side of the giants came a wave of horsemen in boiled leather harness with fire-hardened lances, a mass of running archers, hundreds of foot with spears, slings, clubs, and leathern shields. The bone chariots from the Frozen Shore clattered forward on the flanks, bouncing over rocks and roots behind teams of huge white dogs. *The fury of the wild*, Jon thought as he listened to the skirl of skins, to the dogs barking and baying, the mammoths trumpeting, the free folk whistling and screaming, the giants roaring in the Old Tongue. Their drums echoed off the ice like rolling thunder.

He could feel the despair all around him. "There must be a hundred thousand," Satin wailed. "How can we stop so many?"

"The Wall will stop them," Jon heard himself say. He turned and said it again, louder. "The *Wall* will stop them. *The Wall defends itself.*" Hollow words, but he needed to say them, almost as much as his brothers needed to hear them. "Mance wants to unman us with his numbers. Does he think we're *stupid*?" He was shouting now, his leg forgotten, and every man was listening. "The chariots, the horsemen, all those fools on foot . . . what are they going to do to us up here? Any of you ever see a mammoth climb a wall?" He laughed, and Pyp and Owen and half a dozen more laughed with him. "They're *nothing*, they're less use than our straw brothers here, they can't reach us, they can't hurt us, and they don't frighten us, do they?"

"*NO!*" Grenn shouted.

"They're down there and we're up here," Jon said, "and so long as we hold the gate they cannot pass. *They cannot pass!*" They were all shouting then, roaring his own words back at him, waving swords and longbows in the air as their cheeks flushed red. Jon saw Kegs standing there with a warhorn slung beneath his arm. "Brother," he told him, "sound for battle."

Grinning, Kegs lifted the horn to his lips, and blew the two long blasts that meant *wildlings*. Other horns took up the call until the Wall itself seemed to shudder, and the echo of those great deep-throated moans drowned all other sound.

"Archers," Jon said when the horns had died away, "you'll aim for the giants with that ram, every bloody one of you. Loose *at my command*, not before. *THE GIANTS AND THE RAM.* I want arrows raining on them with every step, but we'll wait till they're in range. Any man who wastes an arrow will need to climb down and fetch it back, do you hear me?"

"I do," shouted Owen the Oaf. "I hear you, Lord Snow."

Jon laughed, laughed like a drunk or a madman, and his men laughed with him. The chariots and the racing horsemen on the flanks were well ahead of the center now, he saw. The wildlings had not crossed a third of the half mile, yet their battle line was dissolving. "Load the trebuchet with caltrops," Jon said. "Owen, Kegs, angle the catapults toward the center. Scorpions, load with fire spears and loose at my command." He pointed at the Mole's Town boys. "You, you, and you, stand by with torches."

The wildling archers shot as they advanced; they would dash forward, stop, loose, then run another ten yards. There were so many that the air was constantly full of arrows, all falling woefully short. *A waste,* Jon thought. *Their want of discipline is showing.* The smaller horn-and-wood bows of the free folk were outranged by the great yew longbows of the Night's Watch, and the wildlings were trying to shoot at men seven hundred feet above them. "*Let them shoot,*" Jon said. "Wait. Hold." Their cloaks were flapping behind them. "The wind is in our faces, it will cost us range. Wait." *Closer, closer.* The skins wailed, the drums thundered, the wildling arrows fluttered and fell.

"*DRAW.*" Jon lifted his own bow and pulled the arrow to his ear. Satin did the same, and Grenn, Owen the Oaf, Spare Boot, Black Jack Bulwer, Arron and Emrick. Zei hoisted her crossbow to her shoulder. Jon was watching the ram come on and on, the mammoths and giants lumbering forward on either side. They were so small he could have crushed them all in one hand, it seemed. *If only my hand was big enough.* Through the killing ground they came. A hundred crows rose from the carcass of the dead mammoth as the wildlings thundered past to either side of them. Closer and closer, until . . .

"*LOOSE!*"

The black arrows hissed downward, like snakes on feathered wings. Jon did not wait to see where they struck. He reached for a second arrow as soon as the first left his bow. "*NOTCH. DRAW. LOOSE.*" As soon as the arrow flew he found another. "*NOTCH. DRAW. LOOSE.*" Again, and then again. Jon shouted for the trebuchet, and heard the creak and heavy *thud* as a hundred spiked steel caltrops went spinning through the air. "*Catapults,*" he called, "*scorpions. Bowmen, loose at will.*" Wildling arrows were striking the Wall now, a hundred feet below them. A second giant spun and staggered. *Notch, draw, loose.* A mammoth veered into another beside it, spilling giants on the ground. *Notch, draw, loose.* The ram was down and done, he saw, the giants who'd pushed it dead or dying. "*Fire arrows,*" he shouted. "I want that ram burning." The screams of wounded mammoths and the booming cries of giants mingled with the drums and pipes to make an awful music, yet still his archers drew and loosed, as if they'd all gone as deaf as dead Dick Follard. They might be the dregs of the order, but they were men of the Night's Watch, or near enough as made no matter. *That's why they shall not pass.*

One of the mammoths was running berserk, smashing wildlings with his trunk and crushing archers underfoot. Jon pulled back his bow once more, and launched another arrow at the beast's shaggy back to urge him on. To east and west, the flanks of the wildling host had reached the Wall unopposed. The chariots drew in or turned while the horsemen milled aimlessly beneath the looming cliff of ice. "*At the gate!*" a shout came. Spare Boot, maybe. "*Mammoth at the gate!*"

"Fire," Jon barked. "Grenn, Pyp."

Grenn thrust his bow aside, wrestled a barrel of oil onto its side, and rolled it to the edge of the Wall, where Pyp hammered out the plug that sealed it, stuffed in a twist of cloth, and set it alight with a torch. They shoved it over together. A hundred feet below it struck the Wall and burst, filling the air with shattered staves and burning oil. Grenn was rolling a second barrel to the precipice by then, and Kegs had one as well. Pyp lit them both. "*Got him!*" Satin shouted, his head sticking out so far that Jon was certain he was about to fall. "*Got him, got him, GOT him!*" He could hear the roar of fire. A flaming giant lurched into view, stumbling and rolling on the ground.

Then suddenly the mammoths were fleeing, running from the smoke and flames and smashing into those behind them in their terror. Those went backward too, the giants and wildlings behind them scrambling to get out of their way. In half a heartbeat, the whole center was collapsing. The horsemen on the flanks saw themselves being abandoned and decided to fall back as well, not one so much as blooded. Even the chariots rumbled off, having done nothing but look fearsome and make a lot of noise. *When they break, they break hard*, Jon Snow thought as he watched them reel away. The drums had all gone silent. *How do you like that music, Mance? How do you like the taste of the Dornishman's wife?* "Do we have anyone hurt?" he asked.

"The bloody buggers got my leg." Spare Boot plucked the arrow out and waved it above his head. "The wooden one!"

A ragged cheer went up. Zei grabbed Owen by the hands, spun him around in a circle, and gave him a long wet kiss right there for all to see. She tried to kiss Jon too, but he held her by the shoulder and pushed her gently but firmly away. "No," he said. *I am done with kissing.* Suddenly he was too weary to stand, and his leg was agony from knee to groin. He fumbled for his crutch. "Pyp, help me to the cage. Grenn, you have the Wall."

"*Me?*" said Grenn. "*Him?*" said Pyp. It was hard to tell which of them was more horrified. "But," Grenn stammered, "b-but what do I do if the wildlings attack again?"

"Stop them," Jon told him.

As they rode down in the cage, Pyp took off his helm and wiped his brow. "Frozen sweat. Is there anything as disgusting as frozen sweat?" He laughed. "Gods, I don't think I have ever been so hungry. I could eat an aurochs whole, I swear it. Do you think Hobb will cook up Grenn for us?" When he saw Jon's face, his smile died. "What's wrong? Is it your leg?"

"My leg," Jon agreed. Even the words were an effort.

"Not the battle, though? We won the battle."

"Ask me when I've seen the gate," Jon said grimly. *I want a fire, a hot meal, a warm bed, and something to make my leg stop hurting,* he told himself. But first he had to check the tunnel and find what had become of Donal Noye.

After the battle with the Thenns it had taken them almost a day to clear the ice and broken beams away from the inner gate. Spotted Pate and Kegs and some of the other builders had argued heatedly that they ought just leave the debris there, another obstacle for Mance. That would have meant abandoning the defense of the tunnel, though, and Noye was having none of it. With men in the murder holes and archers and spears behind each inner grate, a few determined brothers could hold off a hundred times as many wildlings and clog the way with corpses. He did not mean to give Mance Rayder free passage through the ice. So with pick and spade and ropes, they had moved the broken steps aside and dug back down to the gate.

Jon waited by the cold iron bars while Pyp went to Maester Aemon for the spare key. Surprisingly, the maester himself returned with him, and Clydas with a lantern. "Come see me when we are done," the old man told Jon while Pyp was fumbling with the chains. "I need to change your dressing and apply a fresh poultice, and you will want some more dreamwine for the pain."

Jon nodded weakly. The door swung open. Pyp led them in, followed by Clydas and the lantern. It was all Jon could do to keep up with Maester Aemon. The ice pressed close around them, and he could feel the cold seeping into his bones, the weight of the Wall above his head. It felt like walking down the gullet of an ice dragon. The tunnel took a twist, and then another. Pyp unlocked a second iron gate. They walked farther, turned again, and saw light ahead, faint and pale through the ice. *That's bad*, Jon knew at once. *That's very bad.*

Then Pyp said, "There's blood on the floor."

The last twenty feet of the tunnel was where they'd fought and died. The outer door of studded oak had been hacked and broken and finally torn off its hinges, and one of the giants had crawled in through the splinters. The lantern bathed the grisly scene in a sullen reddish light. Pyp turned aside to retch, and Jon found himself envying Maester Aemon his blindness.

Noye and his men had been waiting within, behind a gate of heavy iron bars like the two Pyp had just unlocked. The two crossbows had gotten off a dozen quarrels as the giant struggled toward them. Then the spearmen must have come to the fore, stabbing through the bars. Still the giant found the strength to reach through, twist the head off Spotted Pate, seize the iron gate, and wrench the bars apart. Links of broken chain lay strewn across the floor. *One giant. All this was the work of one giant.*

"Are they all dead?" Maester Aemon asked softly.

"Yes. Donal was the last." Noye's sword was sunk deep in the giant's throat, halfway to the hilt. The armorer had always seemed such a big man to Jon, but locked in the giant's massive arms he looked almost like a child. "The giant crushed his spine. I don't know who died first." He took the lantern and moved forward for a better look. "Mag." *I am the last of the giants.* He could feel the sadness there, but he had no time for sadness. "It was Mag the Mighty. The king of the giants."

He needed sun then. It was too cold and dark inside the tunnel, and the stench of blood and death was suffocating. Jon gave the lantern back to Clydas, squeezed around the bodies and through the twisted bars, and walked toward the daylight to see what lay beyond the splintered door.

The huge carcass of a dead mammoth partially blocked the way. One of the beast's tusks snagged his cloak and tore it as he edged past. Three more giants lay outside, half buried beneath stone and slush and hardened pitch. He could see where the fire had melted the Wall, where great sheets of ice had come sloughing off in the heat to shatter on the blackened ground. He looked up at where they'd come from. *When you stand here it seems immense, as if it were about to crush you.*

Jon went back inside to where the others waited. "We need to repair the outer gate as best we can and then block up this section of the tunnel. Rubble, chunks of ice, anything. All the way to the second gate, if we can. Ser Wynton will need to take command, he's the last knight left, but he needs to move *now*, the giants will be back before we know it. We have to tell him—"

"Tell him what you will," said Maester Aemon, gently. "He will smile, nod, and forget. Thirty years ago Ser Wynton Stout came within a dozen votes of being Lord Commander. He would have made a fine one. Ten years ago he would still have been capable. No longer. You know that as well as Donal did, Jon."

It was true. "You give the order, then," Jon told the maester. "You have been on the Wall your whole life, the men will follow you. We have to close the gate."

"I am a maester chained and sworn. My order serves, Jon. We give counsel, not commands."

"Someone must—"

"You. You must lead."

"No."

"Yes, Jon. It need not be for long. Only until such time as the garrison returns. Donal chose you, and Qhorin Halfhand before him. Lord Commander Mormont made you his steward. You are a son of Winterfell, a nephew of Benjen Stark. It must be you or no one. The Wall is yours, Jon Snow."

ARYA

She could feel the hole inside her every morning when she woke. It wasn't hunger, though sometimes there was that too. It was a hollow place, an emptiness where her heart had been, where her brothers had lived, and her parents. Her head hurt too. Not as bad as it had at first, but still pretty bad. Arya was used to that, though, and at least the lump was going down. But the hole inside her stayed the same. *The hole will never feel any better*, she told herself when she went to sleep.

Some mornings, Arya did not want to wake at all. She would huddle beneath her cloak with her eyes squeezed shut and try to will herself back to sleep. If the Hound would only have left her alone, she would have slept all day and all night.

And dreamed. That was the best part, the dreaming. She dreamed of wolves most every night. A great pack of wolves, with her at the head. She was bigger than any of them, stronger, swifter, faster. She could outrun horses and outfight lions. When she bared her teeth even men would run from her, her belly was never empty long, and her fur kept her warm even when the wind was blowing cold. And her brothers and sisters were with her, many and more of them, fierce and terrible and *hers*. They would never leave her.

But if her nights were full of wolves, her days belonged to the dog. Sandor Clegane made her get up every morning, whether she wanted to or not. He would curse at her in his raspy voice, or yank her to her feet and shake her. Once he dumped a helm full of cold water all over her head. She bounced up sputtering and shivering and tried to kick him, but he only laughed. "Dry off and feed the bloody horses," he told her, and she did.

They had two now, Stranger and a sorrel palfrey mare Arya had named Craven, because Sandor said she'd likely run off from the Twins the same as them. They'd found her wandering riderless through a field the morning after the slaughter. She was a good enough horse, but Arya could not love a coward. *Stranger would have fought.* Still, she tended the mare as best she knew. It was better than riding double with the Hound. And Craven might have been a coward, but she was young and strong as well. Arya thought that she might be able to outrun Stranger, if it came to it.

The Hound no longer watched her as closely as he had. Sometimes he did not seem to care whether she stayed or went, and he no longer bound her up in a cloak at night. *One night I'll kill him in his sleep,* she told herself, but she never did. *One day I'll ride away on Craven, and he won't be able to catch me,* she thought, but she never did that either. Where would she go? Winterfell was gone. Her grandfather's brother was at Riverrun, but he didn't know her, no more than she knew him. Maybe Lady Smallwood would take her in at Acorn Hall, but maybe she wouldn't. Besides, Arya wasn't even sure she could *find* Acorn Hall again. Sometimes she thought she might go back to Sharna's inn, if the floods hadn't washed it away. She could stay with Hot Pie, or maybe Lord Beric would find her there. Anguy would teach her to use a bow, and she could ride with Gendry and be an outlaw, like Wenda the White Fawn in the songs.

But that was just stupid, like something Sansa might dream. Hot Pie and Gendry had left her just as soon as they could, and Lord Beric and the outlaws only wanted to ransom her, just like the Hound. None of them wanted her around. *They were never my pack, not even Hot Pie and Gendry. I was stupid to think so, just a stupid little girl, and no wolf at all.*

So she stayed with the Hound. They rode every day, never sleeping twice in the same place, avoiding towns and villages and castles as best they could. Once she asked Sandor Clegane where they were going. "Away," he said. "That's all you need to know. You're not worth spit to me now, and I don't want to hear your whining. I should have let you run into that bloody castle."

"You should have," she agreed, thinking of her mother.

"You'd be dead if I had. You ought to thank me. You ought to sing me a pretty little song, the way your sister did."

"Did you hit her with an axe too?"

"I hit you with the *flat* of the axe, you stupid little bitch. If I'd hit you with the blade there'd still be chunks of your head floating down the Green Fork. Now shut your bloody mouth. If I had any sense I'd give you to the silent sisters. They cut the tongues out of girls who talk too much."

That wasn't fair of him to say. Aside from that one time, Arya hardly talked at all. Whole days passed when neither of them said anything. She was too empty to talk, and the Hound was too angry. She could feel the fury in him; she could see it on his face, the way his mouth would tighten and twist, the looks he gave her. Whenever he took his axe to chop some wood for a fire, he would slide into a cold rage, hacking savagely at the tree or the deadfall or the broken limb, until they had twenty times as much kindling and firewood as they'd needed. Sometimes he would be so sore and tired afterward that he would lie down and go right to sleep without even lighting a fire. Arya hated it when that happened, and hated him too. Those were the nights when she stared the longest at the axe. *It looks awfully heavy, but I bet I could swing it.* She wouldn't hit him with the flat, either.

Sometimes in their wanderings they glimpsed other people; farmers in their fields, swineherds with their pigs, a milkmaid leading a cow, a squire carrying a message down a rutted road. She never wanted to speak to them either. It was as if they lived in some distant land and spoke a queer alien tongue; they had nothing to do with her, or her with them.

Besides, it wasn't safe to be seen. From time to time columns of horsemen passed down the winding farm roads, the twin towers of Frey flying before them. "Hunting for stray northmen," the Hound said when they had passed. "Any time you hear hooves, get your head down fast, it's not like to be a friend."

One day, in an earthen hollow made by the roots of a fallen oak, they came face to face with another survivor of the Twins. The badge on his breast showed a pink maiden dancing in a swirl of silk, and he told them he was Ser Marq Piper's man; a bowman, though he'd lost his bow. His left shoulder was all twisted and swollen where it met his arm; a blow from a mace, he said, it had broken his shoulder and smashed his chain-mail deep into his flesh. "A northman, it was," he wept. "His badge was a bloody man, and he saw mine and made a jape, red man and pink maiden, maybe they should get together. I drank to his Lord Bolton, he drank to Ser Marq, and we drank together to Lord Edmure and Lady Roslin and the King in the North. And then he killed me." His eyes were fever bright when he said that, and Arya could tell that it was true. His shoulder was swollen grotesquely, and pus and blood had stained his whole left side. There was a stink to him too. *He smells like a corpse.* The man begged them for a drink of wine.

"If I'd had any wine, I'd have drunk it myself," the Hound told him. "I can give you water, and the gift of mercy."

The archer looked at him a long while before he said, "You're Joffrey's dog."

"My own dog now. Do you want the water?"

"Aye." The man swallowed. "And the mercy. Please."

They had passed a small pond a short ways back. Sandor gave Arya his helm and told her to fill it, so she trudged back to the water's edge. Mud squished over the toe of her boots. She used the dog's head as a pail. Water ran out through the eyeholes, but the bottom of the helm still held a lot.

When she came back, the archer turned his face up and she poured the water into his mouth. He gulped it down as fast as she could pour, and what he couldn't gulp ran down his cheeks into the brown blood that crusted his whiskers, until pale pink tears dangled from his beard. When the water was gone he clutched the helm and licked the steel. "Good," he said. "I wish it was wine, though. I wanted wine."

"Me too." The Hound eased his dagger into the man's chest

almost tenderly, the weight of his body driving the point through his surcoat, ringmail, and the quilting beneath. As he slid the blade back out and wiped it on the dead man, he looked at Arya. "That's where the heart is, girl. That's how you kill a man."

That's one way. "Will we bury him?"

"Why?" Sandor said. "He don't care, and we've got no spade. Leave him for the wolves and wild dogs. Your brothers and mine." He gave her a hard look. "First we rob him, though."

There were two silver stags in the archer's purse, and almost thirty coppers. His dagger had a pretty pink stone in the hilt. The Hound hefted the knife in his hand, then flipped it toward Arya. She caught it by the hilt, slid it through her belt, and felt a little better. It wasn't Needle, but it was steel. The dead man had a quiver of arrows too, but arrows weren't much good without a bow. His boots were too big for Arya and too small for the Hound, so those they left. She took his kettle helm as well, even though it came down almost past her nose, so she had to tilt it back to see. "He must have had a horse as well, or he wouldn't have got away," Clegane said, peering about, "but it's bloody well gone, I'd say. No telling how long he's been here."

By the time they found themselves in the foothills of the Mountains of the Moon, the rains had mostly stopped. Arya could see the sun and moon and stars, and it seemed to her that they were heading eastward. "Where are we going?" she asked again.

This time the Hound answered her. "You have an aunt in the Eyrie. Might be she'll want to ransom your scrawny arse, though the gods know why. Once we find the high road, we can follow it all the way to the Bloody Gate."

Aunt Lysa. The thought left Arya feeling empty. It was her mother she wanted, not her mother's sister. She didn't know her mother's sister any more than she knew her great uncle Blackfish. *We should have gone into the castle.* They didn't really *know* that her mother was dead, or Robb either. It wasn't like they'd seen them die or anything. Maybe Lord Frey had just taken them captive. Maybe they were chained up in his dungeon, or maybe the Freys were taking them to King's Landing so Joffrey could chop their heads off. They didn't *know*. "We should go back," she suddenly decided. "We should go back to the Twins and get my mother. She can't be dead. We have to help her."

"I thought your sister was the one with a head full of songs," the Hound growled. "Frey might have kept your mother alive to ransom, that's true. But there's no way in seven hells I'm going to pluck her out of his castle all by my bloody self."

"Not by yourself. I'd come too."

He made a sound that was almost a laugh. "*That* will scare the piss out of the old man."

"You're just afraid to die!" she said scornfully.

Now Clegane *did* laugh. "Death don't scare me. Only fire. Now be quiet, or I'll cut your tongue out myself and save the silent sisters the bother. It's the Vale for us."

Arya didn't think he'd *really* cut her tongue out; he was just saying that the way Pinkeye used to say he'd beat her bloody. All the same, she wasn't going to try him. Sandor Clegane was no Pinkeye. Pinkeye didn't cut people in half or hit them with axes. Not even with the flat of axes.

That night she went to sleep thinking of her mother, and wondering if she should kill the Hound in his sleep and rescue Lady Catelyn herself. When she closed her eyes she saw her mother's face against the back of her eyelids. *She's so close I could almost smell her . . .*

. . . and then she could *smell her.* The scent was faint beneath the other smells, beneath moss and mud and water, and the stench of rotting reeds and rotting men. She padded slowly through the soft ground to the river's edge, lapped up a drink, the lifted her head to sniff. The sky was grey and thick with cloud, the river green and full of floating things. Dead men clogged the shallows, some still moving as the water pushed them, others washed up on the banks. Her brothers and sisters swarmed around them, tearing at the rich ripe flesh.

The crows were there too, screaming at the wolves and filling the air with feathers. Their blood was hotter, and one of her sisters had snapped at one as it took flight and caught it by the wing. It made her want a crow herself. She wanted to taste the blood, to hear the bones crunch between her teeth, to fill her belly with warm flesh instead of cold. She was hungry and the meat was all around, but she knew she could not eat.

The scent was stronger now. She pricked her ears up and listened to the grumbles of her pack, the shriek of angry crows, the whirr of wings and sound of running water. Somewhere far off she could hear horses and the calls of living men, but they were not what mattered. Only the scent mattered. She sniffed the air again. There it was, and now she saw it too, something pale and white drifting down the river, turning where it brushed against a snag. The reeds bowed down before it.

She splashed noisily through the shallows and threw herself into the deeper water, her legs churning. The current was strong but she was stronger. She swam, following her nose. The river smells were rich and wet, but those were not the smells that pulled her. She paddled after the sharp red whisper of cold blood, the sweet cloying stench of death. She chased them as she had often chased a red deer through the trees, and in the end she ran them down, and her jaw closed around a pale white arm. She shook it to make it move, but there was only death and blood in her mouth. By now, she was tiring, and it was all she could do to pull the body back to shore. As she dragged it up the muddy bank, one of her little brothers came prowling, his tongue lolling from his mouth. She had to snarl to drive him off, or else he would have fed. Only then did she stop to shake the water from her fur. The white thing lay facedown in the mud, her dead flesh wrinkled and pale, cold blood trickling from her throat. *Rise*, she thought. *Rise and eat and run with us.*

The sound of horses turned her head. *Men.* They were coming from downwind, so she had not smelled them, but now they were almost here. Men on horses, with flapping black and yellow and pink wings and long shiny claws in hand. Some of her younger brothers bared their teeth to defend the food they'd found, but she snapped at them until they scattered. That was the way of the wild. Deer and hares and crows fled before wolves, and wolves fled from men. She abandoned the cold white prize in the mud where she had dragged it, and ran, and felt no shame.

When morning came, the Hound did not need to shout at Arya

or shake her awake. She had woken before him for a change, and even watered the horses. They broke their fast in silence, until Sandor said, "This thing about your mother . . ."

"It doesn't matter," Arya said in a dull voice. "I know she's dead. I saw her in a dream."

The Hound looked at her a long time, then nodded. No more was said of it. They rode on toward the mountains.

In the higher hills, they came upon a tiny isolated village surrounded by grey-green sentinels and tall blue soldier pines, and Clegane decided to risk going in. "We need food," he said, "and a roof over our heads. They're not like to know what happened at the Twins, and with any luck they won't know me."

The villagers were building a wooden palisade around their homes, and when they saw the breadth of the Hound's shoulders they offered them food and shelter and even coin for work. "If there's wine as well, I'll do it," he growled at them. In the end, he settled for ale, and drank himself to sleep each night.

His dream of selling Arya to Lady Arryn died there in the hills, though. "There's frost above us and snow in the high passes," the village elder said. "If you don't freeze or starve, the shadowcats will get you, or the cave bears. There's the clans as well. The Burned Men are fearless since Timett One-Eye came back from the war. And half a year ago, Gunthor son of Gurn led the Stone Crows down on a village not eight miles from here. They took every woman and every scrap of grain, and killed half the men. They have *steel* now, good swords and mail hauberks, and they watch the high road—the Stone Crows, the Milk Snakes, the Sons of the Mist, all of them. Might be you'd take a few with you, but in the end they'd kill you and make off with your daughter."

I'm not his daughter, Arya might have shouted, if she hadn't felt so tired. She was no one's daughter now. She was no one. Not Arya, not Weasel, not Nan nor Arry nor Squab, not even Lumpyhead. She was only some girl who ran with a dog by day, and dreamed of wolves by night.

It was quiet in the village. They had beds stuffed with straw and not too many lice, the food was plain but filling, and the air smelled of pines. All the same, Arya soon decided that she hated it. The villagers were cowards. None of them would even look at the Hound's face, at least not for long. Some of the women tried to put her in a dress and make her do needlework, but they weren't Lady Smallwood and she was having none of it. And there was one girl who took to following her, the village elder's daughter. She was of an age with Arya, but just a *child*; she cried if she skinned a knee, and carried a stupid cloth doll with her everywhere she went. The doll was made up to look like a man-at-arms, sort of, so the girl called him Ser Soldier and bragged how he kept her safe. "Go away," Arya told her half a hundred times. "Just leave me be." She wouldn't, though, so finally Arya took the doll away from her, ripped it open, and pulled the rag stuffing out of its belly with a finger. "Now he *really* looks like a soldier!" she said, before she threw the doll in a brook. After that the girl stopped pestering her, and Arya spent her days grooming Craven and Stranger or walking in the woods. Sometimes she would find a stick and practice her needlework, but then she would remember what had happened at the Twins and smash it against a tree until it broke.

"Might be we should stay here awhile," the Hound told her, after a fortnight. He was drunk on ale, but more brooding than sleepy. "We'd never reach the Eyrie, and the Freys will still be hunting survivors in the riverlands. Sounds like they need swords here, with these clansmen raiding. We can rest up, maybe find a way to get a letter to your aunt." Arya's face darkened when she heard that. She didn't want to stay, but there was nowhere to go, either. The next morning, when the Hound went off to chop down trees and haul logs, she crawled back into bed.

But when the work was done and the tall wooden palisade was finished, the village elder made it plain that there was no place for them. "Come winter, we will be hard pressed to feed our own," he explained. "And you . . . a man like you brings blood with him."

Sandor's mouth tightened. "So you do know who I am."

"Aye. We don't get travelers here, that's so, but we go to market, and to fairs. We know about King Joffrey's dog."

"When these Stone Crows come calling, you might be glad to have a dog."

"Might be." The man hesitated, then gathered up his courage. "But they say you lost your belly for fighting at the Blackwater. They say—"

"I know what they say." Sandor's voice sounded like two woodsaws grinding together. "Pay me, and we'll be gone."

When they left, the Hound had a pouch full of coppers, a skin of sour ale, and a new sword. It was a very old sword, if truth be told, though new to him. He swapped its owner the longaxe he'd taken at the Twins, the one he'd used to raise the lump on Arya's head. The ale was gone in less than a day, but Clegane sharpened the sword every night, cursing the man he'd swapped with for every nick and spot of rust. *If he lost his belly for fighting, why does he care if his sword is sharp?* It was not a question Arya dared ask him, but she thought on it a lot. Was that why he'd run from the Twins and carried her off?

Back in the riverlands, they found that the rains had ebbed away, and the flood waters had begun to recede. The Hound turned south, back toward the Trident. "We'll make for Riverrun," he told Arya as they roasted a hare he'd killed. "Maybe the Blackfish wants to buy himself a she-wolf."

"He doesn't know me. He won't even know I'm really me." Arya was tired of making for Riverrun. She had been making for Riverrun for years, it seemed, without ever getting there. Every time she made for Riverrun, she ended up someplace worse. "He won't give you any ransom. He'll probably just hang you."

"He's free to try." He turned the spit.

He doesn't talk like he's lost his belly for fighting. "I know where we could go," Arya said. She still had one brother left. *Jon will want me, even if no one else does. He'll call me "little sister" and muss my hair.* It was a long way, though, and she didn't think she could get there by herself. She hadn't even been able to reach Riverrun. "We could go to the Wall."

Sandor's laugh was half a growl. "The little wolf bitch wants to join the Night's Watch, does she?"

"My brother's on the Wall," she said stubbornly.

His mouth gave a twitch. "The Wall's a thousand leagues from here. We'd need to fight through the bloody Freys just to reach the Neck. There's lizard lions in those swamps that eat wolves every day for breakfast. And if we did reach the north with our skins intact, there's ironborn in half the castles, and thousands of bloody buggering northmen as well."

"Are you scared of them?" she asked. "Have you lost your belly for fighting?"

For a moment, she thought he was going to hit her. By then the hare was brown, though, skin crackling and grease popping as it dripped down into the cookfire. Sandor took it off the stick, ripped it apart with his big hands, and tossed half of it into Arya's lap. "There's nothing wrong with my belly," he said as he pulled off a leg, "but I don't give a rat's arse for you *or* your brother. I have a brother too."

TYRION

"Tyrion," Ser Kevan Lannister said wearily, "if you are indeed innocent of Joffrey's death, you should have no difficulty proving it at trial."

Tyrion turned from the window. "Who is to judge me?"

"Justice belongs to the throne. The king is dead, but your father remains Hand. Since it is his own son who stands accused and his grandson who was the victim, he has asked Lord Tyrell and Prince Oberyn to sit in judgment with him."

Tyrion was scarcely reassured. Mace Tyrell had been Joffrey's good-father, however briefly, and the Red Viper was . . . well, a snake. "Will I be allowed to demand trial by battle?"

"I would not advise that."

"Why not?" It had saved him in the Vale, why not here? "Answer me, Uncle. Will I be allowed a trial by battle, and a champion to prove my innocence?"

"Certainly, if such is your wish. However, you had best know that your sister means to name Ser Gregor Clegane as *her* champion, in the event of such a trial."

The bitch checks my moves before I make them. A pity she didn't choose a Kettleblack. Bronn would make short work of any of the three brothers, but the Mountain That Rides was a kettle of a different color. "I shall need to sleep on this." *I need to speak with Bronn, and soon*. He didn't want to think about what this was like to cost him. Bronn had a lofty notion of what his skin was worth. "Does Cersei have witnesses against me?"

"More every day."

"Then I must have witnesses of my own."

"Tell me who you would have, and Ser Addam will send the Watch to bring them to the trial."

"I would sooner find them myself."

"You stand accused of regicide and kinslaying. Do you truly imagine you will be allowed to come and go as you please?" Ser Kevan waved at the table. "You have quill, ink, and parchment. Write the names of such witnesses as you require, and I shall do all in my power to produce them, you have my word as a Lannister. But you shall not leave this tower, except to go to trial."

Tyrion would not demean himself by begging. "Will you permit my squire to come and go? The boy Podrick Payne?"

"Certainly, if that is your wish. I shall send him to you."

"Do so. Sooner would be better than later, and now would be better than sooner." He waddled to the writing table. But when he heard the door open, he turned back and said, "Uncle?"

Ser Kevan paused. "Yes?"

"I did not do this."

"I wish I could believe that, Tyrion."

When the door closed, Tyrion Lannister pulled himself up into the chair, sharpened a quill, and pulled a blank parchment. *Who will speak for me?* He dipped his quill in the inkpot.

The sheet was still maiden when Podrick Payne appeared, sometime later. "My lord," the boy said.

Tyrion put down the quill. "Find Bronn and bring him at once. Tell him there's gold in it, more gold than he's ever dreamt of, and see that you don't return without him."

"Yes, my lord. I mean, no. I won't. Return." He went.

He had not returned by sunset, nor by moonrise. Tyrion fell asleep in the window seat to wake stiff and sore at dawn. A serving man brought porridge and apples to break his fast, with a horn of ale. He ate at the table, the blank parchment before him. An hour later, the serving man returned for the bowl. "Have you seen my squire?" Tyrion asked him. The man shook his head.

Sighing, he turned back to the table, and dipped the quill again. *Sansa*, he wrote upon the parchment. He sat staring at the name, his teeth clenched so hard they hurt.

Assuming Joffrey had not simply choked to death on a bit of food, which even Tyrion found hard to swallow, Sansa must have poisoned him. *Joff practically put his cup down in her lap, and he'd given her ample reason.* Any doubts Tyrion might have had vanished when his wife did. *One flesh, one heart, one soul.* His mouth twisted. *She wasted no time proving how much those vows meant to her, did she? Well, what did you expect, dwarf?*

And yet . . . where would Sansa have gotten poison? He could not believe the girl had acted alone in this. *Do I really want to find her?* Would the judges believe that Tyrion's child bride had poisoned a king without her husband's knowledge? *I wouldn't.* Cersei would insist that they had done the deed together.

Even so, he gave the parchment to his uncle the next day. Ser Kevan frowned at it. "Lady Sansa is your only witness?"

"I will think of others in time."

"Best think of them now. The judges mean to begin the trial three days hence."

"That's too soon. You have me shut up here under guard, how am I to find witnesses to my innocence?"

"Your sister's had no difficulty finding witnesses to your guilt." Ser Kevan rolled up the parchment. "Ser Addam has men hunting for your wife. Varys has offered a hundred stags for word of her whereabouts, and a hundred dragons for the girl herself. If the girl can be found she will be found, and I shall bring her to you. I see no harm in husband and wife sharing the same cell and giving comfort to one another."

"You are too kind. Have you seen my squire?"

"I sent him to you yesterday. Did he not come?"

"He came," Tyrion admitted, "and then he went."

"I shall send him to you again."

But it was the next morning before Podrick Payne returned. He stepped inside the room hesitantly, with fear written all over his face. Bronn came in behind him. The sellsword knight wore a jerkin studded with silver and a heavy riding cloak, with a pair of fine-tooled leather gloves thrust through his swordbelt.

One look at Bronn's face gave Tyrion a queasy feeling in the pit of his stomach. "It took you long enough."

"The boy begged, or I wouldn't have come at all. I am expected at Castle Stokeworth for supper."

"Stokeworth?" Tyrion hopped from the bed. "And pray, what is there for you in Stokeworth?"

"A bride." Bronn smiled like a wolf contemplating a lost lamb. "I'm to wed Lollys the day after next."

"Lollys." *Perfect, bloody perfect.* Lady Tanda's lackwit daughter gets a knightly husband and a father of sorts for the bastard in her belly, and Ser Bronn of the Blackwater climbs another rung. It had Cersei's stinking fingers all over it. "My bitch sister has sold you a lame horse. The girl's dim-witted."

"If I wanted wits, I'd marry you."

"Lollys is big with another man's child."

"And when she pops him out, I'll get her big with mine."

"She's not even heir to Stokeworth," Tyrion pointed out. "She has an elder sister. Falyse. A *married* sister."

"Married ten years, and still barren," said Bronn. "Her lord husband shuns her bed. It's said he prefers virgins."

"He could prefer goats and it wouldn't matter. The lands will still pass to his wife when Lady Tanda dies."

"Unless Falyse should die before her mother."

Tyrion wondered whether Cersei had any notion of the sort of serpent she'd given Lady Tanda to suckle. *And if she does, would she care?* "Why are you here, then?"

Bronn shrugged. "You once told me that if anyone ever asked me to sell you out, you'd double the price."

Yes. "Is it two wives you want, or two castles?"

"One of each would serve. But if you want me to kill Gregor Clegane for you, it had best be a damned *big* castle."

The Seven Kingdoms were full of highborn maidens, but even

the oldest, poorest, and ugliest spinster in the realm would balk at wedding such lowborn scum as Bronn. *Unless she was soft of body and soft of head, with a fatherless child in her belly from having been raped half a hundred times.* Lady Tanda had been so desperate to find a husband for Lollys that she had even pursued Tyrion for a time, and that had been *before* half of King's Landing enjoyed her. No doubt Cersei had sweetened the offer somehow, and Bronn *was* a knight now, which made him a suitable match for a younger daughter of a minor house.

"I find myself woefully short of both castles and highborn maidens at the moment," Tyrion admitted. "But I can offer you gold and gratitude, as before."

"I have gold. What can I buy with gratitude?"

"You might be surprised. A Lannister pays his debts."

"Your sister is a Lannister too."

"My lady wife is heir to Winterfell. Should I emerge from this with my head still on my shoulders, I may one day rule the north in her name. I could carve you out a big piece of it."

"If and when and might be," said Bronn. "And it's bloody cold up there. Lollys is soft, warm, and close. I could be poking her two nights hence."

"Not a prospect I would relish."

"Is that so?" Bronn grinned. "Admit it, Imp. Given a choice between fucking Lollys and fighting the Mountain, you'd have your breeches down and cock up before a man could blink."

He knows me too bloody well. Tyrion tried a different tack. "I'd heard that Ser Gregor was wounded on the Red Fork, and again at Duskendale. The wounds are bound to slow him."

Bronn looked annoyed. "He was never fast. Only freakish big and freakish strong. I'll grant you, he's quicker than you'd expect for a man that size. He has a monstrous long reach, and doesn't seem to feel blows the way a normal man would."

"Does he frighten you so much?" asked Tyrion, hoping to provoke him.

"If he didn't frighten me, I'd be a bloody fool." Bronn gave a shrug. "Might be I could take him. Dance around him until he was so tired of hacking at me that he couldn't lift his sword. Get him off his feet somehow. When they're flat on their backs it don't matter how tall they are. Even so, it's chancy. One misstep and I'm dead. Why should I risk it? I like you well enough, ugly little whoreson that you are ... but if I fight your battle, I lose either way. Either the Mountain spills my guts, or I kill him and lose Stokeworth. I sell my sword, I don't give it away. I'm not your bloody brother."

"No," said Tyrion sadly. "You're not." He waved a hand. "Begone, then. Run to Stokeworth and Lady Lollys. May you find more joy in your marriage bed than I ever found in mine."

Bronn hesitated at the door. "What will you do, Imp?"

"Kill Gregor myself. Won't *that* make for a jolly song?"

"I hope I hear them sing it." Bronn grinned one last time, and walked out of the door, the castle, and his life.

Pod shuffled his feet. "I'm sorry."

"Why? Is it your fault that Bronn's an insolent black-hearted rogue? He's always been an insolent black-hearted rogue. That's what I liked about him." Tyrion poured himself a cup of wine and took it to the window seat. Outside the day was grey and rainy, but the prospect was still more cheerful than his. He could send Podrick Payne questing after Shagga, he supposed, but there were so many hiding places in the deep of the kingswood that outlaws often evaded capture for decades. *And Pod sometimes has difficulty finding the kitchens when I send him down for cheese.* Timett son of Timett would likely be back in the Mountains of the Moon by now. And despite what he'd told Bronn, going up against Ser Gregor Clegane in his own person would be a bigger farce than Joffrey's jousting dwarfs. He did not intend to die with gales of laughter ringing in his ears. *So much for trial by combat.*

Ser Kevan paid him another call later that day, and again the day after. Sansa had not been found, his uncle informed him politely. Nor the fool Ser Dontos, who'd vanished the same night. Did Tyrion have any more witnesses he wished to summon? He did not. *How do I bloody well prove I didn't poison the wine, when a thousand people saw me fill Joff's cup?*

He did not sleep at all that night.

Instead, he lay in the dark, staring up at the canopy and counting his ghosts. He saw Tysha smiling as she kissed him, saw Sansa naked and shivering in fear. He saw Joffrey clawing his throat, the blood running down his neck as his face turned black. He saw Cersei's eyes, Bronn's wolfish smile, Shae's wicked grin. Even thought of Shae could not arouse him. He fondled himself, thinking that perhaps if he woke his cock and satisfied it, he might rest more easily afterward, but it was no good.

And then it was dawn, and time for his trial to begin.

It was not Ser Kevan who came for him that morning, but Ser Addam Marbrand with a dozen gold cloaks. Tyrion had broken his fast on boiled eggs, burned bacon, and fried bread, and dressed in his finest. "Ser Addam," he said. "I had thought my father might send the Kingsguard to escort me to trial. I am still a member of the royal family, am I not?"

"You are, my lord, but I fear that most of the Kingsguard stand witness against you. Lord Tywin felt it would not be proper for them to serve as your guards."

"Gods forbid we do anything *improper*. Please, lead on."

He was to be tried in the throne room, where Joffrey had died. As Ser Addam marched him through the towering bronze doors and down the long carpet, he felt the eyes upon him. Hundreds had crowded in to see him judged. At least he hoped that was why they had come. *For all I know, they're all witnesses against me.* He spied Queen Margaery up in the gallery, pale and beautiful in her mourning. *Twice wed and twice widowed, and only sixteen.* Her mother stood tall to one side of her, her grandmother small on the other, with her ladies in waiting and her father's household knights packing the rest of the gallery.

The dais still stood beneath the empty Iron Throne, though all but one table had been removed. Behind it sat stout Lord Mace Tyrell in a gold mantle over green, and slender Prince Oberyn Martell in flowing robes of striped orange, yellow, and scarlet. Lord Tywin Lannister sat between them. *Perhaps there's hope for me yet.* The Dornishman and the Highgardener despised each other. *If I can find a way to use that ...*

The High Septon began with a prayer, asking the Father Above to guide them to justice. When he was done the father below leaned forward to say, "Tyrion, did you kill King Joffrey?"

He would not waste a heartbeat. "No."

"Well, that's a relief," said Oberyn Martell dryly.

"Did Sansa Stark do it, then?" Lord Tyrell demanded.

I would have, if I'd been her. Yet wherever Sansa was and whatever her part in this might have been, she remained his wife. He had wrapped the cloak of his protection about her shoulders, though he'd had to stand on a fool's back to do it. "The gods killed Joffrey. He choked on his pigeon pie."

Lord Tyrell reddened. "You would blame the bakers?"

"Them, or the pigeons. Just leave me out of it." Tyrion heard nervous laughter, and knew he'd made a mistake. *Guard your tongue, you little fool, before it digs your grave.*

"There are witnesses against you," Lord Tywin said. "We shall hear them first. Then you may present your own witnesses. You are to speak only with our leave."

There was naught that Tyrion could do but nod.

Ser Addam had told it true; the first man ushered in was Ser Balon Swann of the Kingsguard. "Lord Hand," he began, after the High Septon had sworn him to speak only truth, "I had the honor to fight beside your son on the bridge of ships. He is a brave man for all his size, and I will not believe he did this thing."

A murmur went through the hall, and Tyrion wondered what mad game Cersei was playing. *Why offer a witness that believes me innocent?* He soon learned. Ser Balon spoke reluctantly of how he had pulled Tyrion away from Joffrey on the day of the riot. "He did strike His Grace, that's so. It was a fit of wroth, no more. A summer storm. The mob near killed us all."

"In the days of the Targaryens, a man who struck one of the blood royal would lose the hand he struck him with," observed the Red Viper of Dorne. "Did the dwarf regrow his little hand, or did you White Swords forget your duty?"

"He was of the blood royal himself," Ser Balon answered. "And the King's Hand beside."

"No," Lord Tywin said. "He was *acting* Hand, in my stead."

Ser Meryn Trant was pleased to expand on Ser Balon's account, when he took his place as witness. "He knocked the king to the ground and began kicking him. He shouted that it was unjust that His Grace had escaped unharmed from the mobs."

Tyrion began to grasp his sister's plan. *She began with a man known to be honest, and milked him for all he would give. Every witness to follow will tell a worse tale, until I seem as bad as Maegor the Cruel and Aerys the Mad together, with a pinch of Aegon the Unworthy for spice.*

Ser Meryn went on to relate how Tyrion had stopped Joffrey's chastisement of Sansa Stark. "The dwarf asked His Grace if he knew what had happened to Aerys Targaryen. When Ser Boros spoke up in defense of the king, the Imp threatened to have him killed."

Blount himself came next, to echo *that* sorry tale. Whatever mislike Ser Boros might harbor toward Cersei for dismissing him from the Kingsguard, he said the words she wanted all the same.

Tyrion could no longer hold his tongue. "Tell the judges what Joffrey was *doing*, why don't you?"

The big jowly man glared at him. "You told your savages to kill me if I opened my mouth, that's what I'll tell them."

"Tyrion," Lord Tywin said. "You are to speak only when we call upon you. Take this for a warning."

Tyrion subsided, seething.

The Kettleblacks came next, all three of them in turn. Osney and Osfryd told the tale of his supper with Cersei before the Battle of the Blackwater, and of the threats he'd made.

"He told Her Grace that he meant to do her harm," said Ser Osfryd. "To hurt her." His brother Osney elaborated. "He said he would wait for a day when she was happy, and make her joy turn to ashes in her mouth." Neither mentioned Alayaya.

Ser Osmund Kettleblack, a vision of chivalry in immaculate scale armor and white wool cloak, swore that King Joffrey had long known that his uncle Tyrion meant to murder him. "It was the day they gave me the white cloak, my lords," he told the judges. "That brave boy said to me, 'Good Ser Osmund, guard me well, for my uncle loves me not. He means to be king in my place.'"

That was more than Tyrion could stomach. "*Liar!*" He took two steps forward before the gold cloaks dragged him back.

Lord Tywin frowned. "Must we have you chained hand and foot like a common brigand?"

Tyrion gnashed his teeth. *A second mistake, fool, fool, fool of a dwarf. Keep your calm or you're doomed.* "No. I beg your pardons, my lords. His lies angered me."

"His truths, you mean," said Cersei. "Father, I beg you to put him in fetters, for your own protection. You see how he is."

"I see he's a dwarf," said Prince Oberyn. "The day I fear a dwarf's wrath is the day I drown myself in a cask of red."

"We need no fetters." Lord Tywin glanced at the windows, and rose. "The hour grows late. We shall resume on the morrow."

That night, alone in his tower cell with a blank parchment and a cup of wine, Tyrion found himself thinking of his wife. Not Sansa; his *first* wife, Tysha. *The whore wife, not the wolf wife.* Her love for him had been pretense, and yet he had believed, and found joy in that belief. *Give me sweet lies, and keep your bitter truths.* He drank his wine and thought of Shae. Later, when Ser Kevan paid his nightly visit, Tyrion asked for Varys.

"You believe the eunuch will speak in your defense?"

"I won't know until I have talked with him. Send him here, Uncle, if you would be so good."

"As you wish."

Maesters Ballabar and Frenken opened the second day of trial. They had opened King Joffrey's noble corpse as well, they swore, and found no morsel of pigeon pie nor any other food lodged in the royal throat. "It was poison that killed him, my lords," said Ballabar, as Frenken nodded gravely.

Then they brought forth Grand Maester Pycelle, leaning heavily on a twisted cane and shaking as he walked, a few white hairs sprouting from his long chicken's neck. He had grown too frail to stand, so the judges permitted a chair to be brought in for him, and a table as well. On the table were laid a number of small jars. Pycelle was pleased to put a name to each.

"Greycap," he said in a quavery voice, "from the toadstool. Nightshade, sweetsleep, demon's dance. This is blindeye. Widow's blood, this one is called, for the color. A cruel potion. It shuts down a man's bladder and bowels, until he drowns in his own poisons. This wolfsbane, here basilisk venom, and this one the tears of Lys. Yes. I know them all. The Imp Tyrion Lannister stole them from my chambers, when he had me falsely imprisoned."

"*Pycelle*," Tyrion called out, risking his father's wrath, "could any of these poisons choke off a man's breath?"

"No. For that, you must turn to a rarer poison. When I was a boy at the Citadel, my teachers named it simply *the strangler*."

"But this rare poison was not found, was it?"

"No, my lord." Pycelle blinked at him. "You used it all to kill the noblest child the gods ever put on this good earth."

Tyrion's anger overwhelmed his sense. "Joffrey was cruel and stupid, but I did not kill him. Have my head off if you like, I had no hand in my nephew's death."

"*Silence!*" Lord Tywin said. "I have told you thrice. The next time, you shall be gagged and chained."

After Pycelle, came the procession, endless and wearisome. Lords and ladies and noble knights, highborn and humble alike, they had all been present at the wedding feast, had all seen Joffrey choke, his face turning as black as a Dornish plum. Lord Redwyne, Lord Celtigar, and Ser Flement Brax had heard Tyrion threaten the king; two serving men, a juggler, Lord Gyles, Ser Hobber Redwyne, and Ser Philip Foote had observed him fill the wedding chalice; Lady Merryweather swore that she had seen the dwarf drop something into the king's wine while Joff and Margaery were cutting the pie; old Estermont, young Peckledon, the singer Galyeon of Cuy, and the squires Morros and Jothos Slynt told how Tyrion had picked up the chalice as Joff was dying and poured out the last of the poisoned wine onto the floor.

When did I make so many enemies? Lady Merryweather was all but a stranger. Tyrion wondered if she was blind or bought. At least Galyeon of Cuy had not set his account to music, or else there might have been seventy-seven bloody verses to it.

When his uncle called that night after supper, his manner was cold and distant. *He thinks I did it too.* "Do you have witnesses for us?" Ser Kevan asked him.

"Not as such, no. Unless you've found my wife."

His uncle shook his head. "It would seem the trial is going very badly for you."

"Oh, do you think so? I hadn't noticed." Tyrion fingered his scar. "Varys has not come."

"Nor will he. On the morrow he testifies against you."

Lovely. "I see." He shifted in his seat. "I am curious. You were always a fair man, Uncle. What convinced you?"

"Why steal Pycelle's poisons, if not to use them?" Ser Kevan said bluntly. "And Lady Merryweather saw—"

"—*nothing!* There was nothing to see. But how do I prove that? How do I prove *anything*, penned up here?"

"Perhaps the time has come for you to confess."

Even through the thick stone walls of the Red Keep, Tyrion could hear the steady wash of rain. "Say that again, Uncle? I could swear you urged me to confess."

"If you were to admit your guilt before the throne and repent of your crime, your father would withhold the sword. You would be permitted to take the black."

Tyrion laughed in his face. "Those were the same terms Cersei offered Eddard Stark. We all know how *that* ended."

"Your father had no part in that."

That much was true, at least. "Castle Black teems with murderers, thieves and rapists," Tyrion said, "but I don't recall meeting many regicides while I was there. You expect me to believe that if I admit to being a kinslayer and kingslayer, my father will simply nod, forgive me, and pack me off to the Wall with some warm woolen smallclothes." He hooted rudely.

"Naught was said of forgiveness," Ser Kevan said sternly. "A confession would put this matter to rest. It is for that reason your father sends me with this offer."

"Thank him kindly for me, Uncle," said Tyrion, "but tell him I am not presently in a confessing mood."

"Were I you, I'd change my mood. Your sister wants your head, and Lord Tyrell at least is inclined to give it to her."

"So one of my judges has already condemned me, without hearing a word in my defense?" It was no more than he expected. "Will I still be allowed to speak and present witnesses?"

"You *have* no witnesses," his uncle reminded him. "Tyrion, if you are guilty of this enormity, the Wall is a kinder fate than you deserve. And if you are blameless ... there is fighting in the north, I know, but even so it will be a safer place for you than King's Landing, whatever the outcome of this trial. The mob is convinced of your guilt. Were you so foolish as to venture out into the streets, they would tear you limb from limb."

"I can see how much that prospect upsets you."

"You are my brother's son."

"You might remind *him* of that."

"Do you think he would allow you to take the black if you were not his own blood, and Joanna's? Tywin seems a hard man to you, I know, but he is no harder than he's had to be. Our own father was gentle and amiable, but so weak his bannermen mocked him in their cups. Some saw fit to defy him openly. Other lords borrowed our gold and never troubled to repay it. At court they japed of toothless lions. Even his mistress stole from him. A woman scarcely one step above a whore, and she helped herself to my mother's jewels! It fell to Tywin to restore House Lannister to its proper place. Just as it fell to him to rule this realm, when he was no more than twenty. He bore that heavy burden for *twenty years*, and all it earned him was a mad king's envy. Instead of the honor he deserved, he was made to suffer slights beyond count, yet he gave the Seven Kingdoms peace, plenty, and justice. He is a just man. You would be wise to trust him."

Tyrion blinked in astonishment. Ser Kevan had always been solid, stolid, pragmatic; he had never heard him speak with such fervor before. "You love him."

"He is my brother."

"I ... I will think on what you've said."

"Think carefully, then. And quickly."

He thought of little else that night, but come morning was no closer to deciding if his father could be trusted. A servant brought him porridge and honey to break his fast, but all he could taste was bile at the thought of confession. *They will call me kinslayer till the end of my days. For a thousand years or more, if I am remembered at all, it will be as the monstrous dwarf who poisoned his young nephew at his wedding feast.* The thought made him so bloody angry that he flung the bowl and spoon across the room and left a smear of porridge on the wall. Ser Addam Marbrand looked at it curiously when he came to escort Tyrion to trial, but had the good grace not to inquire.

"Lord Varys," the herald said, "master of whisperers."

Powdered, primped, and smelling of rosewater, the Spider rubbed his hands one over the other all the time he spoke. *Washing my life away*, Tyrion thought, as he listened to the eunuch's mournful account of how the Imp had schemed to part Joffrey from the Hound's protection and spoken with Bronn of the benefits of having Tommen as king. *Half-truths are worth more than outright lies.* And unlike the others, Varys had documents; parchments painstakingly filled with notes, details, dates, whole conversations. So much material that its recitation took all day, and so much of it damning. Varys confirmed Tyrion's midnight visit to Grand Maester Pycelle's chambers and the theft of his poisons and potions, confirmed the threat he'd made to Cersei the night of their supper, confirmed every bloody thing but the poisoning itself. When Prince Oberyn asked him how he could possibly know all this, not having been present at any of these events, the eunuch only giggled and said, "My little birds told me. Knowing is their purpose, and mine."

How do I question a little bird? thought Tyrion. *I should have had the eunuch's head off my first day in King's Landing. Damn him. And damn me for whatever trust I put in him.*

"Have we heard it all?" Lord Tywin asked his daughter as Varys left the hall.

"Almost," said Cersei. "I beg your leave to bring one final witness before you, on the morrow."

"As you wish," Lord Tywin said.

Oh, good, thought Tyrion savagely. *After this farce of a trial, execution will almost come as a relief.*

That night, as he sat by his window drinking, he heard voices outside his door. *Ser Kevan, come for my answer,* he thought at once, but it was not his uncle who entered.

Tyrion rose to give Prince Oberyn a mocking bow. "Are judges permitted to visit the accused?"

"Princes are permitted to go where they will. Or so I told your guards." The Red Viper took a seat.

"My father will be displeased with you."

"The happiness of Tywin Lannister has never been high on my list of concerns. Is it Dornish wine you're drinking?"

"From the Arbor."

Oberyn made a face. "Red water. Did you poison him?"

"No. Did you?"

The prince smiled. "Do all dwarfs have tongues like yours? Someone is going to cut it out one of these days."

"You are not the first to tell me that. Perhaps I should cut it out myself, it seems to make no end of trouble."

"So I've seen. I think I may drink some of Lord Redwyne's grape juice after all."

"As you like." Tyrion served him a cup.

The man took a sip, sloshed it about in his mouth, and swallowed. "It will serve, for the moment. I will send you up some strong Dornish wine on the morrow." He took another sip. "I have turned up that golden-haired whore I was hoping for."

"So you found Chataya's?"

"At Chataya's I bedded the black-skinned girl. Alayaya, I believe she is called. Exquisite, despite the stripes on her back. But the whore I referred to is your sister."

"Has she seduced you yet?" Tyrion asked, unsurprised.

Oberyn laughed aloud. "No, but she will if I meet her price. The queen has even hinted at marriage. Her Grace needs another husband, and who better than a prince of Dorne? Ellaria believes I should accept. Just the thought of Cersei in our bed makes her wet, the randy wench. And we should not even need to pay the dwarf's penny. All your sister requires from me is one head, somewhat overlarge and missing a nose."

"And?" said Tyrion, waiting.

By way of answer, Prince Oberyn swirled his wine, and said, "When the Young Dragon conquered Dorne so long ago, he left the Lord of

Highgarden to rule us after the Submission of Sunspear. This Tyrell moved with his tail from keep to keep, chasing rebels and making certain that our knees stayed bent. He would arrive in force, take a castle for his own, stay a moon's turn, and ride on to the next castle. It was his custom to turn the lords out of their own chambers and take their beds for himself. One night he found himself beneath a heavy velvet canopy. A sash hung down near the pillows, should he wish to summon a wench. He had a taste for Dornish women, this Lord Tyrell, and who can blame him? So he pulled upon the sash, and when he did the canopy above him split open, and a hundred red scorpions fell down upon his head. His death lit a fire that soon swept across Dorne, undoing all the Young Dragon's victories in a fortnight. The kneeling men stood up, and we were free again."

"I know the tale," said Tyrion. "What of it?"

"Just this. If I should ever find a sash beside my own bed, and pull on it, I would sooner have the scorpions fall upon me than the queen in all her naked beauty."

Tyrion grinned. "We have that much in common, then."

"To be sure, I have much to thank your sister for. If not for her accusation at the feast, it might well be you judging me instead of me judging you." The prince's eyes were dark with amusement. "Who knows more of poison than the Red Viper of Dorne, after all? Who has better reason to want to keep the Tyrells far from the crown? And with Joffrey in his grave, by *Dornish* law the Iron Throne should pass next to his sister Myrcella, who as it happens is betrothed to mine own nephew, thanks to you."

"Dornish law does not apply." Tyrion had been so ensnared in his own troubles that he'd never stopped to consider the succession. "My father will crown Tommen, count on that."

"He may indeed crown Tommen, here in King's Landing. Which is not to say that my brother may not crown Myrcella, down in Sunspear. Will your father make war on your niece on behalf of your nephew? Will your sister?" He gave a shrug. "Perhaps I should marry Queen Cersei after all, on the condition that she support her daughter over her son. Do you think she would?"

Never, Tyrion wanted to say, but the word caught in his throat.

Cersei always resented being excluded from power on account of her sex. *If Dornish law applied in the west, she would be the heir to Casterly Rock in her own right.* She and Jaime were twins, but Cersei had come first into the world, and that was all it took. By championing Myrcella's cause she would be championing her own. "I do not know how my sister would choose, between Tommen and Myrcella," he admitted. "It makes no matter. My father will never give her that choice."

"Your father," said Prince Oberyn, "may not live forever."

Something about the way he said it made the hairs on the back of Tyrion's neck bristle. Suddenly he was mindful of Elia again, and all that Oberyn had said as they crossed the field of ashes. *He wants the head that spoke the words, not just the hand that swung the sword.* "It is not wise to speak such treasons in the Red Keep, my prince. The little birds are listening."

"Let them. Is it treason to say a man is mortal? *Valar morghulis* was how they said it in Valyria of old. *All men must die.* And the Doom came and proved it true." The Dornishman went to the window to gaze out into the night. "It is being said that you have no witnesses for us."

"I was hoping one look at this sweet face of mine would be enough to persuade you all of my innocence."

"You are mistaken, my lord. The Fat Flower of Highgarden is quite convinced of your guilt, and determined to see you die. His precious Margaery was drinking from that chalice too, as he has reminded us half a hundred times."

"And you?" said Tyrion.

"Men are seldom as they appear. You look so very guilty that I am convinced of your innocence. Still, you will likely be condemned. Justice is in short supply this side of the mountains. There has been none for Elia, Aegon, or Rhaenys. Why should there be any for you? Perhaps Joffrey's real killer was eaten by a bear. That seems to happen quite often in King's Landing. Oh, wait, the bear was at Harrenhal, now I remember."

"Is that the game we are playing?" Tyrion rubbed at his scarred nose. He had nothing to lose by telling Oberyn the truth. "There *was* a bear at Harrenhal, and it did kill Ser Amory Lorch."

"How sad for him," said the Red Viper. "And for you. Do all nose-less men lie so badly, I wonder?"

"I am not lying. Ser Amory dragged Princess Rhaenys out from under her father's bed and stabbed her to death. He had some men-at-arms with him, but I do not know their names." He leaned forward. "It was Ser Gregor Clegane who smashed Prince Aegon's head against a wall and raped your sister Elia with his blood and brains still on his hands."

"What is this, now? Truth, from a Lannister?" Oberyn smiled coldly. "Your father gave the commands, yes?"

"No." He spoke the lie without hesitation, and never stopped to ask himself why he should.

The Dornishman raised one thin black eyebrow. "Such a dutiful son. And such a very feeble lie. It was Lord Tywin who presented my sister's children to King Robert all wrapped up in crimson Lannister cloaks."

"Perhaps you ought to have this discussion with my father. He was there. I was at the Rock, and still so young that I thought the thing between my legs was only good for pissing."

"Yes, but you are here now, and in some difficulty, I would say. Your innocence may be as plain as the scar on your face, but it will not save you. No more than your father will." The Dornish prince smiled. "But I might."

"You?" Tyrion studied him. "You are one judge in three. How could you save me?"

"Not as your judge. As your champion."

JAIME

Awhite book sat on a white table in a white room. The room was round, its walls of whitewashed stone hung with white woolen tapestries. It formed the first floor of White Sword Tower, a slender structure of four stories built into an angle of the castle wall overlooking the bay. The undercroft held arms and armor, the second and third floors the small spare sleeping cells of the six brothers of the Kingsguard.

One of those cells had been his for eighteen years, but this morning he had moved his things to the topmost floor, which was given over entirely to the Lord Commander's apartments. Those rooms were spare as well, though spacious; and they were above the outer walls, which meant he would have a view of the sea. *I will like that,* he thought. *The view, and all the rest.*

As pale as the room, Jaime sat by the book in his Kingsguard whites, waiting for his Sworn Brothers. A longsword hung from his hip. *From the wrong hip.* Before, he had always worn his sword on his left, and drawn it across his body when he unsheathed. He had shifted it to his right hip this morning, so as to be able to draw it with his left hand in the same manner, but the weight of it felt strange there, and when he had tried to pull the blade from the scabbard the whole motion seemed clumsy and unnatural. His clothing fit badly as well. He had donned the winter raiment of the Kingsguard, a tunic and breeches of bleached white wool and a heavy white cloak, but it all seemed to hang loose on him.

Jaime had spent his days at his brother's trial, standing well to the back of the hall. Either Tyrion never saw him there or he did not know him, but that was no surprise. Half the court no longer seemed to know him. *I am a stranger in my own House.* His son was dead, his father had disowned him, and his sister . . . she had not allowed him to be alone with her once, after that first day in the royal sept where Joffrey lay amongst the candles. Even when they bore him across the city to his tomb in the Great Sept of Baelor, Cersei kept a careful distance.

He looked about the Round Room once more. White wool hangings covered the walls, and there was a white shield and two crossed longswords mounted above the hearth. The chair behind the table was old black oak, with cushions of blanched cowhide, the leather worn thin. *Worn by the bony arse of Barristan the Bold and Ser Gerold Hightower before him, by Prince Aemon the Dragonknight, Ser Ryam Redwyne, and the Demon of Darry, by Ser Duncan the Tall and the Pale Griffin Alyn Connington.* How could the Kingslayer belong in such exalted company?

Yet here he was.

The table itself was old weirwood, pale as bone, carved in the shape of a huge shield supported by three white stallions. By tradition the Lord Commander sat at the top of the shield, and the brothers three to a side, on the rare occasions when all seven were assembled. The book that rested by his elbow was massive; two feet tall and a foot and a half wide, a thousand pages thick, fine white vellum bound between covers of bleached white leather with gold hinges and fastenings. *The Book of the Brothers* was its formal name, but more often it was simply called the White Book.

Within the White Book was the history of the Kingsguard. Every knight who'd ever served had a page, to record his name and deeds for all time. On the top left-hand corner of each page was drawn the shield the man had carried at the time he was chosen, inked in rich colors. Down in the bottom right corner was the shield of the Kingsguard; snow-white, empty, pure. The upper shields were all different; the lower shields were all the same. In the space between were written the facts of each man's life and service. The heraldic drawings and illuminations were done by septons sent from the Great Sept of Baelor three times a year, but it was the duty of the Lord Commander to keep the entries up to date.

My duty, now. Once he learned to write with his left hand, that is. The White Book was well behind. The deaths of Ser Mandon Moore and Ser Preston Greenfield needed to be entered, and the brief bloody Kingsguard service of Sandor Clegane as well. New pages must be started for Ser Balon Swann, Ser Osmund Kettleblack, and the Knight of Flowers. *I will need to summon a septon to draw their shields.*

Ser Barristan Selmy had preceded Jaime as Lord Commander. The shield atop his page showed the arms of House Selmy: three stalks of wheat, yellow, on a brown field. Jaime was amused, though unsurprised, to find that Ser Barristan had taken the time to record his own dismissal before leaving the castle.

Ser Barristan of House Selmy. Firstborn son of Ser Lyonel Selmy of Harvest Hall. Served as squire to Ser Manfred Swann. Named "the Bold" in his 10th year, when he donned borrowed armor to appear as a mystery knight in the tourney at Blackhaven, where he was defeated and unmasked by Duncan, Prince of Dragonflies. Knighted in his 16th year by King Aegon V Targaryen, after performing great feats of prowess as a mystery knight in the winter tourney at King's Landing, defeating Prince Duncan the Small and Ser Duncan the Tall, Lord Commander of the Kingsguard. Slew Maelys the Monstrous, last of the Blackfyre Pretenders, in single combat during the War of the Ninepenny Kings. Defeated Lormelle Long Lance and Cedrik Storm, the Bastard of Bronzegate. Named to the Kingsguard in his 23rd year, by Lord Commander Ser Gerold Hightower. Defended the passage against all challengers in the tourney of the Silver Bridge. Victor in the mêlée at Maidenpool. Brought King Aerys II to safety during the Defiance of Duskendale, despite an arrow wound in the chest. Avenged the murder of his Sworn Brother, Ser Gwayne Gaunt. Rescued Lady Jeyne Swann and her septa from the Kingswood Brotherhood, defeating Simon Toyne and the Smiling Knight, and slaying the former. In the Oldtown tourney, defeated and unmasked the mystery knight Blackshield, revealing him as the Bastard of Uplands. Sole champion of Lord Steffon's tourney at Storm's End, whereat he unhorsed Lord Robert Baratheon, Prince Oberyn Martell, Lord Leyton Hightower, Lord Jon Connington, Lord Jason Mallister, and Prince Rhaegar Targaryen. Wounded by arrow, spear, and sword at the Battle of the Trident whilst fighting beside his Sworn Brothers and Rhaegar Prince of Dragonstone. Pardoned, and named Lord Commander of the Kingsguard, by King Robert I Baratheon. Served in the honor guard that brought Lady Cersei of House Lannister to King's Landing to wed King Robert. Led the attack on Old Wyk during Balon Greyjoy's Rebellion. Champion of the tourney at King's Landing, in his 57th year. Dismissed from service by King Joffrey I Baratheon in his 61st year, for reasons of advanced age.

The earlier part of Ser Barristan's storied career had been entered by Ser Gerold Hightower in a big forceful hand. Selmy's own smaller and more elegant writing took over with the account of his wounding on the Trident.

Jaime's own page was scant by comparison.

Ser Jaime of House Lannister. Firstborn son of Lord Tywin and Lady Joanna of Casterly Rock. Served against the Kingswood Brotherhood as squire to Lord Sumner Crakehall. Knighted in his 15th year by Ser Arthur Dayne of the Kingsguard, for valor in the field. Chosen for the Kingsguard in his 15th year by King Aerys II Targaryen. During the Sack of King's Landing, slew King Aerys II at the foot of the Iron Throne. Thereafter known as the "Kingslayer." Pardoned for his crime by King Robert I Baratheon. Served in the honor guard that brought his sister the Lady Cersei Lannister to King's Landing to wed King Robert. Champion in the tourney held at King's Landing on the occasion of their wedding.

Summed up like that, his life seemed a rather scant and mingy thing. Ser Barristan could have recorded a few of his other tourney victories, at least. And Ser Gerold might have written a few more words about the deeds he'd performed when Ser Arthur Dayne broke the Kingswood Brotherhood. He *had* saved Lord Sumner's life as Big Belly Ben was about to smash his head in, though the outlaw had escaped him. And he'd held his own against the Smiling Knight, though it was Ser Arthur who slew him. *What a fight that was, and what a foe.* The Smiling Knight was a madman, cruelty and chivalry all jumbled up together, but he did not know the meaning of fear. *And Dayne, with Dawn in hand . . .* The outlaw's longsword had so many notches by the end that Ser Arthur had stopped to let him fetch a new one. "It's that white sword of yours I want," the robber knight told him as they resumed, though he was bleeding from a dozen wounds by then. "Then you shall have it, ser," the Sword of the Morning replied, and made an end of it.

The world was simpler in those days, Jaime thought, *and men as well as swords were made of finer steel.* Or was it only that he had been fifteen? They were all in their graves now, the Sword of the Morning and the Smiling Knight, the White Bull and Prince Lewyn, Ser Oswell Whent with his black humor, earnest Jon Darry, Simon Toyne and his Kingswood Brotherhood, bluff old Sumner Crakehall. *And me, that boy I was . . . when did he die, I wonder? When I donned the white cloak? When I opened Aerys's throat?* That boy had wanted to be Ser Arthur Dayne, but someplace along the way he had become the Smiling Knight instead.

When he heard the door open, he closed the White Book and stood to receive his Sworn Brothers. Ser Osmund Kettleblack was the first to arrive. He gave Jaime a grin, as if they were old brothers-in-arms. "Ser Jaime," he said, "had you looked like this t'other night, I'd have known you at once."

"Would you indeed?" Jaime doubted that. The servants had bathed him, shaved him, and washed and brushed his hair. When he looked in a glass, he no longer saw the man who had crossed the riverlands with Brienne . . . but he did not see himself either. His face was thin and hollow, and he had lines under his eyes. *I look like some old man.* "Stand by your seat, ser."

Kettleblack complied. The other Sworn Brothers filed in one by one. "Sers," Jaime said in a formal tone when all five had assembled, "who guards the king?"

"My brothers Ser Osney and Ser Osfryd," Ser Osmund replied.

"And my brother Ser Garlan," said the Knight of Flowers.

"Will they keep him safe?"

"They will, my lord."

"Be seated, then." The words were ritual. Before the seven could meet in session, the king's safety must be assured.

Ser Boros and Ser Meryn sat to his right, leaving an empty chair between them for Ser Arys Oakheart, off in Dorne. Ser Osmund, Ser Balon, and Ser Loras took the seats to his left. *The old and the new.* Jaime wondered if that meant anything. There had been times during its history where the Kingsguard had been divided against itself, most notably and bitterly during the Dance of the Dragons. Was that something he needed to fear as well?

It seemed queer to him to sit in the Lord Commander's seat where Barristan the Bold had sat for so many years. *And even queerer to sit here crippled.* Nonetheless, it was his seat, and this was his Kingsguard now. *Tommen's seven.*

Jaime had served with Meryn Trant and Boros Blount for years; adequate fighters, but Trant was sly and cruel, and Blount a bag of growly air. Ser Balon Swann was better suited to his cloak, and of course the Knight of Flowers was supposedly all a knight should be. The fifth man was a stranger to him, this Osmund Kettleblack.

He wondered what Ser Arthur Dayne would have to say of this lot. *"How is it that the Kingsguard has fallen so low,"* most like. *"It was my doing,"* I would have to answer. *"I opened the door, and did nothing when the vermin began to crawl inside."*

"The king is dead," Jaime began. "My sister's son, a boy of thirteen, murdered at his own wedding feast in his own hall. All five of you were present. All five of you were *protecting* him. And yet he's dead." He waited to see what they would say to that, but none of them so much as cleared a throat. *The Tyrell boy is angry, and Balon Swann's ashamed,* he judged. From the other three, Jaime sensed only indifference. "Did my brother do this thing?" he asked them bluntly. "Did Tyrion poison my nephew?"

Ser Balon shifted uncomfortably in his seat. Ser Boros made a fist. Ser Osmund gave a lazy shrug. It was Meryn Trant who finally answered. "He filled Joffrey's cup with wine. That must have been when he slipped the poison in."

"You are certain it was the *wine* that was poisoned?"

"What else?" said Ser Boros Blount. "The Imp emptied the dregs on the floor. Why, but to spill the wine that might have proved him guilty?"

"He knew the wine was poisoned," said Ser Meryn.

Ser Balon Swann frowned. "The Imp was not alone on the dais. Far from it. That late in the feast, we had people standing and moving about, changing places, slipping off to the privy, servants were coming and going . . . the king and queen had just opened the wedding pie, every eye was on them or those thrice-damned doves. No one was watching the wine cup."

"Who else was on the dais?" asked Jaime.

Ser Meryn answered. "The king's family, the bride's family, Grand Maester Pycelle, the High Septon . . ."

"There's your poisoner," suggested Ser Oswald Kettleblack with a sly grin. "Too holy by half, that old man. Never liked the look o' him, myself." He laughed.

"No," the Knight of Flowers said, unamused. "Sansa Stark was the poisoner. You all forget, my sister was drinking from that chalice as well. Sansa Stark was the only person in the hall who had reason to want Margaery dead, as well as the king. By poisoning the wedding cup, she could hope to kill both of them. And why did she run afterward, unless she was guilty?"

The boy makes sense. Tyrion might yet be innocent. No one was any closer to finding the girl, however. Perhaps Jaime should look into that himself. For a start, it would be good to know how she had gotten out of the castle. *Varys may have a notion or two about that.* No one knew the Red Keep better than the eunuch.

That could wait, however. Just now Jaime had more immediate concerns. *You say you are the Lord Commander of the Kingsguard,* his father had said. *Go do your duty.* These five were not the brothers he would have chosen, but they were the brothers he had; the time had come to take them in hand.

"Whoever did it," he told them, "Joffrey is dead, and the Iron

Throne belongs to Tommen now. I mean for him to sit on it until his hair turns white and his teeth fall out. And not from poison." Jaime turned to Ser Boros Blount. The man had grown stout in recent years, though he was big-boned enough to carry it. "Ser Boros, you look like a man who enjoys his food. Henceforth you'll taste everything Tommen eats or drinks."

Ser Osmund Kettleblack laughed aloud and the Knight of Flowers smiled, but Ser Boros turned a deep beet red. "I am no food taster! I am a knight of the Kingsguard!"

"Sad to say, you are." Cersei should never have stripped the man of his white cloak. But their father had only compounded the shame by restoring it. "My sister has told me how readily you yielded my nephew to Tyrion's sellswords. You will find carrots and pease less threatening, I hope. When your Sworn Brothers are training in the yard with sword and shield, you may train with spoon and trencher. Tommen loves applecakes. Try not to let any sellswords make off with them."

"You speak to me thus? *You?*"

"You should have died before you let Tommen be taken."

"As you died protecting Aerys, ser?" Ser Boros lurched to his feet, and clasped the hilt of his sword. "I *won't* . . . I won't suffer this. You should be the food taster, it seems to me. What else is a cripple good for?"

Jaime smiled. "I agree. I am as unfit to guard the king as you are. So draw that sword you're fondling, and we shall see how your two hands fare against my one. At the end one of us will be dead, and the Kingsguard will be improved." He rose. "Or, if you prefer, you may return to your duties."

"*Bah!*" Ser Boros hawked up a glob of green phlegm, spat it at Jaime's feet, and walked out, his sword still in its sheath.

The man is craven, and a good thing. Though fat, aging, and never more than ordinary, Ser Boros could still have hacked him into bloody pieces. *But Boros does not know that, and neither must the rest. They feared the man I was; the man I am they'd pity.*

Jaime seated himself again and turned to Kettleblack. "Ser Osmund. I do not know you. I find that curious. I've fought in tourneys, mêlées, and battles throughout the Seven Kingdoms. I know of every hedge knight, freerider, and upjumped squire of any skill who has ever presumed to break a lance in the lists. So how is it that I have never heard of you, Ser Osmund?"

"That I couldn't say, my lord." He had a great wide smile on his face, did Ser Osmund, as if he and Jaime were old comrades in arms playing some jolly little game. "I'm a soldier, though, not no tourney knight."

"Where had you served, before my sister found you?"

"Here and there, my lord."

"I have been to Oldtown in the south and Winterfell in the north. I have been to Lannisport in the west, and King's Landing in the east. But I have never been to Here. Nor There." For want of a finger, Jaime pointed his stump at Ser Osmund's beak of a nose. "I will ask once more. *Where have you served?*"

"In the Stepstones. Some in the Disputed Lands. There's always fighting there. I rode with the Gallant Men. We fought for Lys, and some for Tyrosh."

You fought for anyone who would pay you. "How did you come by your knighthood?"

"On a battlefield."

"Who knighted you?"

"Ser Robert . . . Stone. He's dead now, my lord."

"To be sure." Ser Robert Stone might have been some bastard from the Vale, he supposed, selling his sword in the Disputed Lands. On the other hand, he might be no more than a name Ser Osmund cobbled together from a dead king and a castle wall. *What was Cersei thinking when she gave this one a white cloak?*

At least Kettleblack would likely know how to use a sword and shield. Sellswords were seldom the most honorable of men, but they had to have a certain skill at arms to stay alive. "Very well, ser," Jaime said. "You may go."

The man's grin returned. He left swaggering.

"Ser Meryn." Jaime smiled at the sour knight with the rust-red hair and the pouches under his eyes. "I have heard it said that Joffrey made use of you to chastise Sansa Stark." He turned the White Book around one-handed. "Here, show me where it is in our vows that we swear to beat women and children."

"I did as His Grace commanded me. We are sworn to obey."

"Henceforth you will temper that obedience. My sister is Queen Regent. My father is the King's Hand. I am Lord Commander of the Kingsguard. Obey us. None other."

Ser Meryn got a stubborn look on his face. "Are you telling us not to obey the king?"

"The king is eight. Our first duty is to *protect* him, which includes protecting him from himself. Use that ugly thing you keep inside your helm. If Tommen wants you to saddle his horse, obey him. If he tells you to kill his horse, come to me."

"Aye. As you command, my lord."

"Dismissed." As he left, Jaime turned to Ser Balon Swann. "Ser Balon, I have watched you tilt many a time, and fought with and against you in mêlées. I'm told you proved your valor a hundred times over during the Battle of the Blackwater. The Kingsguard is honored by your presence."

"The honor's mine, my lord." Ser Balon sounded wary.

"There is only one question I would put to you. You served us loyally, it's true . . . but Varys tells me that your brother rode with Renly and then Stannis, whilst your lord father chose not to call his banners at all and remained behind the walls of Stonehelm all through the fighting."

"My father is an old man, my lord. Well past forty. His fighting days are done."

"And your brother?"

"Donnel was wounded in the battle and yielded to Ser Elwood Harte. He was ransomed afterward and pledged his fealty to King Joffrey, as did many other captives."

"So he did," said Jaime. "Even so . . . Renly, Stannis, Joffrey, Tommen . . . how did he come to omit Balon Greyjoy and Robb Stark? He might have been the first knight in the realm to swear fealty to all six kings."

Ser Balon's unease was plain. "Donnel erred, but he is Tommen's man now. You have my word."

"It's not Ser Donnel the Constant who concerns me. It's you." Jaime leaned forward. "What will you do if brave Ser Donnel gives his sword to yet another usurper, and one day comes storming into the throne room? And there you stand all in white, between your king and your blood. What will you do?"

"I . . . my lord, that will never happen."

"It happened to me," Jaime said.

Swann wiped his brow with the sleeve of his white tunic.

"You have no answer?"

"My lord." Ser Balon drew himself up. "On my sword, on my honor, on my father's name, I swear . . . I shall not do as you did."

Jaime laughed. "Good. Return to your duties . . . and tell Ser Donnel to add a weathervane to his shield."

And then he was alone with the Knight of Flowers.

Slim as a sword, lithe and fit, Ser Loras Tyrell wore a snowy linen tunic and white wool breeches, with a gold belt around his waist and a gold rose clasping his fine silk cloak. His hair was a soft brown tumble, and his eyes were brown as well, and bright with insolence. *He thinks this is a tourney, and his tilt has just been called.* "Seventeen and a knight of the Kingsguard," said Jaime. "You must be proud. Prince Aemon the Dragonknight was seventeen when he was named. Did you know that?"

"Yes, my lord."

"And did you know that I was *fifteen*?"

"That as well, my lord." He smiled.

Jaime hated that smile. "I was better than you, Ser Loras. I was bigger, I was stronger, and I was quicker."

"And now you're older," the boy said. "My lord."

He had to laugh. *This is too absurd. Tyrion would mock me unmercifully if he could hear me now, comparing cocks with this green boy.* "Older and wiser, ser. You should learn from me."

"As you learned from Ser Boros and Ser Meryn?"

That arrow hit too close to the mark. "I learned from the White Bull and Barristan the Bold," Jaime snapped. "I learned from Ser Arthur Dayne, the Sword of the Morning, who could have slain all five of you with his left hand while he was taking a piss with the right. I learned from Prince Lewyn of Dorne and Ser Oswell Whent and Ser Jonothor Darry, good men every one."

"Dead men, every one."

He's me, Jaime realized suddenly. *I am speaking to myself, as I was, all cocksure arrogance and empty chivalry. This is what it does to you, to be too good too young.*

As in a swordfight, sometimes it is best to try a different stroke. "It's said you fought magnificently in the battle . . . almost as well as Lord Renly's ghost beside you. A Sworn Brother has no secrets from his Lord Commander. Tell me, ser. Who was wearing Renly's armor?"

For a moment, Loras Tyrell looked as though he might refuse, but in the end he remembered his vows. "My brother," he said sullenly. "Renly was taller than me, and broader in the chest. His armor was too loose on me, but it suited Garlan well."

"Was the masquerade your notion, or his?"

"Lord Littlefinger suggested it. He said it would frighten Stannis's ignorant men-at-arms."

"And so it did." *And some knights and lordlings too.* "Well, you gave the singers something to make rhymes about, I suppose that's not to be despised. What did you do with Renly?"

"I buried him with mine own hands, in a place he showed me once when I was a squire at Storm's End. No one shall ever find him there to disturb his rest." He looked at Jaime defiantly. "I will defend King Tommen with all my strength, I swear it. I will give my life for his if need be. But I will never betray Renly, by word or deed. He was the king that should have been. He was the best of them."

The best dressed perhaps, Jaime thought, but for once he did not say it. The arrogance had gone out of Ser Loras the moment he began to speak of Renly. *He answered truly. He is proud and reckless and full of piss, but he is not false. Not yet.* "As you say. One more thing, and you may return to your duties."

"Yes, my lord?"

"I still have Brienne of Tarth in a tower cell."

The boy's mouth hardened. "A black cell would be better."

"You are certain that's what she deserves?"

"She deserves death. I told Renly that a woman had no place in the Rainbow Guard. She won the mêlée with a trick."

"I seem to recall another knight who was fond of tricks. He once rode a mare in heat against a foe mounted on a bad-tempered stallion. What sort of trickery did Brienne use?"

Ser Loras flushed. "She leapt ... it makes no matter. She won, I grant her that. His Grace put a rainbow cloak around her shoulders. And she killed him. Or let him die."

"A large difference there." *The difference between my crime and the shame of Boros Blount.*

"She had sworn to protect him. Ser Emmon Cuy, Ser Robar Royce, Ser Parmen Crane, they'd sworn as well. How could anyone have hurt him, with her inside his tent and the others just outside? Unless they were part of it."

"There were five of you at the wedding feast," Jaime pointed out. "How could Joffrey die? Unless you were part of it?"

Ser Loras drew himself up stiffly. "There was nothing we could have done."

"The wench says the same. She grieves for Renly as you do. I promise you, I never grieve for Aerys. Brienne's ugly, and pighead stubborn. But she lacks the wits to be a liar, and she is loyal past the point of sense. She swore an oath to bring me to King's Landing, and here I sit. This hand I lost ... well, that was my doing as much as hers. Considering all she did to protect me, I have no doubt that she would have fought for Renly, had there been a foe to fight. But a shadow?" Jaime shook his head. "Draw your sword, Ser Loras. Show me how *you'd* fight a shadow. I should like to see that."

Ser Loras made no move to rise. "She fled," he said. "She and Catelyn Stark, they left him in his blood and ran. Why would they, if it was not their work?" He stared at the table. "Renly gave me the van. Otherwise it would have been me helping him don his armor. He often entrusted that task to me. We had ... we had prayed together that night. I left him with her. Ser Parmen and Ser Emmon were guarding the tent, and Ser Robar Royce was there as well. Ser Emmon swore Brienne had ... although ..."

"Yes?" Jaime prompted, sensing a doubt.

"The gorget was cut through. One clean stroke, through a steel gorget. Renly's armor was the best, the finest steel. How could she do that? I tried myself, and it was not possible. She's freakish strong for a woman, but even the Mountain would have needed a heavy axe. And why armor him and *then* cut his throat?" He gave Jaime a confused look. "If not her, though . . . how could it be a *shadow*?"

"Ask her." Jaime came to a decision. "Go to her cell. Ask your questions and hear her answers. If you are still convinced that she murdered Lord Renly, I will see that she answers for it. The choice will be yours. Accuse her, or release her. All I ask is that you judge her fairly, on your honor as a knight."

Ser Loras stood. "I shall. On my honor."

"We are done, then."

The younger man started for the door. But there he turned back. "Renly thought she was absurd. A woman dressed in man's mail, pretending to be a knight."

"If he'd ever seen her in pink satin and Myrish lace, he would not have complained."

"I asked him why he kept her close, if he thought her so grotesque. He said that all his other knights wanted things of him, castles or honors or riches, but all that Brienne wanted was to die for him. When I saw him all bloody, with her fled and the three of them unharmed . . . if she's innocent, then Robar and Emmon . . ." He could not seem to say the words.

Jaime had not stopped to consider that aspect of it. "I would have done the same, ser." The lie came easy, but Ser Loras seemed grateful for it.

When he was gone, the Lord Commander sat alone in the white room, wondering. The Knight of Flowers had been so mad with grief for Renly that he had cut down two of his own Sworn Brothers, but it had never occurred to Jaime to do the same with the five who had failed Joffrey. *He was my son, my secret son . . . What am I, if I do not lift the hand I have left to avenge mine own blood and seed?* He ought to kill Ser Boros at least, just to be rid of him.

He looked at his stump and grimaced. *I must do something about that.* If the late Ser Jacelyn Bywater could wear an iron hand, he should have a gold one. *Cersei might like that. A golden hand to stroke her golden hair, and hold her hard against me.*

His hand could wait, though. There were other things to tend to first. There were other debts to pay.

SANSA

The ladder to the forecastle was steep and splintery, so Sansa accepted a hand up from Lothor Brune. *Ser Lothor,* she had to remind herself; the man had been knighted for his valor in the Battle of the Blackwater. Though no proper knight would wear those patched brown breeches and scuffed boots, nor that cracked and water-stained leather jerkin. A square-faced stocky man with a squashed nose and a mat of nappy grey hair, Brune spoke seldom. *He is stronger than he looks, though.* She could tell by the ease with which he lifted her, as if she weighed nothing at all.

Off the bow of the *Merling King* stretched a bare and stony strand, windswept, treeless, and uninviting. Even so, it made a welcome sight. They had been a long while clawing their way back on course. The last storm had swept them out of sight of land, and sent such waves crashing over the sides of the galley that Sansa had been certain they were all going to drown. Two men had been swept overboard, she had heard old Oswell saying, and another had fallen from the mast and broken his neck.

She had seldom ventured out on deck herself. Her little cabin was dank and cold, but Sansa had been sick for most of the voyage ... sick with terror, sick with fever, or seasick ... she could keep nothing down, and even sleep came hard. Whenever she closed her eyes she saw Joffrey tearing at his collar, clawing at the soft skin of his throat,

354   GEORGE R.R. MARTIN

dying with flakes of pie crust on his lips and wine stains on his doublet. And the wind keening in the lines reminded her of the terrible thin sucking sound he'd made as he fought to draw in air. Sometimes she dreamed of Tyrion as well. "He did nothing," she told Littlefinger once, when he paid a visit to her cabin to see if she were feeling any better.

"He did not kill Joffrey, true, but the dwarf's hands are far from clean. He had a wife before you, did you know that?"

"He told me."

"And did he tell you that when he grew bored with her, he made a gift of her to his father's guardsmen? He might have done the same to you, in time. Shed no tears for the Imp, my lady."

The wind ran salty fingers through her hair, and Sansa shivered. Even this close to shore, the rolling of the ship made her tummy queasy. She desperately needed a bath and a change of clothes. *I must look as haggard as a corpse, and smell of vomit.*

Lord Petyr came up beside her, cheerful as ever. "Good morrow. The salt air is bracing, don't you think? It always sharpens my appetite." He put a sympathetic arm about her shoulders. "Are you quite well? You look so pale."

"It's only my tummy. The seasickness."

"A little wine will be good for that. We'll get you a cup, as soon as we're ashore." Petyr pointed to where an old flint tower stood outlined against a bleak grey sky, the breakers crashing on the rocks beneath it. "Cheerful, is it not? I fear there's no safe anchorage here. We'll put ashore in a boat."

"Here?" She did not want to go ashore here. The Fingers were a dismal place, she'd heard, and there was something forlorn and desolate about the little tower. "Couldn't I stay on the ship until we make sail for White Harbor?"

"From here the *King* turns east for Braavos. Without us."

"But ... my lord, you said ... you said we were sailing home."

"And there it stands, miserable as it is. My ancestral home. It has no name, I fear. A great lord's seat ought to have a name, wouldn't you agree? Winterfell, the Eyrie, Riverrun, those are *castles*. Lord of Harrenhal now, that has a sweet ring to it, but what was I before?

Lord of Sheepshit and Master of the Drearfort? It lacks a certain something." His grey-green eyes regarded her innocently. "You look distraught. Did you think we were making for Winterfell, sweetling? Winterfell has been taken, burned, and sacked. All those you knew and loved are dead. What northmen who have not fallen to the ironmen are warring amongst themselves. Even the Wall is under attack. Winterfell was the home of your childhood, Sansa, but you are no longer a child. You're a woman grown, and you need to make your own home."

"But not here," she said, dismayed. "It looks so . . ."

". . . small and bleak and mean? It's all that, and less. The Fingers are a lovely place, if you happen to be a stone. But have no fear, we shan't stay more than a fortnight. I expect your aunt is already riding to meet us." He smiled. "The Lady Lysa and I are to be wed."

"Wed?" Sansa was stunned. "You and my aunt?"

"The Lord of Harrenhal and the Lady of the Eyrie."

You said it was my mother you loved. But of course Lady Catelyn was dead, so even if she had loved Petyr secretly and given him her maidenhood, it made no matter now.

"So silent, my lady?" said Petyr. "I was certain you would wish to give me your blessing. It is a rare thing for a boy born heir to stones and sheep pellets to wed the daughter of Hoster Tully and the widow of Jon Arryn."

"I . . . I pray you will have long years together, and many children, and be very happy in one another." It had been years since Sansa last saw her mother's sister. *She will be kind to me for my mother's sake, surely. She's my own blood.* And the Vale of Arryn was beautiful, all the songs said so. Perhaps it would not be so terrible to stay here for a time.

Lothor and old Oswell rowed them ashore. Sansa huddled in the bow under her cloak with the hood drawn up against the wind, wondering what awaited her. Servants emerged from the tower to meet them; a thin old woman and a fat middle-aged one, two ancient white-haired men, and a girl of two or three with a sty on one eye. When they recognized Lord Petyr they knelt on the rocks. "My household," he said. "I don't know the child. Another of Kella's bastards, I suppose. She pops one out every few years."

The two old men waded out up to their thighs to lift Sansa from the boat so she would not get her skirts wet. Oswell and Lothor splashed their way ashore, as did Littlefinger himself. He gave the old woman a kiss on the cheek and grinned at the younger one. "Who fathered this one, Kella?"

The fat woman laughed. "I can't rightly say, m'lord. I'm not one for telling them no."

"And all the local lads are grateful, I am quite sure."

"It is good to have you home, my lord," said one old man. He looked to be at least eighty, but he wore a studded brigantine and a longsword at his side. "How long will you be in residence?"

"As short a time as possible, Bryen, have no fear. Is the place habitable just now, would you say?"

"If we knew you was coming we would have laid down fresh rushes, m'lord," said the crone. "There's a dung fire burning."

"Nothing says *home* like the smell of burning dung." Petyr turned to Sansa. "Grisel was my wet nurse, but she keeps my castle now. Umfred's my steward, and Bryen—didn't I name you captain of the guard the last time I was here?"

"You did, my lord. You said you'd be getting some more men too, but you never did. Me and the dogs stand all the watches."

"And very well, I'm sure. No one has made off with any of my rocks or sheep pellets, I see that plainly." Petyr gestured toward the fat woman. "Kella minds my vast herds. How many sheep do I have at present, Kella?"

She had to think a moment. "Three and twenty, m'lord. There was nine and twenty, but Bryen's dogs killed one and we butchered some others and salted down the meat."

"Ah, cold salt mutton. I *must* be home. When I break my fast on gulls' eggs and seaweed soup, I'll be certain of it."

"If you like, m'lord," said the old woman Grisel.

Lord Petyr made a face. "Come, let's see if my hall is as dreary as I recall." He led them up the strand over rocks slick with rotting seaweed. A handful of sheep were wandering about the base of the flint tower, grazing on the thin grass that grew between the sheepfold and thatched stable. Sansa had to step carefully; there were pellets everywhere.

Within, the tower seemed even smaller. An open stone stair wound round the inside wall, from undercroft to roof. Each floor was but a single room. The servants lived and slept in the kitchen at ground level, sharing the space with a huge brindled mastiff and a half-dozen sheepdogs. Above that was a modest hall, and higher still the bedchamber. There were no windows, but arrowslits were embedded in the outer wall at intervals along the curve of the stair. Above the hearth hung a broken longsword and a battered oaken shield, its paint cracked and flaking.

The device painted on the shield was one Sansa did not know; a grey stone head with fiery eyes, upon a light green field. "My grandfather's shield," Petyr explained when he saw her gazing at it. "His own father was born in Braavos and came to the Vale as a sellsword in the hire of Lord Corbray, so my grandfather took the head of the Titan as his sigil when he was knighted."

"It's very fierce," said Sansa.

"Rather too fierce, for an amiable fellow like me," said Petyr. "I much prefer my mockingbird."

Oswell made two more trips out to the *Merling King* to offload provisions. Among the loads he brought ashore were several casks of wine. Petyr poured Sansa a cup, as promised. "Here, my lady, that should help your tummy, I would hope."

Having solid ground beneath her feet had helped already, but Sansa dutifully lifted the goblet with both hands and took a sip. The wine was very fine; an Arbor vintage, she thought. It tasted of oak and fruit and hot summer nights, the flavors blossoming in her mouth like flowers opening to the sun. She only prayed that she could keep it down. Lord Petyr was being so kind, she did not want to spoil it all by retching on him.

He was studying her over his own goblet, his bright grey-green eyes full of . . . was it amusement? Or something else? Sansa was not certain. "Grisel," he called to the old woman, "bring some food up. Nothing too heavy, my lady has a tender tummy. Some fruit might serve, perhaps. Oswell's brought some oranges and pomegranates from the *King*."

"Yes, m'lord."

"Might I have a hot bath as well?" asked Sansa.

"I'll have Kella draw some water, m'lady."

Sansa took another sip of wine and tried to think of some polite conversation, but Lord Petyr saved her the effort. When Grisel and the other servants had gone, he said, "Lysa will not come alone. Before she arrives, we must be clear on who you are."

"Who I . . . I don't understand."

"Varys has informers everywhere. If Sansa Stark should be seen in the Vale, the eunuch will know within a moon's turn, and that would create unfortunate . . . complications. It is not safe to be a Stark just now. So we shall tell Lysa's people that you are my natural daughter."

"Natural?" Sansa was aghast. "You mean, a bastard?"

"Well, you can scarcely be my trueborn daughter. I've never taken a wife, that's well known. What should you be called?"

"I . . . I could call myself after my mother . . ."

"Catelyn? A bit too obvious . . . but after *my* mother, that would serve. Alayne. Do you like it?"

"Alayne is pretty." Sansa hoped she would remember. "But couldn't I be the trueborn daughter of some knight in your service? Perhaps he died gallantly in the battle, and . . ."

"I have no gallant knights in my service, Alayne. Such a tale would draw unwanted questions as a corpse draws crows. It is rude to pry into the origins of a man's natural children, however." He cocked his head. "So, who are you?"

"Alayne . . . Stone, would it be?" When he nodded, she said, "But who is my mother?"

"Kella?"

"Please no," she said, mortified.

"I was teasing. Your mother was a gentlewoman of Braavos, daughter of a merchant prince. We met in Gulltown when I had charge of the port. She died giving you birth, and entrusted you to the Faith. I have some devotional books you can look over. Learn to quote from them. Nothing discourages unwanted questions as much as a flow of pious bleating. In any case, at your flowering you decided you did not wish to be a septa and wrote to me. That was the first I knew of your existence." He fingered his beard. "Do you think you can remember all that?"

"I hope. It will be like playing a game, won't it?"

"Are you fond of games, Alayne?"

The new name would take some getting used to. "Games? I ... I suppose it would depend ..."

Grisel reappeared before he could say more, balancing a large platter. She set it down between them. There were apples and pears and pomegranates, some sad-looking grapes, a huge blood orange. The old woman had brought a round of bread as well, and a crock of butter. Petyr cut a pomegranate in two with his dagger, offering half to Sansa. "You should try and eat, my lady."

"Thank you, my lord." Pomegranate seeds were so messy; Sansa chose a pear instead, and took a small delicate bite. It was very ripe. The juice ran down her chin.

Lord Petyr loosened a seed with the point of his dagger. "You must miss your father terribly, I know. Lord Eddard was a brave man, honest and loyal ... but quite a hopeless player." He brought the seed to his mouth with the knife. "In King's Landing, there are two sorts of people. The players and the pieces."

"And I was a piece?" She dreaded the answer.

"Yes, but don't let that trouble you. You're still half a child. Every man's a piece to start with, and every maid as well. Even some who think they are players." He ate another seed. "Cersei, for one. She thinks herself sly, but in truth she is utterly predictable. Her strength rests on her beauty, birth, and riches. Only the first of those is truly her own, and it will soon desert her. I pity her then. She wants power, but has no notion what to do with it when she gets it. Everyone wants something, Alayne. And when you know what a man wants you know who he is, and how to move him."

"As you moved Ser Dontos to poison Joffrey?" It *had* to have been Dontos, she had concluded.

Littlefinger laughed. "Ser Dontos the Red was a skin of wine with legs. He could never have been trusted with a task of such enormity. He would have bungled it or betrayed me. No, all Dontos had to do was lead you from the castle ... and make certain you wore your silver hair net."

The black amethysts. "But ... if not Dontos, who? Do you have other ... pieces?"

"You could turn King's Landing upside down and not find a single man with a mockingbird sewn over his heart, but that does not mean I am friendless." Petyr went to the steps. "Oswell, come up here and let the Lady Sansa have a look at you."

The old man appeared a few moments later, grinning and bowing. Sansa eyed him uncertainly. "What am I supposed to see?"

"Do you know him?" asked Petyr.

"No."

"Look closer."

She studied the old man's lined windburnt face, hook nose, white hair, and huge knuckly hands. There *was* something familiar about him, yet Sansa had to shake her head. "I don't. I never saw Oswell before I got into his boat, I'm certain."

Oswell grinned, showing a mouth of crooked teeth. "No, but m'lady might of met my three sons."

It was the "three sons," and that smile too. "*Kettleblack!*" Sansa's eyes went wide. "You're a Kettleblack!"

"Aye, m'lady, as it please you."

"She's beside herself with joy." Lord Petyr dismissed him with a wave, and returned to the pomegranate again as Oswell shuffled down the steps. "Tell me, Alayne—which is more dangerous, the dagger brandished by an enemy, or the hidden one pressed to your back by someone you never even see?"

"The hidden dagger."

"There's a clever girl." He smiled, his thin lips bright red from the pomegranate seeds. "When the Imp sent off her guards, the queen had Ser Lancel hire sellswords for her. Lancel found her the Kettleblacks, which delighted your little lord husband, since the lads were in his pay through his man Bronn." He chuckled. "But it was me who told Oswell to get his sons to King's Landing when I learned that Bronn was looking for swords. Three hidden daggers, Alayne, now perfectly placed."

"So one of the Kettleblacks put the poison in Joff's cup?" Ser Osmund had been near the king all night, she remembered.

"Did I say that?" Lord Petyr cut the blood orange in two with his dagger and offered half to Sansa. "The lads are far too treacherous to be part of any such scheme ... and Osmund has become especially unreliable since he joined the Kingsguard. That white cloak does things to a man, I find. Even a man like him." He tilted his chin back and squeezed the blood orange, so the juice ran down into his mouth. "I love the juice but I loathe the sticky fingers," he complained, wiping his hands. "Clean hands, Sansa. Whatever you do, make certain your hands are clean."

Sansa spooned up some juice from her own orange. "But if it wasn't the Kettleblacks and it wasn't Ser Dontos ... you weren't even in the city, and it couldn't have been Tyrion ..."

"No more guesses, sweetling?"

She shook her head. "I don't ..."

Petyr smiled. "I will wager you that at some point during the evening someone told you that your hair net was crooked and straightened it for you."

Sansa raised a hand to her mouth. "You cannot mean ... she wanted to take me to Highgarden, to marry me to her grandson ..."

"Gentle, pious, good-hearted Willas Tyrell. Be grateful you were spared, he would have bored you spitless. The old woman is not boring, though, I'll grant her that. A fearsome old harridan, and not near as frail as she pretends. When I came to Highgarden to dicker for Margaery's hand, she let her lord son bluster while she asked pointed questions about Joffrey's nature. I praised him to the skies, to be sure ... whilst my men spread disturbing tales amongst Lord Tyrell's servants. That is how the game is played.

"I also planted the notion of Ser Loras taking the white. Not that I *suggested* it, that would have been too crude. But men in my party supplied grisly tales about how the mob had killed Ser Preston Greenfield and raped the Lady Lollys, and slipped a few silvers to Lord Tyrell's army of singers to sing of Ryam Redwyne, Serwyn of the Mirror Shield, and Prince Aemon the Dragonknight. A harp can be as dangerous as a sword, in the right hands.

"Mace Tyrell actually thought it was his own idea to make Ser Loras's inclusion in the Kingsguard part of the marriage contract. Who better to protect his daughter than her splendid knightly brother? And it relieved him of the difficult task of trying to find lands and a bride for a third son, never easy, and doubly difficult in Ser Loras's case.

"Be that as it may. Lady Olenna was not about to let Joff harm her precious darling granddaughter, but unlike her son she also realized that under all his flowers and finery, Ser Loras is as hot-tempered as Jaime Lannister. Toss Joffrey, Margaery, and Loras in a pot, and you've got the makings for kingslayer stew. The old woman understood something else as well. Her son was determined to make Margaery a queen, and for that he needed a king . . . but he did not need *Joffrey*. We shall have another wedding soon, wait and see. Margaery will marry Tommen. She'll keep her queenly crown and her maidenhead, neither of which she especially wants, but what does that matter? The great western alliance will be preserved . . . for a time, at least."

Margaery and Tommen. Sansa did not know what to say. She had liked Margaery Tyrell, and her small sharp grandmother as well. She thought wistfully of Highgarden with its courtyards and musicians, and the pleasure barges on the Mander; a far cry from this bleak shore. *At least I am safe here. Joffrey is dead, he cannot hurt me anymore, and I am only a bastard girl now. Alayne Stone has no husband and no claim.* And her aunt would soon be here as well. The long nightmare of King's Landing was behind her, and her mockery of a marriage as well. She could make herself a new home here, just as Petyr said.

It was eight long days until Lysa Arryn arrived. On five of them it rained, while Sansa sat bored and restless by the fire, beside the old blind dog. He was too sick and toothless to walk guard with Bryen anymore, and mostly all he did was sleep, but when she patted him he whined and licked her hand, and after that they were fast friends. When the rains let up, Petyr walked with her around his holdings, which took less than half a day. He owned a lot of rocks, just as he had said. There was one place where the tide came jetting up out of a blowhole to shoot thirty feet into the air, and another where someone had chiseled the seven-pointed star of the new gods upon a boulder. Petyr said that marked one of the places the Andals had landed, when they came across the sea to wrest the Vale from the First Men.

Farther inland a dozen families lived in huts of piled stone beside a peat bog. "Mine own smallfolk," Petyr said, though only the oldest seemed to know him. There was a hermit's cave on his land as well, but no hermit. "He's dead now, but when I was a boy my father took me to see him. The man had not washed in forty years, so you can imagine how he smelled, but supposedly he had the gift of prophecy. He groped me a bit and said I would be a great man, and for that my father gave him a skin of wine." Petyr snorted. "I would have told him the same thing for half a cup."

Finally, on a grey windy afternoon, Bryen came running back to the tower with his dogs barking at his heels, to announce that riders were approaching from the southwest. "Lysa," Lord Petyr said. "Come, Alayne, let us greet her."

They put on their cloaks and waited outside. The riders numbered no more than a score; a very modest escort, for the Lady of the Eyrie. Three maids rode with her, and a dozen household knights in mail and plate. She brought a septon as well, and a handsome singer with a wisp of a mustache and long sandy curls.

Could that be my aunt? Lady Lysa was two years younger than Mother, but this woman looked ten years older. Thick auburn tresses fell down past her waist, but beneath the costly velvet gown and jeweled bodice her body sagged and bulged. Her face was pink and painted, her breasts heavy, her limbs thick. She was taller than Littlefinger, and heavier; nor did she show any grace in the clumsy way she climbed down off her horse.

Petyr knelt to kiss her fingers. "The king's small council commanded me to woo and win you, my lady. Do you think you might have me for your lord and husband?"

Lady Lysa pooched her lips and pulled him up to plant a kiss upon his cheek. "Oh, mayhaps I could be persuaded." She giggled. "Have you brought gifts to melt my heart?"

"The king's peace."

"Oh, poo to the peace, what else have you brought me?"

"My daughter." Littlefinger beckoned Sansa forward with a hand. "My lady, allow me to present you Alayne Stone."

Lysa Arryn did not seem greatly pleased to see her. Sansa did a deep curtsy, her head bowed. "A bastard?" she heard her aunt say. "Petyr, have you been wicked? Who was her mother?"

"The wench is dead. I'd hoped to take Alayne to the Eyrie."

"What am I to do with her there?"

"I have a few notions," said Lord Petyr. "But just now I am more interested in what I might do with you, my lady."

All the sternness melted off her aunt's round pink face, and for a moment Sansa thought Lysa Arryn was about to cry. "Sweet Petyr, I've missed you so, you don't know, you can't know. Yohn Royce has been stirring up all sorts of trouble, demanding that I call my banners and go to war. And the others all swarm around me, Hunter and Corbray and that *dreadful* Nestor Royce, all wanting to wed me and take my son to ward, but none of them truly love me. Only you, Petyr. I've dreamed of you so long."

"And I of you, my lady." He slid an arm around behind her and kissed her on the neck. "How soon can we be wed?"

"Now," said Lady Lysa, sighing. "I've brought my own septon, and a singer, and mead for the wedding feast."

"Here?" That did not please him. "I'd sooner wed you at the Eyrie, with your whole court in attendance."

"Poo to my court. I have waited so long, I could not bear to wait another moment." She put her arms around him. "I want to share your bed tonight, my sweet. I want us to make another child, a brother for Robert or a sweet little daughter."

"I dream of that as well, sweetling. Yet there is much to be gained from a great public wedding, with all the Vale—"

"*No!*" She stamped a foot. "I want you now, this very night. And I must warn you, after all these years of silence and whisperings, I mean to *scream* when you love me. I am going to scream so loud they'll hear me in the Eyrie!"

"Perhaps I could bed you now, and wed you later?"

The Lady Lysa giggled like a girl. "Oh, Petyr Baelish, you are so *wicked*. No, I say no, I am the Lady of the Eyrie, and I command you to wed me this very moment!"

Petyr gave a shrug. "As my lady commands, then. I am helpless before you, as ever."

They said their vows within the hour, standing beneath a sky-blue canopy as the sun sank in the west. Afterward trestle tables were set up beneath the small flint tower, and they feasted on quail, venison, and roast boar, washing it down with a fine light mead. Torches were lit as dusk crept in. Lysa's singer played "The Vow Unspoken" and "Seasons of My Love" and "Two Hearts That Beat as One." Several younger knights even asked Sansa to dance. Her aunt danced as well, her skirts whirling when Petyr spun her in his arms. Mead and marriage had taken years off Lady Lysa. She laughed at everything so long as she held her husband's hand, and her eyes seemed to glow whenever she looked at him.

When it was time for the bedding, her knights carried her up to the tower, stripping her as they went and shouting bawdy jests. *Tyrion spared me that,* Sansa remembered. It would not have been so bad being undressed for a man she loved, by friends who loved them both. *By Joffrey, though . . .* She shuddered.

Her aunt had brought only three ladies with her, so they pressed Sansa to help them undress Lord Petyr and march him up to his marriage bed. He submitted with good grace and a wicked tongue, giving as good as he got. By the time they had gotten him into the tower and out of his clothes, the other women were flushed, with laces unlaced, kirtles crooked, and skirts in disarray. But Littlefinger only smiled at Sansa as they marched him up to the bedchamber where his lady wife was waiting.

Lady Lysa and Lord Petyr had the third-story bedchamber to themselves, but the tower was small . . . and true to her word, her aunt screamed. It had begun to rain outside, driving the feasters into the hall one floor below, so they heard most every word. "Petyr," her aunt moaned. "Oh, Petyr, Petyr, sweet *Petyr,* oh oh oh. There, Petyr, there. That's where you belong." Lady Lysa's singer launched into a bawdy version of "Milady's Supper," but even his singing and playing could not drown out Lysa's cries. "Make me a baby, Petyr," she screamed, "make me another sweet little baby. Oh, Petyr, my precious, my precious, *PEEEEEETYR!*" Her last shriek was so loud that it set the dogs to barking, and two of her aunt's ladies could scarce contain their mirth.

Sansa went down the steps and out into the night. A light rain was falling on the remains of the feast, but the air smelled fresh and clean. The memory of her own wedding night with Tyrion was much with her. *In the dark, I am the Knight of Flowers,* he had said. *I could be good to you.* But that was only another Lannister lie. *A dog can smell a lie, you know,* the Hound had told her once. She could almost hear the rough rasp of his voice. *Look around you, and take a good whiff. They're all liars here, and every one better than you.* She wondered what had become of Sandor Clegane. Did he know that they'd killed Joffrey? Would he care? He had been the prince's sworn shield for years.

She stayed outside for a long time. When at last she sought her own bed, wet and chilled, only the dim glow of a peat fire lit the darkened hall. There was no sound from above. The young singer sat in a corner, playing a slow song to himself. One of her aunt's maids was kissing a knight in Lord Petyr's chair, their hands busy beneath each other's clothing. Several men had drunk themselves to sleep, and one was in the privy, being noisily sick. Sansa found Bryen's old blind dog in her little alcove beneath the steps, and lay down next to him. He woke and licked her face. "You sad old hound," she said, ruffling his fur.

"Alayne." Her aunt's singer stood over her. "Sweet Alayne. I am Marillion. I saw you come in from the rain. The night is chill and wet. Let me warm you."

The old dog raised his head and growled, but the singer gave him a cuff and sent him slinking off, whimpering.

"Marillion?" she said, uncertain. "You are . . . kind to think of me, but . . . pray forgive me. I am very tired."

"And very beautiful. All night I have been making songs for you in my head. A lay for your eyes, a ballad for your lips, a duet to your breasts. I will not sing them, though. They were poor things, unworthy of such beauty." He sat on her bed and put his hand on her leg. "Let me sing to you with my body instead."

She caught a whiff of his breath. "You're drunk."

"I never get drunk. Mead only makes me merry. I am on fire." His hand slipped up to her thigh. "And you as well."

"Unhand me. You forget yourself."

"Mercy. I have been singing love songs for hours. My blood is stirred. And yours, I know ... there's no wench half so lusty as one bastard born. Are you wet for me?"

"I'm a *maiden*," she protested.

"Truly? Oh, Alayne, Alayne, my fair maid, give me the gift of your innocence. You will thank the gods you did. I'll have you singing louder than the Lady Lysa."

Sansa jerked away from him, frightened. "If you don't leave me, my au—my *father* will hang you. Lord Petyr."

"Littlefinger?" He chuckled. "Lady Lysa loves me well, and I am Lord Robert's favorite. If your father offends me, I will destroy him with a verse." He put a hand on her breast, and squeezed. "Let's get you out of these wet clothes. You wouldn't want them ripped, I know. Come, sweet lady, heed your heart—"

Sansa heard the soft sound of steel on leather. "Singer," a rough voice said, "best go, if you want to sing again." The light was dim, but she saw a faint glimmer of a blade.

The singer saw it too. "Find your own wench—" The knife flashed, and he cried out. "You *cut* me!"

"I'll do worse, if you don't go."

And quick as that, Marillion was gone. The other remained, looming over Sansa in the darkness. "Lord Petyr said watch out for you." It was Lothor Brune's voice, she realized. *Not the Hound's, no, how could it be? Of course it had to be Lothor* ...

That night Sansa scarcely slept at all, but tossed and turned just as she had aboard the *Merling King*. She dreamt of Joffrey dying, but as he clawed at his throat and the blood ran down across his fingers she saw with horror that it was her brother Robb. And she dreamed of her wedding night too, of Tyrion's eyes devouring her as she undressed. Only then he was bigger than Tyrion had any right to be, and when he climbed into the bed his face was scarred only on one side. "*I'll have a song from you*," he rasped, and Sansa woke and found the old blind dog beside her once again. "I wish that you were Lady," she said.

Come the morning, Grisel climbed up to the bedchamber to serve the lord and lady a tray of morning bread, with butter, honey, fruit, and cream. She returned to say that Alayne was wanted. Sansa was still drowsy from sleep. It took her a moment to remember that *she* was Alayne.

Lady Lysa was still abed, but Lord Petyr was up and dressed. "Your aunt wishes to speak with you," he told Sansa, as he pulled on a boot. "I've told her who you are."

Gods be good. "I . . . I thank you, my lord."

Petyr yanked on the other boot. "I've had about as much home as I can stomach. We'll leave for the Eyrie this afternoon." He kissed his lady wife and licked a smear of honey off her lips, then headed down the steps.

Sansa stood by the foot of the bed while her aunt ate a pear and studied her. "I see it now," the Lady Lysa said, as she set the core aside. "You look so much like Catelyn."

"It's kind of you to say so."

"It was not meant as flattery. If truth be told, you look too much like Catelyn. Something must be done. We shall darken your hair before we bring you back to the Eyrie, I think."

Darken my hair? "If it please you, Aunt Lysa."

"You must not call me that. No word of your presence here must be allowed to reach King's Landing. I do not mean to have my son endangered." She nibbled the corner of a honeycomb. "I have kept the Vale out of this war. Our harvest has been plentiful, the mountains protect us, and the Eyrie is impregnable. Even so, it would not do to draw Lord Tywin's wroth down upon us." Lysa set the comb down and licked honey from her fingers. "You were wed to Tyrion Lannister, Petyr says. That vile *dwarf.*"

"They made me marry him. I never wanted it."

"No more than I did," her aunt said. "Jon Arryn was no dwarf, but he was *old.* You may not think so to see me now, but on the day we wed I was so lovely I put your mother to shame. But all Jon desired was my father's swords, to aid his darling boys. I should have refused him, but he was such an old man, how long could he live? Half his teeth were gone, and his breath smelled like bad cheese. I cannot abide a man with foul breath. Petyr's breath is always fresh . . . he was the first man I ever kissed, you know. My father said he was too lowborn, but *I* knew how high he'd rise. Jon gave him the customs for Gulltown to please me, but when he increased the incomes tenfold my lord husband saw how clever he was and gave him other appointments, even brought him to King's Landing to be master of coin. That was hard, to see him every day and still be wed to that old cold man. Jon did his *duty* in the bedchamber, but he could no more give me pleasure than he could give me children. His seed was old and weak. All my babies died but Robert, three girls and two boys. All my sweet little babies dead, and that old man just went on and on with his stinking breath. So you see, I have suffered too." Lady Lysa sniffed. "You do know that your poor mother is dead?"

"Tyrion told me," said Sansa. "He said the Freys murdered her at The Twins, with Robb."

Tears welled suddenly in Lady Lysa's eyes. "We are women alone now, you and I. Are you afraid, child? Be brave. I would never turn away Cat's daughter. We are bound by blood." She beckoned Sansa closer. "You may come kiss my cheek, Alayne."

Dutifully she approached and knelt beside the bed. Her aunt was drenched in sweet scent, though under that was a sour milky smell. Her cheek tasted of paint and powder.

As Sansa stepped back, Lady Lysa caught her wrist. "Now tell me," she said sharply. "Are you with child? The truth now, I will know if you lie."

"No," she said, startled by the question.

"You *are* a woman flowered, are you not?"

"Yes." Sansa knew the truth of her flowering could not be long hidden in the Eyrie. "Tyrion didn't . . . he never . . ." She could feel the blush creeping up her cheeks. "I am still a maid."

"Was the dwarf incapable?"

"No. He was only . . . he was . . ." *Kind?* She could not say that, not here, not to this aunt who hated him so. "He . . . he had whores, my lady. He told me so."

"Whores." Lysa released her wrist. "Of course he did. What woman would bed such a creature, but for gold? I should have killed the Imp when he was in my power, but he tricked me. He is full of low cunning, that one. His sellsword slew my good Ser Vardis Egen. Catelyn should not have brought him here, I told her that. She made off with our uncle too. That was wrong of her. The Blackfish was my Knight of the Gate, and since he left us the mountain clans are growing very bold. Petyr will soon set all that to rights, though. I shall make him Lord Protector of the Vale." Her aunt smiled for the first time, almost warmly. "He may not look as tall or strong as some, but he is worth more than all of them. Trust in him and do as he says."

"I shall, Aunt . . . my lady."

Lady Lysa seemed pleased by that. "I knew that boy Joffrey. He used to call my Robert cruel names, and once he slapped him with a wooden sword. A man will tell you poison is dishonorable, but a woman's honor is different. The Mother shaped us to protect our children, and our only dishonor is in failure. You'll know that, when you have a child."

"A child?" said Sansa, uncertainly.

Lysa waved a hand negligently. "Not for many years. You are too young to be a mother. One day you shall want children, though. Just as you will want to marry."

"I . . . I *am* married, my lady."

"Yes, but soon a widow. Be glad the Imp preferred his whores. It would not be fitting for my son to take that *dwarf's* leavings, but as he never touched you . . . How would you like to marry your cousin, the Lord Robert?"

The thought made Sansa weary. All she knew of Robert Arryn was that he was a little boy, and sickly. *It is not me she wants her son to marry, it is my claim. No one will ever marry me for love.* But lying came easy to her now. "I . . . can scarcely wait to meet him, my lady. But he is still a child, is he not?"

"He is eight. And not robust. But such a good boy, so bright and clever. He will be a great man, Alayne. *The seed is strong*, my lord husband said before he died. His last words. The gods sometimes let us glimpse the future as we lay dying. I see no reason why you should not be wed as soon as we know that your Lannister husband is dead. A secret wedding, to be sure. The Lord of the Eyrie could scarcely be thought to have married a bastard, that would not be fitting. The ravens should bring us the word from King's Landing once the Imp's head rolls. You and Robert can be wed the next day, won't that be joyous? It will be good for him to have a little companion. He played with Vardis Egen's boy when we first returned to the Eyrie, and my steward's sons as well, but they were much too rough and I had no choice but to send them away. Do you read well, Alayne?"

"Septa Mordane was good enough to say so."

"Robert has weak eyes, but he loves to be read to," Lady Lysa confided. "He likes stories about animals the best. Do you know the little song about the chicken who dressed as a fox? I sing him that all the time, he never grows tired of it. And he likes to play hopfrog and spin-the-sword and come-into-my-castle, but you must always let him win. That's only proper, don't you think? He is the Lord of the Eyrie, after all, you must never forget that. You are well born, and the Starks of Winterfell were always proud, but Winterfell has fallen and you are really just a beggar now, so put that pride aside. Gratitude will better become you, in your present circumstances. Yes, and obedience. My son will have a grateful and obedient wife."

JON

Day and night the axes rang. Jon could not remember the last time he had slept. When he closed his eyes he dreamed of fighting; when he woke he fought. Even in the King's Tower he could hear the ceaseless *thunk* of bronze and flint and stolen steel biting into wood, and it was louder when he tried to rest in the warming shed atop the Wall. Mance had sledgehammers at work as well, and long saws with teeth of bone and flint. Once, as he was drifting off into an exhausted sleep, there came a great cracking from the haunted forest, and a sentinel tree came crashing down in a cloud of dirt and needles.

He was awake when Owen came to him, lying restless under a pile of furs on the floor of the warming shed. "Lord Snow," said Owen, shaking his shoulder, "the dawn." He gave Jon a hand to help pull him back onto his feet. Others were waking as well, jostling one another as they pulled on their boots and buckled their swordbelts in the close confines of the shed. No one spoke. They were all too tired for talk. Few of them ever left the Wall these days. It took too long to ride up and down in the cage. Castle Black had been abandoned to Maester Aemon, Ser Wynton Stout, and a few others too old or ill to fight.

"I had a dream that the king had come," Owen said happily. "Maester Aemon sent a raven, and King Robert came with all his strength. I dreamed I saw his golden banners."

Jon made himself smile. "That would be a welcome sight to see, Owen." Ignoring the twinge of pain in his leg, he swept a black fur cloak about his shoulders, gathered up his crutch, and went out onto the Wall to face another day.

A gust of wind sent icy tendrils wending through his long brown hair. Half a mile north, the wildling encampments were stirring, their campfires sending up smoky fingers to scratch against the pale dawn sky. Along the edge of the forest they had raised their tents of hide and fur, even a crude longhall of logs and woven branches; there were horselines to the east, mammoths to the west, and men everywhere, sharpening their swords, putting points on crude spears, donning makeshift armor of hide and horn and bone. For every man that he could see, Jon knew there were a score unseen in the wood. The brush gave them some shelter from the elements and hid them from the eyes of the hated crows.

Already their archers were stealing forward, pushing their rolling mantlets. "Here come our breakfast arrows," Pyp announced cheerfully, as he did every morning. *It's good that he can make a jape of it*, Jon thought. *Someone has to.* Three days ago, one of those breakfast arrows had caught Red Alyn of the Rosewood in the leg. You could still see his body at the foot of the Wall, if you cared to lean out far enough. Jon had to think that it was better for them to smile at Pyp's jest than to brood over Alyn's corpse.

The mantlets were slanting wooden shields, wide enough for five of the free folk to hide behind. The archers pushed them close, then knelt behind them to loose their arrows through slits in the wood. The first time the wildlings rolled them out, Jon had called for fire arrows and set a half-dozen ablaze, but after that Mance started covering them with raw hides. All the fire arrows in the world couldn't make them catch now. The brothers had even started wagering as to which of the straw sentinels would collect the most arrows before they were done. Dolorous Edd was leading with four, but Othell Yarwyck, Tumberjon, and Watt of Long Lake had three apiece. It was Pyp who'd started naming the scarecrows after their missing brothers, too. "It makes it seem as if there's more of us," he said.

"More of us with arrows in our bellies," Grenn complained, but the custom did seem to give his brothers heart, so Jon let the names stand and the wagering continue.

On the edge of the Wall an ornate brass Myrish eye stood on three spindly legs. Maester Aemon had once used it to peer at the stars, before his own eyes had failed him. Jon swung the tube down to have a look at the foe. Even at this distance there was no mistaking Mance Rayder's huge white tent, sewn together from the pelts of snow bears. The Myrish lenses brought the wildlings close enough for him to make out faces. Of Mance himself he saw no sign this morning, but his woman Dalla was outside tending the fire, while her sister Val milked a she-goat beside the tent. Dalla looked so big it was a wonder she could move. *The child must be coming very soon*, Jon thought. He swiveled the eye east and searched amongst the tents and trees till he found the turtle. *That will be coming very soon as well.* The wildlings had skinned one of the dead mammoths during the night, and they were lashing the raw bloody hide over the turtle's roof, one more layer on top of the sheepskins and pelts. The turtle had a rounded top and eight huge wheels, and under the hides was a stout wooden frame. When the wildlings had begun knocking it together, Satin thought they were building a ship. *Not far wrong.* The turtle was a hull turned upside down and opened fore and aft; a longhall on wheels.

"It's done, isn't it?" asked Grenn.

"Near enough." Jon shoved away the eye. "It will come today, most like. Did you fill the barrels?"

"Every one. They froze hard during the night, Pyp checked."

Grenn had changed a great deal from the big, clumsy, red-necked boy Jon had first befriended. He had grown half a foot, his chest and shoulders had thickened, and he had not cut his hair nor trimmed his beard since the Fist of the First Men. It made him look as huge and shaggy as an aurochs, the mocking name that Ser Alliser Thorne had hung on him during training. He looked weary now, though. When Jon said as much, he nodded. "I heard their axes all night. Couldn't sleep for all the chopping."

"Then go sleep now."

"I don't need—"

"You do. I want you rested. Go on, I'm not going to let you sleep through the fight." He made himself smile. "You're the only one who can move those bloody barrels."

Grenn went off muttering, and Jon returned to the far eye, searching the wildling camp. From time to time an arrow would sail past overhead, but he had learned to ignore those. The range was long and the angle was bad, the chances of being hit were small. He still saw no sign of Mance Rayder in the camp, but he spied Tormund Giantsbane and two of his sons around the turtle. The sons were struggling with the mammoth hide while Tormund gnawed on the roast leg of a goat and bellowed orders. Elsewhere he found the wildling skinchanger, Varamyr Sixskins, walking through the trees with his shadowcat dogging his heels.

When he heard the rattle of the winch chains and the iron groan of the cage door opening, he knew it would be Hobb bringing their breakfast as he did every morning. The sight of Mance's turtle had robbed Jon of his appetite. Their oil was all but gone, and the last barrel of pitch had been rolled off the Wall two nights ago. They would soon run short of arrows as well, and there were no fletchers making more. And the night before last, a raven had come from the west, from Ser Denys Mallister. Bowen Marsh had chased the wildlings all the way to the Shadow Tower, it seemed, and then farther, down into the gloom of the Gorge. At the Bridge of Skulls he had met the Weeper and three hundred wildlings and won a bloody battle. But the victory had been a costly one. More than a hundred brothers slain, among them Ser Endrew Tarth and Ser Aladale Wynch. The Old Pomegranate himself had been carried back to the Shadow Tower sorely wounded. Maester Mullin was tending him, but it would be some time before he was fit to return to Castle Black.

When he had read that, Jon had dispatched Zei to Mole's Town on their best horse to plead with the villagers to help man the Wall. She never returned. When he sent Mully after her, he came back to report the whole village deserted, even the brothel. Most likely Zei had followed them, straight down the kingsroad. *Maybe we should all do the same,* Jon reflected glumly.

He made himself eat, hungry or no. Bad enough he could not sleep, he could not go on without food as well. *Besides, this might be my last meal. It might be the last meal for all of us.* So it was that Jon had a belly full of bread, bacon, onions, and cheese when he heard Horse shout, "*IT'S COMING!*"

No one needed to ask what "it" was. Nor did Jon need the maester's Myrish eye to see it creeping out from amongst the tents and trees. "It doesn't really look much like a turtle," Satin commented. "Turtles don't have fur."

"Most of them don't have wheels either," said Pyp.

"Sound the warhorn," Jon commanded, and Kegs blew two long blasts, to wake Grenn and the other sleepers who'd had the watch during the night. If the wildlings were coming, the Wall would need every man. *Gods know, we have few enough.* Jon looked at Pyp and Kegs and Satin, Horse and Owen the Oaf, Tim Tangletongue, Mully, Spare Boot, and the rest, and tried to imagine them going belly to belly and blade to blade against a hundred screaming wildlings in the freezing darkness of that tunnel, with only a few iron bars between them. That was what it would come down to, unless they could stop the turtle before the gate was breached.

"It's big," Horse said.

Pyp smacked his lips. "Think of all the soup it will make." The jape was stillborn. Even Pyp sounded tired. *He looks half dead,* thought Jon, *but so do we all.* The King-beyond-the-Wall had so many men that he could throw fresh attackers at them every time, but the same handful of black brothers had to meet every assault, and it had worn them ragged.

The men beneath the wood and hides would be pulling hard, Jon knew, putting their shoulders into it, straining to keep the wheels turning, but once the turtle was flush against the gate they would exchange their ropes for axes. At least Mance was not sending his mammoths today. Jon was glad of that. Their awesome strength was wasted on the Wall, and their size only made them easy targets. The last had been a day and a half in the dying, its mournful trumpetings terrible to hear.

The turtle crept slowly through stones and stumps and brush. The earlier attacks had cost the free folk a hundred lives or more. Most still lay where they had fallen. In the lulls the crows would come and pay them court, but now the birds fled screeching. They liked the look of that turtle no more than he did.

Satin, Horse, and the others were looking to him, Jon knew, waiting for his orders. He was so tired, he hardly knew any more. *The Wall is mine*, he reminded himself. "Owen, Horse, to the catapults. Kegs, you and Spare Boot on the scorpions. The rest of you string your bows. Fire arrows. Let's see if we can burn it." It was likely to be a futile gesture, Jon knew, but it had to be better than standing helpless.

Cumbersome and slow-moving, the turtle made for an easy shot, and his archers and crossbowmen soon turned it into a lumbering wooden hedgehog . . . but the wet hides protected it, just as they had the mantlets, and the flaming arrows guttered out almost as soon as they struck. Jon cursed under his breath. "Scorpions," he commanded. "Catapults."

The scorpions bolts punched deep into the pelts, but did no more damage than the fire arrows. The rocks went bouncing off the turtle's roof, leaving dimples in the thick layers of hides. A stone from one of the trebuchets might have crushed it, but the one machine was still broken, and the wildlings had gone wide around the area where the other dropped its loads.

"Jon, it's still coming," said Owen the Oaf.

He could see that for himself. Inch by inch, yard by yard, the turtle crept closer, rolling, rumbling and rocking as it crossed the killing ground. Once the wildlings got it flush against the Wall, it would give them all the shelter they needed while their axes crashed through the hastily repaired outer gates. Inside, under the ice, they would clear the loose rubble from the tunnel in a matter of hours, and then there would be nothing to stop them but two iron gates, a few half-frozen corpses, and whatever brothers Jon cared to throw in their path, to fight and die down in the dark.

To his left, the catapult made a *thunk* and filled the air with spinning stones. They plonked down on the turtle like hail, and caromed harmlessly aside. The wildling archers were still loosing arrows from behind their mantlets. One thudded into the face of a straw man, and Pyp said, "Four for Watt of Long Lake! We have a tie!" The next shaft whistled past his own ear, however. "*Fie!*" he shouted down. "I'm not in the tourney!"

"The hides won't burn," Jon said, as much to himself as to the others. Their only hope was to try to crush the turtle when it reached the Wall. For that, they needed boulders. No matter how stoutly built the turtle was, a huge chunk of rock crashing straight down on top of it from seven hundred feet was bound to do some damage. "Grenn, Owen, Kegs, it's time."

Alongside the warming shed a dozen stout oaken barrels were lined up in a row. They were full of crushed rock; the gravel that the black brothers customarily spread on the footpaths to give themselves better footing atop the Wall. Yesterday, after he'd seen the free folk covering the turtle with sheepskins, Jon told Grenn to pour water into the barrels, as much as they would take. The water would seep down through the crushed stone, and overnight the whole thing would freeze solid. It was the nearest thing to a boulder they were going to get.

"Why do we need to freeze it?" Grenn had asked him. "Why don't we just roll the barrels off the way they are?"

Jon answered, "If they crash against the Wall on the way down they'll burst, and loose gravel will spray everywhere. We don't want to rain pebbles on the whoresons."

He put his shoulder to the one barrel with Grenn, while Kegs and Owen were wrestling with another. Together they rocked it back and forth to break the grip of the ice that had formed around its bottom. "The bugger weighs a ton," said Grenn.

"Tip it over and roll it," Jon said. "Careful, if it rolls over your foot you'll end up like Spare Boot."

Once the barrel was on its side, Jon grabbed a torch and waved it above the surface of the Wall, back and forth, just enough to melt the ice a little. The thin film of water helped the barrel roll more easily. Too easily, in fact; they almost lost it. But finally, with four of them pooling their efforts, they rolled their boulder to the edge and stood it up again.

They had four of the big oak barrels lined up above the gate by the time Pyp shouted, "There's a turtle at our door!" Jon braced his injured leg and leaned out for a look. *Hoardings, Marsh should have built hoardings.* So many things they should have done. The wildlings were dragging the dead giants away from the gate. Horse and Mully were dropping rocks down on them, and Jon thought he saw one man go down, but the stones were too small to have any effect on the turtle itself. He wondered what the free folk would do about the dead mammoth in the path, but then he saw. The turtle was almost as wide as a longhall, so they simply pushed it *over* the carcass. His leg twitched, but Horse caught his arm and drew him back to safety. "You shouldn't lean out like that," the boy said.

"We should have built hoardings." Jon thought he could hear the crash of axes on wood, but that was probably just fear ringing in his ears. He looked to Grenn. "Do it."

Grenn got behind a barrel, put his shoulder against it, grunted, and began to push. Owen and Mully moved to help him. They shoved the barrel out a foot, and then another. And suddenly it was gone.

They heard the *thump* as it struck the Wall on the way down, and then, much louder, the crash and *crack* of splintering wood, followed by shouts and screams. Satin whooped and Owen the Oaf danced in circles, while Pyp leaned out and called, "The turtle was stuffed full of rabbits! Look at them hop away!"

"*Again*," Jon barked, and Grenn and Kegs slammed their shoulders against the next barrel, and sent it tottering out into empty air.

By the time they were done, the front of Mance's turtle was a crushed and splintered ruin, and wildlings were spilling out the other end and scrambling for their camp. Satin scooped up his crossbow and sent a few quarrels after them as they ran, to see them off the faster. Grenn was grinning through his beard, Pyp was making japes, and none of them would die today.

On the morrow, though ... Jon glanced toward the shed. Eight barrels of gravel remained where twelve had stood a few moments before. He realized how tired he was then, and how much his wound was hurting. *I need to sleep. A few hours, at least.* He could go to Maester Aemon for some dreamwine, that would help. "I am going down to the King's Tower," he told them. "Call me if Mance gets up to anything. Pyp, you have the Wall."

"Me?" said Pyp.

"Him?" said Grenn.

Smiling, he left them to it and rode down in the cage.

A cup of dreamwine *did* help, as it happened. No sooner had he stretched out on the narrow bed in his cell than sleep took him. His dreams were strange and formless, full of strange voices, shouts and cries, and the sound of a warhorn, blowing low and loud, a single deep booming note that lingered in the air.

When he awoke, the sky was black outside the arrow slit that served him for a window, and four men he did not know were standing over him. One held a lantern. "Jon Snow," the tallest of them said brusquely, "pull on your boots and come with us."

His first groggy thought was that somehow the Wall had fallen whilst he slept, that Mance Rayder had sent more giants or another turtle and broken through the gate. But when he rubbed his eyes he saw that the strangers were all in black. *They're men of the Night's Watch*, Jon realized. "Come where? Who are you?"

The tall man gestured, and two of the others pulled Jon from the bed. With the lantern leading the way they marched him from his cell and up a half turn of stair, to the Old Bear's solar. He saw Maester Aemon standing by the fire, his hands folded around the head of a blackthorn cane. Septon Cellador was half drunk as usual, and Ser Wynton Stout was asleep in a window seat. The other brothers were strangers to him. All but one.

Immaculate in his fur-trimmed cloak and polished boots, Ser Alliser Thorne turned to say, "Here's the turncloak now, my lord. Ned Stark's bastard, of Winterfell."

"I'm no turncloak, Thorne," Jon said coldly.

"We shall see." In the leather chair behind the table where the Old

Bear wrote his letters sat a big, broad, jowly man Jon did not know. "Yes, we shall see," he said again. "You will not deny that you are Jon Snow, I hope? Stark's bastard?"

"*Lord* Snow, he likes to call himself." Ser Alliser was a spare, slim man, compact and sinewy, and just now his flinty eyes were dark with amusement.

"You're the one who named me Lord Snow," said Jon. Ser Alliser had been fond of naming the boys he trained, during his time as Castle Black's master-at-arms. The Old Bear had sent Thorne to Eastwatch-by-the-Sea. *These others must be Eastwatch men. The bird reached Cotter Pyke and he's sent us help.* "How many men have you brought?" he asked the man behind the table.

"It's me who'll ask the questions," the jowly man replied. "You've been charged with oathbreaking, cowardice, and desertion, Jon Snow. Do you deny that you abandoned your brothers to die on the Fist of the First Men and joined the wildling Mance Rayder, this self-styled King-beyond-the-Wall?"

"*Abandoned . . .?*" Jon almost choked on the word.

Maester Aemon spoke up then. "My lord, Donal Noye and I discussed these issues when Jon Snow first returned to us, and were satisfied by Jon's explanations."

"Well, *I* am not satisfied, Maester," said the jowly man. "I will hear these *explanations* for myself. Yes I will!"

Jon swallowed his anger. "I abandoned no one. I left the Fist with Qhorin Halfhand to scout the Skirling Pass. I joined the wildlings under orders. The Halfhand feared that Mance might have found the Horn of Winter . . ."

"The Horn of Winter?" Ser Alliser chuckled. "Were you commanded to count their snarks as well, Lord Snow?"

"No, but I counted their *giants* as best I could."

"*Ser*," snapped the jowly man. "You will address Ser Alliser as *ser*, and myself as *m'lord*. I am Janos Slynt, Lord of Harrenhal, and commander here at Castle Black until such time as Bowen Marsh returns with his garrison. You will grant us our courtesies, yes. I will not suffer to hear an anointed knight like the good Ser Alliser mocked by a traitor's bastard." He raised a hand and pointed a meaty finger at Jon's face. "Do you deny that you took a wildling woman into your bed?"

"No." Jon's grief over Ygritte was too fresh for him to deny her now. "No, my lord."

"I suppose it was also the Halfhand who commanded you to fuck this unwashed whore?" Ser Alliser asked with a smirk.

"*Ser.* She was no whore, *ser.* The Halfhand told me not to balk, whatever the wildlings asked of me, but . . . I will not deny that I went beyond what I had to do, that I . . . cared for her."

"You admit to being an oathbreaker, then," said Janos Slynt.

Half the men at Castle Black visited Mole's Town from time to time to dig for buried treasures in the brothel, Jon knew, but he would not dishonor Ygritte by equating her with the Mole's Town whores. "I broke my vows with a woman. I admit that. Yes."

"Yes, *m'lord!*" When Slynt scowled, his jowls quivered. He was as broad as the Old Bear had been, and no doubt would be as bald if he lived to Mormont's age. Half his hair was gone already, though he could not have been more than forty.

"Yes, my lord," Jon said. "I rode with the wildlings and ate with them, as the Halfhand commanded me, and I shared my furs with Ygritte. But I swear to you, I never turned my cloak. I escaped the Magnar as soon as I could, and never took up arms against my brothers or the realm."

Lord Slynt's small eyes studied him. "Ser Glendon," he commanded, "bring in the other prisoner."

Ser Glendon was the tall man who had dragged Jon from his bed. Four other men went with him when he left the room, but they were back soon enough with a captive, a small, sallow, battered man fettered hand and foot. He had a single eyebrow, a widow's peak, and a mustache that looked like a smear of dirt on his upper lip, but his face was swollen and mottled with bruises, and most of his front teeth had been knocked out.

The Eastwatch men threw the captive roughly to the floor. Lord Slynt frowned down at him. "Is this the one you spoke of?"

The captive blinked yellow eyes. "Aye." Not until that instant did Jon recognize Rattleshirt. *He is a different man without his armor,* he thought. "Aye," the wildling repeated, "he's the craven killed the Halfhand. Up in the Frostfangs, it were, after we hunted down t'other crows and killed them, every one. We would have done for this one too, only he begged f' his worthless life, offered t' join us if we'd have him. The Halfhand swore he'd see the craven dead first, but the wolf ripped Qhorin half t' pieces and this one opened his throat." He gave Jon a cracktooth smile then, and spat blood on his foot.

"Well?" Janos Slynt demanded of Jon harshly. "Do you deny it? Or will you claim Qhorin commanded you to kill him?"

"He told me . . ." The words came hard. "He told me to do *whatever* they asked of me."

Slynt looked about the solar, at the other Eastwatch men. "Does this boy think I fell off a turnip wagon onto my head?"

"Your lies won't save you now, Lord Snow," warned Ser Alliser Thorne. "We'll have the truth from you, bastard."

"I've told you the truth. Our garrons were failing, and Rattleshirt was close behind us. Qhorin told me to pretend to join the wildlings. '*You must not balk, whatever is asked of you,*' he said. He knew they would make me kill him. Rattleshirt was going to kill him anyway, he knew that too."

"So now you claim the great Qhorin Halfhand feared *this* creature?" Slynt looked at Rattleshirt, and snorted.

"All men fear the Lord o' Bones," the wildling grumbled. Ser Glendon kicked him, and he lapsed back into silence.

"I never said that," Jon insisted.

Slynt slammed a fist on the table. "I heard you! Ser Alliser had your measure true enough, it seems. You lie through your bastard's teeth. Well, I will not suffer it. I will not! You might have fooled this crippled *blacksmith*, but not Janos Slynt! Oh, no. Janos Slynt does not swallow lies so easily. Did you think my skull was stuffed with cabbage?"

"I don't know what your skull is stuffed with. My lord."

"Lord Snow is nothing if not arrogant," said Ser Alliser. "He murdered Qhorin just as his fellow turncloaks did Lord Mormont. It would not surprise me to learn that it was all part of the same fell plot. Benjen Stark may well have a hand in all this as well. For all we know, he is sitting in Mance Rayder's tent even now. You know these Starks, my lord."

"I do," said Janos Slynt. "I know them too well."

Jon peeled off his glove and showed them his burned hand. "I burned my hand defending Lord Mormont from a wight. And my uncle was a man of honor. He would never have betrayed his vows."

"No more than you?" mocked Ser Alliser.

Septon Cellador cleared his throat. "Lord Slynt," he said, "this boy refused to swear his vows properly in the sept, but went beyond the Wall to say his words before a heart tree. His father's gods, he said, but they are wildling gods as well."

"They are the gods of the north, Septon." Maester Aemon was courteous, but firm. "My lords, when Donal Noye was slain, it was this young man Jon Snow who took the Wall and held it, against all the fury of the north. He has proved himself valiant, loyal, and resourceful. Were it not for him, you would have found Mance Rayder sitting here when you arrived, Lord Slynt. You are doing him a great wrong. Jon Snow was Lord Mormont's own steward and squire. He was chosen for that duty because the Lord Commander saw much promise in him. As do I."

"Promise?" said Slynt. "Well, promise may turn false. Qhorin Half-hand's blood is on his hands. Mormont trusted him, you say, but what of that? I know what it is to be betrayed by men you trusted. Oh, yes. And I know the ways of wolves as well." He pointed at Jon's face. "Your father died a traitor."

"My father was murdered." Jon was past caring what they did to him, but he would not suffer any more lies about his father.

Slynt purpled. "Murder? You insolent pup. King Robert was not even cold when Lord Eddard moved against his son." He rose to his feet; a shorter man than Mormont, but thick about the chest and arms, with a gut to match. A small gold spear tipped with red enamel pinned his cloak at the shoulder. "Your father died by the sword, but he was highborn, a King's Hand. For you, a noose will serve. Ser Alliser, take this turncloak to an ice cell."

"My lord is wise." Ser Alliser seized Jon by the arm.

Jon yanked away and grabbed the knight by the throat with such ferocity that he lifted him off the floor. He would have throttled him if the Eastwatch men had not pulled him off. Thorne staggered back, rubbing the marks Jon's fingers had left on his neck. "You see for yourselves, brothers. The boy is a wildling."

TYRION

When dawn broke, he found he could not face the thought of food. *By evenfall, I may stand condemned.* His belly was acid with bile, and his nose itched. Tyrion scratched at it with the point of his knife. *One last witness to endure, then my turn.* But what to do? Deny everything? Accuse Sansa and Ser Dontos? Confess, in the hope of spending the rest of his days on the Wall? Let the dice fly and pray the Red Viper could defeat Ser Gregor Clegane?

Tyrion stabbed listlessly at a greasy grey sausage, wishing it were his sister. *It is bloody cold on the Wall, but at least I would be shut of Cersei.* He did not think he would make much of a ranger, but the Night's Watch needed clever men as well as strong ones. Lord Commander Mormont had said as much, when Tyrion had visited Castle Black. *There are those inconvenient vows, though.* It would mean the end of his marriage and whatever claim he might ever have made for Casterly Rock, but he did not seem destined to enjoy either in any case. And he seemed to recall that there was a brothel in a nearby village.

It was not a life he'd ever dreamed of, but it was life. And all he had to do to earn it was trust in his father, stand up on his little stunted legs, and say, "Yes, I did it, I confess." That was the part that tied his bowels in knots. He almost wished he *had* done it, since it seemed he must suffer for it anyway.

"My lord?" said Podrick Payne. "They're here, my lord. Ser Addam. And the gold cloaks. They wait without."

"Pod, tell me true ... do you think I did it?"

The boy hesitated. When he tried to speak, all he managed to produce was a weak sputter.

I am doomed. Tyrion sighed. "No need to answer. You've been a good squire to me. Better than I deserved. Whatever happens, I thank you for your leal service."

Ser Addam Marbrand waited at the door with six gold cloaks. He had nothing to say this morning, it seemed. *Another good man who thinks me a kinslayer.* Tyrion summoned all the dignity he could find and waddled down the steps. He could feel them all watching him as he crossed the yard; the guards on the walls, the grooms by the stables, the scullions and washerwomen and serving girls. Inside the throne room, knights and lordlings moved aside to let them through, and whispered to their ladies.

No sooner had Tyrion taken his place before the judges than another group of gold cloaks led in Shae.

A cold hand tightened round his heart. *Varys betrayed her*, he thought. Then he remembered. *No. I betrayed her myself. I should have left her with Lollys. Of course they'd question Sansa's maids, I'd do the same.* Tyrion rubbed at the slick scar where his nose had been, wondering why Cersei had bothered. *Shae knows nothing that can hurt me.*

"They plotted it together," she said, this girl he'd loved. "The Imp and Lady Sansa plotted it after the Young Wolf died. Sansa wanted revenge for her brother and Tyrion meant to have the throne. He was going to kill his sister next, and then his own lord father, so he could be Hand for Prince Tommen. But after a year or so, before Tommen got too old, he would have killed him too, so as to take the crown for his own head."

"How could you know all this?" demanded Prince Oberyn. "Why would the Imp divulge such plans to his wife's maid?"

"I overheard some, m'lord," said Shae, "and m'lady let things slip too. But most I had from his own lips. I wasn't only Lady Sansa's maid. I was his whore, all the time he was here in King's Landing.

On the morning of the wedding, he dragged me down where they keep the dragon skulls and fucked me there with the monsters all around. And when I cried, he said I ought to be more grateful, that it wasn't every girl who got to be the king's whore. That was when he told me how he meant to be king. He said that poor boy Joffrey would never know his bride the way he was knowing me." She started sobbing then. "I never meant to be a whore, m'lords. I was to be married. A squire, he was, and a good brave boy, gentle born. But the Imp saw me at the Green Fork and put the boy I meant to marry in the front rank of the van, and after he was killed he sent his wildlings to bring me to his tent. Shagga, the big one, and Timett with the burned eye. He said if I didn't pleasure him, he'd give me to them, so I did. Then he brought me to the city, so I'd be close when he wanted me. He made me do such shameful things . . ."

Prince Oberyn looked curious. "What sorts of things?"

"*Unspeakable* things." As the tears rolled slowly down that pretty face, no doubt every man in the hall wanted to take Shae in his arms and comfort her. "With my mouth and . . . other parts, m'lord. All my parts. He used me every way there was, and . . . he used to make me tell him how big he was. *My giant*, I had to call him, *my giant of Lannister.*"

Oswald Kettleblack was the first to laugh. Boros and Meryn joined in, then Cersei, Ser Loras, and more lords and ladies than he could count. The sudden gale of mirth made the rafters ring and shook the Iron Throne. "It's true," Shae protested. "My giant of Lannister." The laughter swelled twice as loud. Their mouths were twisted in merriment, their bellies shook. Some laughed so hard that snot flew from their nostrils.

I saved you all, Tyrion thought. *I saved this vile city and all your worthless lives.* There were hundreds in the throne room, every one of them laughing but his father. Or so it seemed. Even the Red Viper chortled, and Mace Tyrell looked like to bust a gut, but Lord Tywin Lannister sat between them as if made of stone, his fingers steepled beneath his chin.

Tyrion pushed forward. "*MY LORDS!*" he shouted. He had to shout, to have any hope of being heard.

His father raised a hand. Bit by bit, the hall grew silent.

"Get this lying whore out of my sight," said Tyrion, "and I will give you your confession."

Lord Tywin nodded, gestured. Shae looked half in terror as the gold cloaks formed up around her. Her eyes met Tyrion's as they marched her from the wall. Was it shame he saw there, or fear? He wondered what Cersei had promised her. *You will get the gold or jewels, whatever it was you asked for,* he thought as he watched her back recede, *but before the moon has turned she'll have you entertaining the gold cloaks in their barracks.*

Tyrion stared up at his father's hard green eyes with their flecks of cold bright gold. "Guilty," he said, "so guilty. Is that what you wanted to hear?"

Lord Tywin said nothing. Mace Tyrell nodded. Prince Oberyn looked mildly disappointed. "You admit you poisoned the king?"

"Nothing of the sort," said Tyrion. "Of Joffrey's death, I am innocent. I am guilty of a more monstrous crime." He took a step toward his father. "I was born. I lived. I am guilty of being a dwarf, I confess it. And no matter how many times my good father forgave me, I have persisted in my infamy."

"This is folly, Tyrion," declared Lord Tywin. "Speak to the matter at hand. You are not on trial for being a dwarf."

"That is where you err, my lord. I have been on trial for being a dwarf my entire life."

"Have you nothing to say in your defense?"

"Nothing but this: I did not do it. Yet now I wish I had." He turned to face the hall, that sea of pale faces. "I wish I had enough poison for you all. You make me sorry that I am not the monster you would have me be, yet there it is. I am innocent, but I will get no justice here. You leave me no choice but to appeal to the gods. I demand trial by battle."

"Have you taken leave of your wits?" his father said.

"No, I've found them. *I demand trial by battle!*"

His sweet sister could not have been more pleased. "He has that right, my lords," she reminded the judges. "Let the gods judge. Ser Gregor Clegane will stand for Joffrey. He returned to the city the night before last, to put his sword at my service."

Lord Tywin's face was so dark that for half a heartbeat Tyrion wondered if he'd drunk some poisoned wine as well. He slammed his fist down on the table, too angry to speak. It was Mace Tyrell who turned to Tyrion and asked the question. "Do you have a champion to defend your innocence?"

"He does, my lord." Prince Oberyn of Dorne rose to his feet. "The dwarf has quite convinced me."

The uproar was deafening. Tyrion took especial pleasure in the sudden doubt he glimpsed in Cersei's eyes. It took a hundred gold cloaks pounding the butts of their spears against the floor to quiet the throne room again. By then Lord Tywin Lannister had recovered himself. "Let the issue be decided on the morrow," he declared in iron tones. "I wash my hands of it." He gave his dwarf son a cold angry look, then strode from the hall, out the king's door behind the Iron Throne, his brother Kevan at his side.

Later, back in his tower cell, Tyrion poured himself a cup of wine and sent Podrick Payne off for cheese, bread, and olives. He doubted whether he could keep down anything heavier just now. *Did you think I would go meekly, Father?* he asked the shadow his candles etched upon the wall. *I have too much of you in me for that.* He felt strangely at peace, now that he had snatched the power of life and death from his father's hands and placed it in the hands of the gods. *Assuming there are gods, and they give a mummer's fart. If not, then I'm in Dornish hands.* No matter what happened, Tyrion had the satisfaction of knowing that he'd kicked Lord Tywin's plans to splinters. If Prince Oberyn won, it would further inflame Highgarden against the Dornish; Mace Tyrell would see the man who crippled his son helping the dwarf who almost poisoned his daughter to escape his rightful punishment. And if the Mountain triumphed, Doran Martell might well demand to know why his brother had been served with death instead of the justice Tyrion had promised him. Dorne might crown Myrcella after all.

It was almost worth dying to know all the trouble he'd made. *Will you come to see the end, Shae? Will you stand there with the rest, watching as Ser Ilyn lops my ugly head off? Will you miss your giant of Lannister when he's dead?* He drained his wine, flung the cup aside, and sang lustily.

He rode through the streets of the city,
down from his hill on high,
O'er the wynds and the steps and the cobbles,
he rode to a woman's sigh.
For she was his secret treasure,
she was his shame and his bliss.
And a chain and a keep are nothing,
compared to a woman's kiss.

Ser Kevan did not visit him that night. He was probably with Lord Tywin, trying to placate the Tyrells. *I have seen the last of that uncle, I fear.* He poured another cup of wine. A pity he'd had Symon Silver Tongue killed before learning all the words of that song. It wasn't a bad song, if truth be told. Especially compared to the ones that would be written about him henceforth. "*For hands of gold are always cold, but a woman's hands are warm,*" he sang. Perhaps he should write the other verses himself. If he lived so long.

That night, surprisingly, Tyrion Lannister slept long and deep. He rose at first light, well rested and with a hearty appetite, and broke his fast on fried bread, blood sausage, applecakes, and a double helping of eggs cooked with onions and fiery Dornish peppers. Then he begged leave of his guards to attend his champion. Ser Addam gave his consent.

Tyrion found Prince Oberyn drinking a cup of red wine as he donned his armor. He was attended by four of his younger Dornish lordlings. "Good morrow to you, my lord," the prince said. "Will you take a cup of wine?"

"Should you be drinking before battle?"

"I always drink before battle."

"That could get you killed. Worse, it could get *me* killed."

Prince Oberyn laughed. "The gods defend the innocent. You *are* innocent, I trust?"

"Only of killing Joffrey," Tyrion admitted. "I do hope you know what you are about to face. Gregor Clegane is—"

"—large? So I have heard."

"He is almost eight feet tall and must weigh thirty stone, all of it muscle. He fights with a two-handed greatsword, but needs only one hand to wield it. He has been known to cut men in half with a single blow. His armor is so heavy that no lesser man could bear the weight, let alone move in it."

Prince Oberyn was unimpressed. "I have killed large men before. The trick is to get them off their feet. Once they go down, they're dead." The Dornishman sounded so blithely confident that Tyrion felt almost reassured, until he turned and said, "Daemon, my spear!" Ser Daemon tossed it to him, and the Red Viper snatched it from the air.

"You mean to face the Mountain with a *spear*?" That made Tyrion uneasy all over again. In battle, ranks of massed spears made for a formidable front, but single combat against a skilled swordsman was a very different matter.

"We are fond of spears in Dorne. Besides, it is the only way to counter his reach. Have a look, Lord Imp, but see you do not touch." The spear was turned ash eight feet long, the shaft smooth, thick, and heavy. The last two feet of that was steel: a slender leaf-shaped spearhead narrowing to a wicked spike. The edges looked sharp enough to shave with. When Oberyn spun the haft between the palms of his hand, they glistened black. *Oil? Or poison?* Tyrion decided that he would sooner not know. "I hope you are good with that," he said doubtfully.

"You will have no cause for complaint. Though Ser Gregor may. However thick his plate, there will be gaps at the joints. Inside the elbow and knee, beneath the arms . . . I will find a place to tickle him, I promise you." He set the spear aside. "It is said that a Lannister always pays his debts. Perhaps you will return to Sunspear with me when the day's bloodletting is done. My brother Doran would be most pleased to meet the rightful heir to Casterly Rock . . . especially if he brought his lovely wife, the Lady of Winterfell."

Does the snake think I have Sansa squirreled away somewhere, like a nut I'm hoarding for winter? If so, Tyrion was not about to disabuse him. "A trip to Dorne might be very pleasant, now that I reflect on it."

"Plan on a lengthy visit." Prince Oberyn sipped his wine. "You and Doran have many matters of mutual interest to discuss. Music, trade, history, wine, the dwarf's penny . . . the laws of inheritance and succession. No doubt an uncle's counsel would be of benefit to Queen Myrcella in the trying times ahead."

If Varys had his little birds listening, Oberyn was giving them a ripe earful. "I believe I will have that cup of wine," said Tyrion. *Queen Myrcella?* It would have been more tempting if only he did have Sansa tucked beneath his cloak. *If she declared for Myrcella over Tommen, would the north follow?* What the Red Viper was hinting at was treason. Could Tyrion truly take up arms against Tommen, against his own father? *Cersei would spit blood.* It might be worth it for that alone.

"Do you recall the tale I told you of our first meeting, Imp?" Prince Oberyn asked, as the Bastard of Godsgrace knelt before him to fasten his greaves. "It was not for your tail alone that my sister and I came to Casterly Rock. We were on a quest of sorts. A quest that took us to Starfall, the Arbor, Oldtown, the Shield Islands, Crakehall, and finally Casterly Rock . . . but our true destination was marriage. Doran was betrothed to Lady Mellario of Norvos, so he had been left behind as castellan of Sunspear. My sister and I were yet unpromised.

"Elia found it all exciting. She was of that age, and her delicate health had never permitted her much travel. I preferred to amuse myself by mocking my sister's suitors. There was Little Lord Lazyeye, Squire Squishlips, one I named the Whale That Walks, that sort of thing. The only one who was even halfway presentable was young Baelor Hightower. A pretty lad, and my sister was half in love with him until he had the misfortune to fart once in our presence. I promptly named him Baelor Breakwind, and after that Elia couldn't look at him without laughing. I was a monstrous young fellow, someone should have sliced out my vile tongue."

Yes, Tyrion agreed silently. Baelor Hightower was no longer young, but he remained Lord Leyton's heir; wealthy, handsome, and a knight of splendid repute. *Baelor Brightsmile,* they called him now. Had Elia wed him in place of Rhaegar Targaryen, she might be in Oldtown with her children growing tall around her. He wondered how many lives had been snuffed out by that fart.

"Lannisport was the end of our voyage," Prince Oberyn went on, as Ser Arron Qorgyle helped him into a padded leather tunic and began lacing it up the back. "Were you aware that our mothers knew each other of old?"

"They had been at court together as girls, I seem to recall. Companions to Princess Rhaella?"

"Just so. It was my belief that the mothers had cooked up this plot between them. Squire Squishlips and his ilk and the various pimply young maidens who'd been paraded before me were the almonds before the feast, meant only to whet our appetites. The main course was to be served at Casterly Rock."

"Cersei and Jaime."

"Such a clever dwarf. Elia and I were older, to be sure. Your brother and sister could not have been more than eight or nine. Still, a difference of five or six years is little enough. And there was an empty cabin on our ship, a very nice cabin, such as might be kept for a person of high birth. As if it were intended that we take someone back to Sunspear. A young page, perhaps. Or a companion for Elia. Your lady mother meant to betroth Jaime to my sister, or Cersei to me. Perhaps both."

"Perhaps," said Tyrion, "but my father—"

"—ruled the Seven Kingdoms, but was ruled at home by his lady wife, or so *my* mother always said." Prince Oberyn raised his arms, so Lord Dagos Manwoody and the Bastard of Godsgrace could slip a chainmail byrnie down over his head. "At Oldtown we learned of your mother's death, and the monstrous child she had borne. We might have turned back there, but my mother chose to sail on. I told you of the welcome we found at Casterly Rock.

"What I did not tell you was that my mother waited as long as was decent, and then broached your father about our purpose. Years later, on her deathbed, she told me that Lord Tywin had refused us brusquely. His daughter was meant for Prince Rhaegar, he informed her. And when she asked for Jaime, to espouse Elia, he offered her you instead."

"Which offer she took for an outrage."

"It *was*. Even you can see that, surely?"

"Oh, surely." *It all goes back and back,* Tyrion thought, *to our mothers and fathers and theirs before them. We are puppets dancing on the*

*strings of those who came before us, and one day our own children will
take up our strings and dance on in our steads.* "Well, Prince Rhaegar
married Elia of Dorne, not Cersei Lannister of Casterly Rock. So it
would seem your mother won that tilt."

"She thought so," Prince Oberyn agreed, "but your father is not a
man to forget such slights. He taught that lesson to Lord and Lady
Tarbeck once, and to the Reynes of Castamere. And at King's Landing,
he taught it to my sister. My helm, Dagos." Manwoody handed it to
him; a high golden helm with a copper disk mounted on the brow,
the sun of Dorne. The visor had been removed, Tyrion saw. "Elia and
her children have waited long for justice." Prince Oberyn pulled on
soft red leather gloves, and took up his spear again. "But this day they
shall have it."

The outer ward had been chosen for the combat. Tyrion had to
skip and run to keep up with Prince Oberyn's long strides. *The snake
is eager,* he thought. *Let us hope he is venomous as well.* The day was
grey and windy. The sun was struggling to break through the clouds,
but Tyrion could no more have said who was going to win that fight
than the one on which his life depended.

It looked as though a thousand people had come to see if he
would live or die. They lined the castle wallwalks and elbowed one
another on the steps of keeps and towers. They watched from the
stable doors, from windows and bridges, from balconies and roofs.
And the yard was packed with them, so many that the gold cloaks
and the knights of the Kingsguard had to shove them back to make
enough room for the fight. Some had dragged out chairs to watch
more comfortably, while others perched on barrels. *We should have
done this in the Dragonpit,* Tyrion thought sourly. *We could have
charged a penny a head and paid for Joffrey's wedding and funeral
both.* Some of the onlookers even had small children sitting on their
shoulders, to get a better view. They shouted and pointed at the
sight of Tyrion.

Cersei seemed half a child herself beside Ser Gregor. In his armor,
the Mountain looked bigger than any man had any right to be. Beneath
a long yellow surcoat bearing the three black dogs of Clegane, he
wore heavy plate over chainmail, dull grey steel dinted and scarred

in battle. Beneath that would be boiled leather and a layer of quilting. A flat-topped greathelm was bolted to his gorget, with breaths around the mouth and nose and a narrow slit for vision. The crest atop it was a stone fist.

If Ser Gregor was suffering from wounds, Tyrion could see no sign of it from across the yard. *He looks as though he was chiseled out of rock, standing there.* His greatsword was planted in the ground before him, six feet of scarred metal. Ser Gregor's huge hands, clad in gauntlets of lobstered steel, clasped the crosshilt to either side of the grip. Even Prince Oberyn's paramour paled at the sight of him. "You are going to fight *that*?" Ellaria Sand said in a hushed voice.

"I am going to kill that," her lover replied carelessly.

Tyrion had his own doubts, now that they stood on the brink. When he looked at Prince Oberyn, he found himself wishing he had Bronn defending him ... or even better, Jaime. The Red Viper was lightly armored; greaves, vambraces, gorget, spaulder, steel codpiece. Elsewise Oberyn was clad in supple leather and flowing silks. Over his byrnie he wore his scales of gleaming copper, but mail and scale together would not give him a quarter the protection of Gregor's heavy plate. With its visor removed, the prince's helm was effectively no better than a half-helm, lacking even a nasal. His round steel shield was brightly polished, and showed the sun-and-spear in red gold, yellow gold, white gold, and copper.

Dance around him until he's so tired he can hardly lift his arm, then put him on his back. The Red Viper seemed to have the same notion as Bronn. But the sellsword had been blunt about the risks of such tactics. *I hope to seven hells that you know what you are doing, snake.*

A platform had been erected beside the Tower of the Hand, halfway between the two champions. That was where Lord Tywin sat with his brother Ser Kevan. King Tommen was not in evidence; for that, at least, Tyrion was grateful.

Lord Tywin glanced briefly at his dwarf son, then lifted his hand. A dozen trumpeters blew a fanfare to quiet the crowd. The High Septon shuffled forward in his tall crystal crown, and prayed that the Father Above would help them in this judgment, and that the Warrior would lend his strength to the arm of the man whose cause was just.

That would be me, Tyrion almost shouted, but they would only laugh, and he was sick unto death of laughter.

Ser Osmund Kettleblack brought Clegane his shield, a massive thing of heavy oak rimmed in black iron. As the Mountain slid his left arm through the straps, Tyrion saw that the hounds of Clegane had been painted over. This morning Ser Gregor bore the seven-pointed star the Andals had brought to Westeros when they crossed the narrow sea to overwhelm the First Men and their gods. *Very pious of you, Cersei, but I doubt the gods will be impressed.*

There were fifty yards between them. Prince Oberyn advanced quickly, Ser Gregor more ominously. *The ground does not shake when he walks*, Tyrion told himself. *That is only my heart fluttering.* When the two men were ten yards apart, the Red Viper stopped and called out, "Have they told you who I am?"

Ser Gregor grunted through his breaths. "Some dead man." He came on, inexorable.

The Dornishman slid sideways. "I am Oberyn Martell, a prince of Dorne," he said, as the Mountain turned to keep him in sight. "Princess Elia was my sister."

"Who?" asked Gregor Clegane.

Oberyn's long spear jabbed, but Ser Gregor took the point on his shield, shoved it aside, and bulled back at the prince, his great sword flashing. The Dornishman spun away untouched. The spear darted forward. Clegane slashed at it, Martell snapped it back, then thrust again. Metal screamed on metal as the spearhead slid off the Mountain's chest, slicing through the surcoat and leaving a long bright scratch on the steel beneath. "Elia Martell, Princess of Dorne," the Red Viper hissed. "You raped her. You murdered her. You killed her children."

Ser Gregor grunted. He made a ponderous charge to hack at the Dornishman's head. Prince Oberyn avoided him easily. "You raped her. You murdered her. You killed her children."

"Did you come to talk or to fight?"

"I came to hear you confess." The Red Viper landed a quick thrust on the Mountain's belly, to no effect. Gregor cut at him, and missed. The long spear lanced in above his sword. Like a serpent's tongue it flickered in and out, feinting low and landing high, jabbing at groin, shield, eyes. *The Mountain makes for a big target, at the least,* Tyrion thought. Prince Oberyn could scarcely miss, though none of his blows was penetrating Ser Gregor's heavy plate. The Dornishman kept circling, jabbing, then darting back again, forcing the bigger man to turn and turn again. *Clegane is losing sight of him.* The Mountain's helm had a narrow eyeslit, severely limiting his vision. Oberyn was making good use of that, and the length of his spear, and his quickness.

It went on that way for what seemed a long time. Back and forth they moved across the yard, and round and round in spirals, Ser Gregor slashing at the air while Oberyn's spear struck at arm, and leg, twice at his temple. Gregor's big wooden shield took its share of hits as well, until a dog's head peeped out from under the star, and elsewhere the raw oak showed through. Clegane would grunt from time to time, and once Tyrion heard him mutter a curse, but otherwise he fought in a sullen silence.

Not Oberyn Martell. "You raped her," he called, feinting. "You murdered her," he said, dodging a looping cut from Gregor's greatsword. "You killed her children," he shouted, slamming the spearpoint into the giant's throat, only to have it glance off the thick steel gorget with a screech.

"Oberyn is toying with him," said Ellaria Sand.

That is fool's play, thought Tyrion. "The Mountain is too bloody big to be any man's toy."

All around the yard, the throng of spectators was creeping in toward the two combatants, edging forward inch by inch to get a better view. The Kingsguard tried to keep them back, shoving at the gawkers forcefully with their big white shields, but there were hundreds of gawkers and only six of the men in white armor.

"You raped her." Prince Oberyn parried a savage cut with his spearhead. "You murdered her." He sent the spearpoint at Clegane's eyes, so fast the huge man flinched back. "You killed her children." The spear flickered sideways and down, scraping against the Mountain's breastplate. "You raped her. You murdered her. You killed her children." The spear was two feet longer than Ser Gregor's sword, more than enough to keep him at an awkward distance. He hacked at the shaft whenever Oberyn lunged at him, trying to lop off the spearhead, but he might as well have been trying to hack the wings off a fly. "You raped her. You murdered her. You killed her children." Gregor tried to bull rush, but Oberyn skipped aside and circled round his back. "You raped her. You murdered her. You killed her children."

"Be quiet." Ser Gregor seemed to be moving a little slower, and his greatsword no longer rose quite so high as it had when the contest began. "Shut your bloody mouth."

"You raped her," the prince said, moving to the right.

"*Enough!*" Ser Gregor took two long strides and brought his sword down at Oberyn's head, but the Dornishman backstepped once more. "You murdered her," he said.

"*SHUT UP!*" Gregor charged headlong, right at the point of the spear, which slammed into his right breast then slid aside with a hideous steel shriek. Suddenly the Mountain was close enough to strike, his huge sword flashing in a steel blur. The crowd was screaming as well. Oberyn slipped the first blow and let go of the spear, useless now that Ser Gregor was inside it. The second cut the Dornishman caught on his shield. Metal met metal with an ear-splitting clang, sending the Red Viper reeling. Ser Gregor followed, bellowing. *He doesn't use words, he just roars like an animal,* Tyrion thought. Oberyn's retreat became a headlong backward flight mere inches ahead of the greatsword as it slashed at his chest, his arms, his head.

The stable was behind him. Spectators screamed and shoved at each other to get out of the way. One stumbled into Oberyn's back. Ser Gregor hacked down with all his savage strength. The Red Viper threw himself sideways, rolling. The luckless stableboy behind him was not so quick. As his arm rose to protect his face, Gregor's sword took it off between elbow and shoulder. "*Shut UP!*" the Mountain howled at the stableboy's scream, and this time he swung the blade sideways, sending the top half of the lad's head across the yard in a spray of blood and brains. Hundreds of spectators suddenly seemed to lose all interest in the guilt or innocence of Tyrion Lannister, judging by the way they pushed and shoved at each other to escape the yard.

But the Red Viper of Dorne was back on his feet, his long spear in hand. "Elia," he called at Ser Gregor. "You raped her. You murdered her. You killed her children. Now say her name."

The Mountain whirled. Helm, shield, sword, surcoat; he was spattered with gore from head to heels. "You talk too much," he grumbled. "You make my head hurt."

"I will hear you say it. She was Elia of Dorne."

The Mountain snorted contemptuously, and came on . . . and in that moment, the sun broke through the low clouds that had hidden the sky since dawn.

The sun of Dorne, Tyrion told himself, but it was Gregor Clegane who moved first to put the sun at his back. *This is a dim and brutal man, but he has a warrior's instincts.*

The Red Viper crouched, squinting, and sent his spear darting forward again. Ser Gregor hacked at it, but the thrust had only been a feint. Off balance, he stumbled forward a step.

Prince Oberyn tilted his dinted metal shield. A shaft of sunlight blazed blindingly off polished gold and copper, into the narrow slit of his foe's helm. Clegane lifted his own shield against the glare. Prince Oberyn's spear flashed like lightning and found the gap in the heavy plate, the joint under the arm. The point punched through mail and boiled leather. Gregor gave a choked grunt as the Dornishman twisted his spear and yanked it free. "Elia. Say it! Elia of Dorne!" He was circling, spear poised for another thrust. "*Say it!*"

Tyrion had his own prayer. *Fall down and die,* was how it went. *Damn you, fall down and die!* The blood trickling from the Mountain's armpit was his own now, and he must be bleeding even more heavily inside the breastplate. When he tried to take a step, one knee buckled. Tyrion thought he was going down.

Prince Oberyn had circled behind him. "*ELIA OF DORNE!*" he shouted. Ser Gregor started to turn, but too slow and too late. The spearhead went through the back of the knee this time, through the layers of chain and leather between the plates on thigh and calf. The Mountain reeled, swayed, then collapsed face first on the ground. His huge sword went flying from his hand. Slowly, ponderously, he rolled onto his back.

The Dornishman flung away his ruined shield, grasped the spear in both hands, and sauntered away. Behind him the Mountain let out a groan, and pushed himself onto an elbow. Oberyn whirled cat-quick, and *ran* at his fallen foe. "*EEEEELLLLLLIIIIIAAAAA!*" he screamed, as he drove the spear down with the whole weight of his body behind it. The *crack* of the ashwood shaft snapping was almost as sweet a sound as Cersei's wail of fury, and for an instant Prince Oberyn had wings. *The snake has vaulted over the Mountain.* Four feet of broken spear jutted from Clegane's belly as Prince Oberyn rolled, rose, and dusted himself off. He tossed aside the splintered spear and claimed his foe's greatsword. "If you die before you say her name, ser, I will hunt you through all seven hells," he promised.

Ser Gregor tried to rise. The broken spear had gone through him, and was pinning him to the ground. He wrapped both hands about the shaft, grunting, but could not pull it out. Beneath him was a spreading pool of red. "I am feeling more innocent by the instant," Tyrion told Ellaria Sand beside him.

Prince Oberyn moved closer. "*Say the name!*" He put a foot on the Mountain's chest and raised the greatsword with both hands. Whether he intended to hack off Gregor's head or shove the point through his eyeslit was something Tyrion would never know.

Clegane's hand shot up and grabbed the Dornishman behind the knee. The Red Viper brought down the greatsword in a wild slash, but he was off-balance, and the edge did no more than put another dent in the Mountain's vambrace. Then the sword was forgotten as Gregor's hand tightened and twisted, yanking the Dornishman down on top of him. They wrestled in the dust and blood, the broken spear wobbling back and forth. Tyrion saw with horror that the Mountain had wrapped one huge arm around the prince, drawing him tight against his chest, like a lover.

"Elia of Dorne," they all heard Ser Gregor say, when they were close enough to kiss. His deep voice boomed within the helm. "I killed her screaming whelp." He thrust his free hand into Oberyn's unprotected face, pushing steel fingers into his eyes. "*Then* I raped her." Clegane slammed his fist into the Dornishman's mouth, making splinters of his teeth. "Then I smashed her fucking head in. Like this."

As he drew back his huge fist, the blood on his gauntlet seemed to smoke in the cold dawn air. There was a sickening *crunch*. Ellaria Sand wailed in terror, and Tyrion's breakfast came boiling back up. He found himself on his knees retching bacon and sausage and apple-cakes, and that double helping of fried eggs cooked up with onions and fiery Dornish peppers.

He never heard his father speak the words that condemned him. Perhaps no words were necessary. *I put my life in the Red Viper's hands, and he dropped it.* When he remembered, too late, that snakes had no hands, Tyrion began to laugh hysterically.

He was halfway down the serpentine steps before he realized that the gold cloaks were not taking him back to his tower room. "I've been consigned to the black cells," he said. They did not bother to answer. *Why waste your breath on the dead?*

DAENERYS

Dany broke her fast under the persimmon tree that grew in the terrace garden, watching her dragons chase each other about the apex of the Great Pyramid where the huge bronze harpy once stood. Meereen had a score of lesser pyramids, but none stood even half as tall. From here she could see the whole city: the narrow twisty alleys and wide brick streets, the temples and granaries, hovels and palaces, brothels and baths, gardens and fountains, the great red circles of the fighting pits. And beyond the walls was the pewter sea, the winding Skahazadhan, the dry brown hills, burnt orchards, and blackened fields. Up here in her garden Dany sometimes felt like a god, living atop the highest mountain in the world.

Do all gods feel so lonely? Some must, surely. Missandei had told her of the Lord of Harmony, worshiped by the Peaceful People of Naath; he was the only true god, her little scribe said, the god who always was and always would be, who made the moon and stars and earth, and all the creatures that dwelt upon them. *Poor Lord of Harmony.* Dany pitied him. It must be terrible to be alone for all time, attended by hordes of butterfly women you could make or unmake at a word. Westeros had seven gods at least, though Viserys had told her that some septons said the seven were only aspects of a single god, seven facets of a single crystal. That was just confusing. The red priests believed in two gods, she had heard, but two who were eternally at war. Dany liked that even less. She would not want to be eternally at war.

Missandei served her duck eggs and dog sausage, and half a cup of sweetened wine mixed with the juice of a lime. The honey drew flies, but a scented candle drove them off. The flies were not so troublesome up here as they were in the rest of her city, she had found, something else she liked about the pyramid. "I must remember to do something about the flies," Dany said. "Are there many flies on Naath, Missandei?"

"On Naath there are butterflies," the scribe responded in the Common Tongue. "More wine?"

"No. I must hold court soon." Dany had grown very fond of Missandei. The little scribe with the big golden eyes was wise beyond her years. *She is brave as well. She had to be, to survive the life she's lived.* One day she hoped to see this fabled isle of Naath. Missandei said the Peaceful People made music instead of war. They did not kill, not even animals; they ate only fruit and never flesh. The butterfly spirits sacred to their Lord of Harmony protected their isle against those who would do them harm. Many conquerors had sailed on Naath to blood their swords, only to sicken and die. *The butterflies do not help them when the slave ships come raiding, though.* "I am going to take you home one day, Missandei," Dany promised. *If I had made the same promise to Jorah, would he still have sold me?* "I swear it."

"This one is content to stay with you, Your Grace. Naath will be there, always. You are good to this—to me."

"And you to me." Dany took the girl by the hand. "Come help me dress."

Jhiqui helped Missandei bathe her while Irri was laying out her clothes. Today she wore a robe of purple samite and a silver sash, and on her head the three-headed dragon crown the Tourmaline Brotherhood had given her in Qarth. Her slippers were silver as well, with heels so high that she was always half afraid she was about to topple over. When she was dressed, Missandei brought her a polished silver glass so she could see how she looked. Dany stared at herself in silence. *Is this the face of a conqueror?* So far as she could tell, she still looked like a little girl.

No one was calling her Daenerys the Conqueror yet, but perhaps they would. Aegon the Conqueror had won Westeros with three dragons, but she had taken Meereen with sewer rats and a wooden cock, in less than a day. *Poor Groleo.* He still grieved for his ship, she knew. If a war galley could ram another ship, why not a gate? That had been her thought when she commanded the captains to drive their ships ashore. Their masts had become her battering rams, and swarms of freedmen had torn their hulls apart to build mantlets, turtles, catapults, and ladders. The sellswords had given each ram a bawdy name, and it had been the mainmast of *Meraxes*—formerly *Joso's Prank*—that had broken the eastern gate. Joso's Cock, they called it. The fighting had raged bitter and bloody for most of a day and well into the night before the wood began to splinter and *Meraxes'* iron figurehead, a laughing jester's face, came crashing through.

Dany had wanted to lead the attack herself, but to a man her captains said that would be madness, and her captains never agreed on anything. Instead she remained in the rear, sitting atop her silver in a long shirt of mail. She *heard* the city fall from half a league away, though, when the defenders' shouts of defiance changed to cries of fear. Her dragons had roared as one in that moment, filling the night with flame. *The slaves are rising,* she knew at once. *My sewer rats have gnawed off their chains.*

When the last resistance had been crushed by the Unsullied and the sack had run its course, Dany entered her city. The dead were heaped so high before the broken gate that it took her freedmen near an hour to make a path for her silver. Joso's Cock and the great wooden turtle that had protected it, covered with horsehides, lay abandoned within. She rode past burned buildings and broken windows, through brick streets where the gutters were choked with the stiff and swollen dead. Cheering slaves lifted bloodstained hands to her as she went by, and called her "Mother."

In the plaza before the Great Pyramid, the Meereenese huddled forlorn. The Great Masters had looked anything but great in the morning light. Stripped of their jewels and their fringed *tokar*s, they were contemptible; a herd of old men with shriveled balls and spotted skin and young men with ridiculous hair. Their women were either soft and fleshy or as dry as old sticks, their face paint streaked by tears. "I want your leaders," Dany told them. "Give them up, and the rest of you shall be spared."

"How many?" one old woman had asked, sobbing. "How many must you have to spare us?"

"One hundred and sixty-three," she answered.

She had them nailed to wooden posts around the plaza, each man pointing at the next. The anger was fierce and hot inside her when she gave the command; it made her feel like an avenging dragon. But later, when she passed the men dying on the posts, when she heard their moans and smelled their bowels and blood . . .

Dany put the glass aside, frowning. *It was just. It was. I did it for the children.*

Her audience chamber was on the level below, an echoing high-ceilinged room with walls of purple marble. It was a chilly place for all its grandeur. There had been a throne there, a fantastic thing of carved and gilded wood in the shape of a savage harpy. She had taken one long look and commanded it be broken up for firewood. "I will not sit in the harpy's lap," she told them. Instead she sat upon a simple ebony bench. It served, though she had heard the Meereenese muttering that it did not befit a queen.

Her bloodriders were waiting for her. Silver bells tinkled in their oiled braids, and they wore the gold and jewels of dead men. Meereen had been rich beyond imagining. Even her sellswords seemed sated, at least for now. Across the room, Grey Worm wore the plain uniform of the Unsullied, his spiked bronze cap beneath one arm. These at least she could rely on, or so she hoped . . . and Brown Ben Plumm as well, solid Ben with his grey-white hair and weathered face, so beloved of her dragons. And Daario beside him, glittering in gold. Daario and Ben Plumm, Grey Worm, Irri, Jhiqui, Missandei . . . as she looked at them Dany found herself wondering which of them would betray her next.

The dragon has three heads. There are two men in the world who I can trust, if I can find them. I will not be alone then. We will be three against the world, like Aegon and his sisters.

"Was the night as quiet as it seemed?" Dany asked.

"It seems it was, Your Grace," said Brown Ben Plumm.

She was pleased. Meereen had been sacked savagely, as new-fallen cities always were, but Dany was determined that should end now that the city was hers. She had decreed that murderers were to be hanged, that looters were to lose a hand, and rapists their manhood. Eight killers swung from the walls, and the Unsullied had filled a bushel basket with bloody hands and soft red worms, but Meereen was calm again. *But for how long?*

A fly buzzed her head. Dany waved it off, irritated, but it returned almost at once. "There are too many flies in this city."

Ben Plumm gave a bark of laughter. "There were flies in my ale this morning. I swallowed one of them."

"Flies are the dead man's revenge." Daario smiled, and stroked the center prong of his beard. "Corpses breed maggots, and maggots breed flies."

"We will rid ourselves of the corpses, then. Starting with those in the plaza below. Grey Worm, will you see to it?"

"The queen commands, these ones obey."

"Best bring sacks as well as shovels, Worm," Brown Ben counseled. "Well past ripe, those ones. Falling off those poles in bits and pieces, and crawling with . . ."

"He knows. So do I." Dany remembered the horror she had felt when she had seen the Plaza of Punishment in Astapor. *I made a horror just as great, but surely they deserved it. Harsh justice is still justice.*

"Your Grace," said Missandei, "Ghiscari inter their honored dead in crypts below their manses. If you would boil the bones clean and return them to their kin, it would be a kindness."

The widows will curse me all the same. "Let it be done." Dany beckoned to Daario. "How many seek audience this morning?"

"Two have presented themselves to bask in your radiance."

Daario had plundered himself a whole new wardrobe in Meereen, and to match it he had redyed his trident beard and curly hair a deep rich purple. It made his eyes look almost purple too, as if he were some lost Valyrian. "They arrived in the night on the *Indigo Star*, a trading galley out of Qarth."

A slaver, you mean. Dany frowned. "Who are they?"

"The *Star*'s master and one who claims to speak for Astapor."

"I will see the envoy first."

He proved to be a pale ferret-faced man with ropes of pearls and spun gold hanging heavy about his neck. "Your Worship!" he cried. "My name is Ghael. I bring greetings to the Mother of Dragons from King Cleon of Astapor, Cleon the Great."

Dany stiffened. "I left a council to rule Astapor. A healer, a scholar, and a priest."

"Your Worship, those sly rogues betrayed your trust. It was revealed that they were scheming to restore the Good Masters to power and the people to chains. Great Cleon exposed their plots and hacked their heads off with a cleaver, and the grateful folk of Astapor have crowned him for his valor."

"Noble Ghael," said Missandei, in the dialect of Astapor, "is this the same Cleon once owned by Grazdan mo Ullhor?"

Her voice was guileless, yet the question plainly made the envoy anxious. "The same," he admitted. "A great man."

Missandei leaned close to Dany. "He was a butcher in Grazdan's kitchen," the girl whispered in her ear. "It was said he could slaughter a pig faster than any man in Astapor."

I have given Astapor a butcher king. Dany felt ill, but she knew she must not let the envoy see it. "I will pray that King Cleon rules well and wisely. What would he have of me?"

Ghael rubbed his mouth. "Perhaps we should speak more privily, Your Grace?"

"I have no secrets from my captains and commanders."

"As you wish. Great Cleon bids me declare his devotion to the Mother of Dragons. Your enemies are his enemies, he says, and chief among them are the Wise Masters of Yunkai. He proposes a pact between Astapor and Meereen, against the Yunkai'i."

"I swore no harm would come to Yunkai if they released their slaves," said Dany.

"These Yunkish dogs cannot be trusted, Your Worship. Even now they plot against you. New levies have been raised and can be seen drilling outside the city walls, warships are being built, envoys have been sent to New Ghis and Volantis in the west, to make alliances and hire sellswords. They have even dispatched riders to Vaes Dothrak to bring a *khalasar* down upon you. Great Cleon bid me tell you not to be afraid. Astapor remembers. Astapor will not forsake you. To prove his faith, Great Cleon offers to seal your alliance with a marriage."

"A marriage? To me?"

Ghael smiled. His teeth were brown and rotten. "Great Cleon will give you many strong sons."

Dany found herself bereft of words, but little Missandei came to her rescue. "Did his first wife give him sons?"

The envoy looked at her unhappily. "Great Cleon has three daughters by his first wife. Two of his newer wives are with child. But he means to put all of them aside if the Mother of Dragons will consent to wed him."

"How noble of him," said Dany. "I will consider all you've said, my lord." She gave orders that Ghael be given chambers for the night, somewhere lower in the pyramid.

All my victories turn to dross in my hands, she thought. *Whatever I do, all I make is death and horror.* When word of what had befallen Astapor reached the streets, as it surely would, tens of thousands of newly freed Meereenese slaves would doubtless decide to follow her when she went west, for fear of what awaited them if they stayed . . . yet it might well be that worse would await them on the march. Even if she emptied every granary in the city and left Meereen to starve, how could she feed so many? The way before her was fraught with hardship, bloodshed, and danger. Ser Jorah had warned her of that. He'd warned her of so many things . . . he'd . . . *No, I will not think of Jorah Mormont. Let him keep a little longer.* "I shall see this trader captain," she announced. Perhaps he would have some better tidings.

That proved to be a forlorn hope. The master of the *Indigo Star* was Qartheen, so he wept copiously when asked about Astapor. "The city bleeds. Dead men rot unburied in the streets, each pyramid is an armed camp, and the markets have neither food nor slaves for sale. And the poor children! King Cleaver's thugs have seized every highborn boy in Astapor to make new Unsullied for the trade, though it will be years before they are trained."

The thing that surprised Dany most was how unsurprised she was. She found herself remembering Eroeh, the Lhazarene girl she had once tried to protect, and what had happened to her. *It will be the same in Meereen once I march*, she thought. The slaves from the fighting pits, bred and trained to slaughter, were already proving themselves unruly and quarrelsome. They seemed to think they owned the city now, and every man and woman in it. Two of them had been among the eight she'd hanged. *There is no more I can do*, she told herself. "What do you want of me, Captain?"

"Slaves," he said. "My holds are full to bursting with ivory, ambergris, zorse hides, and other fine goods. I would trade them here for slaves, to sell in Lys and Volantis."

"We have no slaves for sale," said Dany.

"My queen?" Daario stepped forward. "The riverside is full of Meereenese, begging leave to be allowed to sell themselves to this Qartheen. They are thicker than the flies."

Dany was shocked. "They *want* to be slaves?"

"The ones who come are well spoken and gently born, sweet queen. Such slaves are prized. In the Free Cities, they will be tutors, scribes, bed slaves, even healers and priests. They will sleep in soft beds, eat rich foods, and dwell in manses. Here they have lost all, and live in fear and squalor."

"I see." Perhaps it was not so shocking, if these tales of Astapor were true. Dany thought a moment. "Any man who wishes to sell *himself* into slavery may do so. Or woman." She raised a hand. "But they may not sell their children, nor a man his wife."

"In Astapor the city took a tenth part of the price, each time a slave changed hands," Missandei told her.

"We'll do the same," Dany decided. Wars were won with gold as much as swords. "A tenth part. In gold or silver coin, or ivory. Meereen has no need of saffron, cloves, or zorse hides."

"It shall be done as you command, glorious queen," said Daario. "My Stormcrows will collect your tenth."

If the Stormcrows saw to the collections at least half the gold would somehow go astray, Dany knew. But the Second Sons were just as bad, and the Unsullied were as unlettered as they were incorruptible. "Records must be kept," she said. "Seek among the freedmen for men who can read, write, and do sums."

His business done, the captain of the *Indigo Star* bowed and took his leave. Dany shifted uncomfortably on the ebony bench. She dreaded what must come next, yet she knew she had put it off too long already. Yunkai and Astapor, threats of war, marriage proposals, the march west looming over all . . . *I need my knights. I need their swords, and I need their counsel.* Yet the thought of seeing Jorah Mormont again made her feel as if she'd swallowed a spoonful of flies; angry, agitated, sick. She could almost feel them buzzing round her belly. *I am the blood of the dragon. I must be strong. I must have fire in my eyes when I face them, not tears.* "Tell Belwas to bring my knights," Dany commanded, before she could change her mind. "My good knights."

Strong Belwas was puffing from the climb when he marched them through the doors, one meaty hand wrapped tight around each man's arm. Ser Barristan walked with his head held high, but Ser Jorah stared at the marble floor as he approached. *The one is proud, the other guilty.*

The old man had shaved off his white beard. He looked ten years younger without it. But her balding bear looked older than he had. They halted before the bench. Strong Belwas stepped back and stood with his arms crossed across his scarred chest. Ser Jorah cleared his throat. "*Khaleesi* . . ."

She had missed his voice so much, but she had to be stern. "Be quiet. I will tell you when to speak." She stood. "When I sent you down into the sewers, part of me hoped I'd seen the last of you. It seemed a fitting end for liars, to drown in slavers' filth. I thought the gods would deal with you, but instead you returned to me. My gallant knights of Westeros, an informer and a turncloak. My brother would have hanged you both." Viserys would have, anyway. She did not know what Rhaegar would have done. "I will admit you helped win me this city . . ."

Ser Jorah's mouth tightened. "We won you this city. We sewer rats."

"Be quiet," she said again . . . though there *was* truth to what he said. While Joso's Cock and the other rams were battering the city gates and her archers were firing flights of flaming arrows over the walls, Dany had sent two hundred men along the river under cover of darkness to fire the hulks in the harbor. But that was only to hide their true purpose. As the flaming ships drew the eyes of the defenders on the walls, a few half-mad swimmers found the sewer mouths and pried loose a rusted iron grating. Ser Jorah, Ser Barristan, Strong Belwas, and twenty brave fools slipped beneath the brown water and up the brick tunnel, a mixed force of sellswords, Unsullied, and freedmen. Dany had told them to choose only men who had no families . . . and preferably no sense of smell.

They had been lucky as well as brave. It had been a moon's turn since the last good rain, and the sewers were only thigh-high. The oilcloth they'd wrapped around their torches kept them dry, so they had light. A few of the freedmen were frightened of the huge rats until Strong Belwas caught one and bit it in two. One man was killed by a great pale lizard that reared up out of the dark water to drag him off by the leg, but when next ripples were spied Ser Jorah butchered the beast with his blade. They took some wrong turnings, but once they found the surface Strong Belwas led them to the nearest fighting pit, where they surprised a few guards and struck the chains off the slaves. Within an hour, half the fighting slaves in Meereen had risen.

"You *helped* win this city," she repeated stubbornly. "And you have served me well in the past. Ser Barristan saved me from the Titan's Bastard, and from the Sorrowful Man in Qarth. Ser Jorah saved me from the poisoner in Vaes Dothrak, and again from Drogo's blood-riders after my sun-and-stars had died." So many people wanted her dead, sometimes she lost count. "And yet you lied, deceived me, betrayed me." She turned to Ser Barristan. "You protected my father for many years, fought beside my brother on the Trident, but you abandoned Viserys in his exile and bent your knee to the Usurper instead. Why? And tell it *true*."

"Some truths are hard to hear. Robert was a . . . a good knight . . . chivalrous, brave . . . he spared my life, and the lives of many others

... Prince Viserys was only a boy, it would have been years before he was fit to rule, and ... forgive me, my queen, but you asked for truth ... even as a child, your brother Viserys oft seemed to be his father's son, in ways that Rhaegar never did."

"His father's son?" Dany frowned. "What does that mean?"

The old knight did not blink. "Your father is called 'the Mad King' in Westeros. Has no one ever told you?"

"Viserys did." *The Mad King.* "The *Usurper* called him that, the Usurper and his dogs." *The Mad King.* "It was a lie."

"Why ask for truth," Ser Barristan said softly, "if you close your ears to it?" He hesitated, then continued. "I told you before that I used a false name so the Lannisters would not know that I'd joined you. That was less than half of it, Your Grace. The truth is, I wanted to watch you for a time before pledging you my sword. To make certain that you were not ..."

"... my father's daughter?" If she was not her father's daughter, who was she?

"... mad," he finished. "But I see no taint in you."

"*Taint?*" Dany bristled.

"I am no maester to quote history at you, Your Grace. Swords have been my life, not books. But every child knows that the Targaryens have always danced too close to madness. Your father was not the first. King Jaehaerys once told me that madness and greatness are two sides of the same coin. Every time a new Targaryen is born, he said, the gods toss the coin in the air and the world holds its breath to see how it will land."

Jaehaerys. This old man knew my grandfather. The thought gave her pause. Most of what she knew of Westeros had come from her brother, and the rest from Ser Jorah. Ser Barristan would have forgotten more than the two of them had ever known. *This man can tell me what I came from.* "So I am a coin in the hands of some god, is that what you are saying, ser?"

"No," Ser Barristan replied. "You are the trueborn heir of Westeros. To the end of my days I shall remain your faithful knight, should you find me worthy to bear a sword again. If not, I am content to serve Strong Belwas as his squire."

"What if I decide you're only worthy to be my fool?" Dany asked scornfully. "Or perhaps my cook?"

"I would be honored, Your Grace," Selmy said with quiet dignity. "I can bake apples and boil beef as well as any man, and I've roasted many a duck over a campfire. I hope you like them greasy, with charred skin and bloody bones."

That made her smile. "I'd have to be mad to eat such fare. Ben Plumm, come give Ser Barristan your longsword."

But Whitebeard would not take it. "I flung my sword at Joffrey's feet and have not touched one since. Only from the hand of my queen will I accept a sword again."

"As you wish." Dany took the sword from Brown Ben and offered it hilt first. The old man took it reverently. "Now kneel," she told him, "and swear it to my service."

He went to one knee and lay the blade before her as he said the words. Dany scarcely heard them. *He was the easy one*, she thought. *The other will be harder.* When Ser Barristan was done, she turned to Jorah Mormont. "And now you, ser. Tell me true."

The big man's neck was red; whether from anger or shame she did not know. "I have tried to tell you true, half a hundred times. I told you Arstan was more than he seemed. I warned you that Xaro and Pyat Pree were not to be trusted. I warned you—"

"You warned me against everyone except yourself." His insolence angered her. *He should be humbler. He should beg for my forgiveness.* "Trust no one but Jorah Mormont, you said . . . and all the time you were the Spider's creature!"

"I am no man's *creature*. I took the eunuch's gold, yes. I learned some ciphers and wrote some letters, but that was all—"

"*All?* You spied on me and sold me to my enemies!"

"For a time." He said it grudgingly. "I stopped."

"When? When did you stop?"

"I made one report from Qarth, but—"

"From *Qarth*?" Dany had been hoping it had ended much earlier. "What did you write from Qarth? That you were my man now, that you wanted no more of their schemes?" Ser Jorah could not meet her eyes. "When Khal Drogo died, you asked me to go with you to Yi Ti and the Jade Sea. Was that your wish or Robert's?"

"That was to protect you," he insisted. "To keep you away from them. I knew what snakes they were . . ."

"*Snakes?* And what are you, ser?" Something unspeakable occurred to her. "You told them I was carrying Drogo's child . . ."

"*Khaleesi* . . ."

"Do not think to deny it, ser," Ser Barristan said sharply. "I was there when the eunuch told the council, and Robert decreed that Her Grace and her child must die. You were the source, ser. There was even talk that you might do the deed, for a pardon."

"A lie." Ser Jorah's face darkened. "I would never . . . Daenerys, it was me who *stopped* you from drinking the wine."

"Yes. And how was it you knew the wine was poisoned?"

"I . . . I but suspected . . . the caravan brought a letter from Varys, he warned me there would be attempts. He wanted you watched, yes, but not harmed." He went to his knees. "If I had not told them someone else would have. You *know* that."

"I know you betrayed me." She touched her belly, where her son Rhaego had perished. "I know a poisoner tried to kill my son, because of you. That's what I *know*."

"No . . . no." He shook his head. "I never meant . . . forgive me. You have to forgive me."

"*Have* to?" It was too late. *He should have begun by begging forgiveness.* She could not pardon him as she'd intended. She had dragged the wineseller behind her horse until there was nothing left of him. Didn't the man who brought him deserve the same? *This is Jorah, my fierce bear, the right arm that never failed me. I would be dead without him, but* . . . "I can't forgive you," she said. "I can't."

"You forgave the old man . . ."

"He lied to me about his name. You sold my secrets to the men who killed my father and stole my brother's throne."

"I protected you. I fought for you. Killed for you."

Kissed me, she thought, *betrayed me.*

"I went down into the sewers like a rat. For you."

It might have been kinder if you'd died there. Dany said nothing. There was nothing to say.

"Daenerys," he said, "I have loved you."

And there it was. *Three treasons will you know. Once for blood and once for gold and once for love.* "The gods do nothing without a purpose, they say. You did not die in battle, so it must be they still have some use for you. But I don't. I will not have you near me. You are banished, ser. Go back to your masters in King's Landing and collect your pardon, if you can. Or to Astapor. No doubt the butcher king needs knights."

"No." He reached for her. "Daenerys, please, hear me . . ."

She slapped his hand away. "Do not ever presume to touch me again, or to speak my name. You have until dawn to collect your things and leave this city. If you're found in Meereen past break of day, I will have Strong Belwas twist your head off. I will. Believe that." She turned her back on him, her skirts swirling. *I cannot bear to see his face.* "Remove this liar from my sight," she commanded. *I must not weep. I must not. If I weep I will forgive him.* Strong Belwas seized Ser Jorah by the arm and dragged him out. When Dany glanced back, the knight was walking as if drunk, stumbling and slow. She looked away until she heard the doors open and close. Then she sank back onto the ebony bench. *He's gone, then. My father and my mother, my brothers, Ser Willem Darry, Drogo who was my sun-and-stars, his son who died inside me, and now Ser Jorah . . .*

"The queen has a good heart," Daario purred through his deep purple whiskers, "but that one is more dangerous than all the Oznaks and Meros rolled up in one." His strong hands caressed the hilts of his matched blades, those wanton golden women. "You need not even say the word, my radiance. Only give the tiniest nod, and your Daario shall fetch you back his ugly head."

"Leave him be. The scales are balanced now. Let him go home." Dany pictured Jorah moving amongst old gnarled oaks and tall pines, past flowering thornbushes, grey stones bearded with moss, and little creeks running icy down steep hillsides. She saw him entering a hall built of huge logs, where dogs slept by the hearth and the smell of meat and mead hung thick in the smoky air. "We are done for now," she told her captains.

It was all she could do not to run back up the wide marble stairs. Irri helped her slip from her court clothes and into more comfortable garb; baggy woolen breeches, a loose felted tunic, a painted Dothraki vest. "You are trembling, *Khaleesi*," the girl said as she knelt to lace up Dany's sandals.

"I'm cold," Dany lied. "Bring me the book I was reading last night." She wanted to lose herself in the words, in other times and other places. The fat leather-bound volume was full of songs and stories from the Seven Kingdoms. Children's stories, if truth be told; too simple and fanciful to be true history. All the heroes were tall and handsome, and you could tell the traitors by their shifty eyes. Yet she loved them all the same. Last night she had been reading of the three princesses in the red tower, locked away by the king for the crime of being beautiful.

When her handmaid brought the book, Dany had no trouble finding the page where she had left off, but it was no good. She found herself reading the same passage half a dozen times. *Ser Jorah gave me this book as a bride's gift, the day I wed Khal Drogo. But Daario is right, I shouldn't have banished him. I should have kept him, or I should have killed him.* She played at being a queen, yet sometimes she still felt like a scared little girl. *Viserys always said what a dolt I was. Was he truly mad?* She closed the book. She could still recall Ser Jorah, if she wished. Or send Daario to kill him.

Dany fled from the choice, out onto the terrace. She found Rhaegal asleep beside the pool, a green and bronze coil basking in the sun. Drogon was perched up atop the pyramid, in the place where the huge bronze harpy had stood before she had commanded it to be pulled down. He spread his wings and roared when he spied her. There was no sign of Viserion, but when she went to the parapet and scanned the horizon she saw pale wings in the far distance, sweeping above the river. *He is hunting. They grow bolder every day.* Yet it still made her anxious when they flew too far away. *One day one of them may not return,* she thought.

"Your Grace?"

She turned to find Ser Barristan behind her. "What more would you have of me, ser? I spared you, I took you into my service, now give me some peace."

"Forgive me, Your Grace. It was only . . . now that you know who I am . . ." The old man hesitated. "A knight of the Kingsguard is in the king's presence day and night. For that reason, our vows require us to protect his secrets as we would his life. But your father's secrets by rights belong to you now, along with his throne, and . . . I thought perhaps you might have questions for me."

Questions? She had a hundred questions, a thousand, ten thousand. Why couldn't she think of one? "Was my father truly mad?" she blurted out. *Why do I ask that?* "Viserys said this talk of madness was a ploy of the Usurper's . . ."

"Viserys was a child, and the queen sheltered him as much as she could. Your father always had a little madness in him, I now believe. Yet he was charming and generous as well, so his lapses were forgiven. His reign began with such promise . . . but as the years passed, the lapses grew more frequent, until . . ."

Dany stopped him. "Do I want to hear this now?"

Ser Barristan considered a moment. "Perhaps not. Not now."

"Not now," she agreed. "One day. One day you must tell me all. The good and the bad. There is *some* good to be said of my father, surely?"

"There is, Your Grace. Of him, and those who came before him. Your grandfather Jaehaerys and his brother, their father Aegon, your mother . . . and Rhaegar. Him most of all."

"I wish I could have known him." Her voice was wistful.

"I wish he could have known you," the old knight said. "When you are ready, I will tell you all."

Dany kissed him on the cheek and sent him on his way.

That night her handmaids brought her lamb, with a salad of raisins and carrots soaked in wine, and a hot flaky bread dripping with honey. She could eat none of it. *Did Rhaegar ever grow so weary?* she wondered. *Did Aegon, after his conquest?*

Later, when the time came for sleep, Dany took Irri into bed with her, for the first time since the ship. But even as she shuddered in release and wound her fingers through her handmaid's thick black hair, she pretended it was Drogo holding her . . . only somehow his face kept turning into Daario's. *If I want Daario, I need only say so.*

She lay with Irri's legs entangled in her own. *His eyes looked almost purple today . . .*

Dany's dreams were dark that night, and she woke three times from half-remembered nightmares. After the third time she was too restless to return to sleep. Moonlight streamed through the slanting windows, silvering the marble floors. A cool breeze was blowing through the open terrace doors. Irri slept soundly beside her, her lips slightly parted, one dark brown nipple peeping out above the sleeping silks. For a moment Dany was tempted, but it was Drogo she wanted, or perhaps Daario. Not Irri. The maid was sweet and skillful, but all her kisses tasted of duty.

She rose, leaving Irri asleep in the moonlight. Jhiqui and Missandei slept in their own beds. Dany slipped on a robe and padded barefoot across the marble floor, out onto the terrace. The air was chilly, but she liked the feel of grass between her toes and the sound of the leaves whispering to one another. Wind ripples chased each other across the surface of the little bathing pool and made the moon's reflection dance and shimmer.

She leaned against a low brick parapet to look down upon the city. Meereen was sleeping too. *Lost in dreams of kinder days, perhaps.* Night covered the streets like a black blanket, hiding the corpses and the grey rats that came up from the sewers to feast on them, the swarms of stinging flies. Distant torches glimmered red and yellow where her sentries walked their rounds, and here and there she saw the faint glow of lanterns bobbing down an alley. Perhaps one was Ser Jorah, leading his horse slowly toward the gate. *Farewell, old bear. Farewell, betrayer.*

She was Daenerys Stormborn, the Unburnt, *khaleesi* and queen, Mother of Dragons, slayer of warlocks, breaker of chains, and there was no one in the world that she could trust.

"Your Grace?" Missandei stood at her elbow wrapped in a bedrobe, wooden sandals on her feet. "I woke, and saw that you were gone. Did you sleep well? What are you looking at?"

"My city," said Dany. "I was looking for a house with a red door, but by night all the doors are black."

"A red door?" Missandei was puzzled. "What house is this?"

"No house. It does not matter." Dany took the younger girl by the hand. "Never lie to me, Missandei. Never betray me."

"I never would," Missandei promised. "Look, dawn comes."

The sky had turned a cobalt blue from the horizon to the zenith, and behind the line of low hills to the east a glow could be seen, pale gold and oyster pink. Dany held Missandei's hand as they watched the sun come up. All the grey bricks became red and yellow and blue and green and orange. The scarlet sands of the fighting pits transformed them into bleeding sores before her eyes. Elsewhere the golden dome of the Temple of the Graces blazed bright, and bronze stars winked along the walls where the light of the rising sun touched the spikes on the helms of the Unsullied. On the terrace, a few flies stirred sluggishly. A bird began to chirp in the persimmon tree, and then two more. Dany cocked her head to hear their song, but it was not long before the sounds of the waking city drowned them out.

The sounds of my city.

That morning she summoned her captains and commanders to the garden, rather than descending to the audience chamber. "Aegon the Conqueror brought fire and blood to Westeros, but afterward he gave them peace, prosperity, and justice. But all I have brought to Slaver's Bay is death and ruin. I have been more *khal* than queen, smashing and plundering, then moving on."

"There is nothing to stay for," said Brown Ben Plumm.

"Your Grace, the slavers brought their doom on themselves," said Daario Naharis.

"You have brought freedom as well," Missandei pointed out.

"Freedom to starve?" asked Dany sharply. "Freedom to die? Am I a dragon, or a harpy?" *Am I mad? Do I have the taint?*

"A dragon," Ser Barristan said with certainty. "Meereen is not Westeros, Your Grace."

"But how can I rule seven kingdoms if I cannot rule a single city?" He had no answer to that. Dany turned away from them, to gaze out over the city once again. "My children need time to heal and learn. My dragons need time to grow and test their wings. And I need the same. I will not let this city go the way of Astapor. I will not let the harpy of Yunkai chain up those I've freed all over again." She turned back to look at their faces. "I will not march."

"What will you do then, *Khaleesi*?" asked Rakharo.

"Stay," she said. "Rule. And be a queen."

JAIME

The king sat at the head of the table, a stack of cushions under his arse, signing each document as it was presented to him.

"Only a few more, Your Grace," Ser Kevan Lannister assured him. "This is a bill of attainder against Lord Edmure Tully, stripping him of Riverrun and all its lands and incomes, for rebelling against his lawful king. This is a similar attainder, against his uncle Ser Brynden Tully, the Blackfish." Tommen signed them one after the other, dipping the quill carefully and writing his name in a broad childish hand.

Jaime watched from the foot of the table, thinking of all those lords who aspired to a seat on the king's small council. *They can bloody well have mine.* If this was power, why did it taste like tedium? He did not feel especially powerful, watching Tommen dip his quill in the inkpot again. He felt bored.

And sore. Every muscle in his body ached, and his ribs and shoulders were bruised from the battering they'd gotten, courtesy of Ser Addam Marbrand. Just thinking of it made him wince. He could only hope the man would keep his mouth shut. Jaime had known Marbrand since he was a boy, serving as a page at Casterly Rock; he trusted him as much as he trusted anyone. Enough to ask him to take up shields and tourney swords. He had wanted to know if he could fight with his left hand.

And now I do. The knowledge was more painful than the beating that Ser Addam had given him, and the beating was so bad he could hardly dress himself this morning. If they had been fighting in earnest, Jaime would have died two dozen deaths. It seemed so simple, changing hands. It wasn't. Every instinct he had was wrong. He had to *think* about everything, where once he'd just moved. And while he was thinking, Marbrand was thumping him. His left hand couldn't even seem to *hold* a longsword properly; Ser Addam had disarmed him thrice, sending his blade spinning.

"This grants said lands, incomes, and castle to Ser Emmon Frey and his lady wife, Lady Genna." Ser Kevan presented another sheaf of parchments to the king. Tommen dipped and signed. "This is a decree of legitimacy for a natural son of Lord Roose Bolton of the Dreadfort. And this names Lord Bolton your Warden of the North." Tommen dipped, signed, dipped, signed. "This grants Ser Rolph Spicer title to the castle Castamere and raises him to the rank of lord." Tommen scrawled his name.

I should have gone to Ser Ilyn Payne, Jaime reflected. The King's Justice was not a friend as Marbrand was, and might well have beat him bloody ... but without a tongue, he was not like to boast of it afterward. All it would take would be one chance remark by Ser Addam in his cups, and the whole world would soon know how useless he'd become. *Lord Commander of the Kingsguard.* It was a cruel jape, that ... though not quite so cruel as the gift his father had sent him.

"This is your royal pardon for Lord Gawen Westerling, his lady wife, and his daughter Jeyne, welcoming them back into the king's peace," Ser Kevan said. "This is a pardon for Lord Jonos Bracken of Stone Hedge. This is a pardon for Lord Vance. This for Lord Goodbrook. This for Lord Mooton of Maidenpool."

Jaime pushed himself to his feet. "You seem to have these matters well in hand, Uncle. I shall leave His Grace to you."

"As you wish." Ser Kevan rose as well. "Jaime, you should go to your father. This breach between you—"

"—is his doing. Nor will he mend it by sending me mocking gifts. Tell him that, if you can pry him away from the Tyrells long enough."

His uncle looked distressed. "The gift was heartfelt. We thought that it might encourage you—"

"—to grow a new hand?" Jaime turned to Tommen. Though he had Joffrey's golden curls and green eyes, the new king shared little else with his late brother. He inclined to plumpness, his face was pink and round, and he even liked to read. *He is still shy of nine, this son of mine. The boy is not the man.* It would be seven years before Tommen was ruling in his own right. Until then the realm would remain firmly in the hands of his lord grandfather. "Sire," he asked, "do I have your leave to go?"

"As you like, Ser Uncle." Tommen looked back to Ser Kevan. "Can I seal them now, Great-Uncle?" Pressing his royal seal into the hot wax was his favorite part of being king, so far.

Jaime strode from the council chamber. Outside the door, he found Ser Meryn Trant standing stiff at guard in white scale armor and snowy cloak. *If this one should learn how feeble I am, or Kettleblack or Blount should hear of it . . .* "Remain here until His Grace is done," he said, "then escort him back to Maegor's."

Trant inclined his head. "As you say, my lord."

The outer ward was crowded and noisy that morning. Jaime made for the stables, where a large group of men were saddling their horses. "Steelshanks!" he called. "Are you off, then?"

"As soon as m'lady is mounted," said Steelshanks Walton. "My lord of Bolton expects us. Here she is now."

A groom led a fine grey mare out the stable door. On her back was mounted a skinny hollow-eyed girl wrapped in a heavy cloak. Grey, it was, like the dress beneath it, and trimmed with white satin. The clasp that pinned it to her breast was wrought in the shape of a wolf's head with slitted opal eyes. The girl's long brown hair blew wild in the wind. She had a pretty face, he thought, but her eyes were sad and wary.

When she saw him, she inclined her head. "Ser Jaime," she said in a thin anxious voice. "You are kind to see me off."

Jaime studied her closely. "You know me, then?"

She bit her lip. "You may not recall, my lord, as I was littler then . . . but I had the honor to meet you at Winterfell when King Robert came to visit my father Lord Eddard." She lowered her big brown eyes and mumbled, "I'm Arya Stark."

Jaime had never paid much attention to Arya Stark, but it seemed to him that this girl was older. "I understand you're to be married."

"I am to wed Lord Bolton's son, Ramsay. He used to be a Snow, but His Grace has made him a Bolton. They say he's very brave. I am so happy."

Then why do you sound so frightened? "I wish you joy, my lady." Jaime turned back to Steelshanks. "You have the coin you were promised?"

"Aye, and we've shared it out. You have my thanks." The northman grinned. "A Lannister always pays his debts."

"Always," said Jaime, with a last glance at the girl. He wondered if there was much resemblance. Not that it mattered. The real Arya Stark was buried in some unmarked grave in Flea Bottom in all likelihood. With her brothers dead, and both parents, who would dare name this one a fraud? "Good speed," he told Steelshanks. Nage raised his peace banner, and the northmen formed a column as ragged as their fur cloaks and trotted out the castle gate. The thin girl on the grey mare looked small and forlorn in their midst.

A few of the horses still shied away from the dark splotch on the hard-packed ground where the earth had drunk the life's blood of the stableboy Gregor Clegane had killed so clumsily. The sight of it made Jaime angry all over again. He had told his Kingsguard to keep the crowd out of the way, but that oaf Ser Boros had let himself be distracted by the duel. The fool boy himself shared some of the blame, to be sure; the dead Dornishman as well. And Clegane most of all. The blow that took the boy's arm off had been mischance, but that second cut ...

Well, Gregor is paying for it now. Grand Maester Pycelle was tending to the man's wounds, but the howls heard ringing from the maester's chambers suggested that the healing was not going as well as it might. "The flesh mortifies and the wounds ooze pus," Pycelle told the council. "Even maggots will not touch such foulness. His convulsions are so violent that I have had to gag him to prevent him from biting off his tongue. I have cut away as much tissue as I dare, and treated the rot with boiling wine and bread mold, to no avail. The veins in his arm are turning black. When I leeched him, all the leeches died. My lords, I must know what malignant substance Prince Oberyn used on his spear. Let us detain these other Dornishmen until they are more forthcoming."

Lord Tywin had refused him. "There will be trouble enough with Sunspear over Prince Oberyn's death. I do not mean to make matters worse by holding his companions captive."

"Then I fear Ser Gregor may die."

"Undoubtedly. I swore as much in the letter I sent to Prince Doran with his brother's body. But it must be seen to be the sword of the King's Justice that slays him, not a poisoned spear. Heal him."

Grand Maester Pycelle blinked in dismay. "My lord—"

"*Heal him,*" Lord Tywin said again, vexed. "You are aware that Lord Varys has sent fishermen into the waters around Dragonstone. They report that only a token force remains to defend the island. The Lyseni are gone from the bay, and the great part of Lord Stannis's strength with them."

"Well and good," announced Pycelle. "Let Stannis rot in Lys, I say. We are well rid of the man and his ambitions."

"Did you turn into an utter fool when Tyrion shaved your beard? This is *Stannis Baratheon.* The man will fight to the bitter end and then some. If he is gone, it can only mean he intends to resume the war. Most likely he will land at Storm's End and try and rouse the storm lords. If so, he's finished. But a bolder man might roll the dice for Dorne. If he should win Sunspear to his cause, he might prolong this war for years. So we will *not* offend the Martells any further, for *any* reason. The Dornishmen are free to go, and you *will* heal Ser Gregor."

And so the Mountain screamed, day and night. Lord Tywin Lannister could cow even the Stranger, it would seem.

As Jaime climbed the winding steps of White Sword Tower, he could hear Ser Boros snoring in his cell. Ser Balon's door was shut as well; he had the king tonight, and would sleep all day. Aside from Blount's snores, the tower was very quiet. That suited Jaime well enough. *I ought to rest myself.* Last night, after his dance with Ser Addam, he'd been too sore to sleep.

But when he stepped into his bedchamber, he found his sister waiting for him.

She stood beside the open window, looking over the curtain walls and out to sea. The bay wind swirled around her, flattening her gown against her body in a way that quickened Jaime's pulse. It was white, that gown, like the hangings on the wall and the draperies on his bed. Swirls of tiny emeralds brightened the ends of her wide sleeves and spiraled down her bodice. Larger emeralds were set in the golden spiderweb that bound her golden hair. The gown was cut low, to bare her shoulders and the tops of her breasts. *She is so beautiful.* He wanted nothing more than to take her in his arms.

"Cersei." He closed the door softly. "Why are you here?"

"Where else could I go?" When she turned to him there were tears in her eyes. "Father's made it clear that I am no longer wanted on the council. Jaime, won't you talk to him?"

Jaime took off his cloak and hung it from a peg on the wall. "I talk to Lord Tywin every day."

"*Must* you be so stubborn? All he wants . . ."

". . . is to force me from the Kingsguard and send me back to Casterly Rock."

"That need not be so terrible. He is sending me back to Casterly Rock as well. He wants me far away, so he'll have a free hand with Tommen. Tommen is *my* son, not his!"

"Tommen is the king."

"He is a boy! A frightened little boy who saw his brother *murdered* at his own wedding. And now they are telling him that *he* must marry. The girl is twice his age and twice a widow!"

He eased himself into a chair, trying to ignore the ache of bruised muscles. "The Tyrells are insisting. I see no harm in it. Tommen's been lonely since Myrcella went to Dorne. He likes having Margaery and her ladies about. Let them wed."

"He is your son . . ."

"He is my seed. He's never called me Father. No more than Joffrey ever did. You warned me a thousand times never to show any undue interest in them."

"To keep them safe! You as well. How would it have looked if my brother had played the father to the king's children? Even Robert might have grown suspicious."

"Well, he's beyond suspicion now." Robert's death still left a bitter taste in Jaime's mouth. *It should have been me who killed him, not Cersei.* "I only wished he'd died at my hands." *When I still had two of them.* "If I'd let kingslaying become a habit, as he liked to say, I could have taken you as my wife for all the world to see. I'm not ashamed of loving you, only of the things I've done to hide it. That boy at Winterfell . . ."

"Did I tell you to throw him out the window? If you'd gone hunting as I begged you, nothing would have happened. But no, you had to have me, you could not wait until we returned to the city."

"I'd waited long enough. I hated watching Robert stumble to your bed every night, always wondering if maybe this night he'd decide to claim his rights as husband." Jaime suddenly remembered something else that troubled him about Winterfell. "At Riverrun, Catelyn Stark seemed convinced I'd sent some footpad to slit her son's throat. That I'd given him a dagger."

"That," she said scornfully. "Tyrion asked me about that."

"There *was* a dagger. The scars on Lady Catelyn's hands were real enough, she showed them to me. Did you . . .?"

"Oh, don't be absurd." Cersei closed the window. "Yes, I hoped the boy would die. So did you. Even *Robert* thought that would have been for the best. 'We kill our horses when they break a leg, and our dogs when they go blind, but we are too weak to give the same mercy to crippled children,' he told me. He was blind himself at the time, from drink."

Robert? Jaime had guarded the king long enough to know that Robert Baratheon said things in his cups that he would have denied angrily the next day. "Were you alone when Robert said this?"

"You don't think he said it to Ned Stark, I hope? Of course we were alone. Us and the children." Cersei removed her hairnet and draped it over a bedpost, then shook out her golden curls. "Perhaps Myrcella sent this man with the dagger, do you think so?"

It was meant as mockery, but she'd cut right to the heart of it, Jaime saw at once. "Not Myrcella. Joffrey."

Cersei frowned. "Joffrey had no love for Robb Stark, but the younger boy was nothing to him. He was only a child himself."

"A child hungry for a pat on the head from that sot you let him believe was his father." He had an uncomfortable thought. "Tyrion almost died because of this bloody dagger. If he knew the whole thing was Joffrey's work, that might be why . . ."

"I don't care *why*," Cersei said. "He can take his reasons down to hell with him. If you had seen how Joff died . . . he *fought*, Jaime, he fought for every breath, but it was as if some malign spirit had its hands about his throat. He had such terror in his eyes . . . When he was little, he'd run to me when he was scared or hurt and I would protect him. But that night there was nothing I could do. Tyrion murdered him in front of me, and *there was nothing I could do.*" Cersei sank to her knees before his chair and took Jaime's good hand between both of hers. "Joff is dead and Myrcella's in Dorne. Tommen's all I have left. You mustn't let Father take him from me. Jaime, please."

"Lord Tywin has not asked for my approval. I can talk to him, but he will not listen . . ."

"He will if you agree to leave the Kingsguard."

"I'm not leaving the Kingsguard."

His sister fought back tears. "Jaime, you're my shining knight. You cannot abandon me when I need you most! He is stealing my son, sending me away . . . and unless you stop him, Father is going to force me to wed again!"

Jaime should not have been surprised, but he was. The words were a blow to his gut harder than any that Ser Addam Marbrand had dealt him. "Who?"

"Does it matter? Some lord or other. Someone Father thinks he needs. I don't care. I will not have another husband. You are the only man I want in my bed, ever again."

"Then *tell* him that!"

She pulled her hands away. "You are talking madness again. Would you have us ripped apart, as Mother did that time she caught us playing? Tommen would lose the throne, Myrcella her marriage . . . I *want* to be your wife, we belong to each other, but it can never be, Jaime. We are brother and sister."

"The Targaryens . . ."

"*We are not Targaryens!*"

"Quiet," he said, scornfully. "So loud, you'll wake my Sworn Brothers. We can't have that, now, can we? People might learn that you had come to see me."

"Jaime," she sobbed, "don't you think *I* want it as much as you do? It makes no matter who they wed me to, I want you at my side, I want you in my bed, I want you inside me. Nothing has changed between us. Let me prove it to you." She pushed up his tunic and began to fumble with the laces of his breeches.

Jaime felt himself responding. "No," he said, "not here." They had never done it in White Sword Tower, much less in the Lord Commander's chambers. "Cersei, this is not the place."

"You took me in the sept. This is no different." She drew out his cock and bent her head over it.

Jaime pushed her away with the stump of his right hand. "*No*. Not here, I said." He forced himself to stand.

For an instant, he could see confusion in her bright green eyes, and fear as well. Then rage replaced it. Cersei gathered herself together, got to her feet, straightened her skirts. "Was it your hand they hacked off in Harrenhal, or your manhood?" As she shook her head, her hair tumbled around her bare white shoulders. "I was a fool to come. You lacked the courage to avenge Joffrey, why would I think that you'd protect Tommen? Tell me, if the Imp had killed all three of your children, would *that* have made you wroth?"

"Tyrion is not going to harm Tommen or Myrcella. I am still not certain he killed Joffrey."

Her mouth twisted in anger. "How can you *say* that? After all his threats—"

"Threats mean nothing. He swears he did not do it."

"Oh, he *swears*, is that it? And dwarfs don't lie, is that what you think?"

"Not to me. No more than you would."

"You great golden fool. He's lied to you a thousand times, and so have I." She bound up her hair again, and scooped up the hairnet from the bedpost where she'd hung it. "Think what you will. The little monster is in a black cell, and soon Ser Ilyn will have his head off. Perhaps you'd like it for a keepsake." She glanced at the pillow. "He can watch over you as you sleep alone in that cold white bed. Until his eyes rot out, that is."

"You had best go, Cersei. You're making me angry."

"Oh, an angry cripple. How terrifying." She laughed. "A pity Lord Tywin Lannister never had a son. I could have been the heir he wanted, but I lacked the cock. And speaking of such, best tuck yours away, brother. It looks rather sad and small, hanging from your breeches like that."

When she was gone Jaime took her advice, fumbling one-handed at his laces. He felt a bone-deep ache in his phantom fingers. *I've lost a hand, a father, a son, a sister, and a lover, and soon enough I will lose a brother. And yet they keep telling me House Lannister won this war.*

Jaime donned his cloak and went downstairs, where he found Ser Boros Blount having a cup of wine in the common room. "When you're done with your drink, tell Ser Loras I'm ready to see her."

Ser Boros was too much of a coward to do much more than glower. "You are ready to see who?"

"Just tell Loras."

"Aye." Ser Boros drained his cup. "Aye, Lord Commander."

He took his own good time about it, though, or else the Knight of Flowers proved hard to find. Several hours had passed by the time they arrived, the slim handsome youth and the big ugly maid. Jaime was sitting alone in the round room, leafing idly through the White Book. "Lord Commander," Ser Loras said, "you wished to see the Maid of Tarth?"

"I did." Jaime waved them closer with his left hand. "You have talked with her, I take it?"

"As you commanded, my lord."

"And?"

The lad tensed. "I . . . it may be it happened as she says, ser. That it was Stannis. I cannot be certain."

"Varys tells me that the castellan of Storm's End perished strangely as well," said Jaime.

"Ser Cortnay Penrose," said Brienne sadly. "A good man."

"A stubborn man. One day, he stood square in the way of the King of Dragonstone. The next, he leapt from a tower." Jaime stood. "Ser Loras, we will talk more of this later. You may leave Brienne with me."

The wench looked as ugly and awkward as ever, he decided when Tyrell left them. Someone had dressed her in woman's clothes again, but this dress fit much better than that hideous pink rag the goat had made her wear. "Blue is a good color on you, my lady," Jaime observed. "It goes well with your eyes." *She does have astonishing eyes.*

Brienne glanced down at herself, flustered. "Septa Donyse padded out the bodice, to give it that shape. She said you sent her to me." She lingered by the door, as if she meant to flee at any second. "You look . . ."

"Different?" He managed a half-smile. "More meat on the ribs and fewer lice in my hair, that's all. The stump's the same. Close the door and come here."

She did as he bid her. "The white cloak . . ."

". . . is new, but I'm sure I'll soil it soon enough."

"That wasn't . . . I was about to say that it becomes you."

She came closer, hesitant. "Jaime, did you mean what you told Ser Loras? About . . . about King Renly, and the shadow?"

Jaime shrugged. "I would have killed Renly myself if we'd met in battle, what do I care who cut his throat?"

"You said I had honor . . ."

"I'm the bloody Kingslayer, remember? When I say you have honor, that's like a whore vouchsafing your maidenhood." He leaned back and looked up at her. "Steelshanks is on his way back north, to deliver Arya Stark to Roose Bolton."

"You gave her to *him?*" she cried, dismayed. "You swore an oath to Lady Catelyn . . ."

"With a sword at my throat, but never mind. Lady Catelyn's dead. I could not give her back her daughters even if I had them. And the girl my father sent with Steelshanks was not Arya Stark."

"*Not* Arya Stark?"

"You heard me. My lord father found some skinny northern girl more or less the same age with more or less the same coloring. He dressed her up in white and grey, gave her a silver wolf to pin her cloak, and sent her off to wed Bolton's bastard." He lifted his stump to point at her. "I wanted to tell you that before you went galloping off to rescue her and got yourself killed for no good purpose. You're not half bad with a sword, but you're not good enough to take on two hundred men by yourself."

Brienne shook her head. "When Lord Bolton learns that your father paid him with false coin . . ."

"Oh, he knows. *Lannisters lie,* remember? It makes no matter, this girl serves his purpose just as well. Who is going to say that she *isn't* Arya Stark? Everyone the girl was close to is dead except for her sister, who has disappeared."

"Why would you tell me all this, if it's true? You are betraying your father's secrets."

The Hand's secrets, he thought. *I no longer have a father.* "I pay my debts like every good little lion. I did promise Lady Stark her daughters . . . and one of them is still alive. My brother may know where she is, but if so he isn't saying. Cersei is convinced that Sansa helped him murder Joffrey."

The wench's mouth got stubborn. "I will not believe that gentle girl a poisoner. Lady Catelyn said that she had a loving heart. It was your brother. There was a trial, Ser Loras said."

"Two trials, actually. Words and swords both failed him. A bloody mess. Did you watch from your window?"

"My cell faces the sea. I heard the shouting, though."

"Prince Oberyn of Dorne is dead, Ser Gregor Clegane lies dying, and Tyrion stands condemned before the eyes of gods and men. They're keeping him in a black cell till they kill him."

Brienne looked at him. "You do not believe he did it."

Jaime gave her a hard smile. "See, wench? We know each other too well. Tyrion's wanted to be me since he took his first step, but he'd never follow me in kingslaying. Sansa Stark killed Joffrey. My brother's kept silent to protect her. He gets these fits of gallantry from time to time. The last one cost him a nose. This time it will mean his head."

"No," Brienne said. "It was not my lady's daughter. It could not have been her."

"There's the stubborn stupid wench that I remember."

She reddened. "My name is . . ."

"Brienne of Tarth." Jaime sighed. "I have a gift for you." He reached down under the Lord Commander's chair and brought it out, wrapped in folds of crimson velvet.

Brienne approached as if the bundle was like to bite her, reached out a huge freckled hand, and flipped back a fold of cloth. Rubies glimmered in the light. She picked the treasure up gingerly, curled her fingers around the leather grip, and slowly slid the sword free of its scabbard. Blood and black the ripples shone. A finger of reflected light ran red along the edge. "Is this Valyrian steel? I have never seen such colors."

"Nor I. There was a time that I would have given my right hand to wield a sword like that. Now it appears I have, so the blade is wasted on me. Take it." Before she could think to refuse, he went on. "A sword so fine must bear a name. It would please me if you would call this one Oathkeeper. One more thing. The blade comes with a price."

Her face darkened. "I told you, I will never serve . . ."

". . . such foul creatures as us. Yes, I recall. Hear me out, Brienne. Both of us swore oaths concerning Sansa Stark. Cersei means to see that the girl is found and killed, wherever she has gone to ground . . ."

Brienne's homely face twisted in fury. "If you believe that I would harm my lady's daughter for a *sword*, you—"

"*Just listen*," he snapped, angered by her assumption. "I want you to find Sansa first, and get her somewhere safe. How else are the two of us going to make good our stupid vows to your precious dead Lady Catelyn?"

The wench blinked. "I . . . I thought . . ."

"I know what you *thought*." Suddenly Jaime was sick of the sight of her. *She bleats like a bloody sheep.* "When Ned Stark died, his greatsword was given to the King's Justice," he told her. "But my father felt that such a fine blade was wasted on a mere headsman. He gave Ser Ilyn a new sword, and had Ice melted down and reforged. There was enough metal for two new blades. You're holding one. So you'll be defending Ned Stark's daughter with Ned Stark's own steel, if that makes any difference to you."

"Ser, I . . . I owe you an apolo—'

He cut her off. "Take the bloody sword and go, before I change my mind. There's a bay mare in the stables, as homely as you are but somewhat better trained. Chase after Steelshanks, search for Sansa, or ride home to your isle of sapphires, it's naught to me. I don't want to look at you anymore."

"Jaime . . ."

"*Kingslayer*," he reminded her. "Best use that sword to clean the wax out of your ears, wench. We're done."

Stubbornly, she persisted. "Joffrey was your . . ."

"My king. Leave it at that."

"You say Sansa killed him. Why protect her?"

Because Joff was no more to me than a squirt of seed in Cersei's cunt. And because he deserved to die. "I have made kings and unmade them. Sansa Stark is my last chance for honor." Jaime smiled thinly. "Besides, kingslayers should band together. Are you ever going to go?"

Her big hand wrapped tight around Oathkeeper. "I will. And I will find the girl and keep her safe. For her lady mother's sake. And for yours." She bowed stiffly, whirled, and went.

Jaime sat alone at the table while the shadows crept across the room. As dusk began to settle, he lit a candle and opened the White Book to his own page. Quill and ink he found in a drawer. Beneath the last line Ser Barristan had entered, he wrote in an awkward hand that might have done credit to a six-year-old being taught his first letters by a maester:

Defeated in the Whispering Wood by the Young Wolf Robb Stark during the War of the Five Kings. Held captive at Riverrun and ransomed for a promise unfulfilled. Captured again by the Brave Companions, and maimed at the word of Vargo Hoat their captain, losing his sword hand to the blade of Zollo the Fat. Returned safely to King's Landing by Brienne, the Maid of Tarth.

When he was done, more than three-quarters of his page still remained to be filled between the gold lion on the crimson shield on top and the blank white shield at the bottom. Ser Gerold Hightower had begun his history, and Ser Barristan Selmy had continued it, but the rest Jaime Lannister would need to write for himself. He could write whatever he chose, henceforth.

Whatever he chose . . .

JON

The wind was blowing wild from the east, so strong the heavy cage would rock whenever a gust got it in its teeth. It skirled along the Wall, shivering off the ice, making Jon's cloak flap against the bars. The sky was slate grey, the sun no more than a faint patch of brightness behind the clouds. Across the killing ground, he could see the glimmer of a thousand campfires burning, but their lights seemed small and powerless against such gloom and cold.

A grim day. Jon Snow wrapped gloved hands around the bars and held tight as the wind hammered at the cage once more. When he looked straight down past his feet, the ground was lost in shadow, as if he were being lowered into some bottomless pit. *Well, death is a bottomless pit of sorts,* he reflected, *and when this day's work is done my name will be shadowed forever.*

Bastard children were born from lust and lies, men said; their nature was wanton and treacherous. Once, Jon had meant to prove them wrong, to show his lord father that he could be as good and true a son as Robb. *I made a botch of that.* Robb had become a hero king; if Jon was remembered at all, it would be as a turncloak, an oathbreaker, and a murderer. He was glad that Lord Eddard was not alive to see his shame.

I should have stayed in that cave with Ygritte. If there was a life beyond this one, he hoped to tell her that. *She will claw my face the way the eagle did, and curse me for a coward, but I'll tell her all the same.* He flexed his sword hand, as Maester Aemon had taught him. The habit had become part of him, and he would need his fingers to be limber to have even half a chance of murdering Mance Rayder.

They had pulled him out this morning, after four days in the ice, locked up in a cell five by five by five, too low for him to stand, too tight for him to stretch out on his back. The stewards had long ago discovered that food and meat kept longer in the icy storerooms carved from the base of the Wall . . . but prisoners did not. "You will die in here, Lord Snow," Ser Alliser had said just before he closed the heavy wooden door, and Jon had believed it. But this morning they had come and pulled him out again, and marched him cramped and shivering back to the King's Tower, to stand before jowly Janos Slynt once more

"That old maester says I cannot hang you," Slynt declared. "He has written Cotter Pyke, and even had the bloody gall to show me the letter. He says you are no turncloak."

"Aemon's lived too long, my lord," Ser Alliser assured him. "His wits have gone dark as his eyes."

"Aye," Slynt said. "A blind man with a chain about his neck, who does he think he is?"

Aemon Targaryen, Jon thought, *a king's son and a king's brother and a king who might have been.* But he said nothing.

"Still," Slynt said, "I will not have it said that Janos Slynt hanged a man unjustly. I will not. I have decided to give you one last chance to prove you are as loyal as you claim, Lord Snow. One last chance to do your duty, yes!" He stood. "Mance Rayder wants to parley with us. He knows he has no chance now that Janos Slynt has come, so he wants to talk, this King-beyond-the-Wall. But the man is craven, and will not come to us. No doubt he knows I'd hang him. Hang him by his feet from the top of the Wall, on a rope two hundred feet long! But he will not come. He asks that we send an envoy to him."

"We're sending you, Lord Snow." Ser Alliser smiled.

"Me." Jon's voice was flat. "Why me?"

"You rode with these wildlings," said Thorne. "Mance Rayder knows you. He will be more inclined to trust you."

That was so wrong, Jon might have laughed. "You've got it backward. Mance suspected me from the first. If I show up in his camp wearing a black cloak again and speaking for the Night's Watch, he'll know that I betrayed him."

"He asked for an envoy, we are sending one," said Slynt. "If you are too craven to face this turncloak king, we can return you to your ice cell. This time without the furs, I think. Yes."

"No need for that, my lord," said Ser Alliser. "Lord Snow will do as we ask. He wants to show us that he is no turncloak. He wants to prove himself a loyal man of the Night's Watch."

Thorne was much the more clever of the two, Jon realized; this had his stink all over it. He was trapped. "I'll go," he said in a clipped, curt voice.

"*M'lord*," Janos Slynt reminded him. "You'll address me—"

"I'll go, *my lord*. But you are making a mistake, *my lord*. You are sending the wrong man, *my lord*. Just the sight of me is going to anger Mance. *My lord* would have a better chance of reaching terms if he sent—"

"Terms?" Ser Alliser chuckled.

"Janos Slynt does not make terms with lawless savages, Lord Snow. No, he does not."

"We're not sending you to *talk* with Mance Rayder," Ser Alliser said. "We're sending you to kill him."

The wind whistled through the bars, and Jon Snow shivered. His leg was throbbing, and his head. He was not fit to kill a kitten, yet here he was. *The trap had teeth.* With Maester Aemon insisting on Jon's innocence, Lord Janos had not dared to leave him in the ice to die. This was better. "Our honor means no more than our lives, so long as the realm is safe," Qhorin Halfhand had said in the Frostfangs. He must remember that. Whether he slew Mance or only tried and failed, the free folk would kill him. Even desertion was impossible, if he'd been so inclined; to Mance he was a proven liar and betrayer.

When the cage jerked to a halt, Jon swung down onto the ground and rattled Longclaw's hilt to loosen the bastard blade in its scabbard. The gate was a few yards to his left, still blocked by the splintered ruins of the turtle, the carcass of a mammoth ripening within. There were other corpses too, strewn amidst broken barrels, hardened pitch, and patches of burnt grass, all shadowed by the Wall. Jon had no wish to linger here. He started walking toward the wildling camp, past the body of a dead giant whose head had been crushed by a stone. A raven was pulling out bits of brain from the giant's shattered skull. It looked up as he walked by. "*Snow,*" it screamed at him. "*Snow, snow.*" Then it opened its wings and flew away.

No sooner had he started out than a lone rider emerged from the wildling camp and came toward him. He wondered if Mance was coming out to parley in no-man's-land. *That might make it easier, though nothing will make it easy.* But as the distance between them diminished Jon saw that the horseman was short and broad, with gold rings glinting on thick arms and a white beard spreading out across his massive chest.

"*Har!*" Tormund boomed when they came together. "Jon Snow the crow. I feared we'd seen the last o' you."

"I never knew you feared anything, Tormund."

That made the wildling grin. "Well said, lad. I see your cloak is black. Mance won't like that. If you've come to change sides again, best climb back on that Wall o' yours."

"They've sent me to treat with the King-beyond-the-Wall."

"Treat?" Tormund laughed. "Now there's a word. Har! Mance wants to talk, that's true enough. Can't say he'd want to talk with *you,* though."

"I'm the one they've sent."

"I see that. Best come along, then. You want to ride?"

"I can walk."

"You fought us hard here." Tormund turned his garron back toward the wildling camp. "You and your brothers. I give you that. Two hundred dead, and a dozen giants. Mag himself went in that gate o' yours and never did come out."

"He died on the sword of a brave man named Donal Noye."

"Aye? Some great lord was he, this Donal Noye? One of your shiny knights in their steel smallclothes?"

"A blacksmith. He only had one arm."

"A one-armed smith slew Mag the Mighty? Har! That must o' been a fight to see. Mance will make a song of it, see if he don't." Tormund took a waterskin off his saddle and pulled the cork. "This will warm us some. To Donal Noye, and Mag the Mighty." He took a swig, and handed it down to Jon.

"To Donal Noye, and Mag the Mighty." The skin was full of mead, but a mead so potent that it made Jon's eyes water and sent tendrils of fire snaking through his chest. After the ice cell and the cold ride down in the cage, the warmth was welcome.

Tormund took the skin back and downed another swig, then wiped his mouth. "The Magnar of Thenn swore t'us that he'd have the gate wide open, so all we'd need to do was stroll through singing. He was going to bring the whole Wall down."

"He brought down part," Jon said. "On his head."

"Har!" said Tormund. "Well, I never had much use for Styr. When a man's got no beard nor hair nor ears, you can't get a good grip on him when you fight." He kept his horse at a slow walk so Jon could limp beside him. "What happened to that leg?"

"An arrow. One of Ygritte's, I think."

"That's a woman for you. One day she's kissing you, the next she's filling you with arrows."

"She's dead."

"Aye?" Tormund gave a sad shake of the head. "A waste. If I'd been ten years younger, I'd have stolen her meself. That hair she had. Well, the hottest fires burn out quickest." He lifted the skin of mead. "To Ygritte, kissed by fire!" He drank deep.

"To Ygritte, kissed by fire," Jon repeated when Tormund handed him back the skin. He drank even deeper.

"Was it you killed her?"

"My brother." Jon had never learned which one, and hoped he never would.

"You bloody crows." Tormund's tone was gruff, yet strangely gentle. "That Longspear stole me daughter. Munda, me little autumn apple. Took her right out o' my tent with all four o' her brothers about. Toregg slept through it, the great lout, and Torwynd . . . well, Torwynd the Tame, that says all that needs saying, don't it? The young ones gave the lad a fight, though."

"And Munda?" asked Jon.

"She's my own blood," said Tormund proudly. "She broke his lip for him and bit one ear half off, and I hear he's got so many scratches on his back he can't wear a cloak. She likes him well enough, though. And why not? He don't fight with no spear, you know. Never has. So where do you think he got that name? *Har!*"

Jon had to laugh. Even now, even here. Ygritte had been fond of Longspear Ryk. He hoped he found some joy with Tormund's Munda. Someone needed to find some joy somewhere.

"You know nothing, Jon Snow," Ygritte would have told him. *I know that I am going to die*, he thought. *I know that much, at least.* "All men die," he could almost hear her say, "and women too, and every beast that flies or swims or runs. It's not the *when* o' dying that matters, it's the *how* of it, Jon Snow." *Easy for you to say*, he thought back. *You died brave in battle, storming the castle of a foe. I'm going to die a turncloak and a killer.* Nor would his death be quick, unless it came on the end of Mance's sword.

Soon they were among the tents. It was the usual wildling camp; a sprawling jumble of cookfires and piss pits, children and goats wandering freely, sheep bleating among the trees, horse hides pegged up to dry. There was no plan to it, no order, no defenses. But there were men and women and animals everywhere.

Many ignored him, but for every one who went about his business there were ten who stopped to stare; children squatting by the fires, old women in dog carts, cave dwellers with painted faces, raiders with claws and snakes and severed heads painted on their shields, all turned to have a look. Jon saw spearwives too, their long hair streaming in the piney wind that sighed between the trees.

There were no true hills here, but Mance Rayder's white fur tent had been raised on a spot of high stony ground right on the edge of the trees. The King-beyond-the-Wall was waiting outside, his ragged red-and-black cloak blowing in the wind. Harma Dogshead was with him, Jon saw, back from her raids and feints along the Wall, and Varamyr Sixskins as well, attended by his shadowcat and two lean grey wolves.

When they saw who the Watch had sent, Harma turned her head

and spat, and one of Varamyr's wolves bared its teeth and growled. "You must be very brave or very stupid, Jon Snow," Mance Rayder said, "to come back to us wearing a black cloak."

"What else would a man of the Night's Watch wear?"

"Kill him," urged Harma. "Send his body back up in that cage o' theirs and tell them to send us someone else. I'll keep his head for my standard. A turncloak's worse than a dog."

"I warned you he was false." Varamyr's tone was mild, but his shadowcat was staring at Jon hungrily through slitted grey eyes. "I never did like the smell o' him."

"Pull in your claws, beastling." Tormund Giantsbane swung down off his horse. "The lad's here to hear. You lay a paw on him, might be I'll take me that shadowskin cloak I been wanting."

"Tormund Crowlover," Harma sneered. "You are a great sack o' wind, old man."

The skinchanger was grey-faced, round-shouldered, and bald, a mouse of a man with a wolfling's eyes. "Once a horse is broken to the saddle, any man can mount him," he said in a soft voice. "Once a beast's been joined to a man, any skinchanger can slip inside and ride him. Orell was withering inside his feathers, so I took the eagle for my own. But the joining works both ways, warg. Orell lives inside me now, whispering how much he hates you. And I can soar above the Wall, and see with eagle eyes."

"So we know," said Mance. "We know how few you were, when you stopped the turtle. We know how many came from Eastwatch. We know how your supplies have dwindled. Pitch, oil, arrows, spears. Even your stair is gone, and that cage can only lift so many. We know. And now you know we know." He opened the flap of the tent. "Come inside. The rest of you, wait here."

"What, even me?" said Tormund.

"*Particularly* you. Always."

It was warm within. A small fire burned beneath the smoke holes, and a brazier smouldered near the pile of furs where Dalla lay, pale and sweating. Her sister was holding her hand. *Val*, Jon remembered. "I was sorry when Jarl fell," he told her.

Val looked at him with pale grey eyes. "He always climbed too fast." She was as fair as he'd remembered, slender, full-breasted, graceful even at rest, with high sharp cheekbones and a thick braid of honey-colored hair that fell to her waist.

"Dalla's time is near," Mance explained. "She and Val will stay. They know what I mean to say."

Jon kept his face as still as ice. *Foul enough to slay a man in his own tent under truce. Must I murder him in front of his wife as their child is being born?* He closed the fingers of his sword hand. Mance was not wearing armor, but his own sword was sheathed on his left hip. And there were other weapons in the tent, daggers and dirks, a bow and a quiver of arrows, a bronze-headed spear lying beside that big black . . .

. . . horn.

Jon sucked in his breath.

A warhorn, a bloody great warhorn.

"Yes," Mance said. "The Horn of Winter, that Joramun once blew to wake giants from the earth."

The horn was huge, eight feet along the curve and so wide at the mouth that he could have put his arm inside up to the elbow. *If this came from an aurochs, it was the biggest that ever lived.* At first, he thought the bands around it were bronze, but when he moved closer he realized they were gold. *Old gold, more brown than yellow, and graven with runes.*

"Ygritte said you never found the horn."

"Did you think only crows could lie? I liked you well enough, for a bastard . . . but I never trusted you. A man needs to earn my trust."

Jon faced him. "If you've had the Horn of Joramun all along, why haven't you used it? Why bother building turtles and sending Thenns to kill us in our beds? If this horn is all the songs say, why not just sound it and be done?"

It was Dalla who answered him, Dalla great with child, lying on her pile of furs beside the brazier. "We free folk know things you kneelers have forgotten. Sometimes the short road is not the safest, Jon Snow. The Horned Lord once said that sorcery is a sword without a hilt. There is no safe way to grasp it."

Mance ran a hand along the curve of the great horn. "No man

goes hunting with only one arrow in his quiver," he said. "I had hoped that Styr and Jarl would take your brothers unawares, and open the gate for us. I drew your garrison away with feints and raids and secondary attacks. Bowen Marsh swallowed that lure as I knew he would, but your band of cripples and orphans proved to be more stubborn than anticipated. Don't think you've stopped us, though. The truth is, you are too few and we are too many. I could continue the attack here and still send ten thousand men to cross the Bay of Seals on rafts and take Eastwatch from the rear. I could storm the Shadow Tower too, I know the approaches as well as any man alive. I could send men and mammoths to dig out the gates at the castles you've abandoned, all of them at once."

"Why don't you, then?" Jon could have drawn Longclaw then, but he wanted to hear what the wildling had to say.

"Blood," said Mance Rayder. "I'd win in the end, yes, but you'd bleed me, and my people have bled enough."

"Your losses haven't been that heavy."

"Not at your hands." Mance studied Jon's face. "You saw the Fist of the First Men. You know what happened there. You know what we are facing."

"The Others . . ."

"They grow stronger as the days grow shorter and the nights colder. First they kill you, then they send your dead against you. The giants have not been able to stand against them, nor the Thenns, the ice river clans, the Hornfoots."

"Nor you?"

"Nor me." There was anger in that admission, and bitterness too deep for words. "Raymun Redbeard, Bael the Bard, Gendel and Gorne, the Horned Lord, they all came south to conquer, but I've come with my tail between my legs to hide behind your Wall." He touched the horn again. "If I sound the Horn of Winter, the Wall will fall. Or so the songs would have me believe. There are those among my people who want nothing more . . ."

"But once the Wall is fallen," Dalla said, "*what will stop the Others?*"

Mance gave her a fond smile. "It's a wise woman I've found. A true queen." He turned back to Jon. "Go back and tell them to open their gate and let us pass. If they do, I will give them the horn, and the Wall will stand until the end of days."

Open the gate and let them pass. Easy to say, but what must follow? Giants camping in the ruins of Winterfell? Cannibals in the wolfswood, chariots sweeping across the barrowlands, free folk stealing the daughters of shipwrights and silversmiths from White Harbor and fishwives off the Stony Shore? "Are you a true king?" Jon asked suddenly.

"I've never had a crown on my head or sat my arse on a bloody throne, if that's what you're asking," Mance replied. "My birth is as low as a man's can get, no septon's ever smeared my head with oils, I don't own any castles, and my queen wears furs and amber, not silk and sapphires. I am my own champion, my own fool, and my own harpist. You don't become King-beyond-the-Wall because your father was. The free folk won't follow a name, and they don't care which brother was born first. They follow fighters. When I left the Shadow Tower there were five men making noises about how they might be the stuff of kings. Tormund was one, the Magnar another. The other three I slew, when they made it plain they'd sooner fight than follow."

"You can kill your enemies," Jon said bluntly, "but can you rule your friends? If we let your people pass, are you strong enough to make them keep the king's peace and obey the laws?"

"Whose laws? The laws of Winterfell and King's Landing?" Mance laughed. "When we want laws we'll make our own. You can keep your king's justice too, and your king's taxes. I'm offering you the horn, not our freedom. We will not kneel to you."

"What if we refuse the offer?" Jon had no doubt that they would. The Old Bear might at least have listened, though he would have balked at the notion of letting thirty or forty thousand wildlings loose on the Seven Kingdoms. But Alliser Thorne and Janos Slynt would dismiss the notion out of hand.

"If you refuse," Mance Rayder said, "Tormund Giantsbane will sound the Horn of Winter three days hence, at dawn."

He could carry the message back to Castle Black and tell them of the horn, but, if he left Mance still alive, Lord Janos and Ser Alliser would seize on that as proof that he was a turncloak. A thousand thoughts flickered through Jon's head. *If I can destroy the horn, smash it here and now . . .* but before he could begin to think that through, he heard the low moan of some other horn, made faint by the tent's hide walls. Mance heard it too. Frowning, he went to the door. Jon followed.

The warhorn was louder outside. Its call had stirred the wildling camp. Three Hornfoot men jogged past, carrying long spears. Horses were whinnying and snorting, giants roaring in the Old Tongue, and even the mammoths were restless.

"Outrider's horn," Tormund told Mance.

"Something's coming." Varamyr sat crosslegged on the half-frozen ground, his wolves circled restlessly around him. A shadow swept over him, and Jon looked up to see the eagle's blue-grey wings. "Coming, from the east."

When the dead walk, walls and stakes and swords mean nothing, he remembered. *You cannot fight the dead, Jon Snow. No man knows that half so well as me.*

Harma scowled. "East? The wights should be behind us."

"East," the skinchanger repeated. "*Something's coming.*"

"The Others?" Jon asked.

Mance shook his head. "The Others never come when the sun is up." Chariots were rattling across the killing ground, jammed with riders waving spears of sharpened bone. The king groaned. "Where the bloody hell do they think they're going? Quenn, get those fools back where they belong. Someone bring my horse. The mare, not the stallion. I'll want my armor too." Mance glanced suspiciously at the Wall. Atop the icy parapets, the straw soldiers stood collecting arrows, but there was no sign of any other activity. "Harma, mount up your raiders. Tormund, find your sons and give me a triple line of spears."

"Aye," said Tormund, striding off.

The mousy little skinchanger closed his eyes and said, "I see them. They're coming along the streams and game trails . . ."

"*Who?*"

"Men. Men on horses. Men in steel and men in black."

"Crows." Mance made the word a curse. He turned on Jon. "Did my old brothers think they'd catch me with my breeches down if they attacked while we were talking?"

"If they planned an attack they never told me about it." Jon did not believe it. Lord Janos lacked the men to attack the wildling camp. Besides, he was on the wrong side of the Wall, and the gate was sealed with rubble. *He had a different sort of treachery in mind, this can't be his work.*

"If you're lying to me again, you won't be leaving here alive," Mance warned. His guards brought him his horse and armor. Elsewhere around the camp, Jon saw people running at cross purposes, some men forming up as if to storm the Wall while others slipped into the woods, women driving dog carts east, mammoths wandering west. He reached back over his shoulder and drew Longclaw just as a thin line of rangers emerged from the fringes of the wood three hundred yards away. They wore black mail, black halfhelms, and black cloaks. Half-armored, Mance drew his sword. "You knew nothing of this, did you?" he said to Jon, coldly.

Slow as honey on a cold morning, the rangers swept down on the wildling camp, picking their way through clumps of gorse and stands of trees, over roots and rocks. Wildlings flew to meet them, shouting war cries and waving clubs and bronze swords and axes made of flint, galloping headlong at their ancient enemies. *A shout, a slash, and a fine brave death*, Jon had heard brothers say of the free folk's way of fighting.

"Believe what you will," Jon told the King-beyond-the-Wall, "but I knew nothing of any attack."

Harma thundered past before Mance could reply, riding at the head of thirty raiders. Her standard went before her; a dead dog impaled on a spear, raining blood at every stride. Mance watched as she smashed into the rangers. "Might be you're telling it true," he said. "Those look like Eastwatch men. Sailors on horses. Cotter Pyke always had more guts than sense. He took the Lord of Bones at Long Barrow, he might have thought to do the same with me. If so, he's a fool. He doesn't have the men, he—"

"*Mance!*" the shout came. It was a scout, bursting from the trees on a lathered horse. "*Mance,* there's more, they're all around us, iron men, *iron,* a *host* of iron men."

Cursing, Mance swung up into the saddle. "Varamyr, stay and see that no harm comes to Dalla." The King-beyond-the-Wall pointed his sword at Jon. "And keep a few extra eyes on this crow. If he runs, rip out his throat."

"Aye, I'll do that." The skinchanger was a head shorter than Jon, slumped and soft, but that shadowcat could disembowel him with one paw. "They're coming from the north too," Varamyr told Mance. "You best go."

Mance donned his helm with its raven wings. His men were mounted up as well. "Arrowhead," Mance snapped, "to me, form wedge." Yet when he slammed his heels into the mare and flew across the field at the rangers, the men who raced to catch him lost all semblance of formation.

Jon took a step toward the tent, thinking of the Horn of Winter, but the shadowcat blocked him, tail lashing. The beast's nostrils flared, and slaver ran from his curved front teeth. *He smells my fear.* He missed Ghost more than ever then. The two wolves were behind him, growling.

"Banners," he heard Varamyr murmur, "I see golden banners, oh . . ." A mammoth lumbered by, trumpeting, a half-dozen bowmen in the wooden tower on its back. "The king . . . no . . ."

Then the skinchanger threw back his head and *screamed.*

The sound was shocking, ear-piercing, thick with agony. Varamyr fell, writhing, and the 'cat was screaming too . . . and high, high in the eastern sky, against the wall of cloud, Jon saw the eagle *burning.* For a heartbeat, it flamed brighter than a star, wreathed in red and gold and orange, its wings beating wildly at the air as if it could fly from the pain. Higher it flew, and higher, and higher still.

The scream brought Val out of the tent, white-faced. "What is it, what's happened?" Varamyr's wolves were fighting each other, and the shadowcat had raced off into the trees, but the man was still twisting on the ground. "What's wrong with him?" Val demanded, horrified. "Where's Mance?"

"There." Jon pointed. "Gone to fight." The king led his ragged wedge into a knot of rangers, his sword flashing.

"Gone? He can't be gone, not now. It's started."

"The battle?" He watched the rangers scatter before Harma's bloody dog's head. The raiders screamed and hacked and chased the men in black back into the trees. But there were more men coming from the wood, a column of horse. *Knights on heavy horse*, Jon saw. Harma had to regroup and wheel to meet them, but half of her men had raced too far ahead.

"The *birth*!" Val was shouting at him.

Trumpets were blowing all around, loud and brazen. *The wildlings have no trumpets, only warhorns.* They knew that as well as he did; the sound sent free folk running in confusion, some toward the fighting, others away. A mammoth was stomping through a flock of sheep that three men were trying to herd off west. The drums were beating as the wildlings ran to form squares and lines, but they were too late, too disorganized, too slow. The enemy was emerging from the forest, from the east, the northeast, the north; three great columns of heavy horse, all dark glinting steel and bright wool surcoats. Not the men of Eastwatch, those had been no more than a line of scouts. An army. *The king?* Jon was as confused as the wildlings. Could Robb have returned? Had the boy on the Iron Throne finally bestirred himself? "You best get back inside the tent," he told Val.

Across the field one column had washed over Harma Dogshead. Another smashed into the flank of Tormund's spearmen as he and his sons desperately tried to turn them. The giants were climbing onto their mammoths, though, and the knights on their barded horses did not like that at all; he could see how the coursers and destriers screamed and scattered at the sight of those lumbering mountains. But there was fear on the wildling side as well, hundreds of women and children rushing away from the battle, some of them blundering right under the hooves of garrons. He saw an old woman's dog cart veer into the path of three chariots, to send them crashing into each other.

"Gods," Val whispered, "gods, why are they doing this?"

"Go inside the tent and stay with Dalla. It's not safe out here." It wouldn't be a great deal safer inside, but she didn't need to hear that.

"I need to find the midwife," Val said.

"You're the midwife. I'll stay here until Mance comes back." He had lost sight of Mance but now he found him again, cutting his way through a knot of mounted men. The mammoths had shattered the center column, but the other two were closing like pincers. On the eastern edge of the camps, some archers were loosing fire arrows at the tents. He saw a mammoth pluck a knight from his saddle and fling him forty feet with a flick of its trunk. Wildlings streamed past, women and children running from the battle, some with men hurrying them along. A few of them gave Jon dark looks but Longclaw was in his hand, and no one troubled him. Even Varamyr fled, crawling off on his hands and knees.

More and more men were pouring from the trees, not only knights now but freeriders and mounted bowmen and men-at-arms in jacks and kettle helms, dozens of men, hundreds of men. A blaze of banners flew above them. The wind was whipping them too wildly for Jon to see the sigils, but he glimpsed a seahorse, a field of birds, a ring of flowers. And yellow, so much yellow, yellow banners with a red device, whose arms were those?

East and north and northeast, he saw bands of wildlings trying to stand and fight, but the attackers rode right over them. The free folk still had the numbers, but the attackers had steel armor and heavy horses. In the thickest part of the fray, Jon saw Mance standing tall in his stirrups. His red-and-black cloak and raven-winged helm made him easy to pick out. He had his sword raised and men were rallying to him when a wedge of knights smashed into them with lance and sword and longaxe. Mance's mare went up on her hind legs, kicking, and a spear took her through the breast. Then the steel tide washed over him.

It's done, Jon thought, *they're breaking*. The wildlings were running, throwing down their weapons, Hornfoot men and cave dwellers and Thenns in bronze scales, they were running. Mance was gone, someone was waving Harma's head on a pole, Tormund's lines had broken. Only the giants on their mammoths were holding, hairy islands in a red steel sea. The fires were leaping from tent to tent and some of the tall pines were going up as well. And through the smoke another wedge of armored riders came, on barded horses. Floating above them were the largest banners yet, royal standards as big as sheets; a yellow one with long pointed tongues that showed a flaming heart, and another like a sheet of beaten gold, with a black stag prancing and rippling in the wind.

Robert, Jon thought for one mad moment, remembering poor Owen, but when the trumpets blew again and the knights charged, the name they cried was "*Stannis! Stannis! STANNIS!*"

Jon turned away, and went inside the tent.

ARYA

Outside the inn on a weathered gibbet, a woman's bones were twisting and rattling at every gust of wind.

I know this inn. There hadn't been a gibbet outside the door when she had slept here with her sister Sansa under the watchful eye of Septa Mordane, though. "We don't want to go in," Arya decided suddenly, "there might be ghosts."

"You know how long it's been since I had a cup of wine?" Sandor swung down from the saddle. "Besides, we need to learn who holds the ruby ford. Stay with the horses if you want, it's no hair off my arse."

"What if they know you?" Sandor no longer troubled to hide his face. He no longer seemed to care who knew him. "They might want to take you captive."

"Let them try." He loosened his longsword in its scabbard, and pushed through the door.

Arya would never have a better chance to escape. She could ride off on Craven and take Stranger too. She chewed her lip. Then she led the horses to the stables, and went in after him.

They know him. The silence told her that. But that wasn't the worst thing. She knew them too. Not the skinny innkeep, nor the women, nor the fieldhands by the hearth. But the others. The soldiers. She knew the soldiers.

"Looking for your brother, Sandor?" Polliver's hand was down the bodice of the girl on his lap, but now he slid it out.

"Looking for a cup of wine. Innkeep, a flagon of red." Clegane threw a handful of coppers on the floor.

"I don't want no trouble, ser," the innkeep said.

"Then don't call me *ser*." His mouth twitched. "Are you deaf, fool? I ordered wine." As the man ran off, Clegane shouted after him, "*Two cups!* The girl's thirsty too!"

There are only three, Arya thought. Polliver gave her a fleeting glance and the boy beside him never looked at her at all, but the third one gazed long and hard. He was a man of middling height and build, with a face so ordinary that it was hard to say how old he was. *The Tickler. The Tickler and Polliver both*. The boy was a squire, judging by his age and dress. He had a big white pimple on one side of his nose, and some red ones on his forehead. "Is this the lost puppy Ser Gregor spoke of?" he asked the Tickler. "The one who piddled in the rushes and ran off?"

The Tickler put a warning hand on the boy's arm, and gave a short sharp shake of his head. Arya read that plain enough.

The squire didn't, or else he didn't care. "Ser said his puppy brother tucked his tail between his legs when the battle got too warm at King's Landing. He said he ran off whimpering." He gave the Hound a stupid mocking grin.

Clegane studied the boy and never said a word. Polliver shoved the girl off his lap and got to his feet. "The lad's drunk," he said. The man-at-arms was almost as tall as the Hound, though not so heavily muscled. A spade-shaped beard covered his jaws and jowls, thick and black and neatly trimmed, but his head was more bald than not. "He can't hold his wine, is all."

"Then he shouldn't drink."

"The puppy doesn't scare . . ." the boy began, till the Tickler casually twisted his ear between thumb and forefinger. The words became a squeal of pain.

The innkeep came scurrying back with two stone cups and a flagon on a pewter platter. Sandor lifted the flagon to his mouth. Arya could see the muscles in his neck working as he gulped. When he slammed it back down on the table, half the wine was gone. "Now you can pour. Best pick up those coppers too, it's the only coin you're like to see today."

"We'll pay when we're done drinking," said Polliver.

"When you're done drinking you'll tickle the innkeep to see where he keeps his gold. The way you always do."

The innkeep suddenly remembered something in the kitchen. The locals were leaving too, and the girls were gone. The only sound in the common room was the faint crackling of the fire in the hearth. *We should go too*, Arya knew.

"If you're looking for Ser, you come too late," Polliver said. "He was at Harrenhal, but now he's not. The queen sent for him." He wore three blades on his belt, Arya saw; a longsword on his left hip, and on his right a dagger and a slimmer blade, too long to be a dirk and too short to be a sword. "King Joffrey's dead, you know," he added. "Poisoned at his own wedding feast."

Arya edged farther into the room. *Joffrey's dead.* She could almost see him, with his blond curls and his mean smile and his fat soft lips. *Joffrey's dead!* She knew it ought to make her happy, but somehow she still felt empty inside. Joffrey was dead, but if Robb was dead too, what did it matter?

"So much for my brave brothers of the Kingsguard." The Hound gave a snort of contempt. "Who killed him?"

"The Imp, it's thought. Him and his little wife."

"What wife?"

"I forgot, you've been hiding under a rock. The northern girl. Winterfell's daughter. We heard she killed the king with a spell, and afterward changed into a wolf with big leather wings like a bat, and flew out a tower window. But she left the dwarf behind and Cersei means to have his head."

That's stupid, Arya thought. *Sansa only knows songs, not spells, and she'd never marry the Imp.*

The Hound sat on the bench closest the door. His mouth twitched, but only the burned side. "She ought to dip him in wildfire and cook him. Or tickle him till the moon turns black." He raised his wine cup and drained it straightaway.

He's one of them, Arya thought when she saw that. She bit her lip so hard she tasted blood. *He's just like they are. I should kill him when he sleeps.*

"So Gregor took Harrenhal?" Sandor said.

"Didn't require much taking," said Polliver. "The sellswords fled as soon as they knew we were coming, all but a few. One of the cooks opened a postern gate for us, to get back at Hoat for cutting off his foot." He chuckled. "We kept him to cook for us, a couple wenches to warm our beds, and put all the rest to the sword."

"*All* the rest?" Arya blurted out.

"Well, Ser kept Hoat to pass the time."

Sandor said, "The Blackfish is still in Riverrun?"

"Not for long," said Polliver. "He's under siege. Old Frey's going to hang Edmure Tully unless he yields the castle. The only real fighting's around Raventree. Blackwoods and Brackens. The Brackens are ours now."

The Hound poured a cup of wine for Arya and another for himself, and drank it down while staring at the hearthfire. "The little bird flew away, did she? Well, bloody good for her. She shit on the Imp's head and flew off."

"They'll find her," said Polliver. "If it takes half the gold in Casterly Rock."

"A pretty girl, I hear," said the Tickler. "Honey sweet." He smacked his lips and smiled.

"And courteous," the Hound agreed. "A proper little lady. Not like her bloody sister."

"They found her too," said Polliver. "The sister. She's for Bolton's bastard, I hear."

Arya sipped her wine so they could not see her mouth. She didn't understand what Polliver was talking about. *Sansa has no other sister.* Sandor Clegane laughed aloud.

"What's so bloody funny?" asked Polliver.

The Hound never flicked an eye at Arya. "If I'd wanted you to know, I'd have told you. Are there ships at Saltpans?"

"Saltpans? How should I know? The traders are back at Maidenpool, I heard. Randyll Tarly took the castle and locked Mooton in a tower cell. I haven't heard shit about Saltpans."

The Tickler leaned forward. "Would you put to sea without bidding farewell to your brother?" It gave Arya chills to hear him ask a question. "Ser would sooner you returned to Harrenhal with us, Sandor. I bet he would. Or King's Landing . . ."

"Bugger that. Bugger him. Bugger you."

The Tickler shrugged, straightened, and reached a hand behind his head to rub the back of his neck. Everything seemed to happen at once then; Sandor lurched to his feet, Polliver drew his longsword, and the Tickler's hand whipped around in a blur to send something silver flashing across the common room. If the Hound had not been moving, the knife might have cored the apple of his throat; instead it only grazed his ribs, and wound up quivering in the wall near the door. He laughed then, a laugh as cold and hollow as if it had come from the bottom of a deep well. "I was hoping you'd do something stupid." His sword slid from its scabbard just in time to knock aside Polliver's first cut.

Arya took a step backward as the long steel song began. The Tickler came off the bench with a shortsword in one hand and a dagger in the other. Even the chunky brown-haired squire was up, fumbling for his swordhilt. She snatched her wine cup off the table and threw it at his face. Her aim was better than it had been at the Twins. The cup hit him right on his big white pimple and he went down hard on his tail.

Polliver was a grim, methodical fighter, and he pressed Sandor steadily backward, his heavy longsword moving with brutal precision. The Hound's own cuts were sloppier, his parries rushed, his feet slow and clumsy. *He's drunk*, Arya realized with dismay. *He drank too much too fast, with no food in his belly.* And the Tickler was sliding around the wall to get behind him. She grabbed the second wine cup and flung it at him, but he was quicker than the squire had been and ducked his head in time. The look he gave her then was cold with promise. *Is there gold hidden in the village?* she could hear him ask. The stupid squire was clutching the edge of a table and pulling himself to his knees. Arya could taste the beginnings of panic in the back of her throat. *Fear cuts deeper than swords. Fears cuts deeper . . .*

Sandor gave a grunt of pain. The burned side of his face ran red from temple to cheek, and the stub of his ear was gone. That seemed to make him angry. He drove back Polliver with a furious attack, hammering at him with the old nicked longsword he had swapped for in the hills. The bearded man gave way, but none of the cuts so much as touched him. And then the Tickler leapt over a bench quick as a snake, and slashed at the back of the Hound's neck with the edge of his short sword.

They're killing him. Arya had no more cups, but there was something better to throw. She drew the dagger they'd robbed off the dying archer and tried to fling it at the Tickler the way he'd done. It wasn't the same as throwing a rock or a crabapple, though. The knife wobbled, and hit him in the arm hilt first. *He never even felt it.* He was too intent on Clegane.

As he stabbed, Clegane twisted violently aside, winning himself half a heartbeat's respite. Blood ran down his face and from the gash in his neck. Both of the Mountain's men came after him hard, Polliver hacking at his head and shoulders while the Tickler darted in to stab at back and belly. The heavy stone flagon was still on the table. Arya grabbed it with two hands, but as she lifted it someone grabbed her arm. The flagon slipped from her fingers and crashed to the floor. Wrenched around, she found herself nose to nose with the squire. *You stupid, you forgot all about him.* His big white pimple had burst, she saw.

"Are you the puppy's puppy?" He had his sword in his right hand and her arm in his left, but her own hands were free, so she jerked his knife from its sheath and sheathed it again in his belly, twisting. He wasn't wearing mail or even boiled leather, so it went right in, the same way Needle had when she killed the stableboy at King's Landing. The squire's eyes got big and he let go of her arm. Arya spun to the door and wrenched the Tickler's knife from the wall.

Polliver and the Tickler had driven the Hound into a corner behind a bench, and one of them had given him an ugly red gash on his upper thigh to go with his other wounds. Sandor was leaning against the wall, bleeding and breathing noisily. He looked as though he could barely stand, let alone fight. "Throw down the sword, and we'll take you back to Harrenhal," Polliver told him.

"So Gregor can finish me himself?"

The Tickler said, "Maybe he'll give you to me."

"If you want me, come get me." Sandor pushed away from the wall and stood in a half-crouch behind the bench, his sword held across his body.

"You think we won't?" said Polliver. "You're drunk."

"Might be," said the Hound, "but you're dead." His foot lashed out and caught the bench, driving it hard into Polliver's shins. Somehow the bearded man kept his feet, but the Hound ducked under his wild slash and brought his own sword up in a vicious backhand cut. Blood spattered on the ceiling and walls. The blade caught in the middle of Polliver's face, and when the Hound wrenched it loose half his head came with it.

The Tickler backed away. Arya could smell his fear. The shortsword in his hand suddenly seemed almost a toy against the long blade the Hound was holding, and he wasn't armored either. He moved swiftly, light on his feet, never taking his eyes off Sandor Clegane. It was the easiest thing in the world for Arya to step up behind him and stab him.

"Is there gold hidden in the village?" she shouted as she drove the blade up through his back. "Is there silver? Gems?" She stabbed twice more. "Is there food? Where is Lord Beric?" She was on top of him by then, still stabbing. "Where did he go? How many men were with him? How many knights? How many bowmen? How many, how many, how many, how many, how many, how many? Is there *gold* in the village?"

Her hands were red and sticky when Sandor dragged her off him. "Enough," was all he said. He was bleeding like a butchered pig himself, and dragging one leg when he walked.

"There's one more," Arya reminded him.

The squire had pulled the knife out of his belly and was trying to stop the blood with his hands. When the Hound yanked him upright, he screamed and started to blubber like a baby. "Mercy," he wept, "please. Don't kill me. Mother have mercy."

"Do I look like your bloody mother?" The Hound looked like nothing human. "You killed this one too," he told Arya. "Pricked him in his bowels, that's the end of him. He'll be a long time dying, though."

The boy didn't seemed to hear him. "I came for the girls," he whimpered. ". . . make me a man, Polly said . . . oh, gods, please, take me to a castle . . . a maester, take me to a maester, my father's got gold . . . it was only for the girls . . . mercy, ser."

The Hound gave him a crack across the face that made him scream again. "Don't call me ser." He turned back to Arya. "This one is yours, she-wolf. You do it."

She knew what he meant. Arya went to Polliver and knelt in his blood long enough to undo his swordbelt. Hanging beside his dagger was a slimmer blade, too long to be a dirk, too short to be a man's sword . . . but it felt just right in her hand.

"You remember where the heart is?" the Hound asked.

She nodded. The squire rolled his eyes. "Mercy."

Needle slipped between his ribs and gave it to him.

"Good." Sandor's voice was thick with pain. "If these three were whoring here, Gregor must hold the ford as well as Harrenhal. More of his pets could ride up any moment, and we've killed enough of the bloody buggers for one day."

"Where will we go?" she asked.

"Saltpans." He put a big hand on her shoulder to keep from falling. "Get some wine, she-wolf. And take whatever coin they have as well, we'll need it. If there's ships at Saltpans, we can reach the Vale by sea." His mouth twitched at her, as more blood ran down from where his ear had been. "Maybe Lady Lysa will marry you to her little Robert. *There's* a match I'd like to see." He started to laugh, then groaned instead.

When the time came to leave, he needed Arya's help to get back up on Stranger. He had tied a strip of cloth about his neck and another around his thigh, and taken the squire's cloak off its peg by the door. The cloak was green, with a green arrow on a white bend, but when the Hound wadded it up and pressed it to his ear it soon turned red. Arya was afraid he would collapse the moment they set out, but somehow he stayed in the saddle.

They could not risk meeting whoever held the ruby ford, so instead of following the kingsroad they angled south by east, through weedy fields, woods, and marshes. It was hours before they reached the banks of the Trident. The river had returned meekly to its accustomed channel, Arya saw, all its wet brown rage vanished with the rains. *It's tired too*, she thought.

Close by the water's edge, they found some willows rising from a jumble of weathered rocks. Together the rocks and trees formed a sort of natural fort where they could hide from both river and trail. "Here will do," the Hound said. "Water the horses and gather some deadwood for a fire." When he dismounted, he had to catch himself on a tree limb to keep from falling.

"Won't the smoke be seen?"

"Anyone wants to find us, all they need to do is follow my blood. Water and wood. But bring me that wineskin first."

When he got the fire going, Sandor propped up his helm in the flames, emptied half the wineskin into it, and collapsed back against a jut of moss-covered stone as if he never meant to rise again. He made Arya wash out the squire's cloak and cut it into strips. Those went into his helm as well. "If I had more wine, I'd drink till I was dead to the world. Maybe I ought to send you back to that bloody inn for another skin or three."

"No," Arya said. *He wouldn't, would he? If he does, I'll just leave him and ride off.*

Sandor laughed at the fear on her face. "A jest, wolf girl. A bloody jest. Find me a stick, about so long and not too big around. And wash the mud off it. I hate the taste of mud."

He didn't like the first two sticks she brought him. By the time she found one that suited him, the flames had scorched his dog's snout black all the way to the eyes. Inside the wine was boiling madly. "Get the cup from my bedroll and dip it half full," he told her. "Be careful. You knock the damn thing over, I *will* send you back for more. Take the wine and pour it on my wounds. Think you can do that?" Arya nodded. "Then what are you waiting for?" he growled.

Her knuckles brushed the steel the first time she filled the cup, burning her so badly she got blisters. Arya had to bite her lip to keep from screaming. The Hound used the stick for the same purpose, clamping it between his teeth as she poured. She did the gash in his thigh first, then the shallower cut on the back of his neck. Sandor coiled his right hand into a fist and beat against the ground when she did his leg. When it came to his neck, he bit the stick so hard it broke, and she had to find him a new one. She could see the terror in his eyes. "Turn your head." She trickled the wine down over the raw red flesh where his ear had been, and fingers of brown blood and red wine crept over his jaw. He *did* scream then, despite the stick. Then he passed out from the pain.

Arya figured the rest out by herself. She fished the strips they'd made of the squire's cloak out of the bottom of the helm and used them to bind the cuts. When she came to his ear, she had to wrap up half his head to stop the bleeding. By then, dusk was settling over the Trident. She let the horses graze, then hobbled them for the night and made herself as comfortable as she could in a niche between two rocks. The fire burned a while and died. Arya watched the moon through the branches overhead.

"Ser Gregor the Mountain," she said softly. "Dunsen, Raff the Sweetling, Ser Ilyn, Ser Meryn, Queen Cersei." It made her feel queer to leave out Polliver and the Tickler. And Joffrey too. She was glad he was dead, but she wished she could have been there to see him die, or maybe kill him herself. *Polliver said that Sansa killed him, and the Imp.* Could that be true? The Imp was a Lannister, and Sansa ... *I wish I could change into a wolf and grow wings and fly away.*

If Sansa was gone too, there were no more Starks but her. Jon was on the Wall a thousand leagues away, but he was a Snow, and these different aunts and uncles the Hound wanted to sell her to, they weren't Starks either. They weren't *wolves.*

Sandor moaned, and she rolled onto her side to look at him. She had left his name out too, she realized. Why had she done that? he tried to think of Mycah, but it was hard to remember what he'd looked like. She hadn't known him long. *All he ever did was play at swords with me.* "The Hound," she whispered, and, "*Valar morghulis.*" Maybe he'd be dead by morning ...

But when the pale dawn light came filtering through the trees, it was him who woke her with the toe of his boot. She had dreamed she was a wolf again, chasing a riderless horse up a hill with a pack behind her, but his foot brought her back just as they were closing for the kill.

The Hound was still weak, every movement slow and clumsy. He slumped in the saddle, and sweated, and his ear began to bleed through the bandage. He needed all his strength just to keep from falling off Stranger. Had the Mountain's men come hunting them, she doubted if he would even be able to lift a sword. Arya glanced over her shoulder, but there was nothing behind them but a crow flitting from tree to tree. The only sound was the river.

Long before noon, Sandor Clegane was reeling. There were hours of daylight still remaining when he called a halt. "I need to rest," was all he said. This time when he dismounted he *did* fall. Instead of trying to get back up he crawled weakly under a tree, and leaned up against the trunk. "Bloody hell," he cursed. "Bloody hell." When he saw Arya staring at him, he said, "I'd skin you alive for a cup of wine, girl."

She brought him water instead. He drank a little of it, complained that it tasted of mud, and slid into a noisy fevered sleep. When she touched him, his skin was burning up. Arya sniffed at his bandages the way Maester Luwin had done sometimes when treating her cut or scrape. His face had bled the worst, but it was the wound on his thigh that smelled funny to her.

She wondered how far this Saltpans was, and whether she could find it by herself. *I wouldn't have to kill him. If I just rode off and left him, he'd die all by himself. He'll die of fever, and lie there beneath that tree until the end of days.* But maybe it would be better if she killed him herself. She had killed the squire at the inn and he hadn't done anything except grab her arm. The Hound had killed Mycah. *Mycah and more. I bet he's killed a hundred Mycahs.* He probably would have killed her too, if not for the ransom.

Needle glinted as she drew it. Polliver had kept it nice and sharp, at least. She turned her body sideways in a water dancer's stance without even thinking about it. Dead leaves crunched beneath her feet. *Quick as a snake*, she thought. *Smooth as summer silk.*

His eyes opened. "You remember where the heart is?" he asked in a hoarse whisper.

As still as stone she stood. "I . . . I was only . . ."

"*Don't lie*," he growled. "I hate liars. I hate gutless frauds even worse. Go on, do it." When Arya did not move, he said, "I killed your butcher's boy. I cut him near in half, and laughed about it after." He made a queer sound, and it took her a moment to realize he was sobbing. "And the little bird, your pretty sister, I stood there in my white cloak and let them beat her. I *took* the bloody song, she never gave it. I meant to take her too. I should have. I should have fucked her bloody and ripped her heart out before leaving her for that dwarf." A spasm of pain twisted his face. "Do you mean to make me beg, bitch? *Do it!* The gift of mercy . . . avenge your little Michael . . ."

"*Mycah.*" Arya stepped away from him. "You don't deserve the gift of mercy."

The Hound watched her saddle Craven through eyes bright with fever. Not once did he attempt to rise and stop her. But when she mounted, he said, "A real wolf would finish a wounded animal."

Maybe some real wolves will find you, Arya thought. *Maybe they'll smell you when the sun goes down.* Then he would learn what wolves did to dogs. "You shouldn't have hit me with an axe," she said. "You should have saved my mother." She turned her horse and rode away from him, and never looked back once.

On a bright morning six days later, she came to a place where the Trident began to widen out and the air smelled more of salt than trees. She stayed close to the water, passing fields and farms, and a little after midday a town appeared before her. *Saltpans*, she hoped. A small castle dominated the town; no more than a holdfast, really, a single tall square keep with a bailey and a curtain wall. Most of the shops and inns and alehouses around the harbor had been plundered or burned, though some looked still inhabited. But the port was there, and eastward spread the Bay of Crabs, its waters shimmering blue and green in the sun.

And there were ships.

Three, thought Arya, *there are three*. Two were only river galleys, shallow draft boats made to ply the waters of the Trident. The third was bigger, a salt sea trader with two banks of oars, a gilded prow, and three tall masts with furled purple sails. Her hull was painted purple too. Arya rode Craven down to the docks to get a better look. Strangers are not so strange in a port as they are in little villages, and no one seemed to care who she was or why she was here.

I need silver. The realization made her bite her lip. They had found a stag and a dozen coppers on Polliver, eight silvers on the pimply squire she'd killed, and only a couple of pennies in the Tickler's purse. But the Hound had told her to pull off his boots and slice open his blood-drenched clothes, and she'd turned up a stag in each toe, and three golden dragons sewn in the lining of his jerkin. Sandor had kept it all, though. *That wasn't fair. It was mine as much as his.* If she had given him the gift of mercy . . . she hadn't, though. She couldn't go back, no more than she could beg for help. *Begging for help never gets you any.* She would have to sell Craven, and hope she brought enough.

The stable had been burnt, she learned from a boy by the docks, but the woman who'd owned it was still trading behind the sept. Arya found her easily; a big, robust woman with a good horsey smell to her. She liked Craven at first look, asked Arya how she'd come by her, and grinned at her answer. "She's a well-bred horse, that's plain enough, and I don't doubt she belonged to a knight, sweetling," she said. "But the knight wasn't no dead brother o' yours. I been dealing with the castle there many a year, so I know what gentleborn folk is like. This mare is well-bred, but you're not." She poked a finger at Arya's chest. "Found her or stole her, never mind which, that's how it was. Only way a scruffy little thing like you comes to ride a palfrey."

Arya bit her lip. "Does that mean you won't buy her?"

The woman chuckled. "It means you'll take what I give you, sweetling. Else we go down to the castle, and maybe you get nothing. Or even hanged, for stealing some good knight's horse."

A half-dozen other Saltpans folks were around, going about their business, so Arya knew she couldn't kill the woman. Instead she had to bite her lip and let herself be cheated. The purse she got was pitifully flat, and when she asked for more for the saddle and bridle and blanket, the woman just laughed at her.

She would never have cheated the Hound, she thought during the long walk back to the docks. The distance seemed to have grown by miles since she'd ridden it.

The purple galley was still there. If the ship had sailed while she was being robbed, that would have been too much to bear. A cask of mead was being rolled up the plank when she arrived. When she tried to follow, a sailor up on deck shouted down at her in a tongue she did not know. "I want to see the captain," Arya told him. He only shouted louder. But the commotion drew the attention of a stout grey-haired man in a coat of purple wool, and he spoke the Common Tongue. "I am captain here," he said. "What is your wish? Be quick, child, we have a tide to catch."

"I want to go north, to the Wall. Here, I can pay." She gave him the purse. "The Night's Watch has a castle on the sea."

"Eastwatch." The captain spilled out the silver onto his palm and frowned. "Is this all you have?"

It is not enough, Arya knew without being told. She could see it on his face. "I wouldn't need a cabin or anything," she said. "I could sleep down in the hold, or . . ."

"Take her on as cabin girl," said a passing oarsman, a bolt of wool over one shoulder. "She can sleep with me."

"Mind your tongue," the captain snapped.

"I could work," said Arya. "I could scrub the decks. I scrubbed a castle steps once. Or I could row . . ."

"No," he said, "you couldn't." He gave her back her coins. "It would make no difference if you could, child. The north has nothing for us. Ice and war and pirates. We saw a dozen pirate ships making north as we rounded Cracklaw Point, and I have no wish to meet them again. From here we bend our oars for home, and I suggest you do the same."

I have no home, Arya thought. *I have no pack. And now I don't even have a horse.*

The captain was turning away when she said, "What ship is this, my lord?"

He paused long enough to give her a weary smile. "This is the galleas *Titan's Daughter*, of the Free City of Braavos."

"Wait," Arya said suddenly. "I have something else." She had stuffed it down inside her smallclothes to keep it safe, so she had to dig deep to find it, while the oarsmen laughed and the captain lingered with obvious impatience. "One more silver will make no difference, child," he finally said.

"It's not silver." Her fingers closed on it. "It's iron. Here." She pressed it into his hand, the small black iron coin that Jaqen H'ghar had given her, so worn the man whose head it bore had no features. *It's probably worthless, but . . .*

The captain turned it over and blinked at it, then looked at her again. "This . . . how . . .?"

Jaqen said to say the words too. Arya crossed her arms against her chest. "*Valar morghulis,*" she said, as loud as if she'd known what it meant.

"*Valar dohaeris,*" he replied, touching his brow with two fingers. "Of *course* you shall have a cabin."

SAMWELL

"He sucks harder than mine." Gilly stroked the babe's head as she held him to her nipple.

"He's hungry," said the blonde woman Val, the one the black brothers called the wildling princess. "He's lived on goats' milk up to now, and potions from that blind maester."

The boy did not have a name yet, no more than Gilly's did. That was the wildling way. Not even Mance Rayder's son would get a name till his third year, it would seem, though Sam had heard the brothers calling him "the little prince" and "born-in-battle."

He watched the child nurse at Gilly's breast, and then he watched Jon watch. *Jon is smiling.* A sad smile, still, but definitely a smile of sorts. Sam was glad to see it. *It is the first time I've seen him smile since I got back.*

They had walked from the Nightfort to Deep Lake, and from Deep Lake to Queensgate, following a narrow track from one castle to the next, never out of sight of the Wall. A day and a half from Castle Black, as they trudged along on callused feet, Gilly heard horses behind them, and turned to see a column of black riders coming from the west. "My brothers," Sam assured her. "No one uses this road but the Night's Watch." It had turned out to be Ser Denys Mallister from the Shadow Tower, along with the wounded Bowen Marsh and the survivors from the fight at the Bridge of

Skulls. When Sam saw Dywen, Giant, and Dolorous Edd Tollett, he broke down and wept.

It was from them that he learned about the battle beneath the Wall. "Stannis landed his knights at Eastwatch, and Cotter Pyke led him along the ranger's roads, to take the wildlings unawares," Giant told him. "He smashed them. Mance Rayder was taken captive, a thousand of his best slain, including Harma Dogshead. The rest scattered like leaves before a storm, we heard." *The gods are good*, Sam thought. If he had not gotten lost as he made his way south from Craster's Keep, he and Gilly might have walked right into the battle ... or into Mance Rayder's camp, at the very least. That might have been well enough for Gilly and the boy, but not for him. Sam had heard all the stories about what wildlings did with captured crows. He shuddered.

Nothing that his brothers told him prepared him for what he found at Castle Black, however. The common hall had burned to the ground and the great wooden stair was a mound of broken ice and scorched timbers. Donal Noye was dead, along with Rast, Deaf Dick, Red Alyn, and so many more, yet the castle was more crowded than Sam had ever seen; not with black brothers, but with the king's soldiers, more than a thousand of them. There was a king in the King's Tower for the first time in living memory, and banners flew from the Lance, Hardin's Tower, the Grey Keep, the Shieldhall, and other buildings that had stood empty and abandoned for long years. "The big one, the gold with the black stag, that's the royal standard of House Baratheon," he told Gilly, who had never seen banners before. "The fox-and-flowers is House Florent. The turtle is Estermont, the swordfish is Bar Emmon, and the crossed trumpets are for Wensington."

"They're all bright as flowers." Gilly pointed. "I like those yellow ones, with the fire. Look, and some of the fighters have the same thing on their blouses."

"A fiery heart. I don't know whose sigil that is."

He found out soon enough. "*Queen's men,*" Pyp told him—after he let out a whoop, and shouted, "Run and bar the doors, lads, it's Sam the Slayer come back from the grave," while Grenn was hugging Sam so hard he thought his ribs might break—"but best you don't go asking where the queen is. Stannis left her at Eastwatch, with their daughter and his fleet. He brought no woman but the red one."

"The red one?" said Sam uncertainly.

"Melisandre of Asshai," said Grenn. "The king's sorceress. They say she burned a man alive at Dragonstone so Stannis would have favorable winds for his voyage north. She rode beside him in the battle too, and gave him his magic sword. Lightbringer, they call it. Wait till you see it. It glows like it had a piece of sun inside it." He looked at Sam again and grinned a big helpless stupid grin. "I still can't believe you're here."

Jon Snow had smiled to see him too, but it was a tired smile, like the one he wore now. "You made it back after all," he said. "And brought Gilly out as well. You've done well, Sam."

Jon had done more than well himself, to hear Grenn tell it. Yet even capturing the Horn of Winter and a wildling prince had not been enough for Ser Alliser Thorne and his friends, who still named him turncloak. Though Maester Aemon said his wound was healing well, Jon bore other scars, deeper than the ones around his eye. *He grieves for his wildling girl, and for his brothers.*

"It's strange," he said to Sam. "Craster had no love for Mance, nor Mance for Craster, but now Craster's daughter is feeding Mance's son."

"I have the milk," Gilly said, her voice soft and shy. "Mine takes only a little. He's not so greedy as this one."

The wildling woman Val turned to face them. "I've heard the queen's men saying that the red woman means to give Mance to the fire, as soon as he is strong enough."

Jon gave her a weary look. "Mance is a deserter from the Night's Watch. The penalty for that is death. If the Watch had taken him, he would have been hanged by now, but he's the king's captive, and no one knows the king's mind but the red woman."

"I want to see him," Val said. "I want to show him his son. He deserves that much, before you kill him."

Sam tried to explain. "No one is permitted to see him but Maester Aemon, my lady."

"If it were in my power, Mance could hold his son." Jon's smile was gone. "I'm sorry, Val." He turned away. "Sam and I have duties to return to. Well, Sam does, anyway. We'll ask about your seeing Mance. That's all I can promise."

Sam lingered long enough to give Gilly's hand a squeeze and promise to return again after supper. Then he hurried after. There were guards outside the door, queen's men with spears. Jon was halfway down the steps, but he waited when he heard Sam puffing after him. "You're more than fond of Gilly, aren't you?"

Sam reddened. "Gilly's good. She's good and kind." He was glad that his long nightmare was done, glad to be back with his brothers at Castle Black ... but some nights, alone in his cell, he thought of how warm Gilly had been when they'd curled up beneath the furs with the babe between them. "She ... she made me braver, Jon. Not *brave*, but ... braver."

"You know you cannot keep her," Jon said gently, "no more than I could stay with Ygritte. You said the words, Sam, the same as I did. The same as all of us."

"I know. Gilly said she'd be a wife to me, but ... I told her about the words, and what they meant. I don't know if that made her sad or glad, but I told her." He swallowed nervously and said, "Jon, could there be honor in a lie, if it were told for a ... a good purpose?"

"It would depend on the lie and the purpose, I suppose." Jon looked at Sam. "I wouldn't advise it. You're not made to lie, Sam. You blush and squeak and stammer."

"I do," said Sam, "but I could lie in a letter. I'm better with a quill in hand. I had a ... a thought. When things are more settled here, I thought maybe the best thing for Gilly ... I thought I might send her to Horn Hill. To my mother and sisters and my ... my f-f-father. If Gilly were to say the babe was m-mine ..." He was blushing again. "My mother would want him, I know. She would find some place for Gilly, some kind of service, it wouldn't be as hard as serving Craster. And Lord R-Randyll, he ... he would never *say* so, but he might be pleased to believe I got a bastard on some wildling girl. At least it would prove I was man enough to lie with a woman and father a child. He told me once that I was sure to die a maiden, that no woman would ever ... you know ... Jon, if I did this, wrote this lie ... would that be a good thing? The life the boy would have ..."

"Growing up a bastard in his grandfather's castle?" Jon shrugged. "That depends in great part on your father, and what sort of boy this is. If he takes after you ..."

"He won't. Craster's his real father. You saw him, he was hard as an old tree stump, and Gilly is stronger than she looks."

"If the boy shows any skill with sword or lance, he should have a place with your father's household guard at the least," Jon said. "It's not unknown for bastards to be trained as squires and raised to knighthood. But you'd best be sure Gilly can play this game convincingly. From what you've told me of Lord Randyll, I doubt he would take kindly to being deceived."

More guards were posted on the steps outside the tower. These were king's men, though; Sam had quickly learned the difference. The king's men were as earthy and impious as any other soldiers, but the queen's men were fervid in their devotion to Melisandre of Asshai and her Lord of Light. "Are you going to the practice yard again?" Sam asked as they crossed the yard. "Is it wise to train so hard before your leg's done healing?"

Jon shrugged. "What else is there for me to do? Marsh has removed me from duty, for fear that I'm still a turncloak."

"It's only a few who believe that," Sam assured him. "Ser Alliser and his friends. Most of the brothers know better. King Stannis knows as well, I'll wager. You brought him the Horn of Winter and captured Mance Rayder's son."

"All I did was protect Val and the babe against looters when the wildlings fled, and keep them there until the rangers found us. I never *captured* anyone. King Stannis keeps his men well in hand, that's plain. He lets them plunder some, but I've only heard of three wildling women being raped, and the men who did it have all been gelded. I suppose I should have been killing the free folk as they ran. Ser Alliser has been putting it about that the only time I bared my sword was to defend our foes. I failed to kill Mance Rayder because I was in league with him, he says."

"That's only Ser Alliser," said Sam. "Everyone knows the sort of man he is." With his noble birth, his knighthood, and his long years in the Watch, Ser Alliser Thorne might have been a strong challenger for the Lord Commander's title, but almost all the men he'd trained during his years as master-at-arms despised him. His name had been offered, of course, but after running a weak sixth on the first day and actually *losing* votes on the second, Thorne had withdrawn to support Lord Janos Slynt.

"What everyone knows is that Ser Alliser is a knight from a noble line, and trueborn, while I'm the bastard who killed Qhorin Halfhand and bedded with a spearwife. The *warg*, I've heard them call me. How can I be a warg without a wolf, I ask you?" His mouth twisted. "I don't even dream of Ghost anymore. All my dreams are of the crypts, of the stone kings on their thrones. Sometimes, I hear Robb's voice, and my father's, as if they were at a feast. But there's a wall between us, and I know that no place has been set for me."

The living have no place at the feasts of the dead. It tore the heart from Sam to hold his silence then. *Bran's not dead, Jon*, he wanted to stay. *He's with friends, and they're going north on a giant elk to find a three-eyed crow in the depths of the haunted forest.* It sounded so mad that there were times Sam Tarly thought he must have dreamt it all, conjured it whole from fever and fear and hunger . . . but he would have blurted it out anyway, if he had not given his word.

Three times he had sworn to keep the secret; once to Bran himself, once to that strange boy Jojen Reed, and last of all to Coldhands. "The world believes the boy is dead," his rescuer had said as they parted. "Let his bones lie undisturbed. We want no seekers coming after us. Swear it, Samwell of the Night's Watch. Swear it for the life you owe me."

Miserable, Sam shifted his weight and said, "Lord Janos will never be chosen Lord Commander." It was the best comfort he had to offer Jon, the only comfort. "That won't happen."

"Sam, you're a sweet fool. Open your eyes. It's been happening for days." Jon pushed his hair back out of his eyes and said, "I may know nothing, but I know that. Now pray excuse me, I need to hit someone very hard with a sword."

There was naught that Sam could do but watch him stride off toward the armory and the practice yard. That was where Jon Snow spent most of his waking hours. With Ser Endrew dead and Ser Alliser disinterested, Castle Black had no master-at-arms, so Jon had taken it on himself to work with some of the rawer recruits; Satin, Horse, Hop-Robin with his clubfoot, Arron and Emrick. And when they had duties, he would train alone for hours with sword and shield and spear, or match himself against anyone who cared to take him on.

Sam, you're a sweet fool, he could hear Jon saying, all the way back to the maester's keep. *Open your eyes. It's been happening for days.* Could he be right? A man needed the votes of two-thirds of the Sworn Brothers to become the Lord Commander of the Night's Watch, and after nine days and nine votes no one was even close to that. Lord Janos *had* been gaining, true, creeping up past first Bowen Marsh and then Othell Yarwyck, but he was still well behind Ser Denys Mallister of the Shadow Tower and Cotter Pyke of Eastwatch-by-the-Sea. *One of them will be the new Lord Commander, surely,* Sam told himself.

Stannis had posted guards outside the maester's door too. Within, the rooms were hot and crowded with the wounded from the battle; black brothers, king's men, and queen's men, all three. Clydas was shuffling amongst them with flagons of goats' milk and dreamwine, but Maester Aemon had not yet returned from his morning call on Mance Rayder. Sam hung his cloak upon a peg and went to lend a hand. But even as he fetched and poured and changed dressings, Jon's words nagged at him. *Sam, you're a sweet fool. Open your eyes. It's been happening for days.*

It was a good hour before he could excuse himself to feed the ravens. On the way up to the rookery, he stopped to check the tally he had made of last night's count. At the start of the choosing, more than thirty names had been offered, but most had withdrawn once it became clear they could not win. Seven remained as of last night. Ser Denys Mallister had collected two hundred and thirteen tokens, Cotter Pyke one hundred and eighty-seven, Lord Slynt seventy-four, Othell Yarwyck sixty, Bowen Marsh forty-nine, Three-Finger Hobb five, and Dolorous Edd Tollett one. *Pyp and his stupid japes.* Sam shuffled through the earlier counts. Ser Denys, Cotter Pyke, and Bowen Marsh had all been falling since the third day, Othell Yarwyck since the sixth. Only Lord Janos Slynt was climbing, day after day after day.

He could hear the birds *quorking* in the rookery, so he put the papers away and climbed the steps to feed them. Three more ravens had come in, he saw with pleasure. "*Snow*," they cried at him. "*Snow, snow, snow.*" He had taught them that. Even with the newcomers, the ravenry seemed dismally empty. Few of the birds that Aemon had sent off had returned as yet. *One reached Stannis, though. One found Dragonstone, and a king who still cared.* A thousand leagues south, Sam knew, his father had joined House Tarly to the cause of the boy on the Iron Throne, but neither King Joffrey nor little King Tommen had bestirred himself when the Watch cried out for help. *What good is a king who will not defend his realm?* he thought angrily, remembering the night on the Fist of the First Men and the terrible trek to Craster's Keep through darkness, fear, and falling snow. The queen's men made him uneasy, it was true, but at least they had *come*.

That night at supper, Sam looked for Jon Snow, but did not see him anywhere in the cavernous stone vault where the brothers now took their meals. He finally took a place on the bench near his other friends. Pyp was telling Dolorous Edd about the contest they'd had to see which of the straw soldiers could collect the most wildling arrows. "You were leading most of the way, but Watt of Long Lake got three in the last day and passed you."

"I never win anything," Dolorous Edd complained. "The gods always smiled on Watt, though. When the wildlings knocked him off the Bridge of Skulls, somehow he landed in a nice deep pool of water. How lucky was that, missing all those rocks?"

"Was it a long fall?" Grenn wanted to know. "Did landing in the pool of water save his life?"

"No," said Dolorous Edd. "He was dead already, from that axe in his head. Still, it was pretty lucky, missing the rocks."

Three-Finger Hobb had promised the brothers roast haunch of mammoth that night, maybe in hopes of cadging a few more votes. *If that was his notion, he should have found a younger mammoth*, Sam thought, as he pulled a string of gristle out from between his teeth. Sighing, he pushed the food away.

There would be another vote shortly, and the tensions in the air were thicker than the smoke. Cotter Pyke sat by the fire, surrounded by rangers from Eastwatch. Ser Denys Mallister was near the door with a smaller group of Shadow Tower men. *Janos Slynt has the best place,* Sam realized, *halfway between the flames and the drafts.* He was alarmed to see Bowen Marsh beside him, wan-faced and haggard, his head still wrapped in linen, but listening to all that Lord Janos had to say. When he pointed that out to his friends, Pyp said, "And look down there, that's Ser Alliser whispering with Othell Yarwyck."

After the meal, Maester Aemon rose to ask if any of the brothers wished to speak before they cast their tokens. Dolorous Edd got up, stone-faced and glum as ever. "I just want to say to whoever is voting for me that I would certainly make an awful Lord Commander. But so would all these others." He was followed by Bowen Marsh, who stood with one hand on Lord Slynt's shoulder. "Brothers and friends, I am asking that my name be withdrawn from this choosing. My wound still troubles me, and the task is too large for me, I fear ... but not for Lord Janos here, who commanded the gold cloaks of King's Landing for many years. Let us all give him our support."

Sam heard angry mutters from Cotter Pyke's end of the room, and Ser Denys looked at one of his companions and shook his head. *It is too late, the damage is done.* He wondered where Jon was, and why he had stayed away.

Most of the brothers were unlettered, so by tradition the choosing was done by dropping tokens into a big potbellied iron kettle that Three-Finger Hobb and Owen the Oaf had dragged over from the kitchens. The barrels of tokens were off in a corner behind a heavy drape, so the voters could make their choice unseen. You were allowed to have a friend cast your token if you had duty, so some men took two tokens, three, or four, and Ser Denys and Cotter Pyke voted for the garrisons they had left behind.

When the hall was finally empty, save for them, Sam and Clydas upended the kettle in front of Maester Aemon. A cascade of seashells, stones, and copper pennies covered the table. Aemon's wrinkled hands sorted with surprising speed, moving the shells here, the stones there, the pennies to one side, the occasional arrowhead, nail, and acorn off to themselves. Sam and Clydas counted the piles, each of them keeping his own tally.

Tonight it was Sam's turn to give his results first. "Two hundred and three for Ser Denys Mallister," he said. "One hundred and sixty-nine for Cotter Pyke. One hundred and thirty-seven for Lord Janos Slynt, seventy-two for Othell Yarwyck, five for Three-Finger Hobb, and two for Dolorous Edd."

"I had one hundred and sixty-eight for Pyke," Clydas said. "We are two votes short by my count, and one by Sam's."

"Sam's count is correct," said Maester Aemon. "Jon Snow did not cast a token. It makes no matter. No one is close."

Sam was more relieved than disappointed. Even with Bowen Marsh's support, Lord Janos was still only third. "Who are these five who keep voting for Three-Finger Hobb?" he wondered.

"Brothers who want him out of the kitchens?" said Clydas.

"Ser Denys is down ten votes since yesterday," Sam pointed out. "And Cotter Pyke is down almost twenty. That's not good."

"Not good for their hopes of becoming Lord Commander, certainly," said Maester Aemon. "Yet it may be good for the Night's Watch, in the end. That is not for us to say. Ten days is not unduly long. There was once a choosing that lasted near two years, some seven hundred votes. The brothers will come to a decision in their own time."

Yes, Sam thought, *but what decision?*

Later, over cups of watered wine in the privacy of Pyp's cell, Sam's tongue loosened and he found himself thinking aloud. "Cotter Pyke and Ser Denys Mallister have been losing ground, but between them they still have almost two-thirds," he told Pyp and Grenn. "Either one would be fine as Lord Commander. Someone needs to convince one of them to withdraw and support the other."

"Someone?" said Grenn, doubtfully. "What someone?"

"Grenn is so dumb he thinks *someone* might be him," said Pyp. "Maybe when someone is done with Pyke and Mallister, he should convince King Stannis to marry Queen Cersei too."

"King Stannis is married," Grenn objected.

"What am I going to do with him, Sam?" sighed Pyp.

"Cotter Pyke and Ser Denys don't like each other much," Grenn argued stubbornly. "They fight about *everything*."

"Yes, but only because they have different ideas about what's best for the Watch," said Sam. "If we explained—"

"*We?*" said Pyp. "How did *someone* change to *we?* I'm the mummer's monkey, remember? And Grenn is, well, *Grenn.*" He smiled at Sam, and wiggled his ears. "You, now . . . you're a lord's son, and the maester's steward . . ."

"And Sam the Slayer," said Grenn. "You slew an Other."

"It was the *dragonglass* that killed it," Sam told him for the hundredth time.

"A lord's son, the maester's steward, and Sam the Slayer," Pyp mused. "*You* could talk to them, might be . . ."

"I could," said Sam, sounding as gloomy as Dolorous Edd, "if I wasn't too craven to face them."

JON

Jon prowled around Satin in a slow circle, sword in hand, forcing him to turn. "Get your shield up," he said.

"It's too heavy," the Oldtown boy complained.

"It's as heavy as it needs to be to stop a sword," Jon said. "Now get it up." He stepped forward, slashing. Satin jerked the shield up in time to catch the sword on its rim, and swung his own blade at Jon's ribs. "Good," Jon said, when he felt the impact on his own shield. "That was good. But you need to put your body into it. Get your weight behind the steel and you'll do more damage than with arm strength alone. Come, try it again, drive at me, but keep the shield up or I'll ring your head like a bell . . ."

Instead Satin took a step backward and raised his visor. "Jon," he said, in an anxious voice.

When he turned, she was standing behind him, with half a dozen queen's men around her. *Small wonder the yard grew so quiet.* He had glimpsed Melisandre at her nightfires, and coming and going about the castle, but never so close. *She's beautiful*, he thought . . . but there was something more than a little unsettling about red eyes. "My lady."

"The king would speak with you, Jon Snow."

Jon thrust the practice sword into the earth. "Might I be allowed to change? I am in no fit state to stand before a king."

"We shall await you atop the Wall," said Melisandre. *We*, Jon heard, *not he. It's as they say. This is his true queen, not the one he left at Eastwatch.*

He hung his mail and plate inside the armory, returned to his own cell, discarded his sweat-stained clothes, and donned a fresh set of blacks. It would be cold and windy in the cage, he knew, and colder and windier still on top of the ice, so he chose a heavy hooded cloak. Last of all he collected Longclaw, and slung the bastard sword across his back.

Melisandre was waiting for him at the base of the Wall. She had sent her queen's men away. "What does His Grace want of me?" Jon asked her as they entered the cage.

"All you have to give, Jon Snow. He is a king."

He shut the door and pulled the bell cord. The winch began to turn. They rose. The day was bright and the Wall was weeping, long fingers of water trickling down its face and glinting in the sun. In the close confines of the iron cage, he was acutely aware of the red woman's presence. *She even smells red.* The scent reminded him of Mikken's forge, of the way iron smelled when red-hot; the scent was smoke and blood. *Kissed by fire,* he thought, remembering Ygritte. The wind got in amongst Melisandre's long red robes and sent them flapping against Jon's legs as he stood beside her. "You are not cold, my lady?" he asked her.

She laughed. "Never." The ruby at her throat seemed to pulse, in time with the beating of her heart. "The Lord's fire lives within me, Jon Snow. Feel." She put her hand on his cheek, and held it there while he felt how warm she was. "That is how life should feel," she told him. "Only death is cold."

They found Stannis Baratheon standing alone at the edge of the Wall, brooding over the field where he had won his battle, and the great green forest beyond. He was dressed in the same black breeches, tunic, and boots that a brother of the Night's Watch might wear. Only his cloak set him apart; a heavy golden cloak trimmed in black fur, and pinned with a brooch in the shape of a flaming heart. "I have brought you the Bastard of Winterfell, Your Grace," said Melisandre.

Stannis turned to study him. Beneath his heavy brow were eyes like bottomless blue pools. His hollow cheeks and strong jaw were covered with a short-cropped blue-black beard that did little to conceal the gauntness of his face, and his teeth were clenched. His neck and shoulders were clenched as well, and his right hand. Jon found himself remembering something Donal Noye once said about the Baratheon brothers. *Robert was the true steel. Stannis is pure iron, black and hard and strong, but brittle, the way iron gets. He'll break before he bends.* Uneasily, he knelt, wondering why this brittle king had need of him.

"Rise. I have heard much and more of you, Lord Snow."

"I am no lord, sire." Jon rose. "I know what you have heard. That I am a turncloak, and craven. That I slew my brother Qhorin Halfhand so the wildlings would spare my life. That I rode with Mance Rayder, and took a wildling wife."

"Aye. All that, and more. You are a warg too, they say, a skinchanger who walks at night as a wolf." King Stannis had a hard smile. "How much of it is true?"

"I had a direwolf, Ghost. I left him when I climbed the Wall near Greyguard, and have not seen him since. Qhorin Halfhand commanded me to join the wildlings. He knew they would make me kill him to prove myself, and told me to do whatever they asked of me. The woman was named Ygritte. I broke my vows with her, but I swear to you on my father's name that I never turned my cloak."

"I believe you," the king said.

That startled him. "Why?"

Stannis snorted. "I know Janos Slynt. And I knew Ned Stark as well. Your father was no friend of mine, but only a fool would doubt his honor or his honesty. You have his look." A big man, Stannis Baratheon towered over Jon, but he was so gaunt that he looked ten years older than he was. "I know more than you might think, Jon Snow. I know it was you who found the dragonglass dagger that Randyll Tarly's son used to slay the Other."

"Ghost found it. The blade was wrapped in a ranger's cloak and buried beneath the Fist of the First Men. There were other blades as well . . . spearheads, arrowheads, all dragonglass."

"I know you held the gate here," King Stannis said. "If not, I would have come too late."

"Donal Noye held the gate. He died below in the tunnel, fighting the king of the giants."

Stannis grimaced. "Noye made my first sword for me, and Robert's warhammer as well. Had the god seen fit to spare him, he would have made a better Lord Commander for your order than any of these fools who are squabbling over it now."

"Cotter Pyke and Ser Denys Mallister are no fools, sire," Jon said. "They're good men, and capable. Othell Yarwyck as well, in his own way. Lord Mormont trusted each of them."

"Your Lord Mormont trusted too easily. Else he would not have died as he did. But we were speaking of you. I have not forgotten that it was you who brought us this magic horn, and captured Mance Rayder's wife and son."

"Dalla died." Jon was saddened by that still. "Val is her sister. She and the babe did not require much capturing, Your Grace. You had put the wildlings to flight, and the skinchanger Mance had left to guard his queen went mad when the eagle burned." Jon looked at Melisandre. "Some say that was your doing."

She smiled, her long copper hair tumbling across her face. "The Lord of Light has fiery talons, Jon Snow."

Jon nodded, and turned back to the king. "Your Grace, you spoke of Val. She has asked to see Mance Rayder, to bring his son to him. It would be a . . . a kindness."

"The man is a deserter from your order. Your brothers are all insisting on his death. Why should I do him a kindness?"

Jon had no answer for that. "If not for him, for Val. For her sister's sake, the child's mother."

"You are fond of this Val?"

"I scarcely know her."

"They tell me she is comely."

"Very," Jon admitted.

"Beauty can be treacherous. My brother learned that lesson from Cersei Lannister. She murdered him, do not doubt it. Your father and Jon Arryn as well." He scowled. "You rode with these wildlings. Is there any honor in them, do you think?"

"Yes," Jon said, "but their own sort of honor, sire."

"In Mance Rayder?"

"Yes. I think so."

"In the Lord of Bones?"

Jon hesitated. "Rattleshirt, we called him. Treacherous and blood-thirsty. If there's honor in him, he hides it down beneath his suit of bones."

"And this other man, this Tormund of the many names who eluded us after the battle? Answer me truly."

"Tormund Giantsbane seemed to me the sort of man who would make a good friend and a bad enemy, Your Grace."

Stannis gave a curt nod. "Your father was a man of honor. He was no friend to me, but I saw his worth. Your brother was a rebel and a traitor who meant to steal half my kingdom, but no man can question his courage. What of you?"

Does he want me to say I love him? Jon's voice was stiff and formal as he said, "I am a man of the Night's Watch."

"Words. Words are wind. Why do you think I abandoned Dragonstone and sailed to the Wall, Lord Snow?"

"I am no lord, sire. You came because we sent for you, I hope. Though I could not say why you took so long about it."

Surprisingly, Stannis smiled at that. "You're bold enough to be a Stark. Yes, I should have come sooner. If not for my Hand, I might not have come at all. Lord Seaworth is a man of humble birth, but he reminded me of my duty, when all I could think of was my rights. I had the cart before the horse, Davos said. I was trying to win the throne to save the kingdom, when I should have been trying to save the kingdom to win the throne." Stannis pointed north. "There is where I'll find the foe that I was born to fight."

"His name may not be spoken," Melisandre added softly. "He is the God of Night and Terror, Jon Snow, and these shapes in the snow are his creatures."

"They tell me that you slew one of these walking corpses to save Lord Mormont's life," Stannis said. "It may be that this is your war as well, Lord Snow. If you will give me your help."

"My sword is pledged to the Night's Watch, Your Grace," Jon Snow answered carefully.

That did not please the king. Stannis ground his teeth and said, "I need more than a sword from you."

Jon was lost. "My lord?"

"I need the north."

The north. "I . . . my brother Robb was King in the North . . ."

"Your brother was the rightful Lord of Winterfell. If he had stayed home and done his duty, instead of crowning himself and riding off to conquer the riverlands, he might be alive today. Be that as it may. You are not Robb, no more than I am Robert."

The harsh words had blown away whatever sympathy Jon might have had for Stannis. "I loved my brother," he said.

"And I mine. Yet they were what they were, and so are we. I am the only true king in Westeros, north or south. And you are Ned Stark's bastard." Stannis studied him with those dark blue eyes. "Tywin Lannister has named Roose Bolton his Warden of the North, to reward him for betraying your brother. The ironmen are fighting amongst themselves since Balon Greyjoy's death, yet they still hold Moat Cailin, Deepwood Motte, Torrhen's Square, and most of the Stony Shore. Your father's lands are bleeding, and I have neither the strength nor the time to stanch the wounds. What is needed is a Lord of Winterfell. A *loyal* Lord of Winterfell."

He is looking at me, Jon thought, stunned. "Winterfell is no more. Theon Greyjoy put it to the torch."

"Granite does not burn easily," Stannis said. "The castle can be rebuilt, in time. It's not the walls that make a lord, it's the man. Your northmen do not know me, have no reason to love me, yet I will need their strength in the battles yet to come. I need a son of Eddard Stark to win them to my banner."

He would make me Lord of Winterfell. The wind was gusting, and Jon felt so light-headed he was half afraid it would blow him off the Wall. "Your Grace," he said, "you forget. I am a Snow, not a Stark."

"It's you who are forgetting," King Stannis replied.

Melisandre put a warm hand on Jon's arm. "A king can remove the taint of bastardy with a stroke, Lord Snow."

Lord Snow. Ser Alliser Thorne had named him that, to mock his bastard birth. Many of his brothers had taken to using it as well, some with affection, others to wound. But suddenly it had a different sound to it in Jon's ears. It sounded . . . real. "Yes," he said, hesitantly, "kings have legitimized bastards before, but . . . I am still a brother of the Night's Watch. I knelt before a heart tree and swore to hold no lands and father no children."

"Jon." Melisandre was so close he could feel the warmth of her breath. "R'hllor is the only true god. A vow sworn to a tree has no more power than one sworn to your shoes. Open your heart and let the light of the Lord come in. Burn these weirwoods, and accept Winterfell as a gift of the Lord of Light."

When Jon had been very young, too young to understand what it meant to be a bastard, he used to dream that one day Winterfell might be his. Later, when he was older, he had been ashamed of those dreams. Winterfell would go to Robb and then his sons, or to Bran or Rickon should Robb die childless. And after them came Sansa and Arya. Even to dream otherwise seemed disloyal, as if he were betraying them in his heart, wishing for their deaths. *I never wanted this,* he thought as he stood before the blue-eyed king and the red woman. *I loved Robb, loved all of them . . . I never wanted any harm to come to any of them, but it did. And now there's only me.* All he had to do was say the word, and he would be Jon Stark, and nevermore a Snow. All he had to do was pledge this king his fealty, and Winterfell was his. All he had to do . . .

. . . was forswear his vows again.

And this time it would not be a ruse. To claim his father's castle, he must turn against his father's gods.

King Stannis gazed off north again, his gold cloak streaming from his shoulders. "It may be that I am mistaken in you, Jon Snow. We both know the things that are said of bastards. You may lack your father's honor, or your brother's skill in arms. But you are the weapon the Lord has given me. I have found you here, as you found the cache of dragonglass beneath the Fist, and I mean to make use of you. Even Azor Ahai did not win his war alone. I killed a thousand wildlings, took another thousand captive, and scattered the rest, but we both know they will return. Melisandre has seen that in her fires. This Tormund Thunderfist is likely re-forming them even now, and planning some new assault. And the more we bleed each other, the weaker we shall all be when the real enemy falls upon us."

Jon had come to that same realization. "As you say, Your Grace." He wondered where this king was going.

"Whilst your brothers have been struggling to decide who shall lead them, I have been speaking with this Mance Rayder." He ground his teeth. "A stubborn man, that one, and prideful. He will leave me no choice but to give him to the flames. But we took other captives as well, other leaders. The one who calls himself the Lord of Bones, some of their clan chiefs, the new Magnar of Thenn. Your brothers will not like it, no more than your father's lords, but I mean to allow the wildlings through the Wall . . . those who will swear me their fealty, pledge to keep the king's peace and the king's laws, and take the Lord of Light as their god. Even the giants, if those great knees of theirs can bend. I will settle them on the Gift, once I have wrested it away from your new Lord Commander. When the cold winds rise, we shall live or die together. It is time we made alliance against our common foe." He looked at Jon. "Would you agree?"

"My father dreamed of resettling the Gift," Jon admitted. "He and my uncle Benjen used to talk of it." *He never thought of settling it with wildlings, though . . . but he never rode with wildlings, either.* He did not fool himself; the free folk would make for unruly subjects and dangerous neighbors. Yet when he weighed Ygritte's red hair against the cold blue eyes of the wights, the choice was easy. "I agree."

"Good," King Stannis said, "for the surest way to seal a new alliance is with a marriage. I mean to wed my Lord of Winterfell to this wildling princess."

Perhaps Jon had ridden with the free folk too long; he could not help but laugh. "Your Grace," he said, "captive or no, if you think you can just *give* Val to me, I fear you have a deal to learn about wildling women. Whoever weds her had best be prepared to climb in her tower window and carry her off at swordpoint . . ."

"*Whoever?*" Stannis gave him a measuring look. "Does this mean you will not wed the girl? I warn you, she is part of the price you must pay, if you want your father's name and your father's castle.

This match is necessary, to help assure the loyalty of our new subjects. Are you refusing me, Jon Snow?"

"No," Jon said, too quickly. It was Winterfell the king was speaking of, and Winterfell was not to be lightly refused. "I mean . . . this has all come very suddenly, Your Grace. Might I beg you for some time to consider?"

"As you wish. But consider quickly. I am not a patient man, as your black brothers are about to discover." Stannis put a thin, fleshless hand on Jon's shoulder. "Say nothing of what we've discussed here today. To anyone. But when you return, you need only bend your knee, lay your sword at my feet, and pledge yourself to my service, and you shall rise again as Jon Stark, the Lord of Winterfell."

TYRION

When he heard noises through the thick wooden door of his cell, Tyrion Lannister prepared to die. *Past time*, he thought. *Come on, come on, make an end to it.* He pushed himself to his feet. His legs were asleep from being folded under him. He bent down and rubbed the knives from them. *I will not go stumbling and waddling to the headsman's block.*

He wondered whether they would kill him down here in the dark or drag him through the city so Ser Ilyn Payne could lop his head off. After his mummer's farce of a trial, his sweet sister and loving father might prefer to dispose of him quietly, rather than risk a public execution. *I could tell the mob a few choice things, if they let me speak.* But would they be that foolish?

As the keys rattled and the door to his cell pushed inward, creaking, Tyrion pressed back against the dampness of the wall, wishing for a weapon. *I can still bite and kick. I'll die with the taste of blood in my mouth, that's something.* He wished he'd been able to think of some rousing last words. "Bugger you all" was not like to earn him much of a place in the histories.

Torchlight fell across his face. He shielded his eyes with a hand. "*Come on*, are you frightened of a dwarf? Do it, you son of a poxy whore." His voice had grown hoarse from disuse.

"Is that any way to speak about our lady mother?" The man moved forward, a torch in his left hand. "This is even more ghastly than my cell at Riverrun, though not quite so dank."

For a moment, Tyrion could not breathe. "You?"

"Well, most of me." Jaime was gaunt, his hair hacked short. "I left a hand at Harrenhal. Bringing the Brave Companions across the narrow sea was not one of Father's better notions." He lifted his arm, and Tyrion saw the stump.

A bark of hysterical laughter burst from his lips. "Oh, gods," he said. "Jaime, I am so sorry, but . . . gods be good, look at the two of us. Handless and Noseless, the Lannister boys."

"There were days when my hand smelled so bad I wished I was noseless." Jaime lowered the torch, so the light bathed his brother's face. "An impressive scar."

Tyrion turned away from the glare. "They made me fight a battle without my big brother to protect me."

"I heard tell you almost burned the city down."

"A filthy lie. I only burned the river." Abruptly, Tyrion remembered where he was, and why. "Are you here to kill me?"

"Now that's ungrateful. Perhaps I should leave you here to rot if you're going to be so discourteous."

"Rotting is not the fate Cersei has in mind for me."

"Well no, if truth be told. You're to be beheaded on the morrow, out on the old tourney grounds."

Tyrion laughed again. "Will there be food? You'll have to help me with my last words, my wits have been running about like a rat in a root cellar."

"You won't need last words. I'm rescuing you." Jaime's voice was strangely solemn.

"Who said I required rescue?"

"You know, I'd almost forgotten what an annoying little man you are. Now that you've reminded me, I do believe I'll let Cersei cut your head off after all."

"Oh no you won't." He waddled out of the cell. "Is it day or night up above? I've lost all sense of time."

"Three hours past midnight. The city sleeps." Jaime slid the torch back into its sconce, on the wall between the cells.

The corridor was so poorly lit that Tyrion almost stumbled on the turnkey, sprawled across the cold stone floor. He prodded him with a toe. "Is he dead?"

"Asleep. The other three as well. The eunuch dosed their wine with sweetsleep, but not enough to kill them. Or so he swears. He is waiting back at the stair, dressed up in a septon's robe. You're going down into the sewers, and from there to the river. A galley is waiting in the bay. Varys has agents in the Free Cities who will see that you do not lack for funds . . . but try not to be conspicuous. Cersei will send men after you, I have no doubt. You might do well to take another name."

"Another name? Oh, certainly. And when the Faceless Men come to kill me, I'll say, 'No, you have the wrong man, I'm a *different* dwarf with a hideous facial scar.'" Both Lannisters laughed at the absurdity of it all. Then Jaime went to one knee and kissed him quickly once on each cheek, his lips brushing against the puckered ribbon of scar tissue.

"Thank you, Brother," Tyrion said. "For my life."

"It was . . . a debt I owed you." Jaime's voice was strange.

"A debt?" He cocked his head. "I do not understand."

"Good. Some doors are best left closed."

"Oh, dear," said Tyrion. "Is there something grim and ugly behind it? Could it be that someone said something *cruel* about me once? I'll try not to weep. Tell me."

"Tyrion . . ."

Jaime is afraid. "Tell me," Tyrion said again.

His brother looked away. "Tysha," he said softly.

"Tysha?" His stomach tightened. "What of her?"

"She was no whore. I never bought her for you. That was a lie that Father commanded me to tell. Tysha was . . . she was what she seemed to be. A crofter's daughter, chance met on the road."

Tyrion could hear the faint sound of his own breath whistling hollowly through the scar of his nose. Jaime could not meet his eyes. *Tysha.* He tried to remember what she had looked like. *A girl, she was only a girl, no older than Sansa.* "My wife," he croaked. "She wed me."

"For your gold, Father said. She was lowborn, you were a Lannister of Casterly Rock. All she wanted was the gold, which made her no different from a whore, so ... so it would not be a lie, not truly, and ... he said that you required a sharp lesson. That you would learn from it, and thank me later ..."

"*Thank* you?" Tyrion's voice was choked. "He gave her to his guards. A barracks full of guards. He made me ... watch." *Aye, and more than watch. I took her too ... my wife ...*

"I never knew he would do that. You must believe me."

"Oh, *must* I?" Tyrion snarled. "Why should I believe you about anything, ever? She was my *wife!*"

"Tyrion—"

He hit him. It was a slap, backhanded, but he put all his strength into it, all his fear, all his rage, all his pain. Jaime was squatting, unbalanced. The blow sent him tumbling backward to the floor. "I ... I suppose I earned that."

"Oh, you've earned more than that, Jaime. You and my sweet sister and our loving father, yes, I can't begin to tell you what you've earned. But you'll have it, that I swear to you. A Lannister always pays his debts." Tyrion waddled away, almost stumbling over the turnkey again in his haste. Before he had gone a dozen yards, he bumped up against an iron gate that closed the passage. *Oh, gods.* It was all he could do not to scream.

Jaime came up behind him. "I have the gaoler's keys."

"Then use them." Tyrion stepped aside.

Jaime unlocked the gate, pushed it open, and stepped through. He looked back over his shoulder. "Are you coming?"

"Not with you." Tyrion stepped through. "Give me the keys and go. I will find Varys on my own." He cocked his head and stared up at his brother with his mismatched eyes. "Jaime, can you fight left-handed?"

"Rather less well than you," Jaime said bitterly.

"Good. Then we will be well matched if we should ever meet again. The cripple and the dwarf."

Jaime handed him the ring of keys. "I gave you the truth. You owe me the same. Did you do it? Did you kill him?"

The question was another knife, twisting in his guts. "Are you sure you want to know?" asked Tyrion. "Joffrey would have been a worse king than Aerys ever was. He stole his father's dagger and gave it to a footpad to slit the throat of Brandon Stark, did you know that?"

"I . . . I thought he might have."

"Well, a son takes after his father. Joff would have killed me as well, once he came into his power. For the crime of being short and ugly, of which I am so conspicuously guilty."

"You have not answered my question."

"You poor stupid blind crippled fool. Must I spell every little thing out for you? Very well. Cersei is a lying whore, she's been fucking Lancel and Osmund Kettleblack and probably Moon Boy, for all I know. And I am the monster they all say I am. Yes, I killed your vile son." He made himself grin. It must have been a hideous sight to see, there in the torchlit gloom.

Jaime turned without a word and walked away.

Tyrion watched him go, striding on his long strong legs, and part of him wanted to call out, to tell him that it wasn't true, to beg for his forgiveness. But then he thought of Tysha, and he held his silence. He listened to the receding footsteps until he could hear them no longer, then waddled off to look for Varys.

The eunuch was lurking in the dark of a twisting turnpike stair, garbed in a moth-eaten brown robe with a hood that hid the paleness of his face. "You were so long, I feared that something had gone amiss," he said when he saw Tyrion.

"Oh, no," Tyrion assured him, in poisonous tones. "What could *possibly* have gone amiss?" He twisted his head back to stare up. "I sent for you during my trial."

"I could not come. The queen had me watched, night and day. I dared not help you."

"You're helping me now."

"Am I? Ah." Varys giggled. It seemed strangely out of place in this place of cold stone and echoing darkness. "Your brother can be most persuasive."

"Varys, you are as cold and slimy as a slug, has anyone ever told you? You did your best to kill me. Perhaps I ought to return the favor."

The eunuch sighed. "The faithful dog is kicked, and no matter how the spider weaves, he is never loved. But if you slay me here, I fear for you, my lord. You may never find your way back to daylight." His eyes glittered in the shifting torchlight, dark and wet. "These tunnels are full of traps for the unwary."

Tyrion snorted. "Unwary? I'm the wariest man who ever lived, you helped see to that." He rubbed at his nose. "So tell me, wizard, where is my innocent maiden wife?"

"I have found no trace of Lady Sansa in King's Landing, sad to say. Nor of Ser Dontos Hollard, who by rights should have turned up somewhere drunk by now. They were seen together on the serpentine steps the night she vanished. After that, nothing. There was much confusion that night. My little birds are silent." Varys gave a gentle tug at the dwarf's sleeve and pulled him into the stair. "My lord, we must away. Your path is down."

That's no lie, at least. Tyrion waddled along in the eunuch's wake, his heels scraping against the rough stone as they descended. It was very cold within the stairwell, a damp bone-chilling cold that set him to shivering at once. "What part of the dungeons are these?" he asked.

"Maegor the Cruel decreed four levels of dungeons for his castle," Varys replied. "On the upper level, there are large cells where common criminals may be confined together. They have narrow windows set high in the walls. The second level has the smaller cells where highborn captives are held. They have no windows, but torches in the halls cast light through the bars. On the third level the cells are smaller and the doors are wood. The black cells, men call them. That was where you were kept, and Eddard Stark before you. But there is a level lower still. Once a man is taken down to the fourth level, he never sees the sun again, nor hears a human voice, nor breathes a breath free of agonizing pain. Maegor had the cells on the fourth level built for torment." They had reached the bottom of the steps. An unlighted door opened before them. "This is the fourth level. Give me your hand, my lord. It is safer to walk in darkness here. There are things you would not wish to see."

Tyrion hung back a moment. Varys had already betrayed him once. Who knew what game the eunuch was playing? And what better place to murder a man than down in the darkness, in a place that no one knew existed? His body might never be found.

On the other hand, what choice did he have? To go back up the steps and walk out the main gate? No, that would not serve.

Jaime would not be afraid, he thought, before he remembered what Jaime had done to him. He took the eunuch by the hand and let himself be led through the black, following the soft scrape of leather on stone. Varys walked quickly, from time to time whispering, "Careful, there are three steps ahead," or, "The tunnel slopes downward here, my lord." *I arrived here a King's Hand, riding through the gates at the head of my own sworn men,* Tyrion reflected, *and I leave like a rat scuttling through the dark, holding hands with a spider.*

A light appeared ahead of them, too dim to be daylight, and grew as they hurried toward it. After a while he could see it was an arched doorway, closed off by another iron gate. Varys produced a key. They stepped through into a small round chamber. Five other doors opened off the room, each barred in iron. There was an opening in the ceiling as well, and a series of rungs set in the wall below, leading upward. An ornate brazier stood to one side, fashioned in the shape of a dragon's head. The coals in the beast's yawning mouth had burnt down to embers, but they still glowed with a sullen orange light. Dim as it was, the light was welcome after the blackness of the tunnel.

The juncture was otherwise empty, but on the floor was a mosaic of a three-headed dragon wrought in red and black tiles. Something niggled at Tyrion for a moment. Then it came to him. *This is the place Shae told me of, when Varys first led her to my bed.* "We are below the Tower of the Hand."

"Yes." Frozen hinges screamed in protest as Varys pulled open a long-closed door. Flakes of rust drifted to the floor. "This will take us out to the river."

Tyrion walked slowly to the ladder, ran his hand across the lowest rung. "This will take me up to my bedchamber."

"Your lord father's bedchamber now."

He looked up the shaft. "How far must I climb?"

"My lord, you are too weak for such follies, and there is besides no time. We must go."

"I have business above. How far?"

"Two hundred and thirty rungs, but whatever you intend—"

"Two hundred and thirty rungs, and then?"

"The tunnel to the left, but hear me—"

"How far along to the bedchamber?" Tyrion lifted a foot to the lowest rung of the ladder.

"No more than sixty feet. Keep one hand on the wall as you go. You will feel the doors. The bedchamber is the third." He sighed. "This is folly, my lord. Your brother has given you your life back. Would you cast it away, and mine with it?"

"Varys, the only thing I value less than my life just now is yours. Wait for me here." He turned his back on the eunuch and began to climb, counting silently as he went.

Rung by rung, he ascended into darkness. At first he could see the dim outline of each rung as he grasped it, and the rough grey texture of the stone behind, but as he climbed the black grew thicker. *Thirteen fourteen fifteen sixteen.* By thirty, his arms trembled with the strain of pulling. He paused a moment to catch his breath and glanced down. A circle of faint light shone far below, half obscured by his own feet. Tyrion resumed his ascent. *Thirty-nine forty forty-one.* By fifty, his legs burned. The ladder was endless, numbing. *Sixty-eight sixty-nine seventy.* By eighty, his back was a dull agony. Yet still he climbed. He could not have said why. *One thirteen one fourteen one fifteen.*

At two hundred and thirty, the shaft was black as pitch, but he could *feel* the warm air flowing from the tunnel to his left, like the breath of some great beast. He poked about awkwardly with a foot and edged off the ladder. The tunnel was even more cramped than the shaft. Any man of normal size would have had to crawl on hands and knees, but Tyrion was short enough to walk upright. *At last, a place made for dwarfs.* His boots scuffed softly against the stone. He walked slowly, counting steps, feeling for gaps in the walls. Soon he began to hear voices, muffled and indistinct at first, then clearer. He listened more closely. Two of his father's guardsmen were joking about the Imp's whore, saying how sweet it would be to fuck her, and how bad she must want a real cock in place of the dwarf's stunted little thing. "Most like it's got a crook in it," said Lum. That led him into a discussion of how Tyrion would die on the morrow. "He'll weep like a woman and beg for mercy, you'll see," Lum insisted. Lester figured he'd face the axe brave as a lion, being a Lannister, and he was willing to bet his new boots on it. "Ah, shit in your boots," said Lum, "you know they'd never fit these feet o'mine. Tell you what, if I win you can scour my bloody mail for a fortnight."

For the space of a few feet, Tyrion could hear every word of their haggling, but when he moved on, the voices faded quickly. *Small wonder Varys did not want me to climb the bloody ladder,* Tyrion thought, smiling in the dark. *Little birds indeed.*

He came to the third door and fumbled about for a long time before his fingers brushed a small iron hook set between two stones. When he pulled down on it, there was a soft rumble that sounded loud as an avalanche in the stillness, and a square of dull orange light opened a foot to his left.

The hearth! He almost laughed. The fireplace was full of hot ash, and a black log with a hot orange heart burning within. He edged past gingerly, taking quick steps so as not to burn his boots, the warm cinders crunching softly under his heels. When he found himself in what had once been his bedchamber, he stood a long moment, breathing the silence. Had his father heard? Would he reach for his sword, raise the hue and cry?

"M'lord?" a woman's voice called.

That might have hurt me once, when I still felt pain. The first step was the hardest. When he reached the bed Tyrion pulled the draperies aside and there she was, turning toward him with a sleepy smile on her lips. It died when she saw him. She pulled the blankets up to her chin, as if that would protect her.

"Were you expecting someone taller, sweetling?"

Big wet tears filled her eyes. "I never meant those things I said, the queen made me. *Please.* Your father frightens me so." She sat up, letting the blanket slide down to her lap. Beneath it she was naked, but for the chain about her throat. A chain of linked golden hands, each holding the next.

"My lady Shae," Tyrion said softly. "All the time I sat in the black cell waiting to die, I kept remembering how beautiful you were. In silk or roughspun or nothing at all . . ."

"M'lord will be back soon. You should go, or ... did you come to take me away?"

"Did you ever like it?" He cupped her cheek, remembering all the times he had done this before. All the times he'd slid his hands around her waist, squeezed her small firm breasts, stroked her short dark hair, touched her lips, her cheeks, her ears. All the times he had opened her with a finger to probe her secret sweetness and make her moan. "Did you ever like my touch?"

"More than anything," she said, "my giant of Lannister."

That was the worst thing you could have said, sweetling.

Tyrion slid a hand under his father's chain, and twisted. The links tightened, digging into her neck. "For hands of gold are always cold, but a woman's hands are warm," he said. He gave cold hands another twist as the warm ones beat away his tears.

Afterward, he found Lord Tywin's dagger on the bedside table and shoved it through his belt. A lion-headed mace, a poleaxe, and a crossbow had been hung on the walls. The poleaxe would be clumsy to wield inside a castle, and the mace was too high to reach, but a large wood-and-iron chest had been placed against the wall directly under the crossbow. He climbed up, pulled down the bow and a leather quiver packed with quarrels, jammed a foot into the stirrup, and pushed down until the bowstring cocked. Then he slipped a bolt into the notch.

Jaime had lectured him more than once on the drawbacks of crossbows. If Lum and Lester emerged from wherever they were talking, he'd never have time to reload, but at least he'd take one down to hell with him. Lum, if he had a choice. *You'll have to clean your own mail, Lum. You lose.*

Waddling to the door, he listened a moment, then eased it open slowly. A lamp burned in a stone niche, casting wan yellow light over the empty hallway. Only the flame was moving. Tyrion slid out, holding the crossbow down against his leg.

He found his father where he knew he'd find him, seated in the dimness of the privy tower, bedrobe hiked up around his hips. At the sound of steps, Lord Tywin raised his eyes.

Tyrion gave him a mocking half-bow. "My lord."

"Tyrion." If he was afraid, Tywin Lannister gave no hint of it. "Who released you from your cell?"

"I'd love to tell you, but I swore a holy oath."

"The eunuch," his father decided. "I'll have his head for this. Is that my crossbow? Put it down."

"Will you punish me if I refuse, Father?"

"This escape is folly. You are not to be killed, if that is what you fear. It's still my intent to send you to the Wall, but I could not do it without Lord Tyrell's consent. Put down the crossbow and we will go back to my chambers and talk of it."

"We can talk here just as well. Perhaps I don't choose to go to the Wall, Father. It's bloody cold up there, and I believe I've had enough coldness from you. So just tell me something, and I'll be on my way. One simple question, you owe me that much."

"I owe you nothing."

"You've given me less than that, all my life, but you'll give me this. What did you do with Tysha?"

"Tysha?"

He does not even remember her name. "The girl I married."

"Oh, yes. Your first whore."

Tyrion took aim at his father's chest. "The next time you say that word, I'll kill you."

"You do not have the courage."

"Shall we find out? It's a short word, and it seems to come so easily to your lips." Tyrion gestured impatiently with the bow. "Tysha. What did you do with her, after my little lesson?"

"I don't recall."

"Try harder. Did you have her killed?"

His father pursed his lips. "There was no reason for that, she'd learned her place ... and had been well paid for her day's work, I seem to recall. I suppose the steward sent her on her way. I never thought to inquire."

"On her way *where*?"

"Wherever whores go."

Tyrion's finger clenched. The crossbow *whanged* just as Lord Tywin started to rise. The bolt slammed into him above the groin and he sat back down with a grunt. The quarrel had sunk deep, right to the fletching. Blood seeped out around the shaft, dripping down into his pubic hair and over his bare thighs. "You shot me," he said incredulously, his eyes glassy with shock.

"You always were quick to grasp a situation, my lord," Tyrion said. "That must be why you're the Hand of the King."

"You ... you are no ... no son of mine."

"Now that's where you're wrong, Father. Why, I believe I'm you writ small. Do me a kindness now, and die quickly. I have a ship to catch."

For once, his father did what Tyrion asked him. The proof was the sudden stench, as his bowels loosened in the moment of death. *Well, he was in the right place for it*, Tyrion thought. But the stink that filled the privy gave ample evidence that the oft-repeated jape about his father was just another lie.

Lord Tywin Lannister did not, in the end, shit gold.

SAMWELL

The king was angry. Sam saw that at once.

As the black brothers entered one by one and knelt before him, Stannis shoved away his breakfast of hardbread, salt beef, and boiled eggs, and eyed them coldly. Beside him, the red woman Melisandre looked as if she found the scene amusing.

I have no place here, Sam thought anxiously, when her red eyes fell upon him. *Someone had to help Maester Aemon up the steps. Don't look at me, I'm just the maester's steward.* The others were contenders for the Old Bear's command, all but Bowen Marsh, who had withdrawn from the contest but remained castellan and Lord Steward. Sam did not understand why Melisandre should seem so interested in *him*.

King Stannis kept the black brothers on their knees for an extraordinarily long time. "Rise," he said at last. Sam gave Maester Aemon his shoulder to help him back up.

The sound of Lord Janos Slynt clearing his throat broke the strained silence. "Your Grace, let me say how pleased we are to be summoned here. When I saw your banners from the Wall, I knew the realm was saved. 'There comes a man who ne'er forgets his duty,' I said to good Ser Alliser. 'A *strong* man, and a true king.' May I congratulate you on your victory over the savages? The singers will make much of it, I know—"

"The singers may do as they like," Stannis snapped. "Spare me your fawning, Janos, it will not serve you." He rose to his feet and frowned at them all. "Lady Melisandre tells me that you have not yet chosen a Lord Commander. I am displeased. How much longer must this folly last?"

"Sire," said Bowen Marsh in a defensive tone, "no one has achieved two-thirds of the vote yet. It has only been ten days."

"Nine days too long. I have captives to dispose of, a realm to order, a war to fight. Choices must be made, decisions that involve the Wall and the Night's Watch. By rights your Lord Commander should have a voice in those decisions."

"He should, yes," said Janos Slynt. "But it must be said. We brothers are only simple soldiers. Soldiers, yes! And Your Grace will know that soldiers are most comfortable taking orders. They would benefit from your royal guidance, it seems to me. For the good of the realm. To help them choose wisely."

The suggestion outraged some of the others. "Do you want the king to wipe our arses for us too?" said Cotter Pyke angrily. "The choice of a Lord Commander belongs to the Sworn Brothers, and to them alone," insisted Ser Denys Mallister. "If they choose wisely they won't be choosing me," moaned Dolorous Edd. Maester Aemon, calm as always, said, "Your Grace, the Night's Watch has been choosing its own leader since Brandon the Builder raised the Wall. Through Jeor Mormont we have had nine hundred and ninety-seven Lords Commander in unbroken succession, each chosen by the men he would lead, a tradition many thousands of years old."

Stannis ground his teeth. "It is not my wish to tamper with your rights and traditions. As to *royal guidance*, Janos, if you mean that I ought to tell your brothers to choose you, have the courage to say so."

That took Lord Janos aback. He smiled uncertainly and began to sweat, but Bowen Marsh beside him said, "Who better to command the black cloaks than a man who once commanded the gold, sire?"

"Any of you, I would think. Even the cook." The look the king gave Slynt was cold. "Janos was hardly the first gold cloak ever to take a bribe, I grant you, but he may have been the first commander to fatten his purse by selling places and promotions. By the end, he must have had half the officers in the City Watch paying him part of their wages. Isn't that so, Janos?"

Slynt's neck was purpling. "Lies, all lies! A strong man makes enemies, Your Grace knows that, they whisper lies behind your back. Naught was ever proven, not a man came forward . . ."

"Two men who were prepared to come forward died suddenly on their rounds." Stannis narrowed his eyes. "Do not trifle with me, my lord. I saw the proof Jon Arryn laid before the small council. If I had been king you would have lost more than your office, I promise you, but Robert shrugged away your little lapses. 'They all steal,' I recall him saying. 'Better a thief we know than one we don't, the next man might be worse.' Lord Petyr's words in my brother's mouth, I'll warrant. Littlefinger had a nose for gold, and I'm certain he arranged matters so the crown profited as much from your corruption as you did yourself."

Lord Slynt's jowls were quivering, but before he could frame a further protest Maester Aemon said, "Your Grace, by law a man's past crimes and transgressions are wiped clean when he says his words and becomes a Sworn Brother of the Night's Watch."

"I am aware of that. If it happens that Lord Janos here is the best the Night's Watch can offer, I shall grit my teeth and choke him down. It is naught to me which man of you is chosen, so long as you *make a choice*. We have a war to fight."

"Your Grace," said Ser Denys Mallister, in tones of wary courtesy. "If you are speaking of the wildlings . . ."

"I am not. And you know that, ser."

"And you must know that whilst we are thankful for the aid you rendered us against Mance Rayder, we can offer you no help in your contest for the throne. The Night's Watch takes no part in the wars of the Seven Kingdoms. For eight thousand years—"

"I know your history, Ser Denys," the king said brusquely. "I give you my word, I shall not ask you to lift your swords against any of the rebels and usurpers who plague me. I do expect that you will continue to defend the Wall as you always have."

"We'll defend the Wall to the last man," said Cotter Pyke.

"Probably me," said Dolorous Edd, in a resigned tone.

Stannis crossed his arms. "I shall require a few other things from you as well. Things that you may not be so quick to give. I want your castles. And I want the Gift."

Those blunt words burst among the black brothers like a pot of wildfire tossed onto a brazier. Marsh, Mallister, and Pyke all tried to speak at once. King Stannis let them talk. When they were done, he said, "I have three times the men you do. I can take the lands if I wish, but I would prefer to do this legally, with your consent."

"The Gift was given to the Night's Watch in perpetuity, Your Grace," Bowen Marsh insisted.

"Which means it cannot be lawfully seized, attainted, or taken from you. But what was given once can be given again."

"What will you do with the Gift?" demanded Cotter Pyke.

"Make better use of it than you have. As to the castles, Eastwatch, Castle Black, and the Shadow Tower shall remain yours. Garrison them as you always have, but I must take the others for *my* garrisons if we are to hold the Wall."

"You do not have the men," objected Bowen Marsh.

"Some of the abandoned castles are scarce more than ruins," said Othell Yarwyck, the First Builder.

"Ruins can be rebuilt."

"Rebuilt?" Yarwyck said. "But who will do the work?"

"That is my concern. I shall require a list from you, detailing the present state of every castle and what might be required to restore it. I mean to have them all garrisoned again within the year, and nightfires burning before their gates."

"Nightfires?" Bowen Marsh gave Melisandre an uncertain look. "We're to light nightfires now?"

"You are." The woman rose in a swirl of scarlet silk, her long copper-bright hair tumbling about her shoulders. "Swords alone cannot hold this darkness back. Only the light of the Lord can do that. Make no mistake, good sers and valiant brothers, the war we've come to fight is no petty squabble over lands and honors. Ours is a war for life itself, and should we fail the world dies with us."

The officers did not know how to take that, Sam could see.

Bowen Marsh and Othell Yarwyck exchanged a doubtful look, Janos Slynt was fuming, and Three-Finger Hobb looked as though he would sooner be back chopping carrots. But all of them seemed surprised to hear Maester Aemon murmur, "It is the war for the dawn you speak of, my lady. But where is the prince that was promised?"

"He stands before you," Melisandre declared, "though you do not have the eyes to see. Stannis Baratheon is Azor Ahai come again, the warrior of fire. In him the prophecies are fulfilled. The red comet blazed across the sky to herald his coming, and he bears Lightbringer, the red sword of heroes."

Her words seemed to make the king desperately uncomfortable, Sam saw. Stannis ground his teeth, and said, "You called and I came, my lords. Now you must live with me, or die with me. Best get used to that." He made a brusque gesture. "That's all. Maester, stay a moment. And you, Tarly. The rest of you may go."

Me? Sam thought, stricken, as his brothers were bowing and making their way out. *What does he want with me?*

"You are the one that killed the creature in the snow," King Stannis said, when only the four of them remained.

"Sam the Slayer." Melisandre smiled.

Sam felt his face turning red. "No, my lady. Your Grace. I mean, I am, yes. I'm Samwell Tarly, yes."

"Your father is an able soldier," King Stannis said. "He defeated my brother once, at Ashford. Mace Tyrell has been pleased to claim the honors for that victory, but Lord Randyll had decided matters before Tyrell ever found the battlefield. He slew Lord Cafferen with that great Valyrian sword of his and sent his head to Aerys." The king rubbed his jaw with a finger. "You are not the sort of son I would expect such a man to have."

"I . . . I am not the sort of son he wanted, sire."

"If you had not taken the black, you would make a useful hostage," Stannis mused.

"He has taken the black, sire," Maester Aemon pointed out.

"I am well aware of that," the king said. "I am aware of more than you know, Aemon Targaryen."

The old man inclined his head. "I am only Aemon, sire. We give up our House names when we forge our maester's chains."

The king gave that a curt nod, as if to say he knew and did not care. "You slew this creature with an obsidian dagger, I am told," he said to Sam.

"Y-yes, Your Grace. Jon Snow gave it to me."

"Dragonglass." The red woman's laugh was music. "*Frozen fire*, in the tongue of old Valyria. Small wonder it is anathema to these cold children of the Other."

"On Dragonstone, where I had my seat, there is much of this obsidian to be seen in the old tunnels beneath the mountain," the king told Sam. "Chunks of it, boulders, ledges. The great part of it was black, as I recall, but there was some green as well, some red, even purple. I have sent word to Ser Rolland my castellan to begin mining it. I will not hold Dragonstone for very much longer, I fear, but perhaps the Lord of Light shall grant us enough *frozen fire* to arm ourselves against these creatures, before the castle falls."

Sam cleared his throat. "S-sire. The dagger . . . the dragonglass only shattered when I tried to stab a wight."

Melisandre smiled. "Necromancy animates these wights, yet they are still only dead flesh. Steel and fire will serve for them. The ones you call the Others are something more."

"Demons made of snow and ice and cold," said Stannis Baratheon. "The ancient enemy. The only enemy that matters." He considered Sam again. "I am told that you and this wildling girl passed beneath the Wall, through some magic gate."

"The B-black Gate," Sam stammered. "Below the Nightfort."

"The Nightfort is the largest and oldest of the castles on the Wall," the king said. "That is where I intend to make my seat, whilst I fight this war. You will show me this gate."

"I," said Sam, "I w-will, if . . ." *If it is still there. If it will open for a man not of the black. If . . .*

"You will," snapped Stannis. "I shall tell you when."

Maester Aemon smiled. "Your Grace," he said, "before we go, I wonder if you would do us the great honor of showing us this wondrous blade we have all heard so very much of."

"You want to see Lightbringer? A *blind* man?"

"Sam shall be my eyes."

The king frowned. "Everyone else has seen the thing, why not a blind man?" His swordbelt and scabbard hung from a peg near the hearth. He took the belt down and drew the longsword out. Steel scraped against wood and leather, and radiance filled the solar; shimmering, shifting, a dance of gold and orange and red light, all the bright colors of fire.

"Tell me, Samwell." Maester Aemon touched his arm.

"It *glows*," said Sam, in a hushed voice. "As if it were on fire. There are no flames, but the steel is yellow and red and orange, all flashing and glimmering, like sunshine on water, but prettier. I wish you could see it, Maester."

"I see it now, Sam. A sword full of sunlight. So lovely to behold." The old man bowed stiffly. "Your Grace. My lady. This was most kind of you."

When King Stannis sheathed the shining sword, the room seemed to grow very dark, despite the sunlight streaming through the window. "Very well, you've seen it. You may return to your duties now. And remember what I said. Your brothers will chose a Lord Commander tonight, or I shall make them wish they had."

Maester Aemon was lost in thought as Sam helped him down the narrow turnpike stair. But as they were crossing the yard, he said, "I felt no heat. Did you, Sam?"

"Heat? From the sword?" He thought back. "The air around it was shimmering, the way it does above a hot brazier."

"Yet you *felt* no heat, did you? And the scabbard that held this sword, it is wood and leather, yes? I heard the sound when His Grace drew out the blade. Was the leather scorched, Sam? Did the wood seem burnt or blackened?"

"No," Sam admitted. "Not that I could see."

Maester Aemon nodded. Back in his own chambers, he asked Sam to set a fire and help him to his chair beside the hearth. "It is hard to be so old," he sighed as he settled onto the cushion. "And harder still to be so blind. I miss the sun. And books. I miss books most of all." Aemon waved a hand. "I shall have no more need of you till the choosing."

"The choosing ... Maester, isn't there something you could do? What the king said of Lord Janos ..."

"I recall," Maester Aemon said, "but Sam, I am a maester, chained and sworn. My duty is to counsel the Lord Commander, whoever he might be. It would not be proper for me to be seen to favor one contender over another."

"I'm not a maester," said Sam. "Could *I* do something?"

Aemon turned his blind white eyes toward Sam's face, and smiled softly. "Why, I don't know, Samwell. Could you?"

I could, Sam thought. *I have to.* He had to do it right away, too. If he hesitated he was certain to lose his courage. *I am a man of the Night's Watch,* he reminded himself as he hurried across the yard. *I am. I can do this.* There had been a time when he had quaked and squeaked if Lord Mormont so much as looked at him, but that was the old Sam, before the Fist of the First Men and Craster's Keep, before the wights and Coldhands and the Other on his dead horse. He was braver now. *Gilly made me braver,* he'd told Jon. It was true. It had to be true.

Cotter Pyke was the scarier of the two commanders, so Sam went to him first, while his courage was still hot. He found him in the old Shieldhall, dicing with three of his Eastwatch men and a red-headed sergeant who had come from Dragonstone with Stannis.

When Sam begged leave to speak with him, though, Pyke barked an order, and the others took the dice and coins and left them.

No man would ever call Cotter Pyke handsome, though the body under his studded brigantine and roughspun breeches was lean and hard and wiry strong. His eyes were small and close-set, his nose broken, his widow's peak as sharply pointed as the head of a spear. The pox had ravaged his face badly, and the beard he'd grown to hide the scars was thin and scraggly.

"Sam the Slayer!" he said, by way of greeting. "Are you sure you stabbed an Other, and not some child's snow knight?"

This isn't starting well. "It was the dragonglass that killed it, my lord," Sam explained feebly.

"Aye, no doubt. Well, out with it, Slayer. Did the maester send you to me?"

"The maester?" Sam swallowed. "I . . . I just left him, my lord." That wasn't truly a lie, but if Pyke chose to read it wrong, it might make him more inclined to listen. Sam took a deep breath and launched into his plea.

Pyke cut him off before he'd said twenty words. "You want me to kneel down and kiss the hem of Mallister's pretty cloak, is that it? I might have known. You lordlings all flock like sheep. Well, tell Aemon that he's wasted your breath and my time. If anyone withdraws it should be Mallister. The man's too bloody *old* for the job, maybe you ought to go tell him that. We choose him, and we're like to be back here in a year, choosing someone else."

"He's old," Sam agreed, "but he's well ex-experienced."

"At sitting in his tower and fussing over maps, maybe. What does he plan to do, write letters to the wights? He's a knight, well and good, but he's not a *fighter*, and I don't give a kettle of piss who he unhorsed in some fool tourney fifty years ago. The Halfhand fought all his battles, even an old blind man should see that. And we need a fighter more than ever with this bloody king on top of us. Today it's ruins and empty fields, well and good, but what will *His Grace* want come the morrow? You think *Mallister* has the belly to stand up to Stannis Baratheon and that red bitch?" He laughed. "I don't."

"You won't support him, then?" said Sam, dismayed.

"Are you Sam the Slayer or Deaf Dick? No, I won't support him." Pyke jabbed a finger at his face. "Understand this, boy. I don't *want* the bloody job, and never did. I fight best with a deck beneath me, not a horse, and Castle Black is too far from the sea. But I'll be buggered with a red-hot sword before I turn the Night's Watch over to that preening eagle from the Shadow Tower. And you can run back to the old man and tell him I said so, if he asks." He stood. "Get out of my sight."

It took all the courage Sam had left in him to say, "W-what if there was someone else? Could you s-support someone else?"

"Who? Bowen Marsh? The man counts spoons. Othell's a follower, does what he's told and does it well, but no more'n that. Slynt . . . well, his men like him, I'll grant you, and it would almost be worth it to stick him down the royal craw and see if Stannis gagged, but no. There's too much of King's Landing in that one. A toad grows wings and thinks he's a bloody dragon." Pyke laughed. "Who does that leave, Hobb? We could pick him, I suppose, only then who's going to boil your mutton, Slayer? You look like a man who likes his bloody mutton."

There was nothing more to say. Defeated, Sam could only stammer out his thanks and take his leave. *I will do better with Ser Denys*, he tried to tell himself as he walked through the castle. Ser Denys was a knight, highborn and well-spoken, and he had treated Sam most courteously when he'd found him and Gilly on the road. *Ser Denys will listen to me, he has to.*

The commander of the Shadow Tower had been born beneath the Booming Tower of Seagard, and looked every inch a Mallister. Sable trimmed his collar and accented the sleeves of his black velvet doublet. A silver eagle fastened its claws in the gathered folds of his cloak. His beard was white as snow, his hair was largely gone, and his face was deeply lined, it was true. Yet he still had grace in his movements and teeth in his mouth, and the years had dimmed neither his blue-grey eyes nor his courtesy.

"My lord of Tarly," he said, when his steward brought Sam to him in the Lance, where the Shadow Tower men were staying. "I am pleased to see that you've recovered from your ordeal. Might I offer you a cup of wine? Your lady mother is a Florent, I recall. One day, I must tell you about the time I unhorsed both of your grandfathers in the same tourney. Not today, though, I know we have more pressing concerns. You come from Maester Aemon, to be sure. Does he have counsel to offer me?"

Sam took a sip of wine, and chose his words with care. "A maester chained and sworn . . . it would not be proper for him to be seen as having influenced the choice of Lord Commander . . ."

The old knight smiled. "Which is why he has not come to me himself. Yes, I quite understand, Samwell. Aemon and I are both old men, and wise in such matters. Say what you came to say."

The wine was sweet, and Ser Denys listened to Sam's plea with grave courtesy, unlike Cotter Pyke. But when he was done, the old knight shook his head. "I agree that it would be a dark day in our history if a king were to name our Lord Commander. This king especially. He is not like to keep his crown for long. But truly, Samwell, it ought to be Pyke who withdraws. I have more support than he does, and I am better suited to the office."

"You are," Sam agreed, "but Cotter Pyke might serve. It's said he has oft proved himself in battle." He did not mean to offend Ser Denys by praising his rival, but how else could he convince him to withdraw?

"Many of my brothers have proved themselves in battle. It is not enough. Some matters cannot be settled with a battleaxe. Maester Aemon will understand that, though Cotter Pyke does not. The Lord Commander of the Night's Watch is a *lord*, first and foremost. He must be able to treat with other lords ... and with kings as well. He must be a man worthy of respect." Ser Denys leaned forward. "We are the sons of great lords, you and I. We know the importance of birth, blood, and that early training that can ne'er be replaced. I was a squire at twelve, a knight at eighteen, a champion at two-and-twenty. I have been the commander at the Shadow Tower for thirty-three years. Blood, birth, and training have fitted me to deal with kings. Pyke ... well, did you hear him this morning, asking if His Grace would wipe his bottom? Samwell, it is not my habit to speak unkindly of my brothers, but let us be frank ... the ironborn are a race of pirates and thieves, and Cotter Pyke was raping and murdering when he was still half a boy. Maester Harmune reads and writes his letters, and has for years. No, loath as I am to disappoint Maester Aemon, I could not in honor stand aside for Pyke of Eastwatch."

This time Sam was ready. "Might you for someone else? If it was someone more suitable?"

Ser Denys considered a moment. "I have never desired the honor for its own sake. At the last choosing, I stepped aside gratefully when Lord Mormont's name was offered, just as I had for Lord Qorgyle at the choosing before that. So long as the Night's Watch remains in good hands, I am content. But Bowen Marsh is not equal to the task, no more than Othell Yarwyck. And this so-called Lord of Harrenhal is a butcher's whelp upjumped by the Lannisters. Small wonder he is venal and corrupt."

"There's another man," Sam blurted out. "Lord Commander Mormont trusted him. So did Donal Noye and Qhorin Halfhand. Though he's not as highly born as you, he comes from old blood. He was castle-born and castle-raised, and he learned sword and lance from a knight and letters from a maester of the Citadel. His father was a lord, and his brother a king."

Ser Denys stroked his long white beard. "Mayhaps," he said, after a long moment. "He is very young, but . . . mayhaps. He might serve, I grant you, though I would be more suitable. I have no doubt of that. I would be the wiser choice."

Jon said there could be honor in a lie, if it were told for the right reason. Sam said, "If we do not choose a Lord Commander tonight, King Stannis means to name Cotter Pyke. He said as much to Maester Aemon this morning, after all of you had left."

"I see." Ser Denys rose. "I must think on this. Thank you, Samwell. And give my thanks to Maester Aemon as well."

Sam was trembling by the time he left the Lance. *What have I done?* he thought. *What have I said?* If they caught him in his lie, they would . . . *what? Send me to the Wall? Rip my entrails out? Turn me into a wight?* Suddenly it all seemed absurd. How could he be so frightened of Cotter Pyke and Ser Denys Mallister, when he had seen a raven eating Small Paul's face?

Pyke was not pleased by his return. "You again? Make it quick, you are starting to annoy me."

"I only need a moment more," Sam promised. "You won't withdraw for Ser Denys, you said, but you might for someone else."

"Who is it this time, Slayer? You?"

"No. A fighter. Donal Noye gave him the Wall when the wildlings came, and he was the Old Bear's squire. The only thing is, he's bastard-born."

Cotter Pyke laughed. "Bloody hell. That would shove a spear up Mallister's arse, wouldn't it? Might be worth it just for that. How bad could the boy be?" He snorted. "I'd be better, though. I'm what's needed, any fool can see that."

"Any fool," Sam agreed, "even me. But . . . well, I shouldn't be telling you, but . . . King Stannis means to force Ser Denys on us, if we do not choose a man tonight. I heard him tell Maester Aemon that, after the rest of you were sent away."

JON

Iron Emmett was a long, lanky young ranger whose endurance, strength, and swordsmanship were the pride of Eastwatch. Jon always came away from their sessions stiff and sore, and woke the next day covered with bruises, which was just the way he wanted it. He would never get any better going up against the likes of Satin and Horse, or even Grenn.

Most days he gave as good as he got, Jon liked to think, but not today. He had hardly slept last night, and after an hour of restless tossing he had given up even the attempt, dressed, and walked the top of the Wall till the sun came up, wrestling with Stannis Baratheon's offer. The lack of sleep was catching up with him now, and Emmett was hammering him mercilessly across the yard, driving him back on his heels with one long looping cut after another, and slamming him with his shield from time to time for good measure. Jon's arm had gone numb from the shock of impact, and the edgeless practice sword seemed to be growing heavier with every passing moment.

He was almost ready to lower his blade and call a halt when Emmett feinted low and came in over his shield with a savage forehand slash that caught Jon on the temple. He staggered, his helm and head both ringing from the force of the blow. For half a heartbeat the world beyond his eyeslit was a blur.

And then the years were gone, and he was back at Winterfell once more, wearing a quilted leather coat in place of mail and plate. His sword was made of wood, and it was Robb who stood facing him, not Iron Emmett.

Every morning they had trained together, since they were big enough to walk; Snow and Stark, spinning and slashing about the wards of Winterfell, shouting and laughing, sometimes crying when there was no one else to see. They were not little boys when they fought, but knights and mighty heroes. "I'm Prince Aemon the Dragonknight," Jon would call out, and Robb would shout back, "Well, I'm Florian the Fool." Or Robb would say, "I'm the Young Dragon," and Jon would reply, "I'm Ser Ryam Redwyne."

That morning he called it first. "I'm Lord of Winterfell!" he cried, as he had a hundred times before. Only this time, *this* time, Robb had answered, "You can't be Lord of Winterfell, you're bastard-born. My lady mother says you can't ever be the Lord of Winterfell."

I thought I had forgotten that. Jon could taste blood in his mouth, from the blow he'd taken.

In the end, Halder and Horse had to pull him away from Iron Emmett, one man on either arm. The ranger sat on the ground dazed, his shield half in splinters, the visor of his helm knocked askew, and his sword six yards away. "Jon, enough," Halder was shouting, "he's down, you disarmed him. *Enough!*"

No. Not enough. Never enough. Jon let his sword drop. "I'm sorry," he muttered. "Emmett, are you hurt?"

Iron Emmett pulled his battered helm off. "Was there some part of *yield* you could not comprehend, Lord Snow?" It was said amiably, though. Emmett was an amiable man, and he loved the song of swords. "Warrior defend me," he groaned, "now I know how Qhorin Halfhand must have felt."

That was too much. Jon wrenched free of his friends and retreated to the armory, alone. His ears were still ringing from the blow Emmett had dealt him. He sat on the bench and buried his head in his hands. *Why am I so angry?* he asked himself, but it was a stupid question. *Lord of Winterfell. I could be the Lord of Winterfell. My father's heir.*

It was not Lord Eddard's face he saw floating before him, though; it was Lady Catelyn's. With her deep blue eyes and hard cold mouth, she looked a bit like Stannis. *Iron,* he thought, *but brittle.* She was looking at him the way she used to look at him at Winterfell, whenever he had bested Robb at swords or sums or most anything. *Who are you?* that look had always seemed to say. *This is not your place. Why are you here?*

His friends were still out in the practice yard, but Jon was in no fit state to face them. He left the armory by the back, descending a steep flight of stone steps to the wormways, the tunnels that linked the castle's keeps and towers below the earth. It was short walk to the bathhouse, where he took a cold plunge to wash the sweat off and soaked in a hot stone tub. The warmth took some of the ache from his muscles and made him think of Winterfell's muddy pools, steaming and bubbling in the godswood. *Winterfell,* he thought. *Theon left it burned and broken, but I could restore it.* Surely his father would have wanted that, and Robb as well. They would never have wanted the castle left in ruins.

You can't be the Lord of Winterfell, you're bastard-born, he heard Robb say again. And the stone kings were growling at him with granite tongues. *You do not belong here. This is not your place.* When Jon closed his eyes he saw the heart tree, with its pale limbs, red leaves, and solemn face. The weirwood was the heart of Winterfell, Lord Eddard always said . . . but to save the castle Jon would have to tear that heart up by its ancient roots, and feed it to the red woman's hungry fire god. *I have no right,* he thought. *Winterfell belongs to the old gods.*

The sound of voices echoing off the vaulted ceiling brought him back to Castle Black. "I don't know," a man was saying, in a voice thick with doubts. "Maybe if I knew the man better . . . Lord Stannis didn't have much good to say of him, I'll tell you that."

"When has Stannis Baratheon ever had much good to say of anyone?" Ser Alliser's flinty voice was unmistakable. "If we let Stannis choose our Lord Commander, we become his bannermen in all but name. Tywin Lannister is not like to forget that, and you know it will be Lord Tywin who wins in the end. He's already beaten Stannis once, on the Blackwater."

"Lord Tywin favors Slynt," said Bowen Marsh, in a fretful, anxious voice. "I can show you his letter, Othell. 'Our faithful friend and servant,' he called him."

Jon Snow sat up suddenly, and the three men froze at the sound of the slosh. "My lords," he said with cold courtesy.

"What are you doing here, bastard?" Thorne asked.

"Bathing. But don't let me spoil your plotting." Jon climbed from the water, dried, dressed, and left them to conspire.

Outside, he found he had no idea where he was going. He walked past the shell of the Lord Commander's Tower, where once he'd saved the Old Bear from a dead man; past the spot where Ygritte had died with that sad smile on her face; past the King's Tower where he and Satin and Deaf Dick Follard had waited for the Magnar and his Thenns; past the heaped and charred remains of the great wooden stair. The inner gate was open, so Jon went down the tunnel, through the Wall. He could feel the cold around him, the weight of all the ice above his head. He walked past the place where Donal Noye and Mag the Mighty had fought and died together, through the new outer gate, and back into the pale cold sunlight.

Only then did he permit himself to stop, to take a breath, to think. Othell Yarwyck was not a man of strong convictions, except when it came to wood and stone and mortar. The Old Bear had known that.

Thorne and Marsh will sway him, Yarwyck will support Lord Janos, and Lord Janos will be chosen Lord Commander. And what does that leave me, if not Winterfell?

A wind swirled against the Wall, tugging at his cloak. He could feel the cold coming off the ice the way heat comes off a fire. Jon pulled up his hood and began to walk again. The afternoon was growing old, and the sun was low in the west. A hundred yards away was the camp where King Stannis had confined his wildling captives within a ring of ditches, sharpened stakes, and high wooden fences. To his left were three great firepits, where the victors had burned the bodies of all the free folk to die beneath the Wall, huge pelted giants and little Hornfoot men alike. The killing ground was still a desolation of scorched weeds and hardened pitch, but Mance's people had left traces of themselves everywhere; a torn hide that might have been part of a tent, a giant's maul, the wheel of a chariot, a broken spear, a pile of mammoth dung. On the edge of the haunted forest, where the tents had been, Jon found an oakwood stump and sat.

Ygritte wanted me to be a wildling. Stannis wants me to be the Lord of Winterfell. But what do I want? The sun crept down the sky to dip behind the Wall where it curved through the western hills. Jon watched as that towering expanse of ice took on the reds and pinks of sunset. *Would I sooner be hanged for a turncloak by Lord Janos, or forswear my vows, marry Val, and become the Lord of Winterfell?* It seemed an easy choice when he thought of it in those terms . . . though if Ygritte had still been alive, it might have been even easier. Val was a stranger to him. She was not hard on the eyes, certainly, and she had been sister to Mance Rayder's queen, but still . . .

I would need to steal her if I wanted her love, but she might give me children. I might someday hold a son of my own blood in my arms. A son was something Jon Snow had never dared dream of, since he decided to live his life on the Wall. *I could name him Robb. Val would want to keep her sister's son, but we could foster him at Winterfell, and Gilly's boy as well. Sam would never need to tell his lie. We'd find a place for Gilly too, and Sam could come visit her once a year or so. Mance's son and Craster's would grow up brothers, as I once did with Robb.*

He wanted it, Jon knew then. He wanted it as much as he had ever wanted anything. *I have always wanted it,* he thought, guiltily. *May the gods forgive me.* It was a hunger inside him, sharp as a dragonglass blade. A hunger . . . he could feel it. It was food he needed, prey, a red deer that stank of fear or a great elk proud and defiant. He needed to kill and fill his belly with fresh meat and hot dark blood. His mouth began to water with the thought.

It was a long moment before he understood what was happening. When he did, he bolted to his feet. "*Ghost?*" He turned toward the wood, and there he came, padding silently out of the green dusk, the breath coming warm and white from his open jaws. "*Ghost!*" he shouted, and the direwolf broke into a run. He was leaner than he had been, but bigger as well, and the only sound he made was the soft crunch of dead leaves beneath his paws. When he reached Jon, he leapt, and they wrestled amidst brown grass and long shadows as the stars came out above them. "Gods, wolf, where have you *been?*" Jon said when Ghost stopped worrying at his forearm. "I thought you'd died on me, like Robb and Ygritte and all the rest. I've had no sense of you, not since I climbed the Wall, not even in dreams." The direwolf had no answer, but he licked Jon's face with a tongue like a wet rasp, and his eyes caught the last light and shone like two great red suns.

Red eyes, Jon realized, *but not like Melisandre's.* He had a weirwood's eyes. *Red eyes, red mouth, white fur. Blood and bone, like a heart tree. He belongs to the old gods, this one.* And he alone of all the direwolves was white. Six pups they'd found in the late summer snows, him and Robb; five that were grey and black and brown, for the five Starks, and one white, as white as Snow.

He had his answer then.

Beneath the Wall, the queen's men were kindling their nightfire. He saw Melisandre emerge from the tunnel with the king beside her, to lead the prayers she believed would keep the dark away. "Come, Ghost," Jon told the wolf. "With me. You're hungry, I know. I could feel it." They ran together for the gate, circling wide around the nightfire, where reaching flames clawed at the black belly of the night.

The king's men were much in evidence in the yards of Castle Black. They stopped as Jon went by, and gaped at him. None of them had ever seen a direwolf before, he realized, and Ghost was twice as large as the common wolves that prowled their southron greenwoods. As he walked toward the armory, Jon chanced to look up and saw Val standing in her tower window. *I'm sorry,* he thought. *I'm not the man to steal you out of there.*

In the practice yard, he came upon a dozen king's men with torches and long spears in their hands. Their sergeant looked at Ghost and scowled, and a couple of his men lowered their spears until the knight who led them said, "Move aside and let them pass." To Jon he said, "You're late for your supper."

"Then get out of my way, ser," Jon replied, and he did.

He could hear the noise even before he reached the bottom of the steps; raised voices, curses, someone pounding on a table. Jon stepped into the vault all but unnoticed. His brothers crowded the benches and the tables, but more were standing and shouting than were sitting, and no one was eating. There was no food. *What's happening here?* Lord Janos Slynt was bellowing about turncloaks and treason, Iron Emmett stood on a table with a naked sword in his fist, Three-Finger Hobb was cursing a ranger from the Shadow Tower ... some Eastwatch man slammed his fist onto the table again and again, demanding quiet, but all that did was add to the din echoing off the vaulted ceiling.

Pyp was the first to see Jon. He grinned at the sight of Ghost, put two fingers in his mouth, and whistled as only a mummer's boy could whistle. The shrill sound cut through the clamor like a sword. As Jon walked toward the tables, more of the brothers took note, and fell quiet. A hush spread across the cellar, until the only sounds were Jon's heels clicking on the stone floor, and the soft crackle of the logs in the hearth.

Ser Alliser Thorne shattered the silence. "The turncloak graces us with his presence at last."

Lord Janos was red-faced and quivering. "The *beast*," he gasped. "Look! The beast that tore the life from Halfhand. A warg walks among us, brothers. A *WARG*! This ... this *creature* is not fit to lead us! This *beastling* is not fit to live!"

Ghost bared his teeth, but Jon put a hand on his head. "My lord," he said, "will you tell me what's happened here?"

Maester Aemon answered, from the far end of the hall. "Your name has been put forth as Lord Commander, Jon."

That was so absurd Jon had to smile. "By who?" he said, looking for his friends. This had to be one of Pyp's japes, surely. But Pyp shrugged at him, and Grenn shook his head. It was Dolorous Edd Tollett who stood. "By me. Aye, it's a terrible cruel thing to do to a friend, but better you than me."

Lord Janos started sputtering again. "This, this is an outrage. We ought to hang this *boy*. Yes! Hang him, I say, hang him for a turncloak and a warg, along with his friend Mance Rayder. Lord *Commander*? I will not have it, I will not suffer it!"

Cotter Pyke stood up. "*You* won't suffer it? Might be you had those gold cloaks trained to lick your bloody arse, but you're wearing a black cloak now."

"Any brother may offer any name for our consideration, so long as the man has said his vows," Ser Denys Mallister said. "Tollett is well within his rights, my lord."

A dozen men started to talk at once, each trying to drown out the others, and before long half the hall was shouting once more. This time it was Ser Alliser Thorne who leapt up on the table, and raised his hands for quiet. "*Brothers!*" he cried, "this gains us naught. I say we vote. This *king* who has taken the King's Tower has posted men at all the doors to see that we do not eat nor leave till we have made a choice. So be it! We will choose, and choose again, all night if need be, until we have our lord . . . but before we cast our tokens, I believe our First Builder has something to say to us."

Othell Yarwyck stood up slowly, frowning. The big builder rubbed his long lantern jaw and said, "Well, I'm pulling my name out. If you wanted me, you had ten chances to choose me, and you didn't. Not enough of you, anyway. I was going to say that those who were casting a token for me ought to choose Lord Janos . . ."

Ser Alliser nodded. "Lord Slynt is the best possible—"

"I wasn't *done*, Alliser," Yarwyck complained. "Lord Slynt commanded the City Watch in King's Landing, we all know, and he was Lord of Harrenhal . . ."

"He's never *seen* Harrenhal," Cotter Pyke shouted out.

"Well, that's so," said Yarwyck. "Anyway, now that I'm standing here, I don't recall why I thought Slynt would be such a good choice. That would be sort of kicking King Stannis in the mouth, and I don't see how that serves us. Might be Snow would be better. He's been longer on the Wall, he's Ben Stark's nephew, and he served the Old Bear as squire." Yarwyck shrugged. "Pick who you want, just so it's not me." He sat down.

Janos Slynt had turned from red to purple, Jon saw, but Ser Alliser Thorne had gone pale. The Eastwatch man was pounding his fist on the table again, but now he was shouting for the kettle. Some of his friends took up the cry. "*Kettle!*" they roared, as one. "*Kettle, kettle, KETTLE!*"

The kettle was in the corner by the hearth, a big black potbellied thing with two huge handles and a heavy lid. Maester Aemon said a word to Sam and Clydas and they went and grabbed the handles and dragged the kettle over to the table. A few of the brothers were already queueing up by the token barrels as Clydas took the lid off and almost dropped it on his foot. With a raucous scream and a clap of wings, a huge raven burst out of the kettle. It flapped upward, seeking the rafters perhaps, or a window to make its escape, but there were no rafters in the vault, nor windows either. The raven was trapped. Cawing loudly, it circled the hall, once, twice, three times. And Jon heard Samwell Tarly shout, "I know that bird! That's Lord Mormont's raven!"

The raven landed on the table nearest Jon. "*Snow*," it cawed. It was an old bird, dirty and bedraggled. "*Snow*," it said again, "*Snow, snow, snow.*" It walked to the end of the table, spread its wings again, and flew to Jon's shoulder.

Lord Janos Slynt sat down so heavily he made a *thump*, but Ser Alliser filled the vault with mocking laughter. "Ser Piggy thinks we're all fools, brothers," he said. "He's taught the bird this little trick. They all say *snow*, go up to the rookery and hear for yourselves. Mormont's bird had more words than that."

The raven cocked its head and looked at Jon. "*Corn?*" it said hopefully. When it got neither corn nor answer, it *quork*ed and muttered, "*Kettle? Kettle? Kettle?*"

The rest was arrowheads, a torrent of arrowheads, a flood of arrowheads, arrowheads enough to drown the last few stones and shells, and all the copper pennies too.

When the count was done, Jon found himself surrounded. Some clapped him on the back, whilst others bent the knee to him as if he were a lord in truth. Satin, Owen the Oaf, Halder, Toad, Spare Boot, Giant, Mully, Ulmer of the Kingswood, Sweet Donnel Hill, and half a hundred more pressed around him. Dywen clacked his wooden teeth and said, "Gods be good, our Lord Commander's still in swaddling clothes." Iron Emmett said, "I hope this don't mean I can't beat the bloody piss out of you next time we train, my lord." Three-Finger Hobb wanted to know if he'd still be eating with the men, or if he'd want his meals sent up to his solar. Even Bowen Marsh came up to say he would be glad to continue as Lord Steward if that was Lord Snow's wish.

"Lord Snow," said Cotter Pyke, "if you muck this up, I'm going to rip your liver out and eat it raw with onions."

Ser Denys Mallister was more courteous. "It was a hard thing young Samwell asked of me," the old knight confessed. "When Lord Qorgyle was chosen, I told myself, 'No matter, he has been longer on the Wall than you have, your time will come.' When it was Lord Mormont, I thought, 'He is strong and fierce, but he is old, your time may yet come.' But you are half a boy, Lord Snow, and now I must return to the Shadow Tower knowing that my time will never come." He smiled a tired smile. "Do not make me die regretful. Your uncle was a great man. Your lord father and his father as well. I shall expect full as much of you."

"Aye," said Cotter Pyke. "And you can start by telling those king's men that it's done, and we want our bloody supper."

"*Supper*," screamed the raven. "*Supper, supper.*"

The king's men cleared the door when they told them of the choosing, and Three-Finger Hobb and half a dozen helpers went trotting off to the kitchen to fetch the food. Jon did not wait to eat. He walked across the castle, wondering if he were dreaming, with the raven on his shoulder and Ghost at his heels. Pyp, Grenn, and Sam trailed after him, chattering, but he hardly heard a word until Grenn whispered, "*Sam* did it," and Pyp said, "Sam *did* it!" Pyp had brought a wineskin with him, and he took a long drink and chanted, "Sam, Sam, Sam the wizard, Sam the wonder, Sam Sam the marvel man, he did it. But when did you hide the raven in the kettle, Sam, and how in seven hells could you be certain it would fly to Jon? It would have mucked up everything if the bird had decided to perch on Janos Slynt's fat head."

"I had nothing to do with the bird," Sam insisted. "When it flew out of the kettle I almost wet myself."

Jon laughed, half amazed that he still remembered how. "You're all a bunch of mad fools, do you know that?"

"Us?" said Pyp. "You call *us* fools? We're not the ones who got chosen as the nine-hundredth-and-ninety-eighth Lord Commander of the Night's Watch. You best have some wine, Lord Jon. I think you're going to need a *lot* of wine."

So Jon Snow took the wineskin from his hand and had a swallow. But only one. The Wall was his, the night was dark, and he had a king to face.

SANSA

S he awoke all at once, every nerve atingle. For a moment she did not remember where she was. She had dreamt that she was little, still sharing a bedchamber with her sister Arya. But it was her maid she heard tossing in sleep, not her sister, and this was not Winterfell, but the Eyrie. *And I am Alayne Stone, a bastard girl.* The room was cold and black, though she was warm beneath the blankets. Dawn had not yet come. Sometimes she dreamed of Ser Ilyn Payne and woke with her heart thumping, but this dream had not been like that. *Home. It was a dream of home.*

The Eyrie was no home. It was no bigger than Maegor's Holdfast, and outside its sheer white walls was only the mountain and the long treacherous descent past Sky and Snow and Stone to the Gates of the Moon on the valley floor. There was no place to go and little to do. The older servants said these halls rang with laughter when her father and Robert Baratheon had been Jon Arryn's wards, but those days were many years gone. Her aunt kept a small household, and seldom permitted any guests to ascend past the Gates of the Moon. Aside from her aged maid, Sansa's only companion was the Lord Robert, eight going on three.

And Marillion. There is always Marillion. When he played for them at supper, the young singer often seemed to be singing directly at her. Her aunt was far from pleased. Lady Lysa doted on Marillion, and had banished two serving girls and even a page for telling lies about him.

Lysa was as lonely as she was. Her new husband seemed to spend more time at the foot of the mountain than he did atop it. He was gone now, had been gone the past four days, meeting with the Corbrays. From bits and pieces of overheard conversations Sansa knew that Jon Arryn's bannermen resented Lysa's marriage and begrudged Petyr his authority as Lord Protector of the Vale. The senior branch of House Royce was close to open revolt over her aunt's failure to aid Robb in his war, and the Waynwoods, Redforts, Belmores, and Templetons were giving them every support. The mountain clans were being troublesome as well, and old Lord Hunter had died so suddenly that his two younger sons were accusing their elder brother of having murdered him. The Vale of Arryn might have been spared the worst of the war, but it was hardly the idyllic place that Lady Lysa had made it out to be.

I am not going back to sleep, Sansa realized. *My head is all a tumult.* She pushed her pillow away reluctantly, threw back the blankets, went to her window, and opened the shutters.

Snow was falling on the Eyrie.

Outside the flakes drifted down as soft and silent as memory. *Was this what woke me?* Already the snowfall lay thick upon the garden below, blanketing the grass, dusting the shrubs and statues with white and weighing down the branches of the trees. The sight took Sansa back to cold nights long ago, in the long summer of her childhood.

She had last seen snow the day she'd left Winterfell. *That was a lighter fall than this,* she remembered. *Robb had melting flakes in his hair when he hugged me, and the snowball Arya tried to make kept coming apart in her hands.* It hurt to remember how happy she had been that morning. Hullen had helped her mount, and she'd ridden out with the snowflakes swirling around her, off to see the great wide world. *I thought my song was beginning that day, but it was almost done.*

Sansa left the shutters open as she dressed. It would be cold, she knew, though the Eyrie's towers encircled the garden and protected it from the worst of the mountain winds. She donned silken smallclothes and a linen shift, and over that a warm dress of blue lambswool. Two pairs of hose for her legs, boots that laced up to her knees, heavy leather gloves, and finally a hooded cloak of soft white fox fur.

Her maid rolled herself more tightly in her blanket as the snow began to drift in the window. Sansa eased open the door, and made her way down the winding stair. When she opened the door to the garden, it was so lovely that she held her breath, unwilling to disturb such perfect beauty. The snow drifted down and down, all in ghostly silence, and lay thick and unbroken on the ground. All color had fled the world outside. It was a place of whites and blacks and greys. White towers and white snow and white statues, black shadows and black trees, the dark grey sky above. *A pure world,* Sansa thought. *I do not belong here.*

Yet she stepped out all the same. Her boots tore ankle-deep holes into the smooth white surface of the snow, yet made no sound. Sansa drifted past frosted shrubs and thin dark trees, and wondered if she were still dreaming. Drifting snowflakes brushed her face as light as lover's kisses, and melted on her cheeks. At the center of the garden, beside the statue of the weeping woman that lay broken and half-buried on the ground, she turned her face up to the sky and closed her eyes. She could feel the snow on her lashes, taste it on her lips. It was the taste of Winterfell. The taste of innocence. The taste of dreams.

When Sansa opened her eyes again, she was on her knees. She did not remember falling. It seemed to her that the sky was a lighter shade of grey. *Dawn,* she thought. *Another day. Another new day.* It was the old days she hungered for. Prayed for. But who could she pray to? The garden had been meant for a godswood once, she knew, but the soil was too thin and stony for a weirwood to take root. *A godswood without gods, as empty as me.*

She scooped up a handful of snow and squeezed it between her fingers. Heavy and wet, the snow packed easily. Sansa began to make snowballs, shaping and smoothing them until they were round and white and perfect. She remembered a summer's snow in Winterfell when Arya and Bran had ambushed her as she emerged from the keep one morning. They'd each had a dozen snowballs to hand, and she'd had none. Bran had been perched on the roof of the covered bridge, out of reach, but Sansa had chased Arya through the stables and around the kitchen until both of them were breathless. She might even have caught her, but she'd slipped on some ice. Her sister came back to see if she was hurt. When she said she wasn't, Arya hit her in the face with another snowball, but Sansa grabbed her leg and pulled her down and was rubbing snow in her hair when Jory came along and pulled them apart, laughing.

What do I want with snowballs? She looked at her sad little arsenal. *There's no one to throw them at.* She let the one she was making drop from her hand. *I could build a snow knight instead*, she thought. *Or even . . .*

She pushed two of her snowballs together, added a third, packed more snow in around them, and patted the whole thing into the shape of a cylinder. When it was done, she stood it on end and used the tip of her little finger to poke holes in it for windows. The crenellations around the top took a little more care, but when they were done she had a tower. *I need some walls now*, Sansa thought, *and then a keep*. She set to work.

The snow fell and the castle rose. Two walls ankle-high, the inner taller than the outer. Towers and turrets, keeps and stairs, a round kitchen, a square armory, the stables along the inside of the west wall. It was only a castle when she began, but before very long Sansa knew it was Winterfell. She found twigs and fallen branches beneath the snow and broke off the ends to make the trees for the godswood. For the gravestones in the lichyard she used bits of bark. Soon her gloves and her boots were crusty white, her hands were tingling, and her feet were soaked and cold, but she did not care. The castle was all that mattered. Some things were hard to remember, but most came back to her easily, as if she had been there only yesterday. The Library Tower, with the steep stonework stair twisting about its exterior. The gatehouse, two huge bulwarks, the arched gate between them, crenellations all along the top . . .

And all the while the snow kept falling, piling up in drifts around her buildings as fast as she raised them. She was patting down the pitched roof of the Great Hall when she heard a voice, and looked up to see her maid calling from her window. Was my lady well? Did she wish to break her fast? Sansa shook her head, and went back to shaping snow, adding a chimney to one end of the Great Hall, where the hearth would stand inside.

Dawn stole into her garden like a thief. The grey of the sky grew lighter still, and the trees and shrubs turned a dark green beneath their stoles of snow. A few servants came out and watched her for a time, but she paid them no mind and they soon went back inside where it was warmer. Sansa saw Lady Lysa gazing down from her balcony, wrapped up in a blue velvet robe trimmed with fox fur, but when she looked again her aunt was gone. Maester Colemon popped out of the rookery and peered down for a while, skinny and shivering but curious.

Her bridges kept falling down. There was a covered bridge between the armory and the main keep, and another that went from the fourth floor of the bell tower to the second floor of the rookery, but no matter how carefully she shaped them, they would not hold together. The third time one collapsed on her, she cursed aloud and sat back in helpless frustration.

"Pack the snow around a stick, Sansa."

She did not know how long he had been watching her, or when he had returned from the Vale. "A stick?" she asked.

"That will give it strength enough to stand, I'd think," Petyr said. "May I come into your castle, my lady?"

Sansa was wary. "Don't break it. Be . . ."

". . . gentle?" He smiled. "Winterfell has withstood fiercer enemies than me. It *is* Winterfell, is it not?"

"Yes," Sansa admitted.

He walked along outside the walls. "I used to dream of it, in those years after Cat went north with Eddard Stark. In my dreams it was ever a dark place, and cold."

"No. It was always warm, even when it snowed. Water from the hot springs is piped through the walls to warm them, and inside the glass gardens it was always like the hottest day of summer." She stood, towering over the great white castle. "I can't think how to do the glass roof over the gardens."

Littlefinger stroked his chin, where his beard had been before Lysa had asked him to shave it off. "The glass was locked in frames, no? Twigs are your answer. Peel them and cross them and use bark to tie them together into frames. I'll show you." He moved through the garden, gathering up twigs and sticks and shaking the snow from them. When he had enough, he stepped over both walls with a single long stride and squatted on his heels in the middle of the yard. Sansa came closer to watch what he was doing. His hands were deft and sure, and before long he had a crisscrossing latticework of twigs, very like the one that roofed the glass gardens of Winterfell. "We will need to imagine the glass, to be sure," he said when he gave it to her.

"This is just right," she said.

He touched her face. "And so is that."

Sansa did not understand. "And so is what?"

"Your smile, my lady. Shall I make another for you?"

"If you would."

"Nothing could please me more."

She raised the walls of the glass gardens while Littlefinger roofed them over, and when they were done with that he helped her extend the walls and build the guardshall. When she used sticks for the covered bridges, they stood, just as he had said they would. The First Keep was simple enough, an old round drum tower, but Sansa was stymied again when it came to putting the gargoyles around the top. Again he had the answer. "It's been snowing on your castle, my lady," he pointed out. "What do the gargoyles look like when they're covered with snow?"

Sansa closed her eyes to see them in memory. "They're just white lumps."

"Well, then. Gargoyles are hard, but white lumps should be easy." And they were.

The Broken Tower was easier still. They made a tall tower together, kneeling side by side to roll it smooth, and when they'd raised it Sansa stuck her fingers through the top, grabbed a handful of snow, and flung it full in his face. Petyr yelped, as the snow slid down under his collar. "That was unchivalrously done, my lady."

"As was bringing me here, when you swore to take me home."

She wondered where this courage had come from, to speak to him so frankly. *From Winterfell*, she thought. *I am stronger within the walls of Winterfell.*

His face grew serious. "Yes, I played you false in that ... and in one other thing as well."

Sansa's stomach was aflutter. "What other thing?"

"I told you that nothing could please me more than to help you with your castle. I fear that was a lie as well. Something else would please me more." He stepped closer. "This."

Sansa tried to step back, but he pulled her into his arms and suddenly he was kissing her. Feebly, she tried to squirm, but only succeeded in pressing herself more tightly against him. His mouth was on hers, swallowing her words. He tasted of mint. For half a heartbeat she yielded to his kiss ... before she turned her face away and wrenched free. "What are you *doing*?"

Petyr straightened his cloak. "Kissing a snow maid."

"You're supposed to kiss *her*." Sansa glanced up at Lysa's balcony, but it was empty now. "Your lady wife."

"I do. Lysa has no cause for complaint." He smiled. "I wish you could see yourself, my lady. You are so beautiful. You're crusted over with snow like some little bear cub, but your face is flushed and you can scarcely breathe. How long have you been out here? You must be very cold. Let me warm you, Sansa. Take off those gloves, give me your hands."

"I won't." He sounded almost like Marillion, the night he'd gotten so drunk at the wedding. Only this time Lothor Brune would not appear to save her; Ser Lothor was Petyr's man. "You shouldn't kiss me. I might have been your own daughter ..."

"Might have been," he admitted, with a rueful smile. "But you're not, are you? You are Eddard Stark's daughter, and Cat's. But I think you might be even more beautiful than your mother was, when she was your age."

"Petyr, please." Her voice sounded so weak. "Please ..."

"A *castle*!"

The voice was loud, shrill, and childish. Littlefinger turned away from her. "Lord Robert." He sketched a bow. "Should you be out in the snow without your gloves?"

"Did you make the snow castle, Lord Littlefinger?"

"Alayne did most of it, my lord."

Sansa said, "It's meant to be Winterfell."

"Winterfell?" Robert was small for eight, a stick of a boy with splotchy skin and eyes that were always runny. Under one arm he clutched the threadbare cloth doll he carried everywhere.

"Winterfell is the seat of House Stark," Sansa told her husband-to-be. "The great castle of the north."

"It's not so great." The boy knelt before the gatehouse. "Look, here comes a giant to knock it down." He stood his doll in the snow and moved it jerkily. "*Tromp tromp I'm a giant, I'm a giant,*" he chanted. "*Ho ho ho, open your gates or I'll mash them and smash them.*" Swinging the doll by the legs, he knocked the top off one gatehouse tower and then the other.

It was more than Sansa could stand. "Robert, *stop that.*" Instead he swung the doll again, and a foot of wall exploded. She grabbed for his hand but she caught the doll instead. There was a loud ripping sound as the thin cloth tore. Suddenly she had the doll's head, Robert had the legs and body, and the rag-and-sawdust stuffing was spilling in the snow.

Lord Robert's mouth trembled. "You *killlllllllled* him," he wailed. Then he began to shake. It started with no more than a little shivering, but within a few short heartbeats he had collapsed across the castle, his limbs flailing about violently. White towers and snowy bridges shattered and fell on all sides. Sansa stood horrified, but Petyr Baelish seized her cousin's wrists and shouted for the maester.

Guards and serving girls arrived within instants to help restrain the boy, Maester Colemon a short time later. Robert Arryn's shaking sickness was nothing new to the people of the Eyrie, and Lady Lysa had trained them all to come rushing at the boy's first cry. The maester held the little lord's head and gave him half a cup of dreamwine, murmuring soothing words. Slowly the violence of the fit seemed to ebb away, till nothing remained but a small shaking of the hands. "Help him to my chambers," Colemon told the guards. "A leeching will help calm him."

"It was my fault." Sansa showed them the doll's head. "I ripped his doll in two. I never meant to, but . . ."

"His lordship was destroying the castle," said Petyr.

"A giant," the boy whispered, weeping. "It wasn't me, it was a giant hurt the castle. She *killed* him! I hate her! She's a bastard and I *hate* her! I don't *want* to be leeched!"

"My lord, your blood needs thinning," said Maester Colemon. "It is the bad blood that makes you angry, and the rage that brings on the shaking. Come now."

They led the boy away. *My lord husband*, Sansa thought, as she contemplated the ruins of Winterfell. The snow had stopped, and it was colder than before. She wondered if Lord Robert would shake all through their wedding. *At least Joffrey was sound of body.* A mad rage seized hold of her. She picked up a broken branch and smashed the torn doll's head down on top of it, then pushed it down atop the shattered gatehouse of her snow castle. The servants looked aghast, but when Littlefinger saw what she'd done he laughed. "If the tales be true, that's not the first giant to end up with his head on Winterfell's walls."

"Those are only stories," she said, and left him there.

Back in her bedchamber, Sansa took off her cloak and her wet boots and sat beside the fire. She had no doubt that she would be made to answer for Lord Robert's fit. *Perhaps Lady Lysa will send me away.* Her aunt was quick to banish anyone who displeased her, and nothing displeased her quite so much as people she suspected of mistreating her son.

Sansa would have welcomed banishment. The Gates of the Moon was much larger than the Eyrie, and livelier as well. Lord Nestor Royce seemed gruff and stern, but his daughter Myranda kept his castle for him, and everyone said how frolicsome she was. Even Sansa's supposed bastardy might not count too much against her below. One of King Robert's baseborn daughters was in service to Lord Nestor, and she and the Lady Myranda were said to be fast friends, as close as sisters.

I will tell my aunt that I don't want to marry Robert. Not even the High Septon himself could declare a woman married if she refused to say the vows. She wasn't a beggar, no matter what her aunt said. She was thirteen, a woman flowered and wed, the heir to Winterfell. Sansa felt sorry for her little cousin sometimes, but she could not imagine ever wanting to be his wife. *I would sooner be married to Tyrion again.* If Lady Lysa knew that, surely she'd send her away ... away from Robert's pouts and shakes and runny eyes, away from Marillion's lingering looks, away from Petyr's kisses. *I will tell her. I will!*

It was late that afternoon when Lady Lysa summoned her. Sansa had been marshaling her courage all day, but no sooner did Marillion appear at her door than all her doubts returned. "Lady Lysa requires your presence in the High Hall." The singer's eyes undressed her as he spoke, but she was used to that.

Marillion was comely, there was no denying it; boyish and slender, with smooth skin, sandy hair, a charming smile. But he had made himself well hated in the Vale, by everyone but her aunt and little Lord Robert. To hear the servants talk, Sansa was not the first maid to suffer his advances, and the others had not had Lothor Brune to defend them. But Lady Lysa would hear no complaints against him. Since coming to the Eyrie, the singer had become her favorite. He sang Lord Robert to sleep every night, and tweaked the noses of Lady Lysa's suitors with verses that made mock of their foibles. Her aunt had showered him with gold and gifts; costly clothes, a gold arm ring, a belt studded with moonstones, a fine horse. She had even given him her late husband's favorite falcon. It all served to make Marillion unfailingly courteous in Lady Lysa's presence, and unfailingly arrogant outside it.

"Thank you," Sansa told him stiffly. "I know the way."

He would not leave. "My lady said to bring you."

Bring me? She did not like the sound of that. "Are you a guardsman now?" Littlefinger had dismissed the Eyrie's captain of guards and put Ser Lothor Brune in his place.

"Do you require guarding?" Marillion said lightly. "I am composing a new song, you should know. A song so sweet and sad it will melt even your frozen heart. 'The Roadside Rose,' I mean to call it. About a baseborn girl so beautiful she bewitched every man who laid eyes upon her."

I am a Stark of Winterfell, she longed to tell him. Instead, she nodded, and let him escort her down the tower steps and along a bridge. The High Hall had been closed as long as she'd been at the Eyrie. Sansa wondered why her aunt had opened it. Normally she preferred the comfort of her solar, or the cozy warmth of Lord Arryn's audience chamber with its view of the waterfall.

Two guards in sky-blue cloaks flanked the carved wooden doors of the High Hall, spears in hand. "No one is to enter so long as Alayne is with Lady Lysa," Marillion told them.

"Aye." The men let them pass, then crossed their spears. Marillion swung the doors shut and barred them with a third spear, longer and thicker than those the guards had borne.

Sansa felt a prickle of unease. "Why did you do that?"

"My lady awaits you."

She looked about uncertainly. Lady Lysa sat on the dais in a high-backed chair of carved weirwood, alone. To her right was a second chair, taller than her own, with a stack of blue cushions piled on the seat, but Lord Robert was not in it. Sansa hoped he'd recovered. Marillion was not like to tell her, though.

Sansa walked down the blue silk carpet between rows of fluted pillars slim as lances. The floors and walls of the High Hall were made of milk-white marble veined with blue. Shafts of pale daylight slanted down through narrow arched windows along the eastern wall. Between the windows were torches, mounted in high iron sconces, but none of them was lit. Her footsteps fell softly on the carpet. Outside the wind blew cold and lonely.

Amidst so much white marble even the sunlight looked chilly, somehow ... though not half so chilly as her aunt. Lady Lysa had dressed in a gown of cream-colored velvet and a necklace of sapphires and moonstones. Her auburn hair had been done up in a thick braid, and fell across one shoulder. She sat in the high seat watching her niece approach, her face red and puffy beneath the paint and powder. On the wall behind her hung a huge banner, the moon-and-falcon of House Arryn in cream and blue.

Sansa stopped before the dais, and curtsied. "My lady. You sent for me." She could still hear the sound of the wind, and the soft chords Marillion was playing at the foot of the hall.

"I saw what you did," the Lady Lysa said.

Sansa smoothed down the folds of her skirt. "I trust Lord Robert is better? I never meant to rip his doll. He was smashing my snow castle, I only . . ."

"Will you play the coy deceiver with me?" her aunt said. "I was not speaking of Robert's doll. I *saw* you kissing him."

The High Hall seemed to grow a little colder. The walls and floor and columns might have turned to ice. "He kissed me."

Lysa's nostrils flared. "And why would he do that? He has a wife who loves him. A woman grown, not a little girl. He has no need for the likes of you. Confess, child. You threw yourself at him. That was the way of it."

Sansa took a step backward. "That's not true."

"Where are you going? Are you afraid? Such wanton behavior must be punished, but I will not be hard on you. We keep a whipping boy for Robert, as is the custom in the Free Cities. His health is too delicate for him to bear the rod himself. I shall find some common girl to take your whipping, but first you must own up to what you've done. I cannot abide a liar, Alayne."

"I was building a snow castle," Sansa said. "Lord Petyr was helping me, and then he kissed me. That's what you saw."

"Have you no honor?" her aunt said sharply. "Or do you take me for a fool? You do, don't you? You take me for a fool. Yes, I see that now. I am not a fool. You think you can have any man you want because you're young and beautiful. Don't think I haven't seen the looks you give Marillion. I know everything that happens in the Eyrie, little lady. And I have known your like before, too. But you are mistaken if you think big eyes and strumpet's smiles will win you Petyr. He is mine." She rose to her feet. "They all tried to take him from me. My lord father, my husband, your mother . . . Catelyn most of all. She liked to kiss my Petyr too, oh yes she did."

Sansa retreated another step. "My mother?"

"Yes, your mother, your precious mother, my own sweet sister Catelyn. Don't you think to play the innocent with me, you vile little liar. All those years in Riverrun, she played with Petyr as if he were her little toy. She teased him with smiles and soft words and wanton looks, and made his nights a torment."

"No." *My mother is dead,* she wanted to shriek. *She was your own sister, and she's dead.* "She didn't. She wouldn't."

"How would you know? Were you there?" Lysa descended from the high seat, her skirts swirling. "Did you come with Lord Bracken and Lord Blackwood, the time they visited to lay their feud before my father? Lord Bracken's singer played for us, and Catelyn danced six dances with Petyr that night, *six,* I counted. When the lords began to argue my father took them up to his audience chamber, so there was no one to stop us drinking. Edmure got drunk, young as he was . . . and Petyr tried to kiss your mother, only she pushed him away. She *laughed* at him. He looked so wounded I thought my heart would burst, and afterward he drank until he passed out at the table. Uncle Brynden carried him up to bed before my father could find him like that. But you remember none of it, do you?" She looked down angrily. "*Do you?*"

Is she drunk, or mad? "I was not born, my lady."

"You were not born. But I was, so do not presume to tell what is true. I *know* what is true. You kissed him!"

"He kissed me," Sansa insisted again. "I never wanted—"

"Be quiet, I haven't given you leave to speak. You enticed him, just as your mother did that night in Riverrun, with her smiles and her dancing. You think I could forget? That was the night I stole up to his bed to give him comfort. I bled, but it was the sweetest hurt. He told me he loved me then, but he called me *Cat,* just before he fell back to sleep. Even so, I stayed with him until the sky began to lighten. Your mother did not deserve him. She would not even give him her favor to wear when he fought Brandon Stark. *I* would have given him my favor. I gave him everything. He is mine now. Not Catelyn's and not yours."

All of Sansa's resolve had withered in the face of her aunt's onslaught. Lysa Arryn was frightening her as much as Queen Cersei ever had. "He's yours, my lady," she said, trying to sound meek and contrite. "May I have your leave to go?"

"You may not." Her aunt's breath smelled of wine. "If you were anyone else, I would banish you. Send you down to Lord Nestor at the Gates of the Moon, or back to the Fingers. How would you like to spend your life on that bleak shore, surrounded by slatterns and sheep pellets? That was what my father meant for Petyr. Everyone thought it was because of that stupid duel with Brandon Stark, but that wasn't so. Father said I ought to thank the gods that so great a lord as Jon Arryn was willing to take me soiled, but I knew it was only for the swords. I had to marry Jon, or my father would have turned me out as he did his brother, but it was Petyr I was meant for. I am telling you all this so you will understand how much we love each other, how long we have suffered and dreamed of one another. We made a baby together, a precious little baby." Lysa put her hands flat against her belly, as if the child was still there. "When they stole him from me, I made a promise to myself that I would never let it happen again. Jon wished to send my sweet Robert to Dragonstone, and that sot of a king would have given him to Cersei Lannister, but I never let them ... no more than I'll let you steal my Petyr Littlefinger. Do you hear me, Alayne or Sansa or whatever you call yourself? Do you hear what I am telling you?"

"Yes. I swear, I won't ever kiss him again, or ... or entice him." Sansa thought that was what her aunt wanted to hear.

"So you admit it now? It was you, just as I thought. You are as wanton as your mother." Lysa grabbed her by the wrist. "Come with me now. There is something I want to show you."

"You're hurting me." Sansa squirmed. "Please, Aunt Lysa, I haven't done anything. I swear it."

Her aunt ignored her protests. "*Marillion!*" she shouted. "I need you, Marillion! I *need* you!"

The singer had remained discreetly in the rear of the hall, but at Lady Arryn's shout he came at once. "My lady?"

"Play us a song. Play 'The False and the Fair.'"

Marillion's fingers brushed the strings. "*The lord he came a-riding upon a rainy day, hey-nonny, hey-nonny, hey-nonny-hey . . .*"

Lady Lysa pulled at Sansa's arm. It was either walk or be dragged, so she chose to walk, halfway down the hall and between a pair of pillars, to a white weirwood door set in the marble wall. The door was firmly closed, with three heavy bronze bars to hold it in place, but Sansa could hear the wind outside worrying at its edges. When she saw the crescent moon carved in the wood, she planted her feet. "The Moon Door." She tried to yank free. "Why are you showing me the Moon Door?"

"You squeak like a mouse now, but you were bold enough in the garden, weren't you? You were bold enough in the snow."

"*The lady sat a-sewing upon a rainy day,*" Marillion sang. "*Hey-nonny, hey-nonny, hey-nonny-hey.*"

"Open the door," Lysa commanded. "*Open* it, I say. You will do it, or I'll send for my guards." She shoved Sansa forward. "Your mother was brave, at least. Lift off the bars."

If I do as she says, she will let me go. Sansa grabbed one of the bronze bars, yanked it loose, and tossed it down. The second bar clattered to the marble, then the third. She had barely touched the latch when the heavy wooden door *flew* inward and slammed back against the wall with a bang. Snow had piled up around the frame, and it all came blowing in at them, borne on a blast of cold air that left Sansa shivering. She tried to step backward, but her aunt was behind her. Lysa seized her by the wrist and put her other hand between her shoulder blades, propelling her forcefully toward the open door.

Beyond was white sky, falling snow, and nothing else.

"Look down," said Lady Lysa. "Look *down.*"

She tried to wrench free, but her aunt's fingers were digging into her arm like claws. Lysa gave her another shove, and Sansa shrieked. Her left foot broke through a crust of snow and knocked it loose. There was nothing in front of her but empty air, and a waycastle six hundred feet below clinging to the side of the mountain. "Don't!" Sansa screamed. "You're scaring me!" Behind her, Marillion was still playing his woodharp and singing, "*Hey-nonny, hey-nonny, hey-nonny-hey.*"

"Do you still want my leave to go? Do you?"

"No." Sansa planted her feet and tried to squirm backward, but her aunt did not budge. "Not this way. Please ..." She put a hand up, her fingers scrabbling at the doorframe, but she could not get a grip, and her feet were sliding on the wet marble floor. Lady Lysa pressed her forward inexorably. Her aunt outweighed her by three stone. "*The lady lay a-kissing, upon a mound of hay,*" Marillion was singing.

Sansa twisted sideways, hysterical with fear, and one foot slipped out over the void. She screamed. "*Hey-nonny, hey-nonny, hey-nonny-hey.*" The wind flapped her skirts up and bit at her bare legs with cold teeth. She could feel snowflakes melting on her cheeks. Sansa flailed, found Lysa's thick auburn braid, and clutched it tight. "My hair!" her aunt shrieked. "*Let go of my hair!*" She was shaking, sobbing. They teetered on the edge. Far off, she heard the guards pounding on the door with their spears, demanding to be let in. Marillion broke off his song.

"*Lysa!* What's the meaning of this?" The shout cut through the sobs and heavy breathing. Footsteps echoed down the High Hall. "Get *back* from there! Lysa, what are you doing?" The guards were still beating at the door; Littlefinger had come in the back way, through the lords' entrance behind the dais.

As Lysa turned, her grip loosened enough for Sansa to rip free. She stumbled to her knees, where Petyr Baelish saw her. He stopped suddenly. "Alayne. What is the trouble here?"

"*Her.*" Lady Lysa grabbed a handful of Sansa's hair. "*She's* the trouble. She *kissed* you."

"Tell her," Sansa begged. "Tell her we were just building a castle . . ."

"*Be quiet!*" her aunt screamed. "I never gave you leave to speak. No one cares about your castle."

"She's a child, Lysa. Cat's daughter. What did you think you were doing?"

"I was going to marry her to *Robert*! She has no gratitude. No . . . no *decency*. You are not hers to kiss. *Not hers!* I was teaching her a lesson, that was all."

"I see." He stroked his chin. "I think she understands now. Isn't that so, Alayne?"

"Yes," sobbed Sansa. "I understand."

"I don't want her here." Her aunt's eyes were shiny with tears. "Why did you bring her to the Vale, Petyr? This isn't her place. She doesn't belong here."

"We'll send her away, then. Back to King's Landing, if you like." He took a step toward them. "Let her up, now. Let her away from the door."

"*NO!*" Lysa gave Sansa's head another wrench. Snow eddied around them, making their skirts snap noisily. "You can't want her. You *can't*. She's a stupid empty-headed little girl. She doesn't love you the way I have. I've always loved you. I've proved it, haven't I?" Tears ran down her aunt's puffy red face. "I gave you my maiden's gift. I would have given you a son too, but they murdered him with moon tea, with tansy and mint and wormwood, a spoon of honey and a drop of pennyroyal. It wasn't me, I never *knew*, I only drank what Father gave me . . ."

"That's past and done, Lysa. Lord Hoster's dead, and his old maester as well." Littlefinger moved closer. "Have you been at the wine again? You ought not to talk so much. We don't want Alayne to know more than she should, do we? Or Marillion?"

Lady Lysa ignored that. "Cat never gave you anything. It was me who got you your first post, who made Jon bring you to court so we could be close to one another. You promised me you would never forget that."

"Nor have I. We're together, just as you always wanted, just as we always planned. Just let go of Sansa's hair . . ."

"I won't! I saw you kissing in the snow. She's just like her mother. Catelyn kissed you in the godswood, but she never *meant* it, she never wanted you. Why did you love her best? It was me, it was always *meeee!*"

"I know, love." He took another step. "And I am here. All you need to do is take my hand, come on." He held it out to her. "There's no cause for all these tears."

"Tears, tears, *tears*," she sobbed hysterically. "No need for tears . . . but that's not what you said in King's Landing. You told me to put the tears in Jon's wine, and I did. For Robert, and for *us*! And I wrote Catelyn and told her the Lannisters had killed my lord husband, just as you said. That was so clever . . . you were always clever, I told Father that, I said Petyr's so clever, he'll rise high, he will, he *will*, and he's sweet and gentle and I have his little baby in my belly . . . Why did you kiss her? *Why*? We're together now, we're together after so long, so very long, why would you want to kiss *herrrrrr*?"

"Lysa," Petyr sighed, "after all the storms we've suffered, you should trust me better. I swear, I shall never leave your side again, for as long as we both shall live."

"Truly?" she asked, weeping. "Oh, *truly*?"

"Truly. Now unhand the girl and come give me a kiss."

Lysa threw herself into Littlefinger's arms, sobbing. As they hugged, Sansa crawled from the Moon Door on hands and knees and wrapped her arms around the nearest pillar. She could feel her heart pounding. There was snow in her hair and her right shoe was missing. *It must have fallen.* She shuddered, and hugged the pillar tighter.

Littlefinger let Lysa sob against his chest for a moment, then put his hands on her arms and kissed her lightly. "My sweet silly jealous wife," he said, chuckling. "I've only loved one woman, I promise you."

Lysa Arryn smiled tremulously. "Only one? Oh, Petyr, do you swear it? Only one?"

"Only Cat." He gave her a short, sharp shove.

Lysa stumbled backward, her feet slipping on the wet marble. And then she was gone. She never screamed. For the longest time there was no sound but the wind.

Marillion gasped, "You . . . you . . ."

The guards were shouting outside the door, pounding with the butts of their heavy spears. Lord Petyr pulled Sansa to her feet. "You're not hurt?" When she shook her head, he said, "Run let my guards in, then. Quick now, there's no time to lose. This singer's killed my lady wife."

EPILOGUE

The road up to Oldstones went twice around the hill before
reaching the summit. Overgrown and stony, it would have
been slow going even in the best of times, and last night's
snow had left it muddy as well. *Snow in autumn in the riverlands, it's
unnatural,* Merrett thought gloomily. It had not been much of a snow,
true; just enough to blanket the ground for a night. Most of it had
started melting away as soon as the sun came up. Still, Merrett took
it for a bad omen. Between rains, floods, fire, and war, they had lost
two harvests and a good part of a third. An early winter would mean
famine all across the riverlands. A great many people would go hungry,
and some of them would starve. Merrett only hoped he wouldn't be
one of them. *I may, though. With my luck, I just may. I never did have
any luck.*

Beneath the castle ruins, the lower slopes of the hill were so thickly
forested that half a hundred outlaws could well have been lurking
there. *They could be watching me even now.* Merrett glanced about,
and saw nothing but gorse, bracken, thistle, sedge, and blackberry
bushes between the pines and grey-green sentinels. Elsewhere, skeletal
elm and ash and scrub oaks choked the ground like weeds. He saw
no outlaws, but that meant little. Outlaws were better at hiding than
honest men.

Merrett hated the woods, if truth be told, and he hated outlaws even more. "Outlaws stole my life," he had been known to complain when in his cups. He was too often in his cups, his father said, often and loudly. *Too true*, he thought ruefully. You needed some sort of distinction in the Twins, else they were liable to forget you were alive, but a reputation as the biggest drinker in the castle had done little to enhance his prospects, he'd found. *I once hoped to be the greatest knight who ever couched a lance. The gods took that away from me. Why shouldn't I have a cup of wine from time to time? It helps my headaches. Besides, my wife is a shrew, my father despises me, my children are worthless. What do I have to stay sober for?*

He was sober now, though. Well, he'd had two horns of ale when he broke his fast, and a small cup of red when he set out, but that was just to keep his head from pounding. Merrett could feel the headache building behind his eyes, and he knew that if he gave it half a chance he would soon feel as if he had a thunderstorm raging between his ears. Sometimes his headaches got so bad that it even hurt too much to weep. Then all he could do was rest on his bed in a dark room with a damp cloth over his eyes, and curse his luck and the nameless outlaw who had done this to him.

Just thinking about it made him anxious. He could no wise afford a headache now. *If I bring Petyr back home safely, all my luck will change.* He had the gold, all he needed to do was climb to the top of Oldstones, meet the bloody outlaws in the ruined castle, and make the exchange. A simple ransom. Even he could not muck it up ... unless he got a headache, one so bad that it left him unable to ride. He was supposed to be at the ruins by sunset, not weeping in a huddle at the side of the road. Merrett rubbed two fingers against his temple. *Once more around the hill, and there I am.* When the message had come in and he had stepped forward to offer to carry the ransom, his father had squinted down and said, "*You*, Merrett?" and started laughing through his nose, that hideous *heh heh heh* laugh of his. Merrett practically had to beg before they'd give him the bloody bag of gold.

Something moved in the underbrush along the side of the road. Merrett reined up hard and reached for his sword, but it was only a squirrel. "Stupid," he told himself, shoving the sword back in its scabbard without ever having gotten it out. "Outlaws don't have tails. Bloody hell, Merrett, get hold of yourself." His heart was thumping in his chest as if he were some green boy on his first campaign. *As if this were the kingswood and it was the old Brotherhood I was going to face, not the lightning lord's sorry lot of brigands.* For a moment he was tempted to trot right back down the hill and find the nearest alehouse. That bag of gold would buy a lot of ale, enough for him to forget all about Petyr Pimple. *Let them hang him, he brought this on himself. It's no more than he deserves, wandering off with some bloody camp follower like a stag in rut.*

His head had begun to pound; soft now, but he knew it would get worse. Merrett rubbed the bridge of his nose. He really had no right to think so ill of Petyr. *I did the same myself when I was his age.* In his case all it got him was a pox, but still, he shouldn't condemn. Whores did have charms, especially if you had a face like Petyr's. The poor lad had a wife, to be sure, but she was half the problem. Not only was she twice his age, but she was bedding his brother Walder too, if the talk was true. There was always lots of talk around the Twins, and only a little was ever true, but in this case Merrett believed it. Black Walder was a man who took what he wanted, even his brother's wife. He'd had Edwyn's wife too, that was common knowledge, Fair Walda had been known to slip into his bed from time to time, and some even said he'd known the seventh Lady Frey a deal better than he should have. Small wonder he refused to marry. Why buy a cow when there were udders all around begging to be milked?

Cursing under his breath, Merrett jammed his heels into his horse's flanks and rode on up the hill. As tempting as it was to drink the gold away, he knew that if he didn't come back with Petyr Pimple, he had as well not come back at all.

Lord Walder would soon turn two-and-ninety. His ears had started to go, his eyes were almost gone, and his gout was so bad that he had to be carried everywhere. He could not possibly last much longer, all his sons agreed. *And when he goes, everything will change, and not for the better.* His father was querulous and stubborn, with an iron will and a wasp's tongue, but he did believe in taking care of his own. *All* of his own, even the ones who had displeased and disappointed him.

Even the ones whose names he can't remember. Once he was gone, though . . .

When Ser Stevron had been heir, that was one thing. The old man had been grooming Stevron for sixty years, and had pounded it into his head that blood was blood. But Stevron had died whilst campaigning with the Young Wolf in the west—"of waiting, no doubt," Lame Lothar had quipped when the raven brought them the news— and his sons and grandsons were a different sort of Frey. Stevron's son Ser Ryman stood to inherit now; a thick-witted, stubborn, greedy man. And after Ryman came his own sons, Edwyn and Black Walder, who were even worse. "Fortunately," Lame Lothar once said, "they hate each other even more than they hate us."

Merrett wasn't certain that was fortunate at all, and for that matter Lothar himself might be more dangerous than either of them. Lord Walder had ordered the slaughter of the Starks at Roslin's wedding, but it had been Lame Lothar who had plotted it out with Roose Bolton, all the way down to which songs would be played. Lothar was a very amusing fellow to get drunk with, but Merrett would never be so foolish as to turn his back on him. In the Twins, you learned early that only full blood siblings could be trusted, and them not very far.

It was like to be every son for himself when the old man died, and every daughter as well. The new Lord of the Crossing would doubtless keep on *some* of his uncles, nephews, and cousins at the Twins, the ones he happened to like or trust, or more likely the ones he thought would prove useful to him. *The rest of us he'll shove out to fend for ourselves.*

The prospect worried Merrett more than words could say. He would be forty in less than three years, too old to take up the life of a hedge knight . . . even if he'd *been* a knight, which as it happened he wasn't. He had no land, no wealth of his own. He owned the clothes on his back but not much else, not even the horse he was riding. He wasn't clever enough to be a maester, pious enough to be a septon, or savage enough to be a sellsword. *The gods gave me no gift but birth, and they stinted me there.* What good was it to be the son of a rich and powerful House if you were the *ninth* son? When you took grandsons and great-grandsons into account, Merrett stood a better chance of being chosen High Septon than he did of inheriting the Twins.

I have no luck, he thought bitterly. *I have never had any bloody luck*. He was a big man, broad around the chest and shoulders if only of middling height. In the last ten years he had grown soft and fleshy, he knew, but when he'd been younger Merrett had been almost as robust as Ser Hosteen, his eldest full brother, who was commonly regarded as the strongest of Lord Walder Frey's brood. As a boy he'd been packed off to Crakehall to serve his mother's family as a page. When old Lord Sumner had made him a squire, everyone had assumed he would be Ser Merrett in no more than a few years, but the outlaws of the Kingswood Brotherhood had pissed on those plans. While his fellow squire Jaime Lannister was covering himself in glory, Merrett had first caught the pox from a camp follower, then managed to get captured by a *woman*, the one called the White Fawn. Lord Sumner had ransomed him back from the outlaws, but in the very next fight he'd been felled by a blow from a mace that had broken his helm and left him insensible for a fortnight. Everyone gave him up for dead, they told him later.

Merrett hadn't died, but his fighting days were done. Even the lightest blow to his head brought on blinding pain and reduced him to tears. Under these circumstances knighthood was out of the question, Lord Sumner told him, not unkindly. He was sent back to the Twins to face Lord Walder's poisonous disdain.

After that, Merrett's luck had only grown worse. His father had managed to make a good marriage for him, somehow; he wed one of Lord Darry's daughters, back when the Darrys stood high in King Aerys's favor. But it seemed as if he no sooner had deflowered his bride than Aerys lost his throne. Unlike the Freys, the Darrys had been prominent Targaryen loyalists, which cost them half their lands, most of their wealth, and almost all their power. As for his lady wife, she found him a great disappointment from the first, and insisted on popping out nothing but girls for years; three live ones, a stillbirth, and one that died in infancy before she finally produced a son. His eldest daughter had turned out to be a slut, his second a glutton. When Ami was caught in the stables with no fewer than *three* grooms, he'd been forced to marry her off to a bloody *hedge knight*. That situation could not possibly get any worse, he'd thought . . . until Ser Pate decided he could win renown by defeating Ser Gregor Clegane. Ami had come running back a widow, to Merrett's dismay and the undoubted delight of every stablehand in the Twins.

Merrett had dared to hope that his luck was finally changing when Roose Bolton chose to wed *his* Walda instead of one of her slimmer, comelier cousins. The Bolton alliance was important for House Frey and his daughter had helped secure it; he thought that must surely count for something. The old man had soon disabused him. "He picked her because she's *fat*," Lord Walder said. "You think Bolton gave a mummer's fart that she was your whelp? Think he sat about thinking, '*Heh*, Merrett Muttonhead, that's the very man I need for a good-father'? Your Walda's a sow in silk, that's why he picked her, and I'm not like to thank you for it. We'd have had the same alliance at half the price if your little porkling put down her spoon from time to time."

The final humiliation had been delivered with a smile, when Lame Lothar had summoned him to discuss his role in Roslin's wedding. "We must each play our part, according to our gifts," his half-brother told him. "You shall have one task and one task only, Merrett, but I believe you are well suited to it. I want you to see to it that Greatjon Umber is so bloody drunk that he can hardly stand, let alone fight."

And even that I failed at. He'd cozened the huge northman into drinking enough wine to kill any three normal men, yet after Roslin had been bedded the Greatjon still managed to snatch the sword of the first man to accost him and break his arm in the snatching. It had taken eight of them to get him into chains, and the effort had left two men wounded, one dead, and poor old Ser Leslyn Haigh short half a ear. When he couldn't fight with his hands any longer, Umber had fought with his teeth.

Merrett paused a moment and closed his eyes. His head was throbbing like that bloody drum they'd played at the wedding, and for a moment it was all he could do to stay in the saddle. *I have to go on*, he told himself. If he could bring back Petyr Pimple, surely it would put him in Ser Ryman's good graces. Petyr might be a whisker on the hapless side, but he wasn't as cold as Edwyn, nor as hot as Black Walder. *The boy will be grateful for my part, and his father will see that I'm loyal, a man worth having about.*

But only if he was there by sunset with the gold. Merrett glanced at the sky. *Right on time.* He needed something to steady his hands. He pulled up the waterskin hung from his saddle, uncorked it, and took a long swallow. The wine was thick and sweet, so dark it was almost black, but gods it tasted good.

The curtain wall of Oldstones had once encircled the brow of the hill like the crown on a king's head. Only the foundation remained, and a few waist-high piles of crumbling stone spotted with lichen. Merrett rode along the line of the wall until he came to the place where the gatehouse would have stood. The ruins were more extensive here, and he had to dismount to lead his palfrey through them. In the west, the sun had vanished behind a bank of low clouds. Gorse and bracken covered the slopes, and once inside the vanished walls the weeds were chest high. Merrett loosened his sword in its scabbard and looked about warily, but saw no outlaws. *Could I have come on the wrong day?* He stopped and rubbed his temples with his thumbs, but that did nothing to ease the pressure behind his eyes. *Seven bloody hells . . .*

From somewhere deep within the castle, faint music came drifting through the trees.

Merrett found himself shivering, despite his cloak. He pulled open his waterskin and had another drink of wine. *I could just get back on my horse, ride to Oldtown, and drink the gold away. No good ever came from dealing with outlaws.* That vile little bitch Wenda had burned a fawn into the cheek of his arse while she had him captive. No wonder his wife despised him. *I have to go through with this. Petyr Pimple might be Lord of the Crossing one day, Edwyn has no sons and Black Walder's only got bastards. Petyr will remember who came to get him.* He took another swallow, corked the skin up, and led his palfrey through broken stones, gorse, and thin wind-whipped trees, following the sounds to what had been the castle ward.

Fallen leaves lay thick upon the ground, like soldiers after some great slaughter. A man in patched, faded greens was sitting crosslegged atop a weathered stone sepulcher, fingering the strings of a woodharp. The music was soft and sad. Merrett knew the song. *High in the halls of the kings who are gone, Jenny would dance with her ghosts . . .*

"Get off there," Merrett said. "You're sitting on a king."

"Old Tristifer don't mind my bony arse. The Hammer of Justice, they called him. Been a long while since he heard any new songs." The outlaw hopped down. Trim and slim, he had a narrow face and foxy features, but his mouth was so wide that his smile seemed to touch his ears. A few strands of thin brown hair were blowing across his brow. He pushed them back with his free hand and said, "Do you remember me, my lord?"

"No." Merrett frowned. "Why would I?"

"I sang at your daughter's wedding. And passing well, I thought. That Pate she married was a cousin. We're all cousins in Sevenstreams. Didn't stop him from turning niggard when it was time to pay me." He shrugged. "Why is it your lord father never has me play at the Twins? Don't I make enough noise for his lordship? He likes it loud, I have been hearing."

"You bring the gold?" asked a harsher voice, behind him.

Merrett's throat was dry. *Bloody outlaws, always hiding in the bushes.* It had been the same in the kingswood. You'd think you'd caught five of them, and ten more would spring from nowhere.

When he turned, they were all around him; an ill-favored gaggle of leathery old men and smooth-cheeked lads younger than Petyr Pimple, the lot of them clad in roughspun rags, boiled leather, and bits of dead men's armor. There was one woman with them, bundled up in a hooded cloak three times too big for her. Merrett was too flustered to count them, but there seemed to be a dozen at the least, maybe a score.

"I asked a question." The speaker was a big bearded man with crooked green teeth and a broken nose; taller than Merrett, though not so heavy in the belly. A halfhelm covered his head, a patched yellow cloak his broad shoulders. "Where's our gold?"

"In my saddlebag. A hundred golden dragons." Merrett cleared his throat. "You'll get it when I see that Petyr—"

A squat one-eyed outlaw strode forward before he could finish, reached into the saddlebag bold as you please, and found the sack. Merrett started to grab him, then thought better of it. The outlaw opened the drawstring, removed a coin, and bit it. "Tastes right." He hefted the sack. "Feels right too."

They're going to take the gold and keep Petyr too, Merrett thought in sudden panic. "That's the whole ransom. All you asked for." His palms were sweating. He wiped them on his breeches. "Which one of you is Beric Dondarrion?" Dondarrion had been a lord before he turned outlaw, he might still be a man of honor.

"Why, that would be me," said the one-eyed man.

"You're a bloody liar, Jack," said the big bearded man in the yellow cloak. "It's my turn to be Lord Beric."

"Does that mean I have to be Thoros?" The singer laughed. "My lord, sad to say, Lord Beric was needed elsewhere. The times are troubled, and there are many battles to fight. But we'll sort you out just as he would, have no fear."

Merrett had plenty of fear. His head was pounding too. Much more of this and he'd be sobbing. "You have your gold," he said. "Give me my nephew, and I'll be gone." Petyr was actually more a great half-nephew, but there was no need to go into that.

"He's in the godswood," said the man in the yellow cloak. "We'll take you to him. Notch, you hold his horse."

Merrett handed over the bridle reluctantly. He did not see what other choice he had. "My water skin," he heard himself say. "A swallow of wine, to settle my—"

"We don't drink with your sort," yellow cloak said curtly. "It's this way. Follow me."

Leaves crunched beneath their heels, and every step sent a spike of pain through Merrett's temple. They walked in silence, the wind gusting around them. The last light of the setting sun was in his eyes as he clambered over the mossy hummocks that were all that remained of the keep. Behind was the godswood.

Petyr Pimple was hanging from the limb of an oak, a noose tight around his long thin neck. His eyes bulged from a black face, staring down at Merrett accusingly. *You came too late,* they seemed to say.

But he hadn't. He *hadn't*! He had come when they told him. "You killed him," he croaked.

"Sharp as a blade, this one," said the one-eyed man.

An aurochs was thundering through Merrett's head. *Mother have mercy*, he thought. "I brought the gold."

"That was good of you," said the singer amiably. "We'll see that it's put to good use."

Merrett turned away from Petyr. He could taste the bile in the back of his throat. "You . . . you had no right."

"We had a rope," said yellow cloak. "That's right enough."

Two of the outlaws seized Merrett's arms and bound them tight behind his back. He was too deep in shock to struggle. "No," was all he could manage. "I only came to ransom Petyr. You said if you had the gold by sunset he wouldn't be harmed . . ."

"Well," said the singer, "you've got us there, my lord. That was a lie of sorts, as it happens."

The one-eyed outlaw came forward with a long coil of hempen rope. He looped one end around Merrett's neck, pulled it tight, and tied a hard knot under his ear. The other end he threw over the limb of the oak. The big man in the yellow cloak caught it.

"What are you doing?" Merrett knew how stupid that sounded, but he could not believe what was happening, even then. "You'd never dare hang a Frey."

Yellow cloak laughed. "That other one, the pimply boy, he said the same thing."

He doesn't mean it. He cannot mean it. "My father will pay you. I'm worth a good ransom, more than Petyr, twice as much."

The singer sighed. "Lord Walder might be half-blind and gouty, but he's not so stupid as to snap at the same bait twice. Next time he'll send a hundred swords instead of a hundred dragons, I fear."

"He will!" Merrett tried to sound stern, but his voice betrayed him. "He'll send a thousand swords, and kill you all."

"He has to catch us first." The singer glanced up at poor Petyr. "And he can't hang us twice, now can he?" He drew a melancholy air from the strings of his woodharp. "Here now, don't soil yourself. All you need to do is answer me a question, and I'll tell them to let you go."

Merrett would tell them anything if it meant his life. "What do you want to know? I'll tell you true, I swear it."

The outlaw gave him an encouraging smile. "Well, as it happens, we're looking for a dog that ran away."

"A dog?" Merrett was lost. "What kind of dog?"

"He answers to the name Sandor Clegane. Thoros says he was making for the Twins. We found the ferrymen who took him across the Trident, and the poor sod he robbed on the kingsroad. Did you see him at the wedding, perchance?"

"The Red Wedding?" Merrett's skull felt as if it were about to split, but he did his best to recall. There had been so much confusion, but surely someone would have mentioned Joffrey's dog sniffing round the Twins. "He wasn't in the castle. Not at the main feast . . . he might have been at the bastard feast, or in the camps, but . . . no, someone would have said . . ."

"He would have had a child with him," said the singer. "A skinny girl, about ten. Or perhaps a boy the same age."

"I don't think so," said Merrett. "Not that I knew."

"No? Ah, that's a pity. Well, up you go."

"*No*," Merrett squealed loudly. "No, *don't*, I gave you your answer, you said you'd let me go."

"Seems to me that what I said was I'd *tell* them to let you go." The singer looked at yellow cloak. "Lem, let him go."

"Go bugger yourself," the big outlaw replied brusquely.

The singer gave Merrett a helpless shrug and began to play, "The Day They Hanged Black Robin."

"*Please*." The last of Merrett's courage was running down his leg. "I've done you no harm. I brought the gold, the way you said. I answered your question. I have *children*."

"That Young Wolf never will," said the one-eyed outlaw.

Merrett could hardly think for the pounding in his head. "He shamed us, the whole realm was laughing, we had to cleanse the stain on our honor." His father had said all that and more.

"Maybe so. What do a bunch o' bloody peasants know about a lord's honor?" Yellow cloak wrapped the end of the rope around his hand three times. "We know some about murder, though."

"Not murder." His voice was shrill. "It was vengeance, we had a right to our vengeance. It was *war*. Aegon, we called him Jinglebell, a poor lackwit never hurt anyone, Lady Stark cut his throat. We lost half a hundred men in the camps. Ser Garse Goodbrook, Kyra's husband, and Ser Tytos, Jared's son ... someone smashed his head in with an axe ... Stark's direwolf killed four of our wolfhounds and tore the kennelmaster's arm off his shoulder, even after we'd filled him full of quarrels ..."

"So you sewed his head on Robb Stark's neck after both o' them were dead," said yellow cloak.

"My father did that. All I did was drink. You wouldn't kill a man for drinking." Merrett remembered something then, something that might be the saving of him. "They say Lord Beric always gives a man a trial, that he won't kill a man unless something's proved against him. You can't prove anything against me. The Red Wedding was my father's work, and Ryman's and Lord Bolton's. Lothar rigged the tents to collapse and put the crossbowmen in the gallery with the musicians, Bastard Walder led the attack on the camps ... they're the ones you want, not me, I only drank some wine ... *you have no witness.*"

"As it happens, you're wrong there." The singer turned to the hooded woman. "Milady?"

The outlaws parted as she came forward, saying no word. When she lowered her hood, something tightened inside Merrett's chest, and for a moment he could not breathe. *No. No, I saw her die. She was dead for a day and night before they stripped her naked and threw her body in the river. Raymund opened her throat from ear to ear. She was dead.*

Her cloak and collar hid the gash his brother's blade had made, but her face was even worse than he remembered. The flesh had gone pudding soft in the water and turned the color of curdled milk. Half her hair was gone and the rest had turned as white and brittle as a crone's. Beneath her ravaged scalp, her face was shredded skin and black blood where she had raked herself with her nails. But her eyes were the most terrible thing. Her eyes saw him, and they hated.

"She don't speak," said the big man in the yellow cloak. "You bloody bastards cut her throat too deep for that. But she remembers." He turned to the dead woman and said, "What do you say, m'lady? Was he part of it?"

Lady Catelyn's eyes never left him. She nodded.

Merrett Frey opened his mouth to plead, but the noose choked off his words. His feet left the ground, the rope cutting deep into the soft flesh beneath his chin. Up into the air he jerked, kicking and twisting, up and up and up.

APPENDIX

THE KINGS AND THEIR COURTS

THE KING ON THE IRON THRONE

JOFFREY BARATHEON, the First of His Name, a boy of thirteen years, the eldest son of King Robert I Baratheon and Queen Cersei of House Lannister,

> — his mother, QUEEN CERSEI, of House Lannister, Queen Regent and Protector of the Realm,
>> —Cersei's sworn swords:
>>> — SER OSFRYD KETTLEBLACK, younger brother to Ser Osmund Kettleblack of the Kingsguard,
>>> — SER OSNEY KETTLEBLACK, youngest brother of Ser Osmund and Ser Osfryd,
> — his sister, PRINCESS MYRCELLA, a girl of nine, a ward of Prince Doran Martell at Sunspear,
> — his brother, PRINCE TOMMEN, a boy of eight, next heir to the Iron Throne,
> — his grandfather, TYWIN LANNISTER, Lord of Casterly Rock, Warden of the West, and Hand of the King,
> — his uncles and cousins, paternal,
>> —his father's brother, STANNIS BARATHEON, rebel Lord of Dragonstone, styling himself King Stannis the First,
>>> — Stannis's daughter, SHIREEN, a girl of eleven,
>> —his father's brother, [RENLY BARATHEON], rebel Lord of Storm's End, murdered in the midst of his army,
>> —his grandmother's brother, SER ELDON ESTERMONT,
>>> — Ser Eldon's son, SER AEMON ESTERMONT,
>>>> — Ser Aemon's son, SER ALYN ESTERMONT,
> — his uncles and cousins, maternal,

—his mother's brother, SER JAIME LANNISTER, called
THE KINGSLAYER, a captive at Riverrun,

—his mother's brother, TYRION LANNISTER, called THE
IMP, a dwarf, wounded in the Battle of the Blackwater,
— Tyrion's squire, PODRICK PAYNE,
— Tyrion's captain of guards, SER BRONN OF THE
BLACKWATER, a former sellsword,
— Tyrion's concubine, SHAE, a camp follower now
serving as bedmaid to Lollys Stokeworth,

—his grandfather's brother, SER KEVAN LANNISTER,
— Ser Kevan's son, SER LANCEL LANNISTER, formerly
squire to King Robert, wounded in the Battle of the
Blackwater, near death,

—his grandfather's brother, [TYGETT LANNISTER], died
of a pox,
— Tygett's son, TYREK LANNISTER, a squire, missing
since the great riot,
— Tyrek's infant wife, LADY ERMESANDE HAYFORD,

— his baseborn siblings, King Robert's bastards:
—MYA STONE, a maid of nineteen, in the service of Lord
Nestor Royce, of the Gates of the Moon,
—GENDRY, an apprentice smith, a fugitive in the riverlands
and ignorant of his heritage,
—EDRIC STORM, King Robert's only acknowledged
bastard son, a ward of his uncle Stannis on Dragonstone,

— his Kingsguard:
—SER JAIME LANNISTER, Lord Commander,
—SER MERYN TRANT,
—SER BALON SWANN,
—SER OSMUND KETTLEBLACK,
—SER LORAS TYRELL, the Knight of Flowers,
—SER ARYS OAKHEART,

— his small council:
—LORD TYWIN LANNISTER, Hand of the King,

—SER KEVAN LANNISTER, master of laws,
—LORD PETYR BAELISH, called LITTLEFINGER, master of coin,
—VARYS, a eunuch, called THE SPIDER, master of whisperers,
—LORD MACE TYRELL, master of ships,
—GRAND MAESTER PYCELLE,

— his court and retainers:
—SER ILYN PAYNE, the King's Justice, a headsman,
—LORD HALLYNE THE PYROMANCER, a Wisdom of the Guild of Alchemists,
—MOON BOY, a jester and fool,
—ORMOND OF OLDTOWN, the royal harper and bard,
—DONTOS HOLLARD, a fool and a drunkard, formerly a knight called SER DONTOS THE RED,
—JALABHAR XHO, Prince of the Red Flower Vale, an exile from the Summer Isles,
—LADY TANDA STOKEWORTH,
    — her daughter, FALYSE, wed to Ser Balman Byrch,
    — her daughter, LOLLYS, thirty-four, unwed, and soft of wits, with child after being raped,
    — her healer and counselor, MAESTER FRENKEN,
—LORD GYLES ROSBY, a sickly old man,
—SER TALLAD, a promising young knight,
—LORD MORROS SLYNT, a squire, eldest son of the former Commander of the City Watch,
    — JOTHOS SLYNT, his younger brother, a squire,
    — DANOS SLYNT, younger still, a page,
—SER BOROS BLOUNT, a former knight of the Kingsguard, dismissed for cowardice by Queen Cersei,
—JOSMYN PECKLEDON, a squire, and a hero of the Battle of the Blackwater,
—SER PHILIP FOOTE, made Lord of the Marches for his valor during the Battle of the Blackwater,
—SER LOTHOR BRUNE, named LOTHOR APPLE-EATER

for his deeds during the Battle of the Blackwater, a former free-rider in service to Lord Baelish,

— other lords and knights at King's Landing:
—MATHIS ROWAN, Lord of Goldengrove,
—PAXTER REDWYNE, Lord of the Arbor,
  — Lord Paxter's twin sons, SER HORAS and SER HOBBER, mocked as HORROR and SLOBBER,
  — Lord Redwyne's healer, MAESTER BALLABAR,
—ARDRIAN CELTIGAR, the Lord of Claw Isle,
—LORD ALESANDER STAEDMON, called PENNYLOVER,
—SER BONIFER HASTY, called THE GOOD, a famed knight,
—SER DONNEL SWANN, heir to Stonehelm,
—SER RONNET CONNINGTON, called RED RONNET, the Knight of Griffin's Roost,
—AURANE WATERS, the Bastard of Driftmark,
—SER DERMOT OF THE RAINWOOD, a famed knight,
—SER TIMON SCRAPESWORD, a famed knight,

— the people of King's Landing:
—the City Watch (the "gold cloaks"),
  — [SER JACELYN BYWATER, called IRONHAND], Commander of the City Watch, slain by his own men during the Battle of the Blackwater,
  — SER ADDAM MARBRAND, Commander of the City Watch, Ser Jacelyn's successor,
—CHATAYA, owner of an expensive brothel,
  — ALAYAYA, her daughter,
  — DANCY, MAREI, JAYDE, Chataya's girls,
—TOBHO MOTT, a master armorer,
—IRONBELLY, a blacksmith,
—HAMISH THE HARPER, a famed singer,
—COLLIO QUAYNIS, a Tyroshi singer,
—BETHANY FAIR-FINGERS, a woman singer,

—ALARIC OF EYSEN, a singer, far-traveled,
—GALYEON OF CUY, a singer notorious for the length of
his songs,
—SYMON SILVER TONGUE, a singer.

King Joffrey's banner shows the crowned stag of Baratheon, black on gold, and the lion of Lannister, gold on crimson, combatant.

THE KING IN THE NORTH
THE KING OF THE TRIDENT

ROBB STARK, Lord of Winterfell, King in the North, and King of
the Trident, the eldest son of Eddard Stark, Lord of Winterfell, and
Lady Catelyn of House Tully,
— his direwolf, GREY WIND,
— his mother, LADY CATELYN, of House Tully, widow of Lord
Eddard Stark,
— his siblings:
— his sister, PRINCESS SANSA, a maid of twelve, a captive
in King's Landing,
— Sansa's direwolf, [LADY], killed at Castle Darry,
— his sister, PRINCESS ARYA, a girl of ten, missing and
presumed dead,
— Arya's direwolf, NYMERIA, lost near the Trident,
— his brother, PRINCE BRANDON, called BRAN, heir to
the north, a boy of nine, believed dead,
— Bran's direwolf, SUMMER,
— Bran companions and protectors:
— MEERA REED, a maid of sixteen, daughter of Lord
Howland Reed of Greywater Watch,
— JOJEN REED, her brother, thirteen,
— HODOR, a simpleminded stableboy, seven feet tall,
— his brother, PRINCE RICKON, a boy of four, believed
dead,
— Rickon's direwolf, SHAGGYDOG,

— Rickon's companion and protector:
    — OSHA, a wildling captive who served as a scullion at Winterfell,
— his half-brother, JON SNOW, a Sworn Brother of the Night's Watch,
    — Jon's direwolf, GHOST,

— his uncles and aunts, paternal:
    — his father's elder brother, [BRANDON STARK], slain at the command of King Aerys II Targaryen,
    — his father's sister, [LYANNA STARK], died in the Mountains of Dorne during Robert's Rebellion,
    — his father's younger brother, BENJEN STARK, a man of the Night's Watch, lost beyond the Wall,
— his uncles, aunts, and cousins, maternal:
    — his mother's younger sister, LYSA ARRYN, Lady of the Eyrie and widow of Lord Jon Arryn,
        — their son, ROBERT ARRYN, Lord of the Eyrie,
    — his mother's younger brother, SER EDMURE TULLY, heir to Riverrun,
    — his grandfather's brother, SER BRYNDEN TULLY, called THE BLACKFISH,
— his sworn swords and companions:
    — his squire, OLYVAR FREY,
    — SER WENDEL MANDERLY, second son to the Lord of White Harbor,
    — PATREK MALLISTER, heir to Seagard,
    — DACEY MORMONT, eldest daughter of Lady Maege Mormont and heir to Bear Island,
    — JON UMBER, called THE SMALLJON, heir to Last Hearth,
    — DONNEL LOCKE, OWEN NORREY, ROBIN FLINT, northmen, .

— his lords bannermen, captains and commanders:
— (with Robb's army in the Westerlands)

—SER BRYNDEN TULLY, the BLACKFISH, commanding the scouts and outriders,

—JON UMBER, called THE GREATJON, commanding the van,

—RICKARD KARSTARK, Lord of Karhold,

—GALBART GLOVER, Master of Deepwood Motte,

—MAEGE MORMONT, Lady of Bear Island,

—[SER STEVRON FREY], eldest son of Lord Walder Frey and heir to the Twins, died at Oxcross,

— Ser Stevron's eldest son, SER RYMAN FREY,

— Ser Ryman's son, BLACK WALDER FREY,

—MARTYN RIVERS, a bastard son of Lord Walder Frey,

— (with Roose Bolton's host at Harrenhal),

—ROOSE BOLTON, Lord of the Dreadfort,

—SER AENYS FREY, SER JARED FREY, SER HOSTEEN FREY, SER DANWELL FREY

— their bastard half-brother, RONEL RIVERS,

—SER WYLIS MANDERLY, heir to White Harbor,

— SER KYLE CONDON, a knight in his service,

—RONNEL STOUT,

—VARGO HOAT of the Free City of Qohor, captain of a sellsword company, the Brave Companions,

— his lieutenant, URSWYCK called THE FAITHFUL,

— his lieutenant, SEPTON UTT,

— TIMEON OF DORNE, RORGE, IGGO, FAT ZOLLO, BITER, TOGG JOTH of Ibben, PYG, THREE TOES, his men,

— QYBURN, a chainless maester and sometime necromancer, his healer,

— (with the northern army attacking Duskendale)

—ROBETT GLOVER, of Deepwood Motte,

—SER HELMAN TALLHART, of Torrhen's Square,

—HARRION KARSTARK, sole surviving son of Lord Rickard Karstark, and heir to Karhold,

— (traveling north with Lord Eddard's bones)
   —HALLIS MOLLEN, captain of guards for Winterfell,
   — JACKS, QUENT, SHADD, guardsmen,

— his lord bannermen and castellans, in the north:
   —WYMAN MANDERLY, Lord of White Harbor,
   —HOWLAND REED, Lord of Greywater Watch, a crannogman,
   —MORS UMBER, called CROWFOOD, and HOTHER UMBER, called WHORESBANE, uncles to Greatjon Umber, joint castellans at the Last Hearth,
   —LYESSA FLINT, Lady of Widow's Watch,
   —ONDREW LOCKE, Lord of Oldcastle, an old man,
   — [CLEY CERWYN], Lord of Cerwyn, a boy of fourteen, killed in battle at Winterfell,
      — his sister, JONELLE CERWYN, a maid of two-and-thirty, now the Lady of Cerwyn,
   — [LEOBALD TALLHART], younger brother to Ser Helman, castellan at Torrhen's Square, killed in battle at Winterfell,
      — Leobald's wife, BERENA of House Hornwood,
      — Leobald's son, BRANDON, a boy of fourteen,
      — Leobald's son, BEREN, a boy of ten,
      — Ser Helman's son, [BENFRED], killed by ironmen on the Stony Shore,
      — Ser Helman's daughter, EDDARA, a girl of nine, heir to Torrhen's Square,
   —LADY SYBELLE, wife to Robett Glover, a captive of Asha Greyjoy at Deepwood Motte,
      — Robett's son, GAWEN, three, rightful heir to Deepwood Motte, a captive of Asha Greyjoy,
      — Robett's daughter, ERENA, a babe of one, a captive of Asha Greyjoy at Deepwood Motte,

— LARENCE SNOW, a bastard son of Lord Hornwood, and ward of Galbart Glover, thirteen, a captive of Asha Greyjoy at Deepwood Motte.

The banner of the King in the North remains as it has for thousands of years: the grey direwolf of the Starks of Winterfell, running across an ice-white field.

THE KING IN THE NARROW SEA

STANNIS BARATHEON, the First of His Name, second son of Lord
   Steffon Baratheon and Lady Cassana of House Estermont, formerly
   Lord of Dragonstone,
   — his wife, QUEEN SELYSE of House Florent,
      — PRINCESS SHIREEN, their daughter, a girl of eleven,
         — PATCHFACE, her lackwit fool,
   — his baseborn nephew, EDRIC STORM, a boy of twelve,
      bastard son of King Robert by Delena Florent,
   — his squires, DEVAN SEAWORTH and BRYEN FARRING,
   — his court and retainers:
      —LORD ALESTER FLORENT, Lord of Brightwater Keep
         and Hand of the King, the queen's uncle,
      —SER AXELL FLORENT, castellan of Dragonstone and
         leader of the queen's men, the queen's uncle,
      —LADY MELISANDRE OF ASSHAI, called THE RED
         WOMAN, priestess of R'hllor, the Lord of Light and God
         of Flame and Shadow,
      —MAESTER PYLOS, healer, tutor, counselor,
      —SER DAVOS SEAWORTH, called THE ONION KNIGHT
         and sometimes SHORTHAND, once a smuggler,
         — Davos's wife, LADY MARYA, a carpenter's daughter,
            — their seven sons:
               — [DALE], lost on the Blackwater,
               — [ALLARD], lost on the Blackwater,
               — [MATTHOS], lost on the Blackwater,

— [MARIC], lost on the Blackwater,
— DEVAN, squire to King Stannis,
— STANNIS, a boy of nine years,
— STEFFON, a boy of six years,
—SALLADHOR SAAN, of the Free City of Lys, styling himself Prince of the Narrow Sea and Lord of Blackwater Bay, master of the *Valyrian* and a fleet of sister galleys,
— MEIZO MAHR, a eunuch in his hire,
— KHORANE SATHMANTES, captain of his galley *Shayala's Dance*,
—"PORRIDGE" and "LAMPREY," two gaolers,

— his lords bannermen,
—MONTERYS VELARYON, Lord of the Tides and Master of Driftmark, a boy of six,
—DURAM BAR EMMON, Lord of Sharp Point, a boy of fifteen years,
—SER GILBERT FARRING, castellan of Storm's End,
— LORD ELWOOD MEADOWS, Ser Gilbert's second,
— MAESTER JURNE, Ser Gilbert's counselor and healer,
—LORD LUCOS CHYTTERING, called LITTLE LUCOS, a youth of sixteen,
—LESTER MORRIGEN, Lord of Crows Nest,

— his knights and sworn swords,
—SER LOMAS ESTERMONT, the king's maternal uncle,
—his son, SER ANDREW ESTERMONT,
—SER ROLLAND STORM, called THE BASTARD OF NIGHTSONG, a baseborn son of the late Lord Bryen Caron,
—SER PARMEN CRANE, called PARMEN THE PURPLE, held captive at Highgarden,
—SER ERREN FLORENT, younger brother to Queen Selyse, held captive at Highgarden,
—SER GERALD GOWER,

—SER TRISTON OF TALLY HILL, formerly in service to Lord Guncer Sunglass,

—LEWYS, called THE FISHWIFE,

—OMER BLACKBERRY.

King Stannis has taken for his banner the fiery heart of the Lord of Light: a red heart surrounded by orange flames upon a yellow field. Within the heart is the crowned stag of House Baratheon, in black.

THE QUEEN ACROSS THE WATER

DAENERYS TARGARYEN, the First of Her Name, *Khaleesi* of the Dothraki, called DAENERYS STORMBORN, the UNBURNT, MOTHER OF DRAGONS, sole surviving heir of Aerys II Targaryen, widow of Khal Drogo of the Dothraki,

— her growing dragons, DROGON, VISERION, RHAEGAL,
— her Queensguard:
—SER JORAH MORMONT, formerly Lord of Bear Island, exiled for slaving,
—JHOGO, *ko* and bloodrider, the whip,
—AGGO, *ko* and bloodrider, the bow,
—RAKHARO, *ko* and bloodrider, the *arakh*,
—STRONG BELWAS, a former eunuch slave from the fighting pits of Meereen,
— his aged squire, ARSTAN called WHITEBEARD, a man of Westeros,
— her handmaids:
—IRRI, a Dothraki girl, fifteen,
—JHIQUI, a Dothraki girl, fourteen,
— GROLEO, captain of the great cog *Balerion*, a Pentoshi seafarer in the hire of Illyrio Mopatis,

— her late kin:
—[RHAEGAR], her brother, Prince of Dragonstone and heir to the Iron Throne, slain by Robert Baratheon on the Trident,
— [RHAENYS], Rhaegar's daughter by Elia of Dorne,

　　　murdered during the Sack of King's Landing,
　— [AEGON], Rhaegar's son by Elia of Dorne, murdered
　　　during the Sack of King's Landing,
—[VISERYS], her brother, styling himself King Viserys, the
　　Third of His Name, called THE BEGGAR KING, slain in
　　Vaes Dothrak by Khal Drogo,
—[DROGO], her husband, a great *khal* of the Dothraki,
　　never defeated in battle, died of a wound,
　— [RHAEGO], her stillborn son by Khal Drogo, slain in
　　　the womb by Mirri Maz Duur,

— her known enemies:
　—KHAL PONO, once *ko* to Drogo,
　—KHAL JHAQO, once *ko* to Drogo,
　　— MAGGO, his bloodrider,
　—THE UNDYING OF QARTH, a band of warlocks,
　　— PYAT PREE, a Qartheen warlock,
　—THE SORROWFUL MEN, a guild of Qartheen
　　assassins,

— her uncertain allies, past and present:
　—XARO XHOAN DAXOS, a merchant prince of Qarth,
　—QUAITHE, a masked shadowbinder from Asshai,
　—ILLYRIO MOPATIS, a magister of the Free City of Pentos,
　　who brokered her marriage to Khal Drogo,

— in Astapor:
　—KRAZNYS MO NAKLOZ, a wealthy slave trader,
　　— his slave, MISSANDEI, a girl of ten, of the Peaceful
　　　People of Naath,
　— GRAZDAN MO ULLHOR, an old slave trader, very rich,
　　— his slave, CLEON, a butcher and cook,
　—GREY WORM, an eunuch of the Unsullied,

— in Yunkai:
　—GRAZDAN MO ERAZ, envoy and nobleman,

—MERO OF BRAAVOS, called THE TITAN'S BASTARD, captain of the Second Sons, a free company,
— BROWN BEN PLUMM, a sergeant in the Second Sons, a sellsword of dubious descent,
—PRENDAHL NA GHEZN, a Ghiscari sellsword, captain of the Stormcrows, a free company,
—SALLOR THE BALD, a Qartheen sellsword, captain of the Stormcrows,
—DAARIO NAHARIS, a flamboyant Tyroshi sellsword, captain of the Stormcrows,

— in Meereen:
—OZNAK ZO PAHL, a hero of the city.

The banner of Daenerys Targaryen is the banner of Aegon the Conqueror and the dynasty he established: a three-headed dragon, red on black.

KING OF THE ISLES
AND THE NORTH

BALON GREYJOY, the Ninth of His Name Since the Grey King, styling himself King of the Iron Islands and the North, King of Salt and Rock, Son of the Sea Wind, and Lord Reaper of Pyke,
  — his wife, QUEEN ALANNYS, of House Harlaw,
  — their children:
    — [RODRIK], their eldest son, slain at Seagard during Greyjoy's Rebellion,
    — [MARON], their second son, slain at Pyke during Greyjoy's Rebellion,
    — ASHA, their daughter, captain of the *Black Wind* and conqueror of Deepwood Motte,
    — THEON, their youngest son, captain of the *Sea Bitch* and briefly Prince of Winterfell,
      — Theon's squire, WEX PYKE, bastard son of Lord Botley's half-brother, a mute lad of twelve,
      — Theon's crew, the men of the *Sea Bitch*:
        — URZEN, MARON BOTLEY called FISHWHISKERS, STYGG, GEVIN HARLAW, CADWYLE,

  — his brothers:
    — EURON, called Crow's Eye, captain of the *Silence*, a notorious outlaw, pirate, and raider,
    — VICTARION, Lord Captain of the Iron Fleet, master of the *Iron Victory*,

—AERON, called DAMPHAIR, a priest of the Drowned God,

— his household on Pyke:
  —MAESTER WENDAMYR, healer and counselor,
  —HELYA, keeper of the castle,
    — his warriors and sworn swords:
    — DAGMER called CLEFTJAW, captain of *Foamdrinker*,
  —BLUETOOTH, a longship captain,
  —ULLER, SKYTE, oarsmen and warriors,
  —ANDRIK THE UNSMILING, a giant of a man,
  —QARL, called QARL THE MAID, beardless but deadly,

— people of Lordsport:
  —OTTER GIMPKNEE, innkeeper and whoremonger,
  —SIGRIN, a shipwright,

— his lords bannermen:
  —SAWANE BOTLEY, Lord of Lordsport, on Pyke,
  —LORD WYNCH, of Iron Holt, on Pyke,
  —STONEHOUSE, DRUMM, and GOODBROTHER of Old Wyk,
  —LORD GOODBROTHER, SPARR, LORD MERLYN, and LORD FARWYND of Great Wyk,
  —LORD HARLAW, of Harlaw,
  —VOLMARK, MYRE, STONETREE, and KENNING, of Harlaw,
  —ORKWOOD and TAWNEY of Orkmont,
  —LORD BLACKTYDE of Blacktyde,
  —LORD SALTCLIFFE and LORD SUNDERLY of Saltcliffe.

OTHER HOUSES GREAT AND SMALL

HOUSE ARRYN

The Arryns are descended from the Kings of Mountain and Vale, one of the oldest and purest lines of Andal nobility. House Arryn has taken no part in the War of the Five Kings, holding back its strength to protect the Vale of Arryn. The Arryn sigil is the moon-and-falcon, white, upon a sky-blue field. The Arryn words are *As High As Honor.*

ROBERT ARRYN, Lord of the Eyrie, Defender of the Vale, Warden of the East, a sickly boy of eight years,
— his mother, LADY LYSA, of House Tully, third wife and widow of Lord Jon Arryn, and sister to Catelyn Stark,
— their household:
—MARILLION, a handsome young singer, much favored by Lady Lysa,
—MAESTER COLEMON, counselor, healer, and tutor,
—SER MARWYN BELMORE, captain of guards,
—MORD, a brutal gaoler,

— his lords bannermen, knights, and retainers:
—LORD NESTOR ROYCE, High Steward of the Vale and castellan of the Gates of the Moon, of the junior branch of House Royce,
— Lord Nestor's son, SER ALBAR,
— Lord Nestor's daughter, MYRANDA,
— MYA STONE, a bastard girl in his service, natural daughter of King Robert I Baratheon,

—LORD YOHN ROYCE, called BRONZE YOHN, Lord of Runestone, of the senior branch of House Royce, cousin to Lord Nestor,
  — Lord Yohn's eldest son, SER ANDAR,
  — Lord Yohn's second son, [SER ROBAR], a knight of Renly Baratheon's Rainbow Guard, slain at Storm's End by Ser Loras Tyrell,
  — Lord Yohn's youngest son, [SER WAYMAR], a man of the Night's Watch, lost beyond the Wall,
—SER LYN CORBRAY, a suitor to Lady Lysa,
  — MYCHEL REDFORT, his squire,
—LADY ANYA WAYNWOOD,
  — Lady Anya's eldest son and heir, SER MORTON, a suitor to Lady Lysa,
  — Lady Anya's second son, SER DONNEL, the Knight of the Gate,
—EON HUNTER, Lord of Longbow Hall, an old man, and a suitor to Lady Lysa,
—HORTON REDFORT, Lord of Redfort.

HOUSE FLORENT

The Florents of Brightwater Keep are Tyrell bannermen, despite a superior claim to Highgarden by virtue of a blood tie to House Gardener, the old Kings of the Reach. At the outbreak of the War of the Five Kings, Lord Alester Florent followed the Tyrells in declaring for King Renly, but his brother Ser Axell chose King Stannis, whom he had served for years as castellan of Dragonstone. Their niece Selyse was and is King Stannis's queen. When Renly died at Storm's End, the Florents went over to Stannis with all their strength, the first of Renly's bannermen to do so. The sigil of House Florent shows a fox head in a circle of flowers.

ALESTER FLORENT, Lord of Brightwater,
— his wife, LADY MELARA, of House Crane,
— their children:
—ALEKYNE, heir to Brightwater,
—MELESSA, wed to Lord Randyll Tarly,
—RHEA, wed to Lord Leyton Hightower,
— his siblings:
—SER AXELL, castellan of Dragonstone,
—[SER RYAM], died in a fall from a horse,
— Ser Ryam's daughter, QUEEN SELYSE, wed to King Stannis Baratheon,
— Ser Ryam's son, [SER IMRY], commanding Stannis Baratheon's fleet on the Blackwater, lost with the *Fury*,
— Ser Ryam's second son, SER ERREN, held captive at Highgarden,

—SER COLIN,

    — Ser Colin's daughter, DELENA, wed to SER HOSMAN NORCROSS,

        — Delena's son, EDRIC STORM, a bastard of King Robert I Baratheon, twelve years of age,

        — Delena's son, ALESTER NORCROSS, eight,

        — Delena's son, RENLY NORCROSS, a boy of two,

    — Ser Colin's son, MAESTER OMER, in service at Old Oak,

    — Ser Colin's son, MERRELL, a squire on the Arbor,

—his sister, RYLENE, wed to Ser Rycherd Crane.

HOUSE FREY

Powerful, wealthy, and numerous, the Freys are bannermen to House Tully, but they have not always been diligent in their duty. When Robert Baratheon met Rhaegar Targaryen on the Trident, the Freys did not arrive until the battle was done, and thereafter Lord Hoster Tully always called Lord Walder "the Late Lord Frey." It is also said of Walder Frey that he is the only lord in the Seven Kingdoms who could field an army out of his breeches.

At the onset of the War of the Five Kings, Robb Stark won Lord Walder's allegiance by pledging to wed one of his daughters or grand-daughters. Two of Lord Walder's grandsons were sent to Winterfell to be fostered.

WALDER FREY, Lord of the Crossing,
— by his first wife, [LADY PERRA, of House Royce]:
— [SER STEVRON], their eldest son, died after the Battle of Oxcross,
— m. [Corenna Swann, died of a wasting illness],
— Stevron's eldest son, SER RYMAN, heir to the Twins,
— Ryman's son, EDWYN, wed to Janyce Hunter,
— Edwyn's daughter, WALDA, a girl of eight,
— Ryman's son, WALDER, called BLACK WALDER,
— Ryman's son, PETYR, called PETYR PIMPLE,
— m. Mylenda Caron,
— Petyr's daughter, PERRA, a girl of five,
— m. [Jeyne Lydden, died in a fall from a horse],

— Stevron's son, AEGON, a halfwit called JINGLEBELL,
— Stevron's daughter, [MAEGELLE, died in childbed],
    m. Ser Dafyn Vance,
        — Maegelle's daughter, MARIANNE, a maiden,
        — Maegelle's son, WALDER VANCE, a squire,
        — Maegelle's son, PATREK VANCE,
— m. [Marsella Waynwood, died in childbed],
— Stevron's son, WALTON, m. Deana Hardyng,
        — Walton's son, STEFFON, called THE SWEET,
        — Walton's daughter, WALDA, called FAIR WALDA,
        — Walton's son, BRYAN, a squire,
—SER EMMON, m. Genna of House Lannister,
    — Emmon's son, SER CLEOS, m. Jeyne Darry,
        — Cleos's son, TYWIN, a squire of eleven,
        — Cleos's son, WILLEM, a page at Ashemark, nine,
    — Emmon's son, SER LYONEL, m. Melesa Crakehall,
    — Emmon's son, TION, a captive at Riverrun,
    — Emmon's son, WALDER, called RED WALDER, fourteen,
        a squire at Casterly Rock,
—SER AENYS, m. [Tyana Wylde, died in childbed],
    — Aenys's son, AEGON BLOODBORN, an outlaw,
    — Aenys's son, RHAEGAR, m. Jeyne Beesbury,
        — Rhaegar's son, ROBERT, a boy of thirteen,
        — Rhaegar's daughter, WALDA, a girl of ten, called
            WHITE WALDA,
        — Rhaegar's son, JONOS, a boy of eight,
—PERRIANE, m. Ser Leslyn Haigh,
    — Perriane's son, SER HARYS HAIGH,
        — Harys's son, WALDER HAIGH, a boy of four,
    — Perriane's son, SER DONNEL HAIGH,
    — Perriane's son, ALYN HAIGH, a squire,

— by his second wife, [LADY CYRENNA, of House Swann]:
—SER JARED, their eldest son, m. [Alys Frey],
    — Jared's son, SER TYTOS, m. Zhoe Blanetree,
        — Tytos's daughter, ZIA, a maid of fourteen,

— Tytos's son, ZACHERY, a boy of twelve, training at
   the Sept of Oldtown,
— Jared's daughter, KYRA, m. Ser Garse Goodbrook,
   — Kyra's son, WALDER GOODBROOK, a boy of
      nine,
   — Kyra's daughter, JEYNE GOODBROOK, six,
— SEPTON LUCEON, in service at the Great Sept of Baelor
   in King's Landing,

— by his third wife, [LADY AMAREI of House Crakehall]:
— SER HOSTEEN, their eldest son, m. Bellena Hawick,
   — Hosteen's son, SER ARWOOD, m. Ryella Royce,
   — Arwood's daughter, RYELLA, a girl of five,
   — Arwood's twin sons, ANDROW and ALYN, three,
— LADY LYTHENE, m. Lord Lucias Vypren,
   — Lythene's daughter, ELYANA, m. Ser Jon Wylde,
      — Elyana's son, RICKARD WYLDE, four,
   — Lythene's son, SER DAMON VYPREN,
— SYMOND, m. Betharios of Braavos,
   — Symond's son, ALESANDER, a singer,
   — Symond's daughter, ALYX, a maid of seventeen,
   — Symond's son, BRADAMAR, a boy of ten, fostered on
      Braavos as a ward of Oro Tendyris, a merchant of that
      city,
— SER DANWELL, m. Wynafrei Whent,
   — [many stillbirths and miscarriages],
— MERRETT, m. Mariya Darry,
   — Merrett's daughter, AMEREI, called AMI, a widow of
      sixteen, m. [Ser Pate of the Blue Fork],
   — Merrett's daughter, WALDA, called FAT WALDA, a wife
      of fifteen years, m. Lord Roose Bolton,
   — Merrett's daughter, MARISSA, a maid of thirteen,
   — Merrett's son, WALDER, called LITTLE WALDER, a
      boy of seven, taken captive at Winterfell while a ward
      of Lady Catelyn Stark,
— [SER GEREMY, drowned], m. Carolei Waynwood,

— Geremy's son, SANDOR, a boy of twelve, a squire to Ser Donnel Waynwood,
— Geremy's daughter, CYNTHEA, a girl of nine, a ward of Lady Anya Waynwood,
—SER RAYMUND, m. Beony Beesbury,
— Raymund's son, ROBERT, sixteen, in training at the Citadel in Oldtown,
— Raymund's son, MALWYN, fifteen, apprenticed to an alchemist in Lys,
— Raymund's twin daughters, SERRA and SARRA, maiden girls of fourteen,
— Raymund's daughter, CERSEI, six, called LITTLE BEE,

— by his fourth wife, [LADY ALYSSA, of House Blackwood]:
—LOTHAR, their eldest son, called LAME LOTHAR, m. Leonella Lefford,
— Lothar's daughter, TYSANE, a girl of seven,
— Lothar's daughter, WALDA, a girl of four,
— Lothar's daughter, EMBERLEI, a girl of two,
—SER JAMMOS, m. Sallei Paege,
— Jammos's son, WALDER, called BIG WALDER, a boy of eight, taken captive at Winterfell while a ward of Lady Catelyn Stark,
— Jammos's twin sons, DICKON and MATHIS, five,
—SER WHALEN, m. Sylwa Paege,
— Whalen's son, HOSTER, a boy of twelve, a squire to Ser Damon Paege,
— Whalen's daughter, MERIANNE, called MERRY, a girl of eleven,
—LADY MORYA, m. Ser Flement Brax,
— Morya's son, ROBERT BRAX, nine, fostered at Casterly Rock as a page,
— Morya's son, WALDER BRAX, a boy of six,
— Morya's son, JON BRAX, a babe of three,
—TYTA, called TYTA THE MAID, a maid of twenty-nine,

— by his fifth wife, [LADY SARYA of House Whent]:
— no progeny,

— by his sixth wife, [LADY BETHANY of House Rosby]:
— SER PERWYN, their eldest son,
— SER BENFREY, m. Jyanna Frey, a cousin,
  — Benfrey's daughter, DELLA, called DEAF DELLA, a girl of three,
  — Benfrey's son, OSMUND, a boy of two,
— MAESTER WILLAMEN, in service at Longbow Hall,
— OLYVAR, squire to Robb Stark,
— ROSLIN, a maid of sixteen,

— by his seventh wife, [LADY ANNARA of House Farring]:
— ARWYN, a maid of fourteen,
— WENDEL, their eldest son, a boy of thirteen, fostered at Seagard as a page,
— COLMAR, promised to the Faith, eleven,
— WALTYR, called TYR, a boy of ten,
— ELMAR, formerly betrothed to Arya Stark, a boy of nine,
— SHIREI, a girl of six,

— his eighth wife, LADY JOYEUSE of House Erenford,
— no progeny as yet,

— Lord Walder's natural children, by sundry mothers,
— WALDER RIVERS, called BASTARD WALDER,
  — Bastard Walder's son, SER AEMON RIVERS,
  — Bastard Walder's daughter, WALDA RIVERS,
— MAESTER MELWYS, in service at Rosby,
— JEYNE RIVERS, MARTYN RIVERS, RYGER RIVERS, RONEL RIVERS, MELLARA RIVERS, others.

HOUSE LANNISTER

The Lannisters of Casterly Rock remain the principal support of King Joffrey's claim to the Iron Throne. They boast of descent from Lann the Clever, the legendary trickster of the Age of Heroes. The gold of Casterly Rock and the Golden Tooth has made them the wealthiest of the Great Houses. The Lannister sigil is a golden lion upon a crimson field. Their words are *Hear Me Roar*!

TYWIN LANNISTER, Lord of Casterly Rock, Warden of the West, Shield of Lannisport, and Hand of the King,
— his son, SER JAIME, called THE KINGSLAYER, a twin to Queen Cersei, Lord Commander of the Kingsguard, and Warden of the East, a captive at Riverrun,
— his daughter, QUEEN CERSEI, twin to Jaime, widow of King Robert I Baratheon, Queen Regent for her son Joffrey,
— her son, KING JOFFREY BARATHEON, a boy of thirteen,
— her daughter, PRINCESS MYRCELLA BARATHEON, a girl of nine, a ward of Prince Doran Martell in Dorne,
— her son, PRINCE TOMMEN BARATHEON, a boy of eight, heir to the Iron Throne,
— his dwarf son, TYRION, called THE IMP, called HALFMAN, wounded and scarred on the Blackwater,

— his siblings:
— SER KEVAN, Lord Tywin's eldest brother,
— Ser Kevan's wife, DORNA, of House Swyft,

—their son, SER LANCEL, formerly a squire to King Robert, wounded and near death,
—their son, WILLEM, twin to Martyn, a squire, captive at Riverrun,
—their son, MARTYN, twin to Willem, a squire, a captive with Robb Stark,
—their daughter, JANEI, a girl of two,
—GENNA, his sister, wed to Ser Emmon Frey,
  —their son, SER CLEOS FREY, a captive at Riverrun,
  —their son, SER LYONEL,
  —their son, TION FREY, a squire, captive at Riverrun,
  —their son, WALDER, called RED WALDER, a squire at Casterly Rock,
—[SER TYGETT], his second brother, died of a pox,
  —Tygett's widow, DARLESSA, of House Marbrand,
  —their son, TYREK, squire to the king, missing,
—[GERION], his youngest brother, lost at sea,
  —Gerion's bastard daughter, JOY, eleven,

—his cousins:
  —[SER STAFFORD LANNISTER], brother to the late Lady Joanna, slain at Oxcross,
  —Ser Stafford's daughters, CERENNA and MYRIELLE,
  —Ser Stafford's son, SER DAVEN,
  —SER DAMION LANNISTER, m. Lady Shiera Crakehall,
    —his son, SER LUCION,
    —his daughter, LANNA, m. Lord Antario Jast,
  —MARGOT, m. Lord Titus Peake,

—his household:
  —MAESTER CREYLEN, healer, tutor, and counselor,
  —VYLARR, captain-of-guards,
    —LUM and RED LESTER, guardsmen,
  —WHITESMILE WAT, a singer,
  —SER BENEDICT BROOM, master-at-arms,

— his lords bannermen:
  —DAMON MARBRAND, Lord of Ashemark,
    —SER ADDAM MARBRAND, his son and heir,
  —ROLAND CRAKEHALL, Lord of Crakehall,
    —his brother, [SER BURTON CRAKEHALL], killed by Lord Beric Dondarrion and his outlaws,
    —his son and heir, SER TYBOLT CRAKEHALL,
    —his second son, SER LYLE CRAKEHALL, called STRONGBOAR, a captive at Pinkmaiden Castle,
    —his youngest son, SER MERLON CRAKEHALL,
  —[ANDROS BRAX], Lord of Hornvale, drowned during the Battle of the Camps,
    —his brother, [SER RUPERT BRAX], slain at Oxcross,
    —his eldest son, SER TYTOS BRAX, now Lord of Hornvale, a captive at the Twins,
    —his second son, [SER ROBERT BRAX], slain at the Battle of the Fords,
    —his third son, SER FLEMENT BRAX, now heir,
  —[LORD LEO LEFFORD], drowned at the Stone Mill,
  —REGENARD ESTREN, Lord of Wyndhall, a captive at the Twins,
  —GAWEN WESTERLING, Lord of the Crag, a captive at Seagard,
    —his wife, LADY SYBELL, of House Spicer,
      —her brother, SER ROLPH SPICER,
      —her cousin, SER SAMWELL SPICER,
    —their children:
      —SER RAYNALD WESTERLING,
      —JEYNE, a maid of sixteen years,
      —ELEYNA, a girl of twelve,
      —ROLLAM, a boy of nine,
  —LEWYS LYDDEN, Lord of the Deep Den,
  —LORD ANTARIO JAST, a captive at Pinkmaiden Castle,
  —LORD PHILIP PLUMM,
    —his sons, SER DENNIS PLUMM, SER PETER PLUMM, and SER HARWYN PLUMM, called HARDSTONE,

—QUENTEN BANEFORT, Lord of Banefort, a captive of Lord Jonos Bracken,
— his knights and captains:
— SER HARYS SWYFT, good-father to Ser Kevan Lannister,
— Ser Harys's son, SER STEFFON SWYFT,
— Ser Steffon's daughter, JOANNA,
— Ser Harys's daughter, SHIERLE, m. Ser Melwyn Sarsfield,
—SER FORLEY PRESTER,
—SER GARTH GREENFIELD, a captive at Raventree Hall,
—SER LYMOND VIKARY, a captive at Wayfarer's Rest,
—LORD SELMOND STACKSPEAR,
— his son, SER STEFFON STACKSPEAR,
— his younger son, SER ALYN STACKSPEAR,
—TERRENCE KENNING, Lord of Kayce,
— SER KENNOS OF KAYCE, a knight in his service,
—SER GREGOR CLEGANE, the Mountain That Rides,
— POLLIVER, CHISWYCK, RAFF THE SWEETLING, DUNSEN, and THE TICKLER, soldiers in his service,
— [SER AMORY LORCH], fed to a bear by Vargo Hoat after the fall of Harrenhal.

HOUSE MARTELL

Dorne was the last of the Seven Kingdoms to swear fealty to the Iron Throne. Blood, custom, and history all set the Dornishmen apart from the other kingdoms. At the outbreak of the War of the Five Kings, Dorne took no part. With the betrothal of Myrcella Baratheon to Prince Trystane, Sunspear declared its support for King Joffrey and called its banners. The Martell banner is a red sun pierced by a golden spear. Their words are *Unbowed, Unbent, Unbroken*.

DORAN NYMEROS MARTELL, Lord of Sunspear, Prince of Dorne,
— his wife, MELLARIO, of the Free City of Norvos,
— their children:
—PRINCESS ARIANNE, their eldest daughter, heir to Sunspear,
—PRINCE QUENTYN, their elder son,
—PRINCE TRYSTANE, their younger son, betrothed to Myrcella Baratheon,
— his siblings:
—his sister, [PRINCESS ELIA], wife of Prince Rháegar Targaryen, slain during the Sack of King's Landing,
—their children:
— [PRINCESS RHAENYS], a young girl, slain during the Sack of King's Landing,
— [PRINCE AEGON], a babe, slain during the Sack of King's Landing,
—his brother, PRINCE OBERYN, called THE RED VIPER,

— Prince Oberyn's paramour, ELLARIA SAND,
— Prince Oberyn's bastard daughters, OBARA, NYMERIA, TYENE, SARELLA, ELIA, OBELLA, DOREA, LOREZA, called THE SAND SNAKES,

—Prince Oberyn's companions:
  — HARMEN ULLER, Lord of Hellholt,
    — Harmen's brother, SER ULWYCK ULLER,
  — SER RYON ALLYRION,
    — Ser Ryon's natural son, SER DAEMON SAND, the Bastard of Godsgrace,
  — DAGOS MANWOODY, Lord of Kingsgrave,
    — Dagos's sons, MORS and DICKON,
    — Dagos's brother, SER MYLES MANWOODY,
  — SER ARRON QORGYLE,
  — SER DEZIEL DALT, the Knight of Lemonwood,
  — MYRIA JORDAYNE, heir to the Tor,
  — LARRA BLACKMONT, Lady of Blackmont,
    — her daughter, JYNESSA BLACKMONT,
    — her son, PERROS BLACKMONT, a squire,

— his household:
  —AREO HOTAH, a Norvoshi sellsword, captain of guards,
  —MAESTER CALEOTTE, counselor, healer, and tutor,

— his lords bannermen:
  —HARMEN ULLER, Lord of Hellholt,
  —EDRIC DAYNE, Lord of Starfall,
  —DELONNE ALLYRION, Lady of Godsgrace,
  —DAGOS MANWOODY, Lord of Kingsgrave,
  —LARRA BLACKMONT, Lady of Blackmont,
  —TREMOND GARGALEN, Lord of Salt Shore,
  —ANDERS YRONWOOD, Lord of Yronwood,
  —NYMELLA TOLAND.

HOUSE TULLY

Lord Edmyn Tully of Riverrun was one of the first of the river lords to swear fealty to Aegon the Conqueror. The victorious Aegon rewarded him by raising House Tully to dominion over all the lands of the Trident. The Tully sigil is a leaping trout, silver, on a field of rippling blue and red. The Tully words are *Family, Duty, Honor*.

HOSTER TULLY, Lord of Riverrun,
— his wife, [LADY MINISA, of House Whent], died in childbed,
— their children:
— CATELYN, widow of Lord Eddard Stark of Winterfell,
— her eldest son, ROBB STARK, Lord of Winterfell, King in the North, and King of the Trident,
— her daughter, SANSA STARK, a maid of twelve, captive at King's Landing,
— her daughter, ARYA STARK, ten, missing for a year,
— her son, BRANDON STARK, eight, believed dead,
— her son, RICKON STARK, four, believed dead,
— LYSA, widow of Lord Jon Arryn of the Eyrie,
— her son, ROBERT, Lord of the Eyrie and Defender of the Vale, a sickly boy of seven years,
— SER EDMURE, his only son, heir to Riverrun,
— Ser Edmure's friends and companions:
— SER MARQ PIPER, heir to Pinkmaiden,
— LORD LYMOND GOODBROOK,

    — SER RONALD VANCE, called THE BAD, and his brothers, SER HUGO, SER ELLERY, and KIRTH,

    — PATREK MALLISTER, LUCAS BLACKWOOD, SER PERWYN FREY, TRISTAN RYGER, SER ROBERT PAEGE,

— his brother, SER BRYNDEN, called The Blackfish,

— his household:
    — MAESTER VYMAN, counselor, healer, and tutor,
    — SER DESMOND GRELL, master-at-arms,
    — SER ROBIN RYGER, captain of the guard,
      — LONG LEW, ELWOOD, DELP, guardsmen,
    — UTHERYDES WAYN, steward of Riverrun,
    — RYMUND THE RHYMER, a singer,

— his lords bannermen:
    — JONOS BRACKEN, Lord of the Stone Hedge,
    — JASON MALLISTER, Lord of Seagard,
    — WALDER FREY, Lord of the Crossing,
    — CLEMENT PIPER, Lord of Pinkmaiden Castle,
    — KARYL VANCE, Lord of Wayfarer's Rest,
    — NORBERT VANCE, Lord of Atranta,
    — THEOMAR SMALLWOOD, Lord of Acorn Hall,
      — his wife, LADY RAVELLA, of House Swann,
      — their daughter, CARELLEN,
    — WILLIAM MOOTON, Lord of Maidenpool,
    — SHELLA WHENT, dispossessed Lady of Harrenhal,
    — SER HALMON PAEGE.
    — TYTOS BLACKWOOD, Lord of Raventree

HOUSE TYRELL

The Tyrells rose to power as stewards to the Kings of the Reach, whose domain included the fertile plains of the southwest from the Dornish marches and Blackwater Rush to the shores of the Sunset Sea. Through the female line, they claim descent from Garth Greenhand, gardener king of the First Men, who wore a crown of vines and flowers and made the land bloom. When Mern IX, last king of House Gardener, was slain on the Field of Fire, his steward Harlen Tyrell surrendered Highgarden to Aegon the Conqueror. Aegon granted him the castle and dominion over the Reach. The Tyrell sigil is a golden rose on a grass-green field. Their words are *Growing Strong*.

Lord Mace Tyrell declared his support for Renly Baratheon at the onset of the War of the Five Kings, and gave him the hand of his daughter Margaery. Upon Renly's death, Highgarden made alliance with House Lannister, and Margaery was betrothed to King Joffrey.

MACE TYRELL, Lord of Highgarden, Warden of the South, Defender of the Marches, and High Marshall of the Reach,
— his wife, LADY ALERIE, of House Hightower of Oldtown,
— their children:
— WILLAS, their eldest son, heir to Highgarden,
— SER GARLAN, called THE GALLANT, their second son,
— his wife, LADY LEONETTE of House Fossoway,
— SER LORAS, the Knight of Flowers, their youngest son, a Sworn Brother of the Kingsguard,
— MARGAERY, their daughter, a widow of fifteen years, betrothed to King Joffrey I Baratheon,

— Margaery's companions and ladies-in-waiting:
  — her cousins, MEGGA, ALLA, and ELINOR TYRELL,
    — Elinor's betrothed, ALYN AMBROSE, squire,
  — LADY ALYSANNE BULWER, a girl of eight,
  — MEREDYTH CRANE, called MERRY,
  — TAENA OF MYR, wife to LORD ORTON MERRYWEATHER,
  — LADY ALYCE GRACEFORD,
  — SEPTA NYSTERICA, a sister of the Faith,
— his widowed mother, LADY OLENNA of House Redwyne, called the Queen of Thorns,
  — Lady Olenna's guardsmen, ARRYK and ERRYK, called LEFT and RIGHT,
— his sisters:
  — LADY MINA, wed to Paxter Redwyne, Lord of the Arbor,
  — their children:
    — SER HORAS REDWYNE, twin to Hobber, mocked as HORROR,
    — SER HOBBER REDWYNE, twin to Horas, mocked as SLOBBER,
    — DESMERA REDWYNE, a maid of sixteen,
  — LADY JANNA, wed to Ser Jon Fossoway,
— his uncles and cousins:
  — his father's brother, GARTH, called THE GROSS, Lord Seneschal of Highgarden,
    — Garth's bastard sons, GARSE and GARRETT FLOWERS,
  — his father's brother, SER MORYN, Lord Commander of the City Watch of Oldtown,
    — Moryn's son, [SER LUTHOR], m. Lady Elyn Norridge,
      — Luthor's son, SER THEODORE, m. Lady Lia Serry,
        — Theodore's daughter, ELINOR,
        — Theodore's son, LUTHOR, a squire,
      — Luthor's son, MAESTER MEDWICK,
      — Luthor's daughter, OLENE, m. Ser Leo Blackbar,
    — Moryn's son, LEO, called LEO THE LAZY,

—his father's brother, MAESTER GORMON, a scholar of the Citadel,

—his cousin, [SER QUENTIN], died at Ashford,
  — Quentin's son, SER OLYMER, m. Lady Lysa Meadows,
    — Olymer's sons, RAYMUND and RICKARD,
    — Olymer's daughter, MEGGA,

—his cousin, MAESTER NORMUND, in service at Blackcrown,

—his cousin, [SER VICTOR], slain by the Smiling Knight of the Kingswood Brotherhood,
  — Victor's daughter, VICTARIA, m. {Lord Jon Bulwer}, died of a summer fever,
    — their daughter, LADY ALYSANNE BULWER, eight,
  — Victor's son, SER LEO, m. Lady Alys Beesbury,
    — Leo's daughters, ALLA and LEONA,
    — Leo's sons, LYONEL, LUCAS, and LORENT,

— his household at Highgarden:
  —MAESTER LOMYS, counselor, healer, and tutor,
  —IGON VYRWEL, captain of the guard,
  —SER VORTIMER CRANE, master-at-arms,
  —BUTTERBUMPS, fool and jester, hugely fat,

— his lords bannermen:
  —RANDYLL TARLY, Lord of Horn Hill,
  —PAXTER REDWYNE, Lord of the Arbor,
  —ARWYN OAKHEART, Lady of Old Oak,
  —MATHIS ROWAN, Lord of Goldengrove,
  —ALESTER FLORENT, Lord of Brightwater Keep, a rebel in support of Stannis Baratheon,
  —LEYTON HIGHTOWER, Voice of Oldtown, Lord of the Port,
  —ORTON MERRYWEATHER, Lord of Longtable,
  —LORD ARTHUR AMBROSE,

— his knights and sworn swords:
  —SER MARK MULLENDORE, crippled during the Battle
    of the Blackwater,
  —SER JON FOSSOWAY, of the green-apple Fossoways,
  —SER TANTON FOSSOWAY, of the red-apple Fossoways.

REBELS, ROGUES, AND
SWORN BROTHERS

THE SWORN BROTHERS OF THE NIGHT'S WATCH

(ranging Beyond the Wall)
   JEOR MORMONT, called THE OLD BEAR, Lord Commander of the Night's Watch,
      —JON SNOW, the Bastard of Winterfell, his steward and squire, lost while scouting the Skirling Pass,
      — GHOST, his direwolf, white and silent,
      —EDDISON TOLLETT, called DOLOROUS EDD, his squire,
    — THOREN SMALLWOOD, commanding the rangers,
      —DYWEN, DIRK, SOFTFOOT, GRENN, BEDWYCK called GIANT, OLLO LOPHAND, GRUBBS, BERNARR called BROWN BERNARR, another BERNARR called BLACK BERNARR, TIM STONE, ULMER OF KINGSWOOD, GARTH called GREYFEATHER, GARTH OF GREENAWAY, GARTH OF OLDTOWN, ALAN OF ROSBY, RONNEL HARCLAY, AETHAN, RYLES, MAWNEY, rangers,
    — JARMEN BUCKWELL, commanding the scouts,
      —BANNEN, KEDGE WHITEYE, TUMBERJON, FORNIO, GOADY, rangers and scouts,
    — SER OTTYN WYTHERS, commanding the rearguard,
    — SER MALADOR LOCKE, commanding the baggage,
      —DONNEL HILL, called SWEET DONNEL, his squire and steward,

—HAKE, a steward and cook,

—CHETT, an ugly steward, keeper of hounds,

—SAMWELL TARLY, a fat steward, keeper of ravens, mocked as SER PIGGY,

—LARK called THE SISTERMAN, his cousin ROLLEY OF SISTERTON, CLUBFOOT KARL, MASLYN, SMALL PAUL, SAWWOOD, LEFT HAND LEW, ORPHAN OSS, MUTTERING BILL, stewards,

— [QHORIN HALFHAND], commanding the rangers from the Shadow Tower, slain in the Skirling Pass,

—[SQUIRE DALBRIDGE, EGGEN], rangers, slain in the Skirling Pass,

—STONESNAKE, a ranger and mountaineer, lost afoot in Skirling Pass,

—BLANE, Qhorin Halfhand's second, commanding the Shadow Tower men on the Fist of the First Men,

—SER BYAM FLINT,

(at Castle Black)

BOWEN MARSH, Lord Steward and castellan,

—MAESTER AEMON (TARGARYEN), healer and counselor, a blind man, one hundred years old,

— his steward, CLYDAS,

—BENJEN STARK, First Ranger, missing, feared dead,

— SER WYNTON STOUT, eighty years a ranger,

— SER ALADALE WYNCH, PYPAR, DEAF DICK FOLLARD, HAIRY HAL, BLACK JACK BULWER, ELRON, MATTHAR, rangers,

—OTHELL YARWYCK, First Builder,

— SPARE BOOT, YOUNG HENLY, HALDER, ALBETT, KEGS, SPOTTED PATE OF MAIDENPOOL, builders,

—DONAL NOYE, armorer, smith, and steward, one-armed,

—THREE-FINGER HOBB, steward and chief cook,

— TIM TANGLETONGUE, EASY, MULLY, OLD HENLY, CUGEN, RED ALYN OF THE ROSEWOOD, JEREN, stewards,

—SEPTON CELLADOR, a drunken devout,
—SER ENDREW TARTH, master-at-arms,
—RAST, ARRON, EMRICK, SATIN, HOP-ROBIN, recruits in training,
—CONWY, GUEREN, recruiters and collectors,

(at Eastwatch-by-the-Sea)
COTTER PYKE, Commander Eastwatch,
—MAESTER HARMUNE, healer and counselor,
—SER ALLISER THORNE, master-at-arms,
—JANOS SLYNT, former commander of the City Watch of King's Landing, briefly Lord of Harrenhal,
—SER GLENDON HEWETT,
—DAREON, steward and singer,
—IRON EMMETT, a ranger famed for his strength,

(at Shadow Tower)
SER DENYS MALLISTER, Commander, Shadow Tower
—his steward and squire, WALLACE MASSEY,
—MAESTER MULLIN, healer and counselor.

THE BROTHERHOOD
WITHOUT BANNERS
AN OUTLAW FELLOWSHIP

BERIC DONDARRION, Lord of Blackhaven, called THE
   LIGHTNING LORD, oft reported dead,
   — his right hand, THOROS OF MYR, a red priest,
   — his squire, EDRIC DAYNE, Lord of Starfall, twelve,
   — his followers:
      —LEM, called LEM LEMONCLOAK, a one-time
        soldier,
      —HARWIN, son of Hullen, formerly in service to Lord
        Eddard Stark at Winterfell,
      —GREENBEARD, a Tyroshi sellsword,
      —TOM OF SEVENSTREAMS, a singer of dubious report,
        called TOM SEVENSTRINGS and TOM O' SEVENS,
      —ANGUY THE ARCHER, a bowman from the Dornish
        Marches,
      —JACK-BE-LUCKY, a wanted man, short an eye,
      —THE MAD HUNTSMAN, of Stoney Sept,
      —KYLE, NOTCH, DENNETT, longbowmen,
      —MERRIT O' MOONTOWN, WATTY THE MILLER,
        LIKELY LUKE, MUDGE, BEARDLESS DICK, outlaws in
        his band,

   — at the Inn of the Kneeling Man:
   —SHARNA, the innkeep, a cook and midwife,

— her husband, called HUSBAND,
— BOY, an orphan of the war,

— at the Peach, a brothel in Stoney Sept:
   — TANSY, the red-haired proprietor,
      — ALYCE, CASS, LANNA, JYZENE, HELLY, BELLA,
         some of her peaches,

— at Acorn Hall, the seat of House Smallwood:
   — LADY RAVELLA, formerly of House Swann, wife to Lord
      Theomar Smallwood,

— here and there and elsewhere:
   — LORD LYMOND LYCHESTER, an old man of wandering
      wit, who once held Ser Maynard at the bridge,
      — his young caretaker, MAESTER ROONE,
   — the ghost of High Heart,
   — the Lady of the Leaves,
   — the septon at Sallydance.

the WILDLINGS, or the FREE FOLK

MANCE RAYDER, King-beyond-the-Wall,
  — DALLA, his pregnant wife,
  — VAL, her younger sister,

  — his chiefs and captains:
    —HARMA, called DOGSHEAD, commanding his van,
    —THE LORD OF BONES, mocked as RATTLESHIRT,
      leader of a war band,
      — YGRITTE, a young spearwife, a member of his band,
      — RYK, called LONGSPEAR, a member of his band,
      — RAGWYLE, LENYL, members of his band,
      — his captive, JON SNOW, the crow-come-over,
        — GHOST, Jon's direwolf, white and silent,
    —STYR, Magnar of Thenn,
    —JARL, a young raider, Val's lover,
      — GRIGG THE GOAT, ERROK, QUORT, BODGER,
        DEL, BIG BOIL, HEMPEN DAN, HENK THE HELM,
        LENN, TOEFINGER, STONE THUMBS, raiders,
    —TORMUND, Mead-King of Ruddy Hall, called
      GIANTSBANE, TALL-TALKER, HORN-BLOWER, and
      BREAKER OF ICE, also THUNDERFIST, HUSBAND TO
      BEARS, SPEAKER TO GODS, and FATHER OF HOSTS,
      leader of a war band,
      — his sons, TOREGG THE TALL, TORWYRD THE
        TAME, DORMUND, and DRYN, his daughter
        MUNDA,

— [ORELL, called ORELL THE EAGLE], a skinchanger slain
  by Jon Snow in the Skirling Pass,
—MAG MAR TUN DOH WEG, called MAG THE MIGHTY,
  of the giants,
—VARAMYR called SIXSKINS, a skinchanger, master of
  three wolves, a shadowcat, and a snow bear,
—THE WEEPER, a raider and leader of a war band,
— [ALFYN CROWKILLER], a raider, slain by Qhorin
  Halfhand of the Night's Watch,

CRASTER, of Craster's Keep, who kneels to none,
  —GILLY, his daughter and wife, great with child,
  —DYAH, FERNY, NELLA, three of his nineteen wives.

ACKNOWLEDGMENTS

If the bricks aren't well made, the wall falls down.

This is an awfully big wall I'm building here, so I need a lot of bricks. Fortunately, I know a lot of brickmakers, and all sorts of other useful folks as well.

Thanks and appreciation, once more, to those good friends who so kindly lent me their expertise (and in some cases, even their *books*) so my bricks would be nice and solid—to my Archmaester Sage Walker, to First Builder Carl Keim, to Melinda Snodgrass my master of horse.

And as ever, to Parris.

Continue reading mo[...]
epic series: A So[...]

ern fantasy's greatest
g of Ice and Fire

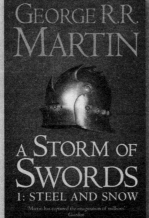

VOLUME THREE

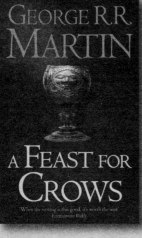

VOLUME FOUR

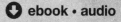